THE PEOPLE'S QUEEN

Vanora Bennett is the author of three novels, *Portrait of an Unknown Woman, Queen of Silks,* and *Blood Royal,* and an award-winning journalist. She has worked around the world for *The Times* of London, the *Los Angeles Times* and Reuters, and contributed to the *Times Lterary Supplement,* the *Guardian,* the *Observer* and the BBC. She lives in London with her husband and two children.

Visit www.vanorabennett.com for Vanora's official website.

Also by Vanora Bennett

Portrait of an Unknown Woman
Queen of Silks
Blood Royal

VANORA BENNETT

The People's Queen

HarperCollins*Publishers*

HarperCollins*Publishers*
77–85 Fulham Palace Road,
Hammersmith, London W6 8JB

www.harpercollins.co.uk

Published by HarperCollins*Publishers* 2010
1

A catalogue record for this book
is available from the British Library

ISBN: 978 0 00 731121 7

Set in Sabon by Palimpsest Book Production Limited,
Grangemouth, Stirlingshire

Printed and bound in Great Britain by
Clays Ltd, St Ives plc

For my mother

Illustration from 'Divided York and Lancaster,' exhibition*
panel outlining the history of the Wars of the Roses.

* The exhibition was 'To Prove a Villain – the Real Richard III', at the
Royal National Theatre, London March 27–April 27, 1991)

FORTUNE'S WHEEL

The picture on the left shows the capricious goddess Fortune, as she was often displayed in the rose window of medieval English churches, teasing her victims with the hope of lasting wealth and power.

The greedy, feverish people rising up Fortune's ever-turning wheel, on the left, are gloating, *regnabo*, boastful Latin for 'I shall reign'.

The person at the top, who has achieved every ambition, crows, *regno*, or 'I reign'.

The terrified people on the right of the wheel, going down, are looking back at their moment of glory, wailing, *regnavi*, or 'I used to reign'.

And the one falling off at the bottom whimpers, *sum sine regno*; 'I am without a kingdom' or 'I have been left with nothing'.

The message understood by every congregation – that pride comes before a fall – took on new significance after the Black Death. This devastating outbreak of plague killed off one-third of the people of Europe in the middle of the 14th century, when my novel begins. The catastrophe ended an era of belief that men were born to fixed and unchangeable positions in society. With survivors everywhere grabbing for a share of the spoils left by the departed, an ambitious few started rushing towards high estate with a speed and determination never seen before. Envious onlookers could only hope that these winners would soon fall from the pinnacle of power, as suddenly and dramatically as they had risen.

CONTENTS

PROLOGUE

A World Ends

Footsteps.

Kate stirred. She was lying on the floor, on her side. She must have managed to fall asleep. She was stiff. Her hip was digging into the packed earth. It was hot already, and there was a burning strip of light coming through the shutters. It took her a moment to understand what she was hearing.

Someone sauntering along the lane outside, with a cheerful, confident, light stride. Whistling.

Kate scrambled heavily to her feet. With the baby inside her kicking and punching, full of energy and raunch, keen to be out and breathing God's air, and with her own heart pounding like the millstream paddles in the spring melt, she rushed to the doorway.

There'd been nearly sixty people living in Great Henney just the other day. They'd all gone. Or that's how it seemed. She'd heard no other footsteps for at least a day, sniffed no smoke on the air, no cooking of broth or eggs last evening. She'd thought she was alone, with just the panicky lowing of lost cows, and the anxious clip of dogs' paws, and the stink. So who could be striding about like that now, whistling the kind of jaunty dance tune you could kick your heels up to?

It was only when she was almost out in the daylight that she stopped. It was too easy to hope. She shouldn't be rash. This person might mean danger.

She dropped to her knees, below a passer-by's eye level, and peered cautiously through leaves and branches. She felt as wild and scared down there as a woodland beast. It was only the hope she couldn't quite suppress that seemed human.

Kate could see brightness in the hedgerow. The midsummer flowers were still glowingly alive, the birds singing, the insects buzzing. There were stripes of corn still yellowing in the field, greener stripes of rye and barley, and the fronds of beans.

But as soon as she was close enough to the doorway to see all the things that seemed so normal, she was also close enough to get a noseful of the stink. It seemed worse every time, but what could you expect? It was a hot day. Not that she could actually see any human bodies from here. But they must be there. What she could see were the corpses of the sheep on the common in front of the field. All dead, hundreds of them. They'd started dropping at the same time as the people. There were flies rising drunkenly in the grass, clouds of flies, buzzing from one still mound to the next.

She and Dad had buried Tom three days ago, and Mum, before Dad went off on the penitents' procession. An hour, he said. But he didn't come back. And the baby would come any day now. Maybe tonight.

But now, in bright daylight, there was this woman, a stranger, who didn't seem to have a care in the world, coming up the lane towards her. Despite herself, despite the possible danger, Kate craned forward.

The stranger was a sharp-faced, tall thing, with pale freckly skin, and ginger hair peeping out under her kerchief, and skinny limbs. She was maybe thirty. The woman didn't bother to pretend she couldn't see Kate staring at her. She just stared back down with frank interest, then nodded, and said, quite matter-of-factly, quite cheerfully, 'That baby's not already started coming, has it?'

The words were so normal that Kate suddenly felt ashamed to be down on her knees, like a wild beast.

Blushing furiously, she shook her head and started to raise herself from the floor, grateful for the warm splintery ordinariness of the door frame under her hands, hot with relief that she wasn't alone any more.

'Backache,' the woman said, still assessing her with that not unfriendly look. 'Terrible, that can be, when you're as far gone as you are. Gah. Tell me about it.' She sniffed and stuck out a hand; she took Kate's arm and hauled the girl the last few inches till they were both standing, not too close, one on each side of the threshold. 'Still,' the woman went on. 'One thing.' She eyed Kate's bump, and Kate thought there was something almost hungry in her look. 'It's not all just dying, whatever they might say. God destroying the race of Adam, my arse. Here's one bit of new life coming in, anyway. So. Not all bad, is it?'

Tremulously, Kate laughed. The woman nodded approvingly. She took a step forward and patted the bump. 'On your own out here, are you?' the stranger said, not unkindly.

For just a moment, Kate had another faint shiver of worry at letting an incomer know just how vulnerable she was. Then she thought: I don't care if she does know. She can see I'm on my own whatever I say. She's got a kind way with her. I need to keep her here.

The woman wasn't from round these parts, that was for sure. Not with that sharp quick way of talking, words all bitten into each other. But she was another living human. 'Tom's dead,' Kate blurted, as trustingly as the girl she'd been before she'd married him, on her fourteenth birthday, six months ago, before the pregnancy showed. 'Mum . . . we buried them. But now Dad . . . he went on the procession. With Sir John. The priest. He was only supposed to be gone an hour or two.'

She was surprised how calm and level her own voice sounded. She knew Dad was dead too, really. She was still scared, but it was ordinary fear now – the watchfulness of two foxes meeting in the forest. She was surprised how grateful she was to this woman just for being here with her.

The woman gave her a bright little look, and shook her head. 'Tom was your man, was he?' she asked, still shaking it, as if the news was a surprise and a sorrow, though one borne lightly. 'And you'd be who, then . . .?' She lifted an enquiring eyebrow.

'Kate,' Kate stammered. 'They call me Young Kate.' She'd never had to explain herself. She'd never met someone who didn't already know her.

'Well, wouldn't you know it,' the woman said. She put down her bundle. There wasn't much in it, maybe a change of linen and a piece of bread, it was that light. She was still shaking her head, as if she couldn't believe something. 'My Tom's little wife,' she said. Then, to Kate's shock, she leaned forward and pinched Kate's cheek. 'A right little beauty he got himself and all,' she added with a sudden, toothy grin.

Kate stepped back, touching her cheek. That jocular pinch had been quite hard. She didn't know if she liked the growing brightness in the woman's voice. Faintly, she said, 'Your Tom?'

'Cousin,' the woman offered. Nothing more. She glanced behind Kate, behind the cottage, behind the open-sided barn where the tiles were drying, to the kiln. A knowing sort of look. In her flat quick voice, she added, 'You must have heard of us. My dad's the one used to take the tiles from the kiln there to market. Way back, we're talking now. Must be twenty years ago.' She nodded again. Her story was taking shape. She was gaining fluency. 'Married a London girl, my dad, didn't he? My mum, that was. Stayed on with her family. Liked the hustle and bustle of town life. Always talked about home though. Brought me here once, when I was a kid. Your Tom and me, thick as thieves we were, back then. Climbing trees, swimming in the river' – she gestured at the landscape – 'smoking out bees for honey. Nicking the broken bits of tiles for skimming stones. A proper little terror he was in those days. Oh, the things he taught me.' She went back to shaking her head, with that tough smile pinned on her face and her bright little eyes fixed very hard on Kate's.

Part of Kate knew there was something wrong. The more she thought about it, the more seemed wrong. Tom had never mentioned having blood in London that Kate remembered. And they'd surely never been kids at the same time, these two. Tom must have been a good ten years younger. Mustn't he?

6

Plus which, most importantly, it wasn't ever Tom's dad, who'd died years ago, who'd worked out what you could do with the clay. The tiles were her dad's business. So there must be a mistake. The woman must be mixing her up with someone else. Some other Essex village. Some other tilery. Some other Tom. But if she pointed that out the woman might go. And the baby was coming, and Kate's back was aching. She told herself: He wasn't a talker, Tom. Perhaps he just never had a chance to tell me about a family in London.

'What's your name?' she said.

The woman only grinned wider. 'Alice . . . Alison,' she said, as if she hadn't quite decided. 'You just call me Aunty.'

Then Aunty put a bony arm around Kate's shoulder and began walking her inside her home. 'Come on, love,' she said, strangely tender. 'Let's us get a fire going. I'm starving, and you need to feed that baby of yours, don't you?'

The next morning, after the baby came, they had eggs and a bit of the pound of bread that was already drying and crumbling away and a few dandelion leaves that Aunty picked and some onion slices from the store. The little girl had been washed and wrapped up in the waiting rags, and Kate, also clean, was lying, still weak and aching and not quite sure what was going on, but with radiant happiness mixed up with her exhaustion and lighting up her plump little face. She held the small breathing bundle in her arms, gazing at her with the disbelief of every new mother, even in circumstances less strange than these, seeing Tom's eyes, and Mum's snub nose, and her own dark hair.

Aunty had fed the hens and made sure they were secured. ('Wouldn't want them to go astray, now, would we?' she said with gallows humour, as if they were hers as much as Kate's. 'Because God only knows where we'd be for food without them eggs.') Then she sat down on the stool by Kate's straw bed, in the band of light cast by the propped-open door, and looked proudly at her charges.

Aunty was tired, after the night of blood and buckets and water and yelled instructions to push. She could feel her eyes prickling under their scratchy lids. But it had all gone well in the end. Alive, all of them. And that was something, at least, she thought. Another one in the eye for the forces of darkness.

Then she began to talk, still very calmly, in a quiet, reminiscent, dreamy monotone, twitching her fingers through the rents and mends in her thin robe, about what she'd walked away from in London, and what she'd walked through on her tramp through Essex. Because she could see this poor little scrap didn't know; didn't have the least idea.

Death hadn't just come stealing into this one village like black smoke. Whatever this girl thought, it wasn't the sins of Kate's mum, or dad, or Tom, or the no-good priest she kept going on about, that had made an angry God decide to smite them all dead, or whatever nonsense it was the priests kept spouting (till they died too).

There were people dying in their hundreds everywhere, Aunty said gently, trying not to shock the girl too much, while not blanketing her in mumbo-jumbo either. There were bodies in the lanes all over Essex: men, women, entire processions of penitents, lying where they'd dropped. Dead people, dead animals. In London they were piling up corpses in burial pits until the pits overflowed before filling them in, a bit. One pit would fill up with the dead before anyone had time to dig the next. Cadavers were dragged out of homes and left in front of the doors. London was no place to be while there was that going on, Aunty said. The air was too foul. They said husband was abandoning wife, wife husband, parents children, and the young their old folk. If you wanted to live, you had to walk. And she wanted to live.

'So I thought, come and look up Tom and his family,' she said, going back into the story from last night, about being some kind of relative.

If the girl was waiting to hear whether Aunty's own family in London had all died, or if she'd been one of the ones who abandoned their own to save herself, she didn't ask. Just sat there, round-eyed, open-mouthed, gawping. Aunty couldn't tell if she was even really taking it in. Even if she was understanding the words, Aunty thought, it was probably too much to absorb their meaning all at once. Even for her, who'd seen it with her own eyes, it was hard enough to believe. So Aunty left the past in the past, and didn't bother with her own story: the kids she couldn't bury; the priest who wouldn't say a Mass over them without money Aunty didn't have. A shrug is all you can offer Fortune, in the end, when nothing will work out; and a calculation: they're dead; nothing more you can do for them. You've got to look out for yourself. Time to go. Aunty just fiddled with the wiry ginger curls under her mended kerchief and went on with her sing-song account of the horror in the rest of the world.

Aunty said she'd heard people were dying even beyond England – all over Christendom, they said. The Mortality was said to have come from the East. People were dying of it in Italy a year ago. Maybe it had come to the ports of Italy in ships; maybe it was the earthquake in Italy that had let the foul sulphurous fumes out from the inside of the earth, from the hellfire below. And now, Aunty said, she'd heard tell of worse on the way. Strange tempests, with sheets of fire and huge murderous hailstones all mixed up together, so you couldn't know whether you'd be burned to a crisp or battered to a pulp first. People said the fish in the seas were dying, and corrupting the air. But it didn't matter whether you blamed the stinking mists and stagnant lakes and poisoned air on the Evil One or the Wrath of God. The important thing was to get away to somewhere clean.

'But where,' Aunty said, almost to herself. She looked round at the flat Essex field, the soft blue and green of the darkening sky, and wrinkled her nose. Surely the stink here was as bad as anything in London. 'There's the rub.'

Aunty paused, and then said, because talking was strangely comforting now she'd started, that she'd heard there were four hundred a day dying just in Avignon, where the Pope's palace was. And all the cardinals were dead. Good riddance to *them*, Aunty added with grim pleasure.

She could see Kate couldn't imagine four hundred people alive, let alone dead, and wasn't sure what a cardinal was.

So instead, timidly, the girl opened her pink lips at last and asked what must have been on her own mind all this time. 'We couldn't find Sir John. Tom, Mum . . . they didn't have any last rites,' she mumbled. 'We prayed. Just the two of us. But I don't think it was enough. And Dad. If he's . . . gone . . . too. Do you think that means they're all . . .' Her voice faded.

'Damned?' Aunty finished for her, grasping her meaning. 'Because there was no priest? Nah. That's been the same everywhere – the priests too scared to minister to the dying. Scared they're heading for hell themselves, after all their years of wickedness. Keen to keep out of their Maker's clutches.' And here, to stop her voice catching, she made it shrill, almost a shout: 'And too greedy to look after the dead without payment, too, half the time. Trying to take money off people even to say a prayer over the bodies.' She shrugged. 'Well, that's priests for you. It's not just your kin. We could all go to bloody Hell, and what would they care?'

She sensed, from the stunned quality of the girl's silence, that she'd gone too far. 'Priests . . . Don't get me started on priests,' Aunty said, a bit apologetically. 'What you need to know is, some bishop's sorted it out so that we *don't* all burn for eternity because of their selfishness. He says laymen can make confession to each other if they can't find a priest. The Apostles did that, didn't they? And if there isn't a man around to confess to, it can even be a woman. And if there's no one around at all, then, they say, faith must suffice. And it does. Suffice. You keep that in your head. Your folks are not in Hell. Your folks are all right.'

The girl nodded, and took her saucer eyes off Aunty and gazed down at the baby. Aunty could see what she was thinking: no baptism, so, also, damned?

'We're all here. That's the main thing. You, and me, and this new little life here,' Aunty broke determinedly into that thought before the girl's terror took hold. 'All alive, all blessed by God, all ready to face tomorrow.' She made the sign of the Cross over the baby. Then she made a wry sort of face. 'No priest,' she said, 'no problem.' She wagged her finger at Kate.

'We don't need them bastards any more to save ourselves, remember?' She dipped her finger in the last bucket of water left and made the holy sign again on the baby's face, and said a made-up blessing. 'Salve Regina, Mater misericordiae,' she muttered against the baby's crying. 'Live long and well, little one. Be happy. Be a beauty. Make others happy, if they deserve it. Be lucky. And be rich if you can! Amen.'

The women smiled tentatively at each other. They both liked the strange little prayer – taking the ordinary chatter that fell from their lips as the Word of God. 'I'm going to call *her* Alice,' the girl said confidingly. 'After you.' Then, quite peacefully, as if Aunty had put her worries to rest: 'Will you sing that song, the one I heard you whistling?' She was just a child herself.

Aunty wrinkled her not-young face till slightly mocking lines criss-crossed it; in the shadows, she felt as though the sorrows of all the world were on it. 'Thought it was a nice cheerful tune, did you?' she said. 'Catchy. Words a bit gloomier though. It was the tramping song I heard on the cattle road out. Toughened everyone up.'

She began to sing it, quietly, breathily, like a lullaby. She had a deepish tuneful voice. She kept her eyes on Kate, whose eyes were drooping as if she didn't mind the words. 'Woe is me of the shilling in the armpit! . . . Seething, terrible, shouting hurt . . . Great is its seething like a burning cinder . . . A grievous thing of ashy hue.'

Looking at the bright square of outside through the door frame, Aunty wondered, as she sang, how many other survivors were also watching the horizon. You couldn't know if there were any; not really. She and these kids might be the last people of all, alone in the desolation.

Well, we're all right, she thought stoutly, shutting out the blackness. We'll get on our feet. And it wouldn't be all bad, a world with just us, and no priests.

Kate let her head start to nod as she listened to the cracked voice, trying not to think of anything except the part of her that was still rejoicing in the touch of the baby, of skin and cloth on her skin. She yawned. She was tired, so tired. The yawn didn't surprise her. But she hadn't expected to start crying. She certainly didn't expect the dirty wash of despair that now broke through her without any warning, the blubbery, snuffly sneezings and coughings, as if she were grieving for her losses and all the woes in the world, now, suddenly, all at once.

Aunty – Alison, Alice – stood up. There was something new in her face, something watchful. She picked the baby up off Kate's breast.

'Going to put her down for a sleep,' Aunty said. With the baby held against herself, she twirled a blanket down over Kate's nakedness without touching her. 'She'll be tired, after what she's been through. You need a bit of quiet too, love. Shut your eyes.'

It was only when Aunty and the baby had stepped outside, into the strong morning light, and Aunty had quietly pushed the door to behind her, that Kate felt, through the aches and bruises of what her body had endured all night, a different kind of pain. There were swellings on either side of her throat, she realised, and where her legs joined her body. She twisted her wet face round, stiffly, because everything ached so much, and squinted into her armpit. It was too shadowy inside to be sure, but she thought the great pulsing engorged mound she saw there was turning black.

PART ONE

Regno

I reign

ONE

They're late for the dinner; late enough that the light is beginning to fade, and the torches are lit, and the ice swans are beginning to melt, rivulets of water running between the silver channels down the table. They've clearly been bickering all the way to Westminster, these two. They look set-faced and stubborn, each in his own fashion. But then they're an odd couple, by anyone's book: the wife tall and graceful and long-necked as the ice swans, visibly at home in these grand surroundings, while the altogether shorter and stubbier husband's only resemblance to a swan is that, like the icy masterpieces starting to sail down the vast table, he's sweating, even before the dancing's begun.

Philippa Chaucer sways down the table to her place, weaving her way among the throng of pages and serving men as if they were invisible, making it clear to her life's companion, as he makes his way more awkwardly down the other side to his parallel place, that she's noting how far they are from the grandees at the top.

'If only,' she mouths, somehow managing to form the chilly words without reducing her chiselled beauty by even a fraction, and indicating the luxury that surrounds them with a small, expert lift of one eyebrow, 'if only you had even a tenth of *that woman's* ambition, how different things might be for us.'

Geoffrey, her husband, only responds by looking around, as if he's surprised by it all, at the eye-popping feast conjured into existence by the ambition of *that woman*, the King's mistress. He furrows his brow in anxiety. He runs his fingers through his hair – or tries to. His fingers connect with the hat he's forgotten he's wearing. They knock it half off his head. He crams it back on, all wrong, and sits down with an embarrassing thump on the bench, interrupting the conversation of the men on either side of him. He goes red. He begins a wordy apology. Philippa looks at him, shakes her head very slightly, and sighs.

Dance, all of you, dance, Alice thinks, watching the crowd of sweating faces below, rather enjoying their sufferings. Go on. Higher, a tiny bit higher.

It's an unusually hot April evening. It's only ten minutes since Alice signalled for the tables to be pushed against the walls. The air's still thick with sheep fat and fowl grease. But how they're all throwing themselves about in the crowd below.

She can't resist taking pleasure in examining them from the superior vantage point of the royal dais. The courtiers have fused into one heaving mass, energetically going through the motions of the saltarello. They're glowing and glistening and panting under their turbans, inside their heavy velvets and silks. They're all doing their best to show their King they're happy to be where they are, and watching Alice where she is, at his side.

Alice fans herself complacently, and examines the rictus smile on the dark face of the Duke of Lancaster. He looked so dignified in his red a few minutes ago, but now his face is the same blood hue as his tunic. It pleases her that even the world's most arrogant man is out there, gritting his teeth and leaping in the air, as determined as the rest of the scarlet-faced courtiers to please the King his father and host by looking delighted with the entertainment laid on by Alice.

She turns a little, enough to murmur into the ear of the King his father and host, in a way that the Duke will be sure to see. (She's wanted to make a relationship with Duke John for years, even though, between his long absences at the war in France, he's not yet shown great interest in her. So it won't

16

do him any harm to show him the extent of her power now. She knows how power attracts.) The lords a-leaping down there won't be able to hear what she's saying to their master, but they'll be able to guess at the tone of her voice from her sly sideways grin. 'I don't know how they all have the energy,' she murmurs, affecting weariness, and fans herself. She has it all worked out. No one will ever expect Edward to dance, unless by some whim he chooses to. His age lets him off: rising sixty-two, and the long golden beard long ago turned silver. So he'll be pleased she wants to sit it out too. And why not? There's no point in her tiring herself out tonight. Her big day will be tomorrow. 'In this heat . . .' she adds, even more languidly. She likes the way the French comes sliding so naturally out of her mouth, as if she'd been born to it, even if, in reality, her French has been learned more at Stratford-atte-Bowe than in Paris. She's had to work hard at it, in her time. But if she's learned anything, it is that the point of hard work is to make things look easy. When Edward chuckles back, and pats her hand, she permits herself a slightly bigger smile.

They haven't always been so eager to please, those courtiers down there. Let them dance to her tune now.

Tomorrow, Edward will show her off to the world, in a burst of glory the like of which England has never seen. Tomorrow, for a week, mercenaries, princes and dukes from all over Christendom will watch a pageant in which the influence of Alice Perrers, who has come so far already in her twenty-five years on this earth, and might yet go further, is finally made plain.

Tomorrow, at mid-morning, the court will walk through London dressed in red and white, the colours she's chosen for the week. With the ladies holding the horses of their gentlemen by their golden bridles, they'll set off from outside this window, from the Hill behind the Tower, and process along Tower Street and Chepe, then out of Aldersgate to the pasture-cum-jousting ground at Smithfield. And then the gentlemen of the court will joust, in her honour, while the people of the City,

17

all dressed in their coloured liveries, watch and cheer. And she, and only she, Alice Perrers, who will be known for the week as Lady of the Sun (a title she's thought of herself), as well as Queen of the Lists, will ride in a golden chariot, at the centre of everything. She'll be wearing a cap encrusted with jewels, and a cloak of Venetian gold lined with red taffeta, on top of the red gown, lined in white, embroidered with seed pearls, and edged in royal ermine, that she's got on tonight. She's going to astonish. She's going to impress.

It's time they realised – all these courtiers, all those Londoners – that a woman who's already, by the grace of God and the generosity of the King of England (and her own financial acumen), one of the richest people in the land, has every intention of shining like the sun for the rest of her days.

She hasn't forgotten her place entirely. Not really. She isn't going to start acting like, or thinking of herself as, a real, born-to-the-throne queen. (Anyway, who would have let her if she tried? They all still worship the memory of dear old Queen Philippa, who's been dead for most of the eight years of Alice's supremacy; and Alice doesn't have a drop of anything like royal blood in her veins, or noble blood, or even knightly blood. She's a different kind altogether. She's not even very interested in thinking of being a helpless, dependent, real queen; she likes her freedom too much to dream of sitting still in an expensive robe, smiling at posturing fools of knights-errant, for the rest of her days.) Still, only an idiot could ignore the meaning of her punning pageant title, and Londoners aren't idiots. Edward's royal symbol is the sun. If Alice Perrers is to be Lady of the Sun, at least for this week of glory, then she will be displaying all the power a queen commands. And power, at least the quiet kind that comes with wealth, she does enjoy.

Even before Edward, even as a very young woman, Alice was busy consolidating her position in this world. Every penny she's ever inherited, or made, has been put back into snapping up leases on this property or that, taking on unconsidered trifles of fields or tenements here, there and everywhere, making improvements, building, putting up rents, and using the profits to buy more. She's got a gift for it. She's done extraordinarily well – far better than she would have if she'd set her sights purely on imitating the real born-to-it ladies of the court and becoming almost indistinguishable from them. But, of course, it's been much easier for her to achieve wealth since the world came to realise that there's a misty, unseen, kingly presence at her back. That knowledge concentrates people's minds. It keeps them honest. No one cheats on a bargain with Alice, as her store of coin and leases grows. No one has, for a long time.

The real point of this week's festivities, as far as Alice is concerned, is to make sure she can continue to enjoy the power that feeds and protects all the wealth she's still building up – even after Edward dies.

For Alice has begun to understand that the enchanted dream she's been living in until now – the best part of a decade as the indulged darling of a dear old man who, himself, has been on the throne for nearly half a century, and is loved, everywhere, as England's greatest king – must soon come to an end. No one else seems to have noticed or to be planning their next move, although when Edward does pass on the end of his reign will surely affect them all. The gentry grumble about paying taxes to fund his war in France, true. But they carry on buying expensive clothes and jewels, far beyond their means, and raiding each other's manor houses when they think they can get away with stealing a few fields, just as the courtiers carry on dancing and jousting and prancing off to the war at vast expense and raiding each other's castles, as if they all thought they could somehow continue for ever in the golden sunset years of Edward's reign, in more or less peace, and more or less prosperity, stuffing their faces with larks' tongues and honeyed peacock breasts, and watching the ice swans melt at an unending succession of banquet tables.

But Alice has heard Edward mumbling in the mornings, unable to shake off the night's dreams; sometimes calling her 'Philippa' after his wife, or 'Isabella' after his favourite, headstrong, high-and-mighty fool of a daughter. He's still most of the time, at least in front of others, the sparkling, charismatic, dynamic man he always was; but, in his unguarded moments, alone with her, she also sees the confused old man he's becoming, or is about to become. She treats the creeping wound on his leg, which won't heal, so she knows the extent of his physical decrepitude too, just as she knows the folly of his having recently restarted the war in France, years after he's past his fighting prime, and of expecting to go on having the luck of the Devil that he enjoyed in his muscular youth, and winning.

So she's formed a view. She needs to think about the future, beyond Edward. And she's decided that the best way to protect herself against that cloudy tomorrow is to cultivate the friendship of one of Edward's sons. Not to become a mistress again, obviously, for Alice doubts that a prince who could have any woman in the land would want his father's cast-off, no longer young; she's realistic enough never to have mistaken her rounded plumpness and dark curls and cheeky freckles for beauty. What Alice wants next is respect and recognition; a relationship that will maintain something of her influence and visibility, while leaving her the freedom of manoeuvre she needs to carry on buying up land and extending her possessions.

Ideally, she'd have preferred this respect and recognition to come from the son who is destined to be the next King of England. But the noble Prince Edward of England, heir to the throne, the former war hero, the ex-ruler of southern France, and as widely admired at court and among the peasants and soldiery as Alice finds him evil-tempered and vindictive, is not an ideal choice of patron for several reasons. One is his wife, Princess Joan, who's made it clear to Alice for years now that she will never have time for a nouveau riche from nowhere. The other is that the Prince of England has been dying, agonisingly slowly, of some Castilian dropsy caught on campaign, for longer than Alice cares to remember. He's still clinging to life for the moment; but Alice doubts he will make it to become King Edward IV. And there's no point in hoping that, when the Prince does die, she'll get anywhere with his little boy, Richard, a child in the nursery, guarded by his disagreeable mother, that bloated ex-beauty of a princess with the pursed lips and nostrils that flare and dent white whenever she sees Alice.

That leaves the other royal son: John of Gaunt, the Duke of Lancaster, the man out there, sweating as he dances. Son number three originally, but since the death of his brother Lionel he's been son number two; and with every chance that his eldest brother Prince Edward hasn't long left in this vale of tears either, he's all too likely, all too soon, to be the King's eldest surviving son.

It's a matter of whispered conjecture whether Duke John might, in that eventuality, try and get the throne for himself, rather than protect it for his little nephew, his brother's son. Some people point to Duke John's innate nobility, the courteous conservatism in every thought and gesture, and say he wouldn't. But most people think he would.

There's no doubt that Duke John's a good-looking man, in body. There's a grace to the way he bows his long lean frame, a beauty in the line of eye and cheekbone, and his voice is deep and authoritative. He has a natural dignity of behaviour. But Alice isn't so sure this beauty extends to his soul. Nor are most other people. After all, Duke John has already claimed one throne, after taking as his second wife a disinherited princess of Castile. He likes to call himself 'We, the King of Castile' in his correspondence, and is always threatening to go and conquer Castile and win back his wife's country (at the expense of the English taxpayer). The suspicious way most people see it is this: would a prince who's so greedy for a crown that he'll go all that way in pursuit of one turn up his nose at the much more glorious Crown of England, if he got a chance to grab it? Of course he wouldn't.

The very fact that people are so ready to believe the worst of the Duke of Lancaster, with no proof one way or the other, shows what an unpopular man this John of Gaunt is. Not without reason, Alice knows. He's the scratchy kind. He rubs people up the wrong way, even when he doesn't mean to; and all too often he does mean to. Even among the aristocrats of this court, he's considered unusually arrogant; considering the competition, Alice thinks wryly, that's quite an achievement.

21

Certainly he's not loved among his social inferiors. He hates his father being so dependent on the merchants of London for money. To the merchants' pained displeasure, he talks too much about the nobility of the nobility and the crawling servility of the lesser orders. And merchants and noblemen alike now have an excuse to dislike and despise Duke John because, in the absence of his sick brother, he's been in charge of the English armies in France in this disastrous past year, so he's the one to carry the can for losing pretty much all of English Gascony and costing the country a mint of money. In fact, it's a good job the Duke's the richest man in England, with territories from the Scottish border to the South, because he has precious few friends anywhere, and if it weren't for his money, he'd have none at all.

John of Gaunt needs more than money. He needs to learn to be popular – especially if, as Alice thinks likely, he's one day going to have a try for the English crown. Alice's nose for money tells her that any king nowadays will need finance from outside his own estates. Rents aren't what they used to be, now that there are only half the number of Englishmen to farm the land and pay the landlords. The nobility is poorer. So the most important lesson the Duke needs to learn is how to get on with the London merchants, who are becoming as powerful as the merchant princes of Italy were right after the Mortality (until Edward bankrupted all of *them* with an earlier lot of colossal war debts). The top few merchants are richer than all the noblemen of England put together. Duke John's got to stop treating them like dirty sheep-shearing tinkerish no-good thieves. He's got to respect them as the financiers of today's England. And it's Alice's private belief that there's only one person who can teach him all that – who understands both court and City, and can explain it right. That person is her.

So Alice has dreamed up this week of glamorous frivolity, this (to her mind) insanely expensive joust in red and gold, with feasts every night for the court and wine flowing instead of water in the conduits of London for the commoners. The week is not so much in honour of the courtly love between swooning knights and the cruel ladies they're fighting to impress, which the tourney's officially supposed to celebrate; Alice has no time at all for the foolishness of chivalry. Nor is it just to amuse and entertain the court, or even to impress on the people of England her own royal-favoured status. What she really wants from it all is to help this man she would like to know better.

'We need to do something to take their minds off the war,' Edward said, back at New Year. He looked at her with his eyes dancing the way they always used to, with his lips and eyebrows slightly raised in a near-smile of expectation, with all his old confidence that the fire in him would communicate itself to her, and that she'd come up with some exuberant, extrovert, extraordinary idea, worthy of the King he was and the life they lived together. 'We need to stop them raging against John.'

She knew exactly how to answer. 'A pageant . . . a joust!' she murmured excitedly back, without a pause, with the golden delight that being with Edward has always brought her, with the sense that, when she's with him, she's breathing in air that tingles with stardust (or devilment – he'd probably prefer her to think of his magic as a bit satanic). 'We'll have a joust – we'll remind them of the glory of England in arms. They'll forget their gripes with my lord of Lancaster in no time, once they're drunk as drowned mice on free wine, watching the knights fight. It'll be all songs and glory talk instead.' He laughed at that. How handsome Edward is, still, when he throws his head back like that and laughs.

'It can't be too obvious,' she warned him. Edward's prone to getting carried away. Sometimes she has to remind him to be more subtle. 'It can't be too much about my lord. With the mood the people of London are in right now, they might not even come if they thought they were just going to have to applaud him for days at a stretch. So . . . we'll give it a theme, not about him at all. Something innocent . . . to do with love, maybe . . . and we'll give them free wine . . . And, on the second or third day of tourneying, he'll win his bout, once they're all in a mood to remember the might of England. And *that's* when everything will calm down.'

Edward accepted that, of course. It's Alice who, soon afterwards, thought of the spring sun-worshipping theme, and
the title of Lady of the Sun, and accepted the role for herself,
graciously, when Edward offered it; of course she did. She
doesn't care, especially, about the title. Titles, in her view,
are an encumbrance; they make you too visible; every jealous
nobody can take a pot-shot at you. Alice runs the royal
households everywhere from Windsor to Sheen to Havering-atte-
Bower, controlling the lives and purses of hundreds of
servants. She's so important that the Pope himself petitions
her for diplomatic favours. Yet in the entire five years since
Philippa died, she's never had any official court status beyond
the shadowy calling of demoiselle to a long-dead queen. She
doesn't altogether mind that, to this day, no one knows
whether to call her 'my lady,' or just 'Mistress Perrers'. But
this title is a piece of glorious frivolity. She'll enjoy it while
it lasts, just as she'll enjoy the wonderful robe and cloak
and cap she gets, worth a king's ransom. It never hurts to
take a gift, she thinks. And it never hurts to ask for a bit
more afterwards either.

It will be fun. It will all be beautifully organised (because
it's been organised by her). But the important thing in her
mind is that, by the end of this week, Alice is determined she
will have made the difficult Duke feel gratitude to her; she'll
have made John of Gaunt her friend.

Watching the heads, Alice's eyes light on Philippa Chaucer,
somehow managing to bring grace even to the saltarello. When
her heart does its usual nervous little leap at the sight of that
lovely, and too familiar, back, it reminds her that she hasn't
always been so phlegmatic about her position at court.

Alice smoothes the red folds of her robe over her knees,
remembering. She touches Edward's arm with a hand; she
leaves it trailing there, against his sleeve, so he can see her
fingers. They aren't particularly beautiful hands, hers – too
square and strong for a lady. How mortified she was, back
at the beginning (sitting very obediently at Queen Philippa's
feet, sewing her tiniest stitches, carefully watching every courtly

female in the room from under her lashes for fear of making a mistake), to realise that the two goddess-like demoiselles sitting on cushions beside her were whispering about her hands. 'Meat cleavers,' she made out, puzzling over the foreign words before she understood the sharp looks her way and sly hints of smiles. 'Wherryman's oars. Bear's paws. Don't you think?' Then, with dawning shame, 'Thick ankles, too . . .' She remembered her eyes widening as her insides turned over. One of them saw she was eavesdropping, and nudged the other, and they both quickly bent over their embroidery. Alice hadn't been there long enough at that stage to be sure which of the sisters was which. They were both blonde and long-limbed and apricot-skinned in that un-English Hainaulter way (Queen Philippa liked to surround herself with other people from the Low Countries). They were both self-assured with it, and so alike they might have been twins. Her first thought was to stick out her chin and make a fight of it with the pair of them. But she wasn't such a fool as that. She knew she didn't know how to fight here, yet. So she just sat on beside them, numb and prickling, fighting alternating desires to hide her shameful hands and to use them to give the smug, beautiful sisters a good slap round the face. She was burning with the slight. But she could feel herself absorbing it too. She thought: I'll bide my time, for now (though I'll get my own back later).

She was wrong to want to hide her hands, at least. She's learned that since. Her hands might not be as white and slender and long-fingered as Katherine or Philippa de Roët's, but they're young. Firm. Fresh-skinned. That's what Edward likes about them. He often holds her hands, even nowadays. He doesn't just hold them. He holds them up, and looks at them with eyes whose pale, pale blue is beginning to go cloudy, and strokes the skin. Alice's hands make him nostalgic.

But that isn't why she wants him to notice her hands tonight; why, next to him, she's fiddling and pleating so insistently at her robe or his sleeve. Or at least it's not the only reason. Perhaps the sight of Philippa de Roët's effortless beauty has made Alice feel insecure, and reminded her of the other small matter on her mind.

Even though Alice's robe is the most splendid in this hall, and has no doubt cost dozens of seamstresses the best of their eyesight to be finished in time, her fingers and wrists are bare.

She should have jewels all over her hands to match the thousands of seed pearls sewn in cloudy swirls all over the silk.

There's nothing glittering at her neck, either. And no jewels dressing her hair, just a thin glitter of gold thread from the caul net holding the dark waves in place under her cap.

It looks shocking to have nothing. Naked. Almost improper.

When Edward doesn't immediately look down at her bare hand, she moves it to cover his. Blue veins; knobbles; big brown freckles. But the face above them, still fine-boned and lean, is so handsome, so noble. He's still a god among men. Her King Arthur.

She's aware of the quizzical look on Edward's face. She thinks: He knows what I'm going to say.

He almost certainly does know what she's up to, and the favour she's going to ask. He's no fool, Edward. They play games about gifts: she begs, or he begs; she holds out, or he holds out. They both like bargaining. They're both fascinated by money. It's one of the things she likes about him.

'Do I look enough the Queen of the Sun in this, do you think?' she asks, raising the hand to his shoulder and running it down his arm with the beginning of sensuality. Edward smiles and shivers pleasurably, like an old cat lying in the sun having its tummy tickled. He's always ready to take pleasure where he finds it. From the floor, she's aware of the Duke of Lancaster's eyes boring into her too. She ignores him. Let him wait his turn. She says, 'My lord . . . truthfully now?'

Edward half smiles, with half-hooded eyes, and inclines his head forward. But he doesn't look at her hands, or her bare throat. 'You are a paragon of loveliness, *mon amour*,' he says, but she's aware of the distance creeping into his playfulness. 'More every day. Today especially. You'll astonish the world.'

'Even', she says delicately, 'without jewels?'

Edward doesn't sigh, quite. But he doesn't meet her eye, either. Less gently, he says, 'Dear girl, you have jewels. Your own jewels. A great many of them too.'

She says, 'But with this robe, Queen Philippa's rubies would be . . .'

Smiling over her head, and bowing to her without hearing her out, Edward rises to his feet. The Duke of Lancaster is on the dais and approaching the table.

'A fine performance, my boy,' Alice hears Edward boom at his son from over her head. He sounds relieved to have a way of ending this conversation with Alice. Yet the dead Queen's jewels aren't official royal gems, not part of the treasury, just Queen Philippa's private collection of trinkets. There's no real reason of state why Edward shouldn't let Alice, or any other commoner, mistress, favourite, or friend, use them. Alice used to have to clean them. It was part of her job as demoiselle, back in the day. She held them up to the light, dreaming. She tried them on. She knows them all. So she keeps nagging him about them, even on the days, like today, when it clearly irritates him. One day, she thinks, without particular rancour, he just might give in – because, after all, why shouldn't she wear them? She's doing the work of a queen, so why shouldn't she have the reward? What good are they doing anyone in their boxes?

She knows, really, why he's reluctant. Edward wants to keep a part of himself, and his memories, separate from her; he wants a place he can remember the big silvery-blonde Queen he loved for so long. He doesn't want another woman wearing Philippa's trinkets. She respects that; she really does. But she can't help herself. It's not in her nature not to ask for more.

'. . . the rubies would be so perfect . . .' Alice finishes, disconsolately. Her voice trails away. There's no point. Neither of the men is listening.

'You're taking a chance, aren't you?' Duke John says with slightly rough familiarity, as they step close in the column of couples. Alice doesn't mind dancing, if it's the stately, dignified basse dance, and if it's with him. They've talked privately before; she's spent many a Christmas with Edward and his family. Her estate at Wendover, north of London, is close to part of the Duke's Lancastrian territory; so they're neighbours. But he's never made a public point like this of acknowledging her before. With him at her side, she doesn't even mind entering the crowd of courtiers who are just a little too impressed by their own noble lineage to enjoy meeting her eye, even though she can see the de Roët women in the line of dancers, and they're both still as terrifyingly lovely as ever. Ah, who cares? she tells herself, suddenly gay. I'm having a better life than either of them. Katherine's now the widow Swynford, with a little estate somewhere up in Lincolnshire and several children running wild. And Philippa's married to one of Edward's esquires, that clever little elf Chaucer, though no one thinks they're happy; she scuttled straight back to work with the Duchess of Lancaster, mean Castilian ladies-in-waiting and all, after both her babies, as if nothing would persuade her to stay home with her husband. They'd probably both rather be in my shoes, Alice thinks.

'My lord?' Alice replies, too innocently. 'What do you mean, taking a chance?'

The Duke of Lancaster steps back in time with the lilting twelve-quaver beat, but with an interested look that suggests the conversation isn't over. A second later, as they lean together again, he goes on, glancing down at her finery: 'Your robe is almost exactly the same as the Princess of England's at Christmas . . . as I'm sure you realise,' and gives her a challenging smile with one eyebrow raised.

Of course I realise, she thinks patiently. I had Princess Joan's dress copied, didn't I? And I did it so you'd notice, didn't I? The Princess never showed herself at a public court dinner at Christmas; she only attended family occasions. So no one outside the royal family will have seen it. And Edward's eyes are failing; he never notices the colour of robes any more. It's a joke for the two of us to share. We're supposed to draw closer, and wink, and enjoy ourselves watching each other enjoying ourselves poking a bit of fun at the Princess, and then you're supposed to think: Why, Alice Perrers, you and I, we're kindred spirits. Two peas in a pod.

But that's not what she says. She just flirts. She lifts her eyebrows and flashes him a smile that's all teeth and daring. Demurely, she says, 'No one else has mentioned a resemblance.' Then she turns the corners of her lips up again.

She's rewarded by a deep snort of scandalised laughter. She's got his attention, all right. He's shaking his head as he goes through the dance step, looking half-disapproving, but half-amused too.

'What will you do if she turns up?' he says. He sounds serious, but she can see that the corners of his lips, like the corners of hers, can't quite stay down.

Alice knows John of Gaunt is said to love his much older sister-in-law and brother, and be sad that, in the past few years, since the Prince's illness, they've gone cold on him. It's obvious to everyone they're scared he's going to wait till his brother's dead, then try and steal the throne from the little boy; but perhaps it isn't obvious to him. People say he misses them. Probably, knowing what a stickler he is for the old ways, the old respect, no one's ever tried lightening his feelings about losing his brother's family's affection by sending that old trout of a Princess Joan up, just a bit.

Alice thinks: I won't let myself be rattled by the idea of Princess Joan coming here. Serenely, she replies, 'Why would she?'

It's unanswerable. They both know Joan of Kent will stay home on her side of the river, in Kennington, with her dropsy-ridden hulk of a husband and her mewling, puking seven-year-old. She was once a beauty, Joan of Kent. They even say she was Edward's mistress, long ago, before she married his son, though Edward's never breathed a word of any such thing to Alice. But Joan certainly isn't the most beautiful woman in England any more, hasn't been for years – certainly not since Alice first clapped eyes on her. She wasn't a beauty any more even in her thirties, when she scandalised Christendom by taking for her third husband her royal cousin – a childhood playmate – in the obvious hope of getting a crown when he became king. And she's fat and forty-five now, and the violet eyes poets wrote about long ago are puffy and mean. She's hardly ever at court.

Alice thinks: She calls me a gold-digger, but what's she? She might be a king's granddaughter, but when it comes down to it, really, she's nothing better than an old, failed gold-digger herself. Fortune has swung Joan up on her wheel, all right, to the dizzying heights of power, but she's swung it down again too, and it's all but destroyed her, poor old thing.

Whereas Alice . . . Alice sometimes feels the wind rushing through her head as she flies upwards through the golden clouds. And the last thing Alice thinks Joan will want to see is a younger woman lording it there in her place – succeeding where Joan failed – especially a younger woman she's made a point of snubbing for so many years.

John of Gaunt's eyes are fixed on Alice. She's intrigued him beyond measure with this little display of insouciance, she sees. She knows it's often the men who talk loudest about respect for the old ways who are most nervous of anything new. But she hasn't expected, until now, to feel timidity behind this man's arrogance. Hearing the music about to reach its final chord, she adds, quickly, almost comfortingly, '. . . so don't worry.'

It would be a mistake to linger after that. But she enjoys the flash of discomfiture in his eyes as she bows and retreats to the dais. She doesn't think her impudence has put him off. She can feel, from the way his eyes are following her across the floor, that he'll be back for more.

By the time it's fully dark, Alice has completely forgotten she wasn't planning to dance. With fresh breezes coming in from the river, and Edward smiling dreamily down at her to the thin skirl of lute and dulcimer, and the stout guardsmen in a living ring of fire around the edge of the hall, each man's feet planted a yard apart on the stone floor, each strong pair of arms holding a torch, a kind of careless magic enters the air.

She's laughing and as pink as the rest of them, skipping in and out of the great wavering round of the carole, even clapping whole-heartedly as that born dancer Katherine Swynford does an especially complicated response to the Duke of Lancaster's advance without losing her poise for a second, and the throng pauses and catches breath so everyone can admire the lovely young widow's skill.

Alice's vis-à-vis at that moment is Philippa de Roët's merry-eyed little husband. She's always rather liked him. He's not from the nobility originally either. His father was a City magnate, a vintner, and she senses, in his slightly mocking smile, that sometimes he might find the endless tempers and savage pride of the courtiers as limiting as she does. He's mopping his brow now and saying hazy but appreciative things of his sister-in-law: 'Terpsichore . . . wouldn't you say? The Muse of the dance . . . it's a divine gift, to dance that well . . . as my own dear wife does too, and' – hastily he twinkles at her, and bows – 'your good self, of course, madame.' Alice bows back. Master Chaucer tails off, in amusing mock-wistfulness: 'Alas . . . if only I had the same gift . . .'

It doesn't for a moment occur to Alice to wonder what the muffled tramp of feet outside, the horns and flutes, might signify.

It's only when the already relaxed line of dancers wavers and breaks up, and, unaccountably, the crowd falls silent, like a group of animals at the approach of a predator, that Alice feels danger.

By then it's too late.

With prickles at her spine, she turns.

Behind her, on the dais, Edward is on his feet, his grey beard streaming down his front, his mouth open. He looks old and dazed. His eyes are fixed on the door.

Through it, walking away from the little troop of musicians and soldiers and rowers she's arrived with, and down the step straight towards Alice, in the middle of the crowded hall, the Princess of England is stumping.

Joan of Kent is carrying a jewelled goblet of wine that a servant must have hastily pressed into her hand. She isn't taking any notice of it.

She's wearing her own red taffeta Christmas robe – just like Alice's, down to the pattern of the seed pearls.

And she's staring at the younger woman with empty, frightening eyes.

The courtiers close quietly in as the two would-be queens, in their identical reds, come face to face. The expression on Joan of Kent's face is that of a woman looking at her reflection in the mirror and hating it. Alice, who's felt the dread start to wash through her at the sight of the Princess, like cold dirty riverwater, senses their suppressed excitement.

They want a fight, she thinks. They want to see me humiliated.

She clutches at the defiance this realisation brings with it. She needs the anger.

Brightly, she smiles, bows a deep bow, and says, in a loud enough voice for half the court to hear, 'The Lady of the Sun welcomes you, madame. I am delighted you were able to honour us with your presence . . .'

Instead of edging back, as every instinct in her body is telling her to, she steps confidently forward, with a gracious hand outstretched towards the bulging silk of the Princess of England's upper arm.

No one breathes. Now Joan will have to answer with a grated politesse of her own – at least, she would if she were minded to recognise Alice as a noblewoman like herself.

The silence continues for an unbearable moment.

Joan doesn't bother with politesses, grated or otherwise. She rasps out one phrase. 'You're wearing my robe.'

There's a little intake of breath. Alice is painfully aware of Edward's eyes on her, from behind. Even he can't help her now. She'll have to deal with it herself.

If Joan's going to insult her, there's no telling how far she might go. Last year at Council, Joan's husband had so lost his temper with the Archbishop of Canterbury, whom he suspected of preferring to obey the Pope than his King, that he'd yelled at the trembling prelate, in front of dozens of noblemen, 'ANSWER, DONKEY!'

Alice squares her shoulders to stop them shaking. She's not going to cut a pitiful figure like the poor Archbishop, whatever the Princess does. Not being frightened, that's the key thing. She learned that years ago. Never show fear.

Bravely, she grins. Looking round to catch Edward's eye,

and draw him, from the dais, into this nightmarish conversation, she quips, brightly, perhaps too brightly: 'Well, you know what they say. There's never a new fashion but it's old.'

Breaths are sucked in.

She waits, hardly daring to breathe herself.

At last, there's a scared eddy of laughter. Alice senses the mood move, the support beginning to flow her way. She sees Edward shake his head in delight, and chuckle. You could always trust Alice to find a good line.

The danger's past now, Alice tells herself, breathing easier. A laugh always eases things. Forcing herself forward again, she begins, with all the grace and charm she can muster: 'My lady, allow me to . . .'

But before she can touch the Princess's sleeve, so tightly packed with coldly furious flesh around taut muscle that the seams are straining, Joan pulls back her arm.

The older woman looks down, almost in surprise, at the jewelled goblet in her hand.

Then she jerks it forward.

At first, Alice feels the cold shock that comes next as just more of the dread and humiliation that swept through her a moment ago, when she first saw the Princess bearing down on her.

Then she realises there actually is dark liquid on her face and running down her front. Her eyes are stinging from it. She can't see.

There's wine all over her.

Alice blinks and breathes, and the claret drips down her hair. Her whole head is wet. She can't move, even her eyes. She can't look down and see how badly the robe is damaged. She's trying to control the surges of humiliation – and rage – rushing through her, the hot and cold of them.

Perhaps the Princess knows she's gone too far. She goes on standing opposite Alice with the goblet in her hand. There's no expression on her face.

Alice goes on standing there too, blinking wine out of her face. After a while, she puts a hand to her sopping wet face and brushes a purplish strand of hair out of her eye. She knows there's nothing she can do that won't be too angry for court. She can only breathe, and blink, and wait for someone else to take the initiative.

Surely this is an insult to the King, as well as to her? Surely someone in this crowd of self-willed, self-regarding donkeys will defend his honour at least?

But it seems no one, even the King, knows what to do.

Until, after what seems an eternity, a completely unexpected voice pipes up, a nasal-ish, confiding, friendly little male voice, followed by Geoffrey Chaucer, stepping out from behind the Princess. 'A thousand pardons. A *thousand* pardons! How could I have been so clumsy? I jogged your elbow, Madame d'Angleterre. There was nothing you could do, nothing at all.'

He's wringing his hands, and bowing his head over them, and twinkling at the Princess, his slightly thin voice so apologetic, so charming, that the court can't help but laugh. He has beautiful eyes, and when his face is animated, dancing with wit and intelligence, as it often is, he becomes handsome. Even Joan, who is perhaps almost as shocked by her transgression as Alice, softens as she looks at him, and almost smiles.

'*Utterly* my fault; *utterly*. Amends, how to make them? A pilgrimage . . . to Jerusalem? No, what good would that be? . . . To Venice, for more silk, to replace your damaged robe, Madame Perrers, to the cloth fairs?'

Alice wipes her hand across her eyes again. She stares through her tangle of wine-dark hair. How has he done it? The little valet has them all laughing, and joining in his cloth-buying fantasy, and forgetting the anger. It's like a miracle. Of course there's no way on earth or in Heaven that Geoffrey Chaucer could ever afford the cloth on the back of Alice Perrers, not on his ten-pound-a-year pension and free pitcher of wine a day, but then it's obviously only a turn of phrase. There's no need for him to worry particularly. Chaucer can say what he likes. He'll never be called to carry out the pilgrimage he's promising. This is pure face-saving improvisation – and a successful improvisation too. Even through the alcohol,

34

Alice can see that the King is grateful to his man for drawing the sting out of the occasion.

Edward steps urbanely forward, bows to Chaucer, and draws his still glowering daughter-in-law up to the dais and out of trouble.

The crowd moves, relaxes and begins to talk (though no one rushes to meet Alice's eye still). The fairy ring at the centre of the hall around her vanishes. The music starts again.

For a moment, Alice doesn't know what to do. It is the Duke of Lancaster who steps up to her, very straight-backed, very long-nosed and serious, to offer her a very white kerchief, with which he dabs away the last of the wine, and then his hand, for the next dance. He's helping her restore appearances, as is proper. Behind his correctness, she sees sympathy in his eyes, and hears it in his voice.

'Joan can be . . .' he begins, as he turns her into the dance. 'Sometimes . . .' But his voice dries up. He's a nobleman, not the type to wink and shrug and laugh things off, she remembers. He's here with her in homage to her gallantry; but all the same, he can't quite bring himself to be verbally disloyal to his sister-in-law.

She nods, so choked with gratitude that, for once, she's also unable to speak. She hasn't expected it to happen like this, but she can sense new beginnings. When she passes Geoffrey Chaucer, she's recovered her poise enough to be able to incline her head and smile. With sparkling eyes, he bows back. And he winks.

'Why did you do that?' Philippa Chaucer asks her husband curiously, materialising through the crowd and taking his arm. Geoffrey tries not to show surprise. His wife doesn't usually stand with him in public. He once heard her say she was embarrassed to have to bend down so low to find his ear to whisper sweet nothings into. It was one of those comments, made sotto voce to her sister over the tapestry, which had, perhaps accidentally, come out just a little too loud.

With all the charm in his armoury, he turns to her, opening his shoulders in an easy-going shrug. 'Oh . . .' he begins non-committally. 'You know . . .' Then he pauses, struck by the fact that he doesn't really know. It's ended well, thank God, but it was obviously insane to risk turning the Princess of England's rage on himself.

It's not even as if he knows Alice Perrers, especially. She's just one of those people who's always been around, at court, pretty much from the time he first came, at nineteen or twenty; he remembers her as rather younger than him, and not from a grand family, one of the waifs the old Queen used to appoint, on a whim, to be snubbed for the rest of their lives by the real nobility. She's always looked a bit mischievous, though, as if it was never going to get her down that much. He's always liked that in her. There's a spark in her pale blue eyes; something that lifts her looks – rounded little limbs, pale skin, curly black hair that often escapes from its headdress – into occasional beauty. Chaucer remembers a younger Alice sitting next to Jean Froissart in church, and whispering something quiet that made the Queen's boyish chronicler (another of those whimsical royal appointments) curl up and snort and rock with laughter, and then looking utterly composed while poor little Froissart desperately tried to control his shaking curls and heaving sides. That sort of thing was probably what made the Queen take Alice on for a bit when the Duke of Lancaster got one of her established demoiselles pregnant. The Queen, God rest her lovely soul, always loved laughter. And being able to make people laugh probably helped Alice cling on afterwards, Chaucer thinks, even though it was obvious she'd never have the instincts of nobility. She's tough. She survived until the King got a soft spot for her, even though the things Chaucer's Philippa said about her, with her sister, both of them looking at each other with those half-closed eyes, like two cats, full of the utter disdain of the born aristocrat for outsiders, which must have been the same sorts of things that other people were saying, were always so unkind . . .

Well, Geoffrey Chaucer thinks ruefully to himself, recalling moments when Philippa has given him that cat look too, and, raising her long and beautiful nose, referred to his own family's background in less than flattering terms. Perhaps *that*'s why. 'I was just easing things along,' he tells his wife quietly.

She half closes her eyes. She half smiles. 'Feeling sorry for the whore,' she says, and though there's no obvious cruelty in her voice he feels belittled by the very gentleness of her contempt. She wafts away.

Geoffrey Chaucer goes on standing there, while the courtiers talk around him, louder and louder. He does know, after all, why he intervened. He felt sorry for Alice Perrers, standing all alone with wine dripping down her face and off her hair, and her shoulders shaking, with that bullying old brute glaring at her as if she wished her dead, and a crowd gathered round staring as if they were at the bear-pit, hoping for blood. You could have all the jaunty courage in the world, and still it would do you no good if no one stood up for you.

TWO

Loyalty, Alice thinks, from her chariot, with its burning hot metallic sides. She's turning her head graciously from side to side. She's ignoring the low mutters from the crowd, and the heat. It's almost like the old days, this spring heat, when she was young, before the weather went so cold, with the skies always lowering, the winters piled with snow, the summers passing in fitful grey. Yes, loyalty's what counts. You stand by the people you've got. You help those who help you.

Chaucer's face keeps swimming into her head, mixed up with fleeting pictures of other people to whom she's had debts of gratitude, whom she's seen right. Her last glance back at the hall last night, when she saw Philippa Chaucer stalk up to her husband and start questioning him, and him politely waving her away – clearly refusing an invitation to gossip about Alice – has only confirmed the warmth she feels. She owes him. He won't regret it.

The procession is passing out of Cripplegate to an especially deafening burst of horns, leaving the worst of the crowds behind. Alice has been focusing her mind on something pleasant she can do for someone, because she hasn't enjoyed her ride through the City one bit as much as she'd expected. The crowd of burghers has been as hostile as any crowd might be on seeing one of its own elevated beyond what Londoners think is her rightful place. She's seen the angry eyes, the men being muscled back from around the chariot by the sergeants-at-arms, the gob of wet landing on the side of the carriage, too close for comfort. She's heard the low hissing, the mutters. Her golden sun-chariot is so low that she's even made out some of the words. Not just the usual perfunctory unpleasantness due any rich nobleman's mistress: 'whore' and 'slack-legs'. Today it's all been angrier and more heartfelt. 'Grave-robber', she's heard; and 'spend-thrift', and 'Lady of the bleeding Night', and 'robbing the poor old King blind'.

Thank God it's over, she thinks. She won't bother with titles again.

Alice looks ahead to the tussocky ground stretching away towards the hill hamlets of Islington and Sadler's Wells. In front of her is glitter and haze: the draperies, the scaffold for the ladies, the reds and golds, the elegantly dressed crowd of waiting gentry and nobility. Behind her, London: the walls of the Priory and Hospital of St Bartholomew and, further back, behind Cripplegate (where, now the citizens' noise is more distant, she can hear the anxious lowing of the cows, moved for the week from their usual pre-slaughter pasture over here at the flat western end of the field), the two vast grave pits dug during the Mortality. Wherever you are, there's no escaping reminders of the Mortality.

But it doesn't trouble her. She's not going to let anything trouble her. The thought of those grave pits only reminds her of her first conversation with Edward, and makes her smile. It seems so long ago, that day, back when she was a girl, even before the Queen had taken her in, sitting on a stool, pretending to be absorbed in needlework, cautiously eavesdropping on him and William of Windsor talking. She was admiring the calm way that handsome, grizzled William of Windsor addressed the monarch, with no sign his heart must be beating faster and his tongue cleaving to the roof of his mouth out of sheer awe at the presence of God's Anointed. She heard William of Windsor say something about the Mortality, one of those pious commonplaces people uttered all the time while she was growing up: God's retribution on the Race of Adam, a curse on sin, some such.

Before she knew what she was doing, Alice remembers, she

found her mouth open and herself piping up, pert as anything: 'Well, it wasn't sent to kill *me*. I was born right in the teeth of it, and I survived,' and she was grinning up at the pair of them, flashing her teeth, all bravado. Then, suddenly realising what she'd done by interrupting the King's conversation, she stopped in terror. Both men were staring curiously at her. She sensed William of Windsor's wide-open eyes were a signal to stop. But she pushed on. Nothing ventured, nothing gained, she told herself. Seize the day. She put the grin back on her face, but she could hear her voice shake a little as she continued, with a smile: '. . . and I've lived to tell the tale through another bout of it, too . . . as we all have, with God's grace. Who's afraid of the Mortality?'

She very nearly went on to say the next things old Aunty Alison always used to say whenever she scoffed at the plague, back at Aunty's kiln where Alice grew up. 'It's an ill wind that blows nobody any good,' that hard old voice echoed in her head. 'God's curse for some; God's blessing for others. So many people gone, but we're still here, thank God, and they left it all behind for us, didn't they? Just waiting to be picked up. The streets are paved with gold, if you only know where to look. Fortunes to be made, a king's ransom many times over. All just waiting for anyone with a head on their shoulders to come along and take it.' But fear overcame her again. She gulped and stopped. Then there was a long pause, during which Alice wished the earth would open and swallow her.

She'd always remember the way Edward's eyes, eventually, softened and his great golden mane started to shake as he laughed. 'Then you must be one of the very few of my subjects to be so blessed by God, little miss,' he said, and his great lustrous eyes sparkled at her until she felt warm all over. He added, with a laugh that included her, 'Or by the Devil, of course, who knows?' and the look in his eyes told her she was allowed to laugh too. In the quietness that followed, he leaned forward, saying, very casually, yet with great courtliness, 'Tell me, to whom do I have the honour . . .?'

She was so lucky in that first conversation with Edward.

At the time, she had no idea that Edward chafed as much

as she did at the notion that the Mortality was divine punishment, and that there was nothing to do but lie down and die
when it struck. Later she found out that the King of England
had lost two children to the sickness himself – in that first
bout of it, about when she, Alice, was born. But Edward was
so reluctant to stay shut away from the world that, after a
fretful winter in the relative safety of Oxford and King's
Langley, he came out at the height of the plague. That April,
on St George's Day, he forced hundreds of terrified knights
to risk their lives coming together at his new castle at Windsor,
for the first great meeting, at the giant Round Table he'd had
built in homage to King Arthur, of the Order of the Garter.
Edward prides himself on defying death. (Later still, once
Alice and Edward were close enough for whispering, he
laughed ticklishly in her ear with his story about how his
ancestor, Count Fulke the Black, had married the daughter of
the Devil, and about Countess Melusine shrieking and flying
out through a window of the chapel, never to be seen again,
when she'd been forced to go to Mass. Alice could see he
very nearly believed he was descended from the Devil. It
explained so much about his devil-may-care bravery, and about
his luck, too. The King's wind, they used to call it, the wind
that blew him straight to France, and victory, every time he
set sail across the Channel.) Of course he liked her death-
defying talk, right from the start.

The chariot's struggling over wooden planks to a platform.

Alice gathers the folds of her robe as the door opens. She
can see Edward waiting for her on the dais, smiling in the
distance. But Duke John is closer, on horseback, right behind
her in the train of noblemen. To her pleasure, it's he who
dismounts and, taking the place of the groom, comes to her
door to hand her down.

'Jewels,' her new friend says in her ear, with the beginnings
of a smile and the beginnings of a compliment. 'Beautiful
ones, too.' Then, in a different voice, looking suddenly taken
aback: 'Oh . . . but . . . isn't that my mother's necklace?'

'Yes . . . your father got it out for me last night,' Alice replies,
feeling slightly apologetic all of a sudden, but trying not to

41

sound it. His mother's jewels – perhaps she should have thought? But it only takes a moment for blessed defiance to come back to her. She's not stealing the jewels, for God's sake, she tells herself. His mother's been dead for years. Why shouldn't she enjoy them? 'And the other rubies. The rings . . . the bracelets . . .' She can't stop herself stretching out her right hand as she says the words.

'By way of an apology,' she adds, when the Duke still doesn't say anything.

How anxious Edward looked, at the end of last evening, with the noise of the dance still going on below, when he came to her, with a sleepy scrivener trying to suppress a yawn bobbing respectfully in his wake. 'I regret . . .' He stumbled over the words, clinging to her hand, as if he feared she might vanish, like the Countess Melusine, leaving him cold and lonely in his last days. 'I very much regret . . . a spirited woman, Joan. Too spirited at times.' He paused. She waited. No point forgiving too fast. After a second, he thrust the letter at her: an order to Euphemia, another ex-demoiselle and now wife to Sir Walter de Heselarton, Knight, who's lodged somewhere here too, that 'the said Euphemia is to deliver the rubies in her keeping to the said Alice on the receipt of this our command'. Alice looked up, only half believing the words dancing on the page, straight into those pale old eyes fixed on hers, mournful, humble, imploring as a dog's, begging for forgiveness.

She blurted, 'You're giving me the jewels? Really?' This man loves me, Alice Perrers, she thought, with a sunburst of gratitude, trying not to notice the slack skin or lean neck or liver spots. His love has made me what I am.

'Oh, only the rubies,' Edward replied quickly, playful again, smiling with relief, but still not giving too much away. (This is why Edward's been so good at making common ground with the merchants, she knows; because he enjoys haggling as much as they do, as much as she does. He will do till his dying day.) Forgetting the old-man's skin, looking into his laughing, knowing eyes, she put her arms around him. 'Only the rubies, my dear,' he repeated, and kissed her.

That's what she should be teaching this Duke, who hasn't had to have dealings with merchants, who as a younger son has been left for longer in the sunlit playground of chivalry and pageantry in which princes once existed, who hasn't had occasion to think about the realities of modern life. He'll need to now, if he's going to make his play for power. He'll have to learn. Drop the ceremonials. No one owes you everything, just because of your noble blood. Pay your way into alliances, if you need those alliances. Do what you need to do. Learn to see things for what they are.

But he's silent, still; perhaps he's taken some terrible princely offence at humble Alice touching his mother's jewels? Perhaps he's too stiff-necked ever to change?

She tries again. She murmurs, with a hint of a twinkle, 'I think your father chose the rubies for the colour of the wine.'

At last, he seems to decide it's all right. He nods, and smiles straight into her eyes. 'They suit you,' he says after a moment, making her a dignified bow, and, after another pause, as if he's looking for the right phrase, full enough of gentillesse: 'She behaved badly. My father did right. I'd have done the same myself.'

Arm in arm, they begin stepping cautiously towards Edward. There's a warmth inside Alice, and it's not just from the lean warmth of the arm in hers.

'Did you enjoy the ride through London?' she hears him murmur politely at her side. Perhaps he's curious. He must have heard the Londoners muttering, too, from where he was, right behind her in the procession.

She nods, as nobly as she can. Hardly thinking, she replies, 'Of course.' Then she stops. If they're to be allies, she should learn to be as honest with him as she'll expect him to be with her. So she dimples up at him and flutters her free hand. 'Well, no . . . to tell the truth, I didn't, really,' she admits candidly. 'They didn't like me much as Lady of the Sun, those Londoners, did they?'

He actually shivers. It's not just for her benefit; his revulsion for the common people of London, tramps, pedlars, fishwives, and the richest merchants in the land alike, shudders right through him, something he feels in every inch of his body and doesn't mind her knowing. 'Terrible people,' he says. His voice is tight. 'Howling like that, at a royal procession, the savages. They should be taught a lesson. Brought under control . . . flogged.'

God be with them all, she thinks, suddenly buoyant again (though she does appreciate the Duke's sympathy). They're right, in a way, those Londoners; she agrees, she shouldn't be out here pretending to be Queen Philippa and Princess Joan rolled into one scarlet silk package. She was asking to be called grave-robber, wearing the Queen's necklace out here. She won't do it again, because she enjoys London. She likes the way the London merchants work: cautiously, by consensus and committee; and purposefully, without the empty showing-off of the court. She shouldn't forget that. She won't next time. She's learned her lesson.

So she shrugs, and grins invitingly, twisting her head sideways like a bird on a bush to include him in her merriment. 'Oh, I don't know,' she differs blithely. 'They're often right, in London. I probably *should* have kept a lower profile. Anyway, they're so good at what they do – making money that can help you. You have to forgive them their outspokenness if only for that, don't you?'

'I can't be doing with them,' he mutters, shaking his head. There's a stubborn look in his eyes, but she now thinks she sees – what, bewilderment? Interest? there too. 'Who do they think they are?'

She murmurs enticingly back: '. . . though London, and its wealth, could be a great support to you, if you could only learn to accept the way the Londoners are.' He turns his eyes to her. He wants to know, she sees. He just doesn't want to admit it. She whispers, 'I could show you how.'

He's definitely interested now. He stops walking. So does she.

'How?' he says, though he can't keep the scepticism out of his voice. 'They don't like me, any more than I like them.'

The idea comes on her like a flash of lightning; she hears the words drop from her lips even as she's thinking it. 'That's because you need some good men who are loyal to you in the big London jobs,' she replies quickly. 'Londoners spend so much time talking to each other, and so much time listening. You need a talker inside the walls, who can influence them; someone who can quietly show them things from your point of view.'

This is how to repay the debt of honour she incurred last night. She's breathless with the cleverness of it. She's thinking of the vacant job checking that Londoners aren't skimping on their payments of wool tax, England's biggest export. It's the most important government job in the City, requiring diplomacy, financial know-how and intimate knowledge of both merchant and court life.

'For instance,' she goes on, startling even herself, 'You need a man you can trust in the wool comptroller's post.' She tightens her grip on the Duke's arm. 'And I know who.'

THREE

Master Geoffrey Chaucer, newly appointed Comptroller of
the Customs and Subsidy on Wool, Sheepskins and Leather
for the Port of London, can tell from the stillness and the
shimmer on the water that it's going to be another hot
June day.

He's early. It's not yet properly light. But then he's nervous.

Any minute now he'll be joined on the jetty at Westminster
by his companions for his first day in his new job – an old
friend and a new. Meanwhile, all he can do is wait and listen
to the bells ring for Lauds behind him in the royal village.

Soon, he knows, there'll be pandemonium at the palace.
All the servants will be up, running around, sweeping, carrying
pails and boxes and bags and piles in and out of every imaginable gate and doorway, feeding horses or killing fowl for the
table, smelling the bread smells rising from the ovens. The
King's court is to move to Sheen in a day or two, now that
the mystery plays and celebrations of Corpus Christi are over.
By St John's Eve, not a fortnight hence, it'll be off again,
having eaten its many-headed way through the local food
supplies, for a midsummer interlude at Havering-atte-Bower.
Chaucer's always liked the peace of Havering. He pulls his
robe around his shoulders and steps on to the jetty, wishing
he could feel more whole-heartedly happy to be leaving behind
that brightly coloured wandering life.

It seems no time at all since Alice Perrers materialised beside him at one of the masques she so energetically organised for her week of spring festivities (one in which the players on the Passion wagon were re-enacting a Crusade, with piercing cries and dramatically flowing crimson blood and a real fire engulfing the mock-castle as Saladin dropped writhing to his death. An incongruous background for conversation, he remembers thinking). She slipped a confiding arm through his, and whispered, with her eyes all persuasively lit up, that the King was minded to give him high Crown office in the City, if he was minded to accept . . .?

He couldn't believe it at first. This is what Philippa most chides him for – failing to seek out preferment – and here it was coming at him without his even trying, in the person of the King's favourite, this chirpy little barrel of fire, who was holding on to his arm and grinning slyly up at him as if they were old friends sharing some tremendous joke.

But going back to the City – even to do this responsible job, which will certainly earn him the King's favour if he's successful – seems in so many ways like a step back into his past that it's thrown him into inner turmoil. This turmoil has gone with him through every one of the meetings with government officials that Alice Perrers has been whisking him through in the past few weeks. Every imagining he has of a future waking up to the cries of the City's streets, and walking through those too-familiar lanes to a job among men he knew as a child, is accompanied by a prickly cloud of difficult memories of the other life he's become accustomed to, these past twenty years.

He might see more of Philippa if he's to be in London all the time – and Alice Perrers has made plain he will be expected to be at his desk at the Customs House every day, checking the merchants' accounts. Philippa's Castilian mistress, the wife of the Duke of Lancaster, likes her long stays at the Savoy (and who wouldn't? Chaucer thinks, as the memories of those bright avenues and splendid halls fill his mind – another soft little knife in his side, another bittersweet sigh). The Lancastrian palace on the Strand, where Philippa spends so much of her time working as demoiselle to the Duchess, is only a boat ride away. Now, seeing Philippa is a mixed blessing at the best of times, but what most concerns Chaucer is that he might also have more time with his children, if he's always in London, than he has while he's been attached to the King's court, as one of thirty esquires kept at my lord's side to be quietly useful, plunging up and down the land on that endless crusade of cushions and silver-gilt cups, not necessarily going the same way, at the same time, as the Duke and Duchess of Lancaster's court, or seeing nearly enough of little Thomas and Elizabeth.

That's a good part of what's made his eyes glitter at the prospect of this new job. What has made Philippa's eyes glitter is learning of the extra pension he'll be getting now for the Customs post, added to the ones the Duke of Lancaster (a better master by far than the tricky old King when it comes to payment) has already secured for both of them for their service to various members of the royal family. Between them, their income will now add up to nearly sixty pounds a year. For the first time, they'll be comfortable by anyone's reckoning. Philippa knows, of course, that she'll be expected to do a little visible wifely duty in return – attending City dinners with him, from time to time, that sort of thing. But he knows her, and her suspicion of merchant ways, too well to expect that she'll do more than the bare minimum. Still, he must be grateful. She's told him, gently enough, that although she won't live with him in the City (he couldn't expect her to give up her life at court for merchants, after all) and she won't hear of Thomas being taken away from court where he does lessons with the Duke of Lancaster's daughters, and being sent instead to St Paul's almonry school in the shadow of the cathedral, to mix with the sons of merchants, (which is where Geoffrey Chaucer got *his* book-learning), she and the children will, at least, spend holidays with him in London. At least sometimes. He's almost sure she'll keep her word. At least, she will if she isn't in a mood, as she too often is, to whisper to the children that their maternal de Roët blood is nobler than their father's, and to have her own coat of arms, not his, embroidered on their clothes.

Geoffrey Chaucer sighs. There's no point in false optimism. He knows that really. She's turned the children against him. More and more, he can see she has. All his absences, all his eager plans to win rewards from the King for his subtle negotiating, have left the children alone with their mother for too long, and Chaucer has come to realise he can't trust her to represent him fairly to them while he's gone. 'You're only nine,' he said to Thomas, when he first noticed that the boy had displayed on his thin chest the three golden Catherine wheels on a red background which Philippa and her sister wear. 'Too young to make decisions like this.' Then he became aware of the plaintive whininess of his voice. Too late, he saw the boy's eyes glaze over with watchful distance and the beginning of boredom. Trying to make a joke of it, Chaucer added, with a miserable attempt at a smile, 'After all, you'll have to get all your clothes reworked if they make me a baron and you start wanting my arms. Think of the expense.'

The boy only blinked his wise blue eyes and said, more dispassionately than Chaucer would have liked, 'Well, let's worry about that if it happens.' Chaucer winces when he remembers the unbearable kindness in the touch of the boy's hand on his arm.

Still, the City's close to the Savoy. That's something to remember. And he's on the path to favour, as it seems he hasn't been till now, despite all those foreign missions for the King that haven't got him anywhere near the state of worldly glory Philippa craves for him. He has to cling to the hope that this will turn out well, and that he might, in the end, make his children proud of their father.

Footsteps. At last.

He turns round with his most gracious smile. He bows, low, as his new friend, Baron Latimer, would expect of a fellow-courtier. It's a practised gesture, but also a sincere one. He's grateful to Latimer, and wants to do him honour. Latimer – the King's chamberlain, an important man, with a glorious war record in France and fingers in every government pie – must have much else on his mind, apart from the well-being of one Master Geoffrey Chaucer, *valettus*. Yet the leathery-faced old baron is making this transition of Chaucer's back to City life so painless that it often seems to the dazzled Chaucer that this is not the case. Latimer's shown no impatience, however many times Alice Perrers has dragged Chaucer in for another briefing. He's sat Chaucer down with him. He's shown him documents. He's explained the intricacies of wool taxation. He's performed introductions. And every act has been performed with exquisite courtesy; charm enough to make Chaucer nearly weep with gratitude.

So Chaucer's glad Latimer's coming today, to introduce him to the merchants in power in the City and settle him into his new role. He's also glad, in a different way, that his old friend Stury has promised to come along. Sir Richard Stury, a knight of the King's household, has been Chaucer's friend since they were youths, boys, almost, and were both taken prisoner near Reims. Their friendship began in earnest in that week they were waiting for the ransom payments to come through. It's never flagged. They're two of a kind. Stury's tall and thin and loves riding and swordplay and dancing and arguing about religion, all unlike Chaucer. But, more importantly, Stury's a thoughtful, intelligent man, who spends most of his spare time nowadays writing poetry, as Chaucer does. They have other things in common. Chaucer and Stury are both part of the circle of young men around the King who also owe allegiance to his younger son, the Duke of Lancaster – for it is the Duke who has stepped in and spoken glowingly of them to his absent-minded royal father, who's reminded the King to arrange pensions for them in return for their services to the Crown, who's suggested marriages for them, and provided this favour or that, and generally smoothed out all the small difficulties that can beset a man making his way at court if he does not have a protector. Chaucer's latest appointment is going to give them one more thing to share. They're about to be neighbours, too. Stury has a house in the City: a riverside mansion in Vintry Ward, which he uses whenever the court's at Westminster. He'll often be in the City with Chaucer. They'll read to each other, sit together of an evening, drinking and talking and looking out over the Thames, side by side.

There are moments when Chaucer feels he's truly going to enjoy what is to come. There are moments when he feels this step back into London is going to connect him more closely to the court than he's ever been connected before. At this moment, overcome by that feeling, he sweeps down into the deepest bow he can manage.

It's only as he rises that he sees it isn't Latimer, or Stury, standing in front of him.

Incomprehensibly, it's Alice Perrers. She's alone. She's dressed in a simple tan travelling robe. The strong sun is casting strong shadows across her face. The breeze has tugged away her flapping veil. She's laughing at the look of utter confusion on his face.

'Well, it's early, and I suppose none of us looks our best at this hour . . . but really, Master Chaucer, it's not gallant to goggle at me like that, as if I were the Grim Reaper come to snatch you away,' she says archly. 'Is it now?'

Feeling foolish, though relieved she seems to find his bewilderment amusing, Chaucer bows again, not sure if he's making things better or worse. As he rises, he stammers, 'Madame Perrers . . . it's just . . . I wouldn't have expected . . . of course, I'm honoured.'

He can see now that she's come purely to see him off – to wish him well, him, Geoffrey Chaucer. And why not? She's been as warm, for all these weeks, as if he were her oldest friend. Still, surely it's natural for him to be flustered at her suddenly appearing here now, with the old boatman he's ordered for far too early spitting and coughing down there and giving him killer looks, with the two men who were supposed to be travelling to London with him still not here, and with him cutting a not very dashing figure hitching up his robes and helplessly waiting and even more helplessly gawping at her as if she were the Grim Reaper, as she says. Too late, he realises that was funny, and his mouth starts to twitch upwards. He still can't believe she's found the time, with all the royal household to run, that she's thought to leave the King's chamber for him.

She nods as the smile gains ground on his face, as if she's

51

pleased he's still got a sense of humour. 'I had to be up early anyway. I'm supervising the packing today,' she says by way of casual explanation. 'And it only takes a minute to run down here.'

Dumbly, he nods, overcome once more.

Before he can mumble, 'I'm honoured,' again, she adds, more seriously, as if it were the question closest to her heart, 'And I had a question for before you go. I wanted to be sure you've ordered a good dinner for your guests today.' She gives him a piercing look, her head on one side, like a plump little bird, and waits.

Chaucer feels his mouth open and close as he stumbles towards the best reply. All his vague but tumultuous hopes for his new life have vanished as soon as he hears that question. He just feels sick. He wonders if she knows how difficult he's finding it, or if she's just hit by chance on his worst fear for the day.

The plan is this. After being shown his desk at the Customs House this morning, he's to play host at dinner in his new home to the Mayor and all the greatest merchants of London.

Geoffrey hopes Philippa understands how elaborate this meal should be, how London citizens are as grand as Florentine merchant princes in their habits and expectations, and how lavish they'll expect the hospitality of the man who will dare to check their books to be.

But he's miserably aware that there was something too dismissive about his wife's shrug when, at their last meeting three days before, as she set off to move their cushions and tapestries and silverware into the new City apartment, he asked for a list of dishes.

'It's all in hand,' Philippa said, refusing to be drawn. When he started to say something more, she just flapped her hands at him. 'It's going to be a Friday,' she added, too calmly. 'Fish. Yes?' And she wafted off.

Unhappily, he thinks: I can influence most people. If only I could my wife. He lifts hangdog eyes to Alice Perrers' face, and sees she understands the whole family drama he isn't going to tell her.

'They'll expect the best,' is all she says. Then she pats his arm, comfortingly, though the gesture reminds him, uncomfortably, of Thomas's similar one during that other conversation. 'But of course you know that, don't you?'

He nods. He'll just have to hope for the best. He's glad to see, behind Alice's back, that the two shapes he's been looking for are finally here, and sauntering closer. He'll feel better once they get started. He doesn't want to have any more time to worry.

Yet unease follows Chaucer on to the river, and beyond.

He tries to relax on the mouldy cushions of the boat. He watches a swan and her cygnets float by, their beaks marked with the two lines of the Vintners' Company, and begin an altercation with a family of ducks. He flexes his fingers. He bites his lips.

Kindly, Latimer lets him be. The chamberlain starts a quiet conversation with Stury, on the other bench. But Latimer's voice, from those earlier briefings, still fills Chaucer's head.

England's biggest export is wool. The wool trade has been booming for decades, even if the last couple of years haven't been so good, what with the war. The merchants who buy wool from farmers around England and sell it overseas at the Flanders cloth markets have become both rich and powerful – the richest among them with incomes greater than those of the mightiest prince, wealth extraordinary enough to take on even the princely traders of Florence and Venice. The King, who understands the ways of his barons and peasants, but doesn't completely understand this new kind of man – a man governed by coin, not chivalry – needs eyes and ears to help explain the merchants to him; explain how best he should love them, and how best to attract their money to him.

The King needs to know, because the King needs those merchants, now he's up to his own eyeballs in war debt; oh, how he needs them. Their wool and their taxes pay for his war. And, because, over time, he's shown himself willing, every now and then, when his need is great, or the opportunity is tempting, to cheat them – just a little, as is his royal right, in the interests of the nation – they don't fully trust him, any more than he fully trusts them. They might want to cheat him back. It's to be Chaucer's job to stop them if they try.

The two hundred English merchants run the wool export trade as a monopoly (from a headquarters that for years before the war was based, for convenience's sake, at Calais, the English-ruled garrison mid-way between England and Flanders; only now that the war's started again, and Flemish buyers can't get across enemy French territory to Calais, the Wool Staple's had to be moved to the safety of Middleburg, in Flanders itself, so the merchants don't go broke). The Merchants of the Staple still finance the King's garrison at Calais, even in these hard times, when they can't actually trade there. They don't have much choice. The King asks for their money, with tears in his handsome Plantagenet eyes, with a tremble in his elegant French, 'for the sake of our beloved England'. Their French isn't as good as his, but they understand. They pay up. They make an agreement with the King as to how he's going to repay them, one day, by letting them off some of their future wool customs dues to the Crown. It's all signed and sealed with many-coloured wax, but no one can really hope to be repaid. But, after that, right here and now, the merchants must provide actual gold and silver, and make coins at the mint they've set up at Calais, and give it over to the soldiers waiting and grumbling in the salt swamps of north France.

So it makes the Merchants of the Wool Staple angry with the King if they find out he's been cheating them – for instance by granting special licences to the Italian merchant community trading out of London, so the foreigners can bypass all the weighing and measuring and customs-paying that English merchants have to endure at Calais or Middleburg. This blithe cheating keeps the Italians happy, as they get to make a bigger profit margin while undercutting the English merchants' sales prices later, at the Flanders wool fairs. It makes the King happy, too, because how can the Italians then refuse when he asks them for a direct loan, to help pay for his war in France?

But there isn't much the Merchants of the Wool Staple can

do about being ripped off by their King, except grin and bear it and, when the King then asks them for a direct loan, too (since the Italians have been so generous), to agree, and ask to take on the Italians' loan, too, on condition the Italians have their special licences cancelled, so the English, at least, get their monopoly of wool exports back. And then they're left shouldering a double debt burden, with no guarantee that the King might not, tomorrow or the next day, take it into his head to do another quiet little deal with another Italian to get off scot free from all taxes for a quick cash payment now. There's nothing the merchants can do openly to let off steam. Sometimes the English merchants' apprentices, having heard unpleasant things said about the Italian merchants of London at their masters' tables, get drunk and go and beat up the nearest Italian. The apprentices are savagely punished. Hanged, often. There's never any question of calling the King to account.

Chaucer's job will not be to call the King to account. It will be to be the royal eyes and ears inside London. He will deal with the pre-exports: what leaves England. London is the last place a King's man can, realistically, get at the wool due for export; after that it's entirely in the hands of the merchants themselves. For almost the entire wool crop leaving England goes through London, where it is packed and weighed and warehoused by merchants; and it's here that the greatest merchants live. It will be Chaucer's job to reweigh the wool crop, sack by sack, and go through the merchants' paperwork, and to form his own view of how big the English trade in wool really is, and how much the merchants should really have paid the King for these exports, or for others, and, generally, to increase the King's income from the City merchants in whatever way he sees fit.

'Be one of them,' Latimer has told Chaucer. 'Make them feel at home with you. Listen to their privy talk. You'll know how. But always remember the reckoning. The bill for these past three years of war has been £200,000, and the truce that's holding now won't last for ever. As long as you're clearing more than 25,000 sacks of wool a year, and getting an annual yield of £70,000 on it, England's still afloat. More or less,' and here, Chaucer recalls, the Baron's face wrinkled into a long, mirthless grin that was more like a snarl. 'At least, as long as the Pope doesn't also come back with his begging bowl. Thirty thousand for his Italian wars, indeed. We can't afford to pay to fight the French and for *him* to wage wars too. Things are far too tight as it is.'

The vast amounts take Chaucer's breath away, even more than the tightness of the royal finances, the narrowness of the margins, and the King's reliance on a mixture of charm and bullying of the entrepreneurs whose language he doesn't even speak (the King sticks to French) to keep England staggering on. He feels naive to be so astonished by these enormous figures. But he is. Chaucer lives in small coin, on graces and favours. The sheer staggering weight of the money being talked about is beyond his ken.

And when they disembark, his welter of conflicting emotions only swirls more wildly.

He shouldn't be surprised, he tells himself. It's years since he's been surrounded like this by his father's acquaintances. He was a child. Watching these half-dozen mostly familiar faces now, the jowls and wrinkles more accentuated than he remembers, the stubble going grey or white on firmly jutting chins (though the furs on their long gowns, worn despite the heat of the day, are more splendid than ever), he feels, almost, a little boy again – the little boy his father used to get in to serve the merchants their wine in the Chaucer house on Thames Street. That smaller Chaucer used to listen admiringly to the talk about pepper imports and mackerel catches and the iniquity of the law allowing foreign merchants to retail their goods on English soil and the quality of this year's wine from Gascony, while outside on the wharves that you could see, dimly, through the glass windows (how proud his father had been of those glass windows), the men running like ants under the winches, watching the barrels swinging down, and the flash and splash of river traffic. Back then, Chaucer knew that any minute he'd feel his father's hand ruffling his head or patting his back. Those quiet, fond, proud touches, which in the manner of small boys trying to be big he never acknowledged, but which he always quietly put himself in the way of, are all that's missing now.

He presses his lips and eyelids together. No point in regrets. John Chaucer, who so wanted to better himself that he spent the Mortality years trailing around France in King Edward's baggage train buying wine for the forces, and then for the King himself, would have been proud to see his son here today, stepping up to the Wool Wharf, the powerhouse where English wealth is made, measured and exported, in the very shadow of the Tower of London, being deferred to by the powerful men he worked so hard to make his own friends.

Chaucer looks around. This year's Mayor is in the welcoming party (a stringy grey man from a lesser guild; Chaucer has no childhood memories of *him*). More importantly, the man who's about to become Mayor for the next year is here too: William Walworth, fishmonger and alderman of Bridge Ward, a tall, ascetic-looking man with spun-gold hair and the innocent face of an angel. Chaucer remembers Walworth's long, thin legs, crossing and uncrossing themselves, the elegant, tendony ankles, the high-arched feet, from a very distant past in which the little Geoffrey played quietly under the table with his ball or top, listening to the men's voices. But it's another of these familiar men – Nicholas Brembre, tall burly Brembre, now alderman for Bread Street Ward – who steps superbly forward from the furry, velvety, bass-voiced cluster and takes it upon himself to reintroduce the rest. Walworth just stands behind Brembre, looking avuncular. Perhaps, now Walworth has secured the mayor's office for himself for a year, he's letting his friend show his paces in time for next year's selection – for, Chaucer knows, Walworth, Brembre, and the stocky, balding man at his side, John Philpot, a grocer like Brembre, are famous for sticking together and protecting each other's interests. Between them, the three victuallers pretty much run the City. They share the mayor's and sheriffs' jobs among themselves, year in, year out. And these are the three London men to whom the King comes, year in, year out, asking for money. Chaucer can see for himself how closely they cooperate. Even now, they're standing together, shoulder to shoulder, making sure he sees their faces first; keeping the lesser men back.

Chaucer remembers Brembre best, from childhood. All that dark energy, those forceful gestures, years ago, once rather frightened little Geoffrey. But now Chaucer has adult eyes in his head, and what he sees with them is that Brembre has become golden. Almost physically golden. The grocer's skin is gilded, as if by the sun, or (perhaps more plausibly for a man who spends his daylight hours in warehouses, checking his inventories of pepper and saffron and pomegranates) just by good fortune and soft living and ambition satisfied. He's smooth and honeyed with success. His blue eyes sparkle as brightly as ever, his face is as animated as Chaucer remembers it being long ago, though his large, regular features seem bigger and smoother, his black hair is silver-streaked, and success has slowed the man's once rapid, excitable speech into a deeper, calmer purr. 'My dear Geoffrey,' he says, very warmly, putting an arm around Chaucer's back, as if claiming ownership. 'We are all delighted to welcome you back to London.'

Chaucer feels the muscle on that arm even through the gown; it's as if Brembre, despite his peaceful calling, is made of iron. Brembre has straight, thick, dark eyebrows too; smooth jet-black, like his smooth hair once was. He raises one of these determined eyebrows, and smiles directly into Chaucer's eyes. Chaucer feels exhilarated by that frank, compelling gaze. 'And I', he says, finding his voice, borrowing the warmth of his tone from that of the merchant, 'am delighted to be once again among the kind of men I can do business with.'

They murmur appreciatively.

Here's where the future will happen, Chaucer sees, as, bowing his big square head in exaggerated respect, Brembre propels him, with a large, warm, clean hand, to where he will sit, inside the Customs House, now he is comptroller.

Across the room, behind the wall of velvet-clad shoulders, stands an enormous desk. Over there, the merchants of London, every day, write down on the Roll exactly how much wool has been weighed and dispatched, and what taxes have

58

been charged on it. Over here, but separately, at a second enormous desk, Chaucer the comptroller will keep his own independent record in the Counter-Roll. Once a year they'll compare Roll and Counter-Roll. With all the tact at his disposal, Chaucer will have to tackle these powerful financiers over any discrepancies, and make the sums add up to the King's satisfaction.

Chaucer takes a deep breath to calm his fast-beating heart. Bowing again to the gathering, he says, skittishly, 'So, masters, let me try my seat for size,' and acknowledges their rumbles of laughter with a bow as he gathers his robes in his hands and sits down behind his desk.

He's glad to be seated while they're standing – all those big, well-covered men with enormous hands and strong bodies that don't notice the heat, despite their long furry gowns. They remind him of a flock of waterfowl – geese, or swans, or herons – all so large, yet so implausibly smooth in every movement. They're tougher than their peaceable gowns make them seem. For all their puffed-up chests and dignity, he can imagine any or all of them mercilessly pecking out the eyes of any impertinent lesser bird, any duck or moorhen or coot that gets in the way of their majestic glide through the waters they rule. And how they're devouring him with their watchful eyes, all of them, he thinks, suddenly. They're no fools. They're wondering if he'll be trouble. Sizing him up.

Behind him, he's aware of Latimer and Stury, his court friends, giving Walworth and his merchant friends the same beady looks the merchants are giving him. They're wondering whether Chaucer will be tough enough to stand up to the merchants. They're sizing *them* up.

Chaucer knows, secretly, that his court friends are right to worry about his loyalty. A part of him feels he's come home as he looks at these smooth merchant faces. When, a moment ago, Brembre has flamboyantly presented his stout friend as 'my worshipful colleague, John Philpot, a grocer like myself . . . alderman for Cornhill Ward . . . you may recall?' Chaucer knows he's only just managed to find it in him to refrain from laughing in pure delight. For of course he knows Philpot, and definitely knows of him – he knows that Philpot and Brembre are financing a fleet for the south coast, and have also just reshaped the City's trade association for victuallers, giving it the new name of grocers and spending fortunes on setting it up grandly.

But that's not why he's having to struggle to keep the merry grin off his face. The grin's because of the memory that pops unbidden into Chaucer's head of Philpot's smooth hand reaching out towards him, passing over a gingerbread man with a silvery crown on its head, and of that soft voice, quivering with amusement, saying, 'Don't make yourself sick now, my boy.'

Chaucer can't choke off that memory altogether. He isn't able not to pronounce the words 'Dear Uncle John' with a rush of real affection, or to refrain from saying, out loud, 'Why, of course. We're old friends.' And even he's surprised to find himself embracing both princes of grocers with such affection that, for a dangerous moment, he feels the mercantile deputation melt and relax, while the courtiers behind him bristle. He'll have to get a grip: to reapply his courtly manners and his air of polite watchfulness, before any of them take him for a pushover. Forget the gingerbread. He has a job to do.

It's only as the group walks across the City to the dinner at Chaucer's new apartment that one of the lesser merchants breaks through the shoulders of Brembre and his friends.

'I hope you will not be offended,' the unfamiliar man says to the comptroller, with the heavy accent of Flanders, 'but I have sent a small gift ahead to your new home, to welcome you to your post. A tun of Gascon wine.'

The man then bows, with a big man's slouching-shouldered imitation of modesty, includes Chaucer in a huge rolling laugh, and introduces himself as Richard Lyons. He's almost unnaturally large and luridly coloured, though without an ounce of fat on him. He makes Brembre look small and weak. He has thighs like tree trunks, a pink face, sly, amused eyes, pale orange hair peeping out from under his hat, and a warm, rich voice that projects without effort over everyone else's. No grey in *his* stubble – he can't be older than forty – and plenty of gold at wrist and chest.

Chaucer never met Lyons while a boy in London, but of course he's heard his name since. Lyons has only emerged as a wealthy man very recently (and, Chaucer remembers, his father, in his latter years, wasn't always too sure that this new wealth was very honestly acquired, though naturally that's the kind of thing almost any Londoner will automatically say about almost any foreigner). Chaucer knows the Fleming is now very rich indeed. Even though he's a foreigner, Lyons is about to serve as one of the next mayor's two sheriffs – high office – which seems to suggest that the London elite walking down this street favour him, except that it's very easy to see that, actually, they don't want him there at all; they feel awkward around him, and are doing everything they can to keep him to the back and dilute his overwhelming presence among them.

Chaucer understands why they'd be nervous. Lyons has been biding his time. He's stayed in the background, and kept his peace for the past hour. But he's been the first, all the same, to get in with his charming little bribe.

'I thank you,' he says, bowing very politely, ending the conversation. Secretly, he's breathing a big sigh of relief that, for the moment at least, Lyons, who's a vintner like Chaucer's own father, is only here for curiosity's sake; he's hoping that this pink-and-orange-and-red-and-gold force of nature doesn't, in the near future, start getting tied up in the wool trade. At least until Chaucer's got everything worked out. He can see, right off, that Lyons is a man on the rise, and a man who does things his own way, and a man who'll always be a focus for trouble.

By the time Lyons bows and moves away, the whole procession, dignitaries, aristocrats, and the new Comptroller of Customs and Subsidy on Wool, Sheepskins and Leather in the Port of London, has passed north and east across half the City – a brisk ten-minute walk, right through the parish of All Hallows Barking, up Water Lane, over Thames Street and

Tower Street, and on up Mark Lane into neighbouring Aldgate parish – and is on Aldgate Street itself, heading for the City wall and the gate. All around them, there's the deafening crash of midday bells for sext.

The City is a democratic place. It's too small for anything but walking, for even the greatest of men, and Geoffrey Chaucer likes the quiet freedom of strolling through the crowds. It's one of the pleasures of London, that you can go everywhere on foot. He clings to this notion of enjoying walking, because he's suddenly a little wobbly inside about how much he really likes London. Travelling has blunted so much of his old pleasure in his home city. Once you've seen honeystone Florence, you're spoiled for ever. Afterwards, how can you feel anything more than slightly pitying affection for this twisty, stinky, thatched, wattle-and-daubed, cobbled, overcrowded, provincial old place? Of course, that isn't a feeling to share with the men now whispering confidingly into his ear, one by one, that they've had a box of pepper, or spices, or fish, or cushions, delivered to his new home as a housewarming gift. True Londoners will always be proud of their White City. They call it the Ringing City, sometimes – all the church bells. It's a place to walk endlessly through the ringing of bells. That's one of the things I'll be doing, from now on, Chaucer thinks, not quite happily.

The apartment above Aldgate was signed over to him last month, as part of his payment for this job. It's a great spacious place, looking out over the cut-throat eastern slum villages beyond the City walls one way, along the Colchester road through to Essex on the horizon, and over the roofs and gardens of Holy Trinity Priory and teeming Aldgate Street the other way, inside the City walls.

The apartment itself is all large echoing rooms, with a solar above and a cellar below the easternmost of the six City gates. It's the only toll-free gate, open to all, beggars included, and there are plenty of those coming from the wild, sparsely popu-lated Essex country beyond. There'll be people coming and going in their carts underneath Chaucer's feet every day, cursing as they try to squeeze through the narrow arch, and the clank of the City gate closing every night at curfew. The apartment has been used as a prison in the past; this is a strategic spot. He's had to swear to use it well and not let enemies of the City enter through the gate below; they've had to swear not to put prisoners in there with him and his family for his life-time. It was a comical little City ceremony, the kind that would have made Philippa smirk. But the apartment's presti-gious enough – as good as Stury's riverside house – so any smirking on her part, right now, is also partly a genuinely happy smile.

Alice Perrers winked when she told him she'd got him the apartment rent-free. 'It's not usually rent-free. But the Mayor said yes, for you.'

'Whatever kindness the worshipful Mayor is doing, it's to impress you, I'm sure, not me,' he replied gratefully. It's her kind of favour, he understands. He's heard a lot of stories about Alice Perrers' ruthless ways with property, exchanging influence and access to the King for favours in land and build-ings, constantly obtaining new leases on still more properties, all on the never-never, feathering her own nest. The stories aren't flattering, but they're probably all true. It's obvious she's minting money. Everyone says the same thing. Chaucer knows he's supposed to be shocked by her greed. Philippa, in particular, keeps telling him so. But he can't help admiring the merry mischief in Alice Perrers' eyes. He likes her for enjoying her tricks and subterfuges so much.

Philippa will have made those empty spaces above Aldgate beautiful in these past days. She'll have hung the tapestries and scattered the cushions artfully to fill the rooms with loveliness and colour. There'll be flowers. All their little wealth will be on brave display. She'll understand the importance of that.

Geoffrey Chaucer finds his hands clutching at his long sleeves. He's wearing merchant robes today, long sweeping things to his feet; he plans to dress like the merchants he'll be living among. But he hasn't reckoned with the heat inside the tube of velvet. He's forgotten that, in his years of aristo-cratic tunics and hosen. He's stifling. His linen undershirt is soaking. He wishes his stomach would stop churning.

If only he could be sure his wife also understands how important it is to treat these merchants like princes, and feed them like kings. If only he knew for certain that she's understood about the dinner.

FOUR

There's a crowd at Aldgate as the merchant procession arrives. Two donkeys, pulling a heavily laden cart, are blocking the traffic while men unload trays from it. They're ignoring other men, who are darting in and out of the gatehouse, complaining, as well as the men on carts trying to come into the City, who are shouting and cat-calling and hooting obscenities in their rustic Essex voices from beyond the gate.

Chaucer winces. He remembers these stubborn City scraps for space so well. It might go on for hours, this slow-motion shouting. It might turn into a fight. He doesn't want *his* dignitaries to be caught up in one of these spats now.

But, after a heart-stopping moment, he realises there's no cause for concern. The aldermen are City folk too. They know, better than he, that there's no need to mix themselves up in this competition among low-lifes. They just puff out their padded chests and glide through the fracas as if unaware of it, making straight for Chaucer's staircase. They don't even seem to see the shaking fists and jutting jaws all around them.

'Warm for the time of year,' Will Walworth opines, velvet-smooth, taking Chaucer's arm and guiding him into the doorway. Only the glint of amusement in his eyes gives away his awareness of the little birds fighting.

It's only when Chaucer is on the narrow stone steps, aware that Walworth has politely taken the narrower side of the spiral yet is so delicate on his long feet that he seems to be flying up the tiny treads, that the new comptroller sees that some of the men with trays are also in the stairwell, both above and below him, and that each of them is carrying a platter on his shoulder.

When Chaucer reaches the top of the stairs, and emerges into the biggest of the stone chambers, he sees, to his unspeakable relief, that it is all decked out with trestles and cushions and benches and the cupboard containing his and Philippa's many silver-gilt Christmas gifts from Countess Elizabeth, his first employer, and both the past and present Duchesses of Lancaster, Philippa's two employers, and Duke John too, and the King himself, each cup bearing one or other noble coat of arms. He sees, too, that the damp back wall is covered by the tapestry his mother worked, a hunting scene she deemed appropriate for his new gentlemanly station in life, and there are nosegays of sweet purple roses and clove-scented pink gillyflowers in small vases everywhere. Only then does he begin to understand what's going on with the food and the platters.

Philippa, in a neat blue robe that she must have considered quite showy enough for City folk, is here, sure enough, with one eyebrow very slightly raised, her gaze passing over Chaucer as she steps forward, with her usual willowy formality, to bow to and welcome the future Mayor to her new home.

But behind her, supervising the men arriving in the room with their trays and platters – on which he can now see, as their coverings are removed, are cooked fishes of every description, and piles of cut oranges and pomegranates and lemons, dates and dried apricots, crumbles and jumbles, pink creamy castles of blancmange and wobbling rivers of posset, and a sugared pastry extravagance in the shape of a swan, until the table resembles nothing so much as the Land of Cockaigne – is another, less familiar, female form.

'Over there,' he hears, as if in a dream. 'And this one, here, in the corner. There's a little bit of space here still.' She has her back to him, but there's something about that strangely confident voice, and about that tan robe. Before the woman has finished and turned round, allowing Chaucer properly to admire the elaborate cauls in which her hair has been arranged over each ear, and the sheer veil sparkling with fine gold threads wafting around her face, he's guessed.

'Madame Perrers,' he mumbles, stepping forward. Then, correcting himself from courtly French to practical English, the language of the City: '*Mistress* Perrers.'

She turns to him. 'Chaucer!' she says familiarly, as if he were her servant. No 'Monsieur' here; no 'Master' either. But who's he to argue with that, when she's saving the day, acting as though she's *his* servant, bringing in food? And she looks so pleased to see him, surrounded by bowing merchants, too. She's smiling, very warm and wide; for a moment, he thinks he sees her wink.

Now he understands Philippa's raised eyebrow. He can see from the colours of the platters – Alice's all of pewter, Philippa's of a jumble of different colours of pottery and metal – that the meal his wife has laid on has been, until Alice got here with these unsolicited reinforcements, a modest affair of herring, sorrel, and strawberries. The relief that surges through Chaucer's innards when he sees the feast now being set out by Alice's servants is like a river flooding its banks. He's intensely aware of the appreciative looks on the merchants' faces, the bright, hungry eyes, inspecting the dishes with pleasurable anticipation. He can almost feel the saliva swirling in every mouth. Everything will be all right now. Except, of course, that behind her cool politeness, Philippa must be fuming at That Woman having so unexpectedly upstaged her.

Hastily, realising Philippa is watching him, as if for signs he's conspired in the Perrers dinner coup, he bows to his un-invited guest, very formally. 'Why, I had no idea . . .' he begins cautiously, so Philippa will understand his innocence. 'I thought the court would be packing up today, for Sheen . . . if I'd realised you might be lingering in London, Mistress Perrers, of course, I would have invited . . .' But then he looks up into Alice Perrers' bold eyes, and sees the ghost of a wink in them, and forgets all his furtive married-man's cunning, and is lost. She's so straightforward in her mischievous do-gooding – understanding everything, saying nothing, and tremendously pleased with herself at having saved the day, all at once – that he abandons caution, takes her hands in his, bobs his head down in a sketchy bow, and says, with all the real happiness and merriment that the sight of this very welcome guest suddenly inspires in him, 'Well, what a wonderful surprise!'

'My modest housewarming gift,' Alice Perrers replies nonchalantly, squeezing his hands, bowing in her turn to Philippa to include her in this circle of warm astonishment, but not batting an eyelid when Philippa's face continues to express nothing more than the minimum of polite gratitude that etiquette demands. 'To you both,' Alice Perrers says, and, to an encouraging rumble of assent from the merchants, 'to wish you health, wealth, and happiness in London.' Then, not trying any further with Philippa, she turns to Walworth, Brembre, and Philpot, and finally to Latimer and Stury (who, Chaucer notices, have struck up a conversation with the flashing-eyed Fleming, Richard Lyons), and greets each group of them in turn with a warm look and a quiet, amusing, private word.

Chaucer notices Alice's poise here, among the merchants, just as he's been noticing her confidence at Westminster ever since she started taking him to meet the officials she clearly knows so well. Chaucer doesn't think she's the child of a London merchant family, because, if she were, surely he'd have known her as a boy? Still, she seems quite at home here – more so than at court. He thinks, vaguely: Haven't I heard something . . . wasn't she married to a merchant, right back at the start? (Perhaps, if she was, the marriage was during his years away, trotting around France and Flanders and Italy . . .) He can't think who the husband can have been, though. He should find out.

Chaucer knows, anyway, that he'll never feel sorry for her in this company – she's too at ease, and too popular. Look at her charming the merchants. Everyone laughs when she whispers in their ear, and it's genuine laughter every time. And they're not usually like this with women, either; they're too sober, and not given to flirting. They must take her seriously. They must be talking about trade; that's what they do talk about. They're treating her like one of themselves.

He's almost laughing himself with the miracle of what she's done for him. They've always said Alice Perrers can organise anything. But it can't have been four hours since he saw her on the jetty, back at Westminster. How in the name of God has she found the time to do her hair like that, and rustle up all these splendid dishes, so far away on the other side of town, and get herself here, all in a morning? He's heard she has a London house in Vintry Ward, like Stury, a proper liveable-in house, as well as all those other London property holdings that people talk about. She must have sent word straight away for her servants there to get to work, then come up to London herself within the hour. But still. He's shaking his head and beaming all over his face, as Philippa seats the party around the table. He can't believe his luck.

Somewhere deep inside, below the grateful hilarity and relief, he can feel just a hint of smugness surfacing too at his own good judgement. If all this is his reward, he thinks, just for stepping in politely to save embarrassment when Princess Joan decided to start throwing goblets of wine around at a ball, he'd better make a resolution to be just as brave every day of the week.

'Can I pass you this dish of sorrel?' Chaucer sees Philippa try with William Walworth at her left, and is grateful to his wife for that good intention, at least. She's sat beside him for twenty minutes without making much effort at conversation, though she's never done anything so obvious as to yawn, or look away. She's just smiled. Walworth appreciates that she's trying, too. He very daintily takes a leaf or two on the end of his knife. His appetite is sated, but *politesse oblige*. He takes a token nibble.

'Have you settled in happily, Mistress Chaucer?' he enquires, beaming virtue at her out of his pale eyes, like a lean, kindly priest. 'Is there anything we can help you with, now you're here? I know my wife would be more than ready . . .' He pauses, full of the will to please, assessing what goods or services Mistress Chaucer might possibly need, or desire.

But Philippa's already shaking her head. Flirtatiously, though not very; but definitely.

'Oh,' she says. Her voice is a little too perfunctory for her polite words to sound sincere. 'You're too kind, Master Walworth. I'm honoured. But I think everything's sorted out, for now . . . though perhaps when I'm next in London I could call on Mistress Walworth . . .' Her voice trails off.

'Ah yes,' Walworth says, not allowing himself to sound disconcerted at the reminder that Mistress Chaucer won't be a regular part of London social life. 'Of course. You're keeping your place as demoiselle to' – and here he can't, for all his good manners, refrain from slightly wrinkling his face – 'my lady the Duchess of Lancaster.'

Walworth is a merchant, so how can he say the name of Lancaster without a bit of a scowl? Because, if there's no love lost between the London rich and my lord the Duke of Lancaster, the merchants know exactly whom they blame. It's the Duke's fault, in their book. The Duke is so jealous of his father's dependence on the rich men of London for loans to finance the war that he insults the merchants, whenever he sees them at court, by telling them to their faces they're not worthy to be there. It was never like this before, he's been heard to say; in the old days, you'd never have seen noblemen kowtowing to the servile classes. The Duke's jealousy of the merchants' influence leads him further still – he also talks openly about wanting to take away the freedoms that the City people enjoy: the right to elect their own leaders and try their own people in their own courts. So naturally the merchants dislike and fear the Duke, in case he destroys London's independence; and naturally any mention of the Duke's wife will cause a certain amount of suppressed upset in Master Walworth's mind. He nods a few more times, bringing a wistful smile back on to his face. 'At least, so I understand,' he adds, with a slightly questioning note in his voice. Philippa Chaucer smiles back, but she's blank-eyed. She's making no further effort at conversation.

Chaucer feels so awkward at his wife's less than enthusiastic treatment of London's greatest merchant that he leans

70

forward himself. 'May I, Master Walworth,' he says hastily, 'draw your attention to the hanap you're drinking from? A very gracious gift to my dear wife from my lord the King himself, for her years of service to his family?' He feels it's important to remind Master Walworth that this awkward independence of spirit that his wife's showing does, at least, bring connections with the greatest in the land. 'I've always admired the beauty of that tracery on the silver-gilt, look . . .' He draws a finger up the chased foliage twining around the stem of the goblet.

Walworth, who no less than Chaucer is a master of smoothing out difficulties in relations, looks as handsomely appreciative as he's supposed to, and clucks warm, admiring praise. It *is* very fine work.

'Mistress Chaucer', Chaucer says, with more warmth than he feels, 'is greatly loved by the royal family. My lady of Lancaster won't think of letting her go . . .' He raises rueful hands to the sky, and shakes his head, making a comedy of Philippa's distance from this new life in London. 'To my great sorrow, of course. I will miss her, and our children; who more?'

Both the men have found a way out of the moment of awkwardness by now. They're leaning towards each other, smiling slightly too much (Chaucer can already feel his jaw muscles begin to ache), waving their arms a little; the picture of affability. Philippa, meanwhile, is drawing back, politely making space for them to talk together. The vague, uninterested look is still on her face.

'Of course,' Walworth replies unctuously, accepting, with apparent delight, the dish of oranges cut into decorative shapes that Chaucer is passing. 'Of course. The price of a good wife is far above rubies. And one who's also as beautiful as your lady is to be treasured most of all.' He and Chaucer laugh at this charming compliment till their eyes fill with tears, then pat each other's hands. Walworth eats a slice of orange. 'Mm,' he mumbles, with mouth full, as Philippa, the hardly noticed object of the compliment, takes the opportunity to slide off her stool and slip away from the table to give the servants some whispered order. 'Delicious, my dear Chaucer. You and your lady wife have done us proud today.'

Yet Chaucer can't help noticing that it's Mistress Perrers whom Walworth seeks out with his eyes as he pays that last compliment.

After the dinner, when the guests have begun to walk around a little, moving to fireplace or window, stretching their legs, Chaucer finds himself at the window with Mistress Perrers, looking out at the golden streaks in the afternoon sky over the quiet fields east of London. He's so full of tender gratitude to her by now that he's only too happy to murmur agreement when she says, 'Isn't it lovely?

'It always gets me right here,' she goes on reflectively, tapping her heart, 'this view. But then I was born in Essex. So I suppose it's only natural.'

Bewildered, and a little disappointed, Chaucer looks again at the shadowy flatlands, the shabby villages. He hadn't realised she was talking about Essex. He thought she meant the sky. There's nothing remarkable that he can see about those fields and forests, the road stretching off into the dusk, the sheep. He's enough of a Londoner that, to him, fields and forest mean boredom, an absence, a place of spectral, hag-faced men and women with skin-covered bones: dead-eyed, earth-smelling, earth-eating, with heads of clay and dung.

'You're from Essex?' he replies, feeling stupid to sound surprised. 'But I thought . . .' He pauses. He really can't remember who the merchant husband could have been, but London is so clearly where Alice feels at home. 'Weren't you married in London, long ago?' he finishes lamely.

She laughs a little, looking down at her hands. 'Oh, husbands,' she says coyly. Then she flashes a quick, mischievous look up at him from under her lashes. When her eyes meet his, he's surprised, after her coyness, by the transparency in them – as if she's looking into his soul, or inviting him to look into hers. 'But, yes, I did have a couple of London husbands,' she adds quietly, still with a little smile on her lips. 'And yes . . . long ago. I was twelve when I took the first one.'

A couple of husbands, Chaucer thinks, dazed. He's only got the one wife, and that's been enough to make his feelings about the married state frighteningly complex. But she sounds so casual.

'They say you should only have one master in life, don't they? Since Christ only went to one wedding in Galilee?' she teases. She knows what's on his mind, he thinks, and feels his cheeks get hot. She adds, even more lightly, 'But, you know, Chaucer, all the Bible actually says is that God told us all to go forth and multiply. It has nothing at all to say about bigamy, or octogamy, either, not that I've heard. Except that, if you think about it, wise old King Solomon gave himself a generous margin when it came to wives, didn't he? More than any of us would take on?' She grins at him. Her hands are on her hips. There's a glint of challenge in her eyes.

Trying to get the right bantering tone, he replies, with a forced chortle, 'So you've had eight husbands, have you?'

As soon as his words are out, he realises he probably hasn't got it right. She shrugs and looks faintly weary for a moment. 'To hear them talk, you'd think I'd had dozens,' she says. 'I've certainly heard people say five.'

For a moment, their eyes meet. There is candidness in hers, he sees with relief. She's sharing her exasperation. As if forgiving him his clumsy remark, she smiles.

'Even one marriage is more than I bargained for,' Chaucer observes, settling for honesty himself, looking out again. His cheeks are warm. 'Sometimes.'

'Experience,' she says lightly. 'That's what you need; give you the upper hand.' And she flashes her eyes at him again, and makes to move away into the throng.

'Well, *my* experience hasn't taught me much,' he mutters, a little rebelliously, as she picks up her skirts, 'except quite a lot about the woe there is in marriage.'

She turns, and for a moment seeks him out again with eyes in which he thinks he sees surprise, and the beginning of amusement. But all she says is a gentle, 'Oh, Chaucer,' and away she goes.

*　　*　　*

A short while later, Chaucer flits back to Walworth, who's standing with his two friends and fellow-magnates Brembre and Philpot, picking at the candied fruits the servants are setting out along the now-empty table, and laughing regretfully. The future Mayor of London leans towards Chaucer to include him in the wry conversation too. 'We're wondering how big the loan I'm about to be asked to make the King will be, Master Chaucer,' Walworth confides without any visible bitterness. 'The price of office, I know . . . every new Mayor gets asked . . . but with the way the war's been going . . .' Then, with a half-laugh: 'We're guessing, maybe . . . £15,000?' He raises an enquiring eyebrow Chaucer's way.

Chaucer, who has no idea, who's never even imagined the possibility of being part of a conversation like this, can only shake his head and try and keep the saucer-eyed look of an innocent off his face. There is loud, though kindly, laughter from the three merchants. 'Ah,' says Brembre wisely, 'you'll learn.'

Maybe it's an instinct of gratitude that makes Chaucer glance around to find Alice Perrers. Maybe he half wants to bow his thanks to her again for helping him make friends with these men so easily. Whatever the reason, he does look around for her. He finds her standing not far away, talking quietly to Lord Latimer, and to Lyons, the florid Flemish merchant. And Chaucer forgets bowing and displaying gratitude. He's too aware of the way they stop what they're saying to listen in to what Brembre and his friends are talking about. There's something a little too furtive in the way they all look as they listen. Then they start their own quieter conversation again, just the three of them. Alice says to Lyons, quietly, hardly moving her lips, as if she doesn't want to be noticed speaking, 'He'd be ready for twice fifteen thousand, at a better rate, too, if you only gave him your promise. I'm telling you.' Her eyes are fixed on Lyons'. Behind her, Latimer's also nodding towards the Fleming. He obviously agrees. He obviously also wants to persuade Lyons to do whatever it is that Alice wants him to do. Lyons looks quickly from Alice Perrers to the chamberlain and back again. He's thinking. Then he also nods.

There's something secret and satisfied on his face when he's done.

Alice's remark itself makes no sense to Chaucer. But the quick, guilty look Lyons gives Chaucer, once Alice has moved off to the next little group of men and the next conversation, makes the comptroller feel as if he's somehow been hoodwinked. He can't imagine how, though; and perhaps it's just the wine, colouring his imagination too rich.

Still, the moment leaves him feeling uneasy. He doesn't like not understanding.

Philippa doesn't stay. As soon as the last guest has bowed and made his exit, Philippa stands up too.

She doesn't want to discuss the dinner. She just says, very politely, that she's expected back at the Savoy tonight. She can make the boat trip before curfew if she hurries.

'But the children. They could stay,' Chaucer mumbles disconsolately. He hasn't even seen them yet. They would have been too young for the dinner. But he's assumed they're here – sleeping, perhaps, in the bedchamber? Or reading? Or walking around London, waiting for the business meeting to be over before the family reunion?

'They're not here,' Philippa replies calmly. 'They've gone down to Sheen early. There was a hunting party they wanted to join.'

He hasn't thought enough, Chaucer realises, crestfallen. He's assumed too much. He should have guessed they weren't here.

Chaucer subsides into defeated silence. He submits when she comes to him and pecks him on the top of his slightly balding head before slipping out. He only remembers to stumble out his thanks to her for coming just in time, before the door shuts. He should be grateful, he knows. Philippa's pragmatic enough to have realised it's important to show a united front to the Londoners, who'll want to see that the marital proprieties are observed in the Chaucer household.

She's done what's expected of her.

There's no reason for him to feel sad, he tells himself, even if she's going, and even if he hasn't seen the children. She has her work. They have their lives. This is how things are done in the courtly world. Perhaps it's only being back among merchants, today, and remembering his own childhood, brought up closer to his parents than any courtier's son could dream of, that's making him chafe . . .

If only the carts weren't rolling quite so loudly through the gate under his feet. If only he hadn't drunk that third cup of wine. Or was it the fourth?

He's slumped at the table, finishing off what's in the bottom of the cup, listening to the servants behind the door, banging and talking as they clear up the trays and plates, with the sense of anticlimax and disappointment gathering strength inside, as the shadows thicken, when there's a knock.

He's astonished to see Alice's face around the door.

She smiles brilliantly, and the shadows retreat. 'I thought I'd drop by for five minutes while my men are picking up the platters out there. I'd ask you for supper at my house . . . but you've probably had enough already, haven't you?' She twinkles at him. Hastily, he straightens up. 'You'd rather sleep, I expect . . .'

He's on his feet before he knows it. 'The *kindness*,' he hears himself chirrup, excitedly, sounding far too eager. 'The *thoughtfulness* . . . finding the time to bring so much . . . your *generosity* . . . I can't begin to tell you how *overwhelmed* I was . . .'

She doesn't say anything. She looks straight into his eyes, almost tenderly. She shakes her head. After a moment, she says, 'I've been thinking about you . . . About how strange it must have felt, for you, today – to be coming back to where you grew up.' She takes his hand, not flirtatiously, more like a sister. 'After everything else you've seen in your life.' Her voice trails away, inviting confidences. 'I could hardly imagine doing that, myself.'

A wave of emotion sweeps him. No one else has understood.

He's felt so alone with those thoughts, until now. Suddenly he longs to pour out all the troubles in his heart. 'A beautiful day,' he begins gratefully; 'I have so much to thank you for.

76

Then: 'I'm only sorry my children weren't here to see it.' He stops. It would have been an even greater pleasure, he's been going to say, if Philippa hadn't kept the children away. But he's not quite a fool, even in his cups. He shouldn't be sharing his troubles. 'They went hunting instead,' he adds hastily, choking off the self-pitying confidence he's nearly shared, and trying to sound proud of his children's courtly friendships. 'At Sheen, Philippa said.'

It must be the memories of his own father that being in London today has awakened – that sudden recollection of a world in which a son's place is at his father's shoulder, learning his business, for all those formative years – that's making him feel this sadness, almost grief, for his own absent children. Or it's the drink. At any rate, Alice is giving him the casually concerned look of someone who doesn't understand the pain he feels. He doesn't think she has children of her own. For a moment he feels almost envious of the freedom from hurt that must represent; she can't be expected to feel the twisting in his heart. He knows he's talking too much.

Mildly, she says, 'And there was me thinking you were going to tell me what it was like travelling in Italy.' She laughs. He feels she's expecting more. But he doesn't know what.

'I'm sorry,' he says. 'Must be a little bit drunk.' She doesn't seem to mind. Her silence goes on being warm and inviting. It's a relief to have been able to confess something so innocuous.

After a pause, she says, 'Oh, well, who isn't, after a splendid dinner like yours? I felt a little tipsy myself.'

Still fuzzily, Chaucer now remembers that he's asked quite a lot of people in this room, since his earlier exchange with Alice by the window, about her husbands. There's been a quiet, nudging, whiskery sort of conspiracy about the answers he's got, and more than one jovial 'oh ho, my boy!' But he senses that no one else really knows, either, what Alice was up to before she became the Queen's demoiselle and the King fell in love with her. 'She's packed a lot into her years in this vale of tears, that one,' someone said knowingly. 'They say she was very friendly with Froissart, the Hainaulter,' Lyons said, 'and, or so I heard, with the knight who went to Ireland, what's-his-name, Windsor.' Lyons tried to wink at Chaucer but Chaucer shifted his eyes. 'There was Champagne, the baker, *I* heard. When she was just a girl. And Perrers, obviously,' someone else said. 'After Champagne. Wasn't she married to Perrers?' Nods all round, though nods that didn't seem to be backed by much precise knowledge as to which Perrers Alice might have lived with. One man opined, hazily, 'Jankyn Perrers, was it? The Fleming?' And, at the same time, another offered, 'Sir Richard Perrers? Hertfordshire?' All merchants know it's a mistake to admit ignorance. Rumours and guesses – even foolish ones – are better than no knowledge at all. But still, this conversation soon petered out. The lack of real interest makes Chaucer see that, even to these men, who like to measure and map and mine every potentially useful relationship and contact, it hardly matters what Alice was before she was touched by the King's grace, or whatever has made her the powerhouse she's become. It's her vivaciousness, and her current web of friendships, and her astonishing Midas touch, that interests them. Now, not the past.

But all those questions come rushing back into Chaucer's mind when he sees her. Suddenly brave, he thinks: No harm in asking.

'So . . .' he says, feeling his tongue thick in his mouth, 'how *did* you come to meet and marry Master Champagne, if you grew up in Essex?'

Country gentry families, in Essex as elsewhere, don't, on the whole, marry their daughters into City trade families, unless they've fallen on hard times and happened upon a temptingly rich merchant suitor already buying land in the countryside near their home. What little Chaucer knows of Master Champagne the baker doesn't seem to fit. If Master Champagne was indeed the first husband.

Then he blushes. He's given away the fact that he's been prying into her past all afternoon now, hasn't he? 'If that isn't an impertinent question,' he adds hastily. But he isn't too mortified. With Alice Perrers, he's beginning to feel, he can ask, at least. She won't hold a spirit of enquiry against him.

He's right. She doesn't look offended. She even hesitates, as if she might confide in him. There are memories in her eyes. For the first time, Chaucer sees the beauty of her.

But all she ends up saying, as Chaucer goes on looking expectantly into her eyes, is, 'Oh . . . I hardly remember. A day on the river . . . cygnets and ducklings . . . liverymen notching their beaks . . . a lot of laughing . . . spring in the air, I expect. But you know how it is. It seems so important at the time, but then you forget . . .'

Her voice grows lighter and more playful with every phrase. The moment has passed. She isn't going to tell him anything.

He shrugs. There's something delicious in this conversation, even without the kind of confidences he's been fishing for. So he doesn't much care.

But she isn't just teasing him. He can tell from the little furrow that now appears on her forehead – which, strangely enough, makes her look very young for a moment, not old – that she's thinking something serious, too.

'You know, Chaucer,' she adds (by now he likes the way she just calls him 'Chaucer'), 'I think people worry far too much about where they're from. It's not the past that counts, or where you're from. It's where you're going, and what you do when you get there. *That's* what matters.'

Chaucer thinks this over, and finds that the honesty in this matter-of-fact statement of her ambition pleases him more than he might have expected it to. This clarity of hers must be what has so impressed the merchants. He thinks: I'll do what they do in future and forget her past. No point asking foolish questions.

There's another pause. The red begins to bleed out of the shadows.

She's staring out again at the greying fields. Without turning towards him, with her eyes fixed out there somewhere, she adds, with that near-wistfulness she's had earlier, that he took for the beginning of sincerity, 'Anyway, you can marry all you want . . . but there's only one person you ever truly love, isn't there?'

Chaucer wonders, but can't for the life of him tell, whether she means the King.

Chaucer goes to sleep in a mostly happy blur of impressions and memories, the majority of them concerning his new friendship with Alice Perrers. But when he wakes up before dawn with a pounding headache, full of worries again, what he remembers most clearly is that quiet, strange moment between Alice Perrers, and Lyons, and Latimer: the three of them muttering together, glancing quickly at each other, egging each other on to something he couldn't grasp.

Even when he thinks back on it now, in the scratchy pre-dawn, tossing in his bed, reaching for the water jug, he can't imagine what that conversation can have been about.

FIVE

'Why was Richard Lyons with us yesterday?' Chaucer asks through his headache. 'When he's a vintner?'

Walworth, who until July, when his mayoral job begins, will represent the City at the wool trade, looks up from his desk across the hall. Chaucer sees the fishmonger's lean jaw clench, and the beautiful peaceful eyes go flinty, so you can see that, despite the angel's golden hair, he'd be a bad man to cross.

Then the merchant's eyes clear and his wry smile comes, transforming the fighter back into a charmer. 'Ah,' Walworth says, easily. 'You mean you don't know why Lyons needed to meet the wool comptroller, since his business has nothing to do with wool?'

The clerks at each man's desk also look up. Chaucer's one puts down his quill. There are faint, expectant smiles on both pink young faces. Chaucer can practically see them craning forward.

Chaucer's feeling a little wary now. He never expected such a strong reaction. But he nods.

'As it happens, we'd all like to know the answer to that question, dear boy,' Walworth says, nodding to the inquisitive clerks to go back to their columns of figures. They bow their heads. Then Walworth smiles a little wider, till his flawlessly ivory teeth glint in the sun. 'Just why *is* Master Lyons so interested in the wool business, when, as you say, he's a vintner?'

* * *

81

Walworth does tell Chaucer what he thinks of the Flemish vintner, but only later, at midday, outside the Customs House, and out of the clerks' earshot. He links arms with Chaucer and walks him up Water Lane to Thames Street. He has to lean down and sideways to reach, and to murmur in, Chaucer's ear. He's tall and wiry, and as strong as a knight in the lists.

'We are very glad,' he begins, with what to Chaucer's ear sounds unnecessary formality, 'all of us, that it is you who have been chosen as comptroller – a man we in the City can talk to without reserve. Someone we can trust.'

Chaucer bows, out of courtesy and pleasure combined. Perhaps he's just being flattered. But his own instinct, likewise, is to trust the three merchants he's trying not to think of as Uncle Will, Uncle Nichol, and Uncle John. Still, he's puzzled. The subtext of everything he's been told in the past few weeks of briefings is that his job in London will be to stop these three men expanding their interests beyond what is proper, and taking for themselves what is rightfully the King's. Yet, in this deep, comforting, familiar voice, he already hears a note of appeal. as if William Walworth and his friends fear that their own rightful interests are being eaten into.

Walworth's saying: 'Ever since I've held office in the City, we merchants have been complaining to the King that he was selling Italians too many special licences to export wool from England without paying customs to you' – he bows at Chaucer the Customs Comptroller – 'as all Englishmen have to. We've complained long and loudly. And, it seems, he heard us. For at least two, maybe three years, no more licences have been granted to Italians.'

Chaucer has to half jog to keep up with Walworth's stride. He puffs, 'Yes?'

'But someone else *has* been granted a special licence.' Walworth turns and arches an eyebrow. He wants Chaucer to guess who. It's a test of Chaucer's wit.

'Lyons,' Chaucer puffs, suddenly seeing it all – exactly how Lyons has become so rich, and why the merchants, who so obviously dislike and mistrust the Fleming, are nevertheless cautiously trying to bind him closer, and buy his loyalty to them, by giving him a post in their City administration. And why they're smarting.

Walworth nods. He looks pleased with Chaucer's quick response.

'We arrested some men at Southampton a week or so ago,' he confirms. 'They were loading cargo there. Sacks and sacks of wool, on a ship bound for Flanders. No stop at London or Middleburg planned, where they would have to pay customs. Naturally we tried to confiscate the cargo. My wool investigators are allowed to, even outside London, whenever they find contraband (and we'd had a tip-off that that's what this would be). But we couldn't, with this cargo, because there was nothing illegal about it. The men had a licence. An absolutely official licence, all green sealing-wax and royal stamps, straight from the King's administration. Made out to Richard Lyons.'

Chaucer wishes he could catch his breath.

'The King . . . wrote . . . Lyons a licence?' he pants. 'Himself?' He doesn't want to believe the King would have done down the merchants if he'd promised them not to sell any more foreigners any more special licences. Like everyone in the King's service, and in the country, he adores the old man. But he's heard about too many slips – and seen that fleeting, amused look in the royal eye too often – to know that loving the King and trusting him, at least with money, can't always be quite the same thing.

The whole business with special licences has always been pure foolishness, in any case. In principle, the King is cheating his own royal coffers – and therefore himself – by selling foreigners the right not to pay England's wool tax. But for a King who's always short of money, right here, right now, who's constantly scrabbling around for the coin to put down on that war-horse, or castle wing, or costume, on top of all the war expenses . . . well, in practice, it's tempting, any offer of a bag of actual gold, in the hand, no questions asked. Of course it is. Chaucer understands that. And as for the King breaking his royal word to Walworth and the other merchants, well, Chaucer can imagine how the King might finesse that, too.

He can see Edward telling himself, with a bit of a grin, that even if he's promised not to sell any more licences to Italians, if it's a *Fleming* who comes along, offering the right price, why, that's quite a different matter . . .

There's resignation in Walworth's laugh. 'Things are never that simple with my lord the King,' he says. 'No, he didn't write the licence himself.'

Chaucer's panting, and guessing, ever more wildly by now. 'A forgery?' he says, trying not to sound too hopeful. He'd rather it was that.

Walworth shakes his head. 'Not that, either . . . the licence was signed', he says sadly, 'by Baron Latimer. It was quite legal. He's the chamberlain. He's authorised to sign on the King's behalf. The King's hand wasn't on it, but he must have known.'

'But then . . .' Chaucer is utterly out of his depth by now. So the licence was legal, and the King just slyly hiding behind his servant's signature. That much he's got straight, now. But what he can't for the life of him see is how Richard Lyons ever met the King to do this private deal in the first place? Flemish merchants don't go running around at court without an introduction, and Walworth, who is sometimes received at court, would obviously never take along a chancer like Lyons. Someone else must have taken him to the King. But who?

It is only now that the other, separate, picture Chaucer woke up with today comes back into his mind. Latimer looking at Lyons, and Lyons looking back across Chaucer's table, groaning with all that food provided by Alice Perrers. And Alice in between them, eyes darting from one to the other, and a little smile on her lips . . .

'. . . Mistress Perrers,' he says flatly. Of course. He's known all along, really, bar the details. It will be Mistress Perrers who's introduced the foreign merchant to the King, or simply made the deal for him without an introduction. She likes money, and she likes stirring things up, just for fun. She enjoyed putting Philippa's nose out of joint with her feast, Chaucer saw yesterday, as much as she enjoyed making sure that the merchants were being properly fed. She'll be taking a cut from this, just as Latimer will be. She has fingers in every pie, doesn't she?

He shakes his head in reluctant admiration. You have to admire Mistress Perrers' sheer audaciousness. Suggesting to him that he should be keeping watch on Walworth and his men, while all along she knows that if there's mischief in the City, it's happening somewhere entirely different; somewhere much closer to her own good self. No, there are no flies on *her* . . .

Chaucer's almost smiling at this new insight into his new patron when Walworth interrupts his reverie by grunting with satisfaction and squeezing his arm.

'You were always a bright boy,' he says. Then, more hesitantly: 'Of course, I can't swear this is true, but they do say that the house Mistress Perrers got in the City last year was a gift from Master Lyons . . .'

He stops walking. He's going to turn left down Thames Street, while Chaucer's going to go straight over. The thoroughfare is crowded with salesmen shouting their wares. Elbows and baskets and carts knock into both men as the streams of human traffic part and sweep on past them. But neither Walworth nor Chaucer notice. Their eyes are locked. Walworth isn't quite ready to bow farewell.

'And of course, what really worries me is who might be behind Mistress Perrers, trying to undermine . . .' Walworth pauses, searching fastidiously for the right word, then settling for, '. . . *us*.' Chaucer understands him to mean *us* narrowly: the trio of merchant princes with power in the City. It doesn't actually include *him*. Still, he's flattered to be honoured by Walworth's confidences so soon in their adult relationship. And he wants to know more, of course. He wants to know why Walworth thinks Alice Perrers has gone to the trouble of putting Chaucer in the City, and of sending him off on this wild-goose chase of suspecting the top merchants are dishonest, while they nurse their own quiet fears about *her*.

Chaucer waits for Walworth to go on.

But then the future Mayor looks down at him, and, almost regretfully, puts his lips together. He begins gently to shake his head, as if wondering at himself. With a visible change of mood, he says, much more briskly, 'Listen to me, gossiping away like a Billingsgate fishwife – and you hungry and looking forward to your dinner. Age, dear boy, age. You'll have to forgive me.' He turns, and, smiling gaily over his shoulder, says, brightly, 'Till tomorrow.'

No point in showing disappointment. Chaucer waves and bobs his own cheerful bow. Thoughtfully he crosses Thames Street. But, on the other side, he stops again, looking back at the crowds packing the busy street without really seeing them. Who was Walworth about to say he suspected of being 'behind' the shifty money-making tactics of Mistress Perrers and Richard Lyons? And what stopped him finishing that thought?

It can't have been, can it, that for some reason, remembered at the last minute, long after he'd started confiding, William Walworth has suddenly got it into his head that he should also be wary of him, Geoffrey Chaucer?

Chaucer shakes his head in wonderment. What would have given the merchant that idea? It can't surely have been something he said?

He shrugs. He can't think what he can have said, or done. He probably won't be able to guess, either. Not yet. He doesn't know enough about the City yet.

So Chaucer's about to turn around again and head on home, towards the dinner he'll buy at a cookshop somewhere (no point in keeping a houseful of cooks if there's just him to look after) when he notices a tall gold-and-silver head back on Thames Street, sticking out above the crowd, a few yards down from where he and Walworth have just parted.

Walworth, like him, has stopped, deep in thought, and is looking back unseeingly at the people, towards where Chaucer was standing a few moments before. Even at this distance, Chaucer can see him slowly shaking his head.

It is later still before Chaucer finally puzzles out what was on Walworth's mind. Late enough that it's dark, and the torches are at their windy last gasp out on the terrace where he's sitting with Stury, looking out over the rushing water at the fire of stars above.

It's Stury who explains. The knight is pouring out more wine with an unsteady hand (unsteady because they have been here for hours, since before sunset, and they haven't bothered much with supper, because what do two poets need with food when they can drink and admire the view?).

'Your merchant friend was going to say he thinks Madame Perrers is the Duke of Lancaster's creature,' Stury says with hazy pronunciation but complete certainty.

'Well,' Chaucer says, after a pause. 'Is she?'

He's not aware of any relationship between Alice Perrers and the King's son; the only time he's ever even seen them talk was at that ball, right after Princess Joan threw the wine. But unravelling what goes on in the City is making him realise how little he knows about anything. Nothing would surprise him any more.

Stury lifts his shoulders. 'Not that I know of, dear boy,' he says blithely. 'Though with her, who can say? Always two steps ahead, that one.' He raises the cup towards the full moon (he's given to toasting the goddess Diana), and then, after drinking the top inch, goes back to talking. 'All I can tell you for sure . . . no love lost between the Duke and Master Walworth and company here in the City, we all know that. If La Perrers and Lyons have got some scheme going, Walworth's automatically going to put one and one together and make three, and see the Duke lurking in the background.'

Chaucer nods. That makes a kind of sense. The Duke's hostility to the big three merchants is well known. He wants them humbled. So Walworth might easily imagine that the Duke is sponsoring a rival clique to unseat his City government, or just that the Duke is turning a quiet penny by protecting that rival clique. Chaucer's immediate reaction is that there can't be any actual truth in any of it, of course. The Duke's not only the soul of honour. He's also the richest man in the land. So he certainly doesn't need money from dubious City deals; and he surely wouldn't take it if it were offered.

Chaucer likes Duke John. The two men are of an age; they've crossed paths often at court; there's always been affection between them. Chaucer remembers the Duke's grief when his first wife died. Chaucer even wrote a poem in memory of that first Duchess. The Duke was grateful. Chaucer knows him for a man who can love deeply. And Chaucer admires that, the more so now that he knows how complicated marriage can be. He doesn't necessarily think the Duke's idea for a wife for him was the right choice; but giving him Philippa as a bride was well meant. He's grateful. He also admires the Duke's loyalty. John of Gaunt looked after him and Philippa (and her sister, Katherine) financially after that first wife's death cost the two girls their jobs as demoiselles. The Duke arranged their pensions. He lets the Chaucer children share the lessons of his daughters, when at court. Chaucer's also grateful that the Duke (unlike Philippa) admires his poetry, and has invited him to more than one court evening to read it out. He's even sympathetic to the Duke's brusqueness of manner, in which he sees shyness, not arrogance. The Duke takes pains. You can't not respect that.

But Chaucer is a man of measure. After a moment, he realises that when it comes to judging whether the Duke might dislike Walworth and his independent-minded London friends enough to encourage a rival clique, just to bring down his enemies . . . to destabilise London's leadership purely out of spite . . . well, Chaucer doesn't really know enough. Yet.

He certainly doesn't understand why Stury's mouth is beginning to twitch.

'You don't know why Walworth got cold feet and ran off in the middle of that conversation, do you?' Stury's saying. He stops, waiting for Chaucer to catch up with the joke, grinning encouragingly at him.

When Chaucer's face fails to lighten, Stury drains the rest of his cup and bangs it down on the table. 'Sharpen your wits, dear boy,' he says mock-warningly. But he's still almost snuffling with barely restrained laughter. 'Welcome to the undeclared war of London. It's because it suddenly occurred to poor Walworth that, even if he likes you, even if he thinks of you as "that clever Chaucer boy, I've always said he'd make good", he can't trust you either . . .'

Chaucer has no idea what's so funny. 'But why?' he says, baffled. 'Why?'

Stury bursts out: 'Because he's bound to think *you're* the Duke of Lancaster's creature too, of course!'

'But . . .' Chaucer begins to stammer through the splutters across the table. He's about to say, in the tones of an injured innocent, 'But I'm not. I'm the King's man.' Which, at least in a formal sense, is true. But then all the other circumstantial things come rushing back into his head too – the pensions and the school lessons and the fact that he's known to admire the Duke and the job obtained for him by Alice, whom Walworth suspects of being in the Duke's pocket – and he realises that, yes, someone who fears the Duke *might* indeed see Chaucer's appointment as just another part of some dark design by the Duke.

Then the sight of Stury, now helpless with laughter at the idea of him, Chaucer, plotting for financial or political gain, gets to him. He picks up his cup. He drains it. He's shaking his head at this first dizzying glimpse of how busily people in this City, peaceful though they seem, actually hate and fear and suspect each other. Stury's right; it *is* all so absurd that it's funny. Whatever happens to him in London, he's beginning to see, at least, that he'll never be bored. After a moment, he too begins, rather hesitantly, to chuckle.

SIX

As far as you can see, forward and back, are horses' rumps, fat and sheeny, some carrying people, some loaded with carpets and hangings and cushions, some pulling carts piled with boxes and cups and dishes, but all ambling forward through Surrey towards the palace at Sheen.

Alice rides along through the spit of rain in a glow of contentment.

She's aware of boys putting sacking over ladies' knees up and down the train, to protect them in case the drizzle gets heavier. There are geese honking in the reeds. A young man somewhere just behind Alice is singing a melancholy love song near the reasonably pretty, and unbelievably rich, Eglantine de la Tour. I know what you're up to, you greedy boy, Alice thinks, not allowing the thought to alter her serene don't-bother-me-I'm-busy smile. She also thinks: Good luck to you; someone's got to get that girl's money; why shouldn't it be you? Let's face it, who, in the normal run of things, does anything but protect their own interests?

Yet, whatever her own doubters and detractors in the City might be thinking about her, the reality is that Alice is not, for now, thinking of any new money-making scams. She's done enough of that in the past.

She's done so well out of so many sharp business ideas, even before she took up with the King nearly ten years ago. She's made a good bit out of property, of course – buying, or begging, or borrowing, or just taking, always on the cheap, then sending in her team of quiet assessors and deputies to make improvements, buy up the next-door bits of land, build stout new buildings, take on good farm men to work the land, push back the forests, and generally shoot up the rental value, which she ploughs back into the next property that comes her way. In her time, she's also done good business advancing scared noblemen the bags of coin they need to pay the ransoms on their poor beloved sons held in France (and relieving the hand-wringing fathers of collateral in the shape of their spare manor houses, so hard to sell or raise money on, or just charging them an excellent rate of interest). And, most recently, she's been coining it, on the quiet, out of the wool trade, along with Richard Lyons.

But you have to be hungry to have the twitchy energy to get rich; you have to be scared of whatever it is, back there, that you're getting away from.

And now Alice is in a kindly, glowing, magnanimous frame of mind, having seen the glimmer of a new future in which her position can be quietly consolidated, and she can feel more sure her wealth will be protected after Edward goes, now she is going to have a new patron in Duke John. It's more of a relief than she expected. She must have been more worried than she knew about what would become of her. Her new serenity means that she is now able to think of other things; of helping people.

Her thoughts turn to Chaucer. Again. She's pleased she's done something good for him. She's paid her debt, more than, by wangling him that job, which will not only help smooth relations between the Duke and London, if Chaucer does that emollient peacemaking thing he's so good at, but will also raise Chaucer's standing. It might even keep that disagreeable wife of his happy that he's got a bit more money coming in, who knows? It feels so good, Alice reflects, to have done someone else a disinterested favour, for once.

It's not just back-patting, what she's thinking about Chaucer. She's also remembering the wistfulness in his eyes as he looked out at Essex, saying 'sometimes even one marriage', and the wry spark in them when he added that second phrase, the one about 'the woe in marriage'.

She likes the way he talks. He's so hopeless at looking after his own interests, so apparently a fool, but then so intriguing to talk to, and therefore not quite the pushover he seems. He isn't like anyone she's ever known. When he says things like that, all sly and mischievous, and his face lights up, he becomes beautiful. She's surprised at how softly she thinks that.

Maybe that's why she's found herself thinking that no one needs to spend their whole life hustling. Of course, if money comes your way, positively asking to be picked up, then why say no? But in the past few days she's realised she can't see the need any longer to make grubbing for gold the whole focus of her existence. No point in getting stuck there. Surely, by now, she's reached a point in life where she can indulge her higher feelings?

Because Alice is happy, she's feeling especially affectionate towards Edward, who is clip-clopping along next to her on his own bay palfrey.

She's been remembering, as she rides, as she steals glances at his slumped old body, so tired now, how magnificent he's looked in the past, tall and thin and energetic in his Garter robes. She's been remembering him in gold, winning the joust – when he could still joust – and triumphantly bringing out her scarf from his sleeve, and waving it for all to see. She's been remembering the thrill of his first embrace, of that then-handsome profile, half-seen from very close through her half-shut eyes, her terrified, thrilled thought: Lips anointed by God . . . touching *me* . . .

She doesn't usually have time for nostalgia. But today she's indulging herself. It's making her kind.

Alice can't wait to get to Sheen, because, once they're there, and she's settled Edward in, she's going to tell him the business idea she's had. (For Alice's kindness to Chaucer has been rewarded. Back there, in London, while she was sorting things out for him, talking to merchants in his hall, she was struck by an inspired plan, one of those bolts from the blue. God's blessings.) It's not a selfish idea, this one; it's not something that will benefit her. It will benefit Edward. It should make Edward happy – very happy indeed – because it should sort out Edward's financial troubles for good. And making Edward happy, she thinks, more earnestly than usual, is what she wants most in life. He's been so good to her. She's treasuring her idea, looking forward to seeing his face when he hears.

Meanwhile, she should entertain him . . . while away the miles . . . make him laugh.

'Look, a dragonfly,' she says. She points it out, and, from astride his horse, Edward's eyes obediently follow. The insect is glittering blue and green above the stream they're crossing. Alice adds, 'Same colours as my robe, do you see?'

Edward's supposed to chuckle at that – to recognise it as the opening gambit in a game of jewellery-giving. But the eyes he turns to her are blank. He's all cloudy and confused this morning. Perhaps she should have insisted on a litter. But he was so excited last night at the idea of seeing how his building works were going at Sheen that it never occurred to her he might be like this by daybreak.

Smiling brightly, because she doesn't know how to behave with Edward except to flirt like a cheeky girl in the presence of the all-powerful, Alice leans over and takes his hand, as if nothing is wrong. 'Look,' she repeats, putting the limp, veined claw to her water-coloured taffeta sleeve. 'I should have a dragonfly brooch made to go with this, shouldn't I?'

He just nods without seeming to understand.

It's not the first time; she can't shake off the unease taking hold of her. Over the next hour, she tries all kinds of things to jog Edward back to his usual self. With that not-worried smile clamped determinedly to her face, she reminds him of how he had the French King John the Good living on English soil as his prisoner for seven years after Poitiers Field, where the Prince of England captured him. England's most glorious victory, she says, and all yours and your son's. You really are the king of kings. There's no reaction. She says, 'Do you remember? They say John and nineteen knights from his guard dressed identically for battle, to confuse our boys. But we got him anyway.' She squeezes Edward's hand. Still limp. 'Do you remember, afterwards, after he got away again, back to France?' she whispers with the brightness fading from her voice. 'How his son escaped too, and the French weren't paying the ransom for him, but he came back to you, all the way to London – of his own accord – because he didn't want to dishonour the King of England, who'd treated him so well?'

Edward smiles vaguely. 'I remember the pageant when he came back . . . and the procession,' she falters. She keeps nodding, like an idiot, trying to force a proper response from him. 'It was the most exciting thing I'd ever seen . . . I worshipped you that day . . . from where I was on the street, at least. No one in that crowd could possibly have been shouting louder than I was. And waving . . .'

He nods, and squeezes her hand weakly back. But she's still not sure he understands.

It's a mood, a vapour, she tells herself determinedly; it will pass as soon as he's rested. She thinks: I'll send him straight off for a nap when we arrive.

This is how Alice has worked out that Edward can get the money he needs if he is to win the war in France – an outcome which, in turn, might bring Edward himself back to his old glory.

It's not simple. But then the problem of getting money for the war has become horribly tangled over the years of fading and failure.

The only reason that England has not been utterly defeated in France is that, after his humiliation overseas last year, the Duke of Lancaster arranged a one-year truce on shaming terms. There is no money for more fighting, so, very soon, Duke John will have to leave England to negotiate another truce, and keep hostilities on hold for another year. The next talks, at Bruges, will be even more humiliating. English pride would prefer a different outcome. But English finances are not in a state to dream of that.

King Edward can't raise enough money for the wars in France nowadays because, back in the good old days of victory, he spent other people's money so lavishly on warships and destriers and scarlet banners and golden trumpets that he bankrupted the finance houses of Florence and brought trading all over Christendom to a standstill.

It's taken decades, but at last the Lombard and Florentine bankers are shakily back on their feet. Yet the Crown of England still owes them thousands upon thousands of pounds, amounts carefully noted in clerk hand on the hundreds of dishonoured bonds and tallies that still flutter on desks and in counting-houses today, bonds as useless for the purposes of trading as the ragged pennants and banners of the knights of England, hanging lifeless and flat in their airless armouries, are for the purposes of war. There will be no new loans from the Italians until those hundreds of old insults to the financiers' honour, those blows to their pockets, are rubbed out of existence.

The whisper blows through the court with every new defeat or humiliation. If only the Italians could be persuaded to lend again . . . if only. But no one knows how to persuade them.

Meanwhile, the only loans the King can raise are ones that come from his own leading merchants. Thank God for the boom in the wool trade; these three Englishmen are richer than ever before. Not just from wool, because they are also traders in cinnamon and anise and coriander, pomegranates and almonds and oranges, shark's fins, swordfish and mermaid's tails, but it's the high price of English wool these last years that has tipped them into grandeur. The King relies very heavily on Master Walworth and his two friends, now there's no one else. Perhaps they should be grateful. But they aren't, particularly. They're honoured to be asked, of course, but . . . they don't think they'll get the money back. They click their beads, and calculate: the King won't pay; the war damages our business interests anyway; the Duke wouldn't win even if we bought him the best army in the world. Alice heard Walworth, back there at Chaucer's, laughing with Brembre, muttering, obviously of the Duke, 'Him? He couldn't lead a pack of choirboys across Chepe – even with a map.' So why throw good money after bad? The London merchants would rather keep their money in their counting-houses than finance the faint hope England can be glorious in victory. Secretly, Alice can understand why. But Edward finds it a mystery. He begs for their money, cheerfully and nobly enough; he relieves each faint-hearted new Mayor, each summer, of another large sum; he laughs behind their backs at their blind spot about glory; but he'd prefer not to have to humble himself.

This, then, is the problem. Italian bankers: fabulously rich again, but not in the least interested in lending to a bad-risk King. England's three mightiest merchants: rich and getting richer, but also clinging anxiously to their money-bags. Look at Walworth, back there, at Chaucer's, tittering so sadly behind his hands for all to see: 'Is my lord going to want fifteen thousand, or more?'

But what if the King could find someone new, in England, who's rich enough to borrow money from in the quantities he wants?

That would be the solution.

And what Alice suddenly saw, back there at Chaucer's house, is that she is in a position to make this happen.

Because, now, there's Richard Lyons, isn't there?

She knows, who better, just how rich Richard Lyons has got. They've done well together out of the special wool licences; and Alice's pay, like Latimer's, has only been a small percentage. Lyons is rolling in it – so rich he could easily afford to lend £15,000 to the King. More, maybe. And the Fleming, unlike the established merchants, would actually *like* to become Edward's backer. Since he got so rich, he's started to crave respectability too. Walworth's half seen the danger of Lyons; he's trying to buy him into the establishment with a little job in the City government at Guildhall. But it's not enough. Lyons is a big powerful man. Nothing would please him better than to bypass Walworth and the City altogether, and make the King his own personal client and friend.

The only obstacle to what Alice has in mind is that Lyons doesn't actually know the King yet. (Those wool licences were all Alice's idea, and it was Alice who, for a consideration, got Latimer's signature on the documents. She didn't see any need, back then, to bother the King with detail.) But now . . . well,

Alice can introduce Edward to Master Lyons, nothing easier. It's time they met.

It will make Alice laugh to put old Walworth's nose out of joint, too. Walworth: so smugly goody-goody, so given to quoting annoying little rules at people, so respectable and pompous and conventional, with his much-paraded friendship with the aristocratic Bishop Courtenay of London and his suspicion of all the new preachers who don't much like the Church of Rome. She knows Walworth isn't really quite the paragon of virtue he likes to pretend, whatever his angel face might suggest. She knows he earns a fortune from his Flemish whorehouses at Southwark. And she can't see why he hasn't been able to live and let live over the question of the tax-free wool exports, when it's been such a nice little earner for her and Lyons for so long. But, with the public fuss Walworth's insisting on making, going blabbing to everyone and their aunt about it, arresting people even, questions are being asked; she's got no real alternative any more but to get Lyons to stop. Just for that, it'll do Walworth no harm to get a bit of a jolt.

Everyone else will be happy. For this is the plan Alice is about to set out.

First, Master Lyons must agree to stop using his special licences to export wool tax free. (Chaucer will be pleased – England's official take from the wool trade will go up, which will make him look good. He might get a pay rise. And it'll be good for Lyons and Alice and Latimer to move on from wool, and stop the talk.)

Next, Alice will introduce Master Lyons to the King. The Fleming will then be allowed to lend the King a first sum of £20,000. (The King will like that bigger, rounder number better than Walworth's grudging £15,000 and lending a bit more, to demonstrate generosity, will be no skin off Lyons' nose).

Third, Lyons will earn a premium of £10,000 on that loan. This means he'll eventually be repaid a total of £30,000. (That very high 50 per cent interest rate will keep him very sweet, and the King never notices the small print.)

Other merchants won't be so envious that Lyons has got into the King's good books when they find out that the Fleming's willing to accept just half his repayments from the King in actual clinking countable gold coin. He'll take the other half in the old, discredited debt paper on which the King made his empty promises to the Italians, years ago. Since the King defaulted on this debt, also many years ago now, those worthless old paper promises will not be exchanged at their face value, but at only half what's written on the page – so any paper signed by the King promising to repay an Italian finance house 100 marks will, now, count as being worth just 50. Even so, prudent City men might feel Lyons was a fool to accept a promise of even 50 from this particular shifty King. (Alice knows Lyons won't care, even if the King never pays a penny back against the debt. Lyons' pay-off will be coming from that fat interest rate he's also getting. Better yet, he'll be building a relationship with the King, which will stand him in good stead later. So he'll have nothing to complain of.)

Best of all, this deal might finally end the festering nastiness between King and Italians.

The Italian financiers, who years ago wrote off their loans to the King of England, will suddenly start getting repayments from the Crown, after all. Only on half of what they originally lent, true, but that's more than they've been expecting for all these years. So they'll be happy. It might be enough to persuade them that the King of England is sorting out the country's finances. It might even just be enough to persuade the Italians to start lending to the King again . . . and then, with a combination of Lyons and Italians at his back, who knows what might not happen with the war?

No wonder Alice is pleased with this plan. It's big. It's public-spirited. It shows her new maturity. And it solves everyone's problems.

Most personally pleasing of all, to Alice, is the knowledge that it all grew out of a chance remark at Chaucer's table, a meeting of eyes between her and Lyons and Latimer while Walworth twittered on about loans; a clear-sighted moment of foreseeing the possible. She's quietly proud that, even now that she's so comfortable, and no longer the dewy young girl she once was, she's still got her wits about her.

How pleased Edward will be, she thinks, as Sheen comes into view through the trees.

It's chaos in the royal chambers: pale bare stone walls, an uncovered bed frame like a lone ship with no sails, a sea of half-open chests and sacks, and a tide of people sweeping over them, whispering furiously. They've turned up late at Sheen. Now tired ladies with muddy hems are doing their best to make up for lost time, pulling out hangings from boxes and pummelling the cushions their demoiselles are yanking from travel bags. Boys with brooms are banging the dust from them. The windows are open, and a chilly summer breeze is gusting at everything. Taller boys on stools and ladders are heaving up heavy brocades and tapestries, stretching to hook the worked cloth from knobs sticking out of the stones, accidentally kicking people passing by carrying clothes or brushes or bed linen or pomanders or perfumes, and hissing and cursing under their breath at all the fiddly effort required to create instant royal splendour.

Alice glides among them with the vague smile she's always found so useful at court, the one that signifies: 'I'm not angry, but don't speak to me just now. I am busy and important. I have better things to do than to be associated with your inefficiency.'

She has a bag in her hand. She doesn't say a word to anyone. She just floats away into the antechamber, where the window looks out over the park with its drowned greens and greys. Despite the season, a fire is burning (he feels the cold, poor old Edward), and the enormous bathtub, hung with cloth and green ribbons for modesty's sake, is already steaming.

Edward's sitting on a stool by the window, still in his sour-smelling travelling cloak, with his shoulders sagging, an old man near the end of his days staring out at nature, to which even a king must one day return. He looks round, startled, when he hears her. But then he smiles – only you – and goes back to his faraway thoughts as she moves about behind him.

Detail matters. Edward loves to wash off the dirt of the journey as soon as he arrives in a new place. It's how he shuts the world out until he's composed himself enough to behave like a king again. So Alice makes a ritual of it.

She's ordered the Sheen servants to have water boiling from midday on, so he wouldn't have to wait. A king shouldn't wait for his pleasures. From the moment they left Westminster, she hasn't for a moment taken her eyes off the man on the horse carrying the bag containing the great sweeps of towel and the bath hangings – the finest embroidered lawn, great cloudy sheets of it, with enough green vines and blue flowers and birds on it to blind a dozen seamstresses. She'd need that bag as soon as they reached Sheen: the moment when, as she knows from experience, the mess of arrival would be at its worst. Edward loves those hangings. They go everywhere with him.

She's kept the little bottle of rose oil in her own saddlebag, and the exotic sponges provided by Brembre and Philpot's grocers' guild, and the gold-backed combs, and the silver-chased scissors, and the oil of lavender to rub the sore on his ankle with, and the strips of bandage. She's also personally carried three red roses plucked this morning from the gardens at Westminster Palace, wrapped in a damp rag, encased in a small wooden box.

Now she arranges all this on the window ledge. She tips a few drops of rose oil through the steam, watching the little ring of it cloud and dissipate in the water, sniffing at the rich scent of gardens in sunlight that suddenly fills the steam.

Finally, she opens the box.

'Look,' she says, and his eyes turn. Neatly, murderously twisting off the heads of each limp rose in turn, she pulls out three great handfuls of dewy pink petals and, with the air of a magician, opens the curtains and throws them on the water.

The mysterious scent of summer happiness wafts out to where the King is sitting. At last Edward smells it, and, now he can see the floating rose petals, seems to understand. Faintly, he smiles. It's the first time today that he's met her eye.

'Beautiful,' he murmurs, and fumbles for her hand. He's as grateful as if it's the first time she's done this, and as surprised, she thinks sadly. 'You're very good to me, my dear.'

She kisses the top of his head. 'I like to make you happy,' she murmurs back as, putting her hands on his shoulders, she eases off the cloak.

Human decline – the slow return of dust to dust and ashes to ashes – is a strange business, she thinks as she undresses him down to the skinny arms and legs, the roughened barrel of chest, the bent back, the privy member hanging uselessly below, and braces herself to half push, half lift him into the water. He's got so thin, but he's still heavy enough to take her breath away.

How long is it since she first saw him like this, with that wondering, uncertain look in his eye? She can't even remember the early shivers of anxiety she must have had when he started to forgot a word here, or a name there.

What she does remember is the time when she was still confident he was all right. She has to work back from those happy moments to find the shadows. For instance, he was definitely all right the day she heard him talking to prim little William of Wykeham. It was a conversation she probably wasn't intended to overhear, but how could she not, since she was in the chamber with them, making them comfortable, pouring out wine, embroidering something in a corner, turning her alert eyes down, keeping herself quiet, keeping her lips tight together, keeping her ears open as she always did? He said, in that mocking way he used to have, in response to one of the Chancellor Bishop's gentle naggings about his failure to make confession often enough, 'But I've had to give up fucking and jousting since I saw sixty on the horizon, dear man, so what would I tell you?' She'll never forget the poor Bishop of Winchester's shocked pink face. She had to bite her own lips tighter together and look down harder than usual at whatever never-to-be-finished piece of work was in her frame to stop herself from laughing. It still makes her smile now to remember it. Of course Edward didn't mind shocking the Bishop. He just went on, with all his old bright brutal cheerfulness, 'Though I still think about them. So you could be right. Perhaps it is time for confession.'

When was that? Before William of Wykeham was sacked as Chancellor, which must be three years ago, for Alice has had his confiscated manor at Wendover for two years already. And not that long before Edward turned sixty. And this greyness of mind has crept up on him since then, she doesn't know when . . . whenever she isn't looking.

It's worse than his body going. That was understandable, at least. She can't remember when she last made love with Edward, but it was certainly some time before that jocular remark of his to William of Wykeham. She doesn't really even want to remember those last bouts of careful, non-jolting, old-man love, with both of them trying their best, and sometimes even having a quiet chuckle together over the slow indignity of age. Those last times have faded and blended in her mind. She prefers to remember the first times: the breathless excitement, the shape of his nakedness, the lion smell of him, before it was medical oils and piss.

Not that he's faded, altogether. Even now, sometimes, Edward can still be so well, and his talk so full of energy and mischief and jest, that it seems as if days like today are only a cloud that has passed. Alice treasures those moments.

'You,' she says lovingly, supporting him back to the stool, catching her breath, then kneeling to towel him vigorously down. She looks up, over the sagging mound of his stomach, into the beautiful long eyes fixed on her above the damp beard. This is intimacy, in the winter of your life. This is all it can be. It must be sad for a man who once so enjoyed the pleasures of the flesh. She makes her voice a little throatier. 'The handsomest man in Christendom, still.' Sensuously, she strokes his blotchy thigh.

He's feeling revived after the bath. He grins with some of his old charm. He even puts a gnarled hand on her head, as if he might push her down on himself. She knows from experience that he won't. He knows that her flirtatiousness doesn't really mean she expects him to make love to her. He just appreciates the make-believe. He's playing along.

102

This is what they've always shared: a love of games; a belief you can play with the realities that no one else has the nerve to question; a faunish, pagan sense of fun. This, she tells herself, is why it doesn't matter what age does to him.

He's humming as she pulls the nightshirt over his head, and slips the slippers on his feet, and leads him away to dress the sore on his ankle.

Once they're alone in the bedchamber, when he's comfortable on the padded armchair before the fire, she puts one of his feet in the basin of lavender water and kneels before the other. She rubs unguent gently over the dry, flaking edges of the scab that won't heal, then winds the bandages she's cut carefully round the ankle whose skin was too old to renew itself, trying to stop the quiet horror inside herself at the thought of the bone just inside there, under the decaying skin, the white mark of death, waiting to come through.

It's only now, when she sees Edward leaning back against the cushions, enjoying the feel of her young flesh rubbing the cold of death away for a moment more, and every now and then grunting a little – but himself again, more or less, with a twinkle in his eye – that she judges the time to be right.

She begins to tell him about her idea.

She goes on rubbing as she speaks. He goes on grunting.

'Lyons will take the Italian debt off your hands,' she says. 'Gnn-h.'

'And you'll sort out the wool problem too – he's promised it will stop.'

'Gnn-h.'

He should sound more excited.

'You'll have the money you need for this year . . . and the Italians may come back too . . .'

With a flicker of impatience, she wonders if those sounds he's making are actually an acknowledgement of what she's saying, or just the sounds of pleasure at being massaged. It's even possible that they're snores. He sometimes does nod off while people are talking to him. And he's just had a bath.

'That would be good,' she goes on experimentally. 'Don't

you think?' She looks up while her hands tie the little knot at the end of the bandage.

His eyes are only half-shut. He's half smiling, like an old alley cat, with torn ears and eyes and scars and a missing limb or two, purring on a sunny wall. It's only when she takes away her hands and takes his bandaged foot out of her lap that he stops. With an air of surprise, he peers down at her.

'Don't you think?' she repeats sharply. She can hardly believe he's taking no notice. She's been so sure he'll be overjoyed. Grateful. He should be. It's the most astute fund-raising idea anyone in his service has come up with in years.

'What, what?' he splutters. 'Oh . . . Yes indeed.'

He hasn't been listening to a word, but thinks he can get away with pretending. All Alice's impressive statesmanlike thought, all that careful weighing of percentages and outcomes, all that convincing herself that, through today's good idea, she's proving herself capable of becoming the intelligent strategist of tomorrow, the good angel at Duke John's shoulder: all gone to waste . . . ignored.

Alice is not always perfectly statesmanlike. The flash of rage she's having that her idea has had such a disappointing response is too vivid to allow measured self-criticism. She doesn't ask herself questions such as: Was this, really, the best moment? Is Edward truly in a state to take in talk of debt today?

Instead, she thinks: Is this all I am to him, after all these years? Someone whose voice he can just ignore? A servant, a nurse, a bloody pair of hands?

Then, mastering herself a little, she moves on to: Well, if he doesn't want to listen, it's not the end of the world. He'd agree all right if he had a sensible bone left in his body. He'd be jumping at the idea.

Finally, taking a deep breath, Alice tells herself that it's up to her to help him make the right decision.

She says, briskly rushing him on, in tones that suggest she'll brook no nonsense, 'Lord Latimer agrees with you – that taking out this loan could be the solution to several problems at the same time.'

Edward answers, 'Latimer . . . a good man, Latimer. Very

good.' But he sounds a little fretful now. He's looking around. He's beginning to understand that the massage is over, the bandage tied. There'll be no more till the morning.

That's assent enough, Alice judges. There's no need to feel exasperated with him. He's agreed.

'You're tired . . . we'll get you into bed,' she says, much more gently. He nods. His eyes are drooping – a child deprived of a treat.

She heaves him up. He stands, helpless, with his arm limp over her shoulder. When she begins to walk, in tiny steps, he shuffles along with her to the bed.

'So shall I tell Latimer to prepare the papers you want drawn up? And send him to you in the morning?' she says as they move.

He nods. He's forgotten the whole conversation already, she can see. He just wants to be stroked and comforted and tucked into bed.

She blows kisses all the slow tiptoeing way to the door, gentle kisses, as if to a baby. His eyes are shut long before she gets there.

But once she's out on the other side, she picks up her skirts and runs, as fast as she can, down the corridor, feeling the power in her legs, pushing her up and away, rejoicing as she goes in the quickness of her breath and the pink on her cheeks and the heat of the blood coursing through her. She can't help herself. After hours of going so slow, she has to celebrate being young and alive.

And she has to find William Latimer, fast.

The candlelight is reflected in his eyes.

The servant has gone.

The lean tanned face is showing its deep lines. Lord Latimer's smile is a lion's casual snarl, eyes half-closed with sheer pleasure, head stretching luxuriously back on the neck, a beast of prey feeling the power of himself. He must have been a devil with the women in his time. 'It doesn't stop here, you know,' he's saying. Quietly – half-growl, half-purr. 'Or it needn't. If you wanted to go further.'

She stays still. What can he mean? They've solved every problem already, haven't they?

But there's always further to go. There's always a refinement. She's always known that. So Alice raises her eyebrows just a self-possessed fraction. It won't do to look naive.

'You mean . . .' she says. Not quite a question. She folds her hands and waits.

The candle flickers on the table between them. Latimer looks around without moving his head, just a flicker of eyes – he has an old soldier's stillness about him – but there are no open doors or windows in this room bare of hangings. He puts his elbows on the table. He leans forward until his eyes are burning so close to Alice that they seem to separate and float, four golden-green circles over very white teeth, bared. He breathes, 'The debt he'll be buying. Lyons. The discounted debt . . .'

Alice waits. His excitement is catching. She's no longer as composed as she would have liked to be. She can feel her body leaning forward, closer and closer, until her face is nearly touching his – as if they're lovers, about to kiss. Her heart beats faster.

'. . . fifty marks for every hundred borrowed from the Crown.'

Alice says, in a monotone, 'Yes.'

'Imagine if you were to buy those debt papers on from Lyons. Pay a bit more. Sixty marks, say. He'd be glad of the profit . . .'

'Yes . . .' Be patient, Alice tells herself. It doesn't do to sound mystified.

'Then, once they were your bonds, you'd cash them in at the King's treasury . . .'

'Yes,' Alice says, nostrils flaring, already scenting the beginning of the answer.

'. . . at face value.'

Alice stops breathing. It seems a long time before she realises her body has stopped obeying her, and tells her chest to expand and take in air, and let it out.

She says, and she no longer cares that her voice is trembling,

'You mean – I'd buy something for sixty marks, and exchange it for a hundred marks straight from the treasury?'

Doubling my money, or just about. Though Latimer would want a cut.

He nods. 'We'd split the profit.'

The candle flickers, but neither of them notices any more. All Alice can see is those golden orbs, dancing before her eyes.

After a long silence, she says, flat-voiced again, 'How?'

But she knows. The three hundred people of the royal household are divided into two layers, the upper one of which, the *domus magnificencie*, numbers more than a hundred people, and centres on the King's chamber. It's run by Latimer. It's Latimer who formally controls access to the royal presence. It's Latimer who chooses the chamber staff of knights and esquires of the body, the King's closest attendants (apart from Alice). He's also in charge of the steward who's in charge of the *domus providencie*, the lower part of the household, that teeming mass of people inhabiting kitchens and butteries and pantries and spiceries and stables, and of the money kept and doled out to the traders and farmers who supply the court, as well as to the King's creditors, by the lower royal purse: the cofferer, the comptroller, and the man in charge of royal finance, the treasurer. Sir Richard Scrope: unruly hair, big bony knees and elbows, flaking skin on a brow furrowed from the counting of coin, a man with anxious, short-sighted eyes.

Somewhere very close to Alice, the white teeth flash again.

'I'm the chamberlain,' Latimer says through his grin. 'I can make it all right with Scrope. He's not a man for trouble.'

'Him . . . yes . . . anything for a quiet life,' Alice agrees, for the sake of saying something pleasant – but almost absent-mindedly. She has blood drumming through her head, a great fast tattoo of it. She's thinking.

They'll . . . They'd make fortunes doing this. If they did it. She and Latimer would be rich beyond their wildest dreams.

But . . . it would also undo so much of the good that the deal she's dreamed up between King and merchants is supposed to bring to Edward, and the merchants, and the Duke of Lancaster, and the whole realm of England. She and Latimer (and probably Lyons, because, realistically, he'd find out, soon enough, and they'd have to cut him in too, wouldn't they?) would be taking at least some of the money meant for the war.

She'd be stealing from Edward, who loves her.

She'd be breaking faith with her new ally, his son, whose protection she wants.

But, then again, they almost certainly wouldn't ever find out. No one ever does, unless you're very unlucky.

And how rich she'd be.

As she ponders, a picture forms behind her eyes. Edward, lying back against his cushions, his beard damp and combed into wet grey seaweed strands, blissfully unaware of her quiet disgust at the sore on his ankle, just enjoying the smell of the lavender oil she's massaging into it, snorting and grunting like an old animal, and not even bothering to listen as she explains how he could save his finances.

The ingratitude of him, she thinks.

And another picture. Edward, exhausted, eyes closing despite himself, and the trusting way he leans his weight on her as she shuffles him to the bed. He doesn't realise that he's so heavy, even now, in his touching helplessness, that she never quite knows if she'll be able to find the strength to heave him forward.

Or perhaps he just doesn't care.

For a moment, she's overwhelmed by the vision of the self-ishness of old age that comes to her. Perhaps he'd be just as carelessly grateful to anyone young and willing, anyone who'd make him feel, for a moment here and a moment there, that he could push back the darkness and grab an extra hour or two of life.

It doesn't matter to him that she's the one beside him, she thinks, with a spike of silent rage. Letting him borrow her vigour and energy. Anyone would do.

'What do you think?' she hears.

She's been so lost in her thoughts – the will-I, won't-I whirligig – that she hasn't realised she's dropped her eyes till, recognising the suppressed impatience in Latimer's voice, she darts them quickly back up to his. A guilty thing surprised.

She shakes her head.

For once, she doesn't care if there's indecision on her face or in her voice. There's indecision in her heart too.

'I don't know,' she says.

Latimer's no fool. She can see, from the velvet look he gives her, that he's following her thoughts.

He purrs, 'My dear. You must think of yourself a little, you know.'

There's a longer silence. She wanted to be told that. She wanted to be cajoled. Still, Alice feels her face grow thoughtful – sullen, almost.

She looks down again. But she hears every word he says next.

'You have to think of your own future. This' – he pauses, giving them both time to hear the unspoken word, *he* – 'isn't going to last for ever, you know.'

She mutters, 'But the war . . . that money was going to help with the war . . .'

But Latimer must hear doubt, or insincerity, in that. He caps her: '. . . which will never be won if Duke John is leading it. There's no point in more war, with him.'

She looks straight at him now. She's beginning to lose the numbness she's felt for all these long moments with Latimer's eyes on her, a paralysis brought on by even contemplating this giant stride towards fully fledged dishonesty. She keeps thinking, instead, about how rich she'll be if she says yes. It's strange what a warming thought that is; how damp her skin, how fast her pulse. He nods encouragingly. His eyes are dancing, inviting her to laugh with him.

'A good peace is better for England than a bad war, isn't it?' he adds, scenting victory, suddenly almost jocular with relief. 'Honestly? And far cheaper, too.'

She'll be rich.

The silence yawns on. His hazel-gold eyes are on hers.

Both of them are almost surprised when Alice laughs, and takes a deep breath, and says, in her firmest, most resolute voice, 'Yes.'

SEVEN

Fortune's Wheel

Alice doesn't sleep well, that first night at Sheen. She tosses and turns. She's up before dawn. She's uneasy enough about what she's said to Lord Latimer that she makes her excuses to Edward, before he's even properly awake, gets his permission, and rides off, back through London, east to Essex.

She needs to talk to Aunty.

When Alice was only a girl, delivering tiles to St Albans with her old Aunty Alison on the cart (she can still hear old Aunty's indulgent voice saying, 'You've been a good girl, show you a bit of the world, why not?'), she saw a picture in stained glass in the church window there that she's kept in her heart all her life.

It's a picture you see all over the place. There are a lot of other people in post-Mortality England who are obsessed with the goddess Fortune and her wheel. She features in the rose window of churches all over the land.

There's nothing very Christian about Fortune, of course. But the priests turn a blind eye to the goddess's inconvenient paganness, because she packs in the crowds at Mass. To the brave, and to the chancers, and the gamblers, and the opportunists, Fortune represents hope: that effortless climb to the top of the wheel. But what she also represents – the capricious destruction of the greedy, later on – suits the gloomy, doomy mood of everyone else.

You see envy in the narrow eyes of every stay-at-home who doesn't dare venture out to try his luck in the rough new game of life, these days. Anyone who isn't making a quick fortune wants anyone who is to get his come-uppance quick. So thinking of the punishment Fortune has waiting at the end of the wheel she spins pleases the dourest of congregations in the churches, looking bitterly up at the rose windows, as much as the promise of hope pleases the people with dreams in their hearts.

What the congregation sees in the window: Fortune, that temptress, that slut, smiles temptingly down, in jewel-bright light, luring people on to take a chance, to jump on her wheel, to make their name, to get rich quick.

And this is what happens next to the humans whirling round their little bubbles of coloured glass, chancing a dance with the goddess: once she's hooked someone in, you'll see her willing victim on her left, clinging to the turning wheel as it moves upwards, clockwise. This happy human figure with everything still to come has sun-kissed hair flying down and back as it floats effortlessly towards the top, with the prideful little word *regnabo*, which Alice likes to translate as 'I'm going to have it all', floating above their prideful little head.

Above Fortune's head, hanging on at the very top of the turning wheel, is a second little human figure who's happier still. This one crows, *regno*, 'I'm at the top!' in the same cramped black letters.

But it's the other side that most interests the losers in the congregation, because the wheel that has brought those human figures up keeps turning, and down they go again.

It's the terror on the face of the little figure to Fortune's right that these people like to gloat over, the terror of someone being whirled back downwards by the wheel, realising it's all over, that day of glory, never to return, and howling, 'I'm finished', *regnavi*. Best of all is the abjectness of the last little person, right at the bottom, dropping off the wheel, being trampled under Fortune's careless feet. 'Sum sine regno,' it whimpers. 'I've been left with nothing.'

Quite right too, says the congregation, through smugly pursed lips. Pride goes before a fall.

Alice remembers looking up at the first of these great glowing stained-glass temptations she ever saw, and saying to Aunty, a bit defiantly, in the way of children trying to find words for a serious idea, but still afraid they'll be laughed at for being naive, 'I don't see why you have to be destroyed by Fortune's wheel. Why can't you just get off when you've got where you want – stop at the top?'

And she remembers Aunty laughing, but kindly, in that way she's always had, of seeming peacefully to know what's what, without even trying, and answering, 'I know just what you mean, dear. The great trick to life is knowing when to stop.'

Alice must already have known, even back then, when she first saw Fortune, when she was, what, nine or ten, that she would try and hitch a lift on the wheel, too, as soon as she possibly could. She must already have been thinking out how.

But she couldn't have guessed how soon her chance would come.

It came on another uncertain day, back in Essex, and Alice a quick girl of eleven or so chasing Johnny and Wat and Tom through a cloud of cow-parsley, and everyone whooping and red-faced and light with laughter, when one of the boys – Wat, maybe, whoever was up ahead – stopped. So they all stopped. They were good like that – took their cues from each other, got the hint as quick as they could, a wink here, a nod there. They trusted each other, all old Alison's brood of waifs and strays, being brought up together, as if they were real brothers and sisters. So now they hunched down in the ditch beside him, stilling their breath, ragged and sharp-eyed, looking to see what he'd seen.

And there they were, a whole family of newcomers, leading horses back from the stream to the road, a lanky mother, complaining in an undertone, a henpecked-looking husband nodding his head and patting hopelessly at the air with his hands, five daughters, walking in order of size, the oldest only a bit smaller than Alice, but all with the same air of yawning

113

discontent, and, still astride on a pony tied by a string to the manservant's nag, a little boy, half-asleep, nodding from side to side with the animal's movement. All in clothes without a tear or a mend in them. And every horse oat-fed and bright and fat as a barrel.

Sometimes it only takes a moment. From the moment Alice stepped out through the tall weeds and, smoothing down her rags, said, in her cheeriest voice, addressing the complaining mother, whom she guessed would be likeliest to respond, 'Need any help, lady?' her future was settled.

The Champagnes let her, and the other dancing-eyed urchins, take them home to the tilery. But it was only her they saw. And when they got home, Aunty Alison took one look at the cut of their clothes and saw them right. Told Alice to mind the little boy, show him the wooden toys on the shelf, make herself useful; got the other kids measuring out drinks and cutting hunks of bread, quickly now. Over a cooling draught of ale, the mum, dusting down the stool she was sitting on with a rag before putting her genteel behind down, told Aunty everything: how they'd left London to inspect the manor she'd inherited from an uncle, who'd died in the latest bout of the Mortality, last year. How lost they'd got with no one to guide them. How they couldn't have asked for directions; they'd feared for their lives in the fleapit inn they'd stopped at last night as it was. Those eyes, staring. It was out Sudbury way, where they were going. She'd been happy enough to bed down at the kiln for the night, the mum. A few fleas in the rushes were nothing to worry about, compared to the eyes of the men out there. The dad was happy too, too. But, oh, how those smeary-faced girls had whined and complained, sniffling and turning away from their food as if it would poison them, looking round with hunted eyes at the thick walls and low roof.

'Never seen anything like it in my life,' Aunty muttered, winking at her own brood, when the little boy, pulled away from the toy Wat had brought him because his mum wanted him and his sisters to wash in the stream, started stamping his feet and shrieking the place down. 'Never been said no to, that one, that's for sure.' Then, as it turned out, the kid wouldn't have anyone but Alice take him to wash. Alice had had him roaring with laughter a minute before, playing with Wat's toy, snuffling, 'Giddyup giddyup!' as she made the imaginary farmer fall off his carved wooden horse. 'Want *her*!' he was howling, and Alice felt old Alison's eyes suddenly thoughtful on her back as she skipped the boy energetically off, away from his grey-faced, relieved parents. She could tell what Alison was thinking. She'd had the same thought already. Alice was the best of old Alison's kids, the sharpest of anyone at spotting whatever it was in the weed-grown manor houses and crumpled Mortality cottages the kids spent their days exploring that might fetch a good price, the best too at remembering what might be useful where, and to whom, and sidling up to the right person on market day to sing out, 'Wasn't it you looking for fire-irons?' or 'Didn't you say you wanted a cook-pot?' So it was natural she'd see this chance as quickly as Alison. She'd heard enough, not just from Alison, but also from the various uncles and cousins who came down from London to take away the tiles to whichever abbey or priory had put in an order, or to take on the other things the kids found, or to leave behind a new child picked up on their travels (old Alison had a soft heart for kids left, as she'd once been, to fend for themselves; and even orphans must be worth something now, with people so desperate for children). Alice had grown up with the knowledge that the streets of London were paved with gold.

She was back with the freshly washed, angelically sleepy toddler in time to hear Aunty Alison's voice, in the twilight, putting her own thought into words: 'You want someone to look after some of them for you, and my Alice, she's a good girl.' They were two of a kind, her and Aunty Alison. And Aunty, who was always telling her there was more to life than a tilery in Essex, that there was a whole world out there, just waiting to be discovered, was winking at her now, winking and grinning, as if she'd struck lucky.

She had. The next morning she was off with the family; Alice leading the little boy's pony, and ignoring the familiar eyes watching from behind the cow-parsley, and not letting herself see the thin boy-arms of Tom and Ham and Wat and Johnny and Jack waving goodbye, because she didn't want to feel sad, and she was already too busy making herself indispensible to these new friends – daisy chains for the girls, stolen apples for the little boy, bright sweet nothings for the mum and dad. She was seizing the moment.

Of course the Champagnes were bitterly disappointed when they actually saw their manor – another of the weed-shrouded ruins Alice knew so well, with its villeins long gone, off hunting higher wages somewhere. She could have told them how it would be before they started, but she was twelve, old enough to know hard truths weren't her business. So she cooed and comforted instead. She trapped them a hare to roast on a little spit. By the end of another week, when the Champagnes, already eager to forget their embarrassingly naive dream of sudden landed wealth, were sighing with relief at the sight of London on the horizon, they still had Alice with them. 'Look,' she was saying to little Tommy Champagne, managing not to look astonished herself at the great wall rearing up ahead, or the gate, or the soldiers. 'Home soon now.'

She'd always thought she would climb high. It had only ever been a question of time, and opportunity.

When, weeping, the silver-haired Master Champagne put his wife into the grave a year later, then turned to Alice the capable maidservant and wept into her hair, and stroked it, and kissed her shoulder, she didn't hesitate for a moment. She knew at once what she'd do. Even if she'd thought that you might only love – truly love – once in your life, and her true love certainly wasn't dear wrinkly old Master Champagne, whose egg always went down his front in a forgetful yellow trail, she also knew there'd be no harm in him. He'd do for now.

A good man he turned out, too, in the rest of his short time in this vale of tears. He let her be the sturdy, independent sort of person she was. He laughed at her stories. In return for her good humour at sharing a bed with a spindle-shanked, grey-skinned old husband, he also became a more willing giver of ribbons from the fair than his daughters remembered him having been before. Also of new robes, not just the old mistress's altered in the details, and (as Alice's knowledge of what she might ask for increased) embroidery silks, and finally even French lessons, so she could act the lady rather than the baker's wife with Master Champagne's well-heeled clients.

Master Champagne loved the idea of his wife chatting in French with the gentry so much that he never said a cross word, or had an ugly thought, either, about the merry friendship Alice had had in those months before he passed away with the curly-haired young French master from Hainault. Young Jean Froissart was glad enough to earn some extra pennies as he set himself up in England, just by spending an afternoon in the City every week or two, chatting to a nicelooking girl so eager to learn; it all worked out well for everyone. As old Aunty Alison always said, 'Pick up whatever you can by the wayside; you never know when it might come in handy.'

The French lessons paid off, all right, though maybe not as Tom Champagne expected. Or Alice, either, come to that.

Eight months after their marriage, he left behind the fuss and bustle of earthly life. He died straining on the chamber pot in the night, an indignity that Alice tactfully tidied up, when she woke up in the morning to find him cold on the floor, before calling for the servants. The poor old dear, she thought, opening the windows, having rearranged him, and wiped him down, and covered and hidden the pot; how he'd hate to have been seen like that. The French lessons were swapped for widow's weeds. But a certain Master Perrers of Hainault, who'd advanced the Champagne family some money so their baking business could be expanded, and thus been part of the discussions with the lawyers that marked the settlement of the estate, had been as impressed by the young widow's few words of elegantly pronounced French as he had by her sudden fortune (or so he said). Master Perrers, a plump lover of the pleasures of the table, who could be reduced to ecstatic groans by a good description of a rich sauce or a fine wine, was old enough, and foolish enough, to enjoy Alice's flattering suggestion that he might be related to the gentry family of Perrers who'd once bought tiles from the kiln. Not that she'd told him, exactly, that this was her connection with that noble family; she couldn't recall exactly, but she just might have teased him with the idea that those Perrerses were distant cousins of her own, for it pleased him so to think she might have a drop of gentry blood in her, and how would he, as a foreigner, ever know the difference? It did no harm. In any event, what with one thing and another, Master Perrers quickly stepped into the baker's shoes, and married her at the church door forty days after Tom Champagne's funeral. Bar a change of address and a different set of servants and the need to go visiting if she wanted to see little Tommy or the rest of the 'children' of her first marriage (the eldest of the girls now grown-up enough to take over the care of the little boy, while an aunt tried to find the daughters husbands), her new life with a different rich, indulgent, older merchant soon became all but indistinguishable from before. Once you got out of the gutter, the Alice of those days was given to thinking, once you didn't have to rush about emptying chamber pots or stealing from ruins any more to keep body and soul together, pleasing people became a much simpler question of vocabulary. Before, in the old house, it had been frisky bed-accented French, all oui, monseigneur, and oh là là, the muscles on the man, morning noon and night, with happy little whiffles of pleasure back from him. Now all she needed to make a new man happy was to talk recipes – the grander and more full of expensive ingredients the better. How intently he listened. How carefully he repeated it all back, imagining every flavour with brain and tongue, and grunting with joy: 'Cream *and* nutmeg *and* cinnamon *and* pepper? Baked *in* the peacock's juices? Gnn-h!'

If poor Jankyn Perrers hadn't died so soon, Alice has sometimes found herself thinking recently (a heart attack over a lobster dinner did for him, less than a year after he moved to England and only a few months after their marriage) – well, who can say? She might have stayed in the City to this day, growing fat with contentment and spending her energy

118

nagging at her husband, or the next one, for a new music teacher or string of beads or bit of silk. She was happy enough, back in those days. You can be happy with so little when you're young, and not in love, and remember enough about being poor to be grateful you've got food in your belly and clothes on your back, and nothing more serious to worry about than the next flirtation, innocent or otherwise.

But another part of her thinks: No, I'd never have stopped there. Not when there's so much more in the world, so much higher to fly. And she's always been right to go on, and take a bit more, and try another thing, and keep her eyes open, until now.

Then again . . .

What she's thinking of doing now . . . with Latimer . . . what she's said she'll do . . .

Well, isn't it dangerous? Isn't it the kind of thing that might tempt Fortune to flip you over the top, and send you down?

Alice sighs, and shakes her head, and nudges her horse on. Aunty will know.

It was after Jankyn Perrers died, and when she got her toehold at court, that Alice first went back to Essex and found Aunty.

Alison was still there, hanging on, by herself. To this day, Alice doesn't know what happened to the boys she grew up with at the Henney tilery, old Aunty's other orphans. All she could work out is that they were long gone. Aunty didn't have much more idea than Alice where. 'People grow up. They make their own luck,' was her phlegmatic comment. All she could tell Alice was that Jack died, Johnny went for a carpenter, on the road, and Wat for a soldier, overseas. That's probably all either of them will ever hear, Alice thinks.

Without the kids' help, Aunty's tilery business wasn't doing so well. She'd got behind with a big order for her best customer, the Abbot of St Albans; he'd cancelled the contract; she'd been left with two thousand expensive tiles to shift. And that was impossible, in those hard new times, with the war gone wrong, and the gentry so tight and short of money. So Alice took Aunty on. It's what the old woman was owed, for Alice's childhood;

and Alice found when she looked at that lined face that Aunty, for all her Essex rusticity, still felt like home.

Alice got the old woman to sell the kiln and the house. 'Don't get bogged down in the past,' she said kindly. And, while they sat together at the old scrubbed table and worked out what Aunty could do next, Alice also told the old woman her own story, and asked for advice about what *she* should be doing next.

While she was talking, she was still thinking to herself: What am I asking her for? A broken-down old stick of a thing from the country? This isn't stuff she knows anything about. It's court: French, and velvet. How can she possibly . . .?

But Aunty knew, all right.

'Seize the moment,' Aunty said, calm and crack-voiced as ever, and without hesitating, as soon as Alice paused. 'Do whatever you need to stay at court. You can; course you can, whatever you put your mind to. Just do it, and stop worrying. No point in agonising half your life away, wondering what to do, when you could have decided already and be off having some fun, is there now?'

And suddenly it all seemed easier; and Alice was grateful to have an adviser to hand who never did hesitate – who knew what she wanted, and just took it.

Alice bought Aunty a manor, further south, but still in Essex. And she's kept Aunty, ever since.

Alice thinks Aunty learned her chirpy ruthlessness on the roads. From various half-understood comments in her childhood, made by neighbours and men at markets, Alice half knows that the tilery wasn't always Aunty's. Aunty probably only got her hands on it through some sort of trick. It's fairly clear, from the droppings-in of the various uncles of long ago, that Aunty came from London. That may not have been the beginning of her story, though; she may have started from somewhere else, before. They've never been able to get it out of her. Alice doesn't blame Aunty for keeping her wits about her, though. People have had to, especially since the Mortality turned every old certainty on its head.

120

Greed, ambition, call it what you will – the spirit of the age – has been set free by so much death. That's what people say. Three bouts of plague since Alice was born, and half of Europe dead: only the naive should be surprised if people's nature changed. Survivors of the Mortality didn't bother to bless God for their astonishing luck (for, as a lot of people muttered, what did it have to do with God, their escape? When the Bishop of Bath and Wells tried to thank God for the plague's passing, at the end of 1349, the howling people of Yeovil kept him and his congregation besieged in the church all night long). People who know what's good for them have, since then, been too busy for God (who at least, as they often say with tough looks, didn't hate *them* enough to strike them dead). They're busy at each other's throats, squabbling over the spoils. That's only natural too.

The Mortality has brought so much change in its wake.

First, plain bewilderment: the glut of merchandise, not enough customers, prices plunging, and anyone still alive and with money in his pocket unable to believe his good fortune. That was the lesson old Alison and her London men friends learned so fast. Move into empty houses, sleep on strangers' beds, take over dead men's work (or don't bother to work at all). Eat off silver.

Then marriages: many more marriages, but much less love. People married orphans, and widows, for greed of goods, then quarrelled their lives away.

Then the fury of litigation, as the courts filled up with inheritance disputes. The notaries were dead. The cases took lifetimes to settle. Meanwhile squatters or the Church took over abandoned property, brigands pillaged the countryside, and fraudsters tricked yet more orphans out of their lands. And all the while, in the background, in the fields (or what had been fields), with the shrinking of land farmed by men, a greening as the forest threatened to come back.

Briefly there was no heriot, no merchet, and no tallage for the unfree, those walking skeletons with the caved-in cheeks and the smudgy under-eye skin and the bare, scratchy, scarred stick legs. For a year or two, till the panic eased, and it became clearer how much could still be farmed, villeins were allowed to keep their pennies. They didn't have to pay an annual cash sweetener to the manor. If their father died, they weren't forced to give the best beast away to the lord and the second best to the priest. For a few precious months, they didn't even have to pay when a daughter married off the manor, to compensate the lord for the loss of her future brood of children – tomorrow's human beasts of burden, each with a cash value in muscle weight, in rendered-down sweat.

It was only later, when the estate managers and the priests and the lords got their nerve again, and went back to demanding their dues from the skinny men-oxen they owned, that they realised there was trouble afoot.

For today there are too few villeins still alive, and too many empty fields needing hands, and too many tempting offers of work for cash. A reasonably brave, or greedy, man (and what's the difference, when it comes to it, between bravery and greed?) can choose to live better than his villein forefathers ever did.

And the men who have escaped out of their ruts talk. On the road, they talk to the other men with tools flocking on to farms and into towns, who've turned their backs on their earthly lords. They talk to the poor hedge-priests on the road, thin men with staring eyes and cheap russet robes – men who don't believe you need the Church of Rome to intercede for you with God, men who tell the crowds they can turn their back on their spiritual lords too, on the chant of the Latin they don't understand, and the fees they've always paid in the belief they're saving themselves from damnation, and yet not suffer for it in Hell. God's waiting, they whisper, in every field and cottage, not just in church, and He's a kindly God, too, not one to fear after all. You can find Him by yourself, if you only look. You don't need to pay. The talk's quiet, among the men who don't fear God or their lords any longer. But the look in every eye is dangerous.

It was all still all right, as far as the rulers of England were concerned – or just about all right – while the news from the war still warmed people's hearts, while drunk men could yell 'St George for Merry England!' in the taverns, and there was still a dream of glory.

But now the King's old. The knights are old. Their banners have faded. Their armour's rusting. And there have been no victories in France for years – just losses, and ransom demands. So the talk on the roads is getting louder, and the looks in the eyes of men no one wants to look at is getting uglier.

But Aunty loves it all: the muttering, the mischief, the men no one wants to look at. She's still taking in waifs and strays, even today, not children any more but furtive men with caps pulled down low on their foreheads to hide whatever burn marks are there. She gets them in to work her fields at her manor at Gaines. She loves that place. She doesn't act anything like a landlord, of course. She pays whatever they want, no questions asked. She shakes her head over their hard-luck stories. She lets them sleep in the barns they put up. She organises rough feasts for them on holy days. She shares her luck with them, and anyone else willing to have a laugh, and a drink, and a dance, and a chat. They love her for it.

So does Alice. However grand Alice has become, these past few years, she's gone on taking her worries to Aunty.

As she goes under the Aldgate, looking up from her horse to see if there's any sign of life at Chaucer's window (there isn't), Alice thinks that it's been good for her to be reminded by Aunty of how things look for the men on the ground. Because there's more and more reason for the stinking, resentful runaways – the men of the road – to be angry. Because the people who are doing well, especially the post-Mortality new rich, who are doing well so very suddenly, are more dangerously, visibly extravagant than anyone has ever been before.

And that's what Alice's personal experience of the changes, in the walk of life she's chosen, has been.

Clothes, for instance, are lovelier and more expensive than ever before, and on backs ever less noble. In the year Alice first came to court, the envious in Parliament were so anxious that the natural, static, eternal order of things was being upended by the shocking vanity of men in curly-toed shoes and women with a hunger for cloth of gold that the Members of Parliament vainly tried to stop the new rich flaunting themselves. They passed a law insisting that everyone dress according to their rightful station in life.

The sumptuary law was an ass, everyone agreed. Yeomen and their wives, for instance, were forbidden to wear cloth of silk or silver, girdles, knives, buttons, rings, garters, brooches, ribbons, chains, or any gold, silver, embroidered or enamelled items. But what fun would it have been for a wealthy yeoman's wife to deny herself all that when she'd extracted the money from somewhere, or someone, and was looking forward to buying it? If you paid heed to the law, it was russet wool only for carters, ploughmen, oxherds, cowherds, shepherds, dairy workers and other keepers of beasts and threshers of corn. But who was going to stop a shepherd who'd found the money to buy a knife, or a ring, and take it off? Naturally, no one took any notice. Naturally, yeomen's wives glittered and preened like peacocks.

'King Canute had no more luck stopping the sea coming in than they'll have enforcing the sumptuary law,' a much younger Alice snickered. A widow, for the second time, but just out of her black and white cowl in time for the one-year mind in her husband's memory. She went on snickering over the sumptuary law for the next four or five years, as her lovers changed, and her own clothes grew more luxurious. By the time she found her way into the King's bed, the law had been repealed.

Alice has tried, in her time, to give Aunty beautiful clothes; jewels. But Aunty only laughs incredulously at them. 'Not me, dear,' she croaks, calm as ever. 'Whatever would I do in one of *them*?' Alice has given up long ago. All she's bringing with her this time is a bunch of flowers she's picked by the roadside, and money for wages.

Aunty's great plus, in Alice's view, is that she's flown a good few rides on Fortune's wheel, but always known when she wants to stop. That's why Alice has gone on asking for the old woman's opinion. She's never met anyone else who knew, so precisely, just how far they could go.

124

It's not just the clothes Aunty doesn't want – the aping of a gentility she doesn't aspire to. There's Gaines, too. When Alice first found the run-down old place, she was only thinking of it as a stopgap. What Alice really wanted, when she bought it, was to bide her time, then get revenge, on Aunty's behalf, on the Abbot of St Albans.

It took Alice's bailiffs at her grand Wendover manor in Hertfordshire (conveniently close to St Albans) months and years of sitting in taverns and listening to gossip to find a man with a grudge against the Abbot that had a cash value, and might stand up in court. When they'd got Thomas Fitzjohn in to see her and he'd told her the Abbot had laid false claim to Oxhey manor – forcing him into the courts to defend his rights, where he might well be cheated of his rights by powerful friends of the abbey, so, effectively stealing it – Alice looked at his light eyes, filled with the familiar hope, the dream of instant money, and something in them reminded her of Jack and Tom and Johnny and Wat and herself, back in the day. Accepting his claim to the property, she bought the lands from him on the spot, for a substantial sum, knowing she was really buying his dispute with the Abbot. Without recourse to any courts, she moved her land agents in. The tenants at Oxhey were happy enough to answer to her, not the grasping Abbot. It was only Abbot de la Mare, that strange old broomstick of twiggy, stringy limbs and white-flecked nose and white eyebrows inside the abbey, who was furious.

Alice's idea was that she'd move old Alison from Gaines into Oxhey manor house, right under the Abbot's nose, and leave her lording it there with peasants who were delighted to have been freed from the Abbot's harsh rule – a triumphant cock-a-snoot that Alice thought would crown Aunty in glory.

But it didn't happen. The old woman refused. 'You shouldn't be doing this, dear,' was all old Alison said. She sounded uneasy. 'De la Mare is a bad enemy to have. Let him have it back. Know when to stop. What do you care about Oxhey?'

Poor old Alison. Losing her will to fight, Alice thought sadly, looking at the other woman's wrinkles and brown-splodged hands. Too scared to seize the moment. And her so tough, before. Perhaps it's age.

Alice has never relinquished the Abbot's lands. She's left the possibility open. She's left her borrowed quarrel with the Abbot simmering, too. She doesn't like giving up. But she's let the question of moving Aunty drop. She doesn't want to upset the old woman, so Aunty's still at Gaines, and always will be. It doesn't matter about Oxhey, really, Alice reassures herself quite often. In some ways, Gaines is a better home for Aunty. More private.

Why Alice wants an entirely private establishment, far from the court, unguessed at by enemies, is nobody's business but her own, she tells herself.

But it's clear enough to her. She needs somewhere where she can feel safe. For all these years, it's been in Alice's mind that, one day, when she loses Edward's protection, she might be stripped of all her most visible possessions. She's never been able to imagine quite how this turn of events will come about, but she feels the possibility everywhere, the need to insure and reinsure herself. All those wealthy farms, all those tenements, all those manors and castles (especially the ones, like Wendover, that Edward has given her): they could vanish into thin air.

Essex is good, because it's a wilder place by far than Wendover and St Albans – less connected to trade routes, and gossip routes too. No one in Essex is going to ask too many questions about an old woman living on a remote settlement. Alice's secrets will always be safe there.

Alice started off with high hopes for the scruffy old house and scrappy fields. She thought she could do the same as she's done with every other property she's got her hands on in this past decade – send money, buy oaks and bricks, build Aunty's home up into a big, efficient, beautiful manor house, expand her land-holdings, bit by bit, take on more labour for the fields . . .

The only difference, with Gaines, is that Alice knew from the start she was never going to do it through her usual team of land agents. Her idea was that Gaines could become her ultimate insurance against disaster, so that, even if everything else in the entire world went wrong for her, she'd still have a home to go back to. The way she envisaged it, even if John Broun and John Vincent and their London colleagues were ever asked about Alice's property holdings there, by some hostile questioner out to wring every last drop of Alice's wealth from her, the land agents would know nothing about that place, and so have nothing to say.

Instead, she's been sending the money directly to Aunty, who she remembers being so good with money – thrifty, with an eye to the main chance, building up the business at the tilery and fencing all those bits and pieces liberated from all those abandoned Mortality houses. Aunty would do the job as well as anyone, or so Alice thought, at first.

But the Gaines improvement plans have never gone quite right. The oaks Alice sends for building work lie for months, years, on the ground, rotting; the barns the men build fall apart; new fields don't get tilled; the real changes she suggests stay firmly in the future tense. 'Not enough money, dear,' is all Aunty says, with her cracked grin, if Alice ever asks; or, 'No time, it was Corpus Christi, the men needed an extra day of rest.'

Alice can see what's happened. Aunty's not bothered about making money these days. She doesn't want to improve anything any more. She's paying all those workers so much over the odds, and feeding them so well, that the money dribbles away through her fingers without her even noticing. Aunty's happy as she is.

Alice doesn't want to argue with happiness. She admires Aunty for knowing it.

But, as she trots through the last of the trees, and sees that the cow-barn roof has caved in again, and there's grass and scrub growing over what should have been the new field by now, and piles of rubbish all over the courtyard, she can't help but sigh.

She can only hope her personal Doomsday never comes. She doesn't want to live here, not like this.

More than ever, when she looks at Gaines these days, she wants to stay at the top.

*   *   *

Aunty's eyes glitter in the firelight as Alice talks. She's thinner than ever, and just as upright, with iron-grey hair sprouting up from her bare head. She's thinking.

The men have gone to sleep; the children too. There's a boy out there, clattering around in the scullery, clearing up the great vat of tasty meat stew.

There are just the two of them left in the kitchen, and no one else listening. Still, Alice mutters out her predicament as if the walls had ears.

She's half afraid Aunty will look shocked, as she did when Alice suggested moving her to Oxhey. She doesn't know what she'll do if the grey head shakes no.

But the first thing Aunty does, when she's understood the details of the plan, is to grin – a small, proud, 'that's my girl' sort of grin. And the first thing she says is 'Who'll ever know?'

Then the old woman puts a stringy arm around Alice's shoulders. 'You get people who are too stupid, or too rich, to feel if their purse is being emptied,' she adds gleefully. 'You don't want to bother worrying for them.'

It's what Alice wanted to hear. Or she thinks it is.

But her shoulders remain tense. There's a doubt she can't quite silence in her mind, still, because Alice isn't used to anyone speaking so baldly about money any more. It sounds more as though Aunty's talking about picking the pockets of some fool herder on market day than offering a judgement on the viability of a complex financial arrangement. Does Aunty mean . . . can she be saying that *Edward* is too stupid to notice his purse being emptied? Can she really see things that simply?

Aunty nods encouragingly, as if she knows exactly what's going through Alice's head. 'It's not so hard as you're making out, dear,' she says. 'Common sense, really. If it's not going to get up anyone's nose, and it'll do you good, then why not?'

Slowly, Alice nods back.

But then words burst out of her that she didn't know herself were coming. 'He's never been a fool about money before,' she stammers. 'Edward.'

She knows, suddenly, what feels wrong about this. She'd

never have been able to deceive Edward before, even if she'd tried. He's always been so knowing about money. It's what they've talked about, money; it's how they've flirted, bickering over houses and jewels. He loves money more than anyone (except possibly Aunty, in her heyday). They've been two of a kind. Until now.

Just saying those words has made her feel lonely. If she can get away with this, it means her kindly, teasing, whimsical, sharp-minded protector is gone; there's only a confused old greybeard, with Edward's face and body but with none of the brightness of wit she's enjoyed so much, still on this earth.

She'd rather have him back as he was before than have this new money, she thinks. Wishing, with all the sharpness of loss, that he'd been in a state to take in the first deal she'd thought out; to appreciate its cleverness; to praise her for it. Wishing she'd never been left to go to Latimer and hear the chancellor's sly proposal for twisting that deal into what it's become. It could have been theirs, hers and Edward's. Between them, they could have saved everything . . .

But Aunty's shrugging. 'No fool like an old fool,' she says, without regret. 'He's lucky to have you. You've been good to him. You'll be around long after he's gone, too. So you have to look after yourself a bit, don't you, dear?'

It's another shock. Aunty can't know it, Alice realises, but she's echoing Latimer's words.

Can it be as simple as they're both saying?

'Seize the day,' Aunty goes on, and her favourite phrase suddenly seems so funny that Alice starts to laugh and can't stop. Gasping with it, leaning against the old woman, feeling her tight muscles relax, Alice has to struggle to get out the expected reply. But she manages it in the end. 'Gold on the streets, if you only know where to look.'

It's night, a week later, at Sheen. King Edward is propped up on pillows, with Alice, returned that afternoon, feeding him broth from a bowl. Downstairs, the sound of supper in the hall.

Alice fanned herself when she came in, as if she thought it

129

was hot and airless in the chamber. The fire's been burning for hours, and is piled high with new logs. But Edward of England's shoulders are wrapped in a quilt. He feels the cold.

She's covered the bedding with white linen, in case he spills it down himself. She has a napkin under her hand.

She's looking thoughtful tonight. She doesn't say anything, beyond automatic murmurs of 'there' and 'mm', as he lets his mouth close over one spoonful after another. He doesn't speak either. He's enjoying the flavour of the chicken soup, enjoying the effort of pushing bits of flesh out from between his teeth with his tongue. For the entire interlude, there's only steam, and silence.

She's been sitting on the side of the bed to feed him. As she twists the top half of her body away from him to put down the empty bowl and spoon on the chest, and to pour him out fresh spring water from the pitcher, he clears his throat, as if to say something important.

She turns back at once at the sound. She moves so fast she spills a drop or two of water. She looks as expectant as though she's been hoping for him to speak. 'Yes?' she breathes, very tenderly.

But all he says, with the pleading, cunning wavering of the old, is: 'Isn't there any wine?' His eyes are bright with his wish for wine. His mouth is watering as he imagines the red of it, the smell of grapes and sunlight, the swooshing round his mouth, the feel of it sharp and strong and resiny on his gullet as he swallows.

He doesn't understand why she sighs.

His heart warms when he sees her in the doorway, a few minutes later, carrying the jug of wine. She's a good girl. She's got the wine he wanted. He says, 'You look after me so well.' She bobs her head in acknowledgement but won't meet his eyes. She's cross about something. He wants to make her happy. So he tries a different tack. He knows how much ladies like compliments. He says, 'That's a pretty necklace.'

She looks up at him. She doesn't smile, exactly, but her face softens. She's always liked her jewels. She fingers the sapphires at her neck. It's true, what he says. They suit her. They match her eyes. He's always liked sapphires on his women, who have always been blue-eyed (although, until Alice, usually blonde).

He says, 'Where is it from?'

She doesn't answer straight away. Instead she turns away and sets the jug down. There's no goblet for the wine, so she pours his water back into the water pitcher, then carefully pours in wine, which, when she's dabbed at the base of the goblet with her cloth, she brings to him.

It's only when she sits down beside him, and proffers the silver-gilt goblet so he can either take it in his hands or let her tip a sip down his throat (he opts to let her bring it to his lips), that she says, 'What, this necklace?' Then she smiles, very wide, so wide that her teeth flash. She has pretty teeth, he thinks, taking another sip – unusually white and strong. 'Oh,' she says, 'it belongs to Richard Lyons, the merchant. We've talked about him, remember?' Edward notices she seems to be pronouncing her words more slowly, and clearly, and carefully, than usual. Or perhaps it's just that he's tired. He remembers now – she was talking about a merchant... someone offering a loan. She goes on, and her voice is merry again now: 'He's thinking of selling it. He's lent it to me to try. He wanted me to show it to you.'

Edward nods, congratulating himself on having chased away her sad mood so easily. He's pleased she's chatting again. He likes ladies to be bright and entertaining – an adornment to their lords – and Alice is quicker-tongued than most, usually. Feeling reinvigorated after his meal, he takes the goblet from her hand in both his, and downs it in one. There's a long gurgle from his throat. Satisfied, he wipes his mouth with the side of his hand, and then yawns.

'You're tired,' she says, and flits around, moving cushions under and around him so he goes from something like a sitting position to something more like a lying position, and piling furs and quilts all around so he won't get cold in his sleep.

'You're very good to me, my love,' he says sleepily.

She carries on whisking bedding over him, with a faint

smile on her face. She's gone quiet again. For a moment, as she moves, her hand strokes at her neck.

The impulse, when it comes, is too strong to resist. And Edward has never tried very hard to resist impulses. He says, joyfully, man-tigerishly, 'It suits you, that necklace – why don't I buy it for you? You deserve a present.'

He loves the look of utter, dazzled, astonishment that comes over her face.

In the privacy of another apartment, with the cool of the night bending the candles around her, Alice removes her necklace and puts it carefully in its box.

She's whistling under her breath. In for a penny, in for a pound, she thinks. She hasn't felt this light and detached – as if she were floating on air – since she was a happy, heartless girl living on her wits, looking out for unattached items in empty houses in Essex.

She has just performed a tiny extra act of dishonesty, which has only confirmed her in her decision to pursue the much bigger act of dishonesty she has also agreed to.

It's freed her and lifted her mood: first making the big decision, and then doing what she's just done. She's started moving away from Edward in her mind, or at least not exactly from her Edward but from this bag of selfish bones who isn't him. Who's yesterday's man. She's never been one for yesterdays. She's leaving behind the uncertainty of all the recent todays, too, now she's decided her path; she's off into a golden tomorrow that he won't be there to share. By the time she left Edward's room, just now, she realises, all her anger with him had gone too – and so had her remaining love. All that's left is a soft, sentimental affection, the pity you might have for a weary old dog, living out its last days in the sun. She'll be good to him; she'll be affectionate; she'll keep him comfortable till he dies. Of course she will. But he won't need money where he's going, will he? And she still will, once he's gone. She owes it to herself to keep her wits about her. She owes it to herself to look to the future. There's no going back now.

Statesmanlike's all very well, she's thinking; but he's proved to her that she's got no business dreaming up highfaluting plans to save England's finances and helping the rest of the world. It's true what they say – it's time she went back to looking out for herself. Defiantly now, grinning at herself till her teeth and eyes flash: I'll have more fun this way.

Edward hardly even flinched when he asked how much Leon, Loyn, whatsisname, Lyons, wanted for the necklace, and she replied, without a moment's hesitation, 'Three hundred.' A king's ransom, if he'd only thought. But as usual he wasn't listening. He didn't even notice the gap in her voice, before she added, experimentally, without realising until she'd said it that she was going to say it, '. . . and ninety-seven pounds.' He just went on nodding and curling himself up in his foetid nest of blankets and grinning, as happy and passive as a sheep being fleeced on a hot day.

The whole trouble is that he never does listen, she thinks with a return of that earlier cold irritation. No wonder people steal from him. He makes it so easy. *He* corrupts *them*. Then the scratchiness passes. She smiles at the faint reflection of her bare neck in the copper mirror. Her teeth smile back. In for a penny . . .

She still can't believe Edward didn't recognise the necklace as the one he gave her last month.

EIGHT

My lord of Lancaster is walking alone in the rose gardens at the Savoy. The first drunken scents of summer are coming from the flowers he's ignoring. He doesn't notice the grandeur of his surroundings: the ornamental railings; the quadrangles; the flattened arches and fan vaulting that he's had Yevele the mason bring to the great hall; the barges waiting, draped in velvet, on the Thames; or the treasures of armour, plate, furs, jewels, and art. This is his favourite palace, but it's familiar too: he's here half the year. The other thirty palaces, or a good many of them, he squeezes into a summer tour, most years, if the state of the war allows him a gallop around his own country. But it's from here he actually governs the Duchy of Lancaster. He sees it all the time. He's not thinking about what it looks like today.

Instead he's looking pensively out over the Surrey marshes beyond the dance of river water and waterfowl, and stroking his neat black beard with one slim hand. How dark he is, and how underfleshed considering his height, with that beak of a nose under piercing eyes as thin as a knife in elegantly hollowed cheeks. How upright he keeps himself, so taut about spine and shoulders that perhaps his gait has given him the headache that he's trying, by pressing points along his eyebrows and forehead with fore-finger and thumb, to banish.

John of Gaunt – self-styled King of Castile, outright ruler of a third of England, the country's first duke, and a richer man, through the Lancastrian inheritance his dead first wife Blanche brought him, than even his elder brother, the Prince of England – is thirty-four. He's feeling his age. He's burdened by responsibilities. He's tired.

Sometimes it seems to him that he has spent a lifetime trying to be a man of honour – and failing.

He's married less to a princess than to a chivalrous cause. He's spent the past three years devoted to winning back the throne stolen from Constance of Castile's father by his bastard brother. But Enrique de Trastamara is still firmly on that throne, and John, on the rare occasions when he now enters Constance's rooms, can understand that the twitter of Castilian from her ladies is not as respectful as it might be.

Castile isn't the only dagger in his side. He's spent the past two years obeying the commands of his father, and his elder brother, those legendary commanders of the past, to win France. There's nothing he wants more than their approval; and there's nothing he more wants their approval for than success in France, the great dream of war that he and his siblings have grown up with. He loves, respects, admires, almost reveres, those two men, no one more, always has; he's done everything in his power to win them the country they want. But . . . he shuts his eyes against the vast futility of it. Weeks of heaving ship decks, the crash of water on mast, the gut-churning, the screams, the forced return to port – for what else can you do when even the seas and the winds turn out to be your enemy? The landscapes he and his men marched through for all those months, golden, silent, smoking, with every village and church abandoned and empty, every crop gone, or burning, and only the hills full of knowing eyes. Gone, now, Gascony, except for Bordeaux and Bayonne. He's lost the lot. And it's not even that he did anything wrong. He spent the money, he raised the armies, he provided the equipment, he led, bravely enough, from the front. There's nothing that even Edward, his brother, who will for ever be a hero in every Englishman's eyes for taking King Jean of France prisoner on the battlefield, can really reproach him with. He just didn't have the right tides, and winds, and weather. He's unlucky at war. That's all there is to it. At the times when his head aches, as now, he stops being able to remember that he's also known as the best, most dutiful, administrator in the country. There's no corruption, no waste, no mess, in John's Lancastrian lands. He's patron to artists and church-builders and castle-builders and writers (Chaucer, of course, whose spry wit he has always admired; and Stury, likewise; but also the morose John Gower; and Yevele the architect, who can make poetry from stone). John of Gaunt rewards the worthy, hurries the tardy, protects the vulnerable, builds and tends his wealth, is prudent with money, and safeguards the North from the Scots. He keeps his nobles from squabbling. He keeps rivers flowing and fields tended. He loves his children. He looks after his soldiers. He treats his wife with honour. But none of it counts, when this mood is on him; the weight of military failure feels too much to bear.

If John were less taken up with his wish to please his father, by doing well at the French war, he might have been better able to examine this dark, inarticulate misery that comes over him whenever he's called south, and remembers France. It might have occurred to him that, deep down, he doesn't want to fight this war any more. He doesn't believe England has the right to France that his father claims; he doesn't believe England can take the French in battle either, if God isn't with them. Yet John doesn't know the words to express that belief – because in a land ruled since before most people were born by a warrior-hero King, the words of war are all people under-stand. Anything else they call failure. People have forgotten the language and virtues of peace, John no less than the rest.

Maybe that's why he's so attracted by men with golden tongues. John loves to listen to Stury, and Chaucer, and Gower, and John Wyclif, his father's eloquent confessor; he's enchanted by the quick play of words between these learned men, like sparks from a fire, or quicksilver. He'll never have that gift, but how intensely he appreciates it in others. If any of those men knew all he knows about the war, he senses, they'd find a way of talking about it that might adequately convey the unease he feels, even to men as passionate about, and defined by, the war as John's father and brother. They'd find the words, if they knew. But they don't know. And they never will, because they don't go to the war.

So John keeps quiet, and soldiers on. That's what he was raised to do. It's what he did, before, when his sister-in-law unexpectedly died, doubling his inheritance from Blanche, and evil tongues said he'd poisoned Maud for the money. And when he has to be in the South, exposed to criticism, he lives with his headaches.

No one likes the truce he's been forced to make, for lack of English money, though he's quietly pleased it's allowed him to be out of France, and home. He's spent the months since tucked away in the North, on his lands, avoiding the court, where he's unpopular for having dissipated England's glory, and London, where he's apparently unpopular for having spent the merchants' money in vain on a failed campaign. (As though those limp-muscled moles of traders have a right to care, down in their burrows, counting their bags of coin; they get their interest paid, so what have they got to complain about?) He's just come south to see his father and brother, and do his business at the Savoy, and take the temperature of relations with France. On that front, everything is still inconclusive. There's no money to go on fighting, and, perhaps mercifully, no sign of money coming. So, at year-end, he'll go back to Bruges and try to negotiate another one-year truce.

But, meanwhile, he can return to the North for the summer, away from the complaints, and be at peace. And not alone.

He scans the trailing roses. He's looking for someone under these arches draped in thorny pink. He's looking for the one person who can charm his worries away; charm out the pain behind his eyes.

Not the knot of secretaries pursuing him from the palace side, thinking they're so clever he can't see them skulking there behind that hedge with their papers; they'll ambush him with their quills and ink as soon as he passes back into their parallel avenue, hardly breathing with the breathless scale of their ambition. Their transparent cunning only makes him grunt, and, almost, grin. They're afraid of him. People often are, though he doesn't intend them to be. Usually. Anyway, they'll wait.

It's only when he hears a rustle from the other side, the river side, that he looks up. In an instant, the strain goes out of his head. If he could see himself from outside, he'd realise that the forbidding look his lean face so easily takes on has gone, too. His cheeks have lost their pallor. There's colour in his face, hope in his eyes. He looks, suddenly, tender . . . happy. He moves as fast as a black wind.

Alice bobs, and lifts laughing eyes to the Duke's face. 'Why, my lord,' she says, guilelessly, 'what a happy coincidence . . . as it happens, I was just thinking, there were a couple of things before you go . . . if you have a moment?' She's happy to have been able to catch him like this, for a few moments of what may seem to him like casual chat. It makes it almost worthwhile having had to accept the honour of being his Duchess's occasional demoiselle last year, even though Constanza, that pinch-faced sallow thing, never said much to Alice when she came, just lisped demurely away in Castilian to the other yellow-faced recluses and pretended Alice wasn't there. The benefit: Alice now knows some of the ways of the Savoy. She knows where people meet, and where they go to be private. It hasn't been hard to come across the Duke by chance.

She knows he's off any day now on his frantic ducal summer jauntings. To Tutbury Castle, by 26 July, where he's scheduled to find his Castilian lady Constanza and be reunited with her and their toddler daughter (and his son and two daughters from his first marriage, the little princesses now looked after by Katherine Swynford, who'll be heading north with him from here, for a meeting that will, come to that, also include the other de Roët sister, Geoffrey Chaucer's disagreeable wife, who'll be there waiting on Duchess Constanza, and the stuck-up sounding Chaucer children too). Perhaps unsurprisingly, after just five days of all those mothers and babies, he'll be hastily off again by month-end, and on to Leicester for the month of August to do some solid work governing his Duchy.

A gallop back to London for 12 September, the anniversary of his first wife's death, the first time he'll have been in England to take part in the procession from the Savoy to St Pauls in the entire six years since she went. Then back north. Tickhill Castle in Yorkshire by 22 September. South to the manor of Gringley in Nottinghamshire by 23 September. South again, thirty more miles in the next two days, to Lincoln for a week. Then – and how grateful Monseigneur must be of this, after all that rushed time in the saddle – to London for the rest of the year.

She's so concerned for his future fatigue after that busy programme, and so pleased at her cleverness in finding him now, that it takes a moment for her to notice that he does not, altogether, share the pleasure.

He's poking at his forehead with his hand, wrinkling his brow, kneading it with his fingers.

She's dimly aware that, for one brief moment when she first appeared through the archway, and caught his eye, he looked happier. As if he'd been expecting someone.

'Do excuse me, Madame Perrers,' he says, rather faintly. He's dignified, though, and as courteous as if she were a queen. 'Splitting headache. But – talk – of course – delighted.'

And then he waits. Not coldly, exactly, but without noticeable warmth either.

Alice says, uncertainly, feeling the chatty brightness in her voice ring false, wondering if she's done the wrong thing by coming, but banishing that thought, 'Well, Chaucer . . . he's settled in. I've been to see him a few times. He's getting on well with Walworth, who's being sworn in this week . . . It's all started off well.'

There's a faint noise from the tall Duke. Alice isn't sure that he's properly listening, but she takes the plunge anyway. He'll be so pleased to hear what she's got to say next; and he'll have all summer to reflect on how it's all thanks to her.

'Secondly, I've negotiated a deal,' she says, modestly lowering her eyes. 'Which I think will help your cause. I don't know if my lord your father mentioned . . .?'

He starts to shakes his head, then winces, and half closes his eyes instead.

'I've been lucky enough to be in a position to arrange a loan to the Crown,' she persists valiantly, 'from Richard Lyons. The Flemish vintner. To be signed in the next few days. Twenty thousand . . .'

She sneaks a look up; Duke John's eyes are closed fully now, his thumb and forefinger pressed above the bridge of his nose. Trying not to be discouraged, she presses on with the detail: the repayments in Italian debt paper, which in turn raise the possibility that the Italians may start lending to England again. She keeps waiting for the joyful smile to break out on his face when he realises he can do what all lords want, as a result of her cleverness, and go back to war.

'. . . So you can be confident, when you go to the peace talks at the end of the year, that you'll be negotiating from a position of strength,' Alice explains carefully, suppressing her impatience to share a moment of triumph with him, giving him an encouraging smile (is he simply not very intelligent? Why isn't he reacting?). 'At the very least. And, if the talks go badly, you'll probably even be in a position to go back to war. You could start planning a new campaign for next spring.'

In one part of her mind, Alice knows that, if she and Lord Latimer do cash in the discounted Italian debt paper at its full face value, there probably *won't* be much spare money in the royal coffers by year-end. But she has shut that knowledge away, almost forgotten it, at least for the purposes of this discussion: they'll cross that bridge when they come to it.

For now, she's just expecting radiant gratitude. Which isn't coming. What's wrong with the man? Why doesn't he do anything?

She's so uncomfortable with her bright voice and her brighter smile by now that she's almost ready to wonder whether he suspects the thing she's not telling him, when John of Gaunt finally nods. She breathes out. But there's no triumph, or even pleasure, in his face. It's the sick, pained nod of someone who's lost in their own physical discomfort, or, possibly, is actually displeased about what he's hearing. Absently, he says, 'Good.' Then, after a few experimental eyebrow wiggles, another 'good'. But what his face seems to be saying, or so it seems to Alice, is 'bad'.

The poor man, Alice thinks, trying to turn her puzzled disappointment at this lacklustre reaction into anxiety for him. His pain must be agonising. She's never had a day's illness in her life and usually she is sceptical about other people's illnesses, assuming they are exaggerating their symptoms, but not now. She has never had a headache like that so, she tells herself sternly, how can she hope to imagine the pain? More's the pity, she's sent her friar who understands medicine to Pallenswick, where she'll be sleeping tonight. But perhaps she should call at an apothecary in London, and send Monseigneur a potion. She's told him about the deal, which is the important thing. For now, he's too sick to express his appreciation. But once he's better, if she's been solicitous enough, he'll appreciate her concern almost as much as her commercial nous.

'I'm so sorry for your pain,' she says with real sympathy. But she can't leave him just yet. 'There was just one other thing.'

The Duke looks at her again with those dead-fish eyes, expecting nothing from her.

She sees she should go. But she has to say this. She knows it for another good idea.

It's Chaucer who first came up with this suggestion, for Alice has been dropping in on Chaucer fairly frequently, on the trips from Sheen to London she's been making to finalise the Lyons deal. He's so sharp-witted and so sweet with her that he's got behind her defences; she likes to sit and chat with him, as if she had nothing better to do. She finds excuses to visit him. It's years since she had a friend like him.

Chaucer doesn't know about the Lyons deal, of course. She's not telling anyone, except the Duke, till it's happened. (Even then, she's not going to tell anyone, ever, about the secret part. That's just for her and Lord Latimer and Lyons to know.) But she likes the way Chaucer worries about the public finances, like the conscientious official he is, and

141

the way he's been talking long and honestly to her about his concerns (especially when he's a little tipsy, she's noticed; so Alice has made a point of making sure he's lavishly supplied with wine). Since Chaucer's started spending so much time with Walworth and the oligarch merchants, he's understood better than before how hard it's always going to be for the Crown to wring money out of either merchants or – if they ever dare call another Parliament – the people: the knights and small landlords. And Chaucer loves the King and the Duke, in that straightforward way that men do love the leaders who've been good to them; he's been putting his mind to helping them.

What Alice is about to suggest to the Duke is, she thinks, the best idea Chaucer's had. She smiles affectionately as she remembers the conversation. Chaucer laughing, with a bright, excited look in his eyes, as he said, 'Well, I can think of another source of money for the King . . . And I can tell you something for nothing: tapping that source would make the King very popular in London – or the Duke, if it was by his order . . .'

'What other source?' Alice said quickly.

'He should be getting money out of the Church, of course.'

Incredulously, Alice laughed back. What, go on bended knee to the Pope, or Archbishop? And come away with bags of money in your hand? She replied, 'Don't be silly, Chaucer. That's about as likely to happen as Hell freezing over.'

But Chaucer wasn't crushed by her friendly scorn. He's braver than you'd think, once he gets going with an idea. He just said, in the voice of someone who enjoyed arguing, 'Well, there are already people saying the Church should be stripped of its wealth. That it should be poor as Christ himself was . . . It's one of the things Stury says, for instance.' He couldn't restrain a grin at Stury's name, for it's hard to take the poetical knight's whimsical religious feelings seriously, so Chaucer rushed on, more earnestly: 'And there are people inside the Church who say the same sort of thing, too. Think of Wyclif.'

Wyclif. At first Alice conjured up the picture of Edward's chaplain without great enthusiasm. John Wyclif is a doctor of divinity at Oxford, a man in his forties, a person of in-different, blunt, mid-height, mid-brown looks, with a chubby curve to his jaw and a fleshiness to his lower lip. He's made it his life's work to disapprove of things. He disapproves of the war, for instance; says it's vainglorious. He disapproves of monks. And he disapproves of his wealthy masters in the Church of Rome. You'd never think Wyclif attractive to look at, even when he opens his plain face to you in a smile of unusual beauty and openness – until he speaks. He has a cultured voice, a dark, rich, melancholy voice, with a tremble of tragedy never quite absent. Women turn round and go thoughtful and a little pink-cheeked at that voice. Men fall silent. Even Alice has felt its power.

People who have heard Wyclif often find themselves enthu-siastically converted to, and preaching and repreaching his passionately expressed belief: that there are too many eccle-siastical foundations, on every street corner, in every field, and each of them rich as Croesus already, yet always with their hands out asking for more. He says it's time the Church gave up these ill-gotten gains, and rediscovered God.

There's a lot of that kind of talk already doing the rounds in London, a city whose walls are lined with monasteries and abbeys, and whose citizens are constantly having to put their hands in their pockets for whitefriars, blackfriars, greyfriars, pinkfriars, anyfriars. But for now, their resentful fundamen-talism is quiet talk in the privacy of homes. The baleful glares of the big three victuallers – especially Walworth, who wants to keep civic and religious life pretty much as it is, doesn't like any kind of dissent, and appears at every ceremony beside William Courtenay, the Bishop of London – stop too much anti-clerical grumbling being heard in public.

Wyclif frightens Alice a bit. She thinks all that humourless magnetism dangerous.

But, as soon as she heard Chaucer say the prelate's name, she liked the inspired idea of having the Duke take Wyclif up and champion him. She liked it partly for the serious reason that Wyclif might indeed show the way to get the Crown a windfall of Church money, if he gave the Crown a template

– a bit of memorable phrasing, a form of reasoning that everyone in the land would agree with – to justify merging some failing monasteries, confiscating some land and gold plate, and enjoying the profits. But Alice liked the idea most of all for its unserious side, because of the mischievous fun she also saw in it: the Duke and Wyclif collecting in money, the war coffers filling from the sale of Church property, Londoners praising the Duke's policy, while Walworth and his tame Bishop, guardians of the status quo, would have to stand crossly by with their noses well and truly out of joint. It was childish, Alice knew, but the idea of annoying them made her splutter with laughter.

She thought at once: Yes, I'll suggest that to the Duke. She knew at once, too, that she wasn't going to credit Chaucer with having had the idea.

Duke John knows it's a good idea too, as soon as she says the word 'Wyclif'.

Now the gratitude's there, all right. His eyes fix on her: rapt attention as he considers the idea; then nods; then, as the smartness of it sinks in, admiring nods. Head to one side, mouth relaxing and broadening into a smile.

He takes her arm. His headache is forgotten. Again, he gives her that warm, surprised, look, that look of intimacy, of – almost – love. It seems to Alice to say, 'You could be my future.'

But all he says is one word. 'How?' he asks.

'Oh, any number of ways,' she replies glibly. She ticks some off on her fingers. 'Have him at your side. Give him a job. At the end of the year, take him with you to the next peace talks . . . to Bruges.'

Duke John murmurs, 'Take him with me . . . have Wyclif at the talks,' as if nothing could give him greater pleasure. He mutters, 'Yes.' She sees colour stealing back into his cheeks.

How strange, she thinks, confused, that he should be so unenthusiastic about one apparently perfect idea, which is actually being put into practice, then so overwhelmed by the next, which is so much vaguer.

It's wrong-footed her, this topsy-turvy reaction. She wants

to understand him. And this . . . well, she doesn't understand it, quite.

But after a moment's suspended breath, she lets her worry go. She tells herself it doesn't matter. All that matters is that he's pleased about one of her ideas. He understands how useful she and her ideas could be in guiding his policy. Looking at his surprise and appreciation now – for she can see he hasn't really expected her to come back with anything this good – she's surprised, too, at the warmth inside herself, the great deep breath she draws into herself and then joyously lets go.

This is just the beginning.

She bows. She knows the rules of flirtation, and, even if this relationship is more about advancement and self-advancement than love, the rules are the same. She'll go now, while he wants more. She says, 'I won't hold you up any longer,' throws him a last smile, and makes off towards the palace, almost dancing through the little gaggle of secretaries hiding behind their bush.

She can feel his eyes, warm on her back. She's not looking, but she knows he's smiling.

There is a rustle from the river side of the walkway.

John of Gaunt looks around.

A tall blonde female form is waiting, motionless, under an archway. There are roses trailing past her shoulders. Katherine Swynford has the gift of quiet. She doesn't smile. There is a happiness inside her that needs no external expression to shine out.

'Were you here all along?' he asks as he reaches her, bending his body towards and around hers. She shakes her head. She has the neck of a swan, he thinks.

She raises an eyebrow towards Alice Perrers' departing back. It is all part of the blessed peace of her that she doesn't ask unnecessary questions. 'A detail,' he explains, and his happiness grows when she nods, as if that's the end of it.

If there is one skill he does believe he is at last beginning to master, it's chivalry. He lost himself, long ago, in the long blonde loveliness of Blanche, his first wife; he'd have obeyed any order she gave, gone on any quest. He was young, then, and everything seemed simple and beautiful. But then she died. And, after that, everything else went wrong for years; there was so much more loss. His mother, gone, years ago now, while he was away in France; his father, so strange and absent-minded in age; his brother Edward, ill, and Joan, whom he used to adore, become cold and hardened by their family pain. Their tight-lipped little boy, Richard, his nephew, who hardly speaks. His own second wife, Constanza, locking herself away with the hard-eyed Castilian ladies and sallow little Catalina. Dust, ashes, ashes . . .

And then, one day, two years ago, with the needling Castilian in the background, a door opened, and there she was, in a shaft of sunlight: dear, familiar Katherine, who's always been underfoot, somewhere around at court, a good bit younger than him, a child. Whose loveliness suddenly looked so breathtakingly strange.

In that moment, John of Gaunt understood he'd found the meaning of his life. France, the war . . . everything else, in these past two years, has become distraction.

He can't be with her all the time, although in his secret heart of hearts a picture has begun to form of the two of them in a rose bower, at peace . . .

The reality of his life is that it hasn't been easy to be quietly together, even for a few days here and there, in the years since they found each other. She has her responsibilities, he has his. It's not just his wife, and France, that come between them. She's a war widow with four children being raised in Lincolnshire. They've taken what precious secret time together they can. It's never been enough.

He was away in France, eighteen months ago, when she gave birth to his son, christened John Beaufort, in secret, from the court at least, at her manor house in Lincolnshire. But they were both back at the Savoy in the spring. She came to London as soon as she was churched – just six weeks after being brought to bed. 'I wanted to see you,' she said simply. And everything was transformed when she was back: the very air brighter. She looked as young and slender as ever; unchanged by childbirth. How he wanted to see the child – his son. But he couldn't, of course. The baby was with a wet nurse at Kettlethorpe.

All he could do to show his love was to free Katherine from the deceit and embarrassment of her job serving his wife Constance. He gave her a separate duty, making her *magistra* to the daughters of his first marriage, giving the two little girls their own household, semi-detached from the rest of his court.

That would be a way to make it easier for him to see Katherine more, or so he thought. How wrong he was about that. By summer, he was off back to France, rushed on by the demands of the Crown, for more duty, more war, and more humiliation – nearly a year of it. By the time he finally took little John in his arms, the child was already walking; almost talking.

John's heard people make up ugly, despicable, whispered motivations for his loss of zeal for France. There's even a ludicrous rumour that he's loitering here in England, making truces with the French, because he's waiting for Edward to die, so he'll be at hand and can seize the moment to steal the throne of England from little Richard, his nephew. His lips thin at that memory. How people – merchants, those non-fighting fools of men, who have wormed their way into his father's trust with their money-bags and their sly eyes and their fat, comfortable, lives – can let filth like this into their minds, he doesn't know. How anyone who has ever talked to *him* could believe such a thing of him is beyond him. No, *this* is the real reason for his private weariness of the business of war: the armies, the expeditions, the sea passages. Not the softness of age, not the slyness of treachery. She is. Love is.

So John is grateful, in a remote way, for hints and tips and nods and policy ideas and bits of advice from these bright-eyed, busy, clever, adviser types pushing themselves forward: the Perrerses, the Latimers. They offer glimpses of possibilities which his father has never dreamed of. They have to be heard out.

147

But all he really wants is to be allowed this rare moment away from duty, alone with his lady, in peace, under a blue sky and a drift of roses, with only the doves breaking the silence, letting her smooth away his headache with her long white fingers.

A part of him is still thinking bits of ordinary, everyday, not unkind thoughts – 'I know a lot of people don't like Madame Perrers . . . pushy . . . common . . . but . . . clever too . . . don't see the harm in her myself' – when Katherine puts her mouth up close to his ear (she's as aware as he is of the secretaries behind the hedge) and whispers, 'Can you believe? We're going to have a baby . . . another baby . . .'

After that, he sees nothing, nothing, but the blue of Katherine Swynford's eyes.

A month later, when the Duke is already at Leicester (or perhaps, secretly, at Kettlethorpe with his lady) and Alice Perrers on her summer circuit between Sheen, or Havering, or Eltham, or Westminster, she is quietly pleased to hear, through her friend Lord Latimer, that John Wyclif has been given the Crown living of Lutterworth in Leicestershire, and has also been invited to accompany the Duke of Lancaster to Bruges next January, for the negotiations over the French truce and the threatened papal taxes.

That idea may bear more fruit later. Meanwhile, for the rest of that summer and autumn, Alice will be busy. Like Wyclif, she's been taking on new property. In 1374, so far, she has personally taken possession of the manor of Pallenswick, west of the riverside village of Hammersmith, and the nearby manor of Gunnersbury. Her business associates, the land agents whose work she directs from her City home, have acquired on her behalf the manors of Culworth in Northamptonshire, Fillyngley in Nottinghamshire, Farndon in Northamptonshire, and Kingham, near Oxford. The papers aren't through yet, but Edward has also promised to grant her several small Crown estates that have come free: the manors of Wantage in Berkshire, Bentham in Salop, Whittington in Salop, Stanton Fitzwarren in Wiltshire, and Crofton in Wiltshire, all from the Fitz Waryn lands. There'll be work to be done on all these properties, sprucing them up for rental.

Mostly, though, Alice is enjoying the first fruits of her other money-raising idea: redeeming the Italian loans from the royal exchequer and taking her cut. She spends the first instalment of cash she receives from Lord Latimer on ordering a very expensive hanging for the great hall at Pallenswick. It is to show Delilah, sneaking up on Sampson, snipping off his hair. She asks for extra gold thread to be worked through everything.

NINE

'I think I'm drunk,' says a surprised Chaucer. 'A littlebit-drunk.'

Alice laughs comfortably. She refills his cup.

How Alice darts around you. She's here, there and everywhere, fetching this, signalling to servants there, showing you one thing or another, affectionately ruffling the top of your head as she passes. There's no stopping her. She must have had his cup filled far more often than he's realised. She's been making him dizzy for a while, all that dashing about. Bewildering. Especially since the walls started waving and wobbling too.

She's been showing him her new manor, at Pallenswick near Hammersmith, which she isn't going to leave her men to manage, but will use herself as a retreat from London and Sheen. The house, unused since the Mortality, is old and decaying, with holes in the roof and buckets on the floor and the mournful smell of damp everywhere. She's going to knock down most of it, and rebuild. But the park behind is full of trees with gold-green leaves, and the river sparkles through the windows ahead. And, even inside, she's already made pockets of portable luxury: a corner of the great hall, where the roof's sound, screened off with thick, lovely, colourful, draught-proof hangings, where she's sitting with Chaucer at a table, feeding and watering him with the gold cups and jewelled knives she's brought here.

These objects, so at odds with the dinge-spotted walls, make Chaucer uneasy. He's been uncomfortable since before the walls started behaving so strangely.

She shouldn't have so much gold on show, he thinks. He knows why, most of the time. It's just now, when he wants to tell her, that the reason escapes him.

She sits down again; there's mischief in her gleaming eyes as she grins up at him. 'Wrong to be drunk, Chaucer,' she's teasing. 'Sinful. Look what drink did to poor old Lot. Drunk as a drowned mouse, lying next two his two daughters, and, before any of them knew where they were . . .' She moves her fingers lewdly, thrusting one through two others, giving him a knowing look. 'So you take care.'

He doesn't care about Lot. Dirty old man. He cares about . . . 'Too mush gold,' he slurs uncertainly. He never manages to tell her this thing, the thing that's always on his mind, except that now he's got her attention he's gone and forgotten it. But he's been trying for weeks now. 'Too mush . . .'

'Too much wine, I'd say,' Alice snips back. 'But never mind . . . I like you even when you're a bit cranberry-eyed.'

She's very pretty, wavering over there. Lovely smile. Lovely shoulders. He stares vaguely in the direction of her breasts.

'Drunk,' he says disconsolately. 'Never should have. Abominable stuff, drink. Sour breath. Foul to embrace. Can't keep secrets. 'Sgusting. Your throat a privy.' Then he says, 'So tired . . . do you mind if I lie down?' He knows she won't. She's his friend. Dearest friend in the world. Wonderful woman, Alice. She's laughing softly as she leads him off to an antechamber with cushions.

Alice leaves him there till morning. No point in sending him up the river after dark. He'd only fall in and drown, or be caught by the guard after curfew.

When she comes to wake him, at dawn, with her candle still lit, he's already hunched on the bench, with the cushions on the floor, energetically writing.

He's unshaven and pallid. He looks shamefaced. He grimaces

151

comically. 'I know,' he says. 'I'm sorry. My punishment: my head aches.'

She laughs very gently. 'You were so lucid,' she replies. 'Even drunk.' She comes a little closer. Aware that he must stink, Chaucer edges shyly back. 'What are you writing there?' she murmurs, craning her neck, peeping.

He tweaks the paper away.

'Oh, let me see,' she pleads playfully. 'Please.'

He gives her a careful look. 'You'll be disappointed,' he says. 'It's not the kind of poetry you probably expect. Not . . . courtly. Chivalrous. Just me.'

'Go on,' she says. 'I don't care.' Her eyes are so inviting. She sits down next to him on the bench and waits.

So he clears his throat. He sits up straighter. He starts to read the words out, in a thin, suffering, self-parodying voice:

> 'O wombe! O bely! O stynkyng cod,
> Fulfilled of dong and of corrupcioun!
> At either ende of thee foul is the soun . . .'

He gets no farther. Their eyes meet. They're already both soundlessly laughing.

But even as he's laughing he remembers that he came to see Alice with a purpose in mind, beyond friendship, beyond this half-flirtation. He was going to tell her some home truths.

He came intending to tell Alice she's not playing her politics as well as she believes.

For a start, he wants her to know that Walworth is angry. Several months into his job, in the autumn of 1374, Chaucer now knows a lot about how Walworth feels. The Mayor may have complained a little, back in the spring, about the need to lend money to the King that he'd probably never see returned, but that was the established tradition for a mayor: lending a lot, and moaning a little. Chaucer knows that Walworth hasn't been happy, since then, to discover Richard Lyons will be making the royal loan instead, and a bigger loan than he was to have made. Chaucer knows because he saw Walworth come back from his much-discussed meeting with Chamberlain Latimer, just before Walworth became Mayor in July, with bright pink splotches in the middle of long pale cheeks, and a tight, closed-off look in his eyes; and, when Chaucer enquired, across the Customs House desk, whether the loan amount suggested by the Crown had been especially onerous this year, Walworth made a ghastly attempt at a smile, and said, tightly, 'Quite the contrary, dear boy. As it turns out, I am to be released from that obligation this year. It appears that my lord the King would prefer to take his loan from' – and here Walworth did that fastidious face-wrinkling thing he's so expressive at – 'Master Lyons.'

Poor Master Walworth. For all his desperate dignity, he must already know what they'd make of it in the taverns, and even in the kitchens of his own house. Since then, as Chaucer's gone on making quiet signs of sympathy, the Mayor has let other small answering remarks drop; ones that suggest that he's trusting Chaucer more and more to be the merchant's son he seems, and not the Duke's proxy; ones that go on making it clear that of course he feels humiliated to have been passed over, and for a foreigner too. Walworth believes that Alice is to blame for the substitution. ('Dear boy, she's as thick as thieves with Lyons, and how else would the man have made the contact with the court?' he's told Chaucer more than once; 'and that idea of swapping back the Italian debt paper – devilish clever – far too clever for that Fleming to have come up with it. It's got her fingers all over it.') Chaucer suspects he's right, because he can see it all began with that conversation he happened to overhear at his own table.

And then there's the other thing. Which, if true, makes it all worse still. But he'd better not start with that. He'd better start gently.

He begins, a little hesitantly, to mumble something along the lines of, 'You know, after all, I've been finding Walworth and his friends very honest business partners; it's Master Lyons whom people talk about with more suspicion . . . and his associates . . . and I've even heard your name come up in that regard . . .'

But Alice isn't in a mood to take advice. She just giggles and lets her eyes twinkle up into his. 'You're sounding far too independent-minded for my taste, Chaucer,' she says. 'And there was me thinking you were coming to the City to be my supporter. Shouldn't I be giving you some food, now, to mop up the wine?'

Chaucer looks disbelievingly at her. Has she really put him in this powerful job, and asked him to keep her informed of how things are in the City, just to laugh at him when he does?

'Look here,' he says, feeling the blood rush to his already throbbing head, as if anger is going straight to his body without passing through his mind, 'you should listen carefully to this. It's no joke. Do you realise how seriously people in this city worry about money – who's spending it, who's making it, who's stealing it? And do you even begin to realise how much there is to worry about?'

She looks back at him, wide-eyed. He takes it as an invitation. He talks on.

'This is the real debt situation in England. Since the war started again five years ago, did you know that more than *half a million pounds* has gone on it, truce or no truce? With not a penny back? And there's no money left to spend?'

She widens her eyes more, looking extra innocent. She's playing with him, he thinks furiously. She thinks him funny. She knows, and she doesn't care.

Hotly he goes on: 'We still like to think it's just possible that if we actually had enough money to deploy our armies, they might come back richer than they set out, just because they used to, once, when the King was young and still had the luck of the Devil. Because back then it seemed there was enough plate and jewellery and coin in every town and every monastery in France to make every Englishman rich. But there's nothing left any more, or if there is we don't have the kind of armies that can find it. We've emptied France of everything it's going to give us. And we're broke.'

She says, in a butter-wouldn't-melt way, 'Dear Chaucer,

154

why are you telling me all this? I know . . . you know . . . and you know I know . . .'

Exasperated, Chaucer barks: 'Because when entire armies of unpaid soldiers come home half-dead to their half-starved families, they don't want to hear that you spent hundreds of pounds on robes for a royal tournament, that's why!'

But it's not just the price of her robes for tournaments that means trouble for her. There's the other thing. All the other things. He takes another breath, almost angry enough to find the resolve to mention them, too.

But not quite. And that one moment of hesitation gives her the advantage again.

She smiles wider. She leans towards him and touches his hand. Can her eyes get any wider? 'But, Chaucer . . . court festivities don't even come out of the government budget,' she coos. How condescending she sounds. 'The King decides on them. And pays.'

Chaucer slumps back on to his bench. She knows, really. He knows she knows. She's just refusing to engage. Stubbornly, he persists: 'But they love the King. They're in awe of him. Even if everyone knows he's extravagant, no one *wants* to blame him. They want to blame someone else. And you're the obvious person. You're the one they all see in the fine robes, wearing the jewels, after all. You're the symbol of the extravagance; and you could be the scapegoat for the anger. It's easy enough to call you loose, and a thief, and a wicked whore, and—' He feels his face flushing from the words, and pulls himself back. 'Well, you can imagine the rest. Because you're an outsider. You're not of the City. You're not of the court. You're no one's responsibility, and no one's wife, and no one's kin. You'd be the easiest person to pin the blame on for every penny spent by the King, or stolen from the King, for all these years. Even if it wasn't you. Surely you see that?'

As he pauses for breath, he's pleased with that speech. He thinks it successfully conveys to her that she could be at risk, without going so far as to insult her by suggesting she might in any way be stealing money herself.

Alice drops the cooing and flirting. There's a hint of sullenness about her mouth, now, and defiance coming into her eyes. But Chaucer likes that better. At least she's being more honest.

'I've got nothing to reproach myself with,' she says truculently. 'The question doesn't arise.'

Oh, Alice Perrers, Chaucer thinks, exasperated. Oh, Alice Perrers.

'But you have,' he says. 'You make enemies, and you don't seem to care. You've angered the most powerful man in the City, for a start. Walworth's furious he's been passed over for that loan. And for Lyons, too – a man he despises.'

Alice pauses. That's surprised her. She looks hard at Chaucer, with assessing eyes. 'Oh,' she says carefully. 'You know about Lyons, do you?'

He nods. 'Of course. Everyone's talking about it. There are no secrets in the City.' He holds her gaze. 'Twenty thousand, they say. Being repaid with discounted Italian debt paper. Right?' She nods again, without expression. He doesn't think she's masking fear, or guilt. He has a nasty feeling she just might grin impishly at him if he lets her, so he rushes on: 'You see? You thought you'd kept that quiet, but it came out anyway. And you must see that you won't get Walworth standing up and defending you, after that, will you?'

She thinks for a minute, then shrugs, as if she really doesn't care. She says, 'Oh, Chaucer. I don't need to worry too much about poor old Walworth's hurt feelings, do I?' and here she does grin, infuriatingly. 'And there'll be no call for him to defend me anyway. That loan is the King's business, not mine. What's it got to do with me?'

Chaucer sighs. She's refusing to have the discussion he wants to force.

'Alice, listen,' he says sadly. 'I went to Westminster to collect my pension from the palace yesterday. And I think you should know that over there, at court, all the courtiers are whispering a whole different lot of rumours.' He puts his head on one side, looking at her, wondering if she'll blush.

She doesn't. She just gazes back, and says, 'You look like

a bird in a hedgerow, Chaucer: sitting there like that with your head on one side, all beady-eyed.'

'Do you know what *they're* saying?' Chaucer persists.

She puts her hands on her hips and goes on meeting his eye. 'Tell me, then,' she says, refusing to look abashed. 'If it's so interesting.'

'Well,' he says. 'My good friend in the treasury said they were short of coin at the moment because a lot of Italian debt paper had suddenly been presented. And been paid off. Not at the discounted rate. At its full face value. Twice as much.'

He's aware he must look ridiculous, but he can't stop his head tilting over a bit more as he examines her face for signs of guilt.

'It cleaned them right out of ready money,' he said. 'They were hard pressed to find my ten pounds.'

Alice shakes her head, with a little smile of mock-pity twitching at the corners of her lips. 'Oh dear,' she says. 'Poor Chaucer.'

'I asked my friend the treasury clerk who presented the paper. He didn't know. He only knew it wasn't Lyons. No big ginger Fleming's ever set foot in the treasury office, he said.'

Alice raises her eyebrows. Coolly, she says, 'Hm. A mystery, then.'

Chaucer's heart is beating like an insane drum. 'I've got to ask you,' he says in a rush of breath, desperate to get it out and have it over with. 'It wasn't you, was it? Because if you *were* to start playing a game like that, it would be exactly the kind of thing I'm warning you about. They'd get you. The City and the court aren't as separate as you think. They all hear each other's rumours in the end. And if you were involved in some sort of bent business, and someone put two and two together . . . they'd all be down on you like a pile of bricks in no time, City, court, wherrymen, the lot.'

'Me?' Alice Perrers says, and now she does grin, openly, with flaring nostrils and wide-open eyes, as if she's invigorated by the cut and thrust of Chaucer's argument. 'But I haven't been near Westminster for days, Chaucer.'

157

She raises her eyebrows higher and spreads empty hands as if to show Chaucer there's no Italian debt paper in them. She's trying to look innocent. But she just looks absurdly pleased with herself.

'So,' Chaucer says, slowly, 'you're saying it really wasn't you? And you know nothing about it?' He doesn't believe her. But he can't help laughing at the mock-affront on her face now.

'Anyone but you who suggested such a thing, you know what I'd say?' she replies robustly. 'I'd say, "That's what you say, you old barrel-full of lies. Now prove your slander." And I'd be safe enough. They never would.'

Baffled, Chaucer nods. Of course he notices she hasn't replied directly to his question. But she's so self-assured that she's beginning to make him feel a blunderer, rushing in with his homespun advice. He thinks: Oh, who knows? Her confidence is catching. Perhaps he's just misunderstood everything. There's so much he doesn't understand about Alice.

So, tentatively, he goes in a new direction. 'Still . . . you lay yourself open to all these accusations . . . because you *are* so interested in money, and so clever about making it. More than other women. More than most men. You are, aren't you?'

She begins another easy don't-bother-me shrug, then, somewhere in the middle of it, pauses. Her shoulders stay up. Her hands are still spread. But above them, her eyes are quietly on him, and the defensiveness in them has gone.

'I suppose I am,' she says, in a different, more honest voice. 'Interested. *More* interested.'

'Why?' he asks.

She goes on looking at him, as if she's surprised by the simplicity of that question – as if she's wondering herself. Chaucer can almost hear her think.

In the end, she says quietly, 'I could tell you about where I started from. Because I didn't start rich, you know; I had to use my wits to get on. And that would be a kind of answer. But . . .'

He waits.

She's in her thoughts, half smiling a couple of times as she remembers things.

'. . . it wouldn't be the real answer,' she says after a while. Quieter still. Looking as if she trusts him. Almost. 'Not any more.'

'Not now you're so rich,' Chaucer prompts in a near-whisper. There's no need to do more than whisper, now they're standing so close.

She nods, acknowledging her present wealth. But absent-mindedly. She's still thinking out her answer, the real answer.

'Other women marry . . . devote themselves to their children . . .?' he prompts.

But she scarcely seems to hear that. 'Oh, I've had husbands,' she says vaguely. Her brow furrows. 'But they're . . . fixed, men, they all have their station in life. Marry a merchant, and you're a merchant's wife for ever. Marry a country knight, and you get a lifetime overseeing dairymaids. No one moves. There aren't many men who could change their lives as much as you just have, Chaucer – court to City, without a quiver. Most people are too scared. But what if it's the movement itself that you've found you enjoy? The freedom to keep trying something new?'

'Freedom . . .' Chaucer repeats, trying the unfamiliar word on his lips, hearing its sound, heady as a rush of fresh wind, inside his mind. He likes the bravery of it – that she isn't frightened to live without the male protection most women seek. He's flattered at the way she seems to be describing him as one of the brave, too. She's right, he finds himself thinking. People don't like change, on the whole. They fear it. *My* wife doesn't like my having changed my life, even this much.

'Because that's what I've found. I'm good at moving . . . thinking on my feet,' she's confiding. 'It's not the point, that I've got enough money (whatever enough is). If I just sat smugly back for the rest of my days, counting my blessings, getting fat – well, what would I *do*? I'd be bored. It's not the money that counts, not in itself. It's the thinking. The truth is, I like living on my wits.'

They're practically touching. Nose to nose. 'And I suppose

that's always going to annoy the people who are scared,' she adds philosophically; pityingly, almost. 'Poor things.'

Chaucer's so transfixed by her candidness, or just by her proximity, that he almost takes that last step forward to kiss her. Catching himself just in time, he steps back instead. And she looks up at him, as if remembering herself too. She grins – her old sharp mocking grin. '*You*'d like to be living on something more solid than your wits, right now, I can see,' she says in her bright, everyday voice. 'Food.'

An hour later, after meat pie and laughter and an enjoyable recitation of some more of his hangover verse ('O dronke man, disfigured is thy face! Sour is thy breeth, foul artow to embrace,' and so on), Chaucer's on the boat home.

Thinking. Because now, with his stomach full and his hangover muffled by pastry, and the river wind blowing his headache away, he's less pleased than he was, back there, about how the conversation with Alice has gone.

Whatever she says, Alice must have a hand in perverting the debt exchange, he's sure. She must be lying to him. There's no point in his hiding the truth from himself, too. For one thing, she's the only person Chaucer can think of (except perhaps Latimer, or himself) who has enough acquaintances both at court and in the City to have been able to work it. And the only one with the wit to think of it.

And if she *is* involved, he thinks, trying to focus on the disapproval he knows it's right to feel, then she's as much a glutton for money as, well, as he's been with her wine. Even if she's just piling it up, as she told him, to prove to herself that she can – in the end, what's it for, all that money? It's not as if she can take it with her to meet her Maker. Or as if she has children to leave it to.

But his disapproval won't quite stay. The hilarity that's always near the surface when Alice is in his mind keeps surfacing instead. Chaucer tries, though not very hard, to turn his thoughts from the cheerfully lewd imaginings that now crowd in, unbidden, about how she's remained childless despite all those husbands and lovers. Perhaps she's chosen it – chosen to keep the girlishness of her face and figure, which are her fortune. Perhaps she's more knowing than other women about sponges and vinegar, about counting days and calculating the cycles of the moon; or perhaps, who can say, she makes the King wear a pig's bladder while he makes love to her. He can't help chuckling to himself at the thought. You can't rule anything out with Alice Perrers.

Or perhaps her barrenness is the private tragedy in her life. Perhaps that's what set her off in the first place on her multiple marriages, and relentless self-enrichment, and general self-willed good-natured entertaining infamy.

Poor Alice Perrers, Chaucer thinks (knowing, at the same time, that he's trying to find excuses for Alice, so he can go on enjoying this friendship; knowing that he needs a bit of compassion, nice, oily, sentimental compassion, to help the bitter pill of her suspected dishonesty go down more easily).

He lets his own two children come to his mind. Whatever the problems that have started to beset his family, he welcomes the tide of tenderness that sweeps through him now at the knowledge of them, the near-drowning intensity of it. Being the father of Thomas and Lizzie is his great pride and consolation in life – more overwhelming than any love for a woman, or advancement at court, or even than the poetry he so enjoys writing.

He's happy not to be a courtier whenever he remembers that lords send their children away at seven, to be trained in the ways of chivalry and courtesy in other men's households. He can think of nothing better than to be of humble merchant stock, where, if all goes well, you keep your beloved children near you, teaching them all you know, until, in their teens, your son marries and brings a wife and, God willing, more children into your home.

If all Alice Perrers' manors and money-bags are only a substitute for the joys of motherhood, he tells himself, half relishing the mawkish twisting of his heart, then they're a poor second best.

After that he lets himself stop thinking. He leans back on the bench, and just enjoys the receding of his headache, and the wind rushing through his hair. Freedom, he's thinking, as he looks up at the circling birds, imagining what their extra dimension of movement must feel like; wishing he knew for sure.

TEN

Alice waits on the jetty until Chaucer has set off east, towards the City, in the boat he's flagged down. She waves until his receding figure turns away.

Then, once his head is only a dot on the glitter of water, she puts her own hand out and stops another boat.

She has her own business downriver, at Westminster, at noon.

She could have shared a boat with Chaucer. But she doesn't want to have to tell him where she's off to, or why. It's exactly the kind of thing that would rile him, and get him preaching again. And she doesn't like being preached to.

She's going east because, last night, after she put sweet, stumbling, apologising, pie-eyed Chaucer to bed on his bench, she got a message from Richard Lyons.

One of his employees was in trouble, said the secretary who rode down to her (and stayed in an entirely different part of the house, sharing quarters with the priest, up in the solar). The man – arrested months ago at Southampton – was finally to come up before the King's Bench tomorrow. The case was being transferred up to Westminster, to the King's own Bench, because the man was known to be employed by a London citizen, had been arrested by London men answering to Mayor Walworth, and the alleged offence had taken place in a royal port. Master Lyons was hoping that she might use her influence to get the man a sympathetic hearing.

The favour Lyons wants from her is exactly the kind of thing Chaucer thinks she shouldn't be doing: interfering with the course of royal justice. Foolhardy, reckless. Blah, blah, blah. But the way she sees it, this is a question of friendship – a matter of honour.

Alice hasn't asked Lyons' secretary the details of the charges, nor has she been told; she can guess it'll be some sort of twisting of trade regulations, but why should she care? Wanting to know too much about the detail, or the employee, wouldn't be in the spirit of the thing. She's off to Westminster to sort things out. Feeling the river run through her fingers; listening to the grunting of the boatman; watching the dance of light on the ripples.

And, as she goes, her gaze is fixed up in front, on Chaucer's little dot of a head.

The case starts, as these things always do, with a quiet word with the judge beforehand. Alice is relieved, as she flits through the hall, having quickly rearranged her own clothing and windswept hair to suggest she's just popped casually in from somewhere upstairs, rather than come up from Pallenswick especially for this, to see that the Justice today is Sir Robert Belknap.

Belknap is a portly, thick-lipped, easy-going man from her own part of the world, with a fat laugh and a younger wife and a good cook. Alice knows him well enough to know he'll do anything to get out in time for dinner. He isn't a man to be held up over the finer points of law.

'Now . . . about your first man,' Alice says, after they've greeted each other and Belknap has asked how the reroofing is going at her aunt's manor at Gaines (not that he's ever been near Gaines, but he's an Essex man, and sits at the Assizes at Brentwood Town, not far away, so he's heard the name; it's a friendly gesture).

Then she pauses. Perhaps she should have paid more attention to the detail, after all. She realises that she isn't even sure what Lyons' man is called. 'Tyler,' Belknap supplies helpfully. She pauses. 'Up before me for . . .' He looks down his roll,

164

whistling in air through his teeth. '. . . extortion – demanding money with menaces? Southampton port? Head of a gang of six?' That'll be the one, Alice thinks, more certain this time. 'Apparently, also for telling his victims that the money he's taking off them is going to Richard Lyons,' Belknap adds with fat delight, wiggling his eyebrows, inviting her to share the laugh. 'The vintner. His employer, too, as it turns out; though the man Tyler's supposed to work as a debt collector, not an out-and-out thief. Still, it's not a bad cover story, all things considered . . . because Lyons actually does have a customs responsibility now, doesn't he? I wonder how *he*'ll feel, when he finds out?'

'I've been asked', she says, 'to put in a word.' She turns her fullest smile on Belknap, flashing her teeth. 'For that prisoner – Tyler.'

Belknap goes on watching her, with the matching smile still firmly on his face but with caution now starting to shadow the corners of his eyes. She can see he's reassessing their chat; repositioning her not as friendly acquaintance but as potential . . . problem? Threat? Perhaps people haven't often asked him for favours before. Perhaps he doesn't know how to respond. 'Uh-huh,' he replies, and he nods his head once or twice, pleating the lardy skin under his chin. 'I see.'

So she bows, ready to move on. If he's not going to ask more, she doesn't need to explain more, does she?

It's only when she's already passed him by, and is wafting on in the general direction of St Stephen's chapel, feeling pleased at how easy influencing people can be, that the Justice finally plucks up the courage to hrmph a couple of times, and then ask the obvious, if tactless, next question. 'If I may ask . . .' his fruity voice calls out. Perhaps it's because he's got his courage back and wants to intimidate her into answering frankly, or perhaps he just hasn't got control of his voice, but for whatever reason it comes out far too loudly for comfort. '. . . who exactly is it who . . .' As she turns, hastily, before he yells out to the entire royal administration in all the different corners of the hall that she's after a favour (which isn't at all the way these things are done), he lowers his voice to a normal speaking tone, but there's still a challenging look in his piggy eyes: '. . . wants Tyler given an easy ride?'

Alice doesn't take kindly to feeling bullied.

So she lets him wait for the answer. She can see, within an instant, that he's wondering whether he's done a dangerous thing by questioning her, or crossed a person more powerful than himself. He isn't brave by nature. He's still meeting her eyes, but he's fiddling with his feet and twitching with his fingers.

Old Alison always used to say Alice was a bit of a bully. She used to get carried away as a kid, taking the boys down a peg or two. She's certainly enjoying the awkward truculence fat old Belknap's trying to keep on his face now.

She doesn't give him the satisfaction of a reply. She leaves him with his uncertainties. She just raises a mocking eyebrow, nods, and moves off, leaving him gaping like a fish.

That would have, should have, been the end of it: the magistrate quelled, the criminal sprung. She'd never have dreamed of going to the hearing herself. That wouldn't be at all the elegant thing. It isn't how power works.

Except that, quite unexpectedly, today, as she leaves the hall, she sees that they're already bringing in the first prisoner for his hearing – *her* man. She notices the two sentries first (and notices, too, with her usual quiet laugh at fate, that the two stocky heavies look at least as villainous as the cowed man roped up between them). This must be him, she thinks. Tailor. Tiler. He'll be grateful to her in due course, though he won't know that yet. She gives way to the group passing through the doorway.

From maybe two or three feet away, she looks up, straight into Tailor-Tiler's face. He looks up, straight into hers.

He's not much taller than her, but thicker-set. He has a not unattractive face under a mess of rope-coloured hair: long, intelligent eyes, a big straight nose (slightly cauliflowered now), some strangely sweet freckles on bridge and cheeks, and a wide sensual mouth ready to turn up into a grin.

I wonder if he still winks when he grins? she thinks, before she realises she's recognised him.

Of course, Tyler. He's taken his name from the tilery, why not?

Then she says, 'Wat?'

The sentries turn, looking alarmed, thinking she's talking to them. 'What, mistress?' one says, absurdly echoing the same sound.

But Wat shakes his head at her, just a fraction.

He's recognised her too, that's obvious (though whether he knows her for the King's mistress is less clear). But his face says, Allie, listen, this isn't the time. No fuss now, it pleads, as it always used to whenever they ran into trouble on their thieving expeditions. Not while these blokes could make my life harder than it need be. Keep a low profile. Keep things simple.

She understands. She shakes her head. 'Nothing, soldier,' she says. 'Carry on.'

Still, she turns and follows them back into the hall, to hear the case going before Belknap. This isn't only a favour to Lyons any more. It's just become personal.

It's astonishing to see the back of Wat's head again – the same squarish flat-topped shape to it that she remembers; the same squared-off fingernails, too. All at once, glancing down at his hands, Alice is a girl of ten, or less, back in the long grass, giggling helplessly, while the boys hold her down and tickle her in the ear with her own long plait and Wat grins at her, winking, holding her down with those same hands, and, with the sun behind him, saying, over and over again, in a treble boy voice, 'So, do you confess?'

He's always been her favourite. They're so alike: the naughtiest of her brood, Aunty always used to say, and the cleverest too.

It's madness, of course, to go back into the courtroom now, when she's already arranged the verdict. But she has to be sure. Now she knows who the prisoner is, she's worried by the flicker of rebellion she thinks she may have detected in old Belknap's eyes.

It isn't every day that Alice Perrers feels it necessary to make use of her position of power. But she doesn't think

167

anyone will dare try and stop her. Belknap? Don't make me laugh, she thinks. And as for Edward – well, if the worst comes to the worst, she can always tell Edward he's told her himself to interfere. He won't remember any different, poor old dear.

Instead of hovering politely on the edge of the court space, leaning against a pillar among the scurrying clerks and scriveners, allowing her influence to be felt quietly, as would have been perfectly proper, Alice, in her bright yellow, standing out against the men in black, consciously drawing all eyes to herself, sweeps out into the middle of the hall.

Holding her head high, making her back straight, she walks to the marble seat in the middle of the floor where Edward would have sat, if he were here: the actual King's bench. She's acutely aware of every footfall as she goes. So is everyone else.

They all know – better than she – that she isn't supposed to be there. But none of them fancies taking her on and telling her.

As she sits regally down on the marble bench, she can almost see the circle of indrawn breaths.

Into the hush, surrounded by O-shaped mouths, she says, 'Proceed, my lord Justice.'

Belknap's eyes are as round as his mouth. But, after a stunned moment, the voices start: the swearing-ins, the formalities. Bowed heads busy about their rituals, eyes turned timidly away, bald patches on display. Ants, below her. She can feel the blood drumming in her ears as the charge is read out.

So this is what it feels like, to be royal.

But she isn't too carried away to notice that Belknap is giving her a very sick look as he leans forward, ready to speak as the first case opens.

'New facts have come to light in this matter,' he begins. His voice is loud and hard.

Her stomach lurches. He looks so hostile – almost as if he might actually get his revenge on Alice for trying to frighten him by announcing to the court what everyone must privately already know. This is the fact that when a man called Wat Tyler

168

is caught with a gang of heavies beating extra money out of exporters at Southampton, but also has a long-term contract as a more conventional type of debt collector with an extraordinarily wealthy vintner called Richard Lyons, he will almost certainly have been sent to do this rather dirtier job by Richard Lyons too. But his pay will have reflected the risk of his work, and his willingness to take the punishment if he's caught, and Richard Lyons' name is not supposed to come up, in any official context, now or ever. It wouldn't be at all in the usual way of business for that to be mentioned now.

Alice thinks, with sudden terror, but Belknap . . . just . . . might. Oh, God's teeth and bloody wounds. He looks so angry. He's practically bristling. Even his paunch has gone from the soft, wobbly, comfortable flab she remembers to a kind of carapace – a great curved breastplate of rage at being dictated to by her. She has a feeling that if someone put a fist into that paunch now, they'd break their knuckles.

So, as Belknap's voice gets louder, Alice leans forward too. She makes her back straighter. She makes her face harsher. And when she speaks, she makes her voice as loud as she can, to compete with the judge's professional boom.

'New facts', she projects back at him, deafening herself, 'which leave no case for the accused to answer.'

Belknap just stares, astonished into silence again. So does everyone else. Have they heard? Perhaps, in her panic, she's thought she's been shouting, but no sound has come out of her mouth?

She booms: 'My lord the King therefore orders the court to release the accused.'

Another muffled silence. It's as if the entire room has had a spell cast on it. It's as if no one can move, or speak, or do anything but stare.

She booms, louder still, addressing herself to the two soldiers around Wat this time, making energetic get-on-with-it-then-go-away gestures with her right hand as she does so: 'Go on, then. Hurry up. Set him loose.'

It's only after the two soldiers have woken up out of their

169

appalled slumber and started hastily fiddling with knots (with their eyes firmly down the whole while) that the rest of the courtroom seems to come back to life too.

She rises to her feet as the others begin to stir around her. She goes and stands in front of the prisoner. Sternly, she says, 'Let this be a lesson to you.'

His eyes, slowly raised, meet hers. He's always had that gift of insolence. He mouths, 'Dancing Bear, Cheapside, in an hour.'

She doesn't acknowledge his words. She's staring at the familiar freckles, and wondering how he's done that to his nose. There'll be so much to catch up on. Loudly, she finishes: 'Do you hear, my man? Don't let the judge find you in his court again. It won't end well another time.'

He winks. She doesn't think anyone else has seen. It makes her smile inside.

She can hear them whisper behind her, then start to mutter, as she sweeps out.

'Bloody marvellous,' Wat says, coming up for air from his tankard of ale. There is scum on his upper lip. 'You were incredible. And there was me thinking, I'm done for this time. Until you showed up.'

They clink cups. He winks. She's grinning like a lunatic, too, drinking him in.

They've already cautiously skirted the question of her status. 'You cleaned up good then,' Wat said, nodding a few times, and then, jerking his head down to her skirts: 'Yellow suits you. Nice bit of stuff, that.' He hasn't said, exactly, that he knows her to be Edward's concubine; but it's obvious, from something in the restraint and respect of him, that he knows. They're waiting to go through some of the lesser stuff before they start on that conversation. They need some jokes they can be sure they share first.

They're in a dark corner in the back of the tavern, in the empty space in the day between sext and the dinner hour. No one is listening as Wat drops his voice and mutters through what got him into trouble. It seems he's worked for Richard Lyons ever since he came back from the wars . . .

170

Before that, Wat has also been telling her, he'd gone from fighting in France for the Duke's older brother, the Prince, back in the day, to the altogether more cheerful robber-baron life of a mercenary in the Free Companies rampaging through Burgundy and Normandy and Champagne and Languedoc and Savoy and the Italian states. Those were the days, he's said reminiscently, out with the King of the Companies, Seguin de Badefol, leaping on some rich merchant or other from Toulouse or La Riolle or Bergerac: 'And never a day that passed without some bit of something falling into our laps to make us richer and happier. It was all ours . . . all just there for the taking. The peasants of Auvergne brought supplies to our castle, wheat and flour and fresh bread and hay for the horses and good wine and beef and mutton and fat lambs and poultry. We ate like kings. And when we rode out the country trembled at the sight of us.'

Alice knows those stories. The routiers and condottieri of the Free Companies, who fight the wars of whichever prince will pay their fees, and amuse themselves in between times, are said to commit every kind of crime: from eating meat in Lent to slitting open pregnant women to kill their unborn and unbaptised children. The countryside of the southern lands is supposed to be full of their victims: a sea of vagabonds – priests without parishes; destitute peasants; artisans looking for work. 'So you', Alice says, 'were one of the famous sons of iniquity . . .' The Pope calls them that when they rob churches. But the Pope also uses them regularly. Alice knows she sounds a little breathless. She can't altogether keep the admiration out of her voice. If she'd been a man, she thinks, she might have done exactly the same thing as Wat, to better herself fast.

Wat winks and, with the feel of a foreigner, says, with rolling r's and suddenly spread-out hands, '*Perfidi e sceller-atissimi* . . . yeah, that's us.' Knowledgeably, he adds, 'If God Himself were a soldier, he'd be a robber.'

So Wat was doing very nicely for himself, until he got into a spot of bother with a man in Mantua. He doesn't say what bother, just touches the side of his damaged nose – meaning a secret – and winks. He had to leave in a hurry and escape home. Leave it all behind: the houses, the lands, the horses, the good clothes, the bags of treasure. 'Still, that's the way it works,' he adds philosophically. 'Easy come, easy go. Plenty more where that came from to be found here, if you only know where to look.'

They look at each other, and grin, remembering Aunty's favourite phrase. It's Alice who starts saying it, though Wat joins in. 'The streets of London are paved with gold, if you only know where to look!'

Back in England, Wat says, when the laughing's done, he couldn't have hoped for a better master than Master Lyons. He's done all kinds of jobs for Lyons in his time, but the latest job has been the best. Lyons, it turns out, has been using his new customs inspection job, which he asked Alice earlier this year to help him secure, to employ large numbers of heavies – under Wat's control – at the south coast ports. Officially, ostensibly, they're there to check on wrongdoing during the loading and unloading of cargoes. But of course there's other stuff going on too, on the side.

Sometimes they take cash bribes. (This is where Wat's come unstuck just now. One of his men picked on the wrong sort – some merchant with an inflated sense of his own honesty, and a bigger gang of heavies than Wat could lay hands on at that moment.) But that's not the only extra deal Lyons has going on. This is the part of Wat's story that most interests Alice. The most important job-on-the-side has been to confiscate and impound a huge proportion of the foreign foodstuffs imported by the big three London merchants, the grocers. Lyons is stockpiling the pepper and the spices entering England – grocers' imports. It's an indirect trade attack, not on Walworth the fishmonger, but certainly on his two closest allies in the City, Brembre and Philpot. Wat doesn't know why Lyons has gone for this, not for sure, but it stands to reason Lyons will try and sell the goods himself, later on, at an inflated price, having cornered the market.

Lyons is always two or three tricks ahead of the rest. You never quite know, with Lyons, where things are going. At first

Alice just thinks, with dawning understanding: So he's taking on the grocers. I see. His war with Walworth and his men is hotting up. Next she thinks, with more resentment than she'd have expected against her City business partner, so charming yet so violently coloured, so orange and pink and purple, the man whose business she's been out doing today: He never told *me* about that. Shouldn't he have?

'Penny for them,' Wat says, still the same boy, tiptilted nose, sunsplotches, aware of her mood, even if he now has this coarser, uglier, stranger's version of his face, and she realises she's been sitting in silence, she doesn't know for how long, wondering about Lyons.

She laughs, a bit uneasily. 'Oh, just thinking,' she says, feeling her own intonations go back to a time before she spoke French, or knew courtiers. 'You never bloody well know with Richard Lyons . . . what he's up to. Do you?'

He grins back, but glassily. He doesn't know. He doesn't care, either, she sees, as long as Lyons pays. He's too happy-go-lucky to bother his head with complications.

Perhaps she should feel the same way.

She tries the same kind of big bland grin. 'Ah well. He's loyal. He got you out today,' she says resignedly. Resentment prickles. 'Or at least, I did.'

She sees Wat's sudden regret at having turned the conversation only to himself. How many chances will he get in life to sit drinking with the King of England's mistress?

'You saved my bacon,' he says hastily. 'I know that.' He's drinking her in again with those cheery dancing eyes. He's practised that merry roguish look over the years, she realises. He uses it to fob off trouble. He goes on: 'Not good at fine words, but you know I'm grateful.' Rather shyly, he adds, in a slower voice, 'I don't know what to ask you about your life. I mean, a lot I know already . . .' He flaps a helpless hand at her rich clothes.

How easy to know about her life, she realises, suddenly sympathetic again. She's famous (or infamous). They make up songs about her in the taverns of London. What can he possibly ask that he doesn't already know?

'Don't know everything, though. How did you . . .' He hesitates, looking a boy again. '. . . meet . . . him?'

Her laugh is short and without much humour. Before she speaks next, she understands with surprise that what she's been feeling, as Wat speaks, is envy.

She's been envying the freedom and straightforwardness of his life: here one day, somewhere else the next, always someone new to shake down, and always a tomorrow to wake up to.

What can she tell Wat about all her yesterdays? A little caustically, she answers, 'Well, obviously, I was always going to end up with some rich old man. Not much else to do, if you're a girl.' And he nods. She can see him imagining that. Not liking the idea much, perhaps. She can even see him sympathising, a little. But not pitying her. Neither of them does pity.

He says, 'I suppose not.'

She misses out the merchant husbands. Wat saw the first one, for a few hours, when the lost, footsore Champagne family stopped that first night at the tilery, once they'd got themselves properly lost in Essex, looking for the manor that some distant relative's death in the Mortality had brought them. He'll have worked out that she married the dad, surely? And that the manor was a hopeless ruin, and that she became a London baker's wife? He can sketch the rest in for himself. She misses out Froissart, too, the French teacher Tom Champagne hired, coming across her again as a comely widow, the resumed French lessons now she had her own money, the cheerful lovemaking now she was her own mistress. Not that little Jean Froissart really wanted her, not for ever. He was in love, by then, once he'd been made the Queen's official chronicler, with the great idea of chivalry, the romance of ladies and knights and impossible quests. And, like everyone else at court, he was at least halfway to being in love with the Queen his employer. He couldn't stop talking about her. The Queen, so beautiful; the Queen, so loving; the Queen, so good. The Queen, fifty if she was a day by then. But she'd given him, a town boy, a job at court. No wonder he loved her. Alice Perrers was ever only an interruption to him, a bit of reality before he went back to his dreams and his stories. Still, Jean knew Alice had her way to make in the world, like him, and he was a generous lad. He got Alice her first taste of court. He took her to a tournament. 'I want you to speak to the Queen in your French,' he said excitedly beforehand. 'I want you to tell her I taught you everything you know. She will be so impressed.'

Alice discards all that, now. 'Someone took me to a joust,' she says calmly, remembering sitting over the street on the ladies' platform as the men charged below, but remembering, better, Queen Philippa's great wrinkled moon of a face, the kindly look in those faded blue eyes, and the gratitude when Alice noticed her little shiver of pain and came forward to attend to her. 'And the Queen took a fancy to me. It was a bit of luck really. One of her sons had got one of her ladies-in-waiting knocked up. There was a vacancy. She gave me the place.'

Wat nods, meditatively, and whistles through his teeth. 'Like you say,' he says, looking at her with slow admiration. 'Your lucky day.'

It's as if all those years since they last talked have been a dream. There are ways she'll never be able to trust anyone as she can trust Wat. They know each other too well to need pretence. They can talk.

Her prickles vanish. She finds herself telling him more, or beginning to: more private things. She tells him about meeting William of Windsor soon after she got to court (though not the shiver when she first felt his quiet blue eyes on her; not the tumultuous feelings that had so astonished her. She thinks Wat will understand other things better). A knight from Northumberland, she says; done well in France. Just back from Ireland with the King's son Lionel of Ulster, the one who died.

'You'd have done well to marry *him*,' Wat says. 'Been a lady. Gone north.'

'But,' she says, and she realises she's never really talked about this to anyone, since the difficult time when she was deciding what to do. Never had cause. It makes her uneasy. 'Then, the King . . .'

175

'Yeah,' Wat says sympathetically. 'You chose different. Course you did. Anyone would, in your shoes.' He laughs. He has a friendly, uncomplicated laugh. It draws her in.

She sees she doesn't need to tell him the rest – the details. He understands the important stuff anyway. Just as well, too, maybe. As old Alison always said, best keep mum unless you need to talk.

She breaks the companionable silence that follows by asking: 'Have you ever come across the others?'

He shakes his head. Not really. He says, 'I heard Johnny's in Kent. Has a bit of land and a family. But . . . no one else.'

The words open up an uncrossable gulf between Johnny, who with Wat used to be her favourite of the nearly 'brothers', and her. She imagines Johnny with peasant children, and a weathered, simple face. None of Wat's deadpan intelligence in that other man's eyes. She thinks: I won't be looking Johnny up.

She says, 'You know I've moved Aunty Alison to live with me?'

She's startled when Wat replies, calmly, 'At Gaines. 'Course.'

'You knew?' she asks. 'Did you?'

He nods. 'Been there, in't I? Couple of times. Saw the kids and all.' His calm face opens. 'Growing up good, they are, all three of them. Nice boy. The little girl. Joan, Jane? The younger one? Got spirit. And she's the dead spit of you.'

There's a glow on both their faces when they leave the Dancing Bear. The jug is empty. There's a glow in Alice's heart too. It's been good to find this man, who's so like kin. She's happy Fortune's sent him her way again.

Before they part, she gives him money: quite a lot of it, in a leather purse that clinks with gold. He weighs it in his hand, raises his eyebrow, then, impulsively, kisses her. She says, 'Now don't get ideas,' and wags a finger in his face. 'There's no more where that came from, not for you. And we'd best not meet, either.'

He nods. He's Lyons' hit-man. He lives in the shadows. Being known to know each other could compromise them both. 'I was thinking that myself,' he says.

176

But it's not good enough, that. She sees his uncertain look. Neither of them have words, or behaviour, that adequately express feelings, those unnecessary luxuries. 'But we can always get in touch if we need to,' she adds, in a half-question. 'Can't we? Through Aunty?'

He nods again. He looks happier with that. 'She'll know where to find me,' he promises thickly. 'She always will. Good old Aunty.' He reaches a hand out to her shoulder. He pats it. He can't bring himself to say goodbye. 'Till next time,' he says, finally, and she sees tears in his eyes.

Lyons leans forward on the leopard-skin rug he's placed on the biggest bench in the room. He has his back to the window, and the late afternoon sun is behind him so Alice can't see into his face; she can just see his silhouette. But he, lord of all he surveys, can stare into her eyes. It's an uncomfortable position to be in.

This room, Lyons' great hall, makes Alice uncomfortable at the best of times, with its mute proofs of its owner's rampant self-importance. Lyons by name, lions by nature, as he likes to say of himself. Since he threw out his wife, and divorced her (poor Isabella, so English, so outraged), it's only got more extreme. There are ermine skins sewn on to borders and fringes in here; royal furs (what would the sumptuary law enforcers have made of *that*?); and, squashed in among the arras that were already hanging everywhere, there are now curtains in the boldest blue and red, embroidered with royal(ish) lions.

'Your man is free,' Alice is telling the shimmering silhouette, wondering as she speaks whether it would be wise to mention what she's found out about some of Lyons' other entrepreneurial tricks while setting Wat free, then opting (for the thousandth time when it came to him) to let sleeping dogs lie. Best not to be seen to know too much. 'Belknap didn't make much fuss.'

Lyons' head nods. He rumbles appreciatively: 'Ach, Belknap, that great coward.'

He laughs his bass laugh. 'You're more than a match for him, Alice.'

Alice is remembering the softness on Wat's hard face when he talked about seeing her children in Essex. She's remembering the tears her nearly-brother couldn't stop when he couldn't say goodbye. She's remembering how Wat, to whom she feels so close, and whom she might never have seen again if he hadn't fallen foul of some Mantuan murderer and escaped home, has been saved from destitution because Richard Lyons decided to employ him.

It doesn't make any difference. She's got to do what she's got to do.

She says, 'Now you have to turn him loose. Your man. Tyler. His cover is blown. If they arrest him again . . .' She draws a finger across her throat.

'. . . it wouldn't be good for me, you mean?' Lyons' voice comes out of the glitter.

Alice says, 'Give him enough money to go away. Abroad, maybe. He'll be fine there. He's a natural recruit for the Free Companies.'

She laughs. She can see the dark head nodding agreement, moving against the gold behind. Lyons doesn't bother to tell her that his heavy has escaped to him *from* the Free Companies. Lyons is as economical with words as Alice is. Words dilute and dissipate intent; words can be dangerous.

Alice goes to bed that night still thinking of Wat, still full of warmth and nostalgia and guilt. She'd have so liked to see him again. If only he hadn't told her so much. If only he hadn't said he'd seen her children.

ELEVEN

Alice has always prided herself on being more alert than most to the first whiff of danger, and quicker than most to neutralise it, too.

But she is far from even imagining the four people walking, very fast, around the cloister of the Abbey of St Albans, in a dusk with snow threatening, as the year 1374 draws to a close. There are three men and a woman in the group. It's the woman who's talking, flashing her eyes, sweeping her long cloak behind her. But all of them, one way or another, are Alice's enemies, or are about to be.

It's the Prince of England who has called these people together. From his stinking, miserable sickbed, he's been planning action ever since the spring night when Joan, his wife, came back, pinch-lipped and angry, from Westminster, with the information that *that woman, the whore*, had been dancing with John.

Edward of England remembers the moment he heard those words like a knife thrust in the side. 'He's going to try and make Perrers his creature,' he remembers saying; and Joan, with her eyes, so like his, long and almond-shaped above high cheekbones, agreeing: 'Or *she* to make him *hers*.'

Edward and his wife, cousins, like as twins, have always shared thoughts that scarcely need to be put into words. But it's only in these last years, the years of his decline, that they've started to share the same all-consuming fear.

Their shared fear is so terrible that, for a long time, they even feared to give it words, a shape, a living, breathing form that might come roaring out of the darkness of the night. But that was the night when it did, finally, emerge.

What they fear, this dying Prince and his Princess, is the Prince's brother.

Not John himself, for there's a part of John they've both always loved, a John who grew up in the same nursery they remembered, even if he came a few years later; a John they recall as a solemn, intense, dark-eyed toddler for whom, as merry twelve- and thirteen-year-olds with life unfolding brightly just ahead, they hid Easter toys in tubs of bran, whom they made jump for honeycakes.

There's a way in which they both still love the present John, too, a prince who shares their slanting Plantagenet beauty and finely honed sense of honour and pride in his own nobility. He's richer than them, but he's never inspired the great love Prince Edward commands from his people, or become the war hero his older brother once was. There's nothing in John, this John, to arouse their fear.

It's the thought of John in the future that makes the Prince and Princess of England wake in the night, more and more often, with their hearts thudding in their chests. It's the choking fear of what John might be moved to do to their only child if Prince Edward were to die before his time.

They both know Prince Edward will die before his time – soon – though they dare not voice that thought to each other. Richard is not yet eight. What grown prince, faced with a throne that would be so easy to steal, would resist the temptation?

So John has become mylordofLancaster in their minds: the implacably waiting enemy, the besieging army, the darkness waiting to come crashing through their walls to destroy their child's life. The change in their feelings has come quietly, imperceptibly. There's never been a harsh word said, never a blow struck. They don't even know if John is aware of their fear.

But, around the sickbed, they talk of nothing else. MylordofLancaster has to be contained, his alliances watched,

180

his every move considered and countered. Fearing him has become the centre of both their lives, a chilly darkness eating away at them from inside.

They've sniffed at, fretted over, ferreted out more information about, considered from every angle and finally decided there's no danger to Richard in John's affair with the pretty widow Madame de Swynford, which he still thinks is a secret.

They've narrowed their eyes at, called in priests over, sent out spies to investigate further and finally decided there's no real danger to Richard in mylordofLancaster's flirtation with Wyclif.

But all kinds of harm might come from mylordofLancaster turning his mind to a friendship with Perrers and the rest of the grubby, gleeful thieves who've come swarming into the palaces of the court like rats ever since the King has grown too feeble of mind to loathe them for the vermin they are, and ever since his oldest son has grown too weak of body to catch them and swing them out by their tails.

Edward can only guess at what the harm might actually be. But each vague picture is more frightening than the last. And the one that stays with him is this. Perrers, he knows, is in cahoots with the merchants. What if she somehow finagled it so John got into the good books of the money-men of London, and made the City his power base? What if the merchants backed John for King?

It's time for action. Or it would be if Edward weren't reduced by the illness he's suffered from for seven years to a sodden, skeletal, exhausted, living corpse.

So Edward and Joan have fretted impotently at how to best to counter the threat of mylordofLancaster's friendship with Perrers, all through the summer, all through the autumn.

The answer, when it does finally occur to them, is blessedly simple. It's a name: that of Prince Edward's old friend, Thomas de la Mare, the Abbot of St Albans.

There's already bad blood between the Abbot and Perrers, he recalls, a land question of some sort. And Thomas de la Mare is full of the energy and relentless drive the Prince once had: a capacity to wait, and plan, for the destruction of his enemies. The Prince knows, as soon as he's thought of it, that this is a mission he can safely delegate to the priest. But he knows, too, that he must be discreet.

So, painfully, they've set off to winter at their estate at Riseberg. St Albans is on the way. Nothing could be more natural than to spend a night there.

Thomas de la Mare, Alice's old foe in a nagging legal battle for the lands of Oxhey manor just by his abbey, is a man without pleasures, unless you count the sting of the scourge on his back in the hours of solitary night prayer, or the itch of the hair shirt chafing at him all day, or the extra, self-imposed hours of foodlessness and sleeplessness he takes on himself beyond what he asks of the men whose worship he directs. That's why the pale flesh of his face has withered and sunk between jaw and cheekbone; why the hand's gristly knuckles seem so enormous.

The Abbot himself would not agree with those acolytes at the abbey who whisper that their master is utterly devoid of *caritas* – that spirit of generous, forgiving, divinely inspired loving-kindness that the Holy Church to which he has devoted his life urges its followers to be guided by. The unfree peasants who cut and hack and plough and dig and shoe and groom and pay on the hundreds of rolling acres of the abbey's land would not dare say anything so bold, even in a whisper. But they might widen their sunken eyes, just for a second, in as close as they dared to agreement. This, after all, is an abbot who has never forgiven a villein an hour's uncompleted work, or a single turnip short of the two-thirds of the harvest demanded, or the fee required when a poor man's relative leaves abbey lands. This man is the reason why the peasants of Oxhey were happy to leave Church jurisdiction and come under Alice's control. This is a man whose discipline borders on ruthlessness, whose ruthlessness borders on obsession, who doesn't stop until he draws blood.

Thomas de la Mare would put the thing differently. What he would say is he has often been disappointed by the men and women – the backsliders, the failures, the faint-hearts – whom it has so often been his unhappy lot to meet. This earthly life is full of bitter disappointments. God moves in mysterious ways.

He's never forgotten the defining disappointment of his life – in his own father, that big, red-cheeked simpleton of a man, who assumed that Thomas' early interest in books meant he should be the one chosen for a career in the Church. Thomas was the second son, a youth who, out of the urgent desire to prove himself, had run the family manor with ruthless efficiency for five years while his elder brother Lionel and father were away at the wars, putting more land under the plough, to better profit, than ever before. So why should he be the one for God? There were two younger brothers who would have made perfectly passable priests, he told his father when the old man came back. But there was no changing things. The old man had his mind made up, and he was stubborn. Thomas took holy orders and, when Lionel was killed in France, John, the third brother, took on the title and the estates and the wife; and their father, grey now, if still red-faced, and hangdog from not having grabbed enough booty in France to give his sons the wealth and destinies they'd have chosen for themselves, couldn't ever meet his disinherited son's eye again. 'You'll make your way faster in the Church,' he'd mumble, scuffing at the dust, eyes on his toecap. 'You'll see.' Thomas de la Mare still fears the shaft of pure savagery that pierces his soul whenever he remembers his father. The old fool.

Yet, as he ponders how best to obey his Prince's command, being conveyed with such force by Princess Joan, his eyes have begun to gleam. He glances from her towards his two surviving brothers, who are keeping pace, more or less, both with the speed of his stride and that of the Princess's speech. He's called them in to advise, with two different purposes, one for each of them. For once in his life, the Abbot is feeling something he hardly knows how to describe. A different sort of man might call it happiness.

Princess Joan, striding forward, has kept her burning eyes turned sideways on the Abbot right through her explanation.

183

'So, my lords,' she says by way of conclusion. She's raking them all with her eyes. 'What now?'.

The Princess can see that encouraging answers from these three brothers will always be problematic. Sir John de la Mare has the family title, but there is something so awkward between him and my lord Abbot that she doesn't like to look at the way the two of them don't look at each other.

She shrugs to herself. It's natural, she thinks. They're men. Men fight.

But for all her hopes of instant wisdom from the Abbot, he remains silent. He has no immediate ideas.

It's the third brother, Sir Peter de la Mare, who has an opinion. Peter is lord of the manor of Yatton in Herefordshire, through his wife, and, more importantly, steward to Edmund Mortimer, Earl of March, who is third in line to the throne – behind little Prince Richard, and in front of Duke John. That association makes Peter de la Mare a man of rank. Peter is also one of the two county leaders for Herefordshire who will go to Parliament whenever the King next dares call it to ask for money. He'll represent the general mass of disgruntled minor nobility and medium-sized landowners called the Commons.

Perhaps it is the weight of all that authority that does it. But certainly Peter de la Mare doesn't seem to know fear. He is walking along, not getting breathless, thinking how to put his answer to the Princess. And everyone, even the Princess, is becoming aware of it.

Sir Peter's tall like his brothers, thin like his brothers, and he doesn't smile much. But he stands upright and looks you straightforwardly in the eye when he talks to you. There is no malice in his gaze, either.

Why is he so different from bitter old Thomas, with his sour comments and hateful judgements, and from me? Sir John de la Mare finds himself wondering a little enviously, as he flicks a sideways glance up at his brother Peter. Why do you find yourself waiting to hear what Peter thinks, and trusting what he says?

It's not that what he says is so different from anyone else.

Since the brothers all turned up at St Albans yesterday, John's heard that Peter de la Mare is as indignant as the next man that the country's in such disarray.

It's not that he's doing anything different with his life from his brother, either. Peter and John: both country lords. Though they say Peter's better than him at running his lands, John thinks anxiously; *he* doesn't rush into the wrong crops, the wrong expenses, punishing the wrong peasants – all the mistakes a lord who prefers war to farming can make.

John digs his bitten nails into his palms to hide them. It's not success, or wit, or efficiency, either, that makes you pay heed to Peter. It's this. In some fundamental way that has passed his brothers by, Peter de la Mare is happy.

Even the Princess seems to relax a little when Peter de la Mare does finally speak, as if that deep-down contentment they can all sense in some way comforts her, even though what he says can't possibly please her.

'If the whore is conspiring with my lord the Duke to the detriment of England,' he says, 'then it's a matter for trial before Parliament.'

The Princess nods, with a grim pleasure that the mention of Parliament doesn't usually arouse in her.

'But what we know now is not enough,' Peter de la Mare continues. Apparently unaware of the Princess's terrible stare, he scratches his head. 'We need facts. Provable facts.'

The Princess's jaw juts out. She grates: 'But you have my word.'

The two other brothers, keeping well clear of each other, one on either side of the talking pair, are staying silent.

But Peter is gently shaking his head. 'That won't take us far in a court of law, dear lady,' he replies, and his eyes twinkle at her with the beginning of humour. 'Not by itself. And that's the problem. Do you see?' He's talking to this great lady as candidly and straightforwardly as if they were equals, brother and sister, husband and wife, which John de la Mare also secretly admires. Where does he get the courage?

Peter pauses, giving the Princess time to acknowledge the

truth of this. Her only response is to increase her pace and look as angry as a caged lion.

John, who is timid behind his countryman's bluster, can scarcely breathe. The heavens move in their appointed orbits; human life too. So there is something uncanny about Peter's confidence in challenging the opinion of a princess.

'But I doubt it would be hard to find legal proofs,' Peter de la Mare goes on, conceding something in his turn, and his voice is as smooth as before. 'God knows there's enough talk about Perrers' private dealings. And as you know so well, dear lady, there's no smoke without fire.'

Sullenly, reluctantly, the Princess grunts. To John's astonishment, she appears to have conceded that Peter is talking sense.

There is a silence. As he catches his breath, and ponders, John realises uncomfortably that he doesn't fully understand why Peter de la Mare would want to apply a higher standard of proof to the question of Alice Perrers' infamy than the Princess does. What does it matter what they say she's done? They all know the woman's a bad lot, and if the Princess wants her punished, then surely they should be working on ways to use what they have against her. There's more going on here than he has understood.

Cautiously, he raises his eyes sideways to snatch a furtive glance at the speaker and see if he can read extra layers of meaning on his brother's face. As he does so, Peter stops walking.

'It's been my ambition, for some time,' he says, looking very searchingly into every one of the faces now turning towards him like flowers to the light, 'to use the next Parliament to put real, serious charges against the court clique, and anyone who has been promoting and supporting them. Perrers is one of the people I'd like to investigate. I want to rid the country of their corruption for once and for all. Like you, madame' – he bows towards the Princess – 'I believe that this corruption may go higher, far higher, than Perrers and her cronies. I suspect that your royal brother-in-law has been . . . unwise, to say the least, in his choice of associates.

186

He may indeed be trying to build secret associations of allies at court, and perhaps also in London, and in the country at large, for reasons of his own that we can only guess at. I agree that he needs to be reined in; and it's my view that if we succeed in framing serious charges against Mistress Perrers and her friends, the Duke will, at the very least, learn from his creatures' fate, and give up whatever his own private plan has been. But *our* plan will only work if we are absolutely clear as to what our purpose is. We must work to frame one clear set of charges. We must be able to prove them. We must be able to condemn Perrers and her friends through the application of the law – which, since we suspect them of acting against the law, should not be difficult. And we mustn't let anything turn us aside from that purpose.'

He pauses. He says, 'Do you agree?'

'Be simpler just to get her for witchcraft, wouldn't it?' barks Sir John, trying to assert himself at last. He's the one with the family title, after all; with the deep lines like gorges through his face to prove his experience in France and knowledge of life. He should be taking charge. He laughs, a whiskery, rustic, drunken, bullying sort of laugh. The kind of laugh he gives when he's trying to impress, or strike fear into people. It seldom works.

It doesn't now. Peter turns to him. 'Only if you can prove her a witch, brother,' he says calmly. 'In a way that everyone in the land would believe, in their hearts, to be true. And even if you could, that isn't the aim we want to achieve, is it? It's the corruption eating away at England that we want to root out, not Mistress Perrers herself. She's only a symptom of the disease. We want to get the cause.'

But John has already dropped his eyes. It's not Peter who's quelled him. It's the utterly malevolent stare his other brother, the Abbot, is bending his way.

'This is a problem of power. It's about the misuse of money and power,' Peter says, and the Princess nods. 'It goes higher than Perrers. It may, Heaven forfend, stretch right up to certain members of the royal family. Likewise, the solution needs to be clearly about power, and money, and corruption.

'What we need now is information about these people's financial dealings, not about their use of magical herbs,' he continues. 'We need information about the way they abuse power they shouldn't have.'

There's a silence, while the brothers look at each other. Sir John shrugs helplessly. 'I don't know anything about financial dealings,' he says, then tries, inanely for a nobleman's joke. 'I'm no bailiff.'

'I think', Peter says, 'that there are certain things I must find out for myself.'

The Princess nods again. 'I see you are the man for the job, Sir Peter,' she says. 'My lord Abbot, you've done well to think of introducing me to your brother.' There's respect in her voice. Even though she hasn't for a moment stopped thinking of, and worrying about, her husband, being moved off his stretcher inside, she almost smiles.

The Abbot nods, with apparent courtesy. But he isn't paying full attention. He's let his eyes slide sideways towards his brother John, who's looking foolishly left out, and knows it; he's scuffing his toes on the flagstones. John, if no one else, saw the fugitive look of satisfaction on the Abbot's face when the Princess humiliatingly ignored him. John is burning inside.

TWELVE

The woods outside Eltham are as dead as world's end. Not a bird, not a rabbit, just the clip of hooves on hardened mud, the rustle of old dead leaves and the creak of harness.

Alice watches the plumes of horse-breath rise, white on white.

She will be glad to be away.

The court's Christmas at Eltham was to have been a joy: three hundred people, with Alice as their female figurehead, in the Queen's jewels. She organised it meticulously: the hunts, the feasts, the fireworks, the minstrels, the troupes of actors, the private moments with Edward, the lavish New Year's gifts. Alice's pleasure at the prospect stemmed largely from the certainty that there would be no need to kow-tow, no need to hide away pretending some other, nobler, lady was in charge. Princess Joan would be safely locked up at Riseberg, nursing her husband. The Duke's Castilian Duchess, Constanza, would spend the holiday locked up at Hertford with her little girl and her Castilian ladies. But the Duke himself, invited on the King's behalf by Alice, months ago, had bowed and declared, graciously, that it would be his great pleasure to be with his father. He'd added, in a laughing, arch, undertone, 'And, of course, with Madame Perrers.' Alice liked that. From the beginning, Alice has thought of the Duke's near-single status as an advantage in making him her patron: his relations with his Duchess are so remote that there's never been the least risk of a hostile, suspicious wife whispering negative things about Alice in his ear.

So, for all the months she was planning Christmas, she was looking forward to having the two most important men in the land, dancing attendance on her alone for two weeks clear, grateful for the elegant festival she'd organised for them.

She doesn't even like to remember that hope now. False, all of it, dust and ashes in her mouth. For, shortly before the retinues began arriving at Eltham Palace, the Duke's steward asked for a private audience and then, squirming and staring at his feet, asked whether she'd thought to invite Madame Swynford. At her politely bewildered headshake – of course she hadn't invited either of the de Roët sisters, for surely they had plans of their own, and in any case wasn't Madame Swynford planning to be with her charges at Hertford, or away in the country with her own children? – the man only squirmed harder, and went pinker. In strangulated tones, he finally brought out the words he'd been told to say: 'My lord of Lancaster . . . my lord the King of Castile . . . asks that Madame Swynford be included.' Alice could see, from the way he was behaving, that the steward, too, had at some point been stung by that swaying, supercilious creature, with her gentle voice and the polite contempt in her eyes. When she stared, then, recovering herself and saying gently, enquiringly, 'I *see* . . .?' the steward refused to be drawn into confidences. Still, Alice couldn't help but feel uneasy.

Not that, at first, there seemed any real cause for that unease. The holiday started as well as she'd ever dreamed it might.

The Duke arrived first, and alone (alone, that is, ducal style – with only a retinue of thirty or forty at his heels). And he was in good health, with roses in his cheeks and a spring in his step, and in good humour, and pleased to see her. His eyes lit up as she came out on to the steps to greet him. He said, 'Ah, Madame Perrers, my dear friend.' He bowed. He kissed her hand.

As soon as he'd seen his rooms and washed the travel dirt off him, she whisked him off to stroll with her in the snowy garden. Her idea was to make little spaces in every day when they could be alone together, and talk freely. In case he proved reluctant this first time, or weary from the road, she told him, in a voice so quiet that he had to draw closer to catch her words, that she needed to talk to him about his father. She was shaking her head sadly to prepare him for what would follow. He came without question. Even before she'd said anything more, he looked concerned. She rushed on with her speech as they stepped out along the scraped paths, between bushes bowed with cloudy white. She did what she could to make my lord comfortable and happy, she said, but the Duke would find him . . . she paused, and searched for a delicate word . . . failing.

The Duke looked stricken at that, as a man of strong family loyalty, not to mention respect for a King who'd been so great, easily might. Slowly, he shook his head, and Alice could see him being overwhelmed by memories of Edward in his glory. Alice warmed to the Duke's obviously genuine sorrow, shared it even, while at the same time a hidden part of her thrilled, secretly, that she and this other man had such a natural starting-point for their murmured, intimate conversation.

'It's hard for me to believe he's getting old, Madame Perrers,' the Duke said wistfully. 'When he's always been so . . .' He paused. He looked helpless. He spread his hands. He's a sincere man, the Duke, open and generous in his emotions, but not one for elegant phrases.

'Glorious . . .' Alice prompted, finding him a word and agreeing with him all at once. Gratefully, he nodded.

She took her cue. It wouldn't do to mention Edward's success in France – such a painful subject for the King's son – but she could dwell a little on other glories.

'Do you remember his fiftieth birthday?' she reminisced, as if they could share the memory. She didn't remember it, as it happened; the jubilee, with its feasting, the special Parliament, and the law making English the language of the law, was before Alice's time. But John wasn't a man for detail. She didn't think he'd notice.

He sighed nostalgically. Alice could see he was proud to

191

remember himself and his brothers, back on that day, being called into Parliament to have the great new titles Edward was creating conferred on them. The new dukedom of Clarence for Lionel, still alive back then; little Edward made Earl of Cambridge; and, of course, John himself elevated from Earl to Duke of Lancaster. A solemn oath, a pass of the sword: Edward's reflected glory.

'And the years when there were jousts every month . . .' the Duke added in the hushed, respectful voice of a hero-worshipping boy: '. . . which he always won . . .?'

'And his hunting . . .' Alice breathed, spinning out the magic thread of narrative a little further for him. Long after Edward stopped being able to win a joust, he went on enjoying his hunting. It's only recently that the King's spending on dogs and his dozens of birds of prey – gerfalcons, goshawks, tiercels, lannerets, you name it – has dipped below £600 a year, as much as the average baron's annual income from rents. He always did look magnificent with a bird on his arm.

Duke John sighed. After a silence, he began to smile. Tenderly, though. He went on: 'And the food . . .'

Alice grinned back. Edward didn't believe servants should eat more than two dishes a day – modesty in everything, he liked to say; don't want them eating me out of house and home. But when it came to his own requirements, well, that was a different matter. Piles of food were required to fuel the jousting, hunting monarch: entire hillocks of beef, and pigeon, and carp. Edward liked eight dishes set before him at every meal, five before the lords eating with him, three before his gentlemen, and two before his grooms. It was a miracle he'd never got fat.

'That's changed now,' she said, bringing them back down to earth. 'He pecks at his food . . . he's been losing weight.'

The Duke shook his head. But he'd got the tempo of the conversation now. 'It's a comfort to know he has you at his side, at least,' he went warmly on, turning his face sideways to meet her eyes, giving her such an affectionate look that she gave his arm a grateful squeeze with the freezing hand she'd slipped through it. 'I'm very aware of your devotion to him.

I know I can be sure that you'll always give him the best possible care.'

Modestly, Alice looked down. Freezing hands or no, there was warmth going right through her at this.

'You must let me know what I can do to help . . . But . . . So much going on . . . There's Bruges coming up; I'll have to leave right after Christmas, as you know . . . unless you think . . .' The Duke paused again, unwilling to voice the next difficult thought. '. . . that the talks should be delayed?'

Alice could see he meant, but couldn't bear to say, 'Unless you think the old man's about to die any day?'

She didn't think he'd want to be overseas when *that* happened.

Reassuringly, she shook her head. 'No, no,' she said, finding herself imitating the Duke's awkward style of speech, 'he's changeable, quite well some days, and, well, wandering, on others, but he's not . . . not yet . . . Well, you'll see for yourself.' She squeezed his arm again. 'He's happy you're off to Bruges,' she added stoutly. 'He'll know everything will be done properly with you in charge. He trusts you, absolutely.'

She glanced up at him again, sideways. Brightly, she went on: 'You're taking Master Wyclif with you, I hear.'

She was thinking: It never does any harm to remind people you've come up with an idea to help them, after all.

She caught him glancing sideways at her. They both smiled. 'A good man,' the Duke said warmly. 'And a wise one. I'm grateful to you for suggesting that.'

Make yourself indispensible, Alice told herself. Make yourself needed.

Alice could already almost see a future in which a slightly older version of herself (quietly, maybe; without titles and pretensions, almost certainly; but with all her present influence and wealth maintained intact) whispered into the ear of a slightly silvered version of this man, to whom she'd long become indispensible as an adviser . . . a future in which her ideas, as if by magic, then became reality. A future in which she was not cut off from power by Edward's death, whenever it came, but brought still closer to it.

By the time they went back inside, so the Duke, now fore-warned, could pay his respects to his father, Alice was so full of confidence that Christmastide would make her and Duke John firm friends that she'd almost forgotten about Katherine Swynford.

But, only an hour later, La Swynford appeared.

When she walked unannounced into the great hall, Duke John – who'd been standing by his father near the fireplace, looking at the old man with anxious affection as he described his journey, clearly wondering just how strange, or sick, the King was likely to be in the next few days – flicked himself round on his heels, saw the newcomer, and let his face soften into an expression of obvious devotion that Alice found embarrassing in a hard-faced man in his thirties. 'Excuse me,' he said, nodding to Alice and his father without looking at either of them, and he made off across the hall towards Katherine.

Alice raised pointedly astonished eyebrows at Edward. She was hoping, at least, to share a moment of mockery with him at the incongruity of it. Duke John, in love with a nursery companion – someone he'd seen when she was a snotty-nosed little girl with tangly hair and dirty face. But Edward was clearly enjoying his son's display of emotion, and, to Alice's worsening disappointment, applauding his choice. He raised puckish eyebrows back, but all he said was, 'Good, excellent,' and then: 'Pretty girl, Katherine.'

There was no respite after that. There were no more quiet walks in the gardens with the Duke, no sense of almost-family deepening. Katherine Swynford stayed to the bitter end, till 2 January. She didn't go out to the big public parties, but she attended every private family event, hanging on John of Gaunt's arm like a limpet. She didn't go out of her way to make Alice feel uncomfortable, either, by being rude, or critical, or mocking. It just happened that, in her presence, Alice was all fingers and thumbs, spilling things or letting them slip or stumbling over them, feeling badly turned out and lumpish, unable to think of charming things to say to keep the conversation turning. Nor was it because Katherine Swynford was unimpressed by Alice's arrangements that she ate next to nothing, she assured everyone. 'An indisposition,' she said faintly, waving away an offer of food in her rooms, 'it's nothing.' When, after the handing-out of family gifts and before she left, she passed out and had to be revived with vinegar, Edward eagerly pressed the sour rag to her nose and said, with blind affection, 'There, you see, my dear, you should have been eating more!'

That was the moment the Duke picked to walk back in, in his cloak, ready to take Alice out for the long-awaited walk in the bare garden that she'd asked for so often. ('I'd like to know your impressions of my lord's state of mind,' she'd murmured persuasively, 'now you've had a chance to talk with him.') One look at the scene sent the Duke, again, running towards Katherine Swynford with concern all over his face. Alice could see at once that there was no blindness about *him. He* knew why she'd fainted, all right. With blackness in her heart, Alice turned towards the window, to look at the white on white of outside.

When the Duke left, alone again but for his retinue, she stood on the steps with them all listening and formally wished him success at Bruges. He, in turn, thanked her formally for welcoming him at Christmas. He didn't seem to be aware that she'd hoped for much more, or that she might be disappointed. He even smiled quite affectionately at her, then stepped forward, and, speaking quietly so they couldn't all hear, said, 'My father seems . . .' and paused, searching for a word. He looked relieved.

'A little better?' she supplied, carefully filleting the impatience she felt out of her voice.

He nodded. 'Please,' he went on, 'send word, as soon as . . . if anything . . . changes.'

That was positive, at least. It just wasn't nearly positive enough.

She let them all leave, even Edward, before setting off herself. She said there were a lot of things at Eltham for her to sort out. She said she'd need a few days in London.

One of the things she did, before leaving, was to seek out Duke John's steward for a private chat and, part-bullyingly, part-cajolingly, part-pretending to know more than she did, extracted the information from him that Madame Swynford, that goddess of beauty and deceit and fertility, was not just bringing up her own four Swynford children in Lincolnshire but had also quietly gone off and given birth, early the previous year, to an earlier son by the Duke of Lancaster. John, the baby was called; John Beaufort. 'Ah, yes,' she said, when the steward finally spat out the name. She managed a mischievous, knowing smile. It felt as though it was cracking her face. 'That's it. Of course. John. I'd half remembered Edward.'

It's not jealousy, exactly, she tells herself firmly as she heads through the trees. It's not passionate love she's felt for her patron-to-be, so why would it be jealousy she's so tormented by now?

But if Duke John's in love with Katherine Swynford – if his heart's one desire is to gaze at Katherine Swynford, and show her off to the court, and make the whole court stare up at the lady he loves with eyes as dazzled as if they're staring at the sun – then he'll never have the time or the inclination for the useful, easy, friendly, flirtatious relationship with Alice that she's seen developing, until now.

(The kind of friendship, she thinks, with a little stab of surprise, that has come about between herself and Chaucer. The kind of friendship where you can talk about everything and nothing, and feel at ease. She's missed that, these past couple of weeks.)

Alice knows she'll never be able to make a friendship with Katherine Swynford, either. The other woman's not exactly an enemy any more, but that's the best light you can cast on their relationship. Katherine Swynford hardly sees Alice; her lovely eyes just don't seem to be made for that. So Alice can forget about getting Katherine Swynford to murmur in her lover's ear that, yes, Alice is right on this, and why not do what Alice suggests about that?

Alice tries to keep her disappointment in check. It's a setback, she tells herself, but it's no worse than that. He still respects me; he's growing fond of me. And he's grateful for my advice.

196

But she can't stop the spiteful little voice in her head, replying: He's a lot fonder of *her*. He hardly noticed you, however hard you tried. You thought you had it all sewn up. But if he's got her, if he loves her, she'll be offering her own advice in between popping out the babies; and who's to say he'll want to support you at all? It's not going to be as easy as you thought, is it?

The thoughts that keep coming back to Alice, as she trails through the woods with her personal servants behind her, are all unpleasant, one way or another.

One thought is personal. She is coming to the end of her twenties, and it's not only her prospects fading. It's her looks. This morning, before setting off, she looked at herself in the mirror and identified wrinkles at eye and mouth that she'd never noticed before.

The other is financial. Until now, she has kept her two plans for the future in careful balance. She wants the profits from the Italian debt, of course, as her insurance against a future in poverty, and taking that profit involves taking money out of the Crown coffers. But she also wants her friendship with the Duke, which might save her from having that future in poverty in the first place. And the Duke is going to need money in the Crown coffers while he's at the peace talks; he'll want to be able to cow the French into offering better terms by threatening to go expensively back to war. She wants him to sit in Bruges, feeling pleased that he has more money than before to play with, and remembering that it's all thanks to Alice Perrers. She'd lose the Duke's friendship in a flash if he ever found out that while she's helping get money in, she's also helping part of it disappear into her own pocket. Knowing that hasn't stopped her, exactly, but it's slowed her down. She's been holding Latimer back from cashing in too much of the Italian debt too fast. Slowly is safely, she's been telling the chamberlain; little and often. Let's not be too greedy.

But what if, when Edward dies, the Duke's friendship fails to materialise? This is the first time Alice has been forced to think of this as a real possibility.

If that *were* to happen, and she *hadn't* maximised her gains from the Italian debt, she's thinking as the horses plod along, wouldn't she look a fool?

Perhaps she should rely less on the prospect of friendship with the Duke?

Perhaps she and Latimer and Lyons should, after all, start taking more?

She wraps the wet hood more tightly around her head, shaking off the snow melting against cheeks and hair. It's bitterly cold today, and, even with the servants' harness chinking and the horses blowing up those great white clouds of air, the loneliness of these grey woods feels eerie.

Her future might feel like this: a howling wilderness.

She knows her thoughts are racing foolishly. She knows she's panicking. Trying to get a grip, she tells herself there's no need to rush into decisions now, in the snow, while she's cold and miserable. That's a question for tomorrow.

Today all she needs is comfort, and a roaring fire.

And a friend.

Out there, in the nowhere country somewhere between Greenwich and Rotherhithe, Alice Perrers suddenly has the first cheering thought of her day. She knows exactly where she can go for all those immediate things. She can take her disappointment, and her wounded pride, and her fears, to the City. She can take them straight to the apartment over Aldgate, where Chaucer, chained to his desk making his daily reckonings of wool taxes like a dog in its kennel, will have spent the holiday lonely and fretful, unaccompanied by his children, resenting his absent Roët-sister wife. Not that Alice can hope to ask Chaucer whether he thinks she should hang on and risk all in the hope of lasting patronage from the Duke or steal more from the treasury. There are limits to the frankness that's possible, even with your dearest friend. Even with Chaucer. But if she sticks to describing her resentment of the Roët sister she's been forced to spend this humiliating Christmas with, why, that's another matter. He'll certainly be in a mood to sympathise with that. He'll listen. He'll lap it up.

198

THIRTEEN

There's a snowstorm blowing through Aldgate. The fierce scurries of hard white on grey have sent most of the traders trying to get back to work after New Year in off the street again, though a few, mostly women, are still sheltering in doorways near their stalls. The snow gives Chaucer's chamber a greyish, unearthly, moonlight glow, even at midday. There is almost no traffic through the gate below as Chaucer and his wife, side by side on the cushioned bench drawn up to the fire, stare into the flames lighting the dark room and say hard things to each other that they wouldn't dare to if forced to meet each other's eyes.

The room is a mess. The table is scattered with quills with blackened ends carelessly laid down, staining the wood. It's piled high with papers, every sheet closely lined with small black squiggles whose uniformity of size suggests they've been written fast, in a frenzy of excitement, by someone who's forgotten the world outside as he works, or at least by someone who's been trying to. There are papers falling off one end of the table that have landed in a parchment snowfall of their own on the floor. There's a bowl of cold stew forgotten under another heap at the other end. There's a piece of bread sticking out from underneath, somewhere in the middle. There'll be mice soon, if no one gets to grips with the chaos. Fastidiously, Philippa Chaucer arranges her very clean white hands on her dove-grey silks. She's not here for long enough to start trying to organise Geoffrey's servants. It would be a waste of effort anyway. The mess will just start building up again as soon as she goes. So she's trying not to look.

On the floor, between them, are the New Year gifts she has brought Geoffrey from the children, who are not with her. Two silver-gilt cups, which she has ordered on their behalf, and, from her, a prettily worked ink-holder. In a bag, ready to go away with her, are the gifts Geoffrey has bought the children – gifts he thought, until she got here alone, that he'd be seeing them open.

The offended silence that followed her solitary entrance into the room has been broken, but the initial skirmishes – 'You've had no luck instilling any filial duty into Thomas and Elizabeth yet, I see; I can imagine how hard you tried' and 'I see you've been writing more poetry' – have been inconclusive. Seasonal greetings have been exchanged through gritted teeth, with averted eyes; the couple's embrace has left three fingers of empty air between their bodies. Chaucer has spent the past few minutes savagely prodding the fire with the poker, glowering.

If asked, neither of them would remember what it was that made them agree to marry. Not that it was ever overwhelming love, exactly, but there must have been a time when they had hopes of each other, and could take pleasure in each other's company, and believe marriage might bring them happiness. Philippa's long forgotten the agony she suffered, at the childlike age of twelve, over the other demoiselles' malicious tittle-tattle that she might be sleeping with Duke John. Likewise, Chaucer's put out of his mind the pleasure it once gave him when the Duke – as uncomfortable as Philippa about that rumour, which was upsetting his adored wife Blanche – took him aside for that awkward chat about marriage. 'Beautiful girl. No money, of course . . . but the bluest blood . . . and the apple of my lady mother's eye. Just the wife you need to set you on your way.' All Philippa now remembers is what the Queen told *her* about *him* in a separate quiet chat on the same day: 'Solid merchant wealth behind him, and one of the brightest and best of my lord's young men. A splendid future in governance,

200

if he chooses it; unless he prefers to go back to the war, in due course. He's served in France already, brave boy . . . a knighthood on the horizon, either way.' It was enough at the time to convince an anxious orphaned girl from Hainault; but Philippa's been throwing that over-optimistic praise back in her husband's face ever after, and nothing, since then, has ever gone right for them. There were only a couple of nights of what Chaucer remembers as maybe inept, possibly puppyish, though interested, love-making, before Philippa was expecting her first child. A year or more later, though with more intensely long-suffering looks this time, there were a few more anxious fumbles; and then there was Thomas. A son. And the battle lines being laid out in earnest. You have an heir. I've done my duty. But what about yours? Where's the fortune, the war record, the knighthood? Philippa's disappointment in her husband is corrosive. It's grown more bitter with every day Chaucer's failed to advance as she expected, and with every comparison she's made, as the years pass, with all the other husbands she might have had. She's even envied her sister her penniless, semi-literate hulk of a spouse, because at least Sir Hugh Swynford was gently born, and believed in bravery, and had a good seat on a horse, and, died gallantly, fighting in France.

The war between the Chaucers has become a matter for concern even outside their family. The Queen is no longer there to see the hostility that husband and wife can barely conceal, even in public. But the Duke's obvious discomfort at having pushed the pair of them together may explain why he's gone on, for all these years, encouraging his second wife to keep employing Philippa as a demoiselle, even though Constanza would really rather only have Castilian ladies around her. It's a relief, Philippa's job, as well as a much-needed extra income. At least the Duchess's travels give the Chaucers the excuse they need to live more or less apart, while preserving the outward decencies. Chaucer went on hoping, at least until he came to the City, that his wife might soften towards him during her long absences, but has given up even that hope in the past few months; he is grateful for the absences, at least. He's grateful, too, for the feelings of guilt he suspects have prompted the Duke to stay hovering on the edge of his life, praising and commissioning his poems, and, periodically, reminding the King to give a man too modest to push for his own advancement at least something in the way of pensions and favours and rewards.

But there's nothing anyone can do to make a real peace between the Chaucers.

Now both of them are marshalling their defences, waiting for the sly ambush they each suspect the other of being about to initiate. It is Philippa's announcement that she and her sister have been corresponding that opens the real hostilities. The sisters have decided, she continues, pleating her skirts, to enrol their daughters, who will both be ten this year, as nuns at Barking Abbey in the summer they both turn twelve – the year after next.

Chaucer is so shocked that, for a moment, he forgets the rules of engagement. Little Elizabeth's face flashes up inside his head – a bit younger than now, back when he saw her all the time, with eyes full of delighted mischief and blonde curls bouncing as she tottered towards his hand to snatch a sweet from it, gloating, 'Lizbeff got daddysweet, Lizbeff got daddysweet,' as he chuckled back down at her, and shrieking with terrified laughter, a moment later, when he swept her up off her feet into a whirling embrace: 'Daddy you tickle!' Thomas is lost to him, he can see that, though he can't begin to understand how the sweetness died out of those other beloved eyes. But Elizabeth is his darling. If she goes to a nunnery, he'll never see her again. He has to be here in London every day; he wouldn't be able to go traipsing off through the Essex countryside on whatever rare occasions the Abbess saw fit to allow visitors. He thinks: I can't lose her too.

He is still holding the poker as he turns to face his wife, suddenly desperately wanting to turn this conversation into a blazing row of the kind Philippa refuses to have. 'What do you mean?' he almost howls, waving the poker emphatically in the air to punctuate his words. 'I don't care what Katherine does with her child. She can marry her to the

202

King of France for all I care. You're not sending my daughter to a nunnery.'

But he can't get in front of Philippa to meet her eye. She's picked her ground too carefully. She keeps her face turned resolutely towards the fire. She purses her lips.

'It's our family tradition,' she says faintly. 'The de Roëts. My sister Elizabeth went. The oldest daughter always does. That's why we named Lizzie for my sister. You know that.'

'She's just a child,' Chaucer shouts, but he's recollected himself enough to lower the poker, and he's shouting at the fire now. With a lurching in his heart, he knows that means she's winning. He lowers his voice, a bit, but he talks faster. 'It's completely different. You can't start talking about sending her away for ever. It's absurd. She's hardly out of the nursery.'

'Children grow up. You know that, Geoffrey.' How dare she sound so condescending?

'Yes,' he says, teeth gritted. 'Of course I know that. I just don't see why I should want to give my little girl away before she's even had her childhood.'

'Traditions are what make a family,' Philippa says, through thin lips. 'Of course it's not always easy, saying goodbye. But it's important to have standards. And you have to plan ahead to get the best. This is an opportunity. Surely even you can see that, Geoffrey. It's – well, Barking, you know. Not just any nunnery.'

That's what's impressed her, Geoffrey thinks, as the sick awareness of defeat he's been trying to keep at bay comes closer. Barking bloody Abbey. Well, it would. Barking is grand. The Abbess has the status of a baron and is the foremost Abbess of England. Only the daughters of the rich and influential can get in. You have to be personally nominated by the King to be accepted.

'She'll never get the nomination, anyway,' he says, voicing the reassuring thought as soon as it comes into his head.

But Philippa has thought of that. 'As it happens, she will,' she ripostes coolly. 'Katherine's already asked my lord the King. He thinks it's a beautiful idea.'

Chaucer suppresses an oath. The blood is beating in his temples.

'She's a Chaucer. She's *my* family. I decide,' he says. He has no other weapon left.

Philippa holds up her beautifully manicured fingers and regards them with interest. They both know she has saved her best blow till last.

She waits. She's a master of timing, Philippa. The room goes so quiet you can hear the logs settle and die.

'Actually, you're wrong,' Philippa finishes. 'Since the King has given his permission, it's not up to you any more. The decision's taken. And Elizabeth's thrilled at the idea of being with Margaret at Barking. She *wants* to go.'

The snowstorm blows out by afternoon. The streets have become magically white and clean.

Chaucer's in no mood to appreciate the joys of nature. He answers the door with glassy eyes.

What Alice sees, from the doorway, is wildly rumpled hair. His usually trim dark beard's longer than it's supposed to be, and there's stubble on his cheeks. His hands are shaking. It's not difficult to work out why. There's an empty flagon of wine on the floor beside the fireside bench he's been lying on, and a half-drunk one beside it. Just one cup.

Recognition dawns only slowly in his eyes as she stalks in, shaking snow on to the floor with the tumble of her cloak.

'You look terrible,' he says. 'What's happened?' She hears sympathy in his voice. She also hears the slur of too much alcohol.

'I could say the same for you,' she replies tartly. She could do without anyone's sympathy making her feel worse than she already does,, especially if it's the sympathy of someone in the state Chaucer's in. She could do without him being drunk, too, if it comes to that. She's been hoping for the comfort of some of his spry wit. Seeing him sodden with drink surprises her, if she's honest. She's always thought he'd be too . . . precise . . . or puckish, to abandon himself alone like this.

He gestures down at the jugs. 'Been worshipping at the temple of Bacchus,' he intones, and then, with such profound gloom that, despite herself, she bursts out laughing: 'drowning my sorrows.'

'We're a right pair,' she says after a moment, through the last of her harsh snorts. For all her own darkness, that moment of laughter has given her the new strength she needs to be at least a bit sympathetic. Something terrible must have happened to him. 'Just look at us. What's the matter with *you*, then?'

'Wife,' Chaucer offers vaguely, sinking back down on to the bench. Or was that 'wine'?

She shakes her head. Then she shrugs. Why not? She can see he's going to be some time telling her his troubles. She sits beside him and sips.

But as he confusedly pours out his troubles, and she strains forward to make sense of the slurred words and meandering phrases, she realises he did mean 'wife', not 'wine'. Her sympathy evaporates when she realises how trivial his trouble is. The only thing that actually seems to be wrong is that his wife has raised the possibility of sending their daughter to the poshest nunnery in the land, and even that only in two years' time – and, for the love of God, even if he hates the idea, how much can change in two years!

All at once, it comes to her that part of the reason she wants to see Chaucer is that she's furious with him. La Swynford is his wife's sister, after all, the very wife he's moaning away about now. And the sisters are thick as thieves, always have been. So Chaucer must have known for years about Katherine and the Duke. But he never breathed a word. Thinking of the disloyalty of it stings the beginning of tears into her eyes. After all she's done for Chaucer, he might have dropped a hint. Even if he doesn't realise how desperately she wants to strengthen her ties to the Duke, he must have seen it would be useful information. For a moment more, she's speechless. But then she's off.

She sits up straight. She breaks through his self-pitying drone. She says, sharp as a needle, 'Master Chaucer, haven't you got anything more useful to tell me than this?'

He stops, staring slack-jawed and uncomprehending at her. He's never seen her angry. He says, 'What?'

She crackles on: 'I've heard quite enough about your wretched

205

daughter. What I *haven't* heard nearly enough about is your wife's sister.'

'What?' Chaucer repeats, dumb as an ox.

'Shouldn't you at least have thought to warn me beforehand that the merry widow Swynford, whom I've just had to spend the full twelve days of Christmas with, is with child? And that it's the Duke's?'

She turns to face him on the bench, putting her hands on his upper arms to drag him round so their eyes meet, so she can make quite sure he's understanding. She's ready to shake him into listening if he's not. But he is. She has his full attention. In fact, he's so startled that he no longer even looks drunk.

'What?' he says, a third time. But his voice is sharp now, sharp with disbelief.

'Their second child,' she finishes – a phrase she'd intended as the final blow of her tongue-lashing. 'And I didn't know.'

But her anger's dissipating, as the truth dawns on her.

'Oh,' she says flatly, realising too that there's more to Chaucer's misery about his wife than a single spat over the daughter. 'You didn't know either.'

For a little while, they go on sitting facing each other, hushed by the enormity of their shared discovery.

Alice finds herself comforted a little by his presence – by the sheer physical warmth of Chaucer's arms under her grasping hands. She's also reassured, in an odd way, to see how the news has shocked Chaucer into his own, separate, suddenly sober state of frantic preoccupation.

Behind Chaucer's dazed eyes, his mind is racing back through his picture of the past two years, taking apart what he knows of his wife and her sister, as if unthreading a tapestry with a mistake in it, and putting the coloured strands back together differently to make a new pattern. Not that he's ever had much to do with Katherine, who's always been disdainful with him, rolling her eyes and turning restively when he talks to her, like a palfrey about to buck off an unwanted rider. He's never enjoyed feeling like that rider. But, he's thinking now, of course, of course. He's had no idea why Katherine

206

has taken to spending so much time in the country these last couple of years when until then she's seemed happy enough, in that careless aristocratic way of the de Roëts, to leave her four Swynford children to grow up wild in the care of nurses and monkish tutors. All those apparently endless trips to Lincolnshire last year to supervise the building works at Kettlethorpe – while the Duke was in the North and Midlands, touring his domains . . . and perhaps she with him. And Philippa's wish to spend the whole of the last two summers at Kettlethorpe with her sister. She probably wanted to be there to play with the Duke's love-child. The first one. It's all beginning to make sense – even, perhaps, his children's growing distance from him. They were at Kettlethorpe last summer. They must be in the secret too.

If his own wife has known this all along, and never told him, then the relationship between the Chaucers must be deader than even he has imagined.

He shakes his head. He's counting months and absences. Katherine got her new job of governess to the Duke's little girls (rather than demoiselle to the Duchess, with Philippa) two years ago, after the first of her long absences at Kettlethorpe. That must be when it started.

It all makes sense, except that he's astonished by the compromise the Duke has made to see his lover more easily. What kind of morality can a man expect his mistress to teach his daughters?

After a long while, he thinks, still wonderingly, but with the first glimmer of resigned amusement, 'Well, I suppose a governess with a secret lover is like a poacher – the best game-keeper.'

It's only when Alice laughs too that he realises he's spoken his thought aloud.

He's almost surprised to find her arms still on his shoulders, and her face, creased into laughter that seems to have come from somewhere else, and doesn't have anything to do with the moistness about her eyes, so close to his. He's so near he can smell her: fur, and musky rose and sandalwood, and snow.

207

They're both almost surprised to find their bodies moving into an embrace. But by the time their lips meet, and their eyes close, the surprise has passed, to be replaced by the blind, questing hunger of the body.

He's lit a candle in the bedchamber. He's sitting up in the bed next to her, wrapped in a quilt, with his hands round his knees. She looks beautiful, naked. She's smaller, and more luxuriantly fleshed, and more pointy-kneed and curvy than he'd thought she would be, and there's something so mischievous about her long eyes and pretty, uptilted, naughtily freckled nose and bouncy black curls, sensuously spread out on the pillow like a dark halo, that he wants to laugh again, out of astonishment and relief, as they've both been laughing through the past hour, just looking at her.

He's surprised again, this time at how easily their friendship, this wish to talk that they've shared from the start, has become physical. He's never realised until now that he wants her. He's surprised, too, at how relaxed she is at finding herself here. She still thinks it's funny. She's laughing up at him from her pillow. She doesn't feel guilty, or sinful, or worried. And he can see from her casual grin that the act of love hasn't made her think she's in love with him any more than he's in love with her. With relief, he understands she's too much of a realist for that.

But their being here together, the touching of their bodies, the ease and languor of satisfied desire, isn't without its worrying aspects. He's trying to banish the thought: I have the King's lover in my bed; but other, almost equally paralysing, anxieties can't be kept off his mind.

He whispers, biting his lip, 'You couldn't, could you, be . . .' but doesn't know how to finish the thought.

'Pregnant, you mean?' she says, impishly. 'Is that what you're worrying about now?' He's relieved and shocked in equal measures by her frankness. He nods. She shakes her head and smiles reassuringly up at him.

He leans down and kisses her forehead. 'Well, thank God for that, anyway,' he says, releasing a whoosh of pent-up breath.

Then, worrying he's sounded unkind, if barrenness really is, as he's sometimes thought, the secret tragedy at the heart of Alice's life, he goes on, more tenderly, 'Did you ever want to have children?'

She gives him a long, thoughtful look. Chaucer looks at the damp dark curls, and the delicious freckles on her nose, and is just thinking he might kiss them, when she answers.

'But I do have children,' she says, and she isn't laughing at all. The confession comes out in a rush of air. 'I just don't tell people about them.'

Chaucer is mid-way down to land his kiss, with one bare flexed arm holding his weight.

But that stops him. He hovers there, staring at her face, trying to see if she's teasing him, imploring her with his eyes to be teasing him. She isn't.

He blinks. Slowly he rises again, and reclasps his hands around his knees, trying, with less success, to rearrange his thoughts. For the past hour, he's felt as though, by making love with Alice Perrers, he's taken back at least a little control of his life, just as, sometimes, finishing a well-made poem makes him feel master of all he surveys, at least for a moment. Not any more. Now life's rushing by again, making shapes and patterns he doesn't understand, and he's back with that dizzying sense of freefall in the pit of his stomach.

'What do you mean?' he says, helplessly. 'What children . . .?'

'Oh, don't give me that lapdog look,' she answers slightly impatiently, though not unkindly. 'I'm trying to tell you, aren't I?'

For a moment, as she starts her story, he thinks: Perhaps she's making it up. But her voice is too steady for that. No, it's clear that what has passed between them tonight has prompted her to trust him with a secret. He should be flattered. But he can't help it: his gut is churning.

The father of her children, Alice is saying through the blood beating its tattoo in his temples, is William of Windsor.

Now, Chaucer knows of William of Windsor. Who doesn't? He's the King's Lieutenant in Ireland, a knight from Westmoreland, did well in France in the old days, became friendly with Lionel of Ulster, has been the King's man in Ireland since Lionel's death, has maintained extremely costly defences there against the French, is said to have treated the Irish savagely, has periodically been recalled to be reprimanded for it . . . Chaucer knows, too, that the man's old – in his forties – though he can see that advanced age might not in itself bar him from Alice's bed. Chaucer tells himself he'll probably be able to remember all kinds of other snippets about William of Windsor too, if he thinks hard enough. But he'd have no reason to, in the normal course of things. This is because, except for the times William of Windsor's been called home to be reprimanded – including one longish visit, several years ago, maybe ten, if Chaucer's remembering right, the year before Chaucer's son was born and his father died, the year when Chaucer himself went overseas, marvelling at the size and aridity of the Pyrenees – the man's been in Ireland for the past fifteen years. Chaucer's never met him.

But ten years ago, he thinks, and his brow furrows as the facts obstinately refuse to fall into place, Alice was just starting at court as the Queen's demoiselle. Alice can't have had much opportunity to meet him either, since then.

'Good God,' he says faintly. 'But . . . how?'

Alice pulls herself up on to one elbow. She's trying to marshal her thoughts. She's never told anyone this story. She doesn't have words prepared. She certainly doesn't have words to explain that once in her life she, who prefers to think of herself as the Queen of Planning and Profit, the Queen of Heartlessness, felt . . . well, that tumult, that torrent of heightened emotions, something so sharp it seemed more like a sickness or a wound than a blessing, something that sent her shamelessly off down corridors and round corners in the hope of just a glimpse of those shoulders, that grizzled head. She's never, before or since, felt that she might faint, just looking at the way a man's fingers grew out of his hand, or at the set of his limbs on his torso.

But facts, she can tell the facts. Some of them, at least. If she tries. That she met William of Windsor at a joust, with Froissart, before she'd even come to court. That soon after

210

the Queen took a fancy to her and gave her a job as a demoiselle, they'd developed an . . . understanding. She feels foolish about the gulp in her voice at that inadequate word. That she fell pregnant, but couldn't tell anyone, because she needed that demoiselle's job if she were to make her way at court, and she'd only been taken on as a replacement because Marie de Saint-Hilaire had conceived a bastard, and *she* hadn't been allowed back, so Alice could see at once that she could never confess the truth to the Queen. So instead she made up a pitiful story about going home for the summer to a sick mother, which touched the Queen so much that she promised Alice she could come back in three months. Then Alice went away to have her baby in the quiet of the countryside . . . twins, as it turned out. A boy and a girl. John and Jane. The next year, she had to make another heart-rending plea to be allowed to tend her sick old mother again. And, after Joan was born, and Alice had recovered from a birth so difficult that they'd told her she'd never have children again, she went back to the Queen, and, with tears in her eyes and black on her back, said her mother, God rest her, had died. And the Queen, bless her, was so moved that she paid for Alice's mourning robe. The best woman in the world, Queen Philippa . . . That then, one day soon after, some chance cheeky remark Alice had made about not being scared of the Mortality had turned the King's eyes towards her.

'And . . .?' Chaucer prompts.

Alice has stopped again. She's wrinkling her nose, so the constellations of freckles change their configuration, and wondering. This is more difficult than she's realised it was going to be. There is so much in this story that makes her uncomfortable.

Will Chaucer, whose wish for self-advancement is so measured, who waits for favour to drop unexpectedly from the skies, who never actively does anything to seek his fortune, have any chance of understanding what came next? That she and William of Windsor, whose love was based from the start on recognising each other as equally hungry and driven, ready to move relentlessly forward to fill the holes and tears left in

211

the tapestry of life by so much death and the changes it brought, both understood the promise of the King's favour being held out to her as the biggest opportunity she might ever get in life? That, a year or two later, when the King's son Lionel of Ulster died of plague, William got his greatest opportunity ever: promotion over the water to do Lionel's job? That they quietly agreed, between themselves, that it would be best to put aside their relationship so she could reap the greater benefit of the King's and he could make his fortune in Ireland? That he gave her a lump sum for the children's care, and left them in her hands? That, because of the way they both were, neither of them could have imagined doing anything else?

She doesn't think so. Chaucer won't ever be able to imagine the purpose of William, though he might understand the bleakness she felt, all those years ago, when the only man she'd loved got on his horse and rode away. William said, 'It's not for ever, we both know that,' and then he kissed her. A dry, regretful kiss. The words a lie; truth in the kiss. They both knew he wouldn't be back. Sometimes, even now, she finds herself hoping that one day, after all, he just might return, and that, if he did, she might again feel . . . that. But she knows it for foolishness. After all these years, that hope has taken on the qualities of a much-fingered pebble; it's become familiar, dry and warm with use, impossible to imagine as it once was, glistening and lovely with water rushing over it. She loved him. He's gone. It's long over.

Alice would like Chaucer's sympathy. She thinks he might like to hear that she kept the King waiting for a while. She doesn't like to remember how short a while it was, in reality. She stretches the time out in her mind. She tells herself that it was for many long months that she devoted herself to her kindly, trusting mistress the Queen's ailments, the gout, the aches and pains and bed rest, and enjoyed only the flash of glances and the occasional stifled laugh at the King's pleasantries, and that it was only when the Queen herself, in her last days, made sure that there was no one around her except her husband, and her youngest son, and one devoted handmaiden, Alice, to nurse her out of this life, and positively pushed the two of them together, as if she wanted them to love each other, that Alice finally let Edward catch her, just outside the sickroom, and . . .

Yes, possibly Chaucer would appreciate that. Especially since he isn't tormented by the memory of the Queen's trusting eyes.

But when it comes to it Alice finds she can't talk too much about the feelings that have no easy names.

Instead she says briskly, winding up her story, 'William was sent back to Ireland. And you know what happened to me.' She shrugs.

Chaucer's brow is wrinkled. Surely he can't think it was really wrong to jump at the chance of the King's bed? But she can see he doesn't like what he's hearing. Or doesn't think he's hearing the right thing. With what sounds like anguish in his voice, he counters: 'But what about the children?'

She sits up beside him. She spreads her hands. 'The children?' she says, rather bewildered by the question. What about the children? 'Well, I see them when I can. They're in Essex. I told you. I have a house there.'

'And he . . . William of Windsor?' he probes. 'Didn't he ever want . . .?'

She feels her heart twist. She makes an effort to keep her face still. That's how she knew, from the start, that William never really meant to come back. He'd have shown more interest in them, if he did, wouldn't he? It was only a young girl's naivety to hope for more. Well, she's learned her lesson. She snaps, 'No.'

Another silence.

She adds, defensively, 'They don't need him.'

Chaucer frowns. 'But children do need their parents. And if yours have no father, surely they need to be with their mother more than ever . . .'

Oh, so that's it. His injured family feelings again.

'They're well looked after,' she protests. But there's only more mutinous wordlessness from the other side of the bed. She senses him drawing away.

213

She tries to explain. 'They're going to need money in life,' she says. 'Money and land and rank. I grew up without any of that and, let me tell you, it's no fun; I don't want them grubbing around in the dirt. I want them to be properly provided for. Able to enter life with a bit of a swagger.'

'But you're their mother. How can you bear not to live with them?' Chaucer insists.

Incredulously, she thinks: He can't mean it. What, go and live at Gaines? Give everything up?

'I do my best for them. Everything I'm doing is for them,' she says, defensive again. But she knows that's not quite true, even as she says it.

She's seeing their three little dark heads in her mind as she speaks; she's feeling the shy tenderness she experiences whenever she's at Gaines, and looks at them laughing together, and holds back from interrupting their play because they look so intent on whatever they're doing, and she doesn't know enough about them to understand what they're up to. Of course she loves them. She enjoys the softness of her thoughts about them.

But that isn't the same as doing everything she does for them. Because she knows, if she's honest, that she's not staying away from Essex just to put clothes on their backs or white chargers between their little legs. She's here piling up money, buying houses and land, dancing between court and City, because she enjoys it. Because she loves being at the centre of everything. Because there's nothing so exciting as the energy and intentness she feels when she's working out some new scheme and making it happen. Because she can.

She's not going to leave Katherine Swynford to take over the court, or Lyons making new fortunes without her. Not while she still has the choice.

'And I couldn't go and bury myself in the country,' she adds flatly.

She hopes that's an end to it. But Chaucer won't give up. He's like a dog, worrying away at a bone.

'Well, why didn't you bring your children to live with *you*?' he says.

214

She sighs. For a moment the old, old sadness seeps back into her. 'Because I got it wrong,' she says wearily. 'Because I imagined for too long that I'd end up as William's lady wife, and by the time he went away . . .' She blinks. 'Well, by then,' she continues, fiercely enough to banish the sadness, 'I couldn't very well tell my new lover the King that I had a family full of someone else's babies, could I? And forgotten to mention it? And told his wife the Queen a pack of lies about my dying mother, into the bargain?'

When she sees his frown, she softens her voice before going on: 'It was too late. Don't you see? It all snowballed. I couldn't unpick the lies . . .'

At last Chaucer seems to be beginning to understand. He shakes his head. She thinks she sees tenderness comes back into his eyes. Or is it pity?

'And before you say anything else, it's much too late now,' she adds briskly. She doesn't want pity. 'You know that, Chaucer. Court children turn seven. They get sent away. They get educated. And mine are nine and ten. Even if I had managed to bring them to live with me at court when they were babies, they'd be too old now. I'd be putting them into some other household for a bit of polish. I wouldn't be sitting around dandling them on my knee all day long, would I now?'

Chaucer puts an arm around her and draws her close. He's not going to lecture her any more, she can see. He's looking too mournful for that. She sees he's thinking of his own family again. His pity's turning to self-pity. 'Philippa always says it's proof I'm not noble that I'm so soft about children. She says, your merchant roots are showing,' he murmurs. He kisses the top of her head. 'And perhaps she's right. Perhaps you are. But having my children near is what I want most in the world. It's the cruellest thing she's done to me, keeping them away.'

Then he turns her round so he can look into her eyes. He's having an idea. She sees his face brighten with it. 'At least with you it won't be for ever,' he says, as if he's holding out a wonderful hope. One which, he doesn't mind her knowing, is denied to him.

What does he mean? But she already thinks she knows. She sighs.

'Because after . . .' He pauses. He can't think of the right delicate phrase.

'After Edward dies, you mean?' she prompts patiently.

He nods gratefully. That's it. 'And when you've left court. You'll have a new life. You won't have to be separated from them any more then.'

He's so pleased for her, that he's worked it all out. He's practically bursting with happiness at the idea that she'll soon be cast out from the life she loves, with all the time in the world to spend with her children. For a moment, she's rigid with irritation. He hasn't been listening at all, has he? He's just thinking what *he* might feel like, or want to do, if he were her; not what *she* might want. She almost bursts out: 'But who says I'll be going anywhere? I might not have to . . . if I can go on making my way under the Duke.'

Still, she doesn't like to burst his bubble. He means well. She likes his softness. 'Let's cross that bridge when we come to it,' she adds gently. 'It's too soon to say.'

FOURTEEN

A soft breeze ruffles the papers on the table. It is golden after-noon, and peaceful, and Chaucer, who hasn't ventured away from Aldgate and the Customs House for three months or more, is smiling reminiscently over the verses under his pen.

'Fair was this young good-wife, and therewithal, As graceful as a weasel was her body small.' He likes these lines. It's her to a T. And these:

> Her broad headband of silk was very high,
> And for a fact she had a flirty eye.
> Her eyebrows plucked into two narrow rows,
> Which both were angled and as black as sloes.
> She was a lovelier sight by far to see,
> Than is the early-ripe pear tree.

He sighs, though this sigh is not without pleasure. He scrib-bles more lines.

> Brighter the pink that on her cheeks did glow,
> Than any new-mint coins fresh from the Tower . . .
> Her mouth as sweet as honey mead,
> Or hoards of apples laid in hay or heath.

It's only when he finds he's also written: 'She was a primrose, a sweet piglet's eye, For any lord to lure into his bed, Or else for any common man to wed,' that he begins to look anxiously at the words on the page, and lays his pen down.

A thick, speechless embarrassment has kept Chaucer to himself as the spring sets in. He can't think now what can have possessed him, in the darkness of the New Year, to do the wild, mad thing he knows he did with Alice Perrers. He's kept well clear of his wife ever since, though that hasn't been hard. Until this week she's been away at Hertford Castle with the Duchess's household; she's to visit him for the first time later this afternoon. He's steered clear of Alice, too.

Especially Alice. Through tightly squeezed eyes, he remembers the great joyous laughter that came bubbling through him, both of them, during all that thrusting and grinding he's trying to banish from his mind. He can understand, now, the pull she has on her lovers; the wish they must all share to be close again to the sheer life-energy of her. But he doesn't mind, either, that she kissed him chastely on the forehead as she left, and said, with the kindest imaginable look, straight into his heart, 'That's us, Chaucer; no more; we both know that, don't we?'

He knows she's right. He agrees. Of course it's impossible for them to be lovers again. Lovers at all. Madness, for people in their present positions: he married, and she so far from free (especially now he knows there are those children whom she'll one day want to bring back to her. Nothing about Alice is uncomplicated. Never has been). He'd do best to forget it ever happened. Still, there's no controlling his thoughts, which, every moment of every day, keep straying back to *that*. And to her. And to the carefree bliss of lying in that bed with her, that evening, laughing. And whenever he does find himself thinking of it, he can't stop smiling.

Chaucer's been sitting over this verse for some time this afternoon.

He's put in his day's work at the Customs House. He has nothing to reproach himself with. He isn't shirking duty. The working day ended early only because the merchants – Brembre and Philpot, who are at the wool office this month – excused themselves to go to a dinner.

218

Chaucer's intrigued by what their dinner can have been about. It wasn't the usual sort of event. Usually formal City dinners are arranged months ahead. This one came out of the blue, but was even grander than most merchant junkets. At noon, Brembre and Philpot put on their livery robes and went out to the jetty to meet the mayoral boat, coming downriver from the Prince of England's palace at Kennington on its way to the Guildhall. The boat was carrying Walworth in full mayoral fig, assorted servants, and another man Chaucer didn't know: a tall, thin, distinguished man in travelling clothes, silver at the temples, with a knightly dash to his movements, wearing a sword.

'Who's your guest?' Chaucer asked curiously, looking out through the window as the boat drew near, while he helped John Philpot struggle with his sleeves.

From inside the furred robe, Philpot's voice: 'De la Mare, a good sort . . . up from Herefordshire on business . . . do you know him, my boy?' Then: 'Brother of the Abbot of St Albans . . . and he'll be a county knight for Hertfordshire at the next Parliament . . . if the King ever gets round to calling it.'

He didn't offer any more explanations, just rushed off to be ready at the jetty before the boat tied up. There's nothing like a wealthy merchant for his dignity, Chaucer knows. So he's been left wondering. Future MP or not, Chaucer can't imagine what business a gentleman from Herefordshire would have with the Mayor of London that would require the three most important men in town to wine and dine him. Not that he minds. It's given him a free afternoon to dream his private dreams.

He's still smiling over his verse, knowing that his pleasure, and the mess, will infuriate his wife, and taking refuge in that mischievous knowledge from the guilt he might otherwise be feeling over having done . . . *that* . . . with Alice Perrers, when, bang on time, Philippa walks in.

Being with his wife sucks the sunlight right out of the air. Within moments, Philippa and he are back in the same angry discussion they were having at New Year, though he realises, as he listens in dull surprise to his own voice, that he's developed new plans and new pleas when it comes to the fate of his daughter.

'At least if she has to go to a nunnery, let her go to one near me, in London,' he finds himself asking. He doesn't like the whining, begging tone of his own voice. 'St Helen's in Bishopsgate, maybe. It's Benedictine too. So what's the difference? If she doesn't like it, she could always move to Barking later . . .'

Perhaps Philippa doesn't like the whining and begging in his voice any more than he does. She certainly doesn't like the look of the paper flapping under his hand. She's getting up, with lips pursed as tight as a cat's behind, nodding a small, displeased nod.

'We're going to stay with Katherine at Kettlethorpe for the summer,' she says coolly, and he thinks she's playing for time because she's can't think of a reason to refuse. 'I'll talk to Elizabeth then. She may be interested, I can't say. We can take a decision when I get back.'

'Ah,' Chaucer hears himself say, and now his voice has modulated into a mean, thin sarcasm that astonishes him. 'Kettlethorpe. So you're planning to visit Katherine's new royal baby, are you?'

He has to hand it to Philippa. She has poise. She gives him a nasty look back, for sure, but there's no fear or discomfiture in it. It's more resigned than that, more of a just-the-kind-of-low-blow-I-might-have-expected-from-you look.

'I hear we also have to congratulate your patron Madame Perrers,' she ripostes without a pause, and without deigning to answer his accusation about Katherine. 'It appears *she* has a nest full of children hidden away in the country.'

Her back is straight.

Chaucer is miserably aware that he hasn't countered her blow half as well as she did his. Too late, he composes his face.

'What?' he finds he's already blurted. He rushes to add, 'Nonsense.' After a pause for reflection, he adds a third comment: 'How do you think you know that?'

Philippa is nodding, as if he's only confirmed her worst suspicions. 'Oh,' she says with infuriating calm, 'only the way these things always come out. Some man the Flemish merchant Lyons fired, detained at a tavern . . . drunk, of course, after an affray. And loose-tongued from the drink.'

Chaucer flares his nostrils. 'And . . .?' he says.

'Apparently he was howling for revenge. Saying he'd get Madame Perrers on to Lyons.'

Maintaining his appearance of disdain, Chaucer asks, 'Why her?'

Philippa laughs, just a little, and raises her eyebrows. 'He said, because she was his sister. As close as two pages in a book, he said. He lives in her house in Essex. She trusts him absolutely. He's teaching her children to ride . . . or so he said.'

'A lunatic, then,' Chaucer says stoutly into the ensuing silence.

Philippa raises her eyebrows a little more. 'Certainly not the kind of kin whose existence she would want bruited abroad,' she remarks, so politely that it's almost as if she's agreeing with him.

It's that sneery politeness that is Philippa's worst trait, Chaucer thinks. He clenches his fists.

'So there we are. If we're going to start repeating tavern gossip' – Philippa delivers her final neat thrust with delicate pleasure – 'perhaps we should be wondering if *she's* not hiding a few royal bastards?'

She smiles as Chaucer feels his face – his whole self – go red and heady. Whatever Katherine's up to, skulking in the country with her babies, why would Alice hide any child of the King that she'd borne? It's not in her nature. She'd have them at court in a flash, surely, decked out in velvet and jewels. She'd be boasting and getting them advantages. It's typical of Philippa to insinuate this to try and turn the conversation away from Katherine. She knows how to get behind his defences, all right. She knows how to make him seethe and explode.

'That's pure spite!' Chaucer cries. 'Stupid, too! They're too old!'

He knows, as soon as it's out, that he's made a mistake. But he can't call it back.

Philippa's eyebrows are off up her forehead again. She couldn't look more delighted at how he's just exposed himself. 'Mmm. So you *know* about these children?' she asks, in honeyed tones. 'You *know* how old they are?'

Chaucer scuffs and mumbles, as the seriousness of his mistake is borne in on him. He's as furious with himself as he is with her. He hopes she'll take his half-shaken head to mean 'no'. But he knows she won't. She knows him too well.

Her lovely cat's-eyes are motionless on him. 'Then how can you possibly know that their father *isn't* the King?' she pursues, even more sweetly.

'Because it's William of Windsor,' he snarls. 'There. Nothing to get your claws into after all.'

She blinks, but maintains her composure. She says, peaceably enough, 'I see . . . and I remember now . . . we did wonder, long ago, about the two of them.'

I bet you did, Chaucer thinks savagely. Probably made her life hell about it, too. He remembers the viciousness of the demoiselles' talk, who better? It was one outbreak of that girlish cruelty that shackled him to Philippa for life.

Still, he wishes he hadn't said what he said. Better to have acted ignorant. Kept faith with Alice . . . kept her secret . . . He knows the ways of diplomacy. He just wishes he could be more of a diplomat with his wife.

Her voice breaks into that uneasy thought. 'And how interesting,' she adds in what sounds like a tentative exploration of a possible new front in hostilities, 'that you should be so well informed about Madame Perrers' family life.'

Again, he curses his loose tongue. He counts to three. It's time for a truce.

'Oh, well, I'm not really,' he backtracks, as soon as he's mastered himself enough to try for calm indifference. 'Just something I heard in the City. Wagging tongues. I couldn't swear to it. I should stop repeating gossip. I suppose we all should.' He manages a smile. The armies are disengaging now, the swords being sheathed.

'I do so agree,' she says with charm. 'We're all too easily led astray.' She looks at him alertly and nods several times. He understands: he will not be permitted to discuss Katherine's babies by the Duke, unless he wants to risk more marital war.

He smiles wider. He can accept those terms. 'Though I'm interested,' he adds. 'Where did you hear *your* piece of gossip?'

She doesn't mind that. She tells him, readily enough. It was at a dinner given by the Princess of England for her sister-in-law of Castile. Of course, Chaucer thinks. Someone's servant in the tavern; the rough scrap of a story picked up, dusted down and served to the court with a relish of malice. The scene floats into Chaucer's mind: the whispers spreading among the Castilian ladies; their shocked laughter behind hands; the gleeful smirking of the English. Sometimes he's glad to be away from court.

'Foolishness, of course,' Philippa says as she gets up to go. 'As you say, we should close our ears to idle talk.'

She pecks him on the cheek in the doorway. She seems glad he's understood. She even says, with a smile that's almost warm, 'I'll talk to Lizzie about St Helen's.'

When she's left, he leans against the door and breathes out.

At first, all he's aware of is his overpowering relief that she's gone off sounding so much more positive about St Helen's, and Elizabeth. It's a moment or two before he goes back to considering her story about Alice.

That could have gone much worse too, he thinks.

If only he'd known, that servant could have gone back to court with much more damaging City stories about Alice. The speculation in most London taverns these days is about where she's getting the money to buy so much new property.

In the first three months of 1375, the King of England, in the forty-eighth year of his reign, has granted Alice Perrers two new manors: Frome Valeys, in Somerset, and Brampford Speke, in Devon. Privately, her team of administrators, including John Bernes, citizen of London, William Mulsho, clerk, Edward de Chirdestoke, clerk, John de Freton, clerk, and Robert Brown of Warwick, have also taken over on Alice's behalf the manors of Southcote in Middlesex, Powerstock in Dorset, Litton Cheney in Dorset, Knole in Somerset, Lydford in Somerset, Stoke Mandeville in Buckinghamshire, Morton Pinkney in Northamptonshire and three manors in Sutton Veny, Wiltshire. Ten new manors in all. That's a lot of rolling acres, and a lot of clinking crowns and nobles. She's coining it, somehow.

Which is strange, considering how poor the rest of England is getting. Chaucer now knows this from close up. Receipts from wool, the country's only big export, have gone on relentlessly falling, even though the loophole of special export licences for Richard Lyons and his kind has been closed off. Although a decade ago 32,000 sacks a year of raw wool regularly went overseas, Chaucer's only seen 28,000 in his first year in office. And revenues from indirect taxes on wool and woollen cloth have, likewise, dropped from levels a decade ago of over £80,000, and the account books' last entry of £70,000, to just under £60,000.

Chaucer hasn't spotted any criminal reason for these dwindling returns. There's no fraud by the wool-exporting merchants that he's aware of. His only explanation is that landowners must be having such a hard time of it, what with ever-rising costs and labour bills, that they can't afford to keep so many sheep at pasture on so much grassland as before. Still, it worries him. He well remembers Lord Latimer telling him, this time last year, that £70,000 was the minimum needed to keep England afloat, 'more or less'. He feels disaster in the air.

Even from the City, he's hearing that the royal coffers are, once again, all but empty. Stury says the King is living on the pawn value of his treasures, as well as on the huge loans that Lyons has cheerfully gone on making. But almost all the money his officials get in seems to pour out of the treasury again straight away, as if through holes gnawed by invisible rats in the bottom of the sacks.

These shortfalls must be making things harder for the Duke of Lancaster, who's away at Bruges negotiating war or more truce with the French (though the City's full of hostile mutterings about him, too, and about the amount of borrowed money he's pouring away, over there, on lavish displays of English grandeur that he thinks will impress the enemy).

There'll be nothing for it, soon, but for the King to grit his teeth and call a Parliament. If the government of England is to make ends meet, in these harder times, it will, within a year, have to ask Parliament's permission to tax the citizens of England directly.

And even that desperate solution isn't without its problems. Traditionally, a direct tax on movable property, which a Parliament might occasionally, in times of war, grant a king the right to levy, would cost citizens one-tenth of the value of that property in towns and one-fifteenth in rural areas; a good collection might bring in £37,000. But the countryside is still relatively empty after the Mortality. There hasn't been a good collection for years. Worse yet, Chaucer knows that the knights of the shires – who are already paying much more than they want for men to till their lands, and receiving much less than they've traditionally expected in rents and services, but will have to bear the burden of any such tax – bitterly resent the prospect of footing the bills of an extravagant King.

Except that the King isn't extravagant any more. He hasn't got the strength. The King sits in his chambers, in his twilight, attended by his doctors. He's too befuddled to enjoy hunts, or dances, or feasts, or golden robes (though there are still hunts, and dances, and feasts, from time to time, and Alice organises them). For the moment, there isn't even a war on which to pour away his money.

So it's anyone's guess where the money is all going, and why England's government is grinding to a halt.

There are so many people quietly taking out their bit from the general wealth. He can hardly bear to look at Scrope the treasurer's pale face these days, as he sits over his books, totting up the figures, chewing at a quill.

But Chaucer's guess is that, whatever she says, Alice is somehow involved.

Chaucer remembers both the City gossip that it's Alice who's behind Lyons' loan to the Crown, and she who arranged the exchange with Italian debt paper and the discount; and the treasury gossip that the Italian paper is, in reality, being exchanged not at the agreed discount, but at full face value, costing the government twice as much as it expected. He sees Alice's hand in that, all right – taking at both ends, probably.

And how many other schemes might there not be, either involving her, or not?

Poor Scrope, trying so hard to look correct, yet unable to keep the fear out of his eyes. There's greed everywhere, and nothing stopping all the mice from playing now the cat's away.

Chaucer should report his suspicion of Alice to officials at court, of course. To Lord Latimer. But he can't imagine how he could ever be disloyal enough to denounce Alice, especially to Latimer, who's her friend. After she's been so good to him. And, especially, now, after . . . *that*. (And who's to say that Latimer's so perfectly honest and pure, or any other court official, come to that? Everyone is suspect.) So he frets, and prevaricates, and puts it off, and writes more poems about her sloe eyes. It's only a possibility, he tells himself. He has no proof.

His guesswork boils down to this. Alice is the only other person he knows of, apart from himself, who's so at home both at court and in the City. He's almost sure she must in some way be taking advantage of that dual citizenship. He's still almost sure it's the thing he's already asked her about, and she's denied: that she's making a profit from the treasury, and taking a cut from the merchants, too, for recycling that Italian debt.

If she is, she'll be relying on the fact that court and City don't in general overlap; that merchants and courtiers don't mix, or gossip together; and that it's all but impossible for anyone firmly in one world to know what's going on in the other.

Yet, every now and then, there *is* a leak of information between court and City – like the one Chaucer's just heard about from his wife.

Alice is over-confident. It takes a worrier like Chaucer to see the dangers.

Chaucer sits down by the fire and pours himself wine. For a moment, as he watches the thick red liquid gurgle into the cup, he lets himself contemplate just how much worse things could have gone for Alice, if only that court servant had been smart enough to listen to the real City gossip being whispered all around him, not gone gawping at some maudlin drunk.

Philippa could have been sitting here telling him how Alice was bankrupting the Crown, a far more serious – and, unfortunately, plausible – charge than the absurd one that she's been secretly bearing the King's bastards. (Absurd, that idea, because however discreetly the perfectly ladylike Katherine Swynford might be hiding her illegitimate offspring, at least you can see why. She's doing it to protect a lover with a damaged reputation, and a living wife. Whereas if the far more flamboyant Alice had managed to conceive a son with her old, still popular, and safely widowed, King, she would have been waving her baby triumphantly in the faces of every lord at court, and she'd have got the boy at least a dukedom by now, too.)

Remembering the King, Chaucer shakes his head. Yes, it could have been worse. Those ladies-in-waiting could have been enjoyably picking over exactly how many thousands Alice had stolen from the sick old man who loves her.

'Quit, Alice,' Chaucer says earnestly. 'Quit while you're still ahead.'

Or that's what he would be saying, if he could only get half a chance.

It's the next day, and he's woken up so anxious on her behalf that he's taken a boat up to Hammersmith village and beyond, to find her at Pallenswick and warn her. This seems so important that he's even postponed going to see the Benedictines at St Helen's about taking in Elizabeth.

(Or, he wonders uneasily, as he wishes the boatman forward, is he making too much of his fears – and making an excuse to ignore Alice's command to leave things where they were between them – just because he wants to see her?)

But she's not taken the blindest bit of notice of his serious face and his request for an important talk. She's just thrown her arms around him and squealed, 'Chaucer!' and 'My dear old friend!' and 'It's been too long!' with every appearance of delight, and absolutely not a blush or a quiver to suggest she even remembers . . . *that*, and insisted on having dinner prepared while she's showing him the house, and how she's improved it in just a year.

He's got wet feet from the boat. He doesn't want to be doing this. He loathes discomfort. He's squelching miserably as she walks him round the sheltered gardens, the sapling orchards, the windbreak trees she's planting to protect them better from the river winds, and pointing out the forty acres of arable land and sixty acres of pasture and one-and-a-half acres of meadow. 'And if we come back *this* way,' she prattles on, drawing him towards the cluster of buildings around the great hall, where some sort of building work is about to begin, and a pile of great oak timbers is lying covered in tarpaulins, 'you'll see . . .' and indeed he does: chapels, kitchens, bakehouses, stables and barns, all repaired and painted, and brand-new gates leading out to the track through the woods behind.

He'll say this for Alice. The serfs look well fed. No sunken faces and bare stick legs and quiet son-of-the-soil anger in eyes here. The fields look well tended, too. And the food that comes out of the kitchen is magnificent.

The main house, though still unfinished, will soon be elegant. There are new hangings, fresh from the workshops, lying on chests on all sides, ready for the walls. 'If only you'd come a month later,' Alice is saying, bright-eyed, 'you'd have seen it finished. But for now, you'll just have to imagine the glorious future.'

Chaucer's forgotten everything except that he's glowing with pleasure at her pleasure. By the time he does, finally, get a chance to talk, over a tender little suckling pig with an apple in its mouth and its side carved neatly off into slices, he's realised how thin an excuse he's got for coming here and what a mountain he's made of a molehill. He doesn't even like to mention the tavern story. It seems so inconsequential now.

So he sticks to general tavern worries: about the King's drifting; and the hash the Duke's said to be making a hash of the peace talks, over in Bruges; and that there's so little money . . . that there might have to be a Parliament . . .

Alice just laughs. Especially when he finishes: 'And most of all I'm worried for *you*, Alice. I hear such hard things about you. People don't like it that you're doing so well, so obviously, when no one else is. Shouldn't you at least think of . . . stepping back? Spending less . . . keeping a lower profile? . . . Or keeping away from the City? . . . Or even retiring to be with your family?'

'Oh, I'm not ready to go anywhere yet,' she says blithely. 'You're always fretting over something, Chaucer.'

He feels snubbed. He falls silent.

She piles more food on his platter. She refills his glass. She flashes her teeth at him. She adds, with kindness, 'But I like it that you worry about me.'

And, when he pushes the platter away, she sweeps him excitedly up again. 'If you're sure you've had enough, then come and see. My best hanging's just come.'

Even Chaucer has to put aside his forebodings and laugh when, puffing and dusty, they've finally got the stiff embroidered thing out and flat on the floor.

It's an extraordinary piece of work. It's Alice through and through.

Sampson, asleep on a bed of pearls, has golden hair and a long golden beard. Real gold: great, flowing locks of Cyprus thread that glitter under the dust motes.

Delilah, scissors in hand, is black-haired and blue-eyed and curvy. She has a wicked little grin as she advances on her victim, ready to cut off his hair and steal his strength. She's wearing scarlet. For a Biblical character, her costume looks strangely like that of the Lady of the Sun.

Oh, Alice Perrers, he thinks, lost in admiration, you brave little minx. Against his will, he finds himself hoping that, somehow, she can safely hang on, picking people's pockets and playing them off against each other and plotting and

229

dancing around and laughing and being intoxicating, for as long as she wants. For ever.

She turns and dimples up at him. 'Do you like it?' she says innocently.

He nods, several times. She's standing too close, for someone who told him, months ago, that they shouldn't think again of . . . *that*. He's got her rose-oil scent in his nostrils. He's on the point of stepping back when she comes closer still, snakes herself round him until he starts to melt and harden against her. Standing on tiptoe, she presses her lips up against his, and says, 'I've missed you, Chaucer.' Again, he finds himself forgetting to breathe.

For a while, Chaucer can't think of anything but what his body's doing. But, as he gets his breath back, and removes his nose and elbows from the prickly gold embroidery and the bobbly seed pearls of Delilah's scarlet skirts, and rushes to lace himself back up, and to pull down Alice's skirts over her legs (because she's just going on lying there, on one elbow, grinning mischievously at him), and to pick up the hat that's fallen on Sampson's fig leaf, he's appalled again, shocked again, at what he's done. Again.

'But I thought you said,' he mutters breathlessly, 'that we shouldn't . . .'

Her dimples show when she smiles. He wants to kiss them.

She lifts her shoulders, which are still bare and deliciously rosy, in a charmingly helpless shrug. 'Well,' she says, and her gesture forgives them both, 'we just did. And it wasn't so bad, was it? No harm done?'

He can't help smiling back. But he has to ask, all the same: 'So what changed your mind?'

She sits up now, and begins calmly to restore order to her own lacings, humming though her teeth as she does. After a moment, she glances up at him – an outrageously intimate look. She's smiling, though more softly. 'Well . . . back then, I was surprised it happened . . . and I thought I couldn't be two men's mistress at once . . . that really would be immoral, even for me. But now? I don't know. Things just look different.

Because, to be honest, I'm not really *his* mistress, not any more, haven't been for a long time . . . and it's true what I said, Chaucer. I missed you. And anyway, why do we always think we have to choose between things? Why not have it all?'

She stands up. Right next to him. He can see he's supposed to react with joy. And he is joyful, of course he is, but he's alarmed, too, that he's come here to warn her to be more careful, but she's only got more foolhardy. But then, what's he blaming her for, when he was only too eager, a few minutes ago, to rush in . . .?

He swallows.

'It must have cost a pretty penny,' he says, changing the subject. 'That hanging.'

She gives him that careful, squinty, narrow-eyed look that he's seen from her once or twice before. She's measuring him, he thinks; seeing if she can trust him.

He holds his breath. Whatever it is, he wants to know.

She nods. 'Mm-hm,' she says. She glances carefully up at him again, and then turns her attention to her sleeves, to get them just so. 'Well, I can afford it. I've made some money recently.'

'Mm-hm?' he enquires. But something in that last look is making his stomach turn. Suddenly he's not so sure he does want to know.

'On the debt paper,' she finishes carelessly. 'A bit of speculation. Only, of course, that's for your ears only, Chaucer, because I trust you. You mustn't tell a soul.' She looks up again, more boldly this time. She wants to see the effect this confession is having on him.

It's explosive. Chaucer's Adam's apple is gyrating up and down his throat as he swallows, and swallows again. She's admitted it. He feels sick. 'But I asked you. Last year. And you said' – he chokes – 'you weren't doing it.'

She isn't bothered. She's still looking pleased with herself, still talking. He forces himself to make sense of the carefree words coming from her mouth. She's saying something about how, last year, she was only dabbling. It didn't really count.

She wasn't really lying to him, back then. But after New Year she decided she could be making more exchanging debt paper. Much more.

'. . . because it really struck me, over Christmas, that there might not be much longer with Edward,' she's saying. 'And that the Duke might not be the kind of master I needed afterwards, either. So I thought, in for a penny, in for a pound . . . time to hurry up.'

Chaucer's shocked. Before New Year, Alice always used to sound so full of hope that she could make the Duke her future protector . . . mentor . . . patron; and she'd seemed so excited about her plan to put the war finances on a better footing, which she thought would do it. Chaucer's always thought it would, too. He's spent all this time trying, dutifully, to help Alice's cause by trying to promote a better relationship between the Duke and the City, and always speaking well of the Duke to Walworth (not with that much success, admittedly, as Walworth is still deeply suspicious of the King's son; but at least the Duke has been away for most of this year, and so, to Chaucer's pleasure, there've been no actual clashes between my lord of Lancaster and the City, these last months).

Can she really have had this more criminal second plan on the go the whole time – a 'plan' that seems to amount to no more than helping herself from the treasury and hoping no one notices? A 'plan' that, when she's caught, as she inevitably will be, will wipe out all the good her clever financial thinking has done her? And can it really be that seeing the Duke only had eyes for his mistress at Christmas has been enough to make her give up on all those earlier hopes – intelligent hopes, too – of the future she could perhaps have earned by serving him well? Can Alice be such a faint-heart?

He can't believe his disappointment. He thought she was better than this.

Her voice is still chirruping on. 'And now I've got almost all my properties rebuilt and in good order. My rental income's going to be up substantially from now on, and I've even been able to buy some new places. I'm in good shape for the future.' She beams proudly.

232

'You fool,' Chaucer says, slowly. 'You gave up all the good you were doing and opted for stealing just out of pique? Because he's sleeping with Katherine?'

She looks at him, as if he's shocked her. Then she shakes her head. 'No,' she says, more seriously. 'It's not that, Chaucer. Not at all.' She stops fiddling with her bodice. She faces him, fair and square. 'Look, I always thought I had to choose: serve him, or steal from him. If I served him well, I'd impress him, and be able to stay on at court. If I stole from him, I'd have to leave court after Edward . . . but I might at least go richer. And I didn't know which to choose. I spent all last year worrying, which would be my best course of action?

'But after Christmas, when the Duke just wasn't interested in knowing anything about the detail of the good work I'd done, as long as there was some vague picture of things getting better that he could enjoy (while the Duke stuffed his face with honeyed peacock and whispered sweet nothings in Madame de Swynford's ear), I realised I'd been wrong. I suddenly saw that I didn't have to choose. I could do both.'

She puts a soft hand on Chaucer's arm. 'He hasn't stopped liking me now he's got her,' she goes persuasively on. 'He still thinks I'm a good adviser, you know. I saw him again in January, on his way to Bruges, when she wasn't there, and he was all charm and gratitude. He just can't be bothered with detail, any more than his father can. They're princes. They only see the big picture. They want life served up to them like a great big golden pageant. How it all actually happens, how the mock-castle bursts into flames without setting the real hall alight, how the ice swans get on the table on a hot April night – well, they leave that for the servants to worry about. So he'll never know if I'm taking a bit on the side. Even if it's quite a big bit. He can't possibly find out, not for a long time, now he's stuck at Bruges talking. And even if, when he gets back, he does find out some money's been going, maybe even too much for any more war plans, he won't have the eye for detail to work out where it's gone or who's taken it. He certainly won't suspect *me*. He trusts me. I can tell him what I like. I can say, "Oh, those government clerks, always got their hands in the money-bags, nothing you can do to stop them, or check," or, "Perhaps Master Walworth's had a hand in it," or anything I like, and he'll believe me. He might even be secretly relieved if there's not enough money for the war – he doesn't really *want* to fight. He'd rather have peace, if he had an excuse that wouldn't make him look cowardly.'

She gazes at Chaucer, with something between defiance and anxiety in her eyes. 'So,' she finishes, 'I've seen the light. I can steal a bit, *and* stay. I can do it all.'

Chaucer's lost for words.

'Oh, Alice Perrers,' he says, in the end. 'You think you're being clever. But you're not. Just greedy. The Duke won't need to go through the books himself to find out you've been stealing. You've got enemies all over the place. They'll be more than willing to take care of the detail for him – point out how. And if they do catch you out, you'll have lost him, and all your money too.'

She lifts her shoulders. He can't dent her confidence. 'But they won't,' she replies quickly. 'They can't. There's no proof I'm involved.'

'Of course there must be proof!' he cries, and he's astonished that she can possibly not have thought of this. Shock tingles through every careful clerkish bone in him. 'The prices that the treasury paid for your paper will have been written down every time, in their account books. Quite openly. Yes?'

She nods, mutely. But there's still a glimmer of impudence on her face.

'And the prices that the Italians paid will have been written down in *their* account books. Also quite openly. Yes?'

She nods again. But she's still not looking abashed.

'So all anyone needs to do is compare the two. And see the profit you've made. Yes?' Chaucer insists. He's almost shouting, he's so eager for her to get the point.

She shrugs. 'But so what?' she says carelessly. 'They never will. No one ever does do that sort of thing, really. You know that. People are lazy. They always mean to check up, but then they just . . . you know . . . go for dinner, or something.'

'Unless they really hate someone,' Chaucer says lugubriously. 'They do then.'

An indulgent smile is coming on to her face. She turns to face him and takes his shoulders. 'You've been listening to too much tavern gossip. You should drink less,' she says more gently. 'I'm not a fool, I promise. Whatever you think. It's all sewn up. Foolproof. All the paper that's been redeemed at the treasury is in Latimer's name. It was his idea in the first place; officially, he profits. And all the paper that's been bought up from the Italians is in Richard Lyons' name. The paper loss is in his name. So there's no connection between them, or the two sets of transactions; and no paperwork involving me at all. Just a little bag of money, every now and then. My savings' – she pulls her eyes down at the corners, turning her face into a comic old-woman mask – 'for my declining years.'

Chaucer is feeling sick again. Latimer too. He's glad he didn't go to Latimer now. In a way, he thinks, perhaps she's right: there's nothing linking her to it. Still, he wishes she hadn't told him. After all, he doesn't want to know all this.

Weakly, he says, 'But what if, say, someone starts investigating Latimer? Won't he just throw you to the wolves?'

She stretches out her hands on plump little arms. She looks bewildered. 'But why would they?' she says simply. 'Seriously, who would want to hurt Latimer? Don't be naive, Chaucer. Everyone's on the make. There's not a soul in the royal household who hasn't helped himself to something at some time. It's honour among thieves. There's no one who'd do the dirty on anyone else, in case someone came sniffing through their own dirty linen. They wouldn't take the risk. You can always find a bit of dirt on anyone, if you dig deep enough.'

It sounds so simple.

'No, you can't,' Chaucer says mutinously.

'I reckon even you're not too noble to have taken a sweetener every now and then.'

'Yes I am,' he says. But she only laughs.

'I must go,' he says. He's feeling offended. He doesn't like being laughed at, or accused of corruption.

But she steps up to him again and pulls his arms around her.

'You should be pleased I've stopped thinking you have to choose your pleasures in life, Chaucer,' she whispers in his ear. 'And you don't have to, either. You know that really. Look. Here we are, the two of us. Here you are, being offered me, as well as . . .' She twinkles. '. . . whatever else you love. So are you going to turn it down?'

As she turns her face up to his, and her lips seek his out, Chaucer knows he's not.

FIFTEEN

Peter de la Mare's hair is greyer than before. There's the beginning of a stoop in his back. He hasn't got eyes for the luminous evening sky, however deliriously the birds are dipping and swooping, however sweetly the waves are lapping on the riverbank beyond the terrace at Kennington Palace.

He's feeling discouraged.

He's been in and around London and Westminster for weeks, on this latest visit alone. Yet he can't find the killer facts he needs. Just rumours, so many rumours.

He can guess that the government's money must be draining away because of some illicit connection between City and court – the two money centres of the kingdom. But that's a hard thing to pin down. For who knows both worlds well enough to see how they might be brought together to the detriment of the kingdom? Certainly not Peter de la Mare, who knows neither world very well.

He sighs.

In the City, all they do is mutter about Alice Perrers stealing, or being behind other people's thefts, as if every other soul in London were a model of irreproachable probity (except possibly the Fleming, Lyons; they don't seem to like *him* much, either, but then who does like foreigners?). The top merchant, Walworth, can't stop himself; he almost twitches with dislike when he hears Mistress Perrers' name. And it's no better at court, where Sir Peter's met at every turn by a wall of polite, smiling hostility. They show him the account books, but they explain nothing. It's clear they don't want outsiders sticking their noses in.

Yet Sir Peter knows, without needing any financial expertise, that if he is to honestly try to improve the state of the nation's finances he will need to present to the Parliament he will lead a charge sheet that features something more precise than vague accusations against a woman of known loose morals with ideas above her station, and a foreigner. They're such obvious scapegoats. They can't, alone, have brought England to the pass it's in. He'd be a laughing-stock if he settled for that trite explanation. There'd be people snickering behind their hands up and down this London river. And it wouldn't improve the finances or cut out the moral rot he senses everywhere if he did take that easy option.

But that's just the point of principle. It doesn't help him with the detail.

If only he could find an ally, an insider. If only someone who understands these matters from close up could talk him through exactly how the government's accounts translate into reality. Who takes what, how and why; who has to nod and wink when.

Without that . . .

He sighs again.

When the boat comes to take him to his final interview of the day, it's a moment before he can summon the strength of purpose to disengage himself from the post he's leaning against, and step down.

Lord Latimer's face is splendidly relaxed as de la Mare walks into his office. He's at his desk, writing, but that doesn't diminish his animal vigour, the rippling power of his shoulders as the pen scratchily chases words across the page.

A magnificently furred dark green velvet coat, thrown over the back of his chair, slips down as he straightens. Lord Latimer turns, raises an eyebrow, and, with a powerful movement of his arm, pushes the offending item down out of sight.

De la Mare is too much of a gentleman to do anything so

obvious as to suppress a sigh at being called in and then kept waiting. He knows the virtue of discipline.

So he waits. But the hair on the back of his neck is prickling, as it always does in Latimer's presence. Discipline is one thing, but you can't altogether suppress instinctive dislike. Latimer was a good soldier once, de la Mare has heard. But back then he probably didn't cultivate this deliberately splendid, sun-kissed, jewel-winking appearance, or have that hypocritical smile forever on his lips.

'Ah, Sir Peter,' Latimer finally purrs, looking up at the gentleman from Herefordshire as if he's only just noticed his guest's arrival. 'Do take a seat.' And he gestures. But he's still fiddling with the papers on his desk, demonstrating the amount, and the importance, of the work before him. De la Mare is increasingly certain that the lord chamberlain is nervous.

'Now, to business,' Latimer says, bestowing a joyous, sharp-toothed smile on de la Mare. 'You'd like to see the schedule of the treasury's Italian debt repayments, I understand?'

De la Mare nods, and bows. His letters of introduction from the Prince of England have opened many doors. A clerk is dispatched for the books.

Latimer, meanwhile, rises, and, with great affability, leads de la Mare over to the window for a little sack while they watch the sunset and wait. The chamberlain lets his arm linger, warm and confiding, on the Herefordshire gentleman's unrelaxed back. He sips, and gazes into de la Mare's eyes, and asks solicitous questions in a velvet voice. Are his rooms comfortable? Are his preparations advancing for the Parliament? Does he have any idea, yet, when it will be?

Leaning even closer, Lord Latimer murmurs, 'I don't envy you the task you've set yourself, Sir Peter. It's never easy to find the source of corruption anywhere, of course. But in London, where every merchant is so very private in his dealings, and yet so demanding of respect and courtesy, it must be all but impossible...' The chamberlain's face expresses utter admiration for de la Mare's dedication to duty, but also an invitation to share a bit of a sly laugh at the merchants.

239

De la Mare allows himself a smile. 'I hope to make progress,' he says evenly.

'I know more now, after all these years,' Latimer goes smoothly on. 'But oh, how deceptive I found appearances in London at first.' He chuckles. Then he starts shaking his head, as if some highly amusing memory has come back to him, quite by chance. He continues, reminiscently: 'For instance, I remember how utterly astonished I was to hear that William Walworth's air of angelic innocence didn't stop him running his little sideline in brothels, over Southwark way. Flemish tarts: less talk that way than with London chatterboxes.' He looks brightly at de la Mare, like a fisherman at a fish, to make sure Sir Peter's swallowed the hook inside that bit of bait. He shakes his head again. 'You'd never guess he was that type to look at him, though, would you?'

More rueful headshakes. Then there's another story, this time about the King's man in Ireland, William of Windsor, who, according to Latimer, has been taking vast sums from London to pay for the defence of Ireland, and, at the same time, wringing vast sums out of the locals – with nothing much to show, in terms of castle walls or soldiers, for either input of money. 'All vanished,' Latimer says. He opens bewildered arms. 'You'd never guess it to look at *him*, either. Soldierly type. Seems honest as the day is long.' He smiles. 'No, you never can tell.'

At last the books come. Latimer retreats, after solicitously settling de la Mare at a table, with light, and wine, and a clerk to hand. 'Take all the time you need,' he breathes, as he withdraws. And: 'If there's anything further I can do, please don't hesitate . . . '

'Thank you,' de la Mare says shortly.

But he leaves an hour later, and has himself rowed back to Kennington, without further comment. He's searched the accounts thoroughly. He's been unable to find even a hint of dishonesty. Again.

He just has two new random rumours to add to the collection of slanders that everyone living in these overcrowded buildings on this stinking river seems to spend their time passing on. Walworth was just as bad, earlier on. Telling him Lyons the Fleming was illegally using his heavies in the ports to confiscate imported spices from the grocers' ships, so he could do Brembre and Philpot out of business by letting scarcity force up the prices, then selling the stuff on himself. Telling him, too, that Alice Perrers and the Duke of Lancaster were secretly and illegally funding a mercer candidate for mayor, to get him and his cronies out of office. But then everyone's got a rumour to tell about Alice Perrers.

De la Mare has heard that she's getting a cut out of the treasury thefts, too. He's heard that her property holdings have trebled in size this year alone. Walworth thinks she must have spent three thousand on houses. He's even heard that she goes and sits on the King's Bench, in the King's own place, and dictates the outcomes of court cases. To hear them all talk, she's the mastermind. In league with the Duke. In league with Lyons. In league with the Devil himself.

They don't seem to realise that he's not unaware that she's the easiest person to blame.

Peter de la Mare is a man of principle. He'll carry on working at this task until he succeeds. But he's so weary of all this London dishonesty. Court, City: each lot as bad as the other. Rotten to the core, all of them; scampering around like human rats, growing fat on what they've stolen.

He can hardly bring himself to bow to the preoccupied-looking official who walks him back out to the jetty. Baron Scrope, the treasurer: tall and stooped and furrow-browed.

'All was well, I hope?' Scrope murmurs, as de la Mare steps stiffly down into the boat. De la Mare closes his eyes. His head aches. He just wants to be away, over this river of sewage, and into the privacy of his room. Through thin lips, he replies, 'No discrepancies.' Then, as the boatman turns, and Scrope tightens his cloak, ready to go too, de la Mare adds: '. . . that I could see.'

He feels Scrope's eyes, steady on him, as the boat pulls out.

Peter de la Mare has felt honoured, ever since he was elected to Parliament as a Herefordshire knight, to represent the

241

people he lives among, and to lead them. He's been waiting two years since then for the King to actually call the Parliament, true; but when the time finally does come for the assembly to meet, here, he wants to be ready to speak out in the name of justice for his kind.

Peter de la Mare has no pretensions to earthly greatness. He doesn't want a life at court, or in the King's armies – the dangers of both seem to him far to outweigh the advantages. He's not interested in fabulous wealth. He doesn't really understand the courtly lords, like Latimer, who, while of not much greater estate than himself, make it their life's work to better themselves, and absent themselves from their country homes for years on end, as if they were no more than landless, rootless merchants, interested only in money. He's more than content with the life God has sent him to this earth to lead, out on his lands. What Peter de la Mare wants to achieve, from the Parliament he's preparing so carefully for, is the preservation of that way of life for country gentlemen like himself. For, as he sees it, the activities of the lords of the court have become noxious enough to threaten the destruction of the modest hopes and dreams of the country gentry. And he's a brave enough man to want to root out the evil.

Thanks to his marriage, he's well off: a lucky turn of events for a younger son, and one for which he is thankful to God. He's master of a compact, efficient estate of three thousand acres, with woods, and fishing, and a rabbit warren, and a park, and corn, and sheep, centred on Yatton, in the Wye Valley, where he lives with Matilda and young Roger and little Janey. He also owns a second estate, bigger yet at five thousand acres, and given over almost in its entirety to sheep and cattle husbandry, over at Little Hereford. His net income has shrunk, as everyone's has, with the rise in wage demands from the peasantry, from near £400 a year in his youth to just over half that now. But he still has no serious financial worries for himself, even if, every time a Parliament has taxed him one-fifteenth of his movable property to pay for the war, he's been forced to sell off a few more fields, to raise the cash money, and whittled a bit more off the estate he hopes one day to leave to Roger.

But his years as the Earl of March's seneschal (another piece of divine providence, for which he gives more thanks), riding out as far as the Welsh border with the county elite to negotiate disputes over land rights, and collecting iron ore dues from the mines in the Forest of Dean, have given him first-hand knowledge of the parlous state other gentlemen of his county find themselves in.

There are fewer and fewer knights today who can afford the privilege of kitting themselves out for war, which, when Peter de la Mare was a young man, was the surest way of earning yourself advancement in life and a profitable lifelong allegiance to a greater lord, such as he himself now enjoys, with its fees and annuities in return for duties done. Now, he sees fathers everywhere, especially the poorer ones, saying, What's the point? All that expense, and then all you do is twiddle your thumbs and polish your plate armour and wait for a call-up that never comes . . . or, if it does, brings you no financial reward, since there have been no victories, and no spoil, for so many years. For a knight whose landed income from rents is already down near twenty pounds, the minimum needed to qualify for shire offices, it's a finely balanced question, these days, whether there's any advantage at all to be got from laying out money to equip their sons for war.

Yet there's not much point, either, in hoping for wealth from farming, when the peasants demand as much as fourpence a day in labour, and the price of corn is dropping every year.

Some of the lesser knights have chosen to seek out tenant farmers, rather than manage their fields themselves. But the tenant farmers are stuck in the same double bind of paying more for labour and earning less from their crops; and if your tenant farmer's a reliable man, but his crop's smaller than he'd hoped, and has sold for less, what can you do but accept two-thirds of his rent, or less?

So there are gentlemen all over Herefordshire facing decline. Men who hold manors on boggy land that won't quite do for pasture; men who find their position undermined by vacant tenancies and mounting arrears of rent. Men who've given up hope that the war will save them. Men, like Sir Peter's old friend Sir John Verney, driven distracted by the fear that their meagre estates won't provide a living for their younger sons; any more than war will, or the legal education they can't afford, which might turn a boy into a good administrator, or the Church, which will swallow the child up. Men forced to entertain the thought that beloved sons like Roger Verney, with his fresh pink cheeks, schooled in the rudiments of church Latin and a good deal more chivalric literature, may, one day, if a willing heiress can't be found (and where can a willing heiress be found, if you can't afford to leave your dwindling lands?), be forced to follow the plough.

Peter de la Mare has spent so many years thanking God for his own lucky escape from genteel poverty – in the shape of Matilda's blue eyes and lavish marriage portion – that he's only recently realised, as his own son grows up, how much worse things are getting for the country gentry of today.

His class is the backbone of England, he's always known. He's always been proud of that fact, and deeply aware of his duty. But it's only in his middle years that he's understood what this now means to the officials who rule the land in the King's name: that his is the class on whom England's tax burden must fall.

Since Peter de la Mare was a boy, in King Edward's early years, the national tax burden has trebled. The officials at Westminster now expect to be kept afloat by impoverished gentlemen such as the ones from Herefordshire – even men who can only pay the tax if they sell their land, and lose their status, and, with tears in their eyes, put their sons back to till the soil.

'If it's for the good of England . . .' de la Mare always used to say to Verney (trying not to see the mute plea in Verney's eyes, but wouldn't my Roger and your little Janey, so pretty, so prosperous, be a good match?), 'then, however hard it seems, we have to pay the King his tax, and keep hope in our hearts.'

But that naive acceptance was before his eyes were opened . . .

. . . which they were, three years ago, during his annual visit to St Albans, to his elder brother Thomas, the Abbot there. Thomas, whose obsessive following of the affairs of the nation stems, probably, from his futile lifelong rebellion against their father's decision to take him out of the world and settle him in the Church. Ambitious Thomas, now almost a prince of the Church, whose frequent court cases and elaborate financial arrangements on his wealthy abbey's behalf have given him an insider's view of what's going on in London, and at court. Well-connected Thomas, whose long-standing friendship with the Prince means his opinions have often been tested against the greatest in the land. If anyone understands what's going on at the heart of England, Peter knows, it's Thomas.

'You think it's all for the good of England?' Thomas said, with that hard look that twists his face into ugliness. 'All the sufferings of good, honest men like John Verney?'

And, without another word, he took Peter off to the scriptorium, to look at the abbey's chronicle of current events, kept by the young brother with the fat pink cheeks by whom he seems to set so much store.

What Peter read there changed his life for ever. The chronicle's account, down in plain black and white for anyone to see, talked of the carryings-on at court, the senile King, the grasping Devil's-spawn whore, and the cabal of courtiers stealing every penny of his own and John Verney's money that has gone into the royal coffers for years, to spend it on their own ill-deserved comforts and misbegotten brats. As he read it, Peter felt his heart beat faster, and his blood throb in his temples, out of sheer fury at the injustice, the outrageous wrongness, of it.

He went straight back to Hereford and got himself elected to represent the Commons of England – the esquires, the gentlemen, the minor nobility, and the City rich – at the next Parliament.

It's been his one ambition, ever since, to stop the criminals in their tracks, and make the honest folk of England safe again from that greed.

Not that he can have much realistic hope that the voice of the Commons will make much difference to the future of England; the Commons are usually told, without excess formality, to know their place and keep to it. Still . . . Peter draws his hope from this. He knows the King's a good king, led astray, not the kind to take it amiss if the best and truest of his people step forward to guide him back to the path. Peter's dream – private at first – has been that, if the knights and burgesses of the Parliament were led by a man of integrity, who'd found out the whole ugliness of the canker attacking the state, who could put the details to them and tell them exactly how to stop the rot, the King would pay heed. Peter wants to be the man who can do that. And his dream seems to have come closer to reality ever since the Princess sought him out.

He's grateful to Thomas – who, for all his flinty appearance, is a good man deep down, and wants virtue to triumph over evil in this world – for putting him in touch with the Princess Joan. The Princess, with her husband, has been funding his research into government corruption for the past year.

Of course, the Princess has her own ideas about the cause of the corruption. She and her husband believe it's sponsored by the Duke of Lancaster, who, they think, wants to steal not only money but the very throne of England from their son.

Peter de la Mare is inclined to suspect that the Prince's fears on that score are no more than the night terrors of a terminally ill man, who knows he won't be around to protect his child into adulthood. Of course the Prince fears for his little boy, just as Sir John Verney fears for his son, but, in de la Mare's mind, it's Sir John Verney who has more reason to fear. Privately, he doubts that there's much real link between the corruption of the court and the activities of the Duke of Lancaster. But, since it's the Prince of England who's paying for him to root out the corruption, he's willing – more than willing – to keep an open mind.

If only he could find something definite, quickly.

If only he could get home to Yatton. The corn will be ripening by now. He wants to sleep with his wife, confess to his priest, and ride out around his lands with his own boy Roger and with Roger Verney, who, of course, he *has*, in the end, reluctantly agreed can marry Janey, once she turns fourteen. He wants to look into honest country eyes, blue as a clear sky, and breathe pure air.

Even once Sir Peter's inside, stalking along the stone corridors to report to the Princess, London clings to him, the creeping putrefaction that the city trails. He can't get its stink out of his nostrils. Whether the root of the evil lies in the City with the merchants, or at marshy Westminster with the government officials, he can't be sure. But they're clever, all of them, so damnably clever, with their elaborate deceptions and their paper trails that peter out into nothingness . . .

Princess Joan's face is alive with a question.

He spreads his hands. 'Nothing.'

The Princess is stony-faced. 'Sir Peter,' she says. 'It's midsummer. They say a deal is imminent at Bruges. A disgraceful deal. Another shameful truce. We're going to give in to the Pope, too, and pay him money England doesn't owe. A Parliament is more and more likely to follow. My lord the King will need money. You must have a case to put. You must hurry.'

De la Mare suddenly hears his brother John's voice. 'I told you,' John's saying truculently, 'it would be far easier just to get Perrers for witchcraft.'

Peter's head is pounding. Perhaps John was right all along. Perhaps it's not the means that matters; the triumph of good over evil, through virtue. Perhaps you do just have to squash the evil, hard, fast, however you can . . .

Quietly, he puts a hand up to his temple and begins to massage his skin. He says, in a monotone, to his own wrist, 'It's a matter of principle. If this is to be done, it must be done right.' He looks up, into the Princess's eyes. 'Trust me,' he says. 'I'll find what we need.'

SIXTEEN

'I told you nothing would happen,' Alice says. 'And here I still am. Safe.'

Besides her, Chaucer stirs. He sees that she's sitting up, hands clasped round her knees, thinking, shivering every now and then as the blankets move. Even inside the bedcurtains, at dawn, in this freezing spring of 1376, it's cold enough for her breath to be rising in a white plume from her mouth. It started to snow last night, to mark the quarter-day. And the servants don't come and stoke up the fire in the mornings, out of embarrassment, when Alice makes her occasional visits. It must have gone out.

Enjoying the warmth of his cosy space under the quilts, Chaucer thinks: Well, perhaps she's right.

Duke John certainly doesn't seem to have checked the finances. He doesn't seem to have cared, either, that Alice's pick of negotiator, John Wyclif, turned out to be no good; he just lost his temper, walked out of the talks at Bruges, and came home. That didn't stop the Duke trusting Alice again. He took her next bit of advice with alacrity: that he should travel with his pregnant wife to Bruges for the next instalment of talks, to show off to the world the bulge that might be the next King of Castile. After the ducal delegation left the Savoy for the coast, Alice rushed straight round to Chaucer's apartment. She had roses in her cheeks. Her first words were about poor Katherine, the left-behind mistress. 'I bet', she said

248

cheerfully, 'that it's mighty cold and lonely up there in Kettlethorpe.'

Chaucer's getting used to the idea that he scarcely sees Philippa any more, only for the occasional tight-lipped encounter on the rare occasions she and the Duchess are at the Savoy; because a truce has developed. He doesn't ask her about Katherine's family circumstances (though he's heard, from Alice, that his sister-in-law called the second ducal baby Henry). In what he sees as a tacit trade-off, Philippa has agreed that Elizabeth can become a novice, next year, at St Helen's, where Chaucer will be able to visit her once a month.

To Chaucer's great sorrow, Thomas hasn't come once to the City in the past year. Philippa just says he's too taken up with his riding and his studies. But Elizabeth – a tall, thin, silent, downcast-eyed, tongue-tied version of the giggling, tumbling child he loves – has been to visit, with her mother, three times. Chaucer is quietly hopeful that, once he starts getting to meet her on her own next year, he'll be able to rekindle some of the old affection he used to see in his daughter's eyes.

Meanwhile, there's Alice. She comes, quite often. He never knows when she will.

He pulls her down, lays her head on his chest. 'Well, maybe you were right,' he concedes sleepily. 'But who am I to say? I'm only a poet in love.'

'Ahhh, poetry,' she says indulgently. 'Saps the common sense.' Alice has no time for fancy. But she looks pleased that, for once, he doesn't sound worried.

In his heart, Chaucer doesn't share Alice's conviction that no one will find her out, however triumphant she's taken to sounding, however right she seems to be.

He certainly feels guilty enough on her behalf. And his instinct is to whisper through these winter days, avoiding all but the most cursory conversation with anyone, bar clerks, servants and family.

It may just be his uneasy conscience, but Chaucer smells threat in the air.

He's relieved, at least, that the mystery knight from Herefordshire, who for months has been in and out of London, and in and out of Westminster, asking nosy questions of everyone about the public finances (he says at the behest of the Prince, though no one's quite sure whether that story's true, or just a front to hide the identity of some other powerful enquirer), seems to have left town again.

No one's been visited by the knight, that Chaucer knows of, for the past two days.

Peter de la Mare's been to the Wool Wharf and checked the merchants' books, and Chaucer's Counter-Roll too, so Chaucer's had a better chance to inspect the knight from close up. He's a great gaunt skeleton of a man, who you'd think might be frightening in anger, though he turned out to be quiet and straightforward enough as he went through Chaucer's work in weary, but thorough, style.

Chaucer even rather liked it when Peter de la Mare looked up from the Counter-Roll, after an hour or so, and gave him a quizzical sort of look. Raised eyebrows, head cocked on one side; as if he were waiting. 'Sir?' Chaucer said deferentially. 'Can I help you with something?' His heart was racing. Had the man found some terrible error he'd made?

Sir Peter began to smile, as if to himself. 'I don't know . . . Don't you have anything to tell me, Master Chaucer?' he replied, and at Chaucer's bewildered headshake, he almost smiled. 'I don't mean to alarm you,' the knight went on. 'But to tell you the truth I do feel there's something missing. Not that it's your fault; good God, no. Nothing you need worry about. It's just that with almost everyone else I've talked to, down in London, there's always been a moment, about an hour in, when they've started telling me, as if it's sheer coincidence they've just thought of it, some story suggesting that their own business rival is the most dishonest man ever to walk God's earth, and needs to be investigated. But you've just been sitting there, silent as a lamb.' There was a glint in his eye that, if he'd seen it on the face of someone less tall and less serious, Chaucer might have taken for the beginning of laughter.

'No enemies, sir,' Chaucer replied smartly, feeling relieved at this hint of humour. 'At least, I try not to have.'

But he breathed more easily, all the same, after the knight made his formal, gracious, countrified farewells and went off to sniff at Walworth, or Lyons, or at Westminster instead.

Everyone's rattled. Perhaps that's because no one is quite sure who stands behind the spectral knight with his silver hair, and what the purpose of these inquiries really is. (There's a story that he's just preparing himself, in case there is a Parliament, and in case, if there is, he ends up spokesman for the Commons, though that's obviously nonsense, because the Commons never get much of a chance to say anything at Parliament, they just get lumped into a corner of the chamber, behind the Lords, and told to hurry up with their speeches and complaints and let the important people get on with the real business; and, besides, what country knight could possibly afford to wander around London for all these months on such a fool's errand?) Still, people are rattled, because everyone feels guilty about something. Whose conscience is clear?

Only Alice knows no fear. In fact, she's behaving more outrageously than ever.

She's come to Chaucer, this time, after a Mayor's Lady Day banquet yesterday at the Guildhall. Chaucer went to it, expecting good food but dull company – chit-chat with merchants' wives, uneasy talk among the men about how long the King can hold out without calling a parliament – without knowing she'd be there. He certainly didn't expect to get there and find her on Richard Lyons' arm, as the divorced Fleming's guest, with every eye in the room on them. Lyons was in vintners' livery, though his own colouring, the pink and the orange of him, took all attention from his muted claret-coloured furred robes. Loose though the robes were, the sheer muscly well-fleshed size of him made his long tunic seem to strain and heave at arm and shoulder seams. Alice was equally ostentatious in fluttering pea-green silks, with silver worked through her veil and emeralds at her throat. Chaucer tried all through the afternoon not to feel jealous of Lyons' flesh against hers. With Alice, what would be the point of that?

But he couldn't help but cringe for Alice at the expression in most of those watching eyes. She was smiling, flirting, working the crowd; apparently unaware of the hateful glances behind her back.

Chaucer doesn't know if she was even aware of him listening in while she talked to Walworth. He kept his back turned the whole time (though of course every fibre of him was straining to catch her teasing words, and Walworth's prickly, pompous replies).

ALICE. They say the government inspector has now visited everyone who's anyone, and left. The knight from Herefordshire, I mean. De la Mare. Has he been to you, at all, Master Walworth?
WALWORTH. Mistress Perrers. He has indeed. Many times.
ALICE. Well, then, Master Walworth, you're uniquely honoured, for I've heard of no one else he's been to more than twice. [*Bright laughter.*]
WALWORTH. You will have your little joke, Mistress Perrers. Very amusing. Though in reality I found him charming. Very eager to know more about government business in London. I was able to help him on that, I think. You'll have spent time with him too, I've no doubt.
ALICE. Well, no. None, actually. Should I feel slighted, do you think? [*Bright laughter.*]
WALWORTH [*after a pause*]. Well, they say he's looking for wrong-doing in high places.
ALICE. Then I can't say I'm surprised a mere woman such as myself hasn't come to his attention. Let alone [*bright laughter*] *many times*, like you, Master Walworth. He sounds far too serious to be interested in female foolishness.

Stop, Alice, Chaucer was pleading inwardly, imagining Walworth's strained, angry face, and Alice's cheerfully mocking eyes. Please stop. Let him be.

But she didn't move away.

When Chaucer couldn't bear it any more, another second later, he turned around and let his eyes light up, first, prudently, at the sight of Master Walworth, then at the sight of Alice. 'Why, Master Walworth! Why, Mistress Perrers! What a great pleasure!' he heard himself flute in his peacemaker's voice.

To his relief, Walworth bowed gratefully towards him, as if to a liberator, and said, with what good grace he could muster, 'Do excuse me, Master Chaucer, I must see my wife is all right. I sent her off dancing with Master Lyons a while ago. Who knows what's become of them?' and made off, at a goodish speed, through the crowd.

'Alice,' Chaucer warned, in an agonised whisper. But she just grinned.

She said, 'But I was enjoying myself.' And she wafted away.

When, a little later, he came across Walworth back at the table, putting himself outside a cream pudding with angry intensity, Chaucer said, sympathetically, almost apologetically, 'Mistress Perrers being tricky, was she?' He's friendly enough with Walworth, these days, to be that honest, at least.

'That Woman,' Walworth said, swallowing the last mouthful as if biting something's head off. 'had the nerve to suggest that the Herefordshire knight, the one who's been . . . well, you know the one, Master Chaucer . . . that he was investigating me. Just because I've been helping him with his work.'

He paused. He scraped at his empty dish. Chaucer wondered, rather enviously, how he stayed so thin. Chaucer also wondered what Walworth had insinuated, an hour into his conversation with the knight, if that was what everyone but Chaucer himself had been doing; whom Walworth had casually implicated. Alice Perrers herself, probably; that must be why he was so angry now.

'Ah, well, we all know you've got nothing to worry about,' Chaucer said comfortingly, trying not to think the uncomfortable thought that Walworth might just possibly have been dropping some casual slander about *him* into a conversation with the knight; and that *he* might have missed his turn in the dance of the investigation to counter-implicate Walworth.

253

Guilt: an ugly emotion, Chaucer thought. We're all behaving badly. All guilty.

He was surprised when, much later, after dark, just as the curfew bells were ringing, Alice turned up at his door. She knew exactly when his servants left. She lifted carefully plucked eyebrows at him across the threshold, mocking his nightcap, and said, 'If the auditor's not with you, is there any room at the inn?'

The illusion of comfort Chaucer managed to sustain through a sleepy moment at dawn while covered in a warm quilt, with Alice confident at his side, is chilled off him again by the time he's broken the ice on the water jug and splashed his face and under his arms and between his legs, and towelled himself dry, and pulled on yesterday's linen. It doesn't take much.

Because by this time he's remembered everything else that's been on his mind recently, and he's as worried as he was before she got here last night. She's scared too, he realises. All her jokes about the knight and his mission: they're a way of dealing with fear. She's just pretending everything's all right.

He goes to the fireplace, shivering as he picks up the tinderbox lying ready by the bucket of leaves and twigs. Just one spark, he tells himself, as his stiff fingers push at the flint. Then the whole thing goes up.

'Look,' he says as the fire blossoms, colouring the cold grey room with gold and copper. He hears her stir behind him. 'Mmm,' he hears. 'Lovely.' But Chaucer isn't seeing loveliness. He's seeing hot light, licking along defenceless fingers and limbs of wood, devouring them as it devours the darkness. The way of the world.

Carefully he places a log on top of the little blaze, and another one across it. Then, as the flames rise, he goes back to the bed, where Alice is lying, watching. She looks so small. She must see from his face that he's serious. After one glance, she seems to shrink even further into herself.

He says, without preamble, 'There's no point in deceiving ourselves.'

Her eyes are all he can see of her above the sheet. Her dark eyes are big and round. She keeps very quiet.

'It doesn't matter that you haven't actually been caught cheating yet,' he says, staring back down into her owl-eyes. 'Even if it's not the knight from Herefordshire, someone, sooner or later, will get you. You have to stop.'

He goes on: 'It doesn't even matter whether or not the knight's here for some serious purpose. His being here is just reminding us of what we already know. We can't go on like this for ever – the court and the City, drinking Gascon wine like there's no tomorrow, stuffing our faces on larks' tongues and posset, while the war never gets anywhere, or ends, either, and the poor stand howling outside the windows, in limbo. Wondering how to pay for our appetites. Even that knight. He's one of the ones who's being asked to pay.'

She blinks. Under the linen, she stirs. He takes no notice.

'You've got to change,' he says. He doesn't know where his hard eloquence has come from. But he knows it's time for it. 'You should not touch any more Italian debt. You must go through your affairs, and make sure everything you do, and own, is strictly legal, and there's legal paperwork explaining everything. I don't know how much you own, and how clear your title is, but get rid of anything that's in the least . . . hazy . . . and get rid of some of it anyway; they'll be less likely to attack you if you're not one of the richest people in the land. And you should make one sensible preparation for a future after the King dies: this. Get him to knight your son, and gift the estate in Essex, and wherever else you can think of, to him. That will give you a clear reason to come back to court, or stay at court, whichever seems better, whoever's on the throne – to look after a young knight with a future. And then, once you've done all that, sit tight.'

Alice sits up, wrapping quilts around herself.

She nods at that last idea, at least. 'I'll want to go on being at court.' She mutters, 'I'll be able to go on seeing you, that way.'

Then she goes back to gazing, irresolutely, at him.

'There will be a Parliament,' she says finally, in a small voice, in the contrite manner of a child admitting misbehaviour. 'There'll have to be. The Duke's on his way home. After all that talk, he's only managed to get another truce. For one more year. And it doesn't look good for after that. And there's not enough money to rearm. So there'll have to be a tax. Latimer's going to tell Edward in the next few days. And Edward will be summoning the Parliament within a week.'

Chaucer shakes his head. The silence deepens. He's so overwhelmed by his yearning to somehow protect Alice, to save this oddly fragile creature cowering there, both from herself, and from her enemies, that he doesn't know what to say.

But at least he understands, now, why she's looking scared.

While Alice is irritating William Walworth at the Lady Day dinner in the City, Sir Richard Scrope, first Baron Scrope of Bolton, is setting out across the choppy grey river from the jetty at Westminster Palace. His raw red hands are clutching tightly on to the big sack on his knees. He doesn't want to let any river water splash it.

The boatman wonders if my lord treasurer has valuables in that bag, he's treating it so gently. But all he can see is bits of parchment peeping out of the top.

'Where to, my lord?' he asks cautiously. Sir Richard's skinny face is even sterner than usual. The man starts to row as soon as Scrope says, 'Kennington.'

Peter de la Mare is packing – or preparing to pack. He's looking at the changes of linen, and his two spare tunics and hosen, and his riding cloak, and the boots he's had cleaned of London mud, and the collection of notes he's amassed, all lined up neatly on the chest in his austere room at the top of Kennington Palace, and imagining them in a bag, on the back of his esquire's horse – and wondering how he can phrase a request to spend a short time at home, on his estates, if he requests leave from his task of the Princess. It will look like giving up, he knows.

He restrains a sigh. It will feel like giving up.

But then the one reliable thing he's learned in all his trips here, in all his fruitless journeyings and wasted days, is that he doesn't know enough about these London people to recognise the ways in which they cheat.

He doesn't like to admit it, even to himself. But it will be giving up, if he goes.

He's so bowed down, so weary with self-reproach, that he hardly turns his head when his esquire knocks at the door. 'I'm working,' he says. God won't be able to detect one more small lie in this polluted air.

'A visitor, sir,' the young voice says back.

Peter de la Mare doesn't remember, for a moment, where he's met this man, younger than him, but with a frame as lean as his, a face as tired.

'Scrope,' the man reminds him briefly, shifting the weight of the leather bag he's carrying.

'Of course,' Sir Peter says, with formality. 'My lord treasurer.'

He's rising from his formal bow when he realises Scrope is shaking his head.

'Not any more,' the younger man says. 'I've just been dismissed.'

A quiet fire kindles inside Sir Peter. 'I'm sorry to hear that,' he murmurs with more animation. He pulls out two stools from under the table. 'Well, sit down, sit down.' He sits down himself, and gestures at Scrope, who follows suit. A terrible impatience is dawning in him. But Scrope's just looking back at him, as if he doesn't know how to go on. 'Now, sir, what brings you to me?' he prompts.

Scrope takes off his hat; rumples his pepper-and-salt hair with skinny fingers. 'I thought we should talk,' he says baldly. 'And I had to come now. Before I leave, you see. I'm to return north, at first light, to my lands. Bolton. I'm to be escorted to the Great North Road by my lord Latimer's men. As a courtesy. So he says.' He smiles mirthlessly. 'Though one could plausibly think that he just wants to make sure I leave Westminster without talking to a soul,' he adds. There's bitterness in his voice. 'That's what he wants, you see. That must

257

be the real reason I'm out – I'm sure of it – because he's worried. I know every detail of every entry in the accounts, you see. And he doesn't want anyone here who knows what I know. Anyone who might tell.'

There's nothing in that for Sir Peter to comment on. He can only give quiet thanks that the man's come straight to him like this, straight away, before Latimer's had the wit even to assemble his guard of honour. As to why Latimer wouldn't have been more thorough about getting Scrope out of town more efficiently, Sir Peter can only surmise that the man must have got smug and soft from all these years of easy living. And perhaps he never expected his underling to take such prompt action. Sir Peter asks, 'What exactly happened?' He knows better than to say more.

'Lord Latimer didn't say. Just that the King had appointed Sir Robert Ashton in my place.' Scrope's forehead wrinkles. 'So he said.'

'But you don't believe it was the King's idea,' Sir Peter probes. 'You think it was Lord Latimer who wanted to be rid of you. So – why?'

Scrope puts big clean hands with big knuckles on the table. This is hard for him. 'Well,' he says. Then he stops, and shakes his head, and takes a big breath. 'I imagine because of you, sir, coming around and asking your questions.' As if to excuse himself for this boldness, he hunches his back; he's not a man to try and tower over whoever he's talking to, or dominate a conversation. 'Or else because the letters are to go out this week, summoning a parliament. It makes no difference. They're cleaning up.'

Sir Peter's eyebrows rise. 'Parliament!' he can't help exclaiming.

'April,' Scrope replies. A man of few words.

Next month, Sir Peter thinks, and his heart speeds up. But that isn't what's most important now. He must concentrate. 'Cleaning up,' he says, returning to the matter in hand. 'What do you mean?'

Scrope doesn't answer directly. Or perhaps he does, and Peter de la Mare just doesn't understand. He says, 'I'm not supposed to be here. But I thought you might like to see some of the detail of how my department has been run. I've been making copies of the household accounts I've prepared for the past two years – before they were corrected by my master for the fair copy that's gone on record. That's the record you've seen, sir. But my accounts are different. Parts get . . . struck out. Often. I thought you might be interested to make the comparison.'

'Aha,' says Peter de la Mare. He can hardly believe his luck. This is the missing piece in the puzzle. This is what he's been looking for all these months. This man, who doesn't look a bad sort, now he comes to think of it, who has conscience in the rumples of his brow, must have been uneasy with the way things were for a long time to have been keeping copies that differ from the recorded version of the truth, and to have them at hand, ready to bring him as soon as Latimer dismissed him. Scrope must have felt slighted that his careful accounting was changed; maybe, at first, purely from professional pride; later, with the dawning awareness that something must be gravely amiss within the government for his master to make those repeated changes. Even if Sir Peter doesn't understand everything yet about why, he sees the calculation that has brought this shy, correct man here. Wounded pride, of course; but also, the possibility of a future in some new government, if Latimer goes. So there must be some discrepancy in the two versions of these accounts – Scrope's raw ones, and Latimer's finished ones – that could topple Latimer.

He holds out his hand for the bag of documents. He puts a warm hand on Scrope's shoulder. His heart is racing. This man is volunteering to teach him the language of Londoners cheating. In time for Parliament. He can't believe his luck.

He even cracks a smile. To think he was about to try and get away.

But he shouldn't crow too soon. Humbly, he adds, 'I'm no expert, of course.' And: 'Perhaps you'll talk me through the changes?'

SEVENTEEN

Alice goes back to Edward, at Havering, and sits out the wintry last days of March. At least, with the King at her side, she feels safe, for now.

The letters of summons are going out across the shires. The Commons and Lords will soon be making their way to Westminster. Parliament will begin in a month. By then it will be late April. And Alice will be prepared: her affairs tidied up, her business papers transparent. There'll be spring, and hope, in the air.

She mustn't rush around, meanwhile, losing her nerve, doing things differently from usual, looking guilty. Chaucer has said she must just sit tight.

No one has ever tried to protect her as Chaucer is doing now, even though he disapproves of what she's done. Knowledge of his support sustains her; keeps her panic at bay. She doesn't want more any more – more houses, more money – because, as it is, she sees, her cup overflows. She's at the top of Fortune's wheel, and all she wants to do now is to stay there. If she can only do as he says, and wipe out as many traces as she can of her most recent manoeuvres, perhaps they will go unnoticed . . . and perhaps then she can go on living just as she is, and seeing him sometimes. In her present anxiety, that seems more than enough.

So she's quietly getting it all worked out. She's written to her land agents to tell them which leases to sell, which paperwork to clarify, and which to destroy; she'll meet them next month to make sure they've carried out her orders right.

She'll wait here at Havering till the Duke is back and Edward goes to Westminster to hear his son's account of this year of inconclusive peace talks. Then she'll slip off to Gaines to re-assure herself that, failing all else, that escape route's still open; and see her children. It was a good idea of Chaucer's, that: getting Edward to knight Johnny; giving herself a route back to court, as a mother if not in her own right, whatever happens next. But doubts have surfaced in Alice's mind since that comforting talk with Chaucer. What will have Johnny and the girls become, running wild out there in Aunty's care? Chaucer can't know how little she's . . . Though she'd like to bring Johnny back with her, if he . . . And Edward's so far gone now that she might never even have to explain who the child is; she could probably sweet-talk Edward into knighting a young gentleman without his ever asking. But she needs to check. See for herself if Johnny will pass muster as a young gentleman.

Edward will never notice her absence. He'll be looking forward too much to the biggest moment of his own year: St George's Day, on 23 April, after Council, just before Parliament, when he'll be off leading the other doddery old men of the court, the ageing knights and grey-haired heroes of France, and his son the Duke, and even perhaps his skeletal dying eldest son, to Windsor to play at being parfit gentil Knights of the Round Table. They'll sit at the giant round table, letting their grey beards trail in the wine, and talk in cracked voices about all their vanished glories.

So, for now, Alice has nothing to do but to look after her old companion. She baths Edward and talks to him, but he's not really with her very often any more. It's hard not to feel impatient with him. He dribbles food down his front. Of course he does. He's lost all his teeth. And he spends most days in bed, not because of any particular illness but just because he lacks the energy to get up. Once, he catches her eye with a little of his old vigour, and says, 'It's not that I don't think of drinking and fucking any more,' but by the time she's laughed at that old joke, and patted his hand, she can see he's forgotten.

Experimentally, she says, '*Cher ami*, will you knight my Johnny soon?' He nods, vacantly.

'Johnny,' he says. He doesn't say, 'Who?' It's assent, of a sort; but Alice doesn't feel reassured.

Fear spreads. Once you've let it in, it gets everywhere. Like love, perhaps.

For the first time, Alice finds she's leery of travelling alone. She takes an escort of palace servants because she'll have to leave the London road for the last few miles of her journey, and you can't trust the woods, these days. The woods are dripping, rustling refuges for violent companies of men and archers back from the wars, out from their tied fields, shifting and making shift, living wild. No money to clear them out, and no one with the will to, either. People are quoting the Bishop of Rochester's latest thundering sermon: England, inundated by homicides, where men are swift to the shedding of blood. Nowhere is safe.

But she leaves the servants at the wayside inn at Upminster, a mile away from Gaines, because, even though the innkeeper says there are murderous footpads everywhere round here, she can't trust palace people either. Servants talk.

'Wait for me here,' she says, more bravely than she feels. 'I'll be back in two days.'

And she walks her horse on, slowly, through the silent drizzle, thankful for the wet that muffles the sound of hooves. Every crack and rustle in the undergrowth sets her heart racing. Once she thinks she hears the snorting of another horse. She freezes. She waits. Nothing. There is no birdsong, either, though she hears a very occasional whir of flight. The woods still have the deadness of winter. Only the stream is full and racing. Yet, as the trees begin to thin out, she sees there are after all a few buds fattening and straining on the twigs slapping at her arms.

There will be spring. She'll just sit tight, as Chaucer said. She'll be all right.

She can't believe the exquisite sweetness of getting out of the woods; or the pearly afternoon light still in the sky as she lets herself through the gate and plods on up the track through the field.

Her breath comes more gently. Joy fills her at this flat, barren vista.

She thought, once, that she'd plant a great avenue of shade trees along the sides of this track, and that they would lead visitors to a warm, commodious, beautiful manor house, surrounded by gardens of waving roses and gillyflowers, with bees in the rosemary and lavender and doves fluttering through the orchards.

Tumbledown though it is, in reality, with those piles of timbers and broken-down carts and boxes and old cracked tiles that Aunty can never bear to throw out ('You never know, they might come in handy, love'), the windswept house ahead represents safety. Love. Home. And, today, that makes it beautiful enough.

Until, over there at the other end of the great field, she spots two young girls skipping. Even from here, she can see they're in rags, like peasant children. Their legs are muddy. Their rope's muddy. Even from here, she can see they're hers.

Her heart leaps with a painful, toxic rush of feelings.

Last time she came, she sent word to Aunty Alison beforehand. And the place was all scrubbed up, the priest in attendance, the children nicely turned out, if silent and careful in front of the stranger they knew to be their mother.

They weren't bare-legged and muddy when they knew she was coming.

But perhaps this is what everything's usually like when she's not around, she thinks with a rush of shame and understanding. Deep down, she realises, she's always known it must be – because how would old Alison know any different?

She stops and looks. Her joy in what she sees is fading as fast as the light.

A tall scarecrow of a figure comes out of the house up ahead and moves through the complicated gloom of the courtyard to stand, silhouetted against the sky, staring out across

263

the eastern field. Then Alice hears Aunty's remote voice hollering, off towards something – someone – approaching her from over that way: 'It's late – what kept you?' and 'Whatcha get?'

The little girls begin to chirrup in thin, excited voices. Aunty's got her back turned to them, but they're excited too at whoever's coming home. Alice sees them pick up their rope and run, heels flashing, rat's-tail hair flying, to the farmhouse.

Alice carries on plodding quietly forward on her tired horse, watching them all watch the eastern field.

She's quite close before she sees who it is they're waiting outside for.

There's a boy's head, bobbing along in the bare furrow of a turned strip of field. Dark hair, brown jerkin, brown soil, but she makes out a pale face and white hands. She sees Johnny's thin little legs working hard, lifting up high at each step, to avoid getting stuck in the claggy soil. That must be making him tired, walking like that. With the painful tenderness of recognition, she thinks: How tall he's got.

Behind him, a man. Taller than Johnny, a bit taller than Alice too, maybe, but not tall as men go; and stocky, with a big mess of hair. He's got a bag on his shoulder. He's got a big stick in his hand.

'Not bad for an afternoon's work!' she hears the distant, excited answering cry, as his head goes back. 'Five nobles!'

Five nobles, Alice thinks. That's nearly two pounds. You don't get that kind of money for honest farm work.

'Who from?' Aunty's just yelled back at him with gusto when, hearing the cautious clip-clop of a horse approaching from an entirely different direction, she shuts up, smartish, and turns towards Alice.

'Alice,' Aunty says. Her face goes still, her body too. Her voice is without emotion. She's not giving anything away. She's obviously not planning to, either. There's a sullenness in the set of her shoulders that says: Don't even bother asking awkward questions.

The little girls have heard the old woman speak and caught on too. When they see where Aunty's looking, they both turn and stare at Alice, as expressionlessly as Aunty, but more uncertainly, as if they don't know how to greet this visitor.

At the same time, Alice hears the man-voice calling his reply from not so far away in the squelchy field any more: 'A posse of fat priests!'

A moment later, there's a high boy-laugh, too: 'Scared stiff, they were! Shittin' themselves!'

Alice holds Aunty's gaze a moment longer, making clear that she's heard everything, and understood everything.

Then she dismounts, and leads the horse to the trough, and lets it drink, and loosens its saddle, and ties up the reins.

Her hands are shaking. She closes her eyes.

Only when she's splashed freezing water on her own face, and composed herself a little, and heard the panting breath and steady tread of man and boy coming right up, almost to the edge of the yard, is she able to open her mouth.

Her voice is still trembling as she says, 'Aunty. Children.' And as she says, 'Wat.'

They're silent enough as they troop into the kitchens. Alice hopes it's shame that's got their tongues, because she's ashamed, too, now she's seeing them through other eyes, Chaucer's maybe, and seeing how far she's let things slide. But once they're inside, where there's a pot on the fire and chicken in the stew, they quickly thaw out in the golden glow, in the bustle of getting the boots and sodden outer layers off, and the silence turns into barely suppressed pleasure and the beginning of talk. They're not ashamed at all, Alice sees; they were just shocked, for a moment, to be caught. But now they've decided it's all right; because Alice is one of them. 'Here, let me do that, your fingers are frozen,' Aunty tells Johnny, and he turns willingly, with a bit of a grin, even, to let her strip off his jerkin. Jane and Joan are ladling out stew and putting steaming bowls on the table. Wat's back from the larder with cups and a jug of ale. They know they shouldn't be, but they're all still pleased with their afternoon's work. There's a cheery light in every pair of eyes.

Alice shakes her head. She hasn't the strength to walk

straight in and tell them it's all wrong. So she just sits tight and lets the children's stories start coming out, which they soon do, in those high, excited little voices. She hears, first, that Wat's taken Johnny out robbing on the roads three or four times already. He's nearly twelve. High time, Wat says. There's a proud light in the boy's blue eyes when Wat tousles his hair and says proudly, 'Got ourselves a good little fighter here.' Then she hears that Aunty's taught Joan and Jane to climb through windows, and wriggle under cracks in doors, and pick pockets, and set snares for hares, just as she taught Alice, long ago.

Aunty's voice cracks with pride as, forgetting her watchfulness earlier, she says, 'Yeah, they're as good as you ever were, by now, dear. Could send them out any day to earn themselves a living, if they had to.'

Alice asks: But where's the priest who was supposed to be teaching the children their letters and Latin?

'Oh, gone, dear,' Aunty replies blithely. 'No loss, either. We couldn't be doing with him. A right old woman, he was. Always nagging us to give everything we grew to the Bishop and spend our Sundays on our knees. Well, I said to him, we got no time for that. Too busy. And if we give you all our turnips, what'll we eat ourselves? So he went.'

Alice says weakly, 'But, Aunty . . .'

But Aunty's never had any time for priests. Alice has always known that, too. So she has no real right to be shocked now.

'There's a lovely young man comes to the village sometimes, dear. Much better,' Aunty confides. 'They lock him up sometimes, but he always gets out. Pops up in the market place. Gets a good crowd, he does. Preaches a lovely sermon.'

It's little Joan who picks up Aunty's story. In a deep imitation-man voice, the ten-year-old intones: 'My good friends, things cannot go well in England, nor ever will, until everything shall be in common.' Wat and Aunty start to laugh and clap their big raw hands against their thighs.

It would be enough to make anyone howl with laughter, if anyone weren't a mother who'd somehow managed to convince herself that her children were turning into little ladies and gentlemen out here in the countryside, and not the budding Lollards and thieves she now sees stuffing themselves with stew.

Alice keeps quiet. She's thinking. Thinking wearily of the unbridgeable gap between here and Aldgate; of the impossibility of explaining to Chaucer, or anyone else she knows in that other life in the centre, how things are here. Not knowing, herself, which of her own selves to be, because a part of her would like to be laughing along with the rest of them, not giving a damn about anything outside these walls. She's spent all these years working so hard at getting rich, but how rich does she need to be, really? And what for? She's flown so high, yet she'll never be truly respectable, however far she climbs. At least, she'll never, despite that dizzying ascent she's already made, have the grand worldly position that truly noble blood brings. And suddenly she's weary of the fear and anxiety that her strivings have brought her along with the wealth. Wouldn't she be happier just stopping trying, and joining in with her family's roars instead, and embracing their view of things?

No one notices her silence. There are tears of mirth coming into everyone else's eyes as Alice's child goes on, grinning and enjoying the attention she clearly knows she'll get, because this is clearly something she often does: '. . . when there shall be neither vassal nor lord and all distinctions levelled . . . when lords shall be no more masters than ourselves.'

You can't send Johnny out with Wat, she whispers to Aunty, in the darkness, inside the bedcurtains, when she thinks the children, and Wat, in the other two beds, are asleep, when the whole world, outside, has gone that velvet quiet of a country night. What were you thinking? Robbing priests, indeed.

Aunty knows that, at least, really. She just doesn't want to admit it.

You never even said you had Wat living here, Alice goes on. He's got to go. Get rid of him.

Aunty wriggles, rebelliously, at her side.

Well, I will then, Alice hisses. First thing tomorrow. And I'm sending another priest down here, too, for the schooling. So don't you scare that one off.

Wat knows, really, too. She catches him in the morning, first thing, shakes him up from his bed and takes him out into the yard, bundled up in any old clothes that came to hand in a hurry, to talk. 'Ow, all right, Allie,' he mumbles, grinning sheepishly as she tweaks his shoulder and nudges him along, 'only stop that pinching, do, I'm coming.' He'd like to make her laugh, and relent. But even as he tries to jolly her along, he's avoiding her eye, because of course he's ashamed to have been caught here, taking advantage of her hospitality on the sly.

The awful thing is, she almost does laugh. It's not that she can't see the funny side herself, at least while she's out here. She just can't afford to.

So she hardens her heart and takes Wat off to the squeaking gate, and they both lean on it, and look out at the big sky, while she says, 'Right, you. A joke's a joke, but you've got to move on.'

Wat just nods. He didn't really think she'd let him off, teaching her kid to be a highwayman. He's already thought out what he'll do next. He says, straight away, 'Yeah . . . I know . . . I'll go to Johnny.'

'What, *our* Johnny?' Alice says, caught out of breath again. She knows Wat doesn't mean her son this time. He means the smallest of Aunty's kids, Johnny with the red freckly nose and the perpetual sniffs. Johnny with the stag beetle collection in his purse, who could turn cartwheels. Johnny who grew up and went for a carpenter on the road. The Johnny Wat told her once he'd found again, grown up. With a bit of land, and a family, in Kent. Grown dull and respectable.

'Yeah. He's settled down. In Dartford. Married, children, working, everything. I told you, didn't I? He'll put me up for a bit, help me find my feet.'

Doubtfully, Alice says, 'What, you, farming with Johnny? You'd be better off overseas.' She's thinking: *I'd* be better off if you were safely back overseas. Didn't I do my best to get Richard Lyons to send you back over the water? But Wat's not interested in foreign parts any more.

'Don't fancy it. Plenty to be getting on with here. And Kent's a good place. Down by the sea. Busy. Plenty on the roads.' So you won't be farming, then, Alice thinks; but it's not for her to criticise. She hasn't helped his career, so why turn her nose up if he makes his crust from the roads? 'Anyway,' he adds truculently, 'I've got a reason to stay.' She must have looked blank. 'Lyons,' he explains. 'I don't take kindly to being humiliated. And he fired me. Made a fool of me in front of my men. I want my own back. I'm biding my time, mind. But one of these days I'll get him. And I can't do that from overseas.'

She laughs a bit at that. 'No chance,' she says. 'Not with Richard Lyons.' Still, there's admiration in the kiss she gives him. He's right. Lyons, back then, took no notice of her idea to set Wat up with money to go back abroad. So no wonder Wat feels resentful that the man just discarded him when Wat could be of no more use to him in England. He's got spirit, Wat. Always had.

He's gone within the hour. 'Well, 'bye,' is all he says. They watch him stride off towards the river with his bag on his shoulder. Presumably the five nobles are in there with his clothes, as no one has mentioned them again. The house seems quiet without him. Aunty clanks reproachfully around the kitchen. The children are quiet too. Johnny disappears. The girls sit by the fire, playing pick-up sticks, muttering something that Alice hopes isn't betting talk. No one meets Alice's eye.

Alice sits at the table, feeling unpopular. Making alternative plans. Because she can't bring Johnny with her to London now. Not the way these children have got.

But the idea of letting go of any of the solutions Chaucer's thought of brings back the panic. So she needs to make compromises; make it all still seem possible.

She's thinking she'll send her old friar down here for a couple of months. She'll tell him not to bother Aunty with priest-talk: no lectures about Mass, or tithes. Then perhaps

Aunty will return the favour and leave him in peace too. And Friar John will school the kids a bit. Maybe before the end of Parliament he'll have undone the damage. Taught them some manners. Bring Johnny back with him, possibly. She can think about trying to get him his knighthood then.

She stays the night. She leaves the next morning. Those servants waiting at Upminster will be fretting, at the Boar.

But first she gets the children to sit up in their bed and gathers them all awkwardly into her arms for an experimental embrace. This might be what Chaucer might imagine her doing, she thinks. They're surprised, though not unwilling. They melt sleepily against her. Just for a moment, touching their hot animal little bodies, she lets herself be lost in might-have-beens. But she stops herself getting emotional. What good would that do?

Instead, she pats them, and gets up again, and says, briskly, 'I'll be sending another priest along. You make sure you do your studies with him, mind. And don't let Aunty bully him into going this time, do you hear?' The eyes that look back at her are wild eyes – the same wild watchful eyes she and Wat and Johnny and the others must have had, years ago – and the heads that nod 'yes' have other ideas in them. They look like her, true. Alice loves the way she recognises her own fingers and toes and nose and sharp eyes on their grubby bodies; but at the same time, she thinks wearily, they're strangers. They're not the children she should have raised, knowing what she knows now, having become who she is now; they're just another brood of Aunty's kids. The thought of changing them – turning them into clean, groomed, well-schooled playmates for Chaucer's children, say, lapping up their Latin and a dab hand with a sword – seems impossible in that discouraged moment. She's failed them, she thinks. She can only hope there's still time for the errors of the past to be reversed.

EIGHTEEN

They come face to face in the King's antechamber, Alice and the Duke.

Alice has dressed for the occasion of coming accidentally across the Duke again (dark, modest clothes; no jewels). She's picked her moment: a quiet early afternoon, after Council's over and done with, when he's just coming in to see his father out of filial devotion and has nothing in particular on his mind. To him, meeting her is happenstance. But when she sees the tension in his body, she realises, all the same, that he's thought about this moment too.

They approach each other watchfully.

In the Duke's eyes: fear that she'll know what his father has said about him and how he's handled the peace talks, at times when the old man's been more lucid than he is now – and that it won't be approving.

In Alice's eyes: nervousness that he'll have found out she's been stealing. And that he won't be happy.

So they're both scared, and both trying to pretend they're not. Brazening it out. As she steps closer, Alice sees that the Duke looks older, with grey dusting his dark hair. Sadder, though of course he'd be sad. Never mind the French, and the Parliament. He's just buried the baby son his wife gave birth to at Ghent, before the peace talks. So they say.

You don't grieve publicly for a child so young. Condolences would be wasted.

271

But Alice puts her hands in his, as she rises from her swoop of a bow, trying to convey mute comfort. He's become so bleak, so bloodless, so lean. The skin on his hands is papery. With a flash of compassion she hasn't expected to feel, she murmurs, 'How glad I am, we are, to see you back . . . After all those months of tireless work . . . The whole of England is grateful . . . We've missed you . . . I know my lord the King has missed you.'

She wishes she'd done better by him. The way he looks wrings her heart. He's a good man, put upon by Fate. Still, it's best not to dwell on that now. A few gracious words are enough, for the moment. Just sit tight. She's comforted by the brief, grateful look the Duke bestows on her, in return.

She'd like to say she saw only warm friendship in his face, of course. That's not exactly true. There are lines of bitterness and disappointment drawn all over it.

Not for her, though. And that's what counts.

She gestures him towards Edward's bedchamber. 'He's awake.' She indicates, with a brave, sad expression, that the King is not going to be capable of much in the way of talk. 'If you want to go in . . .'

The Duke is relieved that Alice Perrers is sidling up to him like this, with her round little face so eager and full of intelligent understanding, her hands so warm.

He breathes more easily. He can see loyalty, and the wish to please, shining in her eyes. He sees now that *she* won't have been criticising his every step at Bruges, from his negotiating style to his hospitality bills.

He's had enough of that, from the savaging he got at Council last week to his trip to the City this morning to meet the fat, insolent new Mayor, Warde the grocer. His coats of arms were hung along Chepe beforehand in what was supposed to be a mark of respect. But by the time he rode by they'd all been turned upside down: the mark of a traitor. He could see idlers by the roadside smirking all over their downturned faces at their practical joke. The dishonour of it made his flesh creep and his hackles rise . . . the malice. But when he strode in and furiously told Warde to have someone flogged for it, the Mayor only smirked too, until his flesh wobbled, and said, far too indulgently, and with an edge of malice of his own, a hint of criticism, 'Dear me, some wag . . . some scallywag . . . of course there's been bad feeling about the truce, but this is disrespect . . . I'll look into it.'

It took the Duke's breath away. It wasn't for Warde-the-grocer to comment on his truce, and as for the beggars of Chepe . . . Who do these City nobodies think they are? That's the trouble with merchants. No one born without blue blood in their veins has any conception of what a fighting nobleman has to do, and risk, to keep them safe in their counting-houses. They've no idea of honour, any more than a rat in a granary does. Yet they've got so puffed up with pride, just because my lord father has allowed them to contribute money to the war, that they've taken to thinking they can dictate to a prince of England how to conduct relations with England's enemy.

At least Perrers knows her place, the Duke's thinking approvingly as he steps through the curtains and approaches his father's bed. She's enjoyed her clothes and her jewels and her parties in the past, true; she interests herself in politics. She's quietly stacked up money, too, he knows. (He's heard them blame her money-making for half the country's woes, in the City, since he's got back, though he's ignored all that; he's actually inclined to think the better of anyone whom those thieving granary rats criticise . . . which he suspects that they're only doing to cover their own trails of stolen grain anyway.) What he enjoys about his father's mistress is that, gifted though she obviously is at handling men and money, in all *his* dealings with her, she's never presumed to know better than him, never criticised, and never carped at his princely choices or underestimated the princely burden he carries on his shoulders. She's not the type to get ideas above her station. He likes it, too, that she's gone on sitting here quietly nursing my lord through his twilight years. A change from the gaiety of before. Sad sort of life. Other women might have married, or retired from court. He values loyalty.

His father is propped up on a mound of pillows. The sour

smell of old age hangs in the air. Duke John leans down, kisses his father's familiar forehead, and looks into the beloved eyes. He's expecting a stranger's eyes: no recognition. But they light up. For a moment, the Duke thrills at that pleasure. 'Edward,' the King says, with weak joy. 'My dearest boy.'

Gently, the Duke shakes his head. 'John,' he says with sinking heart, sitting down on the bed, taking his father's hands. 'I'm John.' Hoping the excitement won't go out of those pale old eyes. Knowing it will.

Once John has gone in to his father, Alice stands quiet for a moment, letting the waves of relief pour through her as she remembers how trustingly Duke John looked at her.

He's not angry, after all. She can rely on him. He's still her best hope for the future.

Then she turns her attention to the Duke's entourage. She shows the men the wine and cakes prepared for while they wait, whisking off the muslins that have kept the baked goods fresh, letting the smell of them rise invitingly into the air. Out of sheer relief, or perhaps just to remind herself that she can, she smiles invitingly up at the steward John's brought – the same awkward Leicester gentleman she once wheedled information about Katherine Swynford's children out of, she sees – and pats the stool beside hers as she sinks back down and takes up her needlework.

The man sits down with her, looking bashful but flattered to be singled out. John de Stafford, she remembers he's called. Dark, big, perhaps shy behind his muscle. She can see he's got a soft spot for her, or is ready to have.

'Now, Monsieur de Stafford,' she begins, and puts down her needlework again, and serves him wine and cake herself, with a rush of hospitable housewife talk about the saffron and fruit in the creamy buns, as if she'd baked them with her own hands. He chomps appreciatively as she nods at the goblet to make him drink up. 'And how have you been up in Leicester, and how is my lady Swynford?' she twinkles at him, reminding him of the private moment they shared at Christmas. He shakes a rueful head back. She can see at once he still doesn't like La Swynford. It took only those few words to make them fellow-conspirators, ready to whisper pleasurably together, even flirt a little, maybe, because, after all, life's not all fear and fretting.

So she's surprised when, after a moment of blushing and nodding and agreeing with everything she's saying, he leans right over to her and mutters in her ear, worriedly, without a trace of the bashful flirtatiousness she's just seen on his face, 'Madame Perrers, may I tell you what I heard with my master in the City this morning?'

'Of course . . .?' she breathes back, looking encouragingly into his eyes.

As the story comes hesitantly out – he feels uncomfortable repeating other people's conversations, she sees, but he does, suddenly, terribly want her to know – she feels so overwhelmed, so close to shaky, that she's glad she's seated.

For what John de Stafford has to say is this. Warde, the Mayor, made it clear this morning during his meeting with the Duke that he's getting a City plot going against Alice Perrers. Apparently the man's managed to get the London merchants to forget their usual squabbles with each other over money and join forces in a financial investigation. On the face of it, it sounds like just the usual London viciousness towards foreigners – the grocer said they were planning to bring a legal case at the Guildhall against the Italians who'd been benefiting from getting part of their loans repaid. For usury, he said (as if they weren't all usurers themselves). But Warde was half mad with excitement – far too excited for an everyday bit of Italian-bashing. Rubbing his hands, gleeful looks: 'I can tell you right now, my lord, that it's not going to end well for anyone who was involved in setting up the debt swaps, either.' When the Duke asked, 'And who do you mean by *that*, Master Warde?' Warde wriggled with pride. 'Well, the trail leads to Richard Lyons, for one thing . . .' he said happily, as if he really thought the Duke would care, one way or another, whether the money-grubbers of London turned on a money-grubber from Flanders. Then he fixed Duke John with a still more significant gaze: 'It may even lead to court, and formal punishment. For him. And for others too.' The Duke knows, of course, that Alice Perrers thought up that debt exchange; he's been grateful to her for the past year for her clever idea. His household knows, too. So he asked, 'You're not suggesting . . .' and: '. . . Madame Perrers?' There was no answer direct, just more noddings and excited wrigglings. And John de Stafford can't swear to it, but he thinks that, for a moment, the City man even had the unspeakable temerity to wink.

'They want to destroy you,' he says sadly, shaking his head. 'They really do. You should watch your back.'

Alice shakes her head too. The shock's passing, and with it the cold dread. After all, she's known for so long there's something brewing. Some attack, some ambush. This confirmation is – almost – a relief.

'But why?' she wonders aloud, allowing herself to sound helpless. She wants a little comfort from this man with strong shoulders; a little reassurance.

John de Stafford, who's better at accounts books than he is at the human heart, is naive enough to think Alice might genuinely not know the answer to her rhetorical question. 'Because you're so powerful,' he says earnestly. 'And because you've made your own power, and your own money. They don't like someone beating them at their own game. Especially a woman.' He's embarrassed himself now. Hastily, he adds, sketching a little bow, 'Especially a beautiful woman.'

Slowly, she nods. It's the comfort she wanted.

Yet how strange it is, she's thinking as she gives the anxious man at her side a pitiful wounded-lapdog look. She still so often thinks of herself as small, an ant or mouse or shadow, some unnoticed creature shifting crumbs no one sees or needs off to its hole. It was only the other day, at Gaines, watching her family laughing at things she can't find funny any more, that she got a first real inkling of how far she's moved from her early days of insignificance. She's part of a bigger landscape now, and a bigger beast in it. It's hard to grasp, even for her, how close to power she is, and should continue to be – look at her just now, murmuring together with the King's son, who may become the next ruler of the land, who eats out of her hand . . . It's difficult to realise how large she seems to loom, especially since she's never been one for titles and visible attempts at grandeur. Yet there it is. People notice her. Perhaps they've been noticing her more than she realises for years. And oh, what an irritant she must be to all those who'd like the world to have stayed the way it used to be, with people in their proper places. Or those who'd like to have done what she's done, but don't know how.

After all, no one, and certainly no woman, has ever climbed as high as she has, from a starting place so low (not that any of them know quite how low she started). She's got more energy than any of them. She's a winner: queen of the climbers, and a queen from the humblest of the people, too.

So perhaps she can understand why Walworth's merchants, no strangers to self-enrichment themselves, would hate and envy her, just like the Princess, and half the court; why they'd all want to bring her down.

Suddenly feeling tough, invincible, almost, she dimples mischievously up at the worried John de Stafford. 'Well, I'm not going to let them beat me,' she says with utter calm, assurance. 'You're very kind, but you mustn't worry. They're not going to win.' She means it, she thinks as she picks up her embroidery again, and says, with composure, 'Now do tell me about the Duke's wonderful building project at Kenilworth . . .'

She's not going to let them bring her down, and stop her enjoying the fruits of her success.

She's not going to let them stop her children enjoying those fruits either, she thinks a moment later. That's what it's all been for, hasn't it?

The Duke doesn't stay long with his father. What would be the point?

He comes quietly back into the antechamber, soundlessly moving the curtains aside.

Alice Perrers has been busy in his absence. She's given his men refreshments, and they're standing around looking pleased and licking cake crumbs off their fingers. And there's a steaming bowl of food on a table, and a flagon of drink waiting for the King. She's sitting by it, head bowed dutifully over her sewing. Waiting, as a good royal servant should.

The sight of this modest virtue cheers him a little.

It also reminds him that loyalty obliges him, too. He'd meant to warn Madame Perrers about something earlier, but he'd been thinking mostly about how his father would be, and it slipped his mind.

Now it's back. Something Warde-the-grocer said in the City. A plot in the offing, against her and her friends. She should know. Forewarned is forearmed.

When she looks up, humbly, and her face softens into pleased excitement at his presence, he's ready to tell her.

'My lord,' she says, rising to her feet, putting aside her needlework, bowing her head. He clears his throat.

But before he can say a word, she's started talking herself. And there's something wheedling, beseeching, even, in the little smiles she's giving him as the words rush out. A favour, then. He knows that look. He composes himself, ready to nod, to listen, to understand, and, probably, to grant it. He owes her so much.

Self-preservation is urgently on Alice's mind, now she's talked to John de Stafford. When she sees the Duke come through the door, she finds herself – can't stop herself – separating him from his men, waiting till they're streaming off out of the room to wait in the corridor, so she can whisper in his ear, and ask him to intercede with Edward, and get Johnny knighted with the next crop of boys who are honoured. By that time, Johnny will be . . . better. And the Duke is so efficient at getting granted the favours that the King promises, but forgets. Always was.

Even before she starts, she's expecting his brow to shadow for a moment. She's expecting the fretful question, 'But whose son . . .?' But she's thought it all out in these last few heady minutes. He won't remember what she was before Edward. And he won't want detail. She knows that. That's the beauty of asking him. So . . .

'Oh, long ago,' she replies with vague charm. 'My first husband. Long before . . .'

She's not expecting this thunderous look deepening and darkening on his face.

There's blood pounding through the Duke's head.

Knighthood is glory, he's thinking, not just grace in the saddle and at swordplay, but courage enough to give your life to defend what you hold dear. A noble reward, for noble men. A badge of honour.

He'd never ennoble a merchant. Even Chaucer, whom he admires, but knows to be a fool on a battlefield. Not Chaucer's fault, that; just his merchant blood.

Knighthood's not for the likes of these people; for Madame Perrers' brood. He thought she knew her place. But she's over-reached herself; she's as grasping as the rest of them, after all. Do these people think they can buy or steal *everything*?

Alice falters. Her eyes drop. His are so angry. She doesn't understand why.

'Madame Perrers,' the Duke says, and his voice is as steely as his gaze. 'Knighthood is a mark of nobility.'

She tries not to cringe or look crestfallen. She stares at the floor. She's given offence. Her short-lived sunny relief is replaced, instantly, by quiet dread.

So much for her power and visibility. All that's not hers, not really, is it? It's this man's, to whom she's linking her future, or hopes she is. She's just a shadow dancing behind him, not a person of the stature to bask in the light of power herself. One frown from this man, and she's back to being a crumb on the floor.

She squeezes anxious hands together till the knuckles go white and she can feel half-moons of fingernail burn into the backs of fingers.

He's being pompous, of course. She can think of half a dozen rich merchants who've retired to country estates with knighthoods; whose sons will be noble. No harm in that. Why not her, and her son?

She didn't mean anything bad. She didn't think . . . Surely he can see that?

But he's still staring accusingly at her, as if her words were so outrageous that they've robbed him of the power of speech.

She swallows, and then nods. Best agree. Best drop it, quick. 'I understand,' she mutters appeasingly, thinking: What can I say next, to make him forget I asked?

But he's not staying for more. He's off towards the door.

There's a game children play, cutting away flour from a heap, slice by careful slice, trying not to let the coin perched at the top of the flour fall. The loser is the one whose hands start to shake, and whose cut finally topples the coin. Alice feels she's playing that game now. She sees the thin column of flour wavering after an injudicious cut, with the coin wobbling precariously at the top. She's made a few bad plays recently.

'You made a good Lady of the Sun,' he adds bitingly over his shoulder. 'But leave it at that.'

Alice shuts her eyes. As the door shuts, she's trying to visualise that coin. It's still up there, she tells herself. It hasn't fallen yet.

NINETEEN

They're waiting for him. They're all at the Customs House, perched on the sides of the big table, companionably chatting, when Chaucer walks in.

Brembre has that muscular sun-kissed bronzed look, Philpot is bald and smooth, and Walworth, relaxed now he's no longer having to perform the daily duties of Mayor, seems taller and paler and more angelic than ever. Chaucer looks at these three, his father's friends, his own mentors, and wonders at the slight dislike in his heart.

Their eyes light up as he comes in. The big beaming smiles come out.

It makes him uncomfortable. He's spent an hour writing this morning, only remembering to rush over here when he saw how high the sun was in the sky. He knows what his father would have said about slacking, when his job is so responsible. He wishes now that he'd stopped to get his cheeks shaved, at least.

Walworth clears his throat. Chaucer sees he's got a roll open on the table.

'My dear Master Chaucer,' he says kindly, and his gold hair shimmers above pale eyes. 'We've been looking at your work. We wanted to talk to you about *this*.'

He puts a clean slim finger on the parchment. Peeping forward, Chaucer can see where it's fallen: on the name John Kent, one of the many caught trying to export wool without

281

paying customs. Kent has had the entire cargo, worth £71 4s. 6d., confiscated. It's in the warehouse now.

Chaucer isn't sure what he's done wrong, but he can't help it. The finger stabbing at the parchment is making him feel guilty. He feels sure they think he's done something wrong.

Anxiously he says, 'Master Walworth' – for they've settled on formality in the ways they address each other – 'we talked about this. You remember, don't you? You agreed that the cargo had to be impounded.'

Walworth looks carefully at him – the others do too – then they all begin to chuckle reassuringly.

'You misunderstand me, dear boy,' Walworth says. 'You did absolutely the right thing.'

There's a little pause. It's Walworth who breaks the silence. Still smiling, he says, 'As a matter of fact, dear boy, we were just saying how very *well* your appointment is turning out . . .'

Philpot chimes in: '. . . and how we've come to depend on you. Reliable and hard-working; quick to spot errors, like this one.'

They all nod, and twinkle. But it's Walworth who makes the offer.

'In fact,' he says merrily, 'we think it's time we offered you a reward for all your unremitting labour and diligence.'

The others nod again. Chaucer's hardly breathing.

'So we've decided. We're going to make over the value of this confiscated property to you,' Walworth finishes.

Chaucer can't believe it. Seventy-one pounds! It's more than seven times his year's pay – more than enough to pay Elizabeth's bride-price to the Church, if she does go to St Helen's, without having to dip into his savings. His heart expands in his chest until it feels he might burst.

'Thank you,' he stammers. 'Thank you.'

He senses, rightly, that there's more to come.

He wants to believe that this isn't a bribe. He doesn't think of himself as buyable. He once told Alice he'd never taken a bribe. He wants to believe they really are just thanking him for his exceptionally good work. Only he isn't sure it has been so exceptional.

So he thinks there will be more, because, if they are buying him, they'll have to explain why.

'You're a loyal man, Chaucer,' Walworth adds warmly, after giving him a moment for his piece of good fortune to sink in. 'Always have been. We didn't quite know what to expect when you came back from court, in all your glory . . .'

Chaucer translates in his head: 'As the protégé of Alice Perrers and the Duke.' Suddenly watchful, he stands a little straighter.

'But you've done us proud. Your father would be proud of you.'

For a moment, the mention of his father's pride brings grateful tears prickling into Chaucer's eyes. But then he realises they knew that would happen. And it makes him more watchful still. He smiles, a sentimental smile, to show how he appreciates the compliment. But inside, he's on his guard.

'You understand better than most that sometimes it pays to keep your head down and your mouth closed, and just get on with the job,' Walworth finishes. He leans closer, gazing hypnotically into Chaucer's eyes, as if willing him to nod along with Walworth's own beautiful head, which is already going up and down.

'Whatever else is going on outside,' Chaucer agrees tactfully. 'Yes indeed.'

'Now,' Brembre says briskly. 'There'll be a lot of commotion for the next few months, what with the Parliament and everything else. People's eyes wandering; work left undone; who knows what trickery being swept into corners.'

Is *that* it? They're bribing me to keep quiet during the Parliament? But why, when I wouldn't have anything to do with Parliament anyway? Chaucer's puzzled. He's heard the rumours. Everyone in town is suddenly talking about how the City aldermen are about to go after the Italians over the debt scandal – and, if they can, drag Lyons and Alice and their friends at court into admitting complicity, too. He can see that these three might easily want him to keep clear of Alice while that's going on. They know Alice is his benefactor. They wouldn't want Chaucer coming up with clever defences for her.

He could understand they'd try to buy him to keep his nose out of the aldermen's courtroom at Guildhall. But why Parliament?

'You want me to keep my head down and keep concentrating on my work,' he says, and he makes his voice extra docile. 'During the Parliament.' He needs to be sure it is actually the Parliament he's being told to keep his nose out of.

Walworth laughs cosily and claps him on the back. 'Yes indeed,' he replies, all bonhomie and charm. 'Though you must do as I say, not as I do, of course, because I'll be at Parliament myself, as you know. One of the two men for London. Forgetting my normal work. Sweeping things under the carpet. You'll have to keep an eye on *me*!'

The future parliamentary representative for London laughs. They all laugh. They all clap Chaucer on the back. They leave together.

After they've gone, and he's alone with the clerks, Chaucer sighs.

He knows they're out to get Alice. He just can't quite yet see how Walworth plans to drag the case to Parliament.

It pains him, the rank injustice of it. He knows (who better than he?) that Alice is, or has been, greedy, and venal, and out for herself. But it also seems clear to him that Alice is just a symptom of all the troubles England's gripped by, not the cause they're going to make her out to be. Greed is in the air. Who doesn't take a little, or a lot, if there's no one to say no? If it's so easy that saying no seems madness? He can't think of anyone in the land who hasn't, these last years . . . even he, now . . .

If only she'd take his advice and go away. Lie low in the country. But she won't. And perhaps it's already too late. Chaucer can sense that the hungry, eager look on Walworth's features doesn't bode well for her. He doesn't want her to be the sacrificial lamb, the offering of repentance for everyone else's gluttony and avarice. He's so . . . *fond*, he tells himself, cautiously . . . of her. But he's frightened, too. He can't help thinking: what if she goes down, and he's dragged with her? He's done nothing he can be reproached with; he's taken no bribes (not counting this gift he's just been made by Walworth) and covered up no truths, but what if he's weeded out of the City job she got him, and is then too tainted by association with her to get a place back at court?

He knows that, if he were a proper knight-errant, the most honourable thing to do, in his present circumstances, would be to graciously thank the merchants and turn down their money, and then defend his lady in whatever way he could against whatever charges were laid against her. But, even if he were brave enough to defend her, whatever could he do to ward off the enemies massing on every side?

Anyway, he can't. He's a merchant's son, among merchants, in a greedy world. He needs the money, for Lizzie. And who, in this greedy world, ever takes the chivalrous course? He says to himself, out loud, trying out the words, and the thought, for size: 'I've never been a particularly brave man; why draw attention to myself now?' Then: 'What's more, how she'd laugh at my naivety if I did.'

That evening Chaucer goes to Vintry Ward and knocks at the house of Sir Richard Stury, his old friend from the wars. It's been months. Too long.

By happy coincidence, Sir Richard is in London. He's delighted to see Chaucer. He flings a long arm over Chaucer's shoulder and guides him in for supper, knightly style.

Over the first pitcher of Rhenish wine ('Can't get Gascon for less than an arm and a leg these days,' Sir Richard apologises), the knight tries to interest Chaucer in the religious theorising he's gone in for recently – a passionate support for Lollardy. 'You should come and hear Wyclif preach one day,' he says, wild-eyed and fervent. 'He talks about freeing ourselves from the tyranny of Rome, and with such eloquence . . . I can't begin to convey it . . . but you'd understand as soon as you heard him.' But when he sees Chaucer sigh and, very faintly, yawn (a gesture Chaucer realises, as he performs it, that he's borrowed from Alice Perrers) he lets that subject drop.

Over the second pitcher of wine, they talk poetry. Sir Richard fetches out the beautifully illuminated, and expensive, copy he's just bought of *The Romance of the Rose*, and, after they've oohed and ahed over it, and read a few passages, he asks Chaucer searching, intelligent questions about the verse he's been writing.

The friendly atmosphere, the refinement of the conversation, and the quality of the wine bring a not unpleasing melancholy to Chaucer's heart.

It's drizzling. It only stopped snowing a month ago, and there's been non-stop rain ever since. It's a monotonous, miserable sound, water beating on windows. 'Do you remember', Chaucer says, 'when we were young, how spring always seemed to come earlier?' And Stury laughs, as wistfully as Chaucer, and says, 'And summer seemed to last for ever? Of course I do . . . but what can you expect, my friend? We live in evil days.' For a few minutes, the pair of them sit, nodding gently, perfectly satisfied with the nostalgia they're sharing, nursing their wine.

After an hour or so more, as they broach the third pitcher and start to indulge in reminiscences about their days shut up together as hostages in the same castle tower all those years ago, sharing one cup of wine and half a loaf of bread, utterly cast down at the prospect of indefinite imprisonment, and then about various old friends in the King's service, and then about the fine times they've had on one trip on the King's business or another, Chaucer also finds the courage to broach the other subject on his mind.

'Old man,' he says tentatively, 'it's not that I'm unhappy with my work at the Customs House, but sometimes I have to confess I miss the old diplomatic days in the King's service, too . . .' He sighs nostalgically. 'Italy . . .'

He's thinking of the wide, smooth streets and great domes and portals of Genoa. He's thinking of the double belt of stone walls encircling Florence, and the loveliness of the great, dim, mysterious baptistry of St John, within those walls: the white and green marble; the glowing mosaics of the cupola.

He's been thinking thoughts like this, thoughts of escape, all day. He's uncomfortable with the sense of foreboding he's carrying in him through the winding streets and wooden houses of London. He'd like it to go away; but if it won't, he'd like to take to heart, for himself, the advice Alice won't hear, and go away from it. It wouldn't be ideal, of course, going back to the King's service now, when the King is so infirm, and perhaps not long for this world . . . but it would feel safer than sitting here waiting for whatever it is that's brewing up in the stormclouds. Putting some distance between himself and this trouble would ease his mind.

Stury laughs. 'I've been wondering how long you'd be able to bear the wool sacks, day in, day out. I won't say I'm not sympathetic. Do you really have to go in there every day?' he answers lightly, filling Chaucer's cup. 'Would you like me to put a few feelers out? See if you can't be excused from the accounts and sent back to work at the King's service?'

Carefully, Chaucer picks up the cup. He examines the wine, rolls the cup in his hands, and sniffs the rich bouquet, as his father taught him. 'A well-made wine,' he says diplomatically, before adding, with a slow nod, knowing his casualness won't fool Stury for a second, 'Well, dear fellow, of course there's no hurry . . . but if something came up, I'd certainly be interested in knowing.'

TWENTY

It is the last day before Parliament convenes at Westminster, 27 April, 1376. The City, glistening with chilly rain long after spring should have come, is crowded with incomers. Every inn is packed.

The King is nowhere near. He's exhausted after the Garter ceremonies. He's gone back to Havering, out in the east, to rest. The Duke has announced publicly that he'll attend Parliament on his father's behalf.

Alice is neither in the tumult of London or safely with Edward at Havering.

She's gone where no one will look for her. She's at her estate at Hammersmith, west of London, upriver even from Westminster, in the gentle flatlands of Middlesex. She wants peace and quiet, for the last hasty task she's set herself before the Parliament: bringing her account books to order.

There are six men seated at the table, watching Alice.

Solid-looking men, all of them, in plain black clothes, with impassive, indeterminate faces; a twisted nose here, a thickened ear there, but nothing to make them stand out in a crowd.

Alice has chosen her people carefully over the years, from the tide of defrocked priests and ambitious nobodies that has swept the land. John Bernes, William Mulsho, John Freford, Robert Broun, John Vyncent and Hugh Cotyngham: skilled

288

mercenaries of the pen, one and all (and not bad, either, at a bit of sheer physical intimidation). She pays accordingly. They've done very well from their work.

They're loyal to her from necessity, maybe, but they are utterly loyal. They have no families that they're willing to acknowledge, and no homes they want to return to. They live on the move. They don't put down roots. Because this, for them, is what passes for home – wherever their fellows are, wherever she is, where the ideas come from which they spend their days implementing. It's their work for Alice that gives meaning to their lives; brings a sly chuckle to their lips.

So, even if they aren't saying a word, just contemplating her, inspecting her own impassive business face, waiting to hear what she has to tell them, she can sense the confusion in their minds.

It's a big change since last time they met, after New Year, in their usual place at her house in London, when she was so full of plans for them. She's looking at Mulsho and Freford, in particular, with their monkish whey-faces and bruisers' knuckles, who've spent the later part of the winter following up her ideas for new land-buying in Northamptonshire. They must have been thinking, for all those months, that she'd be pleased that they've managed to get their hands on every last one of the manors she wanted to buy. Hitchin. Plumpton End. Moor End Castle. Lillington Dansey. They must already have been wondering, pleasurably, how big their bonuses would be.

The rest of them, too, working to improve the other recently acquired places in Dorset, or Devon. Ironing out problems caused by reluctant sellers or litigious lords. Ensuring good reductions in the price of raw materials for building. Getting workers and seed to the land. By fair means or foul, without differentiating; because, as Alice always tells them, with her flat, frightening business voice, 'I'm not interested in excuses. I'm interested in results.'

And then they got her last letters. Stop. Liquidate. Sell.

No explanations.

They may even be scared at the speed of the change.

But they're too well trained to mutter among themselves,

or betray any curiosity or unease. At least in front of her. There's not a raised eyebrow among them. Not a shaking head. They're just sitting there, hands in their laps, waiting for her clarification.

She can't bring herself to explain, even now. They're intelligent enough to know that her position must have become insecure. They can't not know of the Parliament convening tomorrow. They'll have put two and two together.

And anyway, she can't quite bear to admit that this great adventure they've all been having is over, even though, at the same time, she's almost itching with the desire to have today's settling of accounts done. But . . . all the hopes she's had . . . they've all had . . . the price they got for all those Somerset lands last year . . . She bites her lip.

'Thank you for carrying out your new instructions so promptly,' is all she says. 'The first thing I have to tell you today is that you will all receive the rewards I'd been planning for implementing the earlier programme.'

She's aware of the slight shifting of shoulders, the lowering of tension.

Broun lets out his breath, and then turns that lapse of discipline into a cough.

Tersely, she says, 'Let's start, then. With Northamptonshire.' She opens the big ledger on the table in front of her, and picks up her pen. 'Master Mulsho, Master Freford . . .'

They stand, and come up to her, and start taking out the small bags of money at their belts, or sewn into their hems, or secreted in their boots – all kept separate for safety's sake on the roads – as well as the lists on the scraps of parchment in their accounts.

'Twenty pounds intended to buy oaks to extend the hall at Lillington Dancey,' Mulsho says in a thin monotone. 'Returned.' She counts the money and crosses the item off her list. 'Five marks spent on paying the seneschal at Lillington Dancey to alter documentation, as discussed,' he goes on. She marks item two. 'Fifteen marks spent on paying the bailiff at Lillington Dancey to agree to the alteration of documentation, as discussed.' She makes another mark.

Alice's idea is to rid herself of any possessions more than a day or two's ride from London. She wants a neat, manageable set of landholdings, ten estates in all. The other forty-six, in the North Country, in the West Country, are going. She's going to give one small manor each to these lieutenants, near the places she's keeping. She'll set all her men up, buying their continued loyalty; they'll go on minding her business. But . . . quietly, and on a small scale.

It's midday and several pages of the ledger have been filled before the intricacies of the latest aborted Northampton project have been fully unravelled, and all the money accounted for; before the sale or transfer of her many other Northamptonshire properties has been reported, or set in motion.

They stop for bread and cheese.

At three or four of the clock, when moneys have been exchanged for the sale of the West Country estates that have already gone, they hear the clap of hoofs in the courtyard, coming in from the farm road, behind the river. A moment later, there are voices from down there, calling up to the windows.

'Where's the friar? The one who can do physic?' she hears. A cultured man's voice; knightly tones of command; but pitiful, too.

Alice goes to the window. Through the rivulets running down the glass and lead, she makes out two shining forms down below, with spurs on their heels, and the grey horses with their heads in the trough behind both wet to blackness.

Knights don't often come calling in these parts, and if they do they come by river.

It's only when Alice sees the urinals they're both carrying, glass vessels for the collection and analysis of piss by physicians, like her Friar John, who can cure all ills by looking into the human body's waste water, that she understands, and feels reassured, and goes back to her seat to pay attention again to Master Broun's detailed disquisition on the messuages at Lower Chicksgrove.

But she keeps half an ear on the much louder and livelier conversation outside, all the same.

The shouting goes on. The yardman tries to hush the knights. She hears him tell them, 'Not so much noise, now, my lords, hush now,' but weakly. Naturally they ignore him, as (she can imagine them believing) is their lordly right.

Finally there's the thin, reluctant bleat of Friar John's voice from his window, in the solar one floor up.

'I'm the physician, travellers . . . What do you want from me?'

Dear old Friar John. He's old and not well – touches of gout, touches of rheumatism. He feels the cold terribly, and the wet. But a good, kind man, and a learned physician. She's told him a good week ago that he's to go to Gaines to teach three children there, without explaining that these are her own children. (She hasn't found the courage, or the words, for that. Not yet.) She hasn't altogether given up the idea of getting a knighthood for Johnny, just because the Duke was hostile, as long as the boy can be taught a few gentlemanly ways; she's just too frantic doing what she's doing with her land agents, for now; she's going to think again about how to make it happen once she's hurried all this property business out of the way. Perhaps Edward will come to enough to take his own decisions; or perhaps she can just slip Johnny's name on to a list; or perhaps (though she's reluctant to do this) she could take the risk of confiding her secret in Latimer? Still, because the Johnny business will need finessing, and Father John's so frail, she hasn't hurried him off. She's been hoping the weather will change, and the spring arrive, at least, before she has to send him off. He'll suffer in the damp, before the sun comes.

'A remedy, Father, just a few herbs . . . we're all aches and pains, and they say you're good at healing the sick,' one of the voices yells back in a strong bass voice. For a sick man, he certainly has a good pair of lungs on him, that one, Alice thinks, laughing a bit to herself. The voice wheedles: 'Come down and look us over, eh?'

There's a silence.

The friar's probably making his painful way downstairs already. But the men don't understand where he's gone, because they carry on yelling and cajoling.

'We'll pay good money . . . make it worth your while,' shouts one.

'Oh, the agony,' groans the other.

Broun's now summarising work on the London inn near the Thames and the houses adjoining the great gate, all in the parish of All Hallows the Less, that Alice has been having built. That will have to go, too, Alice thinks, unable to avoid regret. In a minute, she'll tell him to sell. Discreetly.

Outside, a door creaks open, and shut. Alice hears the tentative, shuffling footfall of the old man, making his way across the courtyard; hears him say, in his gentle way, 'So, what's all this about then, my lords?'

She doesn't understand what she hears next: a couple of soft thuds, the sound of breaking glass, harsh breath. It's only when Friar John begins to howl, a thin, agonised, outraged and fearful sound – 'You're hurting me, what are you doing, you're *hurting* me!' – that she and all her colleagues drop their papers, knock back their benches, and rush to the window.

What they see: the urinals have been dropped and smashed. They've served their purpose, clearly. They were only ever a trick. And one of the men has the gasping, squealing friar on the ground, face down in the wet, in an armlock. The other is rushing to his horse for the bit of rope hooked round the saddle pommel.

'Stop!' Alice yells, but they're not listening.

She rushes downstairs, holding up her skirts as she runs. Her men come thundering behind her.

The wetness of the air startles her.

The strangers are by now heaving the trussed-up friar roughly to his feet, grunting and snorting as they go, but grinning at each too, with a nasty gleam in their eyes. 'Get moving, you old fraud,' one of them snarls, turning to the friar, working himself up into a bully's rage against his victim. 'Come on. Time someone got the truth out of *you*.' There's muddy water running down poor Friar John's face; a smear of horseshit on his gleaming tonsure; his front is soaking. And there's a look of utter misery on his face, a misery beyond fear.

The sound of the creaking door startles them. They all turn round to face Alice, with the six men in black behind her. She's aware of faces – eyes, breath – at every window; of the terrified yardman behind the men, stepping very quietly backwards, one foot after the other, ready to fade into the background.

In Alice's head, Aunty's unemotional voice is saying: 'Whatever you do, dear, never show fear.'

'Let go of my friar!' Alice yells. 'What the hell do you think you're doing?'

The visitors don't look abashed. Dragging the friar forward like a shield, the bigger of them says, truculently, 'Taking him off to ask him a few questions.' He gives the friar a bit of a shake, until the old man starts to groan and breathe heavily, and all the while the knight's looking her up and down with naked insolence and grinning in a see-what-we-can-do kind of way.

A sound from behind the gates turns Alice's eyes sideways. Suddenly she sees why this man's so brave. She almost stops breathing.

There are more men behind these two, pacing around outside. Men on horseback. Men with glittering points of metal raised. Fifteen, maybe twenty of them. Ready for trouble.

Master Broun's at Alice's side. He hasn't seen the horsemen. He nudges her. There's a question in his eyes. The other land agents are massing: shoulders squaring, fists at the ready. She only has to say the word.

She shakes her head, just a fraction. This mustn't turn into a brawl. Too dangerous. Those men have a troop of horse with them, but that's not the only reason. The point is, they're not footpads. They're here on someone's orders. She has to find out whose.

'By what right?' Alice asks, hands on hips. Shouts, more like. She's comforted enough by the phalanx of solid, disciplined black at her back for that, at least. 'You have no right.'

Gruffly, staring at her with violence in his eyes, the other man says, 'Never you mind.' No 'mistress', no 'my lady'.

'I insist on knowing,' Alice says with the freezing fires of hell in her voice. 'Or I'll have the King himself hound you down to the end of the earth.'

Silence.

Anger takes Alice over; she's hot with it again.

'What are your names?' she grinds out between clenched teeth.

Silence.

The men glance at each other. One – the man holding the friar – nods. The other strides off and mounts his horse. The first man bundles the friar off towards the other horse, and heaves him up over the saddle. The friar's groaning, and moaning, and mumbling prayers now; Alice glimpses his eyes, white all round the edges, fixing imploringly on her as the horse skitters round.

She follows them. She grabs the bridle. But the man grabs it back, making the horse shy. They both jump back to avoid the flailing of hoofs.

The man jerks his head at the friar. '*He*'ll know the witchcraft *you*'ve been working, won't he?'

He stops talking. He sees, after a triumphantly vindictive glare at Alice, that he's silenced her. Seizing the horse's head, he clicks it on.

His parting words, as he walks out of the gate to a thin hurrah from beyond, with his victim moaning pathetically from over the horse's back, are: 'And you'll burn for it, mark my words, you bloody Jezebel.'

When Alice turns back to face her household, the six men at her shoulders and the many servants at the windows see that her face has turned as white as chalk.

Broun says, 'We can go after them.' The men shift on the balls of their feet. The horses are moving away at a walk. They can still hear them.

He wants to. They all want to. She wants them to. No one bullies Alice Perrers and gets away with it . . .

. . . but she daren't. She doesn't for a moment think that ape meant what he said about burning. But still. She can see it's political, this arrest.

She shakes her head. Sucks in her lips. 'I'll raise it at Council,' she says more threateningly than she feels. 'Tomorrow. I'll get Father John back, and these ruffians flogged.' Perhaps, if she says it confidently enough, no one will realise that there's no Council tomorrow. There's just the Parliament. And this arrest must be linked to that.

'Come,' she says less certainly to the saucer eyes and round mouths, trying to put the picture of Father John, bundled over the horse's back, out of her mind. His eyes . . .

And then, seeing the old man's utter dejection in her mind's eye, she suddenly knows fear as well as anger: the black, consuming, treacly tide of fear, lapping at her very weak, very frail, very mortal bones. And what fear does is to concentrate her mind absolutely, and on herself alone. Suddenly she knows exactly what is the most important thing to do, right now. The only thing. She must get the paperwork sorted out. Leave no unexplained business. And she must do it now.

Northamptonshire and Nottinghamshire are dealt with; the West Country holdings are tidied up too. That's the bulk of it. But there are still loose ends, and there could be more men coming, any time. They haven't even begun on Southcote Manor, in Middlesex. Or Stoke Mandeville in Buckinghamshire, or the lands near Oxford. They haven't finished the London properties.

'Back,' she says, faster, trying to turn her rising panic into businesslike briskness, already striding towards the hall. She's thinking: I'll send Broun and Mulsho with the money to London . . . No, too much temptation; I'll put it all behind the stone in the fireplace after all . . . She snaps, over her shoulder: 'We've still got several matters in hand. And you all need to be out of here by nightfall.'

She's still at the top. She has nothing to fear. She tries to reassure herself, as she tucks trembling hands under the table where the men can't see them, by imagining that children's game again: the bright coin, sparkling away on top of that thin column of flour, however close the knife comes.

It's still there. Isn't it?

TWENTY-ONE

There's vindictive joy in the air in the City. It's like a feast day, or what a feast day would be if there were a patron saint of revenge. The taverns are full of gloaters, spilling out into the wet streets, not caring about the gusting rain, shouting: all those incomers, the servants of all those parliamentarians, and all the natives of London, too, chewing over the gossip as if they were brothers in hate, yelling to their friends, spitting hailstorms of chicken legs out into the gutter.

Chaucer leaves work early – he doesn't care any more what he's promised. There is no normal life in the City any more, just this. He goes straight to a corner in the Burning Bush, where he sits, jostled and fearful, to listen to the bloodcurdling talk. There's ice in his heart.

There's talk of only one thing: the opening of Parliament, with the Lords packed into the White Chamber at the palace, and the Commons packed into the chapter house of the abbey. Even the Prince of England has had himself carried into the proceedings, on a stretcher, with death in his face.

Chaucer's no fool. Ever since he heard that the Prince was at Westminster, he's been full of dread. He understands at last. He reads the Prince of England's presence in that chamber as proof that this entire public puppet-show is a battle between two string-pullers: the royal brothers of England. The Prince of England is striking at his over-ambitious younger brother through the Parliament. The ciphers and proxies of one prince are about to be brought low by the ciphers and proxies of the other. And that's a frightening prospect for anyone who owes his position in the world to the Duke – as Chaucer does – and senses defeat in the air.

Already, in a controlled, clever way that speaks of months – years, maybe – of strategy and careful planning, the Commons, that many-headed, many-voiced tool of the Prince of England and his wife, have taken control. The lowly knights and burgesses of the Commons have given their voices nobler weight by demanding and getting four barons included in their number, and four earls, and the bishops. And they've elected the knight from Herefordshire as their Forespeaker: Sir Peter de la Mare, who, because he's the seneschal of one of the chosen earls, Edmund Mortimer, Earl of March, ultimately, like the Earl, owes loyalty to the Prince.

It is this Peter de la Mare who has led his men into the White Chamber to stand among the Lords today, and listened to the Crown asking for money: a first, dry, detailed, inaudible speech from the Chancellor, followed by an address from the scowling, furious Duke of Lancaster, who hates explaining himself to his inferiors, and hates making speeches anyway, and who's mumbled and shouted his way through his own uneasy speech asking for money, which everyone could hear but no one could quite get the drift of.

Tomorrow, it is this Peter de la Mare who will answer the demand of the Crown for a new tax. 'And it'll be fighting talk, I tell you,' the one-eyed drunk next to Chaucer says, elbowing him in the ribs and spitting approvingly into the rushes.

Chaucer knows, before another word is said, that he's somehow going to sneak into the chamber too, just for that speech tomorrow. He has to hear it. He's more afraid of staying here, and not knowing what battle lines are being drawn up between King and Commons, than he is of being caught. He can't not go.

Yet Chaucer feels a shameful coward all the way west. He takes a boat, very early in the morning, before it's properly light, before the crowds get out, covering his head against the rain and also against any eyes that might report him to Walworth. He goes straight to the treasury at Westminster Palace as if about to ask to draw his pension. That's what he'll tell anyone if they ask. He thinks he'd be convincing. He almost convinces himself, on the boat, that this really is his plan. The pension's not actually due for another month, though; he's pretty sure the treasury will be deserted, and then he can just sneak down the corridors . . .

And so, soon, from a dusty gallery above where the Duke and his entourage have taken their places to speak for the Crown, he's able to stick his head out and see the tops of parliamentary heads, a bobbing of faces, the Prince's litter in the far corner, and, rising to his feet at the front of the crowd, the lean grey shape of Peter de la Mare. For a daring moment, Chaucer peers forward for a glimpse of the man's face. The knight looks . . . exalted, he thinks. He sinks back.

Chaucer's cramped between some stacked-up benches. He's fighting sneezes in his nose and pins and needles in his feet. But he can't help but admire the natural beauty of the knight's angry, yet always dignified voice, reaching him through the echo and dust motes, as de la Mare begins his speech.

'Lords and magnates, by whose faith and industry the government of the kingdom ought to be carried out, I will by no means try to conceal from your wisdom how weighed down the common people have been by the burden of taxes, now paying a fifteenth, now a tenth, or even yielding as much as a ninth to the King's use. All of which they would bear cheerfully if the King or the kingdom seemed to gain any advantage or profit from it. It would also have been tolerable to the people if all that money had been spent in forwarding our military affairs, even though these had been unsuccessful. But it is obvious that the King has neither received advantage nor the kingdom any return from it. And so, because the public was never told how such great sums of money were spent, the common people are demanding a statement of accounts from those who received the money, for it is not credible that the King should need such an infinitely large sum if his ministers were loyal.'

Now de la Mare's voice is drowned out by sound. Slightly scared cheers from the knights. Growls of anger from elsewhere. It's breathtaking. Chaucer shakes his head at the sheer bold daring of the man.

'He said no,' Chaucer mutters, trying to take it in. 'The Commons is refusing the King's tax.'

How he wishes he could peep through the boards beneath his own feet and see the Duke's reaction to being told to explain to his inferiors where the last lot of tax money has gone. On the other hand, he thinks, hastily, at almost the same moment, how very glad he is to be up here, safely out of that scrimmage.

Cautiously he pulls back his head right back, crouches down tighter and takes a deep breath of dust.

What follows, once the hubbub dies down, is even more shocking. De la Mare follows up his opening speech by insisting that this Parliament be turned into a trial.

The Commons, he tells the chamber, will not give the King a penny in tax until the Crown has heard the case he wants to bring, on behalf of his fellow-knights and -burgesses, against the highly placed thieves he will identify. He wants the Crown to guarantee to produce every man and woman named by the Commons, so they can have their day standing up in public in this chamber, answering de la Mare's charges.

Chaucer can't believe his ears. There's never been anything like this before. De la Mare is turning the world upside down. The Duke will never . . . will he?

He hugs his knees, waiting for the shouting to die down, or turn violent. This is just the kind of insolence from the lower orders that could send the Duke into a fury.

If the Duke does start raging, Chaucer wonders, what will happen?

He doesn't think it would be right for the Duke to start raging.

It's Chaucer's strong instinct that what's going on here is too highly organised, too purposeful, and too broad, to be deflected by royal anger. Anger might only make things worse.

If the Duke starts raging, Chaucer wonders, should I go down – go to him – try to calm him?

He's often calmed the Duke down before. But now, with Walworth among the members of the Commons, across the room? Chaucer doesn't know the answer.

And there's no need, for now, as it turns out. He doesn't even hear the answer from the Duke's camp, when it comes. It's too quiet. And the Duke is right below where he's crouched, so he can't see why.

But he can guess that the Crown has, reluctantly, agreed, when the knights and burgesses who are just about in his line of vision start grinning and clapping.

As de la Mare rises to his feet again, with his arms outstretched to hush his fellow knightly mutineers – for he's a man who exists to promote order – Chaucer is tiptoeing out of the gallery.

Back on a boat to the City, his head whirling with the extraordinary shape that public events are taking, and the terrifying courage of the knight of Herefordshire in taking on the Duke of Lancaster (even if he's tacitly backed by the Prince), Chaucer somehow also finds space, in a corner of his mind, to think of himself. Partly he's pleased to have whisked in and out so quietly, without being seen. But he's also ashamed of himself. Skulking in the gallery; scurrying through servants' entrances. What a pitiful figure I cut, he thinks.

He doesn't agree with the demands of the Commons, of that he's sure. It's beyond Chaucer to imagine that it can be right to question the Crown's natural authority in the way he's just heard de la Mare do. Yet at the same time he can understand why the knights of the shires and the burgesses of the towns of England are so discontented. And something in Sir Peter, that gravitas, that courage, that voice raised before the crowd, fearlessly expressing the Commons' point of view, has stirred his soul. Sir Peter, today, looked and sounded like an avenging angel.

Now, Chaucer's good enough at quiet diplomacy, and accomplished at reading out poetry he's prepared to a receptive audience, too, but he gets rattled by the eyes on him when he attempts public oratory. So he's surprised to find himself thinking, rather wistfully, as he reviews the tumultuous events of the day in Westminster: If I get a chance, perhaps, soon, I can do my small part too.

In the Burning Bush, on the way back from work that evening, assorted drunks are comparing notes. There's a podgy type who's been here all day, listening to the gossip, and is positively chuckling for joy at de la Mare's outspokenness. His spherical front ripples softly under his tunic again whenever he thinks of it. He's a tanner; he stinks, Chaucer thinks fastidiously, of half-cured hides.

'. . . and let me tell you, brother, he knows what's been going on, all right. He's done his homework. You can see that straight off.' The fatty takes another deep draught of ale. 'So it's going to be a cracking few months, I'd say,' he says with gusto, wiping the foam moustache off his sweaty red face. 'For all of us, right? Watching them get their come-uppance. Best sport we'll have had for years. God speed good Sir bloody Peter, thasswhatIsay.'

'Who,' Chaucer says faintly, 'do you think they'll call?'

The man raises fat fingers. 'Well, Latimer, for a start,' he says knowledgeably, banging two sausages of index fingers together. 'Obviously. And all the rest of the bent little chisellers at court. Then, from over here in the City, Richard Lyons and his lot, I expect. And that's only the start.'

Chaucer stammers: 'But those people are already going to be heard, aren't they? Here in the City . . . I mean, because the aldermen are investigating the rumours about the debt fraud . . . and that's what this is about, really, isn't it?'

The tanner roars with laughter, and, when the gales subside, pats Chaucer so hard on the back he thinks his ribs might crack. 'Nah, mate, you're way behind. That piddling little trial – the alderman one? It's off. I heard down the Dancing Bear at noon – Walworth told the aldermen this morning that they're shutting it down so they can have it all out in Parliament instead. And quite right too. We might actually find out what's been going on, this way. The Parliament way: impeachment, they're calling it. They might all actually get punished. Whereas, leave the case here in the City, and what would happen? Nothing. You know that as well as I do. Lyons would get the little bags of gold coins out, and one of those aldermen would be hushing the whole thing up as soon as someone bunged him a bribe.'

'But why'd he do that?' shrilled a skinny greybeard. 'Walworth? He's got no call letting London cases go out of London. It's up to us to get the bastards, innit? They're our bastards, in'they?' His rheumy eyes pop indignantly with London pride.

'Nah,' a whole chorus of amused voices answers, though kindly enough. 'Come on, use your head, Granddad. Walworth's not Mayor any more this year, is he? But he *is* a member of the Commons, innee? So where would he want the biggest trial of the year to take place?'

The grey head nods. 'Yeah, I see now – he'd want it in Parliament, of course. Better for him. This way, he gets to stuff Warde, and get all the glory for himself. And next year we'll all want him to be Mayor again.'

There is a wave of wise nodding and grunting.

Meanwhile, the numbness in Chaucer's heart is darkening into something like physical pain.

It's not that he wants crime to go unpunished, exactly. He's just frightened of the pent-up rage he can see spilling out, every-where he looks, and whom it will end up being unleashed on.

He hardly dares ask, but at last he gets it out.

'And Alice Perrers?'

It's a fletcher, long and thin as the arrows he makes, who answers, with a smile – an unlovely smile, showing off his black stumps of teeth. He draws in a great gout of unclean tavern air, enjoying the revelation to come.

'The witch, mate?' he says cheerfully. 'Well, I'd say *her* goose is well and truly cooked. Her flesh might be getting a cooking soon too, from what I hear, though we won't know the worst of it till tomorrow. They've got her doctor, see . . . some filthy little friar. De la Mare's brother went after him. Found him down Hammersmith way. He was spilling his guts before they even started roughing him up, that's what they're saying. Magic rings, spells and potions, God knows what. No wonder we're in the state we're in today, with her getting up to all that right under our noses for all these years. They say the friar will be the first up for questioning before the Duke tomorrow.'

Chaucer doesn't often go out of his way to pray. But he does now. He tips his hat to the drunks and goes out of the tavern, through the rain, round the corner to All Hallows church, where he sinks to his knees under the rose window.

His prayer for Alice is without words. He can only hope God will pardon his incoherence and see his sincerity.

This is what he's feared. Worse. This is the plunge into the abyss.

Chaucer sits nailed to his desk from dawn to dusk the next day, hardly daring to look up; every moment an eternity.

By the next evening, however, as he walks home, head down, he realises that the hopes of the City haters that Alice Perrers would be burned for witchcraft have faded out.

He doesn't even have to go to the tavern to find out, they're all shouting so loud about it in the street. His ears prick up; then his head perks up; then his feet go faster. By the time he reaches the first drinking spot, despite all his earlier good resolutions, he's got nothing on his mind more pressing than diving inside again.

The old friar who's been tortured has indeed brought to Parliament his pathetic tales of Alice practising black arts to bewitch the King into unlawful love. But no one could believe the obviously made-up confession. Even the knights felt sorry for the friar. When the Duke cut short the hearing by ordering the Archbishop of Canterbury to take the old man back, and keep him out of harm's way in a friary, the Prince's men, even Peter de la Mare, didn't object.

Chaucer has something else on his mind. He's buying the fat tanner a drink, trying to keep the relief off his own face. He's thinking: It's the Duke's wisdom today that's saved Alice. (Chaucer wouldn't have expected such wise restraint from my lord, to be honest. There've been outbursts of nobleman's fury, more often.) My lord got it so right; cooperate with the

Commons and let their anger dissipate. There'll be plenty more false accusations and climb-downs. He must just sit tight. Because what can a bunch of country squires hope to know, really, about the high finance of the realm?

But it's Chaucer's quiet euphoria, rather than the tanner's good cheer, that dissipates as the evening wears on – as it becomes obvious to him that the crowds in the taverns haven't understood the latest hearing quite as he has.

Chaucer hunches miserably over his tankard, listening helplessly to the wolf-whistles and the cat-calls. He wishes he knew where Alice was, or that he dare send a messenger, or, at least, that there might be something hopeful to send a message about. But not this. 'Witch!' halloo the skinners and fletchers and ropemakers. 'Bitch!' roar the caulkers and the hoopers in response, punching meaty fists into the beery air.

Hating her is making them happier than they've been for years. Even now the charge has been shown to be absurd; even though she's not going to burn, they're still as ecstatic thinking of it as if they'd got Alice chained to a stake, right here, right now, choking in the smoke from the flames devouring her, and were laughing in her dying face. It's as if all the diffuse anger at the state of things that they've felt for so long has been focused, channelled, narrowed; directed at one small target. Chaucer stares at the froth on his ale, wailing, inside his head, at them all, 'But why her? She's only ever done what you've done, had the same fun you've had, helped herself here and there – just like you, only on a bigger scale, because she could. But she's no worse than anyone else. So why pick on her?'

But he knows, deep down. The penny has dropped. They're enjoying howling about Alice because they've been shown, by today's events, that she's the weakest of the high-placed people they blame for their troubles. Vulnerable. Flour on her face; scared eyes in the white. She might not be a witch and therefore easily burnable, but she's still the one Fortune's about to bring down. The victim. Her time at the top is over. Of course it's her blood they're after.

PART TWO

Regnavi

I used to reign

TWENTY-TWO

All through the opening steps of the Parliament, John of Gaunt, Duke of Lancaster, has paced in a thin fury of impotence, glaring out at the crowd in the chamber through the headache pulsing behind his eyes. This afternoon is no different. With every hour that passes, his moments of rage are getting more intense.

The stink of wet wool and greasy leather that these men give off turns his stomach. The figures of the forty-odd shire knights and coming up to a hundred burgesses swim and sway before him, and none of them with the grace to acknowledge their humbleness and the Duke's God-given might. Who do they think they are?

Ever since Chancellor Knyvett read out the Crown's first request for money, and the Commons, with the low cowardice that must be expected of such men, first drew in barons and bishops to hide behind, then pushed forward one of their number to say no on behalf of them all, and then to smear the Duke's real or imagined placemen, starting with Alice Perrers, of imaginary crimes, his rage has simmered and bubbled. Perhaps these people have been stealing; on balance, it's even probable. But that's just what people like that do, because they're merchants, officials; sneaky paper people. It's in their nature. This isn't an attack on corruption; not really. It's an attack on him.

What made him smart first was the way that the Commons

simply ignored his wish when, on the first morning, he ordered them to delegate a few members to come in and hang about at the back of the White Chamber, preserve of the Lords already standing in groups or lying on rugs on the floor, to say whatever they had to say to their betters. That beaky-nosed brute, de la Mare, refused to speak unless all 130 of them came with him. And they just poured in. The impossible self-assurance of it infuriated him, but it rattled him too. He's never before encountered such insouciant insubordination. And they've just stood there ever since, these nobodies, staring insolently round at the Lords, scratching themselves and shaking their heads, while the debate goes on, as if just being free men, as if just having money, gives them rights that the Duke could tell them they never have had, and never will have, either. Their sheer belief that they can has silenced him, until now. He doesn't know how to counter them; how to send them scuttling in terror back to their hills and fields.

There's nothing he can see that he can do. He knows the thought at the back of every mind in this chamber. They all believe he wants to steal the throne, because his brother is dying and his brother's son is a helpless child. If he punishes their impudence – if he gives in to the desire to shake their Forespeaker like the dog he is, or throw over the furniture and draw his sword and declare their wretched gathering null and void and beat them out into the mud and rain outside – it will only confirm in them the belief that he is out for power. He has to tread carefully.

Behind him, on a litter piled high with cushions, lies the unthinkable, skeletal, gurgling, periodically stinking thing his brother Edward has become. The Prince of England, whose good fortune in war has inspired deep dread in all nations, both Christian and pagan, as if he were a second Hector, and in no one more dread and admiration than in his younger brother John, appears to have resolved to defy death for a little longer and be carried in here to watch the proceedings. But John is uncomfortably aware that his brother is really only here to watch *him*. He can feel Edward's baleful eyes

310

boring into him from behind. That unseen gaze sends shivers down his spine.

He can see that this is a battle between brothers, and all these ... *creatures* ... are speaking the mind of Edward. Edward must have orchestrated this attack on him, and his people, for his brother must also believe he wants to seize power.

The shocking injustice of it is a knife in his side. He wants to rush to Edward, to throw himself on his knees before him, to seek through the wasted flesh and lines of pain and humiliation the face he's always revered, to tell his brother that no, he doesn't want the crown that's intended for little Richard's head; never has, never will; that he isn't the man they've taken him for.

But not in front of these swine, these scum, who have no place at Westminster; who have forgotten their rightful place in God's great plan.

He doesn't want Edward to believe this of him. He's always been loyal ... loving. He hero-worships Edward. The very thought of Edward's suspicion agonises him.

But in John of Gaunt's head, at the same time, another thought co-exists, one that doesn't agonise him, because he doesn't let it out from the quiet, shameful place he's locked it up in, deep inside, in an entirely separate part of him. It lurks there, whispering and hissing, clanking its chains. It is this. If Edward were not here, today, or at all, if Edward had departed this life, and if the fate of England boiled down to a choice between himself – a grown man, a prince, a soldier, a statesman, experienced in the bearing of arms and the exercise of power, with years of knowledge behind him and royal blood coursing through his veins; in short, with all the attributes of a warrior prince that will be needed to save a land in the mortal danger England finds herself today – and that spoiled, capricious little boy, his nephew Richard ...

No wonder his head aches, and he hates the trouble-makers of the Commons.

But at least he's persuaded Stury to ask Chaucer to attend today and stay tonight. Chaucer's bright; he knows the ways of diplomacy and argument. And he knows how to explain the ways of the sneaky paper people so a man can understand. Still, can even Chaucer . . .?

John sighs, and focuses his eyes again on the hated figure of the Forespeaker.

When the session ends, the Duke watches his brother the Prince leave on his litter, without so much as a nod of farewell; with his eyes shut. Then he calls his own advisers together in an antechamber. They're as shocked as he is. They crowd around, trembling, waiting to hear his will.

For a few minutes, Duke John can barely speak. His legs carry him here and there. Two paces to the left. Two to the right. A caged lion, pacing.

'What do these degenerates . . . knights of candle-wax . . . What do they think they're up to?' he bursts out in the end. He's beyond strategy. He just wants to voice the howl of rage in his soul. 'Do they take themselves for kings or princes? Where does their pride and arrogance come from?'

The advisers murmur. He sees Stury, taller than most, standing at the back, quietly shaking his head. As if Stury's warning him.

That only makes him angrier.

He shouts, 'I will appear before them tomorrow in so glorious a manner – and raise up such a great force among them – and terrify them with such severity – that neither they nor anybody like them will dare again to provoke my majesty.'

They crowd closer still, at that. There's alarm on every face. Hands start patting the air down, as if the atmosphere itself needs calming. Someone mutters, 'Sssh'. And he sees fearful glances over shoulders, as if they're wondering whether the Herefordshire man's got his ear to the door.

What's got into them all? Has their noble blood been turned to milk?

Furiously, he continues pacing. He won't be silenced. But he does, distractedly, listen when Chaucer's voice, oozing tact, murmurs, 'Lord, don't let your magnificence hide from you how strongly these knights are supported – and by whom.

312

They have the backing of the Lords and, more important still, of Prince Edward your brother.'

At that, the Duke sees Edward's face in his mind again. Eyes shut. Heart shut too.

He stops. He looks down at the smaller man staring so beseechingly at him with his usual surprised respect. Chaucer doesn't look impressive; but, as so often, there's sense in what the man says. Chaucer's gone straight to the nub of things. No one's dared mention Edward's part in this yet, except Chaucer. John pleats his fingers together. He turns, reluctantly, to face his men. Every pair of eyes has the same imploring look that he sees in Chaucer. Be calm, the eyes are all saying. Be mild. Don't give fight.

He turns his face down in a moment of irresolution. He doesn't want to show enmity to Edward, after all . . . He wants Edward to know he bears him no malice. But if he doesn't retaliate against the knights Edward seems to have set on him, then how *is* he to respond? He's a nobleman. A man of the sword, not the word.

Someone else is speaking now. The Duke raises his tormented eyes again. Stury, from the shadows. Stury, who sleeps in London when the court's at Westminster. Stury, who knows what Londoners are saying, who can distil an evening of wild tavern talk into a single careful sentence. And what he's saying now, with a persuasive gleam in his eyes, is: '. . . Neither the Londoners or the common people will let the knights be overwhelmed with insults, or molested with injury, however slight. If these knights are insulted, they'll be driven to undertake all the most extreme steps against your person and your friends . . .'

Duke John thinks, incredulously: He's not saying I should be afraid? Instinctively, his fingers tighten on his sword. But he relaxes, just a little when Chaucer finishes the other man's thought, as if they're agreed (which, since they're friends, they probably are): 'Whereas, if you let them be, they'll most likely do very little.'

Chaucer watches the red on the Duke's thin cheeks. Every diplomatic nerve in Chaucer's knowledgeable body is begging the Duke: Be flexible, be courteous, let calm return, let their anger burn out. He feels this volatile atmosphere is dangerous, but temporary – unless someone fans the flames. But he knows, too, that the Duke, like his royal brother, is prone to occasional, fantastical displays of anger. In this atmosphere, one of those could be the spark that sets the whole bonfire ablaze.

He only realises he hasn't been breathing (can such a thing be?) when the Duke lets the pent-up breath out of his own body. With his sigh, the Duke seems to sag. Weakly, defeatedly, Duke John nods his head and stops pacing. He sits down. With what little dignity he can still muster, he says, 'Very well.'

TWENTY-THREE

When the Duke returns to the chamber to face Parliament the next morning, he seems a different man: smiling, affable, willing to please. There's a murmur of surprise at the gracious, modest, encouraging look on his face, even before he starts to talk to the knights of the Commons.

'I know well how honourable your desires are, as you labour to improve the conditions of the realm,' he says. 'Whatever you think ought to be corrected, you should set forth, and I will apply the remedy you choose.'

Peter de la Mare glances around, drawing his strength from the men at his back. It's clear from their faces that his knights and burgesses are no less grimly suspicious that a portion of all the money stolen from the state by the various miscreants they intend to try has, perhaps, quietly found its way into John of Gaunt's own private purse (for, as de la Mare himself has told them, why else would the Duke have condoned this state of affairs so long?). Like them, he's impressed by the Duke's speech, but not impressed enough. He soldiers on. Today is the day he's been waiting for.

Standing up, he offers the Duke thanks on behalf of the knights. But he doesn't refrain from inviting his fellow-parliamentarians, one by one, to step forward and lay the charges they have prepared.

He goes first. A good commander leads from the front. The words come sonorously to his lips as he voices his ringing

315

accusation against Latimer, the King's chamberlain: 'That he is useless to the King and to the kingdom . . . has often deceived the King and been false – let me not say traitorous – to him. Therefore we most urgently petition that he should be deprived of his office.'

One by one, members of the Commons, speaking in turn at a lectern in the centre of the chamber, add their own charges and complaints. In this quieter but still tense atmosphere, more than sixty charges are laid against Lord Latimer and the vintner Richard Lyons. Alice Perrers' name is often, venomously, mentioned; but charges against her, on these counts, are not formalised.

De la Mare knows they won't be. There never has been much proof, one way or another, when it comes to Alice Perrers, and now his fool of a brother has muddied the waters with that witchcraft business. He doesn't care. She's only a woman. It's Latimer and Lyons he's after: the embodiment of corruption.

The two men are accused of making the King a loan of £20,000 at an exorbitant and unnecessary rate of interest, and of profiting from discounted debt paper.

He can see the Duke looking sceptical, as if he's thinking: Well, anyone can make an accusation. Murmuring to advisers. They're all patting at the air around him, calming him down; no doubt telling him to sit quietly and wait for the parliamentarians to run out of steam; saying, what proof can these rustic nobodies have of anything? It's all just hot air; let the poor fools talk themselves out. De la Mare, who knows better, bides his time. Among the Duke's advisers he recognises smug Sir Richard Stury. There's another one, too, in the shadows, who looks rather like the Customs man . . . Chaucer. Can't be, though. Look at them: shaking their heads. Pitying him, for the fool he's about to make of himself.

But he's not. De la Mare's heart swells and sings as he rises again. The knights stir and murmur. They trust him. They know he's done his preparation properly.

'With my lord's permission, I invite Richard, Baron Scrope of Bolton, the King's former treasurer . . .' he begins. His lips form the final words, 'to testify', but even he can't hear them. The sound is lost in the roaring hubbub.

With quiet joy, de la Mare watches the bewildered eyes of the men around the Duke. They know he means business now, because if anyone knows the truth about the government accounts, it'll be Scrope. They just can't see how he's done it. He can almost see them saying: But Scrope's gone home. North. Hasn't he?

Scrope, when he comes in from the antechamber, is grey-faced. He flinches at the approving calls and whistles from the knights. He turns his eyes away from the Duke, too; and once he's standing by de la Mare, he keeps his gaze fixed on the floor. It's clear he's hating this. But it's clear, too, that he won't shirk his duty.

De la Mare is brief. He waits for silence. He can afford the time. All he says, once the room's quiet enough to hear a pin drop, is: 'Do the copies of the royal accounts that you have kept over the past year confirm the truth of these accusations?'

All Scrope says, in return, is: 'Yes.' Still staring at the floor as the room goes wild.

'Thank you, my lord,' de la Mare says, or mouths, through the noise.

With an awkward bow at his own feet, Scrope sits down.

Then de la Mare gets down to the detailed business of comparisons.

First he reads out from the testimony of City merchants, some of them Florentines, the values written on several Florentine debt agreements that should have been exchanged at the Crown treasury, under the terms of the deal, for half their paper value. The testimony he reads states that the holders of this paper did, as agreed, receive only half the paper value of the debt agreements: £50 paid for every £100 of paper debt.

Then de la Mare turns to the Crown's accounts for the past two years. In the final version of these, as approved by Lord Latimer, the Crown does indeed appear to have paid out only £50 for every £100 of paper debt – the 50 per cent discount formally agreed.

But in Scrope's contemporaneous version of the royal accounts, things look very different.

In Scrope's version of the accounts, a full £100 in gold coin has left the treasury for every £100 of Italian debt paper presented. The total of extra money which has disappeared out of the final version of the accounts, over the past year alone, amounts to many thousands of pounds.

'Who was that extra money paid to, my lord?' de la Mare asks courteously, turning back to Scrope.

The man rushes to his feet. Staring down, he says, 'I can't say, Master Forespeaker. I wasn't present on any of the occasions on which money was paid out. All I can say is that the original entries were made in my lord Latimer's hand. If you want more details, I can only suggest that you ask my lord Latimer himself. Alternatively, you might ask the London agent for the House of Bari, of Florence, who, as I understand, has also been closely involved. He may know.'

'Ah – so the House of Bari still has an agent in London, does it, my lord?' de la Mare asks in a velvety whisper. 'All these years after closing down its offices in England?' He smiles a little. An eyebrow rises delicately.

'Only an informal one, sir,' Scrope replies. 'And I don't believe he bruits the connection abroad. A Flemish merchant, sir, by the name of Richard Lyons.'

There's a stir in the room. From the throne, the Duke watches without moving, while his men buzz and whisper around him in what seems to be soundless panic.

'When did these "corrections" start being regularly made to the treasury accounts, my lord?' de la Mare resumes over the hum.

Scrope hesitates, and then screws his eyes shut and plunges on. 'Only about a year ago, Master Forespeaker . . . when you were first given the task of investigating losses from the treasury,' he says. He opens his eyes. 'Before that, if you go back to last year's or the previous year's books, you'll see the amounts that were actually paid out all written down, plain as a pikestaff. But those books have been lodged in the archives; down in the cellars. They're never brought out.'

'And why do you think the accounting system was changed at that time?' de la Mare asks gently, scenting sweet victory.

Scrope's face is a furious red stain; he's never been so embarrassed. But he doesn't stop now. 'I believe your inquiries must have frightened the perpetrators of this fraud, Master Forespeaker,' he says, giving his own toes a terrible stare. 'I believe they wanted to cover their tracks. But I don't believe they thought you'd do more than glance at the latest accounts. I don't think they realised how deep you'd dig.'

De la Mare lets those words sink in across the chamber. 'Thank you, my lord,' he says sweetly.

De la Mare's having a job suppressing the smile that wants to come to his own face. He's done it. He's proved his knights have the truth with them. He's got the Lords on the run. From his litter, with closed eyes, the dying Prince allows the corners of his mouth to turn up, just a little. For a moment, he even opens his eyes and glances at de la Mare. De la Mare half closes his eyelids and bows his head: the closest he'll allow himself to a celebration. A shared moment of quiet triumph.

It's only later, as the crowds start pushing out through the doors, and the tide of emotion recedes with them, that de la Mare feels his hands begin to shake with delayed emotion. Other men would feast and sing, maybe. But he's tired, so tired. He's longing to be off his feet. Tonight, he tells himself, I'll sleep soundly tonight.

The next morning, with Latimer and Lyons impassive before them, the knights try Latimer and Lyons before the lords of the land. The next morning, after a night at Stury's, Chaucer sneaks back west with him as an extra, unofficial member of the Duke's entourage.

In the chamber, Latimer is accused of all kinds of supplementary crimes, as well as stealing profits from the debt deal. He's accused, among other things, of profiting from the recent unsuccessful military campaign in Brittany by extorting excessive ransoms from a number of Breton towns whilst at the same time surrendering others to the enemy – including

Bécherel and Saint-Sauveur – in return for bribes. He is also accused of cruelty to the people and cities of that land.

Lyons is accused of massive tax evasion, of various forms of customs-farming skulduggery in the ports of southern England, and of trying to corner the market in imported foodstuffs – legally the preserve of the pepperers and grocers – by confiscating, stealing and hoarding enough cargoes to force up prices.

The commoners gaze at Latimer and Lyons hungrily, full of their seething commoners' resentment that the treasury's pockets have been picked by the court and the court's creatures. Peter de la Mare's phrase hangs over the commoners' heads, 'the kingdom impoverished, the Commons ruined . . . for the private advantage of some near the King'. Do justice to these crooks, the Commoners are all thinking, as Peter de la Mare's interrogation begins, and there'll be no need for us to pay you a tax, too.

Chaucer and Stury, likewise, gaze at Latimer and Lyons. But what the pair of them are looking for, in those two faces, is the calm knowledge that this will pass, because Chaucer and Stury are now too rattled to have confidence in what they're telling the Duke.

To Chaucer's relief, it's there, on the faces of the accused, that golden self-assurance. A little comforted, Chaucer thinks: Well, they don't look bothered, at least. He's never seen Latimer ruffled, come to that. And Lyons – it's hard to imagine *him* looking anything but smooth and smug.

It is in Latimer's silky, leonine nature to argue. With his long tawny eyes flashing in his long golden face, the noble lord growls out a demand to know what person accuses him. The Commons, who have sworn vows of secrecy and mutual support, answer, through the mouth of Peter de la Mare, that they make all their charges 'in common'.

Latimer is disconcerted. But not for long. After a moment he says, with the knowledge of triumph dawning in his eyes, 'Ah, but all my actions had the approval of the King and his ministers.'

'Ah,' replies de la Mare, with the knowledge of a different

triumph dawning in his, 'but your actions nevertheless evaded the law of the kingdom, and were against the provisions of the statues made in Parliament, and statutes made in Parliament must be followed as written.' And he brings out the book of statutes he just happens to have about his person, opened at the right page to prove Latimer has broken the law, and he reads out the relevant paragraphs, to howls of approval from his men.

It is also in Latimer's nature to inspire fear by displaying his power. So, after the midday break, he sends his son-in-law, Sir John Neville, the King's seneschal, to defend him to the Commons. Grandly, Neville tells the little hedge-knights from nowhere that it's unseemly for low persons such as themselves to persecute a peer of the realm, privy councillor, and knight of the Garter.

Equally grandly, de la Mare replies, tapping the mountain of parchments in front of him, 'Cease, my lord, to intercede for others. We have not yet discussed you and your misdeeds. You may have enough to do in your own case.'

Latimer leaves the chamber when his part of the hearing is over with his usual slight smile. He looks as though nothing has gone wrong. But Chaucer, lurking in the shadows at the back of the room, is no longer convinced.

It's too much for Stury. He's outraged, that night, by the downfall of his friend Neville, who was also indicted at the end of his testimony and will have to answer charges of his own. Stury drinks himself maudlin. 'You know what this is leading to, don't you, Chaucer?' he keeps asking, looking out at the quiet of the black river with red eyes.

Chaucer keeps his peace. 'Don't take it too much to heart. We're observers, don't forget,' is all he says, in the manner of a man to a child. 'We can offer the Duke advice, if he wants it. But we're not part of it ourselves. We want to keep it that way.'

But Stury only shakes his head and pours himself more wine, and goes on muttering, 'Rebellion, rebellion; this is rebellion.' Stury's getting too close to it all, Chaucer thinks privately. Worried; distancing himself in his mind.

When Lyons' turn comes to face the knights, it emerges that bribery is more his weapon than persuasion or intimidation. He is cynical enough to believe there is no point in trying to bribe Peter de la Mare, that deluded nobody with his gassy talk of justice. Lyons goes straight to the master. He fills a fish barrel with a thousand pounds in gold coin, tops it off artistically with a few choice sturgeon, and has it sent to the Prince of England. Disgusted, the Prince sends the bribe on to the King, in his bed at Havering, to show how low the creature Lyons is. But he counts without his father's sense of humour. King Edward, who's feeling a little better now that he doesn't have to face this Parliament, is said, in the crowd, to have accepted Master Lyons' gift with amusement. He's taking the bribe, he tells his son, with a cheerful cynicism to match Lyons' own, because, after all, it appears to be money that's been stolen from him. 'He offers us nothing but what is our own', men in taverns quote him saying. With approval, too. They've always loved the King.

Neither arguing or bribery works for the accused men. Both Latimer and Lyons are found guilty, as are four subordinates, including Neville. They are dismissed, fined, and imprisoned. The sentences are pronounced by the Duke, who, apparently stunned at the turn events are taking, lets de la Mare hand him the paper on which they're written, and then reads them out in a monotone, without changes. Chaucer, in the shadows, watches Latimer, Lyons, Neville and the others bundled off. They can't believe it either, he sees. Latimer manages a disdainful look for the heavy pushing him. But he sees fear on Lyons' smooth jowl.

The crowds pour into the taverns to celebrate. Stury, hungover and shocked, has hardly spoken all day. Like him, Chaucer feels anxious for the arrested men, even though it was stated in court that they'll be kept in accommodation suitable to their rank, not some fetid cell. Still, Chaucer also senses that the worst is over. 'De la Mare's had his day,' he says as they ride home, thinking to comfort his friend. 'There'll be no more shocks now, Stury. He's done what he came to do, don't you think?' Silence. 'The knights will go home soon . . . it will all be forgotten . . . And perhaps Latimer and Lyons will even learn a few lessons; or the next people in their places be more honest.

'We should count this a success, not a failure,' Chaucer tries more weakly. 'You kept the Duke calm; I played my small part, too . . .' and he pauses, allowing Stury an elegant space in which to thank him for his time and eloquence. But Stury's tweaking at his reins. He's not listening. A hundred or so yards later, Chaucer adds, with rather less warmth, 'I should go back to work tomorrow. I should go home tonight.'

Back at work in the Customs House, from the next morning, Chaucer finds relief in the calm comparison of weights, the minute calculations of pennies and shillings. He drops in at one tavern or another, on his way home, for a Westminster update. But he's lost the urgent need to do nothing but live and breathe the parliamentary sessions. The Duke's still treating the knights with kid gloves, thank God. Alice has wisely gone to ground, and they've passed her by. With luck, it won't be long now before it all peters out.

Over at Westminster, the Parliament grinds on, through April and May. But its flash and energy is wearing low.

De la Mare asks for, and obtains, royal permission for a nine-man council to share in the ruling of England. This, it is implied but not stated, will dilute the influence of John of Gaunt and his creatures. The council will contain old enemies of the Duke of Lancaster, including a former chancellor, William of Wykeham, Bishop of Winchester, and John's cousin, Edmund, the Mortimer Earl of March, who've both been very actively helping the Parliament.

Once the new council is in place, Parliament, still meeting, starts to dissipate its energies in prosecuting lesser men on smaller charges.

Among them is Chaucer's friend Stury. Chaucer thinks, uncharitably: Well, it's his own fault; he should have kept quiet, lain low . . . lived to fight another day.

For Stury – the impulsive fool – seems to have given way to a better-to-do-something-than-nothing knightly impulse, and stuck his neck out. He's ridden off to Havering and told the King, who seems to know nothing, how his friends are being persecuted at Westminster. Stury's always been excitable. And he's over-egged this story. He's told the distressed, confused old man that the Parliament is seeking to depose him – to do to him what was once, long ago, done to the King's father. Irritably, Chaucer thinks that he can just imagine the way Stury will have stood there repeating, 'Rebellion . . . outright rebellion!' When the King asked him, piteously, what he should do to avert the danger, Stury apparently said he should dismiss the Parliament at once. Or so the street talk has it, anyway.

The result of that meeting is tavern talk for a good two or three days. Panicking, the King decides to stumble off to Westminster to consult his eldest son. He doesn't know that Prince Edward of England has been fainting and fitting so much in the chamber that he's retired home to his sickbed at Kennington.

His litter comes into London, under Chaucer's gate, with a troop of a hundred men. When they see the King's insignia on the litter, clusters of people stop what they're doing and form a thin crowd around the slowly jolting parade. It's always been a pleasure to be near the King's movements; he's a man for a smile, and a joke, and leaning over to tip a boy with a coin or a girl with an appreciative kiss. But today the red-and-gold litter curtains remain closed all the way down to the Tower jetty. The King doesn't get out, even then, even when it's being awkwardly manoeuvred on to his waiting barge. Shaking their heads resignedly, as if pausing on the thought that things aren't how they used to be, the goodwives of London put their baskets back on their shoulders and hurry about their business.

There are betrayers everywhere. News of Stury's mission to Havering reaches London before Stury gets back. Stury's dismissal from the King's Council is announced in Parliament. Men are posted at his house to arrest him on his return. Perhaps Stury knows. He vanishes. Gone to ground, like Alice. But the Parliament keeps on.

TWENTY-FOUR

Chaucer has all but stopped bothering to drop in at the Burning Bush, or the Bear, or the Bull, on his way home from the Customs House, to get the very first of the news. He hears it all anyway, one way or another, sooner or later – at work, or on the street, or from the servants. There's no tearing hurry.

He's not even that frightened for Alice when he hears that she's been arrested at Pallenswick. She's now staying, under guard, at Westminster.

If she's wise, and keeps quiet, she'll be fine, he thinks. It's passing.

It's at his workplace, at the beginning of June, that he hears, from one of his clerks, that there is, after all, a new development at Parliament. The man has glee written all over his face. He says, 'You'll never guess what. They've been talking about Alice Perrers again in Parliament. And she's testifying this afternoon.'

Chaucer lifts his face from the Counter-Roll. At the same time he feels his innards contract. He says, 'What?'

Then, trying to put an unconcerned grin on his face, he adds, 'Why?'

'Adultery!' the man replies, rubbing his hands.

'What?' Chaucer says again, stupidly. His innards are tying themselves in knots. But Alice isn't married. She's a widow. The King's a widower. No one would pretend that the pair of them weren't lovers, but they haven't been hurting anyone

325

else with their private sin. In Church terms, what they did was only ever fornication, surely, not the graver sin of adultery that, say, the Duke is quietly committing with Katherine; bringing shame on his neglected wife. What sense can it make to label Alice an adulterer? 'But . . . wasn't it witchcraft . . .' he stammers, 'that they were accusing her of?'

His mind is racing. It was always stupid to try and make Alice out to be a witch. And there hasn't been enough evidence to accuse her of embezzling government money, either, however many times her name has been named in this connection. (She was right about that.) There have been vague accusations from the Commons that the King gave her thousands of pounds a year – three thousand, by one account. There have been accusations that she invaded the courts of justice, sitting on the King's Bench. There have been the usual accusations that she used her position of influence with the King to further her own business interests, and wore the Queen's jewels. A man has even been dragged in who said, with no evidence, that Alice had paid a squire of her retinue to kill an unnamed sailor against whom she had a grudge. But there've been no facts, just stories. And none of the dirt has stuck.

Perhaps de la Mare is despairing of a real charge. Perhaps he just wants to get Alice, somehow, anyhow, before the Parliament ends. But they're angry with her about money, not sex. And to frame one kind of charge in punishment for a different kind of offence doesn't seem in de la Mare's nature. He's been more precise, until now. He hasn't gone in for unsubstantiated slanders.

Especially this one, which as well as being foolish seems impossible to prosecute. They'd have to hand Alice over to the Church for trial, if they pursued adultery . . . and Chaucer can't imagine that de la Mare will be expecting the Church, in the shape of Edward's tame Archbishop Sudbury, to dance to his tune and destroy Alice for mortal sin, just on the Parliament's say-so, or even to have her hair shaved off. It would be absurd.

Chaucer can't make out what the man's game can be.

Because, really, adultery . . . well, it's just one of those holier-than-thou pulpit words, isn't it? Something to accuse your enemies of, if you're minded to be vindictive, while not looking too closely at your own affairs, because everyone . . .

It's only now that something else dawns on Chaucer – an idea so utterly horrifying that he feels the blood draining away from his head until he's dizzy and has to reach for the table to hold his back straight, then rushing back, whooshing in his ears and staining his face the guiltiest possible harlot scarlet.

They can't, can they, they can't possibly be meaning . . .

. . . he conjures up Philippa's sleek head; her scornful smile . . . and he smells the smell of Alice's rose-scented flesh, moving under him . . .

. . . *him?*

Because he knows, who better, whom Alice Perrers *has* recently been committing adultery with. He's just not thought of it like that. Never given it a name at all.

But surely the Parliament doesn't know, or care, about *him*. Surely not even Peter de la Mare, with his uncanny knack of ferreting out hidden knowledge, with his relentless mills-of-God approach to justice, going on and on, grinding more and more exceeding small every day, can possibly think that what Alice Perrers has done, just a few times, in a quiet corner of the City, far from prying eyes . . .

The clerk's shaking his head, enjoying his tale. Pleasurably, he explains, 'Turns out she's been married, for years – to William of Windsor. The one in Ireland.'

Chaucer nods, too stunned to say anything. 'Oh,' he mutters. For now, all he can feel is selfish relief. He's weak with it. He bends over his work, waiting for his flush, and his panic, to recede, thanking God with every ounce of his sullied flesh that, at least, not that; he won't be dragged through the mud . . . disgraced.

It seems a long while before his mind begins to function; before the questions begin again.

But they do.

De la Mare must have dug deep, been forced to dig deep, to accuse her of adultery on the basis of that old relationship

327

with William of Windsor – to have even begun to think that she might once have been the wife of a man who's spent the past decade in Ireland. How can he have found out?

Chaucer knows that this story is more or less true, because Alice has told him. (Though he doubts she and William of Windsor were ever formally blessed in a church; but there are the children; the Church might take their existence as proof of a permanent union, if it were minded to . . . if it knew about the children . . . which de la Mare can't . . . though then again how can he know any of it?)

What puzzles Chaucer most is that he knows Alice doesn't talk about her past love. Chaucer supposes it's possible that little Froissart once knew – she was close to him at that time. But he's not been in England for years. And, after that, Chaucer believes, she's never mentioned it again. To anyone. Until she told him.

It can't even be William of Windsor himself who's talked. He's not here either.

So how can de la Mare know? The man's grim reach seems almost superhuman.

It seems a long time that Chaucer agonises over this.

It seems a long time before he remembers himself blurting out to Philippa, months ago, that Alice's children aren't royal bastards; remembers saying the name, 'William of Windsor'; remembers the answering gleam in his wife's eye.

It's only now that he realises he's known all along that he shouldn't have said it.

It was only a rash comment made in the heat of the moment. It should have died and been forgotten. He shouldn't have to feel responsible.

But he does. Oh, how he does. He's staring into an abyss of wordless, eye-closing, stomach-churning, howling self-reproach that'll be with him for ever.

For all his hopes and good intentions, it's he, Geoffrey Chaucer, who's betrayed Alice to her enemies. It's he, Geoffrey Chaucer, who is to blame.

A few hours later, Alice is brought to the lectern and sworn in. She's spent a week in polite custody – in a good enough room overlooking the river, with clothes cared for and palace food provided, and even hot bathwater, but with men at the door whom she can't make friends with, and watched all the time by servants she doesn't know, who only shake their heads at her falsely casual requests to provide her with writing materials, or carry messages to the King. (She doesn't even ask whether they'll take messages to Richard Lyons or Chaucer.) She's not in despair, exactly; she's been keeping herself light on her toes, whistling under her breath, not letting her mind stop too long on what the Forespeaker might accuse her of. They've got nothing against her, she keeps telling herself, trying not to remember that they didn't seem to have much on Stury or Neville either at the start, but found charges anyway. They're fools, these parliamentarians. Hicks. What can they pin on her? She's also found herself, more than once, taking comfort in the thought that the Duke will intercede to stop them bullying her; she only wishes she could be more certain that this were definitely true. For the opening part of this session, he hasn't looked at her. He hasn't looked at anything much, except the backs of his hands. He looks, she thinks, glancing sideways at him, letting her lungs deflate, rather hopeless . . . defeated, almost.

For the past hour, while the knights troop in and the formalities are completed, she's been kept at the back of the room, between Sir John de la Mare and his unchivalrous knightly friend (who enjoyed arresting her friar and also their miserable ride from Pallenswick with her last week so much that they've volunteered to accompany her to the chamber today, too, as guards, and are still giving her triumphant little looks from mean eyes) during an entire peroration by Peter de la Mare about the allegation that she 'had been preferred in the King's love before the Queen'. Well, she's thinking defiantly, so what if I was? I wasn't the only one, by any manner of means. And you'll never prove, one way or another, when it all started between me and Edward anyway. Is that the worst you can do? She raises her chin.

The King is reclining on his litter. They've asked him to attend today, specially, the servants were saying. He's looking puzzled. Lost. Tentatively, she smiles at him. He throws her a sad answering look. Take me away from here, he seems to be signalling. Let's go home. For a moment, her heart leaps with the possibility of it; with the possibility of all this being over, and her being able to go back to looking after her poor old darling, quietly, with trees outside the windows, and none of these people here. But then she realises he's hardly recognised her. It's not a look specifically intended for her, Alice Perrers, the woman he's loved for so long. It's just a woeful old-man's look, meaning, 'I need peace and quiet . . . why am I here, surrounded by enemies?' Poor Edward. She doesn't think he understands any of it.

She's heard that the Prince of England also comes to the sessions in a litter. But there's no sign of him today.

Peter de la Mare leans forward. She can smell the hatred on him, the expectation of an almost sexual pleasure in her disgrace. She doesn't care. She's been scared long enough. She's fed up with the fear of these past months. It's a surprise, but a not unpleasant one, when she identifies the feeling inside herself as anger. She thinks, almost with relief: How I loathe the sanctimonious look on his grey face.

She grins defiantly at him. Nothing is actually going to happen to her, is it? There's nothing that this bullying man can say that can actually shake her out of the life she's earned, at the top; nothing that can make her world spin and crumble to dust behind her.

'Are you, Alice Perrers . . .' he intones, ignoring her monkey grimace.

Misunderstanding his intonations, she answers, sweetly enough, 'Yes.'

He tuts, and continues, as if she's deliberately obstructing the course of justice by interrupting him: '. . . the wife of Sir William of Windsor, of Greyrigg, Northumberland?'

For a moment she doesn't even take it in. Because there's no way he can know that.

Is there?

There's no one in this land who knows.

Except Chaucer.

That's when she looks at Edward and sees his white beard quiver, and his eyes seek her out and suddenly know who she is; and the pitiful look in them is a betrayed look, a dog shut out of the house and deprived of its bone.

Chaucer? Her friend? Chaucer, whom she trusts?

That's when the world starts to spin.

Chaucer doesn't rejoin the Duke's entourage when he gets off the boat at Westminster. He's too scared. He feels too guilty. He can't be in that room, where Alice might see him. But he does find his way back to the upstairs gallery, and squats there, alone, trying to stifle sneezes and sniffs, above the Duke's head, trying to catch the voices.

He cranes forward when they bring Alice forward to swear her oath. He sees her, all right. She goes white when de la Mare makes his adultery charge. She looks around, as if in panic, as if she's looking for the escape route, or the friend who isn't there. She sways. They put a stool behind her, and she sinks down. She doesn't say anything; doesn't even answer the charge. There's no need, really. Not right now. Her face says it all. Her face stays grey.

He can't see the King, swearing an oath on the Virgin that he's not aware of any marriage. But he hears the weak old voice as the King pleads: '. . . Master Forespeaker, I beg you to have mercy on her, out of love for me.' And, like everyone watching below, he hears the voice waver and crack on those last words. He thinks the King, who for all his nearly fifty years on the throne has been loved for the freedom of his emotions, might be publicly weeping.

The Forespeaker nods, and clears his throat. Not a man of easy emotions himself, he seems embarrassed to be distressing his monarch. From the bottom of his self-dug pit of despair, Chaucer leans forward again as de la Mare turns back to Alice, as if looking at her is easier, and resumes, in that velvety, yet insistent, voice: 'Mistress Perrers, will you answer the charge?'

Alice rises to her feet. She stands there for a long moment without saying anything, just swaying. She's plucking at the stuff of her skirt with one busy hand.

Chaucer remembers he's not breathing, and gulps in air.

Eventually, Alice finds her voice, and a glimmer of her old cheek. She looks up, and meets de la Mare's eye. And she says, with a shrug, and the beginning of her familiar devil-may-care grin: 'Well, Master Forespeaker, all I can tell you is that it was a long time ago . . . and only a marriage at the church door.'

Chaucer can see why she's trying this tack. The Church has never been sure it accepts those vague pledges people some-times make at the church door, without benefit of clergy (without benefit to the clergy either, as there's no marriage fee involved), as real marriages in the eyes of God.

But it comes out wrong. It sounds . . . cheap, that defiance; it sounds like just the kind of wilful tricksiness that these men are trying to eradicate. And, by saying it, she's admitted that at least a form of marriage took place, and that she is, as alleged, an adulterer. He can see that from the small smile de la Mare can't keep from his face. And he can hear it's gone down badly from the sudden hubbub in the room, the excited murmurings and quick movements of triumphant eyes.

He shuts his eyes. He leans back, covering his face with his hands. He doesn't want to have to see Alice's face, as she realises her sally's only made things worse for her. He's heard enough.

On the boat, the boatman gloats: 'If you ask me, they *won't* have mercy. I've heard they're going to call in the Bishop of London tomorrow.'

Chaucer stares fiercely at the ripples, trying to ignore the wrenchings of his gut. He hasn't thought, until now, that anything could make him feel worse. But now he does. If gentle Archbishop Sudbury is being passed over in Alice's case, and William Walworth's pocket churchman coming to judge her instead, then . . .

'Adultery is a crime against God,' he hears the boatman saying from very far away. 'So she'll hang. Bishop Courtenay will tie the noose himself.'

* * *

But something else happens, before the trial of Alice Perrers goes veering off in this altogether more threatening and sinister direction – something that utterly overshadows, and briefly halts, Peter de la Mare's puppet show at Westminster.

TWENTY-FIVE

Muttering, fiddling with his rheumatic fingers, and with tears streaming down his face and into his beard, tears which are not altogether the work of the unkind wind, King Edward has himself rowed across the river from the session at Westminster to the palace at Kennington.

De la Mare, following in a hired boat, watches that frail figure with pity colouring his usual awe. De la Mare feels sorry that he's had to distress his monarch by asking the questions he's had to ask today; but that England needed to have the immorality of the Perrers woman publicly aired he has no doubt, since her dishonest dealings with money, which are proving so hard to pin down, are surely along the same lines as her years of dishonest behaviour with men. Now, he thinks, the King will take comfort with his son; and the rightness of that mixes in his mind with his own dutifully suppressed desire to be home watching his own boy mount a horse and gallop along the riverbank, all freckles and spontaneity, shouting with happiness. De la Mare reveres everything about the King, and now, on this boat, nothing more than the love the old man bears his eldest son. He can well imagine the thoughts chasing through the King's confused head: My son will understand. My son will explain what's going on.

But there is to be no comfort for the King across the water. What awaits the newcomers at Kennington Palace, coming from the darkened bedchamber of the Prince, is the sound of screaming.

The bouts of coma that the Prince has been suffering in recent days are now interspersed with waking periods of agony. Looking up the great stairwell, at the bent old back labouring up those steps towards his daughter-in-law, Sir Peter can see that Princess Joan's face is twisted with anguish. The doctors' faces are twisted with terror.

Edward hastens on, and vanishes with Joan into the noise. The door shuts.

Sir Peter is left in the hall downstairs, ignored by the scurrying servants, alone with his thoughts.

He knows the King has buried four grown-up children in his time; he's lost two boys himself. He can well imagine that the King, too, must feel the continuing pain of each of their deaths like an amputation. But this must be different. Worse. This is King Edward's most beloved child; his treasure, his consolation.

The screaming upstairs stops after a while. But the frantic running-around downstairs persists. Men rushing upstairs with new slops buckets, water, wine, blankets, linen, and braziers to cut the stink; and others rushing downstairs with used articles, which no one wants to look at.

Sir Peter is still there, overwhelmed by pity that's becoming almost unbearable, when a litter bearing the now silent Prince makes its unsteady way down the stairs, followed by King, Princess, little boy, doctors, knights of the body, attendants, and more servants carrying boxes and bags. The King's head is bowed. He makes no attempt to hide the tears pouring down his face.

Sir Peter can see the howling emptiness in the old man's soul as he watches the litter being manoeuvred on to the boat, and the King, with a strange return to majesty, handing Princess Joan down into it after her husband. The King is taking them back to Westminster with him. Sir Peter under-stands, or thinks he does. This is the end, and the King wants only what every good father would, when what is about to happen is something no good father can bear to contemplate. At least, at the last, he wants his family to be together.

So there is no Parliament at Westminster in the days that follow. There are just the screams, which set everyone's teeth on edge, and the silences, which set everyone's teeth on edge worse. And in between there are the busy moments of consciousness, when the Prince sits up and calls the trembling lawyers to his side to dictate that after his death this war-horse will go to that knight, and his bed-furniture embroidered with the deeds of Saladin to his son, and this silver cup to that servant; when he calls the quiet little boy trying not to move next to Princess Joan and asks him to keep on all his retainers; when his long will is finally read over, on 7 June, and more changes and additions made, and his executors named. He is to be buried in Canterbury Cathedral, in the undercroft beneath the shrine of St Thomas the Martyr, with his shield, helmet, sword and surcoat above his grave. He wants a French poem inscribed on his tomb, and also the badge of three ostrich feathers and the Flemish motto *Ich Dien*, which he used at Crécy, his greatest victory. There's a moment when he assembles his family – the Princess, and the scared boy by her side, and the King, and John, Duke of Lancaster, and his two younger brothers – and orders the men of his blood to swear on the Bible to protect his son. He watches his brother, mylordofLancaster, through fierce, narrowed eyes, as John takes the Bible; he's aware of Joan doing the same from her corner. It is important to him to die well, with all his worldly affairs settled.

Only after the will is completed does he order the doors opened. For that evening, and through the night, and through the next morning, and into the next afternoon, the gatemen at the palace entrance allow anyone in who wants to say goodbye. The members of his family are on stools behind the bed, all of them (except the child, who doesn't know what to do, and frets and fidgets) immobile: wet-faced and dead-eyed. The household files through. Then the rest. The Prince's agony is all but over. Only the fear for his little boy's future, which he experiences as a rage against his brother as intense as any of the pains that have racked him, is still there. Mostly he lies quietly, as people move through the chamber, though sometimes he opens his eyes, and once he stirs and shouts, though it's not clear to whom, 'I recommend to you my son, who is still very young and small. I pray that as you have served me so from your heart you will serve him.'

But, even now, there is no meekness in this prince's passing. He will leave this life as superbly and as pridefully as he has lived it. It is generally considered important, when preparing for the flight of the soul from its bodily prison, for a man to ask forgiveness of God and of all those whom he has injured during his life on this earth. But not this man. For hours on end, the Prince of England ignores the requests of the bishops fluttering around him, trying to administer extreme unction, to actually say the words 'I pray pardon of God and man'. The best he can manage is a curt nod. Then a grunt. The bishops eye each other and shake their heads. Between visitors, in moments of quiet, they glide back to him and try again to make him ask for pardon for his sins. 'You must say the words yourself,' they plead. But there's no fear of his Maker in the Prince. He hasn't yet abandoned this life, and the anger that has kept him alive for so long. He purses his lips, and clenches his fists as if to beat the confessors off, and shuts his eyes.

He is almost dead when, at dawn, Sir Richard Stury comes in, wet from the river, or the rain, shrugging off the russet travelling cloak of a poor man. The sight of Stury, whom he's always treated with honour, as a friend and fellow-knight, but whose loyalty he fears lies with mylordofLancaster, skulking in the shadows there, briefly rouses him – but only to new anger. He snarls at the glistening shape before him, the shape of the man who's tried to incite the King of England to dismiss the Parliament intended to destroy mylordofLancaster, the very shape of treachery, who must be here only to gloat at the passing of the Prince he's betrayed. Bitterly, he says, 'Come, Richard, come and look on what you have long desired to see.' He ignores the horrified hushes and the whispered I-have-always-loved-you protests. He shouts, with hatred, 'God pay you according to your deserts. Leave me and let me see your face no more.'

Stury is not there when next he opens his eyes. Just the confessors, buzzing in his ear, begging him, again, to repent, and forgive.

Forgive? He shakes his head. He looks at mylordofLancaster's set wet face. It's not in him. It's only when he sees his father's tormented face beside the clerk's – the red eyes, the white beard drizzled with the tears that flow unnoticed from them – that he feels the softness, and gives in. He still won't say the words. But he does, through gritted teeth, reply, 'I will do it.'

After the death, hours afterwards, after sunset even, the King, who's lapsed into vague torpor, ignoring every whispered request to be allowed to bring him food or drink, asks his servants to call Alice.

But the servants don't call Alice. They whisper among themselves, and vanish.

And, the next morning, the merciless Parliament reconvenes.

TWENTY-SIX

It is dusk, or would be if it wasn't raining – slanting spears and arrows of cold dark water. Over the river the Prince is dying. Over here, creeping down a back alley off deserted, splashy Thames Street, ignoring the City's curfew bells like a bedraggled footpad, is Geoffrey Chaucer.

He knows there are soldiers at the front of Alice's house. He's seen them – half a dozen men at the gatehouse, playing cards. That must mean she's been brought here to wait out the break in the Parliament.

But there's no one at the kitchen-garden gate. Perhaps the soldiers don't know it's there.

He slips up the main path towards the house, with the river gurgling and roaring at his back. He's blinking water out of his eyes. In front of the windows is a big old apple tree, whose blossom has been dashed off it by the harsh weather – a white scatter on the ground. As he approaches, the shutters at the house's downstairs windows are closed by unseen hands, and the garden goes dark.

He doesn't mind. There's one window left unshuttered, upstairs: a square of yellow. Alice must be in her room.

He waits. There's wet seeping through to his bones. Then he climbs the glistening tree, toehold by slippery toehold.

You're always safe if you're holding on in three places. His father's voice comes into his head as he hoists himself carefully up. *Two feet and a hand. Two hands and a foot.* But Chaucer doesn't want to hear that kindly voice now. His problem isn't being safe enough. It's not being brave enough.

Chaucer's never been brave enough. When the merchants tell him, 'Your father would be proud of you,' he knows it's not true. John Chaucer spent his life doggedly following the King around the wars, building up wealth and knowledge of the court, of course, but really just hoping that his son would benefit from lifelong proximity to nobility; what he always wanted was for Geoffrey to bear arms – maybe to become a knight himself. He didn't understand when his son lost his nerve. Even today, Geoffrey Chaucer doesn't like remembering how proudly his father presented him with the sword and buckler he took to France that one time . . . or the bewilderment in John's eyes when Geoffrey, after not even one battle – just one ambush, and one brush with captivity – refused point blank to go back to the war, and left Lionel of Ulster's service rather than be asked. John Chaucer couldn't hope to understand the dread. He was a pure-bred merchant, not a courtly mongrel like his son. He'd never had to try to fight. Not that there were any reproaches. All the older Chaucer said, with a wistful shake of the head, was, 'Well, if it doesn't happen, it doesn't happen,' and within a few months he was letting himself be consoled by the offer of marriage to well-born Philippa. Another route to knightliness, Master Chaucer must have thought. If only, Geoffrey Chaucer sometimes thinks today, his father had realised – or *he'd* realised – how Philippa would always despise his lack of knightly skills, and how his children, almost courtiers themselves, would shy from being associated by blood with a man in a long gown, his only weapon a quill.

But he's trying to prove himself now, at least. He's trying to win his spurs. He's going to tell Alice he's going to save her.

When he's got high enough to be able to peer in at the first-floor window, through the thin upper branches that crack and sway with his weight, he sees with a rush of indescribable relief that there's a small head silhouetted behind those glowing panes of glass. Alice, looking out, through the torrent, at the dark.

'Alice,' he calls, in a low voice, so the soldiers won't hear. 'Alice.'

After a moment, the head rises. Her body comes into view.

He sees her looking out at him: eyes in the rain. Her quiet gaze meets his. He thinks she recognises him.

But there is no answering smile on her face. She closes the shutters.

In the morning, people are saying Stury has been arrested leaving the Prince's palace at Kennington. By then, the passing-bells have started to clang, and they also know the Prince is dead.

Every prudent bone in Chaucer's body tells him to go straight home from the Customs House. There's no point in anything else. What good can he do? He's got a cold. He's shivery. He's chilled inside and out. He hasn't slept. His cloak is still damp. His boots, too.

But instead he goes out and pays a boatman to take him to Westminster.

Honour demands it. He has to try.

They find an empty room somewhere in the warren of corridors and spaces behind the abbey. It's not usually this quiet. But most of the Commons are out on the street, milling about, talking in hushed voices about the Prince's passing.

Chaucer, too, has muttered 'a tragic day' and 'God rest his soul', while introducing himself as a man who, while a courtier, knows the mood of London. He's been rewarded with a single austere phrase, 'I know your work, Master Chaucer.'

From a perch in the window, de la Mare is now gazing down at him like an eagle contemplating its prey. He wastes no words. But he's listening.

Chaucer does his best to keep his breathing light and shallow. He's thought out very carefully what will impress the Forespeaker. He's not going to mess this up.

'This tragedy changes everything, including the work your men will do when Parliament reconvenes,' he begins oratorically. 'What was uppermost in the minds of the Commons, before, will count for less after today . . .'

After a silence, de la Mare nods.

341

'. . . while England's leading men will have new burdens to shoulder,' Chaucer pursues, encouraged.

De la Mare nods again, with the minimum possible movement of the head. He's coiled tight as a spring, Chaucer sees: white at nostril and knuckle, preparing himself for battle. The death of the Commons' royal sponsor lays the Forespeaker and his men open to attack. They must be expecting reprisals from the Duke of Lancaster. De la Mare will be terrified, yet elated, that the moment has come when John of Gaunt may even, as evil tongues have been whispering for so long, try to seize the throne. He'll have no time for anything except the showdown he feels is coming. He'll want to tie up the loose ends of Parliament.

Chaucer's praying this will mean he's lost interest in Alice.

'I speak for many in London who admire your achievements,' Chaucer goes on. 'You've swept the government clean. You've stopped the rot.'

De la Mare permits himself the smallest of smiles.

'Many in London would say your task is already completed,' Chaucer now ventures, hardly daring to breathe. 'There's only Alice Perrers left to deal with. And, with this new weight of grief and sorrow on all of us, the City may grow impatient if a trial into possible long-ago marriages is dragged out at length . . .'

He gasps in air. '. . . a trial that may now seem frivolous,' he finishes.

Silence. De la Mare raises an eyebrow.

Chaucer wishes he could tell what the man is thinking.

But he persists: 'You and I both know that it's not Mistress Perrers who's to blame for all the bad government in the land. She's only a symbol of the corruption you've – so successfully – cut out. It would be merciful – and wise, in today's sadder circumstances – to make her punishment symbolic too.'

What Chaucer dreads is that de la Mare, who only last week locked Neville up for defending Latimer, will turn to him with cold fire in his eyes and say, 'Who are you to defend the whore? Isn't it time we investigated *you*?'

But if the Forespeaker is not a kind man, he's a just one.

When, at last, he speaks, he only says, in a faraway voice, 'What did you have in mind, Master Chaucer?'

Chaucer might not know about swords, but he knows the moment to make a deal. Promptly, he replies, 'Make her agree to leave court and the King. Confiscate the properties the King has given her. Then drop the other charges – and let her go.'

Alice will have her children, at least, he thinks, hopefully. And she'll have properties stashed away, rainy-day money. She'll get by. She'll have the life she might otherwise have lived.

With growing confidence, he waits for the thoughts chasing through the other man's mind to come clear.

He can't begin to imagine the painful, sombre compassion that has been in de la Mare since he saw the King with his son in that litter. He can't imagine that de la Mare would now do almost anything to save the King further distress. That de la Mare simply needs to convince himself that his own strong instinct to heed Chaucer and spare the King's whore is not just the softness of grief: mercy untempered by reason, an emotion he has never allowed himself.

The silence seems to last for ever. But, eventually, the eagle-head nods. De la Mare says, 'Leave it with me.'

TWENTY-SEVEN

There are trumpets when the new heir to the throne of England walks into the Parliament chamber. Peter de la Mare has used his temporary powers to summon the young Prince to be publicly presented to his future subjects.

The blond nine-year-old, tall for his age but still shorter by a head than the shortest man present, blinks a little at the size of the crowd. But he's poised. He's in black, but there are no obvious traces of grief on his face. He's a Plantagenet, for all his tender years. Graciously, he inclines his head. Then the eyes devouring him turn down, and every man in the room drops to his knees. There'll be no chance the Duke can say, after this, that the little Prince was a weakling, and died in his sleep, or a cripple not long for this world, or a bastard. The boy's strength and royal bearing have been noted. Every knight now swearing loyalty has seen.

The only man left standing, for a moment or two, is the Duke of Lancaster. His face is dark. His eyes are dark, too, and unfocused. But they fix on Peter de la Mare as the Forespeaker, on his knees, swears his public vow of loyalty to the boy, first of all the Commons of England. And there's an intensity of hatred in them that makes even the impassive knight of Herefordshire flinch.

Alice takes the crucifix. She stares at it. She's trying not to think of the eyes.

The men are all around, pressing in on her. The chamber is packed.

'I swear,' de la Mare intones.

'I swear,' she repeats, clutching the big metal cross.

They've already heard the list of her sins and crimes. She's already heard her sentence. How unreal it all seems. And how strange, she thinks, almost gaily, that getting Wat off his charge is all they can get her on in the end. Witchcraft, adultery, embezzlement . . . no result. But they've passed a whole law forbidding women to interfere with the course of the King's justice. She can't quite believe they're letting her off. She isn't going to die. She's light-headed with the relief of it. She wants to finger her neck, tell it, 'You escaped.' She just can't imagine what she will do when she walks out of this door.

She wishes her cheeks weren't so hot.

She promises never to return to the King's presence. She promises to return his gifts to her.

There is no more to the ceremony. 'You may go,' de la Mare says. The eyes follow her all the way to the doors and beyond.

In the antechamber she walks into, she stretches out her hands and presses them and one cheek against the nearest bit of cool stone wall. What to do now is, for the first time, coming into focus. She has no idea whether she even has a right to ask for a horse. And she has no idea where to go. She just knows that she has to get away from the eyes. For now, she can do no more than listen to the sound of her own breathing.

This is how the Duke finds her.

He understands that spread-eagled pose; the helplessness.

He feels it too. He's grieving for a brother who he sees has died hating him. He's yelling at him in his head; he's wishing Joan didn't seem to hate him so passionately too; and, above all, he's full of his own poisonous hatred of de la Mare for so humiliatingly demonstrating, by that public vow of loyalty, that the Commons suspect he's about to murder his nephew. And there's nothing he can do. I don't want to be King of England, he's shouting inside; I want revenge.

345

'Madame Perrers,' he says very softly.

She turns her head. Nothing else. She's past caring.

But when she sees it's him, she shakes her head, as if trying to compose herself, and detaches herself from the wall. She even bobs a little bow. Her cheeks are flushed.

'My lord,' she breathes, looking down at his feet.

He has a little bag of money ready.

'My father has been asking for you,' he adds. 'Let's say this is from him.'

She takes it, uncertainly.

She doesn't say anything about the King. He sees she's too overwhelmed to speak. Her silence somehow makes him feel better about his own towering, impotent rage at the gathering of rogues and fools out there. We're both their victims, he thinks. This is what it does to you.

He says, 'This will not last.' There's a promise in his voice. He hasn't sought out Alice Perrers for a long time. But he can no longer remember the anger he once felt when she rashly asked for a noble title for her child. Now, all he sees is a kindred spirit, being mocked, defiled, destroyed, by unworthy enemies.

She raises her eyes to his – a glance of disbelief. He holds her gaze, willing her to believe it. If she does, he'll begin to believe it himself.

'No one will touch you,' he says more firmly. 'Take a horse from my stables. Go to Wendover – it's near my lands at Weston Turville and Chalfont St Peter, so you can always get word to me if need be. And wait.'

She's still looking at him, as if she doesn't know whether to believe him.

'Don't be afraid,' he adds stoutly. 'I'm going to sort all this out.'

She shakes her head. She manages a quick grin. 'Me,' she says, 'I'm never afraid.'

Then she bows her head, low, so he can't see her eyes any more. He has an uncomfortable feeling she might be hiding tears. There's a shakiness in her voice when she mutters, 'Thank you.' There's a shakiness in her gait when, brushing past him, breaching every possible kind of etiquette but without causing him any offence, she backs away to the door.

The Duke emerges from the antechamber feeling marginally better.

Not that grief isn't lashing at him with its monstrous tail; not that he's not feeling crushed by misfortune. So many misfortunes.

John's lost a beloved brother. He still can't believe that he won't see Edward again; that the dark mist that came down between them, for reasons he doesn't understand, will now never be dispelled. He may also have lost his sister-in-law for ever, he realises, for Joan, who's locked herself away at Kennington until now with Edward's body and her son, did accompany the child today to Westminster, but only stared, red-eyed, at her feet when she came across John in the corridor, and refused to say anything but, 'You will excuse me; I am a widow in grief,' before sweeping off. He stared after her. There was nothing he could say.

John's all but lost his father too, at a time when all he wants is loving guidance from the man he most reveres. John hasn't known what to do when that old man with his father's face stares at him with those stranger's eyes, and mumbles, and dribbles down his chin. He's embraced him; he's wiped the tears, very gently, from the withered cheeks. But he can't grieve with his father. He's almost relieved that the King has gone to Eltham with his sorrows; for the King's sorrows are all sorrows, past and present, folded into today's grief, and John can't bear to follow him back through time to so much other buried misery. Edward of England is ordering masses and wildly expensive cloths of gold almost every day, to dress churches in memory of his dead mother, and his dead wife, and his dead son. He's ordered fifty-seven of them for any church that is marking the Prince's obsequies. And every day he asks for Alice. Sometimes he seems to understand that she's not coming back, though not for long. Sometimes he even seems to understand she was (perhaps) married to another man. He has ordered William of Windsor back from Ireland.

347

He's also ordered a small carved chest, in which he's locked the Parliament's accusations against his former Lieutenant in Ireland. Mostly he doesn't seem to understand anything. He just cries, until his beard's wet.

John was born to want to offer his services to England. And now, in this dark hour, of course he wants to be of use, to push himself into a whirl of public-spirited activity in which his grief can find an outlet. He's the only adult left standing with the experience to preserve his family's honour and reputation. He wants to guide the child in the ways of government. He wants to take some of the cares off his father's shoulders. There's so much he could do . . .

But those dogs, those bumpkins in the chamber there, have deprived him even of that. The unconscionable arrogance of them deprives him of speech; their misguided hatred; their suspicions he's out to murder Richard and take power, which only betray the squalid darkness in their own minds. They've prevented him from becoming Regent; they've substituted their own chaotic alternative, that council of his enemies they've dreamed up, for the role that God and nature intended for him. They're shutting him out, as surely as they're shutting out that poor woman, the mistress; exiling him from the birthright that should have been his . . .

Duke John feels cornered, paralysed, by events.

The only action he's successfully managed to plan and carry out for weeks has been this small act of mercy to the disgraced mistress.

It's not much. But it's given him, at least, a moment of hope; a breathing-space. The energy to make his own plans.

When this Parliament is over, when the dogs are back in their kennels, he tells himself as he strides back towards the chamber, he'll take himself north. At least they can't interfere with his summer procession through his own lands, where he'll recover his poise; where he'll plan his next moves; and where Katherine, with her blessedly calm gaze and cool hands massaging away the pains in his head and heart, will understand.

*　　*　　*

It's July. The Parliament is over. The country is being run by the nine-man council that the lawmakers appointed. But the King still hasn't got the money he wanted for war. Even after the corruption trials, de la Mare still said no.

The King will have to call another Parliament soon, and do better at winning it over. There are only nine months left until the truce with France expires, and, unless some miracle can avert it, war resumes.

Westminster and London seem strangely empty now the parliamentarians are gone. Walworth holds a banquet for the great and good of the City; in all but name, it's a celebration of his triumph against his enemies. Geoffrey Chaucer's place stays empty; he sends word that he has an upset stomach and can't leave his bed. For weeks, Chaucer wanders miserably between home to work and back again, not meeting the smugly satisfied eyes of the merchants or their clerks, hating them, despising himself. Alice has gone; no one knows where. He waited a day outside Westminster Palace, hoping for a glimpse of her leaving, and maybe a final word. Nothing. Lyons and Latimer and Stury, and the rest of the victims of the Commons, are in prison of one sort or another. The Duke of Lancaster is about to set off from the Savoy for a quiet summer at Pontefract, hunting and licking his wounds, spending his evenings with his daughters, and his nights with their pretty governess. The Duchess of Lancaster, Philippa Chaucer's mistress, has not yet returned to London, as she was supposed to. She is still grieving for her baby son. So Philippa Chaucer and the Chaucer children are staying at Hertford with her. Geoffrey Chaucer is relieved at his wife's absence, at least. He's too angry with Philippa, and himself, to trust himself to speak to her.

If only he'd managed to see Alice. If only she knew that, at least, he'd done something to right the wrong he'd done her.

If only he didn't have to live with the knowledge of his own contemptible cowardice. If only there was something he could do to redeem himself, in his own eyes, at least, and perhaps in those of his children.

If only he wasn't left behind, having lost everyone, in this miserable clerkly city.

It's only when he hears that a delegation is to leave London for France, to keep open the channels for peace talks, that he realises what he might do.

'Send me too,' he begs the Duke. 'Send me to France.'

The Duke doesn't want to hear. He's watching the cavalcade assemble in the stable courtyards of the Savoy for his trip north. Chaucer can see Duke John can hardly bear to be here in London any more; the man's desperate to be away.

'Why?' he says.

Chaucer's full of inspiration, suddenly: intoxicated by the notion of single-handedly saving England from its enemies; by the picture that presents itself to him of Thomas and Elizabeth gazing wide-eyed at him as he modestly lists his successes. He says, 'The Commons would have no power if you didn't need money from them for war. And there's nine months before the truce expires.'

The Duke says, with his eyes elsewhere, 'The French don't want peace. I've tried.'

'Your admirable efforts have not been well enough understood, or appreciated,' Chaucer says, rushing over that difficult truth. 'Blessed are the peacemakers.' He takes a deep breath. 'But things have changed now,' he persists. 'What if they were offered a marriage with the new Crown Prince of England?'

The Duke looks round. For the first time, he actually seems to see Chaucer.

A week later, Chaucer too is leaving London.

It's only as he steps on board the ship at Southampton that the vague sense of consolation that bustling around organising his departure and settling in his deputy at the Customs House has brought him finally evaporates. Miserably he realises that he hasn't been brave enough after all. Deep down, he knows he won't singlehandedly make peace with France. He can't do anything to make amends to Alice, or peace with Philippa, or to impress his children. He's just running away from his problems.

TWENTY-EIGHT

It is the end of September before John of Gaunt rides back south from Pontefract, in good time for his brother Edward's funeral at Canterbury on 5 October. He's calmer after two months of peace under big skies, in the perfect joy of the blue eyes and the soft Flemish tones of his love, watching her belly swell again, loving the way their two children, John, already talking, Henry, already walking, have his straight nose and long fingers and her straight blondness: living, breathing, fleshly proof of the innocence and loveliness of their private union. 'Joan will find her own peace soon,' Katherine has murmured to him, over and over again, stroking his hair, smoothing his brow. 'Joan knows she has always loved you, just as Edward always loved you. It was only the sickness in him that hated you. She shared that passion because she was a loyal wife. But it will pass, as all things pass, as her grief softens . . . as she sees you taking care of her son . . . putting Richard on the throne. You have nothing to fear. And nothing to regret.'

Katherine believes in love. That's the beauty of her.

As John rides south, through the turning leaves and the crisp harvest sunlight, it all seems so clear. He loves his father. He loved his brother. He will be the strong uncle to little Richard that his family would want. He will find the boy a French princess and save the land from war, or, failing that, he will die a hero's death on the battlefield.

351

But that's before news reaches John that his father is dying. The King's running a fever, the abscess on his ankle has turned poisonous, the bone's showing through skin too thin to heal, the stink is unbearable, gangrene may set in at any moment, the doctors are in despair, the lawyers have been called in to make wills, and the priests are waiting behind the tapestries, and he's considered unlikely to last more than days, perhaps no longer than the Prince's burial.

At that news, unbidden, the other, darker thoughts chained up in John's mind stir and clank again.

He's at Leicester. He leaves Katherine there to return to Kettlethorpe. A thoughtful day or two later, on the road south from Northampton, he sends the train on without him, towards London and the Savoy, and rides off almost alone on a detour. He's going to Wendover to see Alice.

He tells himself this: Whatever vows Alice Perrers has been forced to make to Parliament, surely they can be suspended if his father's really dying? There is nothing that would comfort the old man more, in his last days, than the woman he loves. And who could begrudge a beloved king that final happiness?

He doesn't quite admit to himself that Alice, with her devious mind and eye for the main chance, might understand his darker thoughts about the future better than anyone; better even than Katherine, who sees everything about him as noble, and whose only thoughts are of reconciliation.

He doesn't exactly tell himself: Alice Perrers will understand, and approve, and nudge me on, and help me plan it, if my father's illness forces me to take a more active part in government now, and if I use my power to get vengeance on the people who have humiliated me . . . us. But he does half think it. He knows Alice Perrers will want him to plan revenge against his enemies, because his desires to mete out punishment to his enemies will coincide so precisely with her desires, and their enemies are the same enemies.

But Duke John certainly doesn't tell himself, or even think: Or if it ever came to pass that I were compelled to sit on the throne of England . . . For that idea is far too tightly locked up even to be thought consciously (though it's there all right, in its dungeon, flexing its muscles, clanking its chains).

'They should have let me stay with him,' Madame Perrers says. She's become so thin that she's pointy: elbows and knees and cheekbones and nose, all angles and hollow planes. It suits her, John thinks. He prefers his women unthreatening. But she's still full of energy. Flushed and pink-cheeked and eager, rushing him to basins and cushions and refreshments. 'I know the poultices; it never bothered him before, that abscess. Doctors are fools. I could have kept it in check.'

John doesn't want to talk about poultices. Perhaps she is a witch, after all, as they said, he reflects. He's not altogether sure he likes her, even now they are allies, but he smiles sympathetically at her fluttering, busy, practical concern. It's right that she should worry for his father.

She sighs. She pours him more wine. He fears she's about to make demands.

But she doesn't.

'England needs a strong man at the helm,' she says un-expectedly, looking admiringly at him out of eyes that in her shrunken face seem bigger than before. More vulnerable. 'In these times of danger. How glad I am that you're back.'

She hasn't quite said, 'Not a boy of nine.' But John feels himself swell protectively. He thinks: Alice Perrers has a head on her shoulders.

'I'm going to him now,' he tells her. 'I'll take charge.'

He means, or thinks he means, 'of my father's care'.

But he leaves that unsaid, and the unasked question of what he will take charge of unanswered. They are both happy with the vagueness.

'Good,' she says. There's a new hardness in her voice. 'Seize the moment. There are men out there whose insolence should not go unpunished.'

John's eyes narrow. It's as if she can read his mind. He's been going over their names himself. He's thinking: de la Mare, the Earl of March, William of Wykeham . . .

She nods. She has the same list in her head, clearly. There's no need for words.

Before he leaves, John tells her: 'My father deserves some last wishes. And what he wants is to be with you.' He looks at her shabby clothes, her neglected air. 'Be ready,' he adds decisively. 'I'll send word.'

Eltham in persistent drizzle: the King propped up in bed, looking closer to a hundred than sixty-four, with a hutch of sorts over his suppurating leg. John tries not to be aware of it, but he's sitting on the bed holding his father's hand, and, every time he moves, it jogs the mattress and his father winces. The seven doctors in the background fuss and fidget.

'I've called the Council for after the funeral,' he says. He wishes his father's eyes had shown more pleasure at the sight of him. King Edward's eyes are vague. He's an old man, all taken up with his own pain. '*Your* Council, I mean, not the one the Parliament chose,' he continues firmly. 'I'm going to dismiss *that* council.'

His father's not so ill. The old eyes wrinkle and focus, struggling to join him. There's a flash of panic in them, or perhaps it's King Edward's lifelong glee at a fight. It will do him good, John thinks, to give him something new to think about.

John explains: 'Last spring's Parliament's work is null and void. We can't tolerate insubordination. We'll call another one. We need money, for the war.'

He's worried that his father, weak though he is, might object. But when, after a pause, the old man responds, it's only to let a cunning, wheedling expression steal over his face, and, from his mouth, the words: 'If I let you, will I get Alice back?'

A bargain, John thinks, relieved. There's life, and devilment, in the old man yet.

He presses his father's hands tighter. He says, 'Of course.'

It is 22 October by the time Alice comes to Eltham, and what the wags are calling the rout of the rats by the cat of court is well under way. The spring Parliament's decisions have been cancelled. The Parliament's council has been disbanded. Latimer and Stury and Neville are free again (the imprisoned merchants aren't yet, but their time will come). William of Wykeham, Bishop of Winchester, has been stripped of his secular estates and banished from court.

John tells her all this on the walk from the stableyard along the echoing stone corridors to the King's bedchamber. Alice nods. She has a small leather box in her hands, which she insists on carrying herself. From time to time, Alice stops listening to nod at a servant here or a guard there. She's trying to look serious, but there's a little smile that keeps coming to her lips. He sees she can hardly believe she's back.

I brought this about, he thinks proudly. I've done it.

Alice stops an equerry. She seems to know the man's name. Murmuring something polite to the Duke, she breaks off. She tells the man, with composure: 'Prepare a bath for my lord the King.'

Turning back to the Duke, who's paused to wait for her – as he would for any lady – she looks admiringly up at him. 'I had no idea,' she says, and her eyes are glowing, 'that anyone could right so many wrongs so fast.'

Edward is asleep in his chair. The hutch is over his leg, on its stool. His mouth is open. He seems utterly still. For a moment, John's heart leaps, with that fearful anticipation he doesn't altogether understand. It always does this, at this sight. There's always the moment of wondering, is the old man dead? But, as John realises his father's chest is, after all, still rising and falling under the blanket, Edward lets out a little snore. With the familiar mixture of relief and regret that always follows this realisation, John turns to Alice.

But Alice has forgotten him. She's already tripping lightly forward and putting her hands very gently on Edward's shoulders. '*Mon amour*,' she murmurs in her London French, and the King stirs. When, slowly, reluctantly, he opens his eyes to the harsh world, and his gaze falls on her, the set misery on his grey face lightens strangely and, to John's wonderment, a disbelieving smile even comes to his lips.

'Philippa,' he breathes, before seizing one of Alice's hands and pressing it eagerly to those lips, and nuzzling it as if he'll never let go.

She doesn't mind not being recognised. She leaves her hand where it is, and puts her face to his head, carefully avoiding banging against the hutch, and kisses him – the softest little butterfly kisses to silvered crown, to forehead, to cheeks, and, finally, to his lips.

'You're back,' Edward's muttering, still clutching on to her hand.

She laughs, a breathy little laugh, from very close up. 'I've brought the oils, and the ointment. Let's get you into a bath, shall we, and see what we can do about your poor leg?'

She sings to him as she binds his leg. It's a horrible sight. There's white under the purple, angry scabs, and pus everywhere, seeping out from edges, and the whole foot and ankle, nearly up to the knee, are tight and swollen. But she sends away the doctors. They'll be better, just the two of them, for now. She can put him to bed herself, she says firmly. As the doctors take their disappointed faces off, she says to Edward, 'We don't need those old scavengers, do we now?' and, laughing back, he shakes his head.

Love heals everything, she tells him in a sing-song rhythm as she dabs at the wounds and gently rubs in the ointment. He's almost asleep. His hair and beard are freshly washed and combed. He smiles and shuts his eyes. Love heals everything, she hears him murmur.

She wants Edward alive. She isn't going to let him die.

She's there in the chair when he wakes up. She lies beside him on the bed, propped up on one elbow, feeding him little sips of chicken soup and wine. She laughs him into eating. 'One for you, one for me,' she counts, as if he were a child. He gives in, and laughs too, and eats. He holds her hands.

It takes him a day to be sure which of his lady-loves she is. She only knows he has remembered her for sure when his face saddens and he says, mournfully, out of nowhere, 'I've sent for William of Windsor, you know. I know it was all his fault.' He looks pleadingly at her. Then he says, fretfully,

'He should be here any day. He should have come already. I can't think why he's taking so long.'

She puts down the soup, and, with the same arm she's been using to feed him, gently draws him closer on the bed in a half-embrace. The poor old man, she thinks; she doesn't for a moment let herself entertain the thought that he's really ordered William home. 'Oh, *him*,' she whispers, shrugging and snuggling and tenderly stroking Edward's forehead. 'What's *he* to me? I hardly remember what he looks like. It was so long ago . . . a lifetime ago. There's no one for me' – and she leans her head forward, looking into those anxious old eyes with real tenderness, believing what she says as she says it – 'no one but you. Never has been, since I met you.'

She can't think of Chaucer as a lover. She doesn't think of him, off on some hopeless peacemaking mission in France. She doesn't need him. Let him stew out there, alone. There's no place for remembering him in her mind, except as a kind of emptiness. So she doesn't feel guilty. It's not a lie she's telling.

Edward's not altogether reassured. 'They said you had children,' he whispers. His eyes are on her. She closes hers.

'I did you wrong never to tell you about them,' she says quietly, more seriously, into the red haze of her eyelids. 'I know that. I ask your forgiveness.'

'A son,' he persists.

'John,' she mutters. 'He's just twelve.'

It's been so long since she's had anything but despair to finesse. She's lost her touch. It's as if her planning muscles are only just starting to tingle and flex again.

She breathes out when he whispers, 'My dear . . . you meant no harm. I know that.' But she catches her breath again when he goes on: 'A good boy, is he? Your John? Like Richard? A good rider? Good with a sword?'

She mutters, 'Oh yes.'

Her eyes are still shut. So she doesn't see the expression on his face, just hears a sudden return of the old gaiety to his voice when he goes on, 'Then shouldn't I knight him, in the spring, when I knight Richard?'

She opens her eyes. He's smiling, and his eyes are dancing with that devilish sunlight she remembers from long ago. She's so astonished that, for a moment, she can't even smile back. 'Knight him?' she stammers, thinking of that ragged little stranger playing among the weeds and piles of junk, grinning his Essex grin. What, Edward actually offering, spontaneously?

It will probably never happen. Edward will probably die before it does.

But he's saying, 'Once I'm better . . .' He's saying, 'We'll have other celebrations too – a summer season – start planning Christmas – my jubilee next spring . . .'

Making an effort to respond, Alice smiles, and does her stunned best to enter the make-believe. A little faintly, still, she agrees: 'Seasons to remember.' And Edward nods, with new vigour. He's pleased she's joining in with his plan.

She feels like a stray cat who's crept in off the street, only to find a warm place waiting by the fire, and a bowl of cream. It's not a return to the old days, exactly. She knows that all she's got is a short reprieve as royal nursemaid, in this palace-turned-hospital, for the brief remainder of Edward's life. At least that's what she's being offered right now. But she's seen the gleam in the Duke's eye. He's out for more, all right.

And so Alice can't help herself go further, in her thoughts at least. If she can use this time to dig herself back into favour with the Duke, help him neutralise his enemies and erase the disastrous events of the past months from history . . . then she will be at hand, too, to help him when the time comes for Edward . . . when the Duke could rise right to the top . . .

. . . bypass the little boy . . .

Unlike the Duke, Alice isn't afraid to think that thought.

In fact, that thought has always been part of Alice's wish to get close to the Duke. Alice believes that a close relationship with Duke John represents power in the most direct form available to her, because Alice has always believed that the Duke would, one day, find the temptation to seize the throne of England from his child nephew irresistible.

There's more waiting out there for him, surely, if he only has the wit and nerve to see it, and take it.

And now the glittering prospect that Alice has thought, these past months of reverse and disappointment, had moved out of her reach seems, again, temptingly, to be just about within grabbing range.

Could there be more for her too? Couldn't there be?

Couldn't she, after all, become Duke John's adviser . . . couldn't she walk back into power, following his star?

TWENTY-NINE

Edward doesn't die.

The violent colour and swelling ebb, day by day, from his impostume. His mind clears. After ten days, Alice thinks he might be well enough to travel to Havering, their private palace, where she hopes the quiet of the woods and the dreaminess of the sky will help him come fully back to himself.

On each of those ten days, she dines with the Duke, in a parlour, away from the eyes of the household. And, every day, she becomes a little more certain that she has a future, even after Edward.

The Duke confers with Alice, every day, and listens carefully to her advice. The Duke, who has no one else to consult at the moment, since La Swynford is away at Kettlethorpe with another bun in the oven, and he can't reveal his secret hopes to most people, is eating out of her hand.

Her advice is harsh. Alice has found the iron in her soul in the lonely weeks of this rain-sodden summer. She doesn't mind revealing that. She feels her vengeful mood matches that of her dining companion. 'Shouldn't de la Mare be arrested?' she says, narrow-eyed; and straightaway the order goes out for the knight of Herefordshire, sometime Forespeaker of the Good Parliament of 1376, to be flung into a dungeon in the Duke's castle at Nottingham, with no prospect of a trial. 'Shouldn't you send my lord of March away?' she suggests as the knowledge of her new power stirs and thickens in her.

360

Duke John immediately orders his trouble-making cousin to Calais to be governor of the garrison there. When the Earl refuses, fearing for his life in the claustrophobic confines of the castle in the marshes of northern France, the Duke has him stripped of his post as Marshal of England. He gives that honour to March's enemy, Henry, Lord Percy.

'Good,' Alice says, and the Duke glows.

They look at each other through narrowed eyes, planning the next move: the tame Parliament, staffed by John's placemen, whose speaker will be John's own steward, which will cancel the previous Parliament's decisions and grant the King a tax for war.

They're egging each other on to be harder, and harsher, every day.

Alice finds it intoxicating, seeing her enemies fall without having to lift a finger. She only has to breathe a wish for revenge, and it comes true.

She understands that the Duke is shy of discussing the ultimate motive for clearing his opponents out of power. She respects that. She doesn't mention it either. Softly softly, she thinks; we'll prepare the ground now, and then later . . .

When he does get around to making his move, Alice thinks triumphantly, he'll know I've been with him all the way; and how he'll thank me.

John of Gaunt enjoys those weeks of narrow eyes and hard, quick, violent moves. The conversations with Madame Perrers – in which every time a hated name comes up, a terrible solution to the problem of that enemy's existence is quickly broached, he doesn't know quite by whom, and, before he quite realises what's happened, that person is no longer a threat – have restored to him his sense of himself as a man of action. He's lost that frozen immobility that came on him during the Parliament. He's forgotten the feeling he doesn't want to call fear.

It's only after Alice and the King and a slow, slow baggage train have set off for Havering that John returns to the Council, and the Savoy, and his senses.

Perhaps it's the fact that his father's crisis has passed. Madame Perrers' return seems to have saved the old man. He's relieved that the King isn't going to die just yet. He dreads his father's passing, always has, and now more than ever. He dreads the writhing worm in his own gut when he thinks of it; the sense of fateful decisions waiting to be made, ones that he may always regret.

Or perhaps it's the letter that's waiting at the Savoy, from Katherine, which reminds him of the blissful look in her eyes, and the gentleness of the face above her swelling belly, and her peaceable thought on the night they parted as she put his hands on the kicking inside herself. The letter says: 'If this is a boy, we'll call him Richard. And if it's a girl, we'll call her Joan.'

He reads it and understands. Katherine wants him to make his peace with his brother the Prince's family. By offering to name her child after one or other of them, she's suggesting a way.

The relief that comes from that sudden understanding spreads right through his body. John knows – has known for all these weeks, really – that what he's been doing, as he orders arrests and Parliaments, as he strides around, tight-voiced, hard-muscled, allowing Madame Perrers' admiration to push him further, every day, than he might otherwise go, is quietly preparing for the day when, after his father's death, he might try . . .

He can hardly bear to think it.

. . . might try to seize power.

Once the thought's out, once he's had a moment or two to examine it and comprehend how much it's influenced his every move, all autumn, the relief spreads.

It's simply not in him to do that, he realises. He's not that man. It would never have been possible.

However young Richard is, however untested, however unsuited to kingship in time of war, he's still Edward's son: the true heir; God's anointed. And he, John, is a man of honour. A man of action, true; but only virtuous, knightly action. A man of duty. And he knows his duty; always has, deep down. Just as it's his duty to try and win back his wife's kingdom in Castile, and it's his duty to try and deal with the French, it's his paramount duty to protect Richard throughout his minority, to guide and protect his nephew, if he's called to, with his last drop of blood.

John sinks on to a bench. He hasn't felt this happy for a long time.

Vengeance is all very well, he tells himself. But he's had his fill of it now. He's got his enemies: he need go no further. He's not a thief. He's not out to be king. He's not cut out for treachery.

At Council the next morning, the Duke of Lancaster takes the opportunity to name a date in November for the formal investiture of Richard as Prince of Wales. In December, at Westminster, there will be a great feast at Westminster Hall, at which Edward will have Richard on his right hand, and every peer in the land, led by John himself, can kneel and swear allegiance.

How else could he look Katherine in the eye again?

In the peace of Havering, Alice hears the news of Prince Richard's forthcoming investiture late, but with equanimity.

She doesn't read it as a sign that the Duke has pulled back from dreaming of the absolute power she wants for him. She has no tingling awareness that, with this change of heart, the edge might also have gone off his desire to consult with her.

She just thinks, with the hard-eyed expression she's getting used to keeping on her face: Well, he's cleverer than I realised to be doing this. Playing along, calming every suspicion, softly softly. Who'll ever think (until the time comes) . . .?

Alice is content with what she's got, for now. She's enjoying getting used to feeling safe again. She's been given back the title to her properties. Her rents from the ten estates she has kept on are coming in again. In the quiet hours when Edward's asleep, she's written to her team of land agents; she's even brought two of them, Robert Broun and John Vyncent, back to full-time work for her, coordinating the restoration of order to her possessions. To the fury of the new royal chamberlain,

Roger Beauchamp, she's also persuaded the King to pardon Richard Lyons and let him out of jail. Otherwise she's kept a low profile, but she's at Westminster, at Christmas, and Katherine Swynford, big now with the third child, isn't. The Duke is as courteous to her as he was at Eltham, back in October, though, she notices, they no longer discuss politics, except in generalities, and all he says about Richard's investiture is a polite comment that it went well. But that doesn't worry her; they've prepared the ground already, she tells herself. What else is there to say about all that, for now? Meanwhile, she's proud that he doesn't stop telling her how grateful he is that she's looked after the King so well.

In the new year, when Richard, and Duke John's eldest son Henry of Bolingbroke, and the ten-year-old heirs to various earldoms are knighted, her son is brought up to London to join the noble throng. She doesn't insist on this, any more than the Duke, if he knows or notices, complains. It's not that she doesn't want her son knighted (of course she does) she just isn't sure she wants the court (Edward) to see how her children really are. Nor does she want her son, or any of the children, to learn how close she came to the edge, and what a fragile straw she's climbed back out on. She needs them to think of her as successful; as too successful to have time to spend at Gaines. Still, Edward remembers his promise without being prompted, so how can she refuse?

Alice entrusts the task of bringing her child to court to Robert Broun and John Vyncent. She doesn't need to explain the task to them. She just asks them to visit a manor in Essex and escort a young gentleman from there to her home in London. She can't do anything to avoid them finding out John's her son if they're minded to; or, probably, that Gaines is her manor. But if she doesn't tell them that herself, it's deniable. And they're not men for unnecessary questions.

Nervously, she goes to spend the night before the ceremony at her London house, where little John's to sleep. When she walks into the courtyard – she's come by river – he's there, just getting off his pony, in his battered country clothes, staring round. There are other people in the courtyard, too, but it's only him she sees: his shock of black hair, his rough russet wool, his nervous bowed shoulders. Bitten nails. He's taller than she remembers; thinner, too. She's embarrassed for him, so rustic, so untutored, so vulnerable. Thank God she's had suitable clothes made, at least. The servants are staring. She rushes him inside without touching him. She has food waiting in a parlour. She doesn't want them gawping in the hall. 'Well, John,' she says, trying to hide the hammering of her heart, talking in the strict-but-fair manner of a visiting aunt, 'how've you been keeping?' but he only gazes back at her, dumbstruck, and he hardly does any better at mumbling answers when she rushes on, 'Nothing to worry about tomorrow. We'll go to town together. You'll wait with the other boys until you're called. Then a little ceremony. I'll have to stay. But Master Broun will take you back. Understand?'

He nods. He has big eyes. He was never scared of talking when she went to Gaines, she thinks; she's sure she remembers him telling her about snares he'd set and rabbits he'd skinned and toy soldiers Wat had made him. But now the cat's got his tongue. She hopes that isn't because he's heard how near she came to oblivion; they're not going to talk about that, even if it is. 'Hungry?' she asks, feeling a fool rushing about and talking at him so fast, wishing he'd say something, anything, back. He gives her a cautious look from under his long lashes. 'Come on, then, eat up,' she urges, pushing a platter of bread and cheese at him. 'And I'll show you the tunic and hose you're to wear. And crackowes. Have you worn crackowes?' Saucer-eyed, he shakes his head. They're great big things, she worries: they take practice. Some courtiers wear the curled-up pointy shoes with fronts as long as twenty-four inches, held to their calves by ribbons, or chains, though the ones she's ordered for John are a more manageable twelve inches. She's thinking too of the little wooden platforms into which courtiers slip their elegant shoes: pattens. Three or four inches high. What if he falls off them in front of the King? If only he'd speak, it would reassure her. She'd give anything for him to speak.

The child finally does when he's got a first mouthful of

food down his dry throat, and coughed, and taken a tickly draught of small ale. Plucking up courage, looking around at the expensive hanging on the wall, he jerks a finger out towards the courtyard and says, in his anxious little country voice, 'You got a lot of servants up 'ere, mam. Right grand, this 'ouse.'

She can't help it. Sharply, she says, 'Don't call me that!' He cringes back into himself. She wishes she hadn't. It's not as though he's going to show her up at court by chattering away calling her 'mam', is it? But it's too late to recall her words.

Biting his lip and looking scared, he practises mincing about in the crackowes. He tries on the tunic. She tells him to kneel when he sees the King and not to say anything except 'Yes, my lord king'. (In French, too. 'Oui, monseigneur le roi.' Go on, say it: not like that, like this.) Or to the other boys, who are all earls and princes. 'Just keep quiet,' she says. She takes him to the room he's to sleep in. He lifts his cheek obediently for her kiss. 'You be good now,' she says. 'And don't be scared.' She knows it's her own nerves, as much as his, she's trying to calm.

For a moment, their eyes meet and his shyness goes. He grins up at her. 'Me, scared?' he says, with urchin bravado, and she hears old Alison's voice, and her own. 'Never.'

For a moment, she sees herself in him, and him in her, and with that sense of closeness comes . . . Is it pride? she wonders, a feeling she doesn't know the name of, a sense of swelling inside. For a moment, she almost hugs him. But she stops herself. No point spoiling the child; muddying the waters. This is tricky enough as it is. Hastily, she says, 'Sleep well then,' and pulls the door to.

She can't help taking another look back, though. He thinks she's gone. He's already forgotten her. He's putting his candle up close to the bedcurtains, and feeling the embroidered stuff with a knowing, appreciative finger and thumb.

Alice sighs. She remembers that gesture. He probably knows someone who'd give him a good price for it, down Brentwood way.

He does fine the next day. She leaves him, all dressed up,

366

looking bravely insouciant, in the antechamber with the other children. They ignore him. They're busy with each other. She nods brightly at him while Edward puts the sword on his shoulder and whispers in his ear. She sees those big blue eyes, which stay fixed on her, widen; sees his lips mouth, 'Yes, my lord.' Afterwards, she leads him straight out to Robert Broun and John Vyncent. He's quiet. John Vyncent has a cloak for him. Broun has the horses. She pats the boy, awkwardly. 'Hurry now,' she says. 'You'll make Barking by nightfall, no trouble.' It's only afterwards, when Edward's saying, 'A lovely child,' and 'Just like you,' and 'Sad he couldn't stay for the dinner,' and 'How did he enjoy being called "Sir John" afterwards?' that she realises, with a pang, that she doesn't even know. She wishes she'd asked now. But she's also relieved he's gone. Best keep a low profile.

It might have been better for Alice if she'd kept a low profile for longer.

But in the early days of January, as she let out her laces after weeks of rich food and festivities (she's not so pointy now), something about the combined facts of being back in the company of a King who no longer shows any signs of dying imminently, but is about to celebrate his first fifty years on the throne, and of being high in the favour of the son who's really ruling the land, and, what's more, being the mother of a knight of the realm, and having so much to play for when the next stage begins, encourages her to relax her guard.

For the first time in a long time, the confident phrase 'seize the day' starts coming back to her lips.

The Duke of Lancaster is displeased, though he can't explain why, even to himself.

Whenever he goes to see his father at Havering, Madame Perrers is there, hovering in the bedchamber, listening, joining in the private talk between father and son, even. And she's all puffed up with her dark certainties, with knowing eyes he doesn't want to look into. He no longer wants to remember that his own eyes, back in the autumn, when he talked so often with her, were perhaps full of those same dark certainties.

When he looks uncomfortably back, now, on that time with her, he finds it easy to think; She was egging me on to violence. She was using me to get the vengeance she wanted. She's manipulative; devilishly manipulative. It was because of her that I had de la Mare arrested. It was her idea for me to give March the fright of his life and send him running off to Ireland.

Not that he minds having done those things, exactly. Those men deserved punishment. Not that he resents having been influenced to call a Parliament quite as certainly obedient as the one that will meet any day in Westminster, either. No point in allowing inferiors to get insubordinate. Power lies with the Crown, not the scarecrows from the fields of England.

It's just that he doesn't like that look in her eyes, or some of the things she's still saying. Because, even now, now that he's realised he doesn't want discord, he feels she's still trying to push him into further aggression. Unnecessary aggression. And she makes him feel a coward for not wanting it.

For instance, Madame Perrers has been turning up her nose at the thought of the proper peace talks that are to begin this month, to try one more time to avert more war in April. The Duke will not participate personally. The talks will be at a lower level, to save expense, with England represented by Richard's guardian, the Gascon knight Sir Guichard d'Angle, Sir Richard Stury (out of jail now), Lord Thomas Percy, brother of the new Marshal of England, and Chaucer. There are plenty of offers on the table, including Chaucer's idea of a marriage between Richard and the French king's seven-year-old daughter, Marie. Reading Chaucer's dispatches, the Duke has allowed himself hope. It just might work.

But Madame Perrers doesn't seem impressed. She quibbles over the composition of the English delegation, for a start; 'Chaucer?' she sniffs. 'Well, *he* won't do much good, will he?' And she hardly hears the Duke's hopes out before wrinkling her nose as if she smells something off, and asking, with something like disdain, 'But you don't want peace, do you? Don't you want a glorious victory?'

That's not a question he can answer no to, of course. He is a prince, the sword arm of the nation, and every law of chivalry dictates that he should bear arms.

So, as the peace talks begin in Boulogne, John of Gaunt is emphasising in his talks with his father (which means, effectively, talks with Alice Perrers) the activities of the Parliament now meeting at Westminster. This tame Parliament makes no bones at all about voting to give the Crown money for more war. 'Good,' says Alice, when John reports this to his father. 'The glory of Englishmen under arms . . .' And the old man's eyes sparkle, as she must have known they would.

The Commons, after consultations with the Lords, decide on a novel form of tax. Instead of bearing the brunt of payment themselves, as usual, they've proposed sharing the burden out, and charging every man and woman in the land 4d. There's never been a universal tax in England before, but it makes perfect sense to the knights and merchants of the Commons, who've chafed for years at the outrageous wage demands of the lower orders. Let *them* share the burdens, too, the knights mutter to each other; let *them* see life's not always a tranquil river. They're calling it a poll tax in the streets of London. (They're calling this the Bad Parliament, too.)

Now, even though John is still privately hoping the peace talks will get somewhere, he doesn't talk with Alice about those hopes. That she sees them as dishonourable coincides perfectly with what his father and the knights of England have tended to believe, and say, all his life; it undermines his timid sense that England might, in reality, be better served by peace than by war. What he does talk about with Alice is the plans he's also making for war, guided by her. He's preparing to gather a fleet in the Port of London, ready for another naval offensive once the truce expires. He can't tell her about the dread he feels, inside, when he thinks of those ships. Best be prepared, Alice Perrers says cheerfully. Seize the day.

She's a clever woman, Alice Perrers, he thinks discontentedly. He knows her advice is often canny, although, more and more, he's uncomfortable being in a room with her (because what will she think of next?). Best be prepared: you can't argue with that. But there's no doubt about it, she's a hard one. Can't stop pushing; nagging. And how strident her voice can be. It makes his head ache.

He avoids her eye. His visits become shorter. But, in February, when the London merchants' favourite bishop, Courtenay of London, calls in John Wyclif to face heresy charges, Alice does come up with more demands.

'But Wyclif's *your* man,' she tells him from behind his father's shoulder. Flint in her eyes, John thinks unhappily; she's harder than diamonds. 'He was your negotiator at Bruges. This is an attack on *you*. And you've been very soft on the bishops until now. They were against you last year too, you know; it wasn't just the knights. Shouldn't you be punishing them? Defending your honour?'

John knows what she's up to. Alice wants to see Courtenay suffer; she still wants to make those London merchants squirm, he sees; and it's true, there's been no retribution against the City for the merchants' part in last year's Parliament. But John's desires are different now. He wants to go to Kettlethorpe, as soon as the baby's born, before he has to face up to the likelihood of more war, and be with Katherine. He's done enough.

Yet honour is paramount, he knows. And she's called this a question of honour.

Miserably, he nods. He'll go to London, then. He'll support Wyclif at his hearing.

Alice doesn't know why the Duke looks so furious when, unexpectedly, he gallops into the courtyard at Havering a week later, and flings himself down from his horse, and, leaving his escort in the yard, strides straight into his father's rooms.

Alice is putting Edward into a chair by the window, tucking the shawls around him so they prop him up, putting cushions at his back and behind his head.

She sketches a bow; she thinks of smiling and saying gracious words of welcome, but then she sees from his face that this is no time for graciousness. She tries, at least, to catch his eye and share a private glance.

'Leave us, please, Madame Perrers,' he says curtly, looking away. 'I want to talk privately with my lord the King.'

So she goes. She has no choice, now he's been that blunt.

But of course she goes no further than the courtyard, to find out from the snippets of conversation brought by the knights of the body, and the men-at-arms, and the grooms, what's got his goat.

And so she's downstairs, outside, with the steam of horse-breath and the jingle of harness, and the excitable shouting of the men, who seem to have been in some sort of armed conflict she can't make head or tail of, when the second un-expected delegation turns up.

The second lot are City men, in gowns. Not Alice's most direct enemies of yesteryear, she sees with relief, but people she's never had much to do with: this year's Mayor, the mercer Adam Stable, and the draper John de Northampton, and Robert Lounde the goldsmith – his two sheriffs, Alice assumes.

The three merchants are already wringing their hands and looking anxious, but they look more worried still when they see that the other men already stamping around in the court-yard are wearing the S-linked chains of the Duke of Lancaster's livery. They huddle, prudently, to one side, leaving the Lancastrians as much space as possible, and are eager to be taken inside and asked their business.

And so, between one lot and the other, Alice soon estab-lishes what's happened.

The City men say the Duke turned up armed and terrifying at Wyclif's heresy hearing in St Paul's Cathedral, and lost his temper, in public, with Bishop Courtenay. He threatened the Bishop with arrest. A London man was arrested, illegally, by the Duke's men. Rioting ensued.

The Duke's men say that, after their master necessarily dis-ciplined miscreants in London, a howling mob poured out of the City walls and down the Strand to the Savoy, where they were only stopped at the very last minute from burning the whole palace down.

The City men say it was Bishop Courtenay himself who bravely stopped the mob.

The Duke's men say: Because he was scared he'd pay for it with his life if the palace was sacked.

The Duke's men also say their master only escaped with his life by a miracle. By running through the Savoy gardens at full tilt, and throwing himself in a boat, and rowing with all speed over the river.

The City men say they've come here to talk to the King, and beg him to restore peace in their relations with the Duke.

The Duke's men don't say anything. It's clear they don't have peace with the City in mind.

Nodding quietly to herself, Alice says to Mayor Stable, whom she has nothing particular against, and whose gingery cheeks are pink with panic, 'I'll go and have a word with my lord. I'll see whether he's minded to receive you.'

She doesn't let herself sound too optimistic. Let him stew.

Still, this is the excuse she wants to get back into the conversation upstairs.

Quietly, she edges into the room. She can see Edward's face: he's horrified, though at least alert; following what's being said. Shaking his head.

'. . . the worst thing I could imagine,' she hears the Duke saying. 'Losing all that . . .' His voice is hollow; haunted. As he comes into view, she sees his face has lost its earlier fury. He's as pale as death.

Now that she understands, she's furious on his behalf. He's been ambushed. By a mob. Savages. No wonder he wanted privacy in which to pour out his story.

She's aware that there's something negative that comes over his face when he realises she's back in the room. But she's only here to help; discreetly she murmurs, 'My lords . . . a deputation from the City . . . Mayor Stable.'

At that bad news, the Duke immediately launches himself to his feet. The stool he's been perching on rolls over backwards. He doesn't notice. He's too angry. He paces over to the next window and, with pinched lips and white nostrils, stares out at the extra horses that have appeared.

She keeps her eyes down. She lets the Duke be. She takes her place on another stool beside Edward, and reaches for his hand.

Edward looks down at her, as if for guidance. She pats his hand.

'Well, they must be punished,' she says very gently. 'The London rebels. My love, you must see that.'

'But . . .' Edward mumbles. 'But . . .'

She can see that all he's understood is that, if the leaders of London are here, he can call them to him and, somehow, patch things up.

'You can't let them get away with trying to burn down the Savoy,' she says. 'Or threatening to excommunicate your son. You must make an example.'

Edward looks confusedly at her again. Yet, for once, he knows his own mind. After a moment or two, he shakes his head. He says, 'Tell the good men of London to come to me now; I'll hear them.'

She looks uncertainly back.

Edward pats her hand, and then lets it go. 'Please, my dear,' he says, quavering but decided. 'Now. And John; we'll talk again when I've heard what they've got to say.'

He nods at them both. It's dismissal.

Outside in the corridor, heading for the stairs, Alice sees Duke John is more enraged than ever, as wild-eyed and flaring-nostrilled as a sweating horse, pawing the ground, ready to buck or bolt. With his father's decision, she assumes.

She says, 'Don't be downhearted, my lord.'

Silence. He purses his lips. She says, 'Your moment will come.'

His stride lengthens. She's forced into a trot to keep up. 'You'll be able to give these upstarts the drubbing they deserve then,' she says breathlessly.

Perhaps it's because of getting out of breath, or because he's so dejected and so irate; she doesn't know why, exactly. But she adds, in the cosy kind of voice you might use if talking to a child crying over a grazed knee, 'When you're King.'

That does it. He goes berserk. He stops. He glares. He puts hands on hips. He grows even paler. And he snarls with a rage she's never seen before, rage against her: 'King, what do you mean King?' She suddenly sees that he hates her. 'You evil bloody Jezebel, are you trying to make a traitor of me now?'

Alice stops too. She's staring back at him. She has no idea, no idea; is this just caused by his recent fright? What else can have prompted this?

Then their eyes meet. His face is slack with the intensity of his thought, as if he's only just seeing her for what she is, and utterly despises it. 'Tell me this, Madame Perrers. How can I be King,' he says, quieter now, but just as hatefully, 'unless my father dies, and my nephew dies too?'

Alice thinks, with something like panic: But that's what *you* . . .

And: But I've only ever wanted what *you* . . .

And now he's blaming *her* for what he once wanted.

She can't speak. She stares back with her mouth open, hardly aware that she must be cutting a ridiculous figure. He holds her gaze.

When, in a helplessness that comes close to despair, she drops her eyes at last, she senses his head move: a small, hostile, triumphant shake.

Even amid her fear, she's getting a first glimmering of why he might be so full of fury. It's not as if he hasn't thought that thought himself; she's seen it in his eyes too often to be in doubt. But can it be, now, that he's transferring all the blame on to her for having thought it himself privately – so privately that they've never spoken it out loud, even between themselves? For having imagined that boy's deathbed, and his own life afterwards, and the crown on his head, and for having sought her out so she could strengthen him in that desire, encourage him to take all those oblique moves towards making his wish come true? It can . . . it must be. There's no other explanation.

He's had a change of heart since; must have done. Or lost his nerve, which comes to the same thing. He doesn't want the future she's been trying to shape for him. Not any more.

Perhaps she's been pushing him further and faster, all along, than he wanted to go? But, if so, why didn't he just say so? Say, stop. Enough. Peace. Perhaps . . . She pauses as this astonishing possibility occurs to her, because it surely can't be, since he's a prince with the blood royal running in his veins and a dove of divine grace hovering over his head, the closest man comes to God, but what other explanation can there be? Perhaps he's kept quiet and done what she suggested (until this explosion, in any case) because he is, or has been . . . scared? A little bit scared . . . *of her*?

The fool, she thinks, and she opens her mouth to try and justify herself, or talk him down from this unjustified rage, at least; but he interrupts her.

'I won't hear another word from you,' he hisses. 'Get out of my sight. And stay away. Do you hear? You're on your own now. On your own.'

But it's the Duke who stalks off on his own, on thin legs, in a dark wind of his own creation, leaving Alice standing completely still, staring after him.

For the first time in her life, as she feels the mantle of borrowed power she's worn for so long slip from her shoulders, she knows she's gone too far.

THIRTY

Alice Perrers is not invited to the burial of the King.

They say she nailed the old man upright in his chair every time he had visitors, in a cocoon of cloth of gold, so that, despite his empty eyes and drooling mouth, he could go on receiving guests till he dropped. She hammered in the nails herself.

They say she refused to let the confessors see the King, and went on bewitching her speechless victim with sinful talk of hunting and feasting to the end.

They say she stripped the rings off her lover's fingers before she finally fled from Sheen, leaving Edward to die alone.

Alice might have a different story to tell. But she's disappeared.

This is just what Geoffrey Chaucer hears after he rides unhappily back into London in June 1377, on the day after the King's death, on the day the truce he's tried to turn into a peace turns, instead, back into war. Knowing he's failed.

His team, which includes the Chancellor of England, has only just managed to sail into Southampton in time. The ports are now closed, in an attempt to prevent the French finding out about the King's death. From today, ships are to be turned away. Citizen guards are hastily polishing up their rusty weapons, while their wives stockpile food. Everyone is afraid of the invasion to come.

So now Chaucer's horse is carrying him forward at its own ambling pace, and, slumped atop it like a bag of lead, Chaucer's trying to quell the near-nausea he feels as the too-familiar streets and buildings come into view. He doesn't want to go to his apartment. He doesn't want to go to the Customs House. He doesn't even want to hear what the scurrying crowds of Londoners, weighed down with their bags and boxes of emergency provisions, checking bolts and bars on their shutters, are talking about. He can guess: there'll be weeping for the old King; fears about the new boy-King; malice about my lord of Lancaster; more malice about Alice; panicking over tomorrow; and recriminations over all the wasted yesterdays. Including the ones he's wasted. Guiltily, Chaucer bows his head.

When he clicks his horse on, it's to go to Guildhall. Drearily, he thinks he might as well start by paying his respects to the Mayor. The Duke, whom he knows is now hated as the enemy of the City's freedoms, forced the last Mayor out of office to punish him for the riots in February. But that City coup has done the Duke no good. The new Mayor is Nicholas Brembre, the grocer, an altogether more powerful man, and he hates the Duke's oppressive busybodying even more than his predecessor did. Brembre has publicly opposed the Duke's plan this spring to abolish the Mayor's office and replace the Mayor with a puppet leader, with the pompous Latin name of Custos, answerable directly to the Duke himself and the Marshal of England. And Brembre's won. So there is no punishment for anyone disrespecting the Duke's name in the taverns or in the streets. And there are many acts of disrespect.

'You know what they say, dear boy,' Brembre says, looking exaggeratedly relaxed, putting his feet up on a stool and an elbow on his enormous table. (He's been affability itself about the inglorious peace talks; he's complimented Chaucer on his energy and finesse; he's said, 'You did the best possible job in impossible circumstances.' He's even said, with more warmth than Chaucer could possibly have expected, 'And of course we're the winners, here in the City, because we've got you back at your desk at last.') But it's only now, talking about the Duke, that his big mouth curves into an enormous, self-satisfied smile. 'While the cat's away, the mice will play.'

Not, Brembre adds, sounding almost pained at having to mention it, that the Duke has actually put a foot wrong since his father's death. In fact, he's gone out of his way to be amenable. He's let Peter de la Mare out of jail, and he's neither protested at not being named Regent nor disputed the composition of the Grand Council that will rule England until the little King is grown up. It's a neutral council, too. The Duke's friends are in it, including Lord Latimer (*he*'s done all right, then, Chaucer thinks sourly). But so are the Duke's enemies: the Earl of March, now back from Ireland, and Bishop Courtenay of London. 'People *say*', Brembre drawls casually, though Chaucer is aware of the sharp glance the merchant is directing at him as he speaks, 'that his most dangerous time was when he was closest to Mistress Perrers, last year. They say he's lost his claws, now *she*'s gone.' He laughs, and his eyes flash with malice.

'Where *has* Mistress Perrers gone?' Chaucer asks, equally casually. Newer worries have overlaid his guilt on her account; a part of him is relieved she's left, and that, this time at least, it's not his fault. Yet part of him wants to see her, still; to make amends, if he can. He's never been a hero, never will be; but having seen the courage that goes right through Alice has, at least, made him recognise this failing in himself and, sometimes, yearn to be a different, better man. He'd like to be able to dream of becoming that man now, he thinks; it would make this unheroic homecoming less sad.

Brembre only shrugs. His enemy's enemy is not, in this case, his friend. 'Who knows, dear boy, who knows?' he says. 'And, frankly, who cares? She's yesterday's news.'

Alice Perrers does indeed seem like yesterday's news. There are so many more urgent worries once the truce expires.

Every piece of news from the south coast is another stab of guilt in Chaucer's heart. Just five days after the end of the truce, on 29 June, French warships land at Rye. For a day and a night, there's savagery – exactly the same kind of savagery the English have inflicted for so long on the towns of France. Houses go up in flames and are looted. Men are

378

killed, women raped before being killed, and screaming, bloody-mouthed, ripped-up girls carried off in ships. The French admiral, Jean de Vienne, then takes his fleet down the coast to savage Folkestone, Lewes, Portsmouth, Weymouth, Dartmouth, and Plymouth, and, later, the Isle of Wight.

There is no organised defence; no counter-attack. The lords and knights of England let the towns of the south burn. Nothing has been organised. And they're not overly worried about townsfolk anyway. They're busy.

John, Duke of Lancaster, for instance, is busy with his father's funeral and his nephew's coronation and the new Council of England.

And once he's through with all of that, by late July, and has left little King Richard to perform various sweetly un-important duties, including nominating Elizabeth Chaucer to St Helen's Priory in Bishopsgate and her cousin Margaret Swynford to Barking Abbey, the Duke retires to his own terri-tories in the Midlands for the summer. He spends three months at Kenilworth Castle, busying himself hunting around Leicestershire and assessing the defences of his castles. He has Katherine Swynford with him. He plays with his new girl-baby, Joan. He goes out dancing with merry peasants in a meadow at Rathby.

Well, *he's* all right, Chaucer thinks bleakly.

They are less happy in Kent and Sussex, perhaps, rebuilding their houses, or trying to, holding masses in roofless churches for their dead. But how would the Duke know about them?

Chaucer next hears of Alice Perrers only in the autumn of 1377, when a new Parliament opens.

'By the way, have you got any credit notes from La Perrers?' Walworth grins, between rolls of accounts, when he comes to the office for the annual autumn reckoning. It's Walworth who gets to do it this year, now Brembre is Mayor. 'Loans outstanding . . . trinkets missing?'

Chaucer looks up from his own roll of figures. He raises an eyebrow. Non-committally, he asks, 'Why?'

'Only because,' Walworth drawls, 'if you have, this is your

chance to get your money back. Parliament's offering to take on any debt cases against her, and fight her creditors' actions for them. They'll pay costs. It wouldn't cost you a penny.'

Chaucer's eyebrows rise higher. There's real spite in that. Cautiously, clerkishly, he says, '*In*-teresting.' Then, more boldly: 'She's not quite yesterday's news, after all, is she? If there are still people who want to destroy her that much?'

Walworth's watching him. Loyalty is key, now that London is against the Duke of Lancaster. However low-profile Chaucer has kept himself, there's still the faintest of question marks over him. Chaucer's been the Duke's man, in his time, or as good as. Chaucer can see Walworth's not sure of his loyalty to the City oligarchs, but would like to be. This is a test.

Chaucer is wondering: whom *does* he feel loyal to, in his heart?

Not to Philippa, certainly, with whom he's had unpleasantly frank whispered words during their last meeting, in July, as they watched Elizabeth going into St Helen's.

Not to the Duke, at least privately. He's disillusioned with his patron, or former patron (there might still be the pensions, but Chaucer knows those are thanks to Philippa's service to the Duke's family, really; and there have been no invitations to read poems to the court for years). Chaucer tells himself his growing distaste for the Duke is because the Duke left Kent to be burned by the French this summer. But maybe, too, it's because the Duke doesn't seem to have made the effort he might have to protect Alice (who always did her best for him) when she needed him. And, just possibly, the most honest reason of all is because the Duke loves Philippa's sister.

And Alice? He feels desperately sorry for Alice, especially with this latest confirmation that she's still being hunted, wherever it is that she's gone to ground. He feels guilty about Alice, too – of course he does – but he doesn't even know where she is. She's not part of his life any more. She doesn't need him.

In which case, in these dangerous and uncertain times,

Chaucer may have no one to feel loyal to except the City men. That thought doesn't fill him with joy, either.

Lightly, neutrally, Walworth says, 'We heard in the session yesterday that they've confiscated all the moveable property she had at Pallenswick.'

'Was there much?' Chaucer asks, equally lightly and neutrally.

It's hearing that question, in his own non-committal voice, that tells him for sure that he's not going to stick his neck out to defend Alice Perrers. Once again, he's not going to be brave.

Walworth shakes his head and bulges his eyes, projecting disbelief. There's a pleased little smile on his face. He knows, too. Chaucer's a sound man, after all.

'Unbelievable,' he says sanctimoniously, as if everyone didn't have something on his conscience, as if his own life, and Chaucer's too, were one long white sweep of irreproachable virtue. He smacks his lips. 'The amounts. Thousands of pounds' worth. All stolen, of course. An immoral woman, through and through.'

Chaucer's hot with shame inside, but he feels himself smirking knowledgeably as he answers, 'Well, I suppose it will do the treasury some good if the Crown's got extra things to pawn.' It's the latest scandal in the City – that the King's new Council is so short of cash that it's begging the City to advance it money against Crown jewellery and the old King's embroidered cloaks and jackets. The councillors have asked for £5000 worth of royal possessions to be pledged for credit so far, or at least that's the rumour. Walworth, who surely knows, doesn't deny the rumour. Chaucer notes the older man's matching smirk. All at once, he can't bear either Walworth or himself. He turns his head back down to the figures under his hands.

He can't help himself. Talking to the roll, not Walworth, he says, not exactly to the point, 'Though it's a bit absurd to take such a high moral tone about Mistress Perrers . . . taking money, fornicating, or whatever they want to pin on her now . . . when what's so moral about any of us, when it comes to it?' As he speaks, he becomes uncomfortably aware of Walworth drawing back. He realises he's speaking out of turn; it's not what Walworth wants to hear. So, hating himself more than ever, he does what he can to recoup. He can't stop feeling negative; but he can, at least, choose a target Walworth will want to be hit. 'The Duke himself, for instance, nothing so moral about him, either,' he says; and the merchant leans a little closer again. Chaucer goes on: 'We never hear any carping about his three bastards with Katherine Swynford, do we?'

It's not the first time Chaucer's mentioned this fact, privately, like this, one on one, in quiet conversations around London. It's part of his reluctant realignment with the City merchants, as his distaste for the Duke's behaviour, and the people in the Duke's camp, grows. It's what he's started to do, without really thinking why, whenever he's most tormented by his memories, and irritated by the disloyalties and lack of courage of others. Or himself. Perhaps mostly himself. It's only the foolish false bravery of spite; but, for a moment or two, whenever he does it, it makes him feel less of a coward.

He's pleased when, from under his eyelashes, he sees Walworth's eyebrows rise.

That night, alone in his rooms, Chaucer can't concentrate on the poem he's started writing. It sprang, in a playful moment, from his mischievous thought, long ago, that the merchants gliding about the Thames were as sleek and self-satisfied and smooth as geese, and as greedy when it comes to fighting off smaller birds and grabbing the last crust on the water. It's about a parliament of birds, each smaller and sillier than the last, making a raucous, crazy hash of a decision about the marriage of the beautiful noble eagle. He's been enjoying it until now, in a bleak sort of way; it's his own private protest against the foolish insanity of Parliaments. But tonight all he can do is scribble, 'Kek kek!' 'Cuckoo!' 'Quack quack!' and then, crossly, cross out the words.

He puts his head in his hands. He puts down the quill. He goes very quiet.

The candle is getting low, and it's dark outside, before he nods, and, suddenly decisive again, pulls a blank piece of parchment towards him, and starts, very quickly, to write. 'To the estimable Sir William of Windsor, Baron, of Greyrigg, Westmoreland, greetings,' he begins.

Someone needs to help Alice, and Chaucer knows he won't be brave enough. But what about this man?

Chaucer knows Alice's long-ago lover, or husband, recalled from Ireland in the King's last days, went quietly home to his estates up north as soon as he landed rather than come south to face awkward questions from his monarch. He hasn't been seen at the boy-King's court, either, and there's been too much else going on for anyone to think to summon him. There's nothing Chaucer can do now to help Alice, though he can sense another attack on her coming in the new Parliament. But what if he seeks out Windsor, who's said to be a brute, but therefore can't be lacking in courage, and who may still feel loyal to Alice, and who may, just possibly, in the wildness of up there, not even be aware of the latest moves against her? What if Chaucer asks *him* to come south and defend his wife?

THIRTY-ONE

Alice has known for weeks that she must prepare for the worst.

She's known ever since rough-mannered men came banging at the door at Pallenswick to say they represented a new parliamentary commission. They said it was their official task to inventory every item handed over to Alice from the Crown.

The mistress is not here, they were told. No matter, they replied brusquely. Show us the store-rooms. Bring out the clothes and hangings. And they set up at the table in the Great Hall, with a clerk writing lists of everything that's brought out to them. They swilled beer. They belched. They munched on meat and bread and onions that they ordered from Alice's kitchens.

It was clear, as the glistening, winking piles around the commissioners swelled and rose in the hall, in the manner of a fairy-tale castle, that none of these possessions would ever go back up the stairs. The servants could see everything would be confiscated. (Everything, of course, except the golden hanging of Sampson and Delilah. That was already stashed away in a trunk, which the men's leader had two of his followers quietly take away. It never appeared on the list of the Parliament's findings.)

The inventory these gloating commissioners compiled was mean-spirited in the extreme. They listed bed linen, furniture, jewels, clothing and trinkets. They listed the gorgeously expensive green gown Alice had been going to wear in a pageant that never happened. They listed 21,868 pearls. But they also listed a yard of ribbon, and a pair of gloves. Nothing was too insignificant to arouse their hostile interest. They wrote down a value for each item; and they over-valued every-thing by a dizzying percentage. After they'd pawed at and gawped over some jewels the King gave Alice, jewels that were down in the Exchequer's accounts as being worth £400 at the time they were given, they wrote down a bigger, rounder value: £500. It would be better, for the purposes of black-ening her character, to exaggerate the amount of loot she had stashed away.

That, at least, was what the black-haired female servant, wearing nothing special, thought they were up to, as she slipped in and out, taking off platters. Unnoticed.

The new Parliament has sensed from the start that there is will at the top to attack Alice Perrers.

The Commons still want to punish someone for all the wrongs of the past years. And there's no one left, any more, except Alice. The old King is already facing his Maker, and the Duke, the original target of the knights' rage – the source and paymaster of corruption, the coward, the provoker of riots, who's also been presumed, for so long, to be plotting to seize the throne – is keeping his head very carefully down now. He's loyal to his royal nephew. He's friends with his sister-in-law. The Parliament has, reluctantly, had to hold its nose and ask him to join the planning to defend the nation. He's agreed to lead a fighting force to France next year. He isn't putting a foot wrong. Not that he's become popular; not that anyone thinks this quiet state of affairs will last; but, while it's precariously holding, no one has the nerve to make any accusations against *him*. His royal blood is too awe-inspiring; his power too intimidating. They only dared to take him on before because they knew his older, senior brother was nudging them on. Yet the anger that was unleashed last year is still floating on the air, the bloodlust, the hunger for revenge. They need a victim.

Alice Perrers is out there, somewhere. And she's the ideal scapegoat. She's lost her main patron, the King. She also seems to have come adrift from her second patron, the Duke. She's become weak. Her name makes the current crop of parliamentarians lick their lips. They carry on hunting, and researching.

At the request of the Commons, the Lords announce that Alice Perrers must appear before them for a second trial.

It's wishful thinking, of course. It doesn't make Alice Perrers come out of hiding.

The whole month of November, and half of December, goes by before she is found. Christmas is in the air before the yardman at Pallenswick comes to London and reports to the parliamentary commission boss, who's now back in his usual place of work at Kennington Palace, that the mistress is hiding out in the servants' quarters. She's been there all along, right under the commissioners' noses.

The yardman receives enough money to get drunk on right through Christmas. There will be no one, now, to notice that several small household items, too humble for the commissioners to bother about, have gone missing from Pallenswick at the same time as him.

A day later, word gets about in London that the whore is now lodging at Westminster Palace, under guard.

The Lords put off their departure for the shires. Her trial begins on 22 December.

When Alice looks at her face in the pail of water they give her to wash in – the closest she has to a mirror – she's shocked by the grey-white circle looking back. Something irreversible happens to a face when the last hope goes. She's pale. Her eyes have white all around the edges. And she's so cold. Her blood seems to have turned to ice. She stares at the water. She can't think.

The first person Alice Perrers sees when they shuffle her into the crowded parliamentary chamber is the Duke of Lancaster. She's pinched red into her cheeks and forced nonchalance on to her face, but as soon as she's confronted with those dark, un-focused eyes, looking slightly past her, brimful of destruction, she feels herself going grey and papery and insubstantial again. She can see she's lost.

Those are enemy eyes. The eyes of a man trying to destroy a piece of his own past.

She knows why. She's the one person who's seen his darkest and most secret desire. And, now he's turned his back on that desire, and the self he might have been, he wants to destroy her. It's not a reasoned wish; he just wants her out of any world he's part of, eradicated, so that he can forget what he almost became. If throwing Alice to the wolves will appease knights and merchants alike, the very groups of men who've been so hostile to him, then so much the better. He could do with a bit less unpopularity. But appeasing them is not the true reason why he's going to find her guilty.

Surreptitiously, with the hands she keeps folded in front of her, she feels the swish of her legs moving under her, as if to remind herself that she is, for now, still flesh and muscle and bone, still capable of fight and flight. But her hands are dry and white; ghosts already.

Everything seems very far away. The speeches echo, as if in a dream. Shouldn't they be talking about fraud, or treachery? She can't hear any charges she can understand. She's vaguely aware that the real danger isn't here, in these words, these voices. The real danger is over there, in the black-haired Duke's eyes.

It doesn't take long for Alice to realise she hasn't just been daydreaming and failing to understand the charges. There are no formal accusations that would stand in law. These parlia-mentarians are too confident of their prey to bother overmuch with the niceties of framing charges. It's bad law, what they're doing, and rough justice, but (for them) good sport. The room sizzles with malice.

This Parliament claims Alice Perrers disobeyed the orders passed by last spring's Parliament, to keep away from the King, and returned to the old man on a whim.

This Parliament also claims that Alice Perrers illegally

influenced the King to pardon Richard Lyons and get him released from the Tower of London.

When Alice, with colour returning to her cheeks and feeling to her fingers, rises to say she is innocent on both counts, since it was the Duke of Lancaster, sitting here today as judge of this court, who ordered her back to the King's side last year, and also the Duke of Lancaster who, acting in the King's name, formally authorised Lyons' release, she realises why the parliamentarians are so careless of legal detail.

The Duke of Lancaster is not just the judge of this court. He is also a hostile witness.

With that glazed, hateful expression, he shakes his head at everything she says. He doesn't even answer.

The parliamentarians murmur, but subside. They're taking their lead from him.

Alice thinks faster on her feet. She stands before the Duke, considering him. His eyes shift and burn. He'll never admit to sending for her to return to the King, that much is obvious; the knight he sent won't admit it either; and there are no other witnesses. But she wasn't alone with him when they discussed springing Richard Lyons from his cell. Half Edward's household was there, lurking around, curious ears flapping, as he suggested she ask the King to sign the release form he'd prepared. Surely someone will say it was his idea. And surely there's paperwork, at the Tower if nowhere else, showing who authorised the release.

It can't be impossible. She says, with strength that surprises her in her voice, 'Let me find witnesses. There are officials who will confirm what I say. Give me time to prove my case.'

The simple ways are best. Even if she's got to take her guards with her, she'll be out. She'll go to the Tower. She'll ask directly. Even the thought of London air on her cheeks again invigorates her.

There's another uncomfortable murmur through the room.

They all know she's right, really. And it's midday. They want to break for dinner.

The eyes turn from her, expectantly, towards the Duke.

The Duke looks sick. He fiddles with his rings. He steeples

his fingers, as if in prayer. 'Very well,' he growls in the end, looking past her, over the fingers.

The next, louder, murmuring seems to anger him. The last thing he wants is to look weak. He turns his head, trying to quell the muttering. 'Appoint a representative to make your inquiries,' he adds brusquely, raising his voice above the rest. 'You're not going gadding about on your own.'

Alice gawps. 'But', she says, equally loudly, not giving up, knowing that her best hope is to keep the whole chamber listening, 'who? And how?'

He stands up. He spreads his arms. He doesn't give an answer. He makes only the smallest pretence of giving anything. He says, 'I give you this afternoon, and tonight. We resume in the morning.'

That's no time at all. It's hopeless. In the ensuing uproar, he walks out.

They take Alice from the chamber as the grey comes back over her. She lets them half tug her along the corridor. It's crowded. The men jostling all want to stare.

For a moment, she's let herself hope. And hope is so cruelly close to despair. She's trying to get herself back under control. Trying to think . . . but her mind won't obey her, and even her feet feel unsteady; she mustn't trip over her skirts, she mustn't humiliate herself.

She blanks out the voices. She blanks out the eyes. She shuts hers, and concentrates on gliding forward, as if there were no one but her here.

It's only when she feels a hand on her arm – a new hand, as well as those of the two men-at-arms – that she half opens her eyes again.

She can hardly believe what she sees. It's not some oaf of a knight, mocking her. It's Chaucer, bobbing anxiously along, trying to catch her eye, as if he's been mouthing at her for ages. Perhaps he has. He doesn't look like a man who once betrayed her friendship, and whom she's put out of her mind. He's taller than she remembers, but with the same elfin looks, and the same worried, guilty, affectionate half-frown. There is no sound coming from his lips. He doesn't want to be heard. Well, he was never a lion among men, she thinks, from far away.

But he's forming silent words. After a while, she realises he's saying: 'Shall I try?'

Mutely she nods. Chaucer falls back. She and her minders turn a corner. The noise recedes.

She never cries. Never has, till today. So she's astonished to find her eyes are pricking and brimming again, and her lips trembling so hard she has to purse them to keep her whole face from dissolving.

THIRTY-TWO

Chaucer can hardly believe he's suddenly so brave.

But something has changed in him. Yesterday, when, after Nones at St Helen's, he asked for and was again refused permission to see Elizabeth (whose lovely voice he'd heard soaring into the heavens from behind the screen, but who again didn't seem to have seen him in the brief moments when the novices filed into their places, and out again), the person he did see as he trailed disconsolately back towards the gate, and the street, and ordinary life, was his wife.

Philippa had lost all her usual condescending calm. She was white-faced and black-eyed with rage, striding along with her arms swinging. He nearly laughed, until he saw she was heading straight for him, and the rage appeared to be connected with him. She was looking at him as if she wanted to kill him.

It was only then that Chaucer noticed the Lady Prioress, lurking with her psalter back there in the cloister, where Philippa must be coming from. The nun was trying to pretend she was reading it as she walked, but was unable to stop herself sneaking curious glances at the couple.

Philippa may have been aware of their audience too. She didn't speak until she got near enough Chaucer to whisper. But the whisper came out as a furious hiss: 'You'll never see me, or Elizabeth, again. Don't think you will.'

'What? Why?' Chaucer said back, utterly baffled (though,

in the way of the unhappily married, he also, almost automatically, did all he could to make himself look as visibly woebegone and wrongly accused as possible, just in case that helped whatever case he might be called upon to make, or persuaded stray watchers that he was being mistreated).

It didn't cut any ice with Philippa, his play-acting. She just narrowed her eyes even further, and shook her head in extreme irritation, as if fighting down an urge to hit him.

How strange, he thought, I've never seen her really angry, like this.

'She asked me when I came in if it was true about Katherine and the Duke,' Philippa said. It was clear she meant the Lady Prioress. 'So I asked Elizabeth. And *she* says it's common talk in London that you've been spreading the word. Disgracing Katherine. She never wants to see you again.'

Geoffrey Chaucer paused. He ignored the bigger threat in what his wife was saying. It was a tactic, obviously. For the moment, he was only thinking tactics. This was going to be a tricky one to get himself out of.

He knew, just as Philippa knew, that this was worse, much worse, than the previous ugly whispered argument between them, the one begun back in July as they stood side by side watching Elizabeth being kissed by the Mother Prioress and ushered away through the gate. Back then, they'd at least been pretending to be a couple, at least preserving the external appearances of domestic harmony, even if what they'd been saying, in their guarded mutters, was savage. That time, at least, he'd had the moral high ground. The earlier conversation, as he recalled it, had gone something like this:

HIM. You gave Alice away; why did you have to do that to her? What harm did she ever do you?
HER. What, that slut? So what? She deserves everything she gets. It's time she got her just deserts. Why would you care, anyway?
HIM. Who are you to talk like that, sheltering a sister who's no better than she ought to be either?'

It had ended inconclusively, like all their arguments, because there was nowhere for it to go. Neither of them would state their interest, or fight openly for a declared cause. So neither of them could win. They'd tossed their heads like restive war-horses and retreated, as always, in different directions.

This conversation, however, was worse, because the accusation Philippa was flinging at him, through those clenched teeth, was undeniably true. He *had* been telling people about Katherine and the Duke and their children. He *had* given way to spite and foolishness. He *had* committed the great sin of the merchant caste and loosened his lips. But only out of frustration, and only a few times, he told himself, trying to feel innocent (though not succeeding). Only to Walworth, and the servants, and one of the clerks . . . and a man in a tavern . . . It just hadn't occurred to him that he'd get caught.

He caught himself on all these disingenuous thoughts. He recognised the lies he was telling himself. Of course he must have known that he'd likely be caught. Of course a part of him must have wanted to hurt his wife, and her sister.

What really had never occurred to him was that he'd get caught by his daughter, of all people. How could he know that London gossip travelled so fast that even the novices in the religious houses knew everything?

Opting for denial, because, for the moment, he couldn't think what else to do, he said, very coldly, 'Don't be ridiculous. You're hysterical. Get yourself under control. I don't know what you're talking about. You shouldn't spend your time getting over-excited about street gossip. It's bad for your health.' He drew himself up to his full height (as usual resenting the fact that this still didn't make him as tall as Philippa), raised his eyebrows coolly at her, turned around, and walked off without looking back.

It wasn't until he'd flung himself through the streets and slammed his own door shut that he realised the significance of what Philippa was saying.

He'd felt he was simply righting the wrongs against Alice by whispering here and there about the Duke. But in doing so he'd made himself the enemy of Philippa and her blood, and, he now realised, that might also mean that he'd made enemies of his own children, who were Philippa's blood too.

Was that the real reason the Lady Prioress wouldn't let him see Elizabeth? (Even though he'd said, honestly and practically enough, that he wanted to deliver to her the two new habits he'd had sewn for her, which were waiting in his saddlebag?)

With the dawning of wild, reckless despair, he wondered: Had his own daughter really said she'd never speak to him again? Might she mean it?

There'd be nothing he could do if she did. He might really never see her again.

So he's been up all night, cursing, throwing papers in the fire, snatching them out again, drinking too much, almost howling with grief, realising he's making a fool of himself, imagining himself, sodden and pathetic, through Elizabeth's eyes, castigating himself for making a fool of himself, then drinking more and crying again.

In the morning, with a splitting headache and a sick stomach, he's got as far as Seething Lane on the way to the Customs House before accepting he's not going to work. He strides on down Thames Street instead, heading for the passenger jetty. He can't tell, even now, where he's going, but his feet seem to have decided.

He's thinking: What's the point? What's the point of sucking up to one ambitious man after another, if the very centre of his world is this barren and empty of love? What's the point of a lifetime of self-reproach?

It's only when he's already in the boat, telling the man to let him off at Westminster, that he realises what he's going to do.

He's going to try and see Alice. He's going to try and sneak into her trial, or hang around outside hoping to get a chance to talk to her, and see if he can help her in some way, and to hell with the consequences.

He doesn't care about respectability any more. He doesn't care about his colleagues' possible disapproval, or the Duke's likely anger, or his wife's probable disgust. He's made enough of a mess of enough of his life by skulking in corners, trying idiotically to score points off Philippa, mistaking meanness for manliness.

He's been too busy doing that, and currying favour with men he doesn't respect, to do anything for that other woman, whom he loves, who's being persecuted and has no one to defend her. Even though he's appalled by the trial, and by the Duke's treachery to a woman so loyal, he's done nothing but write a feeble letter to a lover she's parted from long ago, asking him to step in. Even that well-meant, inadequate gesture now seems shameful.

He's probably got nothing left to lose himself, anyway, by now. He's probably about to be as much an outcast from everything he loves as Alice has become.

But Chaucer's full of resolution. He's not going to act out of hate, or malice, or pettiness, any more. He's going to do his bit in the service of love. He's going to try to be true to his better self. He wants to become the man his father would have wanted him to be.

Once Chaucer has seen Alice, and once he has his task to perform for her, he becomes determined as any knight-errant to fulfil his quest to the best of his ability. He's confident, too. He doesn't see the need to run around the court bureaucrats at the Tower, or anywhere else, asking for papers they won't want to part with, because he already knows just the man to help Alice.

The man is John Beverley, who was a personal attendant in King Edward's retinue, and who, since the King's death, has retired to London to live with his widowed daughter. He drinks in the Dancing Bear. He's already told Chaucer Alice Perrers wasn't half as bad as they're painting her. She always tipped him, anyway. No one in London likes the Duke. And Beverley's a sweet old man, as straightforward and honest as the day is long. Surely he will help.

Chaucer finds him nursing his ale, with pale, cloudy eyes lost in the past, trying to tell the landlord some story about the way he folded the King's clothes, with rosemary inside them to help his lordship remember better. It's a story that the busy landlord doesn't really have time to listen to; he's just muttering, 'Well I never,' and, 'Amazing what a few herbs can do,' whenever he passes.

The old man's face lights up at the idea of a moment in the Parliament's courtroom.

'The important thing,' Chaucer says, buying him another drink, 'is to say you never heard Mistress Perrers and the Duke discuss a pardon for Richard Lyons. And that you were there all the time, and would have heard.'

The old man scratches his head. There's nothing wrong with his mind. He's just puzzled. 'But', he says simply, 'I did. They talked about it for weeks.' His eyes brighten. 'It was his idea, though. The Duke's, I mean. It was him wanted it.'

Impatiently, Chaucer shakes his own head. 'Too complicated,' he says firmly. 'Keep it simple. We want the Parliament to understand that the Duke was acting on his own initiative. We want them to realise he never even tried to get the King's approval. We want them to see Alice wasn't involved. So just say, "It was never discussed." Can you do that?'

The old man shakes his head. But, looking confused as he does it, he says yes.

Chaucer only begins to understand that he should have listened more carefully to the old man when John Beverley is already sworn in, with proud eyes shining, and has started to talk to the Parliament.

The Duke, still with that sick, raging look of a man bent on vengeance, turns his dark lanterns of eyes balefully towards the serving man as soon as he begins to speak.

Alice, meanwhile, keeps her gaze down at her feet, in her corner.

John Beverley quavers that he was in constant attendance on the King because of his lord's infirmities. 'Never out of the room,' he adds, a little boastfully. The Duke's eyes glow. Uneasily, Beverley begins to eye him, rather than the crowd of parliamentarians, as he speaks.

'. . . and I never heard the King and Mistress Perrers discuss

396

the question of a pardon for Master Lyons,' the servant says, bravely enough.

He listens to the hubbub calmly enough. He's a little excited, though he's keeping his face still, to be saying something that causes this much talk.

But the Duke's eyes are still on him. And the old man goes quiet when he becomes aware of the intensity of that gaze. Chaucer's heart sinks as Beverley asks permission to sit, then squirms on his bench, and asks for water. Beverley knows he's told a lie. Beverley's watching the Duke's face carefully now; and Chaucer can see he's thinking some new, shamed thought.

Neither of them has fully thought this out. Is Beverley brave enough to withstand that angry-lion look?

Beverley could leave now. He's said his piece.

But the Duke growls dangerously, 'Have you anything to add to your statement, Master Beverley?'

And the servant gives him a sick, anxious look, before rising to his feet again, and giving a kind of military salute, and saying, in an old man's near-shout, 'Yes.'

Chaucer closes his eyes. He can't stop the frail old voice, or the frail old man, who's clearly remembering nothing now but the fact that he's served the royal family all his life, and wants nothing more than to serve the senior surviving member of it still.

'In my conscience,' Beverley shouts suddenly, tipping over his water in his agitation, but not noticing, 'I believe Mistress Perrers *must* have been the prime mover in getting Master Lyons released. And' – he adds with reluctance – 'I suppose I wasn't *always* in the room with them. Often, but not always. Naturally there were times when I was dismissed, but Mistress Perrers stayed . . .' He pauses here. He's a man made for respect. He's bewildered by the hoots and catcalls and lewd arm gestures.

'Naturally,' the Duke replies, smooth as silk, putting out a hand to calm the shouting. 'Thank you, Master Beverley.' He inclines his head towards the old man. He almost smiles.

Chaucer looks up as the old man is led out. Master Beverley averts his eyes and shuffles past. He knows he's messed it up. He'll squirm over what he's said, later.

Alice is completely still, staring at the floor.

Chaucer is utterly crushed. He can't believe how sick he feels.

The committee trying Alice withdraws to deliberate, walking behind the Duke. But the verdict is a foregone conclusion. They return from the antechamber no more than three minutes later.

It's the Duke, as head of the committee, who pronounces her guilty.

In ringing tones, he announces that all her lands and possessions, which have been obtained by fraud (the assumption that all her lands have been obtained by fraud is strong enough, by now, that he doesn't ask for, or provide, any proofs of deceit or dishonesty), will be forfeited. To show he means business, he announces that the rich manor of Wendover will be among those reverting to the King.

It's only as the other members of the committee come back to their seats, and Chaucer sidles up to the nearest triumphant-looking knight for a whispered consultation, that he understands more about what will happen to Alice's property. 'The Duke wants her house in London for himself – and all her rental property along the Ropery,' the man mutters with a smug look. 'He says it's compensation for being so wickedly maligned. But he's promised to give us the first year's rent from the Ropery properties as a reward for our service here.'

Chaucer sighs, feeling sicker than ever and hopeless at the knowledge of so much human frailty. How cheap it is to buy people, he thinks in disgust; how shabby this gathering of men of supposed honour and principle.

He doesn't understand why the Duke would want to be so cruel to Alice. The Duke was once a better man, surely? A man with his heart in the right place. There must have been some terrible falling-out that he can't imagine.

Unless the Duke's enemies have been right all along . . .

The Duke is still talking. There's more.

'Having confirmed her guilt, the committee therefore also confirms the original sentence of banishment on Mistress

Perrers,' he adds, and his voice carries effortlessly over the buzz.

The final words silence the buzz.

There's a moment's puzzled silence. Even the other committee members look surprised.

Eighteen months ago, Alice was sentenced to banishment from the King's presence. They all remember that. But it's impossible to reconfirm that sentence now, surely? Now the King's dead, Chaucer's wondering, and from the intentness of the silence many others must be wondering at the same time, where, exactly, will Alice be banished from, or to?

The war makes the whole notion of banishment unworkable – a vague but inevitable death sentence – for where can an exile be sent that isn't at war with England? What hope could an English person have, in France, of anything except murder at the hands of the French?

It's pure spite. The Duke's own, unnecessary, personal cruelty. In wonder, Chaucer looks at that handsome dark face, with its hard little smile, with the kind of automatic revulsion he normally feels only for the kind of animal you exterminate without thinking: spiders, or rats, or stoats (and, at present, for his own wife). Chaucer wonders: Whatever has become of him? And: How can he?

As the talk begins, as the implications sink in, as the volume rises, he turns his gaze to Alice. She still won't look up. But Chaucer sees her downturned face has gone paler, until it seems so grey and full of dread that it looks dead already.

THIRTY-THREE

She's being led away, down a corridor, and he's following her again, through the crowds.

She's so quiet he has to follow the determined movements of the guards, not the bobbing top of her head. Her head must be bowed. He can't see it.

They put her back in an antechamber, away from the fuss. Chaucer's still behind.

He hardly knows what he's thinking. All he knows is that the fear that has always been his constant companion, the fear that makes his gut churn and heave, and sweat break out on brow and palms and armpits, is absent. Instead, there's a welcome quiet in his body; a tautness. He's walking on air. The world he's passing through seems to be moving more slowly than usual, or perhaps it's his mind that's working faster. He can't tell, for what's bubbling up inside his head is taking shapes he doesn't even recognise. He doesn't care, either.

Alice is so quiet the men start playing cards outside as soon as they've shut the door on her. They don't bother locking it, Chaucer sees.

No one knows what to do next, it seems. Everyone's still too surprised to have thought of the next step to fulfil the Duke's order.

Except Chaucer, that is. Chaucer, with the wind in his nose, and the blue of the sky outside in his eyes; Chaucer, who for some unaccountable reason has the phrase 'it's now or never' singing inside him; Chaucer, who's wondering if the heady feeling in his heart is courage.

Chaucer gives Alice's guards fifteen minutes to relax, while the chaos of men leaving the chamber below and eddying around is at its worst.

It's not his cautious mind that's organising his behaviour any more. If you stopped him now, he wouldn't be able to tell you what he was doing. But the mysterious new impulse governing him prompts him to go quickly and purposefully to the stables, to fetch his saddlebag. It still has Elizabeth's two habits in it.

Then he goes back upstairs to the watchmen, and tells them, as if he's known all along he would say this: 'There's food in the kitchen – a celebration meal, with ale – someone go down and fetch it.'

He hears with surprise that his voice is steady. Calm. Confident. Cheerful, even, as if for some reason he, the Comptroller of Customs for the Port of London, were the natural person to be deputed to bring this news to the guards; as if he might also be enjoying tucking into this dinner for guards in a few minutes. From far away, the usual Chaucer, the careful one, thinks, approvingly: Well, of course they'll trust me. Why wouldn't they? I couldn't sound more trust-worthy.

He's guessed right. They hardly even look at him, they're so pleased to have something to do. And they all pour off down the stairs, every last one of them, with expectant faces. No one wants to be the one left behind while the rest take the best of the pickings.

Chaucer opens the door.

Alice is sitting by the window, with her back to the room. He says, 'Now.' There's no time for talk.

He's got the habit out by the time she looks round. He's holding it open.

She understands at once. He can see that from the light that comes back into her eyes. Alice isn't one to miss a trick, or waste time philosophising. It's no time at all before she's

401

in the habit, doing up the top fastening, with the hood over her head, and they're out of the door and trotting along the corridor, very fast, feeling a couple of inches above the flag-stones, almost before they've had time to breathe.

It's only when she's on his horse, and he's holding the bridle, with his belly full of fire, and they've silently negotiated the gate out of Westminster, and the fields and river and London town are visible ahead, that she seems to breathe out; that she whispers, 'We're away . . .' and then, looking at Chaucer with something like wonder, '. . . are we? Is that really it? You've got me out, just like that?'

It's a moment more before she grins – the old Alice, resur-facing, he thinks with relief – as if she's just heard the best joke she could possibly imagine. She shakes her head. A little louder, though still hoarsely, because after all she still isn't used to talking freely, she adds, 'I'd never have guessed you had it in you, Chaucer.'

Chaucer doesn't explain the nun in his apartment to the servants. She sits quietly by the fire, with her hands clasped and her hood up. There seems no need. Nor does Chaucer feel any need for thanks. He's hardly realised until he's done it that he was planning this wild moment of rebellion.

If he'd had a moment's conscious thought, he might have explained that he thinks the Parliament has gone so far in its wild burst of malice, sanctioned, encouraged even, by the Duke, that it's surprised itself. The lawmakers have no more idea than he or Alice how to implement the sentence they've just passed. They may soon be slightly embarrassed by their own vindictive-ness; and, even if they aren't, they won't make any great effort to actually pursue the woman they've punished. They've had their spectacle; made their kill. They'll probably be quietly relieved that Alice has made off without forcing them to face the consequences of their action. They're more than likely just to let the whole thing drop. And now Chaucer's full of joy, and, unexpectedly, of fun, that he's managed to get Alice out so easily. He's full of fellow-feeling for her, too; full of the idea 'we're two of a kind, so we have to look after each other'. He's racing.

When the servants have gone, leaving dishes of meat and bread, and cups of wine, he says briskly: 'What we need to work out now is where can you go? To be safe?'

What property Alice might still own is unclear. So it is also unclear where she can go and take quiet refuge.

She shakes her head. She still can't bring herself to speak, or eat. She's grateful, so grateful, but all she wants to do, in practice, is look at the fire, and not have to think. But she doesn't mind Chaucer thinking for her.

Chaucer's fizzing with purpose. 'Not Wendover, obviously. Not Pallenswick. And not London. But what about . . .?' He starts to list the manors he remembers her having acquired without the King's help, in the past few years: Hitchin, Plumpton End, Moor End, Lillington Dansey, Frome Valeys, Brampford Speke, Southcote, Powerstock, Litton Cheney, Knole, Stoke Mandeville, Morton Pinkney, Sutton Veny . . . but every time she just shakes her head.

'Why?' he asks, with this brisk new energy that fills him with light. She mumbles something. He waits, until he understands that she let go rights to all but a clump of property-holdings, ten in all, before the first Parliament she was called to. She wanted to rid herself of any possessions more than a day or two's ride from London. Those ten were restored to her, later; and she's managed to move most of the cash from most of the other sales down to Gaines, too. The deeds of these properties are firmly in her name; there's nothing fraudulent about her title to them. It's all as rock solid as Chaucer told her to make it. But now, after the latest Parliament moves against her, and after seeing the Duke's open malice, she suspects that the lawmakers will make it their business to inspect every last one of the properties she's still listed as owning, and will almost certainly requisition them and everything in them – especially now she's run away. And she doesn't want a repeat of what she saw happening at Pallenswick, when the government inspectors came calling.

'Then there's nothing else for it,' he says in the end. She hasn't suggested it herself, so he can see she's reluctant. 'I'll see what I can do about finding out the status of those properties.

But meanwhile, you'll have to go home, to Essex. To Gaines.'

She shakes her head again.

Misunderstanding why, he persists: 'But I remember. You made the manor there over to your son, when he was knighted. At least you were going to. Didn't you?'

That isn't why she was shaking her head, but it's a novel thought, so she stops and considers for a minute. It's true. She did do that. And that means that, technically at least, Gaines can't be confiscated (though there's no predicting whether that will hold good if the Duke decides he wants to take it from her).

Chaucer thinks he's won the argument, she can see.

If only he understood that her children don't mean to her what his must mean to him; that they are strangers to her now, the left-over human relics of a love that's long gone too. They're more Aunty's children, really. If only he understood that, to her, accepting a future at Gaines means accepting she's lost everything. She's not ready to accept that.

If only she could not think about any of it.

He's leaning persuasively forward, saying, 'You must be worried that by being there you'd endanger your children . . . but if you don't actually own it any more, and the Duke and his men have got the best of your property for themselves, it's remote enough that no one's going to bother looking there. Don't you see?'

She shakes her head. But she feels so dazed that she's not surprised he's ignoring her preference.

He says, 'Go there. Let the dust settle. Let the lie of the land emerge.'

He says, 'Get your strength back.'

He says, 'It's not all bad. At least you'll have your children with you.'

She doesn't understand why the mention of children makes his mouth, briefly, twist. She doesn't ask. She's too absorbed in her own problems.

But he's so insistent about sending her to Gaines that, at last, she nods her head. She does see that it might be bad for his prospects, harbouring her right here, under their noses.

When he sees her nod, finally, he puffs out a great sigh of relief. 'Good,' he says with satisfaction. 'Gaines it is. Now, let's get started.'

He's treating her like a child, not a lover. She's grateful for that. She's lost all ability to take decisions.

First, he wraps up bread and meat for her.

Next, he gives her a little bag of money. She takes it without a word. (Last time, last trial, she remembers, numbly, it was the Duke who rescued her and gave her money. How grateful she was then; but how pointless her gratitude has turned out to be.)

Thirdly he hands her a key. 'To here,' he says. 'The door here's always open to you.'

Finally, Chaucer takes her down and puts her on his own horse. She thinks: He's not a rich man. Somewhere inside, she's grateful to him again. More than grateful. It's a grey day, bitterly cold, but mercifully the sleety snow that's been threatening all day is holding off.

It's only when he's heaved her up, and walked her out through the gate, in case of questions, and settled her at the back of a late train of tradesmen making their way to Waltham, that he reaches up, puts a kindly hand on her back, and grins encouragingly at her.

'Life has so many surprises for us all,' he says, squinting up, as if trying to impart some great secret. 'You never know what you'll find at the end of your road.'

She knows he means to be encouraging. She nods, dully. She kicks on the horse. She doesn't mean to be rude. She just doesn't want to leave all this behind. If she doesn't say goodbye, doesn't freeze her feelings into words, she's thinking, it may not be for ever.

A few minutes after Alice has gone, Chaucer's hands start to shake. It's only when he's alone again, picking up the empty goblets and finding them, unaccountably, rattling against each other, that he realises how close he and Alice have been, all day, to being caught. The risks he's taken. He gives up on clearing away. He sits down, feeling suddenly cold, and wraps his arms around his knees, waiting for the trembling to pass. He's seeing, for the first time, how close bravery is to thoughtlessness.

This time, when Alice reaches the quiet road to Gaines, there are no children playing in the fields. There's just a man, with grey hair and a neat grey beard, stiffly tying up a horse at the iron ring in the wall.

She looks warily at him as the horse shakes her forward. Another stranger. She's starting to fear strangers.

He has big broad shoulders. He's very tall. He's well made. Must have been handsome in his time.

She's close, very close, by the time he turns round and gives her an equally suspicious stare from pale, pale blue eyes.

It's only then that she realises whom she's looking at. Was this what Chaucer meant by surprises at the end of the road? Could Chaucer possibly have known?

She reins in the horse. 'Will,' she says, expressionlessly, from six feet away, from high up.

He goes still. He's recognised her voice, all right. He's just not sure . . .

She's in her nun's garb, she remembers. She puts down the hood.

He's never been given to displays of emotion. He looks at her for a long while before he answers, even more blankly, 'Alice.'

He's never been given to displays of emotion, she reminds herself. But she's not sure she can hear the tenderness she might have wanted in her husband's voice.

What follows next is almost enough to make Alice laugh, especially when she imagines Chaucer, sitting in his mess of bits of paper, with his endless flow of talk and ideas, with his generosity of spirit, with his eyes shining, picturing her in some happy-ever-after Christmas moment, being reunited with her lost love, being hugged by clean pretty rejoicing children.

William takes her inside, takes her upstairs, unbuttons himself, pushes her down on a bed, pulls up her skirts, and

406

makes love to her, in no-nonsense military fashion, without a word of endearment.

He smells familiar, like remembered happiness. And everything, for days, has felt so unreal anyway. And she's interested. She lets it happen. This might be the future. Why protest?

But when he sits up and starts to talk – he doesn't seem to expect a word from her, even an explanation of the nun's habit he's just unseeingly desecrated – and she sits meekly listening and watching, relearning his tics of eye and mouth and expression, remembering the timbre of his voice, recalling, now she sees it again, that roll of fat behind his ears that she never liked, she begins to realise that, though he seems a greyer, harder version of the man he was before, she might have changed more. Did she really just sit, in this slumped silence that seems so familiar, while he gave orders, before? Wasn't she ever the centre of attention, back then? Didn't he ever listen while she laughed, and made jokes, and amused him with her wit? She begins to think that the woman she's become, in the years of running things, and planning things, and jollying people along, might never be able to accept that this man – this abrupt-mannered, cold-eyed, order-issuing soldier – could ever bring her the kind of happiness she's come to want.

It seems he's been here at this house for a week, and he's been travelling to find Alice for a good while longer; since soon after he received a letter from Chaucer, who'd thought, but not been sure, that Alice would sooner or later pitch up here. (Chaucer, she thinks, with a burst of nostalgia for her London friend's verve and intelligence; always one step ahead.) Because William didn't know exactly where to find her, he tried Wendover and a couple of her other manors en route. His next stop would have been London, except that when he reached this house, and found the children and Aunty Alison were still here, as they had been all along, he also heard that Alice had been arrested. So he decided to wait out the trial here. He hasn't been doing the things that Chaucer was advising Alice to when she reached Essex: letting the dust settle, getting the lie of the land, gathering strength. That isn't Will's way. He's a soldier. He's been making a thorough investigation of everything, putting everyone here through their paces, and smartening everything up.

'Servants were running wild when I got here,' he barks. 'So – had a few whipped. Discipline, you know. Discipline. All fine now.'

It's true, she realises. It's more orderly here than she remembers. The house is strangely neat. So is the yard. The usual clutter of half-mended farm implements and cracked leather buckets and discarded boxes and big bits of wood that might, one day, be useful for something has vanished from the courtyard. The peasants are in the fields, turning over the earth, ready for spring. The horses are in the stable. The servants are in the kitchen. The chickens are in the hen-run. There are cooking smells in the air.

It no longer looks the kind of place where the lord lives scarcely any better than the peasants he reigns over. Alice thinks, not without admiration, that with someone like Will in charge, who knows? The land at Gaines might actually make some money, for once. Of course, she also thinks, since Will's techniques seem to involve beating his subordinates into submission, the price would be unhappiness all round. But a proper income from the fields might be good.

Alice can scarcely think how Aunty Alison can have taken to this soldierly make-over, though she can imagine a good many tart comments that might have come from the old woman's lips.

'Whatever did Aunty say?' she asks with the beginning of a smile. She'll break the ice between them, she thinks, suddenly hopeful. She imagines she's going to hear about an epic tussle of wills. Then she'll tell Will a few stories about Aunty and her odd ways, perhaps; it will be the first laugh they'll share.

Will looks back, not registering the laugh. 'Your old nurse?' he replies seriously. 'Complained. Lippy type. I've moved her off to sleep with the servants. Right place for her. Been getting above herself; taken over running the house. Gossiping with serfs. Egging them on. Whatever next.'

Alice's eyes widen, though she stays tactfully silent. Poor Aunty. How furious she must be.

Will continues, even more sternly: 'She should watch herself. That old woman. Talks too much. No discipline. I've got half a mind to get her flogged too. Set an example.'

There is a moment's pause.

I must find Aunty, as soon as possible, Alice thinks, feeling her hands already flapping around uneasily on the quilts. I must find out what's been going on.

But she smiles up appeasingly at her husband. Cautiously, with sinking heart, she asks the next question. 'And the children . . . where are the children?'

He hasn't mentioned them, either. Not that he's ever shown much interest in them, in all those years in Ireland. But still . . . they're his own children . . . and his only children that she's aware of. They must be on his mind?

He looks blankly out of the window. She thinks, hopes, that he isn't too angry with her for letting them grow up such wild little peasants. It takes her a moment to realise that he might be feeling the same mixture of worry and guilt she does. He's been away all their lives too, after all. And he's their father.

'Sent them up to Greyrigg,' he says guardedly. 'No choice. Boy can't hold a bow, let alone a sword. Girls can't sew. No priest to teach them, here. They can hardly read. No French. And they can't so much as mumble a prayer in Latin. Best they go home. Get a bit of schooling.'

With the light on his granite face catching his pale eyes, he's handsome, as statues are handsome. How strange, Alice thinks; he's taken them on as his, then. She wanted that once. But now all she can think is how sad Aunty will be.

'They can come back in the summer,' he adds. 'Maybe. With a tutor. If they've done well.'

For all the harshness of his tone, Alice thinks she's hearing an apology, or the nearest he can come to it: a concession to the presumed maternal instinct in her that he thinks he must have gone against.

She lowers her head. She doesn't know what she feels.

She thinks she's relieved. This is difficult enough as it is. So she nods.

'But, Will,' she says, giving in to the way things are going, since there's nothing else to do, and asking him for leadership, as she can now see she must always have done in the past, 'what will *we* do?'

She means, 'now that I've lost everything'. She means, too, 'now that you've lost everything'. Because, since he was sent home in disgrace from Ireland, he has no cosy government position, no favours from on high; just his rents from his northern manors, just obscurity, like her. Desolately, she thinks: All those years of effort, wasted.

He knows the answer. He's a leader of men. He always knows the answer. Will doesn't do might-have-beens, or regrets. He's accepted the way things are, after defeat in the last battle. But he'll always want to fight on.

'Let the dust settle,' he says firmly. 'See how the land lies. Then, see what we can get back.'

Alice recognises those phrases. William must have taken them from whatever Chaucer wrote to him. He's quoting, though he probably doesn't even realise that he is. For the first time, Alice feels just a little comforted.

But, in the weeks that follow, there's little else to comfort Alice. Over a muted Christmas, while she's trying not to think of the splendid style in which she's celebrated previous Christmases, running the court, William has a list made of her properties. Aunty, meanwhile, makes a list of gifts she's going to send after the children, from her and, as she tells Alice, 'from their mum. They'll like that.' There isn't a hint of reproach in her voice. She's obviously always said this. After Christmas, William sends clerks to each of the manors Alice so recently owned. Then William strides around, shouting at the clerks when they return, one by bedraggled one, with their separate pieces of inevitable bad news. William shouts at Aunty, that bristling stick of resentment, stuck away upstairs and in the kitchens, seething. William scarcely speaks to Alice, except to update her on the property news, or to order her to order Aunty to change the way the house is run, or to find grease for his armour, or better oats for his horses, or a priest, for God's sake, why is there no proper priest in this place?

He wants to do something to fight back. But he's lost, away from his troops and garrisons. He's not a man of the mind. He doesn't know how to fight, except with a sword.

Alice is too grateful to be alive, and free, too relieved no one has come after her, to feel as desolate, yet, as she thinks she will when she really begins to believe it's going to go on for ever. Still, time hangs more heavy on her hands every day. She tiptoes around. She rides around the bare winter fields, noticing how quiet the peasants have gone (they've never had serfs at Gaines; 'Can't see the point of it,' Aunty's always said). The servants' pay's been cut, she knows. Their hours have been raised. Aunty's seething (though only in a whisper). Those peasants were her friends.

She sneaks off to the solar and kitchens, sometimes, and talks to Aunty – tells her, in a whisper, the story of the trial, and the escape, and Chaucer's unexpected and triumphant rising to the occasion. 'He sounds a good boy, your Chaucer,' Aunty says, putting aside her own woes, and considering. 'We both like a lad with a bit of wit and mischief in him, don't we, dear?' Then her thin old face darkens, and her loose old-lady mouth tightens, as she mutters, rebelliously: 'Not like old Lord Misery-guts out there.'

Aunty has nothing much else to say about Will. But she tells Alice that the children knew, before they went north, that their mum was on trial. That they were worried. That they asked Aunty all the time, 'Will she be safe?' and that they had tears in their eyes.

Alice doesn't know exactly what the confusing feeling is, churning inside her, when she hears that. She just nods. 'It's for the best,' she says, wondering why her voice feels so choked.

'They'll have heard you're out and safe, at least, dear,' the old woman says reassuringly, and her thin turkey-jowls quiver. 'The boy will have got there by now. That'll be a weight off. Poor little mites.'

Alice can't talk to Aunty all the time, because Aunty's so

411

often out these days. To keep out of Will's hair, the old woman trots off to Brentwood every few days to hear the hedge-priest's insurrectionary sermons in the cemetery, outside church, on the days the real priests don't come out and chase him away. 'You should come too,' Aunty says with wickedness in her grass-green eyes. 'Ooh, how that man can talk. You'd enjoy it. I can tell.' But Alice knows Aunty just wants to rile Will with this invitation, because Will makes no secret of the fact that he wants to get the ranting revolutionary, who's called John Ball, locked up for preaching that there should be no more lords, and no more princes of the church either, and certainly no taxes. Alice doesn't want to rile Will, so she stays put. And when Aunty tells her that there's a bit of a society being formed among the hedge-priest's supporters, a secret sort of thing called the Magna Societas, and that they're doing a bit of letter-writing to spread the word among the people, because the collectors are out gathering this new poll tax, and it's an outrage, dear, just imagine, a groat a head, from the poorest in the land, when the wages have been cut back to twopence a day (by Lord Misery-guts and his land-lord friends), and so Aunty's promised to help with the letters, because of course it's a good cause, and worth the time, only she's not that good with a pen, so perhaps Alice might . . .? Alice just smiles, a bit sadly, and shakes her head. Aunty's never allowed herself to be bored, however unpromising her circumstances. That hasn't changed. But Aunty's flirtation with a new form of risk isn't for Alice.

Sometimes Alice is so at a loss for ways to occupy herself that she even reads. Aunty scoffs, 'Well, look at *you*,' when she catches her, but Alice thinks that's because the only book she has is a Bible. She can only half understand the Latin. Sometimes she wishes she'd asked Chaucer for some of his work. He writes in English. She's never read his poems.

Once every few days, Will unbuttons himself and pushes Alice down on the bed, with never an endearment, never a soft word. She opens her eyes, sometimes, and looks wearily around as he labours over her, grunting energetically. Was this really what she's swooned to remember all her life, this muscular, dull coupling? Surely she enjoyed herself more, laughed more, on those few snatched nights with Chaucer, talking half the night; Chaucer, whom she's always taken so lightly, whom she's always thought of as a friend more than a lover. Why didn't she notice at the time?

There's no lightness now, that's for sure. Even if Will's not admitting it himself, even if his mind doesn't admit of might-have-beens, or deal in fancies, she can see he's angry with life for this reversal, angry with God, and angry with her.

What Will wants more than anything else, she comes to see as the estate visits go on, and the list-making, and the futile shouting, isn't her, it's getting the property back. All those estates she might have brought him; all those estates she had in her hand, and lost. He thinks of nothing else. He recites the names, and the fates, of each unknown manor. He knows the acreage. He knows the yield. He knows the rents. He knows who's taken over. He knows whom he'd get revenge on, if he could. But he doesn't know how.

It's February, or March, and the first green fuzz of buds is appearing on the bare branches, before she realises that she actively dislikes her husband. She doesn't want to hear him muttering the names of the estates she's lost any more, or shouting at any more clerks, as if it were their fault the lands have gone. She's lost in her numb grey cloud here; she's got no use for the rents she's lost, now she's got to be here. And nor does he. Yet he wants those lands more than she does, even though it was she who earned them, and on her back, too, half the time. With the first stirrings of conscious resentment, she thinks: It's wrong that he's so much more desperate than me for the profit he feels he should have made from pimping his wife, all those years ago, to another monstrously selfish old greybeard like himself.

She looks at that grey head, and the neat grey beard, and the too-broad shoulders, and she imagines him in another few years, bent, and frail, with aches and pains and weeping, stinking sores, demanding warmth, attention, time, respect, ointment and bandages, sucking the life out of her, out here in the mud and biting wind. They're all the same, old men.

Their selfishness destroys you. And there was me, thinking I was using *them*, when all along, my old men have been having the last laugh on *me* . . .

She almost laughs, at that, though joylessly. It's true. Here she is, right at the bottom again, in Essex with Aunty, with mud on her boots, nostalgically howling 'regnavi' – 'my reign is over' . . . And none of it need have happened, none of it might have happened, if she hadn't spent so much of her life trying so hard to manipulate all those old men.

None of her old men have done her any real good. Chaucer – clever, bright-eyed, young, unconfident Chaucer – is the only man who's been her friend, and who's actually helped her. He saved me, she says, out loud, trying out the words. No, he *noticed* me, she corrects herself a moment later; that's what she's most grateful for, now she's with another unthinking old monster, who treats her as if she were invisible, unless she's being useful. Chaucer noticed me, and he thought about me, and so he saved me, and I've done nothing in return. I never even really thanked him.

If only she had, she thinks with painful nostalgia for him, and for the busy cheerfulness of those days rushing between court, and London, and Westminster, and Chaucer's rumpled bed. She's trying to make a kind of bargain with a God who she's pretty sure isn't listening: she should have thanked him . . . and she still could, if only, even just one more time, even for a moment, she could come out of this strange dull afterlife, this punishment for flying too high; if only she could see Chaucer again.

THIRTY-FOUR

It will be nearly two years before Alice's wish to see Chaucer again, and thank him, comes true.

Meanwhile, Chaucer's advice to lie low and let the dust settle proves sound. The wheel keeps turning, bringing if not a return to Fortune's embrace at least another summer, and a harvest of sorts, and then, in the next bleak wintertime, when the only fruit on the skeletal trees is the crows with their melancholy cawing, black as ink blots, dropping like ghostly pears to swoop through the grey air, a new Parliament at Westminster.

Until she finds out what will be discussed at the Parliament, until she understands William's preoccupation, and the reason for his exchanges of messengers and letters with London, Alice doesn't feel the momentum of change. She's aware only of what stays the same. She knows, for instance, that Aunty still misses the children, who are still up north, because Aunty talks about them so often, and so softly. These aren't the stories Alice might have expected, either. There's never a word about training the kids up to be thieves, as Aunty once trained her: slipping in and out of windows, sliding through openings in sheds and barn, picking up unconsidered trifles and slipping them into poachers' bags. Instead, Alice has learned that stubborn little Joan has nightmares, but that when she wakes up from them, trembling and clinging to you in the bed, she's stoical enough to pretend they never happened. That Jane is a natural-born tree-climber, and kind-hearted enough with servants to save food to share with Hamo the ploughman's daughter, who's the same age as her. That Jane and her friend had to be stopped, when they were toddlers, from eating earthworms. That Joan's as light and wiry to hold as a ratting dog, while Jane's body has always been warm and barrel-shaped. That Johnny's freckles started to appear on his face soon after his sixth birthday, and that he's embarrassed by them. That the little boy has the pure voice of an angel. That he can ride like the wind. That he had a wooden whistle made for him by Hamo, and that the girls liked dancing to the tunes he plays on it by the bonfires they lit in the autumn. And that Jane once leapt right through a bonfire, so high she didn't catch fire.

'They're better where they are,' Will grunts whenever Aunty asks, meekly enough, when the children will be back.

So Aunty's keeping herself busy with her hedge-priests instead. Not John Ball, at the moment; he's been clapped into Maidstone jail after an outing to Kent. But there's always someone floating through Essex on the tide of angry human flotsam and jetsam sweeping the roads of England, who's got a rousing sermon in him. Aunty takes food to them all in her basket. Alice has also seen her going to Will's little bag of money and filching coins from him, sometimes right under his nose, with a grin on her face. She knows the coins go to the hedge-priests too. Alice never stops Aunty. She just pretends not to see.

It's through Aunty and her friends that Alice hears her news these days – all the latest vicious stories about the Duke of Lancaster, who's the man everyone in the land, more than ever, loves to hate, as things get worse. These are stories she doesn't comment on, neither with Aunty nor Will. She won't let herself be drawn into conspiracy with Aunty; and with Will she's found that the sharp tongue and quick wit that once earned her her fortune just aren't there any more. He silences and intimidates her; he doesn't mean to, perhaps, but she can't talk easily to him, any more than his stern face seems able to soften when he addresses a rare comment to her. There's nothing between them. He's out supervising the farming, or he rides into Colchester to spend his days with his friends at the garrison there. He eats with her at the same table once every couple of days. They make quick, wordless love once a week. So when she hears the stories about the Duke, the last person she's going to share her feelings with is her husband. She just smiles with grim private satisfaction, and thinks: The Duke's made his bed, and now let him lie on it. He can't blame me for any of *this*.

The Duke has put aside all shame of man and fear of God, she hears; he sleeps with an unspeakable concubine named Swynford, a witch as well as a whore. He's so under her spell, or so cowardly, or both, that he's failed to sail for France . . .

The Duke sent his knight, Sir Ralph Ferrers, bursting into Westminster Abbey during Mass to violate sanctuary and murder a squire who was seeking refuge after escaping from the Tower of London, where the Duke had had him wrongfully imprisoned. The abbey has had to be closed, and reconsecrated. But the Duke's making no bones about defending Ferrers . . .

God's against the Duke, who's lost another siege, and another king's ransom in Englishmen's money, now he's finally set sail for Saint-Malo to fight the French . . .

The Duke's still out for revenge on Londoners for scaring him silly by trying to burn down his great big bloody palace. The latest: he's trying to destroy angel-face Walworth, the fishmonger. He's scrapped the fishmongers' trade monopolies. He's kicked Walworth out of his government job as war treasurer, too . . .

They say the Duke hates Londoners, and this really proves it. He's also kicked John Philpot, the most powerful of the grocers, out of his government job. John Philpot, to whom he should be grateful; John Philpot, who's paid, out of his own pocket, for a private fleet of warships to protect the coast from pirates . . .

You'll never guess what. The Duke's plotting with the Genoese to destroy the London merchants. He's always with the ambassador, Janus Imperial (and what kind of two-faced foreign name is that?); they say they're about to announce that England's trade centre will be moved, permanently, from London to Southampton . . .

Alice listens to the next story, too, with only her usual dark dream-like pleasure, right up to the incomprehensible punchline. For what seems an eternity, she doesn't even begin to understand the amazed, expectant look in Aunty's eyes.

How about this, then? They're so fed up with the Duke that the next Parliament's going to reconsider one of his cases. It's your case, Alice. Will's bringing an appeal.

'It's your case, Alice,' Aunty repeats. 'Will's bringing an appeal.'

As the moments pass, as the room spins, Alice realises Aunty's still staring at her, half-excited, but half-hurt, too, at having been kept out of the secret.

'Did you know?' Aunty asks.

'Didn't he tell you?' Aunty asks a little later, reading Alice's face more accurately. But Alice has picked up her heels and fled in search of Will.

'That's right,' Will says, shortly. 'Appeal in January. I'll be leaving for Westminster right after Christmas.' He looks as square and military and phlegmatic as ever; she can't see even a flicker of excitement in his eyes.

'But . . . why didn't you *tell* me?' Alice asks. She hears her voice, soft and trembling. She's had no idea. He's been doing something useful all this time, after all. He's been thinking about her. He's known how to make her case, in the right places. She's misjudged him. 'How . . .? When . . .?' she mutters, humbly.

He stands up. 'Men's business,' he says, even more shortly. 'I wrote in. I said I was your husband. They agreed at once to an appeal.'

Alice becomes aware of a little golden glow inside her chest.

After all these years, he's publicly acknowledged that he's my husband, she's thinking. There was something that touched him, after all, about our putting our hands together at the church door, in the dawn of time. Something he remembered. He's taken the children on . . . and now this, too. How little I've understood.

She tries to look into his eyes. She'd like to lose herself in them, as she once did; to enjoy feeling truly loved, and protected, and cherished, as she now thinks she may have been all along. She'd like to throw herself into his arms and surrender herself to his knowledge and wisdom, as utterly as she had all those years ago.

But Will's clearing papers, making things into orderly piles with big hands. He's not looking at her. He doesn't see the need for a loving moment. Now he's started, he's going to complete his staccato explanation.

He says, 'I told them they'd made a mistake to try you as a single woman. I told them they'd made a second mistake, arising out of the first. They were wrong to confiscate your property. As my wife, what you own rightfully belongs to me. And I've done nothing wrong, so they shouldn't have been punishing *me*. So I've asked them to return your estates to me.'

Slowly, the rosy-gold feeling fades inside Alice. 'Oh,' she says flatly. Is that it? No exoneration for her, no vindication, no head held high? He's been far cleverer than she expected to get the case reheard at all. But, after all, has he really only wanted one thing all along: to make sure he gets the money she's earned him?

He has, hasn't he?

'They will, I think,' Will finishes. He nods, as if she should now be satisfied with his explanation; as if dismissing her from the environs of his business table. 'Don't worry your head about it. It's a formality. I'm dealing with it.'

Alice doesn't go. 'But,' she stammers. 'What about . . .?' Her voice trails away.

He looks impatient. 'What?'

She wrestles with the words. If only she could talk to this man she lives with, and is married to, who's such a stranger to her. The phrase 'a pardon' sticks in her throat. She wants to go triumphantly back to court, of course; she wants to be presented to the new King as my lady Alice of Greyrigg, a respectable matron who's been wronged. Why can't he see for himself?

'. . . *ME*?' she says in the end: an undignified sound, a kind of strangulated squeak, half-pain, half-fury.

He moves towards the door. 'This *is* about you,' he says,

with no great interest or affection, from the doorway. 'I'm cleaning up your mess. I'm saving you from yourself.'

The door shuts. But he was already gone, Alice thinks, long before he left the room. If, that is, you could ever really say he'd been there with her at all.

Just to show she's actually there, just to give vent to her suppressed anger, she starts ruffling through the piles of documents he's been putting in order, messing up the neat military squares, making them human again.

Which is how she sees Chaucer's writing: a letter, and another, and another; a whole correspondence. She picks one up. A phrase leaps out. 'With feeling turning so sharply away from the Duke, now might be a good moment to request an appeal,' she reads. She drops it. She picks up another. At once, she sees: 'As far as recovering property is concerned, I would suggest you argue that they made a first mistake in trying your wife as a single woman, while knowing her to be married, and a second mistake in punishing her by confiscating her property, when doing so in fact constituted punishing you, an innocent man.'

So that's it. Chaucer's been writing to her husband. Chaucer's been framing the arguments Will's going to use. Naturally, Will hasn't mentioned he's had help. That's not in his nature. But this explains how her husband suddenly sounds so well informed. This is how he got the appeal lodged.

Dear Chaucer . . .

Thoughtfully, she picks up another page. She's looking for some other clue in that small, neat, speedy writing: some message, some hint, some flicker of affection, just for her. She reads:

I suggest your primary request should be for the Parliament to reverse all previous judgements, and give Alice a full pardon. You could make the following two arguments. Alice should have been heard by the King's Bench in a case involving public funds, rather than by Parliament. Secondly, she wasn't given enough time to prepare a case, or locate witnesses.

420

'. . . "give Alice a full pardon,"' she repeats in a whisper. Chaucer understands what she wants. But then, he always has. The soft golden glow steals back into her (though it's not for the stranger she's married to, this time); as well as a not unpleasant breathlessness, and that dangerous dampness around the eyes that she's hardly ever felt, except in exceptional circumstances . . . except around Chaucer.

Aunty tells Alice the Parliament's decision, long before Will gets back from Westminster. It's a non-answer, though a fairly hopeful one.

'They say they need a year to decide,' she says, breaking the news gently.

They're going to collect another poll tax first. The war has eaten up all the money from the first tax. Or rather, the Duke's eaten it up.

But the Parliament hasn't left Will, or Alice, quite empty-handed. Aunty says the little King's formally commanded Alice's husband to accept the post of Governor of Cherbourg while the legislators deliberate – a lucrative sinecure. 'They'll want you to go too,' Aunty says with an encouraging grin. 'Out of sight, out of mind, I suppose. But what do you care? You'll be able to gad about in your silks and satins again for a year, ruling the roost. Nice work if you can get it, that's what I say. And at the end of that, they're hardly going to clap the Lady of Cherbourg in irons, are they?'

Alice shakes her head. She can't imagine anything worse than being locked up in some fortified French town, listening to the waves breaking on the walls and the gulls keening, with no one for company but her husband and a few hundred soldiers. She'd far rather spend the rest of her days in Essex, alone with Aunty. Firmly, she says, 'I'm not going anywhere.'

She's aware of the bright flicker in Aunty's eyes. But Aunty keeps quiet.

She says the same thing again to Will, when he breaks the news of the posting on his return a week later. Politely, she thanks him for his efforts, and his success, and says she'd prefer to stay in these safe, familiar, surroundings while the

421

Parliament's deliberating. Once her pardon is through, of course, she'll come and join him.

Will doesn't ask more. 'Very well,' he says, equally formally. 'I'll go alone.' She thinks he's relieved. He's started preparing for his departure before nightfall. She hears him whistling on the stairs. He sounds as happy as she feels, to be about to be free of him.

'We'll have fun, with him gone,' Aunty says, hopefully, as they watch Will jog off with his men. The crows are cawing. There's a wild freshness in the wind. 'We could get the kids back.'

Alice shakes her head. 'I can't just disobey him, after all he's done,' she replies disingenuously, feeling shabby. She knows Aunty wants the children. Aunty's told her enough, and lovingly enough, that Alice, or a part of Alice, also wants to see them, with their freckles and nightmares and barrel chests. But Alice can't face them yet. She wants them to respect her; she wants them to know she's a successful woman, not a failure, a whore, a has-been. 'Let's see how it goes with the pardon first.'

Aunty's face falls. But she composes herself within seconds. She's not going to bully; she takes what life doles out, and never complains. 'Well then . . . you could help me write my letters,' she goes on chirpily enough, 'my eyes not being what they were . . . and me having never been so good with a pen?'

Alice laughs, and embraces Aunty. Her spirits are lightening with every step the tiny horseback figures take towards the horizon. Aunty's 'letters' are nothing of the kind, of course. They're insurrectionary concoctions with thoughts from the hedge-priests' sermons, which are circulated among the free peasants, the ones who've got a bit of book-learning from somewhere, enough to read. They're disguised as letters, in that they're addressed to 'Piers Plowman' and signed from 'John Carter' or 'Henry Hooper'. They're how members of the Magna Societas, Aunty's trouble-making secret society, think they'll persuade the peasantry to rise up against their oppressors, when the time comes. For now, they're just mustering. The letters are nailed to church doors, or tree trunks, or passed from hand to hand among the disaffected on the road. Alice isn't unsympathetic to the peasants' miseries; how could she be, considering where she's come from? And she's pleased it all keeps Aunty busy. But she thinks it's a nonsense, too – they'll never rise up, really. And she's a landlord, so why encourage them rise up against herself? 'No, I'm not writing your letters for you either,' she says affectionately, and the old woman's pale eyes laugh back at her. 'You just want to get me into trouble, don't you, you old rogue?'

'Nothing for it then,' Aunty replies, sly and swift. She's always liked a bit of banter. 'We'll just have to get Wat out here to tell us some tall stories.'

She gives Alice a beady look. This is what she's really been bargaining for. She wants more of her kids with her. Alice grins, feeling suddenly reckless, and raises her hands. 'All right,' she says cheerfully, seeing a future opening up of long card evenings and shady visitors by firelight, after long days on the farm, and not caring. It will pass the time. 'Find him. Why not?'

Alice busies herself once Will has gone and the energy that being with him leeched out of her comes back. She takes over running the farmland, and the repairs, and the women making butter and cheese, and the team of men gathering in the rents. She does it more kindly than Will has, and she pays better. The mood around Gaines lightens with every passing week. But she's more thorough than Aunty used to be, too. And the profits keep coming in. When spring comes, she even goes back to her original plan to beautify Gaines, and plants what will one day become a great avenue of beech trees along the sides of the track – weedy-looking saplings, for now, but by the time John has children, God willing, who knows? And she plants other, more immediately rewarding plants too: gardens of waving roses and gillyflowers, with bees in the rosemary and lavender, and doves fluttering through the orchards.

If only she could get her hands on the money she left behind the stones behind the fireplace at Pallenswick, she sometimes

423

muses (her profits from several of those last-minute property sales), she'd buy up land all around, and turn this old hall into a manor to be proud of . . . but that money's gone. She'll never have a chance to get Pallenswick back. She's heard the Duke's got it.

So she tries not to think about that money, hidden away; a vestige of her past.

She tries to live in the present.

And, once Wat starts coming, Alice comes to date her months by the gossip he brings.

He's leaner and more ragged around the edges; he doesn't talk about how, exactly, he spends his days. But he's as entertaining as he ever was, and Alice, relaxing into Aunty's raffish rustic life, enjoys seeing him again. Wat's road to Essex from Johnny's in Kent takes him round the edge of London. He hears everything. He passes it all on: (other) brigands attacking travellers; women being kidnapped; despair in London at the failure of the Parliament to stop the new King's Council spending; the latest war failures; the Council pawning the old King's embroidered cloaks in the City; the plague breaking out in the North; the second poll tax being collected; the second poll tax, all £27,000 that's been collected, vanishing. Don't give me robbers, Wat says, sententiously, the biggest robbers aren't the men on the roads (though he would say that, of course); they're the men of the Council. And, of course, the biggest robber of all is the man who leads the Council: the Duke.

They sit by the fire, of an evening, with the account books, and cider, and meat, and Wat's talk of the world outside; with Aunty nodding sententiously, and Alice poking the fire.

It's August 1379 when Wat remarks: 'You remember how I was saying that the Duke and the Genoese ambassador are plotting to screw the London merchants by moving the trade port to Southampton? The man with the funny name, Janus Imperial? Well, how about this, then? Proof. Someone's murdered the ambassador, right on his doorstep in St Nicholas Acon Street, in broad daylight.'

Someone must be worried, then. No smoke without fire.

424

He comes back later in August, full of it: 'Here we go. Mayor Philpot's had two men picked up for knocking off Janus Imperial. Bruisers from the guilds. Londoners. John Kirkby and John Algor, they're called. Algor says he picked the fight with the Genoese servants. Kirkby says he stabbed Janus Imperial in the head. Twice. They say the wound went seven inches deep. Nasty, that. Angry.'

By the autumn Wat is rubbing his hands with glee: 'You'll never credit it. The Duke doesn't want those killers tried for murder – because he's got something worse lined up. He says Janus Imperial was ambassador to the Crown, so killing him was *lèse-majesté*. He wants those blokes tried for treason – a hanging, drawing and quartering job. What they're saying in the City is, this is going to be how he fingers the merchants . . .'

Returning in January of the new year, Wat tells his fireside family of the new Parliament meeting at Westminster. The King begs for more money. Money is somehow granted, through a mix of appeals to merchants and more sell-offs of royal property. But the Parliament makes the little boy who rules England, thirteen now, promise to hold off for at least another eighteen months before asking again for the people of England to pay his bills for him. What he gets off his own vast acreage of royal estates must, surely, be enough till then.

All this gossip about the government being short of money worries Alice. They'll never give up the estates they've confiscated from her, not now, will they?

But at last, in March 1380, they do.

Remarkably, considering the temptation it represents in this time of financial troubles, Alice's confiscated property is all (bar what the Duke has taken for his own people) made over to her husband, who's still in Cherbourg. The banishment order on her is formally revoked, too.

And Alice gets her chance to thank Chaucer.

THIRTY-FIVE

Alice goes to London to receive her pardon. It is made out to her, and stamped, signed, sealed and delivered into her hand, at Westminster, in the Painted Chamber, on 15 March.

She has Wat bring her to London, not on horseback, but on his quiet river route up the Thames. It's how he gets over to Kent, these days, hopping on fishing boats south to Dartmouth. He knows the ways of the watermen. This time he isn't going on to Kent until he's seen her home afterwards. He'll be waiting for her here, south of the river, in some fleapit inn in the shadow of St Mary Overie in Southwark, listening to the choirboys sing in their wavering trebles, remembering being a boy. She doesn't want to stick around, she says grate-fully; she'll maybe spend a night in town, though; visit a few old friends; but she'll be quick. Wat understands how strange this partial reprieve must feel to her. She knows that when she realises he can't bear to set foot in London; won't cross the bridge, even. Not in the state he's in now: as a no one, a has-been. London's a place for a man in his glory days, he says, with a bit of money to spend and a dash to cut. Southwark's near enough, for now. But she buys him a meal, and he cheers up a bit, and they both look north, imagining the rooftops of the City proper, and he squeezes her hand, and says, 'One day, though, Allie love, we'll be back in all our glory. You know that, don't you?'

It's a soft day, with flashes of sun between dancing clouds.

426

But Alice's mood is neither soft nor flashing with sunlight as she slinks through the streets. She's got an hour to kill, and, even though there's no need, she finds her feet taking her away from the river, up to Aldgate. She looks up at Chaucer's windows, but there's no familiar head behind the glass, waving. Shaking her head, she heads back to the river for a Westminster boat. For the entire walk, she doesn't see a soul she knows. She's just looking at the scene in front of her as if through glass. In ways she can't quite put her finger on, things have changed. For the first time, walking down to the jetty, she realises she's not altogether sure that she still belongs here. As she fails to recognise men on guard, or on boats, or, once she gets to Westminster, the new King's new officials scurrying through the corridors, she's numb with the possibility that she might not. Alice is modestly dressed, like a country lady, and she does her best to comport herself quietly, as befits a wronged but respectable matron. But the worm turning in her gut is screaming for attention. No one seems to see her. They're all so busy. There are uniforms she's never seen; new passwords; new rituals.

She comforts herself: It will all change once I have the pardon in my hand. I'll stay a little, visit a little, begin to gather my team about me again . . . and surely the little King will remember that I held out his New Year gift to him, with Edward, last time we met; he'll smile; he'll say something gracious . . . it will be a beginning. Very soon, all the new things will seem familiar. I won't even remember the strangeness of this morning. I'm going to start living again.

But nothing happens quite as she imagines. Her case is not news any more, that much is clear. It's just a moment's adjustment of paperwork; an old story. That might have felt a relief, considering how terrifying she once found all those hostile eyes fixed on her in the chamber at the height of the scandal. But now, ignored by everyone, she almost misses the terror she felt before. She's only called into the session for a few moments. Briefly, she's shocked to see the Duke, the author of all her woes, standing beside the little boy she hardly knows, who is now King. She holds her breath, and steels herself: she might have expected this, after all. She's heard enough about how the Duke and Princess Joan are competing with each other, politely (for now), to be the power behind the throne. And it might have been just as bad, or worse, if it had been the Princess standing there. Alice ignores the Duke as she bobs her curtsey to the King; he ignores her too.

But she can't stop herself glancing up from under her lashes when she thinks no one's paying attention. And so, inevitably, sooner or later her eyes do meet the Duke's. And when he sees her looking, he makes a point of moving protectively closer to the young Richard II and saying, loudly, with tremendous emphasis, 'our beloved nephew, whom we hold so dear,' all the while looking significantly at her through those narrowed, angry eyes she remembers so well.

Alice lets the stirrings of long-forgotten rancour settle. She tries for a jocular, jaunty, 'what, he's *still* blaming me for all that?' frame of mind. She tries to make herself laugh at the Duke's black gaze. She doesn't want to let this man's hostility distress her, just at the moment when things are coming a bit more right for her again. He's nothing to her any more. Why should she care?

So she looks away. She lets her shoulders perform the smallest of shrugs.

She's aware he's noticed her insouciance. She can sense his indrawn breath.

But so what? It doesn't matter if he feels cheeked. She'll be out of here in a minute, with her papers.

Won't she?

At the very last, as the pardon's actually being handed to her, the Duke speaks.

He says, in an exhausted, peevish voice, 'Let the woman return to her son's manor in Essex, and not come back to London, on pain of our displeasure.' He nudges the little King. The little King looks sideways, briefly puzzled, as if this wasn't in the plan. But then he nods – what's it to him, after all? He hardly knows Alice, and he won't have heard anything good – and the paper is taken back, and a new line is added to the pardon.

Not come back to London? No glory days? Alice's gut is churning at this unexpected extra mark of the Duke's spite, or displeasure, or indifference, or whatever it is. But she's trapped, behind her glass. She can do nothing but narrow her eyes and bob again. At least the Duke can't see inside her mind, where horrible scenes are being played out. If I had a knife . . . she thinks, and lets herself, just for a moment, imagine his startled eyes fixed on her as 'the woman' drove it up under his ribcage. That would make him look, all right, even if it was the last thing he did. But in real life she doesn't have a knife. And in real life his gaze is fixed grandly else-where. So Alice meekly takes her paper and leaves, walking behind a guard, who sees her down to the jetty and calls a boat. 'Thank you,' she says, almost timidly (she's always been friendly with servants), trying to make a connection, hoping to see an answering flash of warmth in the other eyes; but the man just nods, without looking, and sets off back towards the palace.

As Alice glances back at the splendour of Westminster, she recognises, painfully, that this may be the last time she sees the domain she once more or less ruled. Every stone and bench looks familiar, but it no longer feels familiar. Looking at it now reminds her of seeing Will for the first time after all those years. This place has become separate from her, and she has become invisible.

Alice is aware of all sorts of uncomfortable personal things as she sits in the bobbing boat in the uncertain sunshine. She feels the dryness of the skin under her eyes, the limpness of the skin under her neck, and the tightness of the laces around her waist. Her hands are no longer soft; she's been checking on too many furrows ploughed badly, and counting the feed bags. How could they have stayed soft? There has been no one, in these gloomy country months, whose attention she has wanted to attract; no one to notice if she's looking beauti-ful, or not. Perhaps, without even realising, she has just stopped being a woman whom people look at. And perhaps she was always worthless; perhaps the gloss has gone off her, and the rot of age beneath is becoming visible . . .

Vigorously, she shakes her head. Stop that, she tells herself, stop that right now.

She pushes down the rising panic and stokes up her anger. Anger makes her feel alive. If she's going down, she might as well go down fighting. Once again, the Duke's spoiled every-thing for her. She can't go and spend a couple of days in the City, now. Her own house in Vintry Ward hasn't been returned to her as part of the pardon, but given to the King's half-brother, so she'd have had to stay at the Dancing Bear; but at least she could have found John Broun and the rest of her men and made plans for a future she can see now isn't going to happen. She can't go and visit her old friends; she can't do anything. She's supposed to scurry straight back off to Essex with her tail between her legs.

But how will they know? Defiance grips her. She doesn't have to meet stupidity halfway, surely. There are still things she can do. She can, at least, go and see Chaucer. She can show him her pardon. She sees his hand in every line of it, after all. Surely the Duke won't know, and couldn't complain even if he did, if she at least paid her debt of honour to her old friend by thanking him for remembering her, even at the bottom of the wheel, and for saving her. Who could argue with that? He's at Aldgate. It's on her way home. Well, not really, not if she's going to Southwark, over the river, to meet Wat. But it might be.

She doesn't call the servants. No point seeking trouble. She lets herself in. She still has the key.

It's strangely neat in Chaucer's rooms. There are no traces of paper anywhere. There are no festering jugs of drink. There are spring meadow flowers in the jugs, and a small fire burning, and the cushions plumped up, and fresh rushes on the floor, and food laid out on the table.

When Chaucer comes in, he's strangely neat too. He has a new tunic on. His beard is trimmed. His skin looks fresher. He smells of lavender.

'Chaucer,' Alice says, turning towards him from the window, where she's been looking back at Essex, and feeling suddenly shy. Perhaps he won't want to see her either.

For a moment, he looks confused. He still has anxious eyes. Her heart stops. Then they light up, and he cries, 'Alice!' and he rushes to her, and embraces her, very tenderly, but correctly too, like an old friend, and all her shyness drops away. 'I didn't realise it was today, your hearing,' he says. 'No one said.' Her heart stops again at that. They're not even gossiping about her in the taverns. But then she hears his voice again, from somewhere near her ear, and it's cheerful, as if a weight's been lifted off his mind at the sight of her, and she starts to breathe again: 'So are you done with the Parliament?' Then, pulling his face back so he can look into her eyes from close up: 'Have you got the pardon?'

Here, in the rippling sunlight on these familiar walls, Alice finally knows she's safe. She laughs. She kisses his nose. Not leaving this embrace, she lifts her right hand and holds up the pardon, which she's kept treasured in her hands all this way, not even in a bag, cradled gently as a baby bird. She's going to offer to return the money he laid out on her escape: the bag of coins, the price of the horse. She's always paid her debts. And she's going to make the speech of thanks she's been thinking out: careful, gracious, grateful.

But she can't. He's already talking. As usual, she thinks fondly. 'Forgive me,' he says, 'if I looked puzzled to see you just now.' His arms are warm and tight round her back. He's holding her very close. She's always liked that in him, the way his body seems to expect that they'll mould to each other until they merge. She's so grateful to him for being pleased to see her; so grateful that he's looking at her at all. 'For a moment I thought you were Philippa, come early. I'm expecting her, you see . . .'

'Oh,' she says, disappointed, but not stepping back; still relishing the warmth.

'She lives at Kettlethorpe, these days,' Chaucer's explaining, and as usual she's astonished at the speed with which words and explanations and ideas pour from his lips. How does he move them that fast? 'When she's not with the Duchess. You won't know any of this, will you? Well, she's through with me. Not to worry, though. Old history now. It's for the best

431

for everyone, really. And we've patched things up a bit, over time, enough to be going on with, anyway. We don't disgrace ourselves, or each other; we don't let scandal touch our names; I keep my nose clean, and my rooms tidy, and do my job properly; I pick up one of her pensions for her, at Westminster; and we go to see Elizabeth together, at the convent, around every quarter day, and divide the money over dinner.'

He laughs, a little regretfully. 'My reward, you see. For good behaviour. Being allowed to see my daughter.'

'I was wondering why you'd got so tidy,' she says affectionately, entering his story, relieved to leave the emptiness of her own day behind.

'Not easy,' Chaucer admits. 'For me.' He pulls a tragicomic face. 'But then I'm not allowed to get drunk any more, either. Which makes it easier, I suppose.' He steps back, but keeps an arm round her waist. 'You're looking so well,' he says appreciatively. (Or is he just being kind?) 'If only we could talk now. I want to hear everything. *Everything*. But . . .' He suddenly looks anxious again, and glances round at the door.

'I know,' she says, looking into the fire, at all those dancing possibilities, changing shape. They all burn out in the end. 'Philippa.'

She steps back. She can't interfere with Chaucer's new life. There's no space in it for her. She'd better go.

But then she sees he's looking at her with his old glinting mischief, and not saying goodbye at all. 'We *could* talk, of course, only it would have to be later,' he rushes on, brimful of his new idea. 'If you had time, that is?' She nods. What else does she have to do? If she's this invisible to everyone, perhaps, she can even stay at an inn after all. No one will know, or care, will they? 'Listen: wouldn't you go and eat dinner at the Dancing Bear? They're doing delicious pork stew there today. I know, because I've ordered some of it in for Philippa. Kill a couple of hours there. And after she's gone off, clinking her money-bag, come back.' He's nodding at her with imploring lapdog eyes, begging her to agree.

She almost weeps at the warmth and charm of him. She nods. There's a lump in her throat. She can't speak.

He blows her a kiss. 'Thank you,' he says, sounding as light-hearted as she feels, though hurried, and then rushing her towards the door. 'Now, don't let her catch you. Quick, run!'

She's still laughing to herself when she gets back down the stairs. She's still laughing to herself when she reaches the Dancing Bear.

The light's just beginning to steal in from round the shutters. The lovers are as soft and happy together as kittens, twined together in the bed.

'I should go,' Alice said, yesterday, when she came back to Chaucer's door. 'I'm not supposed to be in London, really.'

He just grinned, and pulled her into his stairwell, and up.

She's been here ever since. Wat will wait a night. They've talked, and bathed, talked, and made love, talked, and eaten, talked, and built up the fire, talked, and made love again, talked, and lit the candles, and talked. She's told him about the life she's been living . . . about Aunty, about Wat, about the raggedy children, gone away. ('She loves you, doesn't she? Your Aunty?' he says gently. 'Oh,' she shrugs, unfamiliar with the idea, 'I'm what she has, that's all. We're all realists.' But she's been strangely comforted by the idea of Aunty's love.) They've talked about Will. They've talked about Philippa. They've shrugged their unsatisfactory marriages away. It doesn't matter, any of that, with someone you . . . Alice hesitates before the word 'love'. It's not as familiar a word to her as it is to this newer, calmer, wiser Chaucer. A night: it can feel like for ever, if you're happy.

'You saved me, you know,' he whispered in her ear, half-jokingly, sometime in that night. 'From staying a coward all my life. I've had one brave moment now. I can die happy.'

'You saved *me*,' she whispered back very seriously.

He only laughed. 'And you have beautiful eyelashes. So long. Like tiny brushes, tickling. Here . . . and *here* . . . and *here* . . .' He stops kissing them long enough to say: 'If Philippa weren't . . . if William . . . if they weren't there, somehow, I'd marry you, you know, Alice.' Then he moves his lips to her

433

hair, so she can't see his face; she has the impression he's startled even himself with those half-serious words. 'I'm only really alive with you.'

'How?' she asks his neck. He's always only half serious. It's an easy enough thing to say, she thinks, not very happily. But to actually do it . . .

He shakes his head above her. 'Oh, I don't know,' he muses. 'We couldn't be here, could we? You couldn't, now, at least; and I couldn't be with you in London . . . but I wouldn't mind that. To be honest, I don't like my life in the City that much, except for seeing Elizabeth. I spend all my time writing poetry these days, you know. Don't want to be at court, either. Too complicated. Philippa . . . and as for the Duke, what he's done to you . . .' She can feel his head shaking again.

When he mentions the Duke, she appreciates his pained bewilderment on her behalf, though she also knows she'll never explain what he doesn't understand: why the Duke will always hate her. Chaucer would never understand that. There's no darkness in him. She wishes there wasn't in her, either, now.

But she sighs anyway. Because for a moment she hoped he had a plan, though she knew all along that he wouldn't. How could he? What he's saying, about being together, is only a playful fantasy. It's stupid to feel disappointed.

'So perhaps we could go away somewhere?' he's murmuring. 'A long pilgrimage, say . . . the Holy Land . . . you can spend years on pilgrimages . . . and you've never seen Italy, either – the golden stone, the sunlight, the colours?'

She sighs again. After all, he's just being a poet.

She doesn't want to go. But there's no choice. She can't stay.

'I must leave,' she says, hating the fresh light, and the absent spouses, and the loneliness of everything that lies ahead, outside this bed, away from this man.

It's only now, now that she knows for sure that the love she'd thought, for all those years, she felt for Will was a wraith of a nothing, a sick thing of the imagination, or of the past, that she understands how important it's become to her

434

to know that Chaucer is here. Alive . . . within reach . . . somehow, hers. But no more. Because of the Duke, not after today. He'll be out of her reach, for ever.

He props his head up on his elbow, looking at her as if he's memorising her.

'I know,' he says sadly.

She dresses, quickly. He watches her.

She's surprised by the treacly blackness moving inside her again, the anger coming back. She's had no time to think, for the past couple of days, about anything except the rush of immediate events. But now, as she pulls on linen, and kirtle, and gown, as she realises there's no more to keep her here in this busy, happy, fleeting moment, she's remembering another conversation from last night: the questions she's been asking about her old friends and fellow-victims of Edward's last Parliament. What's become of Lyons? Where's Latimer? What about Stury?

They're all fine, it turns out. Prospering. Lyons is back in the City, making a new fortune, living in his enormous house in Vintry Ward, over the road from St James' Garlickhithe. Stury is a knight of the privy chamber, close to the new King, and still blithely preaching Lollardy to the court. Latimer, briefly returned to the royal Council before being removed again after Edward died, has recently been made Governor of Calais, and is high in the royal favour in the army in France.

None of them has been forgotten. None of them has been told to keep out of London.

'So it's only me who's lost out,' Alice said, trying to keep bitterness out of her voice.

Chaucer kissed her, and said nothing. She knows he could have crowed: I always told you that might happen. There was nothing kind he could say, she supposes.

And now she can't keep her last picture of the Duke of Lancaster out of her mind: the lustrous black hair, the neat pointed beard, the sharp brows, the very red lips, the long bone-thin limbs, and the sick, hateful black eyes, staring petulantly away from her in the chamber.

The Duke has the face she imagines on Lucifer; the phrase

slips into her mind: the Day Star, the Son of Dawn . . . Aunty's been on about Lucifer a lot, recently. One of Aunty's hedge-priests has been translating Isaiah into English. The old woman can't stop muttering the words in front of the fire. Lucifer, the all-powerful King of Babylon, who thought he could rise higher than God's stars . . . until he was brought down to the abode of the dead to be taunted by the vengeful Israelites he once oppressed. Alice hears the taunts in Aunty's voice. 'How you are cut down to the ground, you who laid the nations low!' And, in Wat's answering bass: 'Is this the man who made the earth tremble, who shook kingdoms, who made the world like a desert and overthrew its cities, who would not let his prisoners go home?'

How Alice longs to bring the Duke low; to be able to say those words to him while he lies, muddy and bloody, grov-elling before her.

It's because of the Duke's hatred that she can't come back to London . . . that she's locked away from the court where she'd found her place . . . that she won't see Chaucer again. The Duke has done so much to ruin her life. And she could see, back at Parliament, that he'd still like to do worse. He still wants to destroy her.

She thinks, and it's a relief to admit the thought: And I'd like to destroy him.

'What are you thinking?' Chaucer says.

She shrugs. She's so full of pent-up anger that she can hardly speak.

'That I'd like to burn down the Savoy, with the Duke right in the middle of the bonfire . . . and his smug mistress, and your smug wife and my husband, too, if only I could think how . . . and then stay here for ever,' she says, finally, in a bloodthirsty rush that, almost at once, embarrasses her.

She shrugs again. 'A fancy,' she half apologises, even managing something close to a rueful smile. A childish one, too, she admonishes herself. It's stupid, worse than stupid, to blame the Duke for all her misfortunes. He's done her wrong. Of course he has. But she's partly to blame too. She remem-bers what she saw in the Duke's eyes all right, when they were close – but only because she was thinking it too. She never told herself, back then, that it was a wicked thought. It never crossed her mind to apply moral rules to her plan; to any of her plans, because in those days she thought she could always get away with everything, for the rest of her days. She somehow felt everything was allowed to her, because she'd come so far that it just must be. But she didn't know, until much later – until now, maybe – how suspicious her giddy rise must have made the people who'd grown up expecting to be at the top, when they found her among them. And she didn't understand her own power, while she had it. She certainly didn't realise how hard they'd all want to kick her once she was down, because they'd seen her in her glory, swanning around, hardly noticing them and their foolish fears and doubts. Perhaps she should have tried harder to understand. She might have saved herself. She might even have clung on . . .

She shakes her head, banishing from her mind the mental picture of flames licking at the Savoy, with the Duke's screaming face in the middle. She wants to shrug all that hatred off. She'll have to leave it behind when she leaves London. Might as well start now.

He shrugs, too. 'That isn't going to happen,' he says, baldly. 'But it's not important. They're not important. The Duke. My wife. Your husband. The world.' He reaches up for her, pulls her down with him, gazes at her from close up. 'What matters is that I love you. Remember that. Knowing it is our comfort. It's what we have to hold on to. And there's nothing any of them can do about that.'

She looks down, too stunned by the word 'love' to be able to move; how does he say, or think, these things, so boldly? Her eyes are suddenly glistening.

'But, Chaucer, don't you *mind* . . .?' she almost shrieks, forgetting, for a moment, to strive to be philosophical. He's been left behind, too, by the capriciousness of Fortune: trapped in the City, when he doesn't want to be. Dumped by his wife. Returned to his father's merchant life, when he's so talented, so brilliant . . . 'Because it's not just me. It's you, too. You should be at court, too . . . glorying.'

Chaucer only smiles, rather sadly. 'We're not the same, Alice,' he says. 'You can change yourself – you have a genius for transformation – but I don't want to become what I'm not. My father tried to make me an aristocrat. But I couldn't fight. I found that out early on; I'm grateful I did. It's not in my nature. If the price of a title, and a court life is to have to live with my wife, and go to France . . . well, it's not for me. So I'm just trying to live the life God sends me, in my station, and be with my children . . .' His face twists. 'Whenever they'll have me.'

He takes a deep breath. Trying to look encouraging, he says, even more softly: 'There is degree above degree, as reason says . . . that's my motto, Alice; I'm trying to be contented living within the degree I was called to.' He shakes his head at her. 'But I know it's not your philosophy. Never has been. You've always wanted to rise; to glory. You must feel trapped. Locked out. But you'll find your consolation somewhere. In Essex even. I promise you that.'

She breathes out. She buries her face in his neck and holds him tight. She'll never feel this close to anyone again, she knows that now. She's saying goodbye to love.

He's murmuring something else, from the lips she can't see, whispering into her hair. He's saying, very softly, something about how she's going to build up Gaines into a vast farm, and become the envy of all her Essex neighbours, or maybe buy them all out, and marry her children off to the best and richest of them, so the kids will become aristocrats in their own right, and Johnny a great man in his prime, with the longest crackowes in England. He's saying no woman has ever risen so far, from so low, as she has – something she's sometimes thought, not without pride, but never said aloud, so, even now, it's strangely comforting to hear it from his lips. He's telling her she should be proud of what she's achieved. He's telling her no one likes to be forced to scale back their ambitions, but she can still make a future she and her children will be proud of, even in Essex.

Still, she doesn't want to hear any of that. It's not import- ant enough. She wants to say the words back to him, the love words, but they won't come.

438

'It's all right,' Chaucer whispers. 'We'll be all right. We both will.'

She lets go, and stumbles up. She nods, with a tremulous smile.

He finds his night-robe, and shucks it on, and follows her to the door.

He takes her hands, gravely, because they're done with kissing, and this is farewell. He says, very tenderly, 'Get your children sent back to Essex to you, at least. Promise me that. You'll get such joy from them . . . you'll never know joy like the love of your children . . . Make them your comfort.'

She's pleating her lips together to stop her lips from quivering; but she can't stop the tears. They're running, hot, down her cheeks.

He kisses them out of her eyes.

He whispers, 'I give good advice, don't I? Usually? So trust me. Take back your children. Promise me you will.'

She can't speak. But she nods her head.

And then he's gone, and she's looking at the door.

She'll do it, once she's back, once she's grown accustomed to the small life that lies ahead. She'll write to William, and to Greyrigg, as soon as she gets to Gaines. They'll come back, a bit educated, a bit better at riding and sewing and Latin and archery than before; the children of a gentleman.

She'll accept that she'll never be able to make them look up to her as the person who brought them a glittering courtly life. She'll accept that they will all be small people, for ever, shut away in the country, though at least they'll be better off than the way she was, when she grew up, and more secure . . . Chaucer was right about that; perhaps she needn't feel she's failed altogether. There's even a bleak sort of comfort in the thought. She *has* risen a long way, even now, from where she started. She *can* do what's demanded of her now.

So, she'll find it in herself to accept all that the future has in store now. She'll learn to take pride in the children. Her shoulders are broad.

Yet, however hard she tries, she can't answer the question of whether doing what she's going to be doing from now on will ever compensate for the yawning abyss inside. Will it even begin to make up for her howling rage at the eyes sliding sideways; the people who no longer want to know her? For the emptiness of a future without Chaucer?

She doesn't think so.

She tries not to think of Chaucer: the smell of him, the tenderness of that last moment in the doorway. She tries not to think: Never again . . . never again . . .

Still, she can't stop her eyes filling with hot, wet liquid that she won't shame herself by letting out, as she sets off for the river, and Wat, and the future she doesn't want.

PART THREE

Regnabo?

Shall I reign again?

THIRTY-SIX

The children – taller, more dignified, Johnny in a well-made tunic and cloak, Jane and Joan in neat dark-green robes under their brown travelling cloaks – look hesitantly down from their horses.

Alice looks hesitantly up.

It's Aunty who rushes past her, and, grabbing all three bridles, pushes the grooms aside. 'Off you go, boys, off to the kitchen, you must be hungry, get some food,' she cries excitedly, walking off towards the stables, pulling the horses, talking over her shoulder. 'I want to see the kids.' Her excitement is infectious; Alice is aware of answering smiles on her children's faces. They're already scrambling down off the ponies, and Johnny, first off, is walking proudly at Aunty's side, putting his left hand round her in a one-armed knightly hug, leaning his head on her shoulder, saying, quietly, but not so quietly that Alice can't hear him, 'Look how tall I've got, I have to lean down to do this now,' ignoring the girls wriggling and jostling and pushing each other, trying to break through between them, from behind, or from the side, for a place under Aunty's arm.

They move off. Alice just stands, watching the glow, feeling left out, with the welcoming smile that's come too late to her face beginning to fade.

Aunty's been rushing round for the past two days, preparing. Aunty's been carrying on like a lunatic. Aunty's been saying, 'They'll be so excited to see you,' and squeezing Alice, and rushing off again, when all along it's been clear that it's her own excitement she's talking about, her own almost uncontainable love. Alice doesn't remember any of this excitement from when she was a kid. Back in those days, there was just the watchfulness, the waiting for the next snatch, the sheer thrill of surviving from one day to the next. But it was always fun, at least, she thinks; they always had a laugh. Alice never felt lost. She doesn't feel lost now, come to that. Not completely. She's grieving for everything else; but she's pleased to be back with Aunty. Perhaps, back then, they just never had the luxury of time, to think about love; or the words. Alice even said to Aunty, last night, 'Do you think people go on learning to love, better, all their lives? Do *you* love these kids . . . *more* . . .?' She didn't need to say more than whom. Aunty understood, and patted her shoulder, and grinned. She shook her head. Then she kissed Alice's forehead, and scurried on; and Alice sat astonished at the table, feeling the papery lip-print still on her forehead. Aunty's never done that.

It's Aunty who turns round now. It's always Aunty who sorts things out – a mother in all but name.

'Come on, love,' she calls with a hint of impatience in her voice. 'Don't get left behind. Because it's their mum they really want to see, isn't that right, kids?'

They tighten to Aunty.

But she pushes them forward. 'Give your mum a kiss,' she urges. And it's Johnny who comes, in the end: a bit shy, but with a cautious smile.

Alice steps forward too. She doesn't want to frighten him. He doesn't look as though he despises her, or knows her to be bad, deep down. She's warmed by that careful wish to please.

And she's pleased, in her own cautious way, when he approaches her from the side and puts his left hand round her back, in that same comradely knight's embrace. They walk into the house side by side.

Alice has spent the past fortnight trying to shut the past out of her mind.

444

It comes back, though. It sneaks up on her when she's alone at night. Aunty doesn't comment on her red eyes in the shadows of the morning. Aunty just gets her busy, out supervising something, or talking to someone. It passes.

Alice wants it to go easily with the children. But she wants it to partly because she hears Chaucer's voice in her head, saying, 'Make them your comfort,' and she's trying to follow his advice. And whenever she thinks that it starts her thinking about Chaucer, standing in his nightgown, just inside his door, on the last day she'd see him, in one of the places she could no longer go . . .

Fiercely she dashes the wet from her eyes. Get a grip on yourself, she says. This is what is meant for you on this earth. Make the best of it.

But, even now the children are here, running around, happily checking on their beds and their favourite climbing tree and Tom the cook's missing finger, all the familiar things they've missed, with a Yorkshire priest vainly following them urging them to sit down quietly and read their psalters with him – even now that a part of her is entering into the merriment of it – a deeper part of her is sad.

She wanted the children to be brought up like ladies and gentlemen. She keeps telling herself that. They should have been pages and demoiselles in a household by now. They should have . . . but that's excuses, not why she's sad. Not really.

She can't help herself. She feels left out. There's a world out there, getting on without her. Chaucer, at his table, writing. Chaucer, lying in the bed she used to—

She knows she's brave. She knows she'll conquer the sadness. She thinks she will, anyway.

The meal's less shy. The priest who's come with the children has been put to bed with supper in his room: broth and bread. No point offering *him* meat, Aunty says derisively. He's supposed to be poor, isn't he? Alice knows she'll have to do something about Aunty's hatred of priests; she knows the children have got to be educated, after all. But she'll do it tomorrow.

445

She's tired. 'Wat'll be here tomorrow,' Aunty's shouting, comfortably, over the din of the fire, and the turning of the spit. (She's had a lamb slaughtered: 'No point not celebrating, eh?' as she said.) 'Up from Kent. Brentwood Assizes in a day or two. Market, too. He never misses the fair there.' She winks.

'Why?' says Joan with wide eyes.

'I like fairs, I like jumbles and ribbons, can we go?' says Jane.

'You'll have to ask him why,' Aunty says. She winks again. 'I'd say there's a girl in it. Wouldn't you?'

Alice sees Johnny, who's fifteen now, after all, and nearly as tall as she is, blush at the idea. But the girls laugh delightedly. 'Is he in love, then?' Jane says, trying out the word, twisting her lips over it.

Aunty only shakes her head. 'You ask him, love,' she says. 'He hasn't told *me* anything.'

Johnny's hovering not far away from Alice, having found her a stool. He gives her another careful, solicitous look. As if she's ill. As if he's going to look after her.

The children have never talked about her past life away from Gaines. They've never asked; she's never said. They have no idea, beyond Yorkshire and Johnny's one trip to London. It's beyond their ken. Still, it must seem strange to them that she's back for good. Especially to him, because he's seen . . . the other thing. The luxury of it. The elegance. Perhaps that's why he's looking at her like that. Or perhaps the servants talked about it, up where they've been – about her disgrace.

'What did you learn up there?' she asks, fumbling for words. It hurts, in a way she doesn't understand, that they might know of her humiliation.

They burst into eager responses, all at once.

'We sewed. For hours every day. Stuck inside. I hate sewing. I hemmed and hemmed and hemmed and I lost my thimble and my fingers are stuck full of pinpricks,' Jane says. 'They kept trying to make me do punching – nasty little holes. It kept going wrong though. And they wouldn't let me on to embroidery or tapestry 'cause I was so bad. Ever.' She doesn't sound as though she cares.

'"Pater noster qui es in caelis sanctificetur nomen tuum adveniat regnum tuum fiat voluntas tua sicut in caelo et in terra,"' Joan lisps, without pauses, and giggles when Aunty purses her lips. Teasingly, she adds: 'Amen!'

Johnny says, a bit hesitantly, 'No one really knew what to do with us. I worked with the reeve on managing the estate, a bit. And Father Thomas taught us some Latin. There was archery practice on Sundays, after church. And I went out riding with a boy from nearby, and his father taught us swords-manship.'

The others have stopped now. They're nodding. He's their spokesman, Alice can see. He's good with words. He goes on: 'We didn't know what to do with ourselves at first. We couldn't understand the way they talked, even. And we didn't know anyone. And it was so cold. It's cold now, up there. There was still snow on the ground when we set out last week, and it's April. But it got better.'

'And it was better than being here . . .' Joan says.

Jane finishes: '. . . with *him*.'

Aunty nods, bright-eyed, and says nothing. Alice nods too.

'They told us he was in France now,' Johnny went on, giving her another of those careful looks. 'They said you'd be going too, to be Lady of Cherbourg.'

Alice keeps the smile on her face – she doesn't want to disrespect their father – but she shakes her head. 'I don't think so,' she says. 'I'm staying here.'

'With us,' Jane says. She turns her eyes softly on to her mother.

They don't say anything for a few minutes, but Alice sees Joan's little dark head is nodding, and Johnny's come closer to Alice's stool. Alice can feel his warmth against her shoulder.

'They said you'd been in trouble,' Johnny says into the quiet. He's a brave boy.

'Over now,' Alice says quickly back, and then wishes she hadn't choked him off. He's braver than she is, perhaps. And she can see he's been worried.

'We prayed for you,' Joan says. She gives Aunty a triumphant nod. 'And, look, it worked, see?'

447

Aunty's over by the spit, prodding at the meat with a skewer. 'Come on, kids,' she calls in her rough rasp of a voice, ignoring Joan's religious enthusiasms. 'Let's get this carved and inside of you.'

They rush over to help. In the ensuing clatter of wooden platters and knives and squeals over spitting fat, with everyone giggling and bumping into each other, Alice gets up from her stool. 'I'll fetch the ale,' she says. She gets down a jug from the shelf and goes towards the cool cupboard where the ale barrel is kept.

Then everything goes round.

From very far away, she hears the bang of metal.

She finds herself slumped, half-lying, half-sitting, on the floor, still holding the pewter jug. It has a big dent in it. She stares at it. How did that happen? It's a moment more before she realises someone's saying, very sharply, 'Are you all right?' When she looks up, she sees them all staring down at her. Aunty bends down and scoops her up.

'I must have tripped up,' Alice says a bit shakily. She kicks at the flagstone. 'Careful of the floor.' She tries for a perky grin. She retreats to her stool, where Johnny brings her the first platter of food.

The meat's greasy. The smell of it turns her stomach. She doesn't want it. She prods at it and pushes it around, cutting bits of gristle off.

'Can I have that bit?' Joan says, growing in confidence. The little girls begin to fight over scraps from Alice's meal.

Alice half closes her eyes, trying to control the nausea. Even looking down, she can feel Aunty's eyes on her.

'Are you all right?' Aunty asks, sticking her head through Alice's bedcurtains with a lighted candle. 'You were white as a sheet, down there.' She clucks and peers closer. 'Looking a bit better now, though.'

Alice nods. She can't speak, because she's afraid any talk will break down the comforting certainty she's clinging to. Aunty knows, she's been thinking with something close to panic; Aunty delivered all the babies. Aunty remembers the last time: the weeks of bleeding, the fever, the panic. Something ruptured, something that nearly killed her. They even joked about it afterwards, deadpan Aunty-style: So God (or the Other One) nearly got you then, eh. Aunty will know, as surely as Alice knows, that she can't have any more babies. Alice has never even worried about getting with child again. It's never happened. Because it can't. And it can't be why she fainted, down there. Can it?

Aunty gives her an even more searching look. But the old woman's never been one to poke her nose in where she's not wanted. When she sees the closed look on Alice's face, she goes on, peaceably enough, 'Coming down with something, maybe. Get a good night's rest, eh?'

The children creep whispering and giggling into Alice's bed at dawn, with big eyes and the smell of outside on them, bringing her a daisy chain and a bunch of primroses in a little jug, chasing away the troubling wisps of her dreams. They sit playing clapping games in the warmth of the quilts. They have muddy feet, crossing over each other an endless kneading and squirming of limbs, like kittens in a basket. It's clear they're happy to be back home. Alice thinks they're also happy to be in this bed, curled up with her. They've never come to her like this before. She doesn't care about the mud, especially once Joan snuggles her head against Alice's shoulder, and then, seeming not to notice what she's doing, lets her arm cross over Alice's front. She curls up with them, sleepily enjoying their talk, trying to empty her mind of everything else.

Chaucer's there, though. Looking through the bedcurtains, nodding his head, grinning at her, one eyebrow up. 'There, you see,' he's saying. The thought's a soft knife-blow to the heart. She raises herself on her elbow, shutting him out; dislodging Joan, too, but the little girl just adjusts her position, leaning against her mother as if she were a comfortable settle, putting a trusting hand on Alice's shoulder.

'What shall we have to eat?' Jane's saying.

'Aunty's ham, of course,' Johnny says, forgetting his grown-up ways, flicking his hair back out of his shining eyes.

449

Joan says, 'With the honey.'

For a moment, Alice feels sick at the thought of that ham, with the muslin on it to keep the flies off, with the great thick crust of white cold fat on the outside, blackened with charred honey. She lies very still. The feeling passes.

It doesn't mean anything, she tells herself while the children go back to chanting 'Yan, tan, tether, mether, pip!' in thin high voices, crossing their hands over each other's as they clap. She hasn't lost her appetite, not really. She's got a great thirst for milk. And cheese. And ginger, she'd like ginger jumbles, only there is no ginger out here, of course.

It's only after they've scampered off to make mischief downstairs, and Alice throws off the bedclothes herself, feeling warmer and more cheerful than on most mornings, and jumps out, that she finds her head rushing and spinning dizzily again. Hastily, she sits down. She tells herself she's sat down, anyway. But she knows it was more like a fall.

It's three days till Wat comes, only after the Brentwood Assizes, and, to the children's disappointment, the market. He must have ridden straight there from Johnny's in Kent, even though the straightest route to Brentwood Town is up this way, through Chafford Hundred, right past Gaines and Upminster, and it would have been no trouble to stop off here.

When he does come, he's got news. He's going to get married. He's looking less ratty and shifty than she's seen him for years: he's scrubbed up, in newish leggings, with his hair and beard trimmed. He swings the children round, making them whoop and wail. But she can see straight off that he's got something on his mind. He tells her and Aunty when the kids are in bed. The girl is Nan, daughter of Tom, the baker, of Fobbing. Alice has never got so familiar with this southern end of Essex, down near Havering-atte-Bower, as she once was with the wild northern flats of her childhood, but she knows Fobbing is not far away, maybe fourteen or fifteen miles west of Gaines, one of the many farming villages of Barstable Hundred whose senior men have to attend every session of the assizes at Brentwood, to hear the King's wishes for them, and the manorial court sessions, too, to know the will of the lords of Essex for them. That's why he's been hanging out at the fair that goes with the assizes, then. He's settling down.

She can't believe the soppy, happy look on Wat's face. It reminds her . . .

It takes a moment to come out of the morass of other half-thoughts, in which Chaucer features, and the other black-bearded face, the Duke's, burning.

She squeezes Wat's arm in hers. Aunty's out in the pantry, clattering around. Looking for cider, Alice supposes. A cele-bration. 'How strange that we've both ended up back here, isn't it?' she ventures a little wistfully. 'As if nothing that happened out *there*' – she gestures west, back towards London and beyond – 'was real at all.'

His eyes are on her now, expressionless, totally attentive. His face has changed. He's probably shocked that she's even invoking that past. No one does. But he's interested, she can also see; more than interested. There's a brooding darkness in him, too, a morass of memories and crushed hopes and resentments, just waiting to come out if anyone gives him half a chance.

His face twists. 'No point remembering,' he says shortly. 'Is there? We're here now. Best make the best of it, that's all.'

But Alice nags on; she can't let go. 'But do you think you can ever forget? Really?' She almost wants him to say yes; to tell her that the past goes away. It might help her to learn to live in the present, if she sees that he can.

He doesn't. He narrows his eyes. He turns so he's fully facing her, and puts both arms on her shoulders. 'No,' he says grimly. 'Well, I never have, anyway. The past's still there, always, somewhere inside, isn't it? I dream about it every night. And not just Italy, the hills, the freedom, the golden light . . . It smelled of rosemary, you know, wherever you went, and of thyme. But that's not what I dream about. It's *him*: Richard Lyons, the richest man in England, humiliating me. Punching me down in front of my men, *disrespecting* me, telling me to get lost. After all I'd done for him. I was done for after

451

that. Shamed. But in my dream, sometimes, it comes out right. I'm chasing him down the street, down Cheapside, running so fast it feels as though I'm flying, and there's a sword in my hand, and people cheering me on. He's running for his life. I'm gaining on him . . .'

His face sags. 'And then I wake up.'

Here.

'I know,' Alice says. 'I dream about the Duke like that.'

They look at each other, a look too deep for words. But what can they do?

It's only after they've all gone away again, leaving just Aunty, grumbling away about the priest upstairs ('Eating us out of house and home, and for what?' 'For their lessons, that's what,' Alice answers firmly, sending the children slowly and miserably up the stairs to their books and their tutor, as Aunty mutters, 'What do they need Latin for? Bloody priests. English is good enough for me. Always has been . . .'), that she has time to think about her current predicament again.

She's managed a dish of eggs at dinner. But she's gone outside and been sick since. She's still dizzy all the time too. And she's tired, so tired; she's had to drag herself out of bed this morning, and she dozes off at every opportunity. She sits staring into the fire in the kitchens, half listening to Aunty going through the pantry and buttery, privately counting the days since her last bleeding, back a good week before she went to London. Six weeks ago tomorrow.

There's no doubt. Not really.

The flames leap and vanish.

Soon she'll have to find the courage to tell Aunty; tell the children, too, and Wat.

She tries to think that through calmly. She's finding it hard to force herself into admitting, even in her private thoughts, that there could be a child growing in her belly. But she has to start. It won't be so bad, she thinks, folding her hands over her stomach, terrified of it yet protecting it at the same time. They'll all be happy, her family. They're good people. They love her. They'll help her hide the baby, keep it safe; they'll work something out, between themselves. They might tell Will it's another of Aunty's foundlings. They might tell Will it's Wat's eldest, with Nan. It's not as if Alice hasn't done something like this before – hidden her babies. It's not as if she doesn't know how. It's not as if she isn't a fighter.

She can't tell Chaucer. She won't see him again.

She lets her eyes lose focus, lost in the flames. A thought pops unbidden into her head. Lewis, she'll call him, if, God grant, he makes it into this world; if he's a boy. Chaucer once told her it means 'famous warrior', in French. He'd like that: his son a famous warrior. The name will keep the child safe; keep enemies at bay.

Because God knows he'll need to fight well, this helpless new little life she's going to bring into the world. He's going to need every scrap of cunning and aggression she can instil in him. Because he won't be raised as Will's child. He's not going to have the same life as Alice's other children – who, for all the threadbare, carefree life they're leading today, do, at least, now have money waiting for them, and a titled father, and a future, of sorts. The hard-faced Essex county leaders will wrinkle their noses at Alice, of course; that's to be expected. But they'll all come sniffing at the money she's earned for her sins. So John and Joan and Jane will, at some point, she imagines, probably be asked to marry the children of one of the Sir Johns – Gildesburgh the parliamentarian, or Sewale the sheriff, or Bampton the ex-sheriff. Which isn't quite becoming princes, but isn't to be sniffed at.

But this little Lewis – if he lives – he's not going to be part of the rich. He's going to be part of the poor: of the army of disgruntled, discontented Wats and Aunties teeming through the land, listening to hedge-priests, pinning up letters on road-side trees, dreaming of rebellion and a fairer ordering of things. The long-ago world they talk about, before the Mortality; before even that. Before the lords and the priests and the lawyers carved everything up, wrote it down in French, and cut out the rest. The ancient Law of Winchester, Wat calls it; the Book of Domesday. Aunty's hedge-priests want to bring it back. Some hope. She'll throw her child what scraps she can, of course she will. But still, it's clear: he'll be one of the ones who struggle.

It clears her mind to think that. It shows her clearly what she's been beginning to see ever since she came back here, knowing she couldn't leave. The pieces of the puzzle in her mind shift and take on new shapes: whom she should count herself with; whom she should value. As the mother of this unborn child, she'll be one of the have-nots again, or as good as. She'd better brush up her fighting skills, for Lewis's sake.

'Aunty,' Alice calls, sitting up straighter. 'Do you still want any help writing those letters?'

THIRTY-SEVEN

'For now is the time to beware,' Alice writes, in big clear letters. The child kicks inside her. Lewis. She sighs and looks up.

There's iron in the earth, and snow on the ground outside, and Christmas is coming, but nothing stops Wat building. He's making a farmstead down the road from here. He and his wife-to-be are going to become Alice's tenants. Men from Fobbing have been coming, even before the summer was out and the harvest in, to help the locals and men from the roads whom Alice and Aunty have drafted in dig foundations, and fill them in with flinty mix, and put together the timber frames. Wat's been back for good since the instant Johnny Tyler's crops were in, down in Kent, directing the work on the new house and barns.

'You didn't need to go to so much trouble,' Alice says sometimes, looking up from her letters as his men pass. 'You could have shared our farm buildings.'

But she doesn't really mean it. The calm of pregnancy has set in (even if it doesn't stop her dreams), and Wat pats her swelling belly every time he passes her and the children, who gather around, softly marvelling, stroking her, feeling the unborn child kick and play inside her. Alice can't think where the money for all this building's come from, if it's not from years of highway theft; but she doesn't ask. Perhaps miracles can be achieved, if you're just calling in favours after years of doing right by village people. Because village people are good people; they stand manfully together; they do right by each other. And anyway, if Wat's to take her child and raise him, just down the hill, on the other side of the stream from her, she wants Wat and his wife to be living as comfortably as they can.

Besides, she likes the non-stop procession of men through Gaines. Men from Fobbing, men from Henney and the next-door village of Bocking, north Essex people Aunty knew, and has given a few weeks' work to, and townsmen, craftsmen of one sort or another, from Brentwood. Alice likes the tramp of feet, and the smell of broth and bread, and the deep voices. It makes her feel alive.

They sing as they work, the men. They sing the songs of an England systematically robbed from the top for as long as they can remember, misruled and mismanaged for years now, decades, ever since the Mortality robbed them of innocence and justice. They hoist the joists up, from shoulder to shoulder, yelling, 'Now lechery is without shame, and gluttony is without blame,' and, bitterly comparing the lords' bullying might with the peasants' forgotten rights in this topsy-turvy state, 'Might is right, light is night, fight is flight.' And Alice can think of nothing that could chime more perfectly with her own quiet bitterness than that melancholy bass chorus in the morning mist.

For everyone who's a part of this remote manor is coalescing and unifying, though not in the quiet, orderly, loving way that an earlier Alice might once have imagined. It's their hatreds (and their guilts) that are starting to bind them together.

Everyone has his secret, and everyone's secret fuels his anger. If Wat, for instance, almost howls with resentment against the thieving noblemen of an evening, it may be partly out of guilt that he's concealed so much from his family-to-be about his own past thieving, whether abroad, in London, in the ports of the south, or down in Kent. It may equally be that Aunty Alison feels guilty that, by keeping the tilery up at Henney for herself, she once, long ago, stole the birthright of the baby Alice; and it may be that, even though she's done right by Alice ever since, this is what makes her so full-throated in her rage against the lordly robbers, who take so much more than she ever did, yet never feel so much as a pang. Alice may well still feel guilty that she once quietly got Wat sacked from his post with Richard Lyons and ruined his prospects. She's doing right by him now, so she can afford to shut out that thought. But it probably makes her more vociferous than she might otherwise have been in her condemnation of the misrule of the Duke and his latest circle of advisers.

(Strangely enough, Alice has never felt guilty for dancing into court on the take in the first place; for having, once upon a time, been right at the heart of the corruption against which these men sing their songs of anger. If it hadn't been her, someone else would surely have come along and done the same thing, wouldn't they? She's only ever been a little person, she tells herself. It isn't her fault if England started going to the dogs. It's theirs – the thieving lords' fault, the cunning lawyers'. The Duke's. And they're the ones who should pay.)

Who knows what private guilts the men from the road are hiding as they come in singing their angry songs? After a lifetime of the blithe hunt for money that the Mortality ushered in – a bribe here, an overcharging there, a swindling somewhere else; or a glib lie, or a dishonest marriage, or a quiet pocketing of some trifle – everyone probably has something on his conscience.

Even Alice's children perhaps feel guilty (in their way) that they've grown up wanting to know their father, but that, when he finally appeared, they couldn't love him; or that they aren't fulfilling the destiny they learned up north should be theirs, to become lords and ladies. If they do have these feelings, however, they remain obscure to those around them. No one asks.

Everyone is busy, this autumn, not just with building Wat a house, but with turning their backs on their own secrets, and pasts, and private regrets and evasions and dishonesties. Everyone wants to find someone else to blame for whatever wrongs have been done in the past. They tell themselves, and each other, that they're hunting for justice. They tell themselves they want the truth.

Truth is the old way. Truth dates back to the time when your word was your bond, and you didn't need papers in a language you couldn't understand to compel you to act honestly. Truth is what governed England in the time of Alfred, in the days of Winchester: truth, and the men of the village. Englishmen could live by truth again, if there was nothing, and no one, standing in their way.

Truth is more necessary than ever, because confusions and corruptions are growing so fast. Even God has become doubtful, for the Church of Rome has split in two. There's a mad pope in Rome, and a French pope in Avignon, and, even though the English acknowledge the mad Roman pope, because he's not French, no one knows who really has God's spiritual authority, or should receive the tithes and taxes taken for the Church; the belief is seeping into every heart that neither of these false foreign popes is the man.

As for the war that's ruining England, back in the spring, at the last Parliament, the King promised not to bring out his begging bowl again for at least another eighteen months. But now there's more talk of a French invasion, and another.

Parliament being called, this November, up at Northampton (the Duke being too unpopular to dare to try calling the legislature to London). The begging bowl's out again. And the lords will soon be wanting the people to pay again.

'Mam,' Johnny says.

Alice is humming one of the workmen's angry songs, as softly as a lullaby, as she writes. His voice, still treble, most of the time, breaks through hers.

'Mm,' she answers, not looking up.

'Mam, not that song again,' Johnny says plaintively. 'Please.' She looks up.

He's sitting on the hearthstone, with his nearly mannish bony knees up against his chin, and his arms wrapped round his legs. He's been sitting there for hours, she realises. And, for all his new height, he's the picture of childish dejection.

The line she's been repeating goes 'envy reigneth with trea-*son*, and sloth is always in sea-*son*.' It's true, she's had

458

it on her mind all day. She may have been singing it all day. That might be annoying, if you were in a mood to be annoyed.

'What's up with you?' she says, not especially sympathetically.

'Bored,' he says. 'Bored of that song. Bored of . . . oh, everything.' Unexpectedly, his eyes fill with baby tears. Furiously he blinks them away.

'Well, go and do something,' she says carelessly. 'Help Wat's men or something.'

'Do a bit more singing out there, you mean?' Johnny says, and she can hear anger in his voice now. 'And bang at a bit of wood?'

She looks curiously at him. She can't think what's got into him.

'You could write a letter for me,' she says, trying to please. 'If you like.'

She's taken over Aunty's letter-writing, and made the old woman's scrawls into art. These letters are supposed to be read by travellers, or men in taverns, or men outside churches. They don't have a specific instruction to deliver, a 'go here' or 'do that'. They offer only general inspiration. They say: 'Be angry', or 'Be aware', or just 'Beware'.

Alice addresses the letters to, and signs them from, the working men whose discontents she's tapping: Piers Plowman, Jack Trueman, Jack Carter, Jack Miller, John Nameless. Sometimes she allows herself to imagine Chaucer, with secret laughter in his eyes, writing at his own table, as she turns out her vague, but stirring, poems to the nobility of the sons of earth, with God at their back.

Jakke Trewman giveth you to understande that falsnes and gyle have regned to long, and trewthe has bene sette under a lokke, and falsnes regneth.

Trewthe shal help you, she writes, day after day.

Be ware or be woeful . . .

Now is the tyme.

Usually Johnny enjoys all this. At least she thinks he does, because he's hardly left his mother's side in weeks and months, except when she sends him out to pin her letters on trees on the highway. Usually he comes back in, pink-faced and exhilarated, chanting, 'Jack the Miller grinds small, small, small!' And he laughs in delight when she (or someone else) calls back the answering catchphrase: 'The King's son of Heaven shall pay for all!'

But not today. Even the offer of writing his own letter hasn't cheered him up this time. He just shakes his head, and slumps lower against his knees.

'Well, do you want to read to me?' she asks in the end.

Perhaps it's just since the priest went last week that Johnny's got so fractious. It hasn't taken long for Aunty to win the campaign she was waging against the priest teaching the kids Latin, the language of 'clerks and con-men', as Aunty puts it (she has equally scathing things to say about French, the language of 'liars and lawyers'). What finally did for the scared little priest was coming into the laundry and finding Aunty pinching diamond marks into the pleats of his sheets. She'd been saying, for weeks, with grim satisfaction and nasty little nods, 'Diamonds . . . the mark of death, they say.' He stared at her, open-mouthed. He was gone by dawn.

If Alice is aware that it was illogical for her to have let the priest go and the children's education stop – to be saying goodbye to the world of the elite, and turning her face against the Gildesburghs and the Bamptons and the Sewales, where her children's best prospects lie, while embracing the interests of the angry men of the fields and the road, and to be bringing the children whose advancement she's claimed all her life to be working for back into the rustic hardscrabble of Essex – she hasn't let the thought in. She hasn't found a new tutor. She's done with priests, she thinks. Aunty was right.

But now, for a moment, she wonders whether she hasn't made a mistake.

'Come on,' she says with a little laugh, trying to jolly his gloom away. 'Tell me. What's biting you?'

He takes a deep breath. He lifts his chin off his knees. 'I wish you'd leave off those letters, that's all,' he says.

Then he stops, and bites his lip, and looks down.

She stares. 'But why?' she says, in bafflement. 'I thought you liked . . .'

460

Timidly, he looks back up, as if he's been expecting her to sound crosser, and is trying to work out whether to trust her. 'I just don't see why you'd want to write them,' he finally confides in a rush. 'Or sing those songs.' There's a pleading softness on his face now that almost hurts her, it's so transparently loving. 'Because we're not serfs, are we? You're the Lady of Gaines. And I'm a knight. And I'm not a bad swordsman, and I was doing all right at my French, and Latin, till Aunty . . .' He blinks again, and hurries on. 'I mean, do we actually want the Law of Winchester, mam? You and me? Isn't all that just what old village men go on about when they're drunk?'

'Oh, Johnny,' she says.

What he's just said is honest enough to make her uncomfortable, though she's not going to show him that. Later, she thinks, she'll talk to him about how the greatest lords – she may even say the Duke's name – think they can take and take and no one will resist; and explain that this is what makes it important to stand together and show the Duke when enough is enough. But for now the best she can manage is a shrug she does her best to make nonchalant. She says, 'It's more complicated than you realise,' and, 'You're too young to understand it all yet.' Appeasingly, she smiles. But she isn't really surprised when he unfolds himself to his full scrawny height, gives her a disappointed look, and mooches out.

'They're talking about a new poll tax,' Wat says, back from Brentwood market, with bags of dowels and big eyes. 'In the Parliament.'

Aunty sniffs. She's stepped out of the kitchen, as soon as she heard the clop of hoofs, to meet him. She's left the door ajar. Alice is inside, listening.

'Well, we've been *there* before,' she says with calm hatred. 'Those bloody swine.'

Everyone in Essex is following the Parliament, even though it's so far away. The Speaker of the Commons this time is their own county's man: Sir John Gildesburgh. And everyone's afraid of a new tax. So news travels.

461

'No,' Wat says, urgently. 'This isn't like before. They want *eight times as much* next year as they got last time. They want £160,000. That's five groats a head.'

The carpenters stop their door-hanging. The tapping falls silent at the windows. The yard goes quiet as all the peasant freemen start calculating how they can possibly pay out an extra two or three weeks' wages for every person in their household to the King, next year, on top of the ten per cent of their income they already pay the Church, and as well as the great tithes – two-thirds of the value of their crops and cattle – and the lesser tithes on everything else from wool to flax to leeks to apples to cheese to chickens to bees and honey. Half of them have houses stuffed with waifs and strays: war widows, old people, grown-up children who can't afford to marry. They'll have to stump up the same amount for each and every one of them. They live on barley bread and cheese as it is. Their worsteds are in rags. Here at Gaines is the only place they ever sniff meat.

If anyone in this yard is reassured by anything, in this bleak moment, it's the knowledge that at least they're not serfs. It will be even worse for the serfs, who pay even more, out of even less, to the lords who own them.

It's cold comfort, though.

'What, that little Sudbury asked for all that?' Aunty scoffs disbelievingly.

No one wants the job of Chancellor of England these days; it's too thankless. So they've forced it on the quiet old Archbishop of Canterbury, the Duke's man, with his gentle Suffolk burr and his unquestioning obedience. Sudbury's a joke. He'll do anything the Duke tells him. Everyone knows that.

But surely, Alice thinks, even the Duke can't really believe he'll get that much? Even he can't be that cruel? Or stupid? He'd have to march an army across England to force all those thousands out of its people. Even he must realise that.

Then she hears Aunty's cracked, chirpy old voice. 'Well then, if they're really going to rob us like that, there'll be no harm in our cheating them a bit in return, will there? We'll just have to tell them our families have got smaller. We'll say our grannies have all died since last time the lawyers came for our money, and our granddads, maybe, and our children too if need be, so we're only going to pay a quarter as much this time.'

Aunty looks expectantly round. She likes an audience. She likes playing the clown. She likes applause, too. But this crowd's too stunned.

'What goes around comes around. Never meet stupidity halfway, that's what I say,' Aunty prods, doing all she can to encourage them to take the news lightly. At last, there's a first, hesitant ripple of laughter.

When Alice looks down at her page, ready to go on writing, she finds she's been writing, all along. The parchment is scored with heavy black lines. And all of them read the same thing.

Now is the tyme.

Now is the tyme.

Now is the tyme.

She's forgotten all about trying to be philosophical about her fate. She's been forgetting it ever since she found out the baby was coming; and this news is the last straw. The picture of fire, and John Duke of Lancaster's burning head, is so vivid in her mind that it's almost hurting her. It *is* hurting her. Or something is. A deep, dark ache is tightening through her gut. She clamps down on herself, crouching on her stool, arms wrapped round her knees.

'Aunty,' she calls quietly, as soon as the pain eases a bit. She knows what it is now. 'Aunty. The baby's coming.'

THIRTY-EIGHT

It's mid-morning, and Chaucer's at his window looking down at the little bands of men in ragged russet and black outside, who are looking back up at him: the peasant rebels' advance guard. They've been slying up since yesterday, from Mile End Meadow, to have a gawp at the City walls. They look in rude good humour, these Essex men. One of them even waves. 'Hey, you!' the man mouths cheekily up. 'Go downstairs and let us in!'

Chaucer steps back, feeling uneasy.

No one knows where the peasant rioting came from, but the whole of Essex and Kent have been up in arms for the past fortnight. And now they've come together, converged around London in two great armies, ready to invade the City itself.

Chaucer's waiting until he knows the outcome of the King's negotiations with the Kentishmen before he goes to Mass at St Helen's. He'll go at Sext if he misses Terce. He wants to have something reassuring to tell Elizabeth when he sees her afterwards. He doesn't like to think of all those poor girls cooped up in there, so scared, waiting; with no way of getting out.

They say it all started at Brentwood Assizes a fortnight ago. They say the tax collectors tested the virginity of a village headman's daughter to see whether she could be counted as a woman and forced to pay. Chaucer can imagine the casual brutality of *that*, the guffawing knights, the terror of the poor girl. They say that was the last straw.

But outrage doesn't explain how coolly intelligent the rioters have been. There hasn't been mass murder, even though thousands of men, armed only with sticks and their anger, have joined the riots and marched all over both counties, seizing towns and castles, even capturing Canterbury and Chelmsford, the county towns. There have only been carefully targeted attacks on the half-dozen men who run each of the counties: the MPs, the poll-tax collectors. Those few knights have been locked away, or murdered, or taken hostage. Their houses have been burned. But no one else has been touched. It's almost as if these unlettered peasants know instinctively whom to attack to decapitate government and stop the authorities in their tracks. Yet their leaders are only supposed to be village men, with rustic names: Jack Straw, Tom Baker, Wat Tyler. So how can they know? It's eerie.

It's also almost miraculous good luck, or organisation, that there are no armies to stop them, either. There's just the small garrison at the Tower of London, a couple of hundred men, and they're not venturing out; they're needed to protect the King. The Duke is away in the North, extending the peace agreement with the Scots. And the main body of the soldiers of the South is far away at in the south-west, at Plymouth, pursuing what is just emerging as the Duke's secret agenda: embarking to spend England's tax money, which was supposed to go on the French war, on another attempt to conquer Castile.

More uncanny still, the two peasant armies seem to be communicating. Just before both of them turned towards London, they held two great public bonfires on the same day, one in Canterbury, the other in Chelmsford, on which they threw every scrap of documentation sealed with green wax – the mark of financial papers – that they'd found in every public official's workplace. So there's no proof, any more, of who's paid, or not paid, their tax.

And now the wild men are all here, just beyond the City walls, again in tandem, howling that they're the true servants

of the King, who's being betrayed by his lords and tax collectors, and demanding that he come to meet them and follow
their advice. The Kentishmen from the South are over the
river, camped beyond Greenwich, and the Essex men Chaucer
keeps seeing are sleeping at Mile End Meadow, just a mile or
so up the road from Chaucer's home at Aldgate.

The King's rowing out along the river this morning – now,
probably – to meet the Kentishmen. Chaucer can only hope
that seeing the King with their own eyes satisfies them, and
that they go home.

If it doesn't, well, the danger could easily spread inside
London too. It's Corpus Christi today, the holiday Thursday
in June when no work is done and everyone is out holding
summer pageants, in which the poor are allowed to dress up
as kings and bishops, and ape their betters for the day – which
means, in practice, that the streets of the City will be thronged
all day with the poorer sorts of city folk, who are no less
disgruntled than the country rioters, and they'll be idle, and
probably drunk, and up for mischief.

So far, with no certain news, everything Chaucer sees is
disquieting in the extreme. The streets downstairs, inside the
City, are already full of crowds. If he crosses the room again,
and looks down at the windows giving on to London, he'll
see them. He chooses not to. He's been pacing from one side
to the other all morning, biting his nails and staring. Some
people in those holiday crowds have been in and out of town
all week, or so people say, telling the wild men with sticks
out there that they'll be welcome in the City when they get
here. And the mood of the street people inside is scarcely less
threatening than that of the lurking peasants outside.

Chaucer shivers. He's glad of the extra guard Mayor
Walworth's put on Aldgate.

An hour later, he gives up on reassuring news of the King's
meeting with the rebels and heads up Bishopsgate to St Helen's
anyway.

On the way, he hears that the King was so scared of the
rebels' yelling from the riverbank at Rotherhithe – or his

advisers were, because the rebels wanted most of the advisers killed – that the royal boat was rowed away without even trying to parlay.

That's torn it, Chaucer thinks, uneasily, as he scrabbles through the rowdy crowds crammed into Aldgate, pushing against burly shoulders, elbowing people in the gut if they won't get out of the way, remembering some of the unsettling stories doing the rounds. He's never liked crowds. When the peasants took Rochester Castle, he's thinking, they say they only had to shout, and the walls came tumbling down, like Jericho. So, that's torn it. If the King won't talk to them, it's obvious: they'll charge in anyway. Who's going to stop them? Didn't anyone tell him to try?

There are people caterwauling outside, right through Mass. In rough voices, they're chanting, 'When Adam delved and Eve span, who was then the gentleman?'

'Are you safe?' he asks Elizabeth as soon as he's shown into the visitor's cell with her. He doesn't care if she knows he's panicking. He's panicking for her.

She nods, but she doesn't look sure. 'They're shuttering up all the windows. Barring them, and the doors,' she says. Babbling. 'Great thick planks. Just in case. I was even thinking I should try and ask them to let *you* join us. It's more secure here than over Aldgate, and you probably don't have enough bread to last you a day, do you? Whereas we have food and water, enough for weeks. There's even firewood.' She laughs, or tries to. It's so hot, and there's damp on her brow. She's trying to be brave. But she looks so young, with that baby face, that peachy skin. So vulnerable. A child. What if those savages get in?

He can spot her straight away, as soon as he enters the church, however dark it is, however identical all the girls' black robes. She's the smallest of the novices by two inches. And today she has bitten nails, just like him.

But, perhaps precisely because of her size, Elizabeth's always made great efforts to be self-possessed. 'At least I'm not at Barking,' she says with another miserable little titter, because even she, shut away inside these big walls, knows that they've been all over Essex for days now, these wild men. Barking's not safe.

He's grateful for that remark; for the grace in it. So he lets her will for calm lead him. She's a wise girl, he thinks, and he tries to lighten his own breathing, and take comfort in what he can.

'Thank God for that, at least, eh?' he answers in as everyday a voice as he can manage, and he raises an eyebrow at her. She used to love it that he could move his eyebrows separately. She nods encouragingly. He thinks she's grateful in her turn. 'And thank God Thomas and your mother are safely at Hertford Castle. They're well out of all this. It's all quiet up there.'

'For now, at least,' Elizabeth says. She sounds suddenly sombre. 'It's them I'm worried about, to be honest, Papa,' she says, and her fingers go up towards her mouth; but she remembers herself in time, and starts fidgeting with her rosary instead. 'More than about myself. Because all these people shouting outside, well, I can't help hearing what they're shouting . . . and it's all bad things about my lord of Lancaster. They hate him, don't they? Really hate him. And I've been thinking, Aunt Katherine was with him for at least part of the ride north. She was going to leave his train at Leicester and go home . . . but you know how she is . . .'

Chaucer shakes his head in genuine ignorance. No one ever tells him about Katherine and the Duke.

'Well, sometimes she doesn't go,' Elizabeth says, as if this is common knowledge and her father's being a bit dense. 'So she might still be with him. And I'm not sure that's safe. Because what if there's more of *this* . . . up *there*?'

Chaucer doesn't care about Katherine; not as he does about this wise, beautiful child. But he doesn't want to look unfeeling. He even senses his voice might be too glib as he says, 'Oh, you mustn't worry about them. If she's with him at the border, there's an army with him too, after all. And if she's not . . . well, then, she's safe enough.'

Elizabeth looks doubtful. He feels doubtful too, in private.

If a ravening mob wanted revenge on the Duke, why wouldn't they descend on the man's mistress, at Kettlethorpe?

But there's more on his daughter's careful mind. She's wrinkling her lovely forehead. He wants to kiss away her worries.

She blurts it out. 'If Mama and Thomas are with my lady of Lancaster – even if the Duke's nowhere near – how safe are they going to be, really?' Suddenly all her grown-up poise has gone. She's got damp eyes and fingers twisted into her mouth.

He takes her in his arms and cradles her. 'Don't worry,' he soothes, so swollen with tenderness he thinks he might burst, 'don't worry, Lizbet. It will all be over in a day or two. They'll be safe. We'll all be right as rain.'

It's years since she's shown him her heart like this. It makes everything worthwhile. His closed-down life; the goodbyes; Alice. For a frivolous moment, he's almost grateful to the rebels.

They let him out through the little door in the gate.

He almost walks under the hoofs of Mayor Walworth, parading down the street through the threatening-looking low-lifes as if he can't see them. The Mayor's at the head of a newly mustered guard of property-owning worthies, who are mostly sat like sacks on their horses, looking uncomfortable in their little-used armour, giving the street people scared little looks from under their metal caps.

'Master Chaucer,' Walworth says, taking off his hat. He doesn't look like an angel today. He looks taut and tight and stern. Walworth's always been an excellent organiser. He's the most successful of this whole generation of men who've made the English merchant's calling a glorious one, almost the equal of the powerful merchant princes of Italy; men who've made friends, and supplicants, of kings. But suddenly Chaucer also sees that, if he'd been born of noble blood, Walworth might have made an excellent soldier, too. He's got a good commanding seat on a horse. He doesn't look as though he'll be afraid to cut down a few wild men. Might enjoy it, judging from that gleam in his usually cautious eye. Walworth might even be a better soldier, and a better general, than the military leaders England has had in recent years. Chaucer almost laughs: Walworth could hardly be a worse commander than most of the lords who've done the job, after all.

Walworth's saying: 'Customs House secured, I hope. Locked, barred, shuttered?'

A slightly intimidated Chaucer nods to cover himself, while making a private note to go and double-check now.

'Then we have to arm,' Walworth continues. For a moment, his war face relaxes, and he laughs, a little shyly, as if he's embarrassed by the aptitude he's showing for flexing his warrior muscles. 'The Mayor's duty, you know.' He leans down, straight-backed. He's far nobler today, Chaucer thinks, than most of those harum-scarum knights you see in the lists at tournaments. He gives Chaucer an eagle's glare. 'You're a man of property, Chaucer. One of us. And a man of duty. So will you ride out with us? Protect London?'

'Oh, I'm not a man of arms,' Chaucer says hastily, aware that he's lowering the high chivalric tone. 'I'd be more of a hindrance than a help.'

Walworth just looks coldly impatient. He thinks Chaucer will find his courage in a minute, and say yes. They both know this is Chaucer's duty. But Chaucer also knows that nothing on God's earth would ever persuade him out into even a possible battle again, not even the thought of Elizabeth's admiration, if it was safely behind him and he could go back in there and tell her about it, pretending to be modest. So he ducks his head awkwardly towards the Mayor, without quite meeting his eye, feeling ashamed, but also relieved to have made his decision, and scurries on. Another friend lost, Chaucer thinks; someone else who thinks less of me. He doesn't much care.

Chaucer doesn't make it home. He's only just finished supervising the full barring of the Customs House, and sent away the two clerks he's called in to help him for an hour, despite the holiday. He's standing on the dock, leaning against the crane, looking out towards Southwark and the bridge, trying not to be too frightened that there's a crowd he's never seen the like of over there, and hearing, with a chill, that they're yelling something that, perhaps distorted as it comes over the water, sounds like, '—ill! —ill! —ill!' when the shouts suddenly change, turning to raucous hoots and hurrahs.

He sees why at once. The drawbridge in the middle of Bridge Ward is going down. Walworth must have given up. They're letting the Kentishmen in. Chaucer turns and starts running up Water Lane as fast as his feet will carry him. If he's quick, if he dodges round the back of the Tower, and through the lanes, he might still make it home before they get here.

But there are so many other people also running at full pelt through the streets that he can't choose his route. This lot aren't running away, like him. They're great oxen of men. Not Kentishmen: London men, but the rough kind, all with sticks and knives. Horribly excited. They keep banging into him, bashing him with their lowered heads. And they're all heading west, and at full pelt. He tries to cut across Thames Street, and continue north, but he can't. He's swept west. He tries to cut north across Tower Street. The same thing happens. There are so many of them. Soon there's no way he can do anything but hang on to his hat and join them, streaming along Cheapside towards Ludgate, running like lunatics for London's western exit. He knows where they're heading because of what they're panting at each other, and even more because of the look in their eye. The Duke's palace on the Strand: the Savoy. It's a magnet for hate, and the London mobsters want to beat the foreigners to it. They want to be the first to destroy the Duke.

A kind of wonder takes Chaucer over as he pants up Fleet Street and past the walled orchards and gardens of this lovely riverside suburb for princes of kingdom and Church.

This isn't mob action, not really, even if there were men back there shouting that they were off to break into Newgate Jail and set the prisoners free.

It's something else. Something he's never seen, or imagined.

471

These men don't loot. They aren't trying to get rich, or even just get fed. They're not remotely interested in picking up a few unconsidered trifles from the palaces they're passing, however lovely the houses are, however manicured the gardens.

They're here to destroy. And they know their targets.

They ignore the Bishop of Salisbury's palace, with all its rich treasures, as if it didn't exist. They ignore the Whitefriars convent. But a huge detachment of men charges yelling into the next great enclosure, the Temple, where the lawyers of London have their chambers and their libraries. Cautiously, Chaucer follows them down Middle Temple Lane and watches, from a safeish distance, from behind a tree. There are men rushing in and out of every building he can see, busy and systematic as ants. They're bringing out book after book of legal documents. They're building them up into a giant bonfire outside the old round church – which is a copy, as Chaucer knows, and perhaps they do too, of the temple on the site of Christ's Sepulchre in Jerusalem, and considered as sacred as the Jerusalem Sepulchre itself – and these men are not in the least bothered that this bonfire that some are setting light to now, and others are cheering on, is almost certainly sacrilege and will have them burning in Hell for ever. Chaucer retreats, carefully, back up to Fleet Street.

He's missed the worst of the crowd pounding down to the Savoy, ignoring the Bishop of Exeter's inn, and the Bishop of Bath's, and the Bishop of Llandaff's, and the Bishop of Coventry's, and the Bishop of Worcester's, too. It's calmer now on the road. And there's no point in hurrying. He already knows what he'll see.

He can smell the smoke.

The Savoy is no longer white.

It is black, and red, and crackling, and there are guards in bloodied uniforms slumped ominously unmoving at the gates, with dark stains under their prone forms.

The same ant-men are inside, surging and scurrying around, thousands of them. There's a crowd of them right in front of Chaucer, just inside the gates, with a beautifully embroidered

472

quilted body-protector stuck up on a pole. They're drawing arrows at it, like archery practice, yelling, after every thwang of the bowstring, as uproariously as if they were drunk (but they're not), 'We will have no king named John!' It must be the Duke's, Chaucer sees; they must have got into the treasury. He should feel sad to be a witness to this festival of hate; but he doesn't feel anything, even fear, even these men's excitement. He's just eyes, for now; just stunned, stunned eyes.

Hesitantly, Chaucer moves on in through the gardens. He doesn't think anyone will notice him. He feels invisible. They aren't interested in him.

Yes, they've got to the treasury. There are dozens of them dragging out gold and silver plate on to the terrace that over-looks the river. It's like a mad workshop out here, in the battering afternoon sun. Men sweating as they swing axes to bash and dent the finest work in Christendom with hideous metallic screeches. Men stuffing jewels into mortars and trying to grind them into knobbly paste. Men jumping on glittering necklaces, trying to smash them to bits with their boots (if they have boots, which many of them don't). Men ripping tapestries and cushions and napery and hangings with their rippling blacksmiths' or ploughmen's arms. Men chopping up furniture, or pulling it apart in obscene games of tug-of-war. There are even two men who've put their hands through the sleeves of robes of cloth of gold, far too small for them, and are mincing about like great hairy ladies, yelling, 'Will you dance, sweet madame?' and tearing at each other's bodices to reach for imaginary breasts, and thrusting their lanky pelvises at each other in quick, rhythmic snuffles of mirth.

Everywhere is the same. Men laughing insanely. Men shouting. Men sweating. Men grabbing at bits of shattered stuff and hurling it into the Thames.

There are rumblings and crashings from below, too: shouts, and the smash of metal on wood. They'll have got into the wine cellars. They'll be breaking open the barrels.

There are two directions the men go in, Chaucer sees, as the logic of the scene shifts and settles in his mind. There's one stream of them throwing the unburnable valuables – what's left of the jewels and metals when the axemen have finished with them – out over the terrace into the Thames. And there's another stream of them carrying account books and papers, great piles of them, from buildings all over the compound into the oak-panelled great hall, where the shredded textiles are also heading.

The great hall is also where the smoke is coming from, and the crackling.

Chaucer's not the only gawper lurking near the terrace, not by any manner of means. They're all around, the other shadows and starers, like ghosts: shaking their heads, mouths hanging open. Mostly, no one notices any of them; they don't even seem to notice each other. Not always, though. 'Be you coming 'long of us?' one of the wreckers yells at one of his audience, cheerfully, without threat, and he's rushed by before the man he's addressed has a chance to fade back, or tremble, or faint with terror, which, Chaucer sees afterwards, were the only options on the watcher's mind. It takes Chaucer another moment to realise, from that dialect, that the Kentishmen have got here too.

But, because he still feels invisible, Chaucer keeps moving on, as if in a trance. And when he comes upon one higgledy-piggledy heap of the Duke's accounts that he recognises – in which his own pension, and those of Philippa, and probably (who knows?) the Duke's various gifts to Katherine, are entered – lying on the terrace, abandoned, perhaps because they're not sealed with green wax, he's even bold enough to lean down and open his bag and stuff the rolls inside, before making a few vague steps in the direction of the men making the paper bonfire, as if to suggest he's on his way there too. There's not much he can save. But this is a God-given chance to do something, at least. It's only after a few more moments, when he's reassured himself that no one is looking at him, that he corrects his course again and goes on gliding inside.

How Alice would rejoice, he's thinking, allowing his mind to consider her for the first time in a long time, because in that strange suspended state his mind is in right now there's no pain. This is almost exactly what she said she wanted to see, the last time they spoke, isn't it? He can almost hear her voice again, now; almost see that bleak look on her face. 'I'd like to burn down the Savoy, with the Duke right in the middle of the bonfire . . . and his smug mistress, and your smug wife and my husband, too, if only I could think how . . .'

He smiles. He misses Alice's energy. He even misses her vindictiveness.

He wishes she could see this for herself.

He hopes she's been safe, out in Essex, where they say it's been worst of everywhere, but there's nothing he can do to protect her now.

Then, because nothing seems quite real right now except what's going on before his eyes, and even that doesn't seem very real at all, Chaucer forgets Alice and moves on. Tranquil. Light on his toes.

He's actually in the hall with more of the intent, dancing, whirling maniacs, with his eyes stinging from the flames licking up over the giant bonfire, with his hands up to protect his face from the heat, wondering if there isn't anything else lying about that he can stuff in his bag and save, when, through the spit and fury of the fire, he hears a scuffle behind him.

He turns. A group of the men hauling barrels towards the fire (wine barrels, he thinks) have dropped them and turned on one of their fellows. They're pummelling the man, pulling at his tunic, grabbing his bag. The victim's screaming like a stuck pig, digging his heels in, clinging on to whatever he can, but they're lifting him up, whacking him as they go, shouting confused, furious words at him. There's a moment of near-quiet – just the crackle, and the man's enormous eyes. Then someone hisses, 'That'll larn you to go a-stealing,' and someone else shouts, 'We told you and told you, we do not do nothing of that like, right?' and a bit of something glittery is thrown into the fire. 'We are not thieves! We are the True Commons: zealots for truth and justice!' yells another voice, a London voice. Then they throw the man in the fire too. A rush of flame and smoke envelops them all.

As the screaming gets louder, Chaucer fades out of the hall, ashen-faced. The bag on his back, crackling with its secret load, feels like a hot coal.

His legs are suddenly moving very fast. If they're going to turn nasty, it's time he got out of here.

It's only as he whisks down a green alleyway outside, making for the Strand and hopefully home, that he hears two more voices, behind the hedge, out of sight. They're breathless voices, busy, but surprised out of the trance-like destruction, for a moment, at least: 'Tom? That's never Tom Piper of Henney?' Then, in a deeper voice, the reply: 'Whoo-oop, Janny, bin heyah since the start, boy,' and a clapping of flesh on cloth.

If they're saying, 'Whoo-oop,' then those are Essex men.

The Essex men must have got in too. Through Aldgate.

Chaucer breaks into a sweat; he's running.

He's still running when he gets up the hill to the cathedral. He doesn't even stop when, far behind him, there's an almighty explosion.

Well, he does, of course. Just for a moment. Though he shouldn't. But a man wouldn't be human without a bit of curiosity. Anyway, everyone else on the crowded hill street has stopped too. They're all craning their necks and shaking their heads. There's awe on every face. There are giant flames and vast black clouds gushing out of the Savoy; as he gazes back, more pops and more vast flying chunks of masonry. 'Gunpowder,' he hears from some know-all.

The greatest palace in Europe, gone in one almighty flash. The Duke of Lancaster's permanent presence in London, obliterated.

Those barrels, he thinks. The ones I was going to watch them chuck on the fire. Thank God he got out in time. Thank God. But there's no time to waste. He turns, heaves in breath, and staggers on east, against the human tide.

It's not just to put as much distance as possible between himself and that scene from Hell, back there.

It's this. If the Essex men are here, they've entered through Aldgate. So what's happened to his home?

*　　*　　*

Aldgate is open. He can see St Botolph's beyond, and the houses of the eastern villages, and the fields. There are still rustics pouring in from the Essex encampment at Mile End, shouting and spitting and charging down the road.

But there are no gate guards that Chaucer can see. No dead men on the ground. No prisoners. No ugly scenes. There's no smoke, either, and no torn masonry. The staircase to Chaucer's apartment is intact.

He wriggles through the crowd and up the stairs. There's danger everywhere outside. All he can do now is bar his door and sit tight. Wait it out, as his daughter's doing. After a while, Chaucer's heart stops thudding and the sweat on his skin dries and cools. He's not exactly sitting tight. He's still pacing around, wild-eyed and wild-haired, revisiting in his mind his most frightening moments out there.

When he's recovered himself a little, he gets the rolls out of his leather bag and spreads them on his table. It's only two years' worth of household accounts, though even that's better than nothing: a splinter of defence against the onslaught of the darkness these . . . *others* . . . are bringing into London. Chaucer's a little cheered by that thought. He even summons up enough ordinary inquisitiveness to go through the rolls he's grabbed and saved quite carefully – for what else is he going to do, here, today? He sees his own name twice a year (and that of his wife, rather more often, including as the recipient of a silver-gilt cup at Christmas that sly Philippa never mentioned to *him* she'd been given, which is listed here as being worth £5 2s. 1d., or half the entire value of Chaucer's ducal pension for the year). He also sees some of the large amounts of money that the Duke seems to spend on fripperies for Katherine, on top of her already lavish allowances. Katherine has received, this spring alone, two tablets of silver and enamel for 7 marks, a silver belt costing more than 40 shillings, a three-legged silver chafing pan worth 33 shillings, a gold brooch in the form of a heart set with a diamond, and a gold brooch set with a ruby and fashioned in the form of two hands.

It seems nothing's too good for the Duke's women, Chaucer

thinks sourly. But then he catches himself on that ungenerous thought, and imagines Katherine hiding wherever she is, with her secret children, and the fear they must feel now, with the peasants gone wild and out for blood, and finds that all he feels for her, really, is pity. Gold brooches won't help her now, poor creature. He wouldn't be in her shoes, if a mob of madmen like the ones he's seen today is after her, too. He hopes she's found a refuge.

Chaucer goes to the window.

There's a nagging voice in his head, telling him he should do something more to defend what he holds dear. Take these rolls to Walworth, maybe. Show willing.

But there are no familiar faces or shapes out there. Just strangers, some yelling in their Essex voices as they head back through the open gates to Mile End, some drunk already, more coming in, with frightening joy on their turnip faces.

Irresolute, he stands and stares.

THIRTY-NINE

They come out of the woods, arising from the greenery like furtive spirits. They must have slept rough. There are at least ten of them, led by a woman with a tattered shawl draped over what may once have been a good robe. She has a baby in her arms, a very still baby. But what Alice notices about her first is her closed black eye and fat lip. And the children trailing behind have brambles in clothes blackened and scorched by fire.

It is nearly noon. There are no men at Gaines. They're long gone, with their big staves and their big talk, following Wat. It's just the women and children left behind: Alice and her baby, and Aunty, and the kids. All Alice knows of what the men are up to is what she hears, via Aunty, from the talk on the road: from the wives whose men come back for a snatched night at home, or those sent to the villages to gather reinforcements. What Aunty said this morning, stirring the pot with dark satisfaction, was that the men had left the green-wax fires burning in Chelmsford and Canterbury, and got straight into London. The King's readily agreed to meet the True Commons. And not a drop of blood shed.

It's Johnny who sees the arrivals first. Johnny, who stayed in the solar while the men were still milling about; who hasn't had a good word for Wat or anyone else for weeks now, even before he stopped talking to Alice and Aunty altogether. Still

479

in his mutinous silence, not meeting anyone's eye, he gets up from the table and stares out of the window.

Then he walks out, across the courtyard, through the gate, across the field.

Alice sees something in the set of his shoulders, so she gives Aunty little Lewis, who's heavily asleep, and follows Johnny out, feeling strange in the hot air of outside after her days in confinement, staring at the approaching woman with the black eye, and the children, and the cowered women behind, supporting a limping figure Alice can't make out, and watching how they cringe down when Johnny, silhouetted against the sky, starts waving to them up ahead. He's tall. A man, they might be thinking. But when they hear his thin boy's voice, full of a concerned warmth Alice hasn't heard in a while, not around her house, the women start moving forward again. Even from her distance, Alice can hear the kids begin to snivel as they stumble across the field towards safety.

Mary Sewale and her family have been in the woods for three days.

They ran out of the burning house when the mob got in. She doesn't know what's happened to her husband, the sheriff of Essex. She pushed the children out through the chicken hole, she says, and ran after them.

There'd been men all around the house for days before. A week. There was no food left by the time the crowd got in.

The Sewale children are wolfing down bread. Stuffing it in. They're staring round Aunty's kitchen with vacant eyes. They jump at every noise.

And the young girl with them, the one the two old servant women have been holding up, the one who was limping with the lost look on her face, and is now huddled down on the floor, crying in a forgetful sort of way, as if she doesn't remember that there's water on her face: she's been . . . well, none of them can describe the outrage done to her. All the old servants can say, with that imploring look that begs you to understand, and with those occasional flashes of rage at the memories they don't want to revive, is that it happened after the mob got into the Sewales' house at Coggeshall, and found this young Jane Ewell there too, and her new husband, the escheator of Essex.

They know what happened to *him,* all right. John Ewell came out of his hidey-hole when he heard his wife screaming. So they got him, and dragged him out. Cut his head off in front of the chapel. Tom Woodcutter did it, with this crazy look on his face. And the old women got Jane out the back, after the others. Into the woods.

'But why were you all still there? Why didn't you get away days ago?' Johnny says very gently, with his hands on Mary Sewale's. 'When the rioting first started? Why didn't he take you to safety?'

Mistress Sewale shakes her head. She can't explain properly, even to this kind lad. Who can explain fear? She's too exhausted; overwhelmed.

Alice, too. She's got her baby back in her arms. She's nestled in her corner, on her stool, doing nothing but staring down into his tiny face, watching his eyes open and gaze at her with that look that goes beyond trust. She's taking refuge in that look. But there's a terrible misgiving swelling somewhere deep inside her.

And not a drop of blood shed, Aunty was saying earlier on. Wasn't she?

This isn't what was supposed to happen, was it?

She peeks up. If Aunty's also feeling a stirring of guilt, she's not letting on. Aunty's face is closed. She's leaving the questions to Johnny.

Aunty's heaving a big pot of water on to the hook over the fire. Then she takes the baby off Mary Sewale. It's tied on, round my lady sheriff's front. Aunty fumbles with the knots, then cuts them. It's still not moving, that lump.

Aunty unwraps the swaddling. She lays the baby on the table to do it. Bluish stick limbs emerge, floppy against the wood. The stink is unbearable. So is the silence.

As if only just remembering her child's existence, Mary Sewale gets up to help. She moves as if she's in a trance. But her voice is strangely ordinary as she says, 'She's been sick for days. We couldn't go, she was so sick. That was why.' Then, leaning over, pale as a ghost, but still with that unnatural calm, 'Is she dead?'

Doubtfully, Aunty shakes her head. But she doesn't seem able to speak to Mary Sewale. 'Janey, Joanie,' she croaks, ignoring the woman and picking up the baby. 'Get me a bucket and a cloth. Move.'

The baby only stirs once Aunty's started dabbing away at the encrusted dirt with the warm water. Once clean, Aunty picks it – her – up, leaving the swaddling bands, streaked with glistening mucus and liquid brown, on the table, and holds the bluish scrap of flesh close. 'Cold as ice,' she says, to no one in particular, as the baby starts to whimper.

At the first gurgle from the child, Mary Sewale sits down, rather suddenly, on the table. But Johnny's at her side, guiding her solicitously back down to the safer perch of the bench.

It's only now that Alice sees what she can do. What she must do, if she wants Johnny, who's avoiding her gaze, as if he holds her personally responsible for every outrage committed by the men, to forgive her for her part in starting this.

With a pang, she realises, that's all she *does* want from life. Her world, which once encompassed kings and palaces, has shrunk to no more than the size and shape and urgency of that desire. It's simple; it may always have been this simple, if only she'd realised. She wants her son to be able to look at her again with that innocent look that goes beyond trust. That's enough. Would be enough. If it's not too late . . . if she hasn't spoiled everything, for ever.

I didn't know, a voice inside her implores Johnny. I told them not to hurt anyone. Don't blame me for this.

But she knows that's not good enough. Not any more. Not for these accusing wraiths, standing so quietly around her kitchen, staring. Not for her son.

Hastily, she passes little Lewis to Janey, who's hovering beside her.

'Give that baby here,' she says, turning to Aunty and holding her arms out for the Sewale infant. It's suddenly blindingly obvious. Mistress Sewale's been scared out of her wits, running for her life. She'll have no milk.

As Alice puts the small stranger to her breast, feeling the unfamiliar ways of this new body, and the chill in those miserable little limbs, she looks up, almost humbly, over her shoulder, at Johnny.

Below her the baby starts searching excitedly for the nipple; finding it, she closes her eyes and clings on, sucking painfully for all she's worth.

Johnny's standing beside Mistress Sewale, who's staring at her baby with painful urgency now, willing her to take milk and live, just beginning to believe she might. For the first time in days, Johnny's actually looking straight at Alice. And a bit, just a bit, of trust, or hope, or something close, is back in his eyes.

Doubtfully, Johnny whispers: 'This isn't what you wanted, is it, mam? This isn't what you meant . . . *them* . . . to do?'

It's evening. The barns are filling up fast. Johnny's spent half the day carrying bedding and water and food around the barns with his sisters, as more bedraggled female strangers, with smashed faces and slashed clothes and horror stories, have crept out of the woods. All of them wives, or widows, or children, or servants of one or another of the officials Wat was going to put out of action. We heard it was quiet here, they say, before they start weeping. Aunty's stone-faced with them, and all but silent in front of Alice and Johnny and the girls, too; she senses they've shifted ground, and doesn't want to hear. But she's sweet with the kids, at least; all those staring-eyed, slack-jawed, silent gentry children whose noses are running, and whose heads are splitting, and who can't sleep without screaming.

It's the first time all day that Alice and Johnny have had a moment to speak.

Johnny looks so grown-up, Alice thinks, yearning to take this burden off his shoulders, the burden she's created. He looks so tired.

'I had no idea, no idea,' Alice says weakly, shaking her head. 'They've all gone mad.'

It's true, in a way. She really can't imagine Wat or his men doing the terrible, bloody things she's heard the women talk about today. She wishes, now – with desperate, guilty sincerity – that she'd never egged him on.

But it's a lie, too, that she had no idea. She knows that, too, even as Johnny sighs his resigned acceptance and puts a hesitant hand on her arm. However much she now wishes she'd never given Wat any of that clever-clever advice about destroying every last trace of tax paperwork and the top half-dozen men in each county, she did say those things. She did egg him on. She just never thought how it would actually be. She's guilty of everything that's happening, because she should have known it would end like this, in horror. She's gone too far, again, despite all those resolutions she made at Chaucer's, in that other life. Chosen the wrong side, the wrong friends; damaged her children and herself. And it's too late for regrets.

FORTY

'We must attack,' says Mayor Walworth.

The lords around the golden-haired boy-King are slumped, hunched, bundles of fear. But there's nothing soft about Walworth's pale eyes. They flash like steel.

The rebels have settled down for the night, most of them, right outside the Tower, where this Council meeting is being held, on St Katherine's Square. You can hear the catcalls and the drunken songs and the demands through the window. They want to know what the Chancellor's been spending the money on for the past five years. They want to see the King. Or else.

Walworth raises his voice over the shouts from outside. 'We wait till midnight,' he says. 'We come out down four different streets. We attack. They're drunk now. They'll be asleep. And there's scarcely one in twenty of them with a proper weapon. We slaughter the whole sixty thousand of them, like pigs.'

Walworth's supposed to be from the servile classes; he's supposed to fear blood. But he has interests to protect, no less than any lord, and a family, and pride. He's standing tall, strung tight as a bowstring – an avenging angel. He's the only one.

The boy with the golden hair, whom they're all addressing, looks interested. But the assembled lords, the nation's experienced fighting arm, the muscle and brawn and sinew of England, only mumble and shake their heads. Archbishop Sudbury is no longer the Chancellor; he's resigned. But he's in fear of his life now he's trapped here, surrounded by those men who want his head. His skin is grey with fear; his hands tremble. Sir Robert Hales, the treasurer, so fine and bold before, is paralysed too. But then he's another one whose blood the crowd wants.

'Sire, if you can appease them by fair words, that would be the better course,' advises the Earl of Salisbury uneasily. He can't meet Walworth's eyes.

The boy isn't sure. He glances questioningly at the Mayor. Young Richard has been up a turret this evening, observing the revellers. He can't see why he couldn't go and talk to them. He can't really see, either, why he shouldn't go and kill them now. Nor does he especially trust Salisbury, that dried-up old stick, whom his mother always laughs at; whom his mother married, for a while, long ago, then left when her first husband Thomas Holland reappeared.

But Salisbury has a long and glorious past in France. He was at Poitiers. He helped negotiate Brétigny. He's the senior soldier here, and a nobleman. He should know best – better than a merchant, anyway. Still, the King would like Walworth to go on arguing for attack. 'Walworth?' he says. His voice squeaks between man and child. Perhaps it's the squeak that does it.

Walworth thins his lips and bows. 'Very well,' he says coldly. 'If you command it, sire, I will remain inactive.'

So the criers go out at first light, telling whoever wants to know that the King will ride out of London to Mile End fields, and there grant the requests of anyone who wishes to speak to him. Everyone between the ages of fifteen and sixty must leave the City to meet the King there at seven of the bell.

It starts well. The City begins to empty out as the innocents still excited by a meeting with the King march back east, under Aldgate and into the fields. The King rides out and meets the simple souls.

But this is not the happy ending it might seem, for not everyone has left London for the Mile End meeting.

Wat Tyler and John Ball are among those who don't bother. They have bigger fish to fry.

Within an hour of the King leaving they're inside the Tower. Their men are tousling the hair of the defeated, dejected guards, and jumping on Princess Joan's bed, and raiding the larders, and hunting down enemies.

They're dragging out poor old Archbishop Sudbury from his chapel, protesting, in his thin goaty voice, that he's done nothing wrong, right to the block, and bashing off his head with an axe blunted from too much use on metal yesterday. The first of eight blows only wounds his neck. He puts up his hand to feel the wound. He says: The hand of God. The second blow cuts off his fingers.

Sir Robert Hales' head is chopped off too; that's Hob Robber gone. They find the Duke of Lancaster's physician, a Brother William, and behead him – a token of intent for when they find the Duke himself.

Only a few nobles are lucky. The Duke's son, Henry of Derby, dresses up as a soldier and gets away with his life. Princess Joan is kissed by a drunk rebel and faints. But she manages to get away by boat, and makes it to the Royal Wardrobe building right at the other end of the City shoreline before collapsing.

Chaucer doesn't bother going to Mile End either.

He ventures out once, at dawn, to check on St Helen's. Five minutes there, five minutes back. All quiet. All safe.

In hope, he watches the crowd stream out for their seven o'clock meeting with the King, enjoying the rhythm of those feet thudding through the gate and away. During a long and wakeful night, he's almost decided several times that he must go to Walworth and volunteer to serve with him against the rebels. But that resolution has left him too sick with fear to sleep. Only the news, at sunrise, of the royal meeting unglues his eyes and cleanses him of the scratchy foreboding that's been gripping his body. Perhaps, if that goes well, he won't need . . .

An hour or so later, with foreboding, he watches many of the rebels stream back.

And then the bloodletting that the King has accidentally permitted begins.

Chaucer doesn't see a lot of it, at first, because he doesn't, after all, arm himself and rush out to find Walworth. The dread comes back. He stays at home, listening. Getting the lie of the land before venturing out, he tells himself (though he knows, really, that he's just hiding from his duty).

At least, from the safety of his window, he hears everything. Everyone does. There are whispers from window to window, for hours more, explaining the latest screams and crashes, the latest plumes of smoke.

There's a mob wandering around with heads on sticks, gone Charing way, towards Westminster. They've nailed Sudbury's red mitre on to his head.

They're allowed, some people whisper. The King's agreed: Sudbury was a traitor. Hales too. No, whisper others; it's the peasants who are the traitors. No one knows who's right and wrong any more. Even the King, hiding out at the Royal Wardrobe with his mother, watching the disembodied heads bob past, and the chanting rebels, may not be sure.

Then it gets too confused. No one can understand the mobs any more. It's just wild cries, and draggings, and the crashing of glass. The windows of Aldgate Street bang shut. The talk stops.

All the same, Chaucer steels himself to go out again at midday to make sure Elizabeth is safe. And, as soon as he's out, he feels strangely calmer. Just going into the street, being active, is less terrifying than sitting inside, alone, feeling a victim, listening, watching . . . waiting.

Yet his heart is still beating many times faster and louder than usual. The atmosphere of threat is palpable. First it's too quiet, just him walking over broken glass, in sinister sunlight, through the no man's land of a city without law. And suddenly, without warning, it's too noisy: screams, a torrent of arms and shouts and blows. These aren't even the big fights; these are private questions: a hasty settling of scores, feuds, and business problems, while no one's paying attention. A smash

488

and grab, netting a silver candlestick or cup. Moments to be forgotten with all speed, afterwards.

Within minutes of venturing out, for instance, Chaucer comes across a band of burly Kentishmen obeying the orders of Sir Robert Allen, the fishmonger: evicting another younger fishmonger. 'My house,' Allen's yelling as the man's dragged kicking out of the door, with pots and pans hurtling after him and a wife still screaming fit to bust somewhere inside. There's a torn-up lease at Allen's feet. 'Not yours. Don't forget it. And don't come back.'

Human nature at its worst, Chaucer thinks wryly. But he's almost cheered by the familiar, petty sight confronting him. This is just everyday spite and opportunism, not the terrifying work of the Devil that the incomers seem to be bent on. Still, he makes himself very small. He knows Allen won't want anyone to have seen him do this.

On Bishopsgate, once he's checked that the gates of St Helen's are still stoutly barred and the walls unattacked, Chaucer breathes so much more easily that he decides not to go straight home.

The flicker of courage he's found burning in himself is strangely exhilarating. He doesn't want to wall himself in again just yet. He's happier out here, where there's no time or space to think; where everything is action, one foot in front of the other. Perhaps he will, after all, try and find Walworth; it's easier to be brave out here than cowering at home. But where? Walworth will be with the King. And, though nothing is certain any more, the last Chaucer heard, from his window, was that the King was at the Royal Wardrobe, right across the City. As he thinks, he's already sneaking off west down Catte Street, across Broad Street and Coleman Street and Chepe Wards, towards Cheapside, the market zone, the centre of everything, flattening himself against walls and in doorways, just in case, whenever he hears the sound of running, or the smash of wood and glass that signals looters.

It's only after he's branched off Catte Street down past the mercers' mansions of Milk Street, thinking that if all goes on being relatively quiet he might brave the conduit on Cheapside and drink some water – he's as dry as a desert – that he sees the real violence consuming the City today.

There are excited screams up ahead, where Milk Street meets Cheapside, and the great rumble of a crowd.

It's almost welcome, the sound of people, after all his tiptoeing around. And Chaucer's confident enough by now of his ability to melt back into the brickwork to keep moving forward.

He's safe enough, he realises, as he inches up. They're all too busy shouting to take any notice of him. It's deafening, on Cheapside.

It takes him a minute to see what's going on through the shifting of shoulders. The men are dragging victims up from Bread Street, in grand Vintry Ward, on the south of Cheapside. The cobbles and slabs of Cheapside are dark and glistening. There's a pile of bodies, lying still, nearby.

They have no heads, he realises with a sudden rush of nausea. The bodies end in brown and red at the neck. Separately, there are heads staring out, dead-eyed, wild-haired, from underfoot, between people's legs, where they've rolled.

They're executing them, here. Chaucer hears the thwack of metal through flesh . . . a groan . . . though it might be just his imagination. He doesn't really know, any more, what he's hearing, and what he's just making up.

'Who,' he whispers, or maybe shouts, at the white-faced woman peeping out from a half-shuttered window upstairs. She's got the view.

'Flemings,' she mouths back.

He knows. He breathes out. Then it's just another bit of private score-settling, he thinks; violence against Flemings always is, in London. The Flemish merchant families are too well-off, and too favoured by the Crown, to be safe in the City. No wonder the London mob's gone hunting them down in Vintry Ward. They set fire to Walworth's brothel in Southwark this morning, too; he's heard that. They chased the Flemish tarts into the fishponds.

It's horrible, this; nauseating. Just the smell of the blood is turning his stomach. He'll go home in a minute. He's had enough.

But at least, he reassures himself, it's the same stuff: just Londoners released from the rule of law into bloody Carnival, giving free rein to their most savage instincts.

'Thirty-five of them, hiding,' the woman shouts, and suddenly, because the noise is shifting, he can hear the roughness of her voice. 'In St Martin in the Vintry, rich bastards.'

She doesn't say more. She's seen something Chaucer can't, from up there. She turns, as if her head's been pulled by an invisible string. At the same time, a murmur goes up across the bloody junction, which swells to a roar.

Chaucer's eyes swivel towards the sound too.

The crowd's yelling, 'Wat! Wat! Wat!' and for a moment, as it shifts and sways, a stringy bareheaded man with his hair all over the place and wild eyes comes into view, muscling a prisoner twice his size forward towards the block, pulling him by his beard. The victim's face is blackened and swollen over what were once fine merchant clothes: a long gown with some sort of damask figuring. He's hopping on one leg, dragging the other painfully behind him.

Then the crowd tightens again, and the vision is lost.

Chaucer looks up. So that's Wat Tyler, and some of this crowd must be Essex men. But seeing the rebel leader he's heard so much about with his own eyes isn't the reason the knot in his stomach is tightening. Something's bubbling up inside – some combination of names and memories. He can't quite grasp it, yet. But it's already making him feel so sick with dread that he thinks he might vomit.

'Lyons,' the woman mouths down at him, jerking her head towards the centre of the crowd.

'What, Richard Lyons?' Chaucer mimes back. That wreck, that condemned man, the magnificent merchant prince he knows? Alice's old ally, back then . . . before?

'Fleming,' she confirms soundlessly. 'Richest bastard of all.' She runs a finger across her throat.

Chaucer closes his eyes as the darkness comes down. He gets round the corner, away from the cheering and screaming, before he's violently sick.

If it were Londoners killing Flemings, it would make sense.

But Wat Tyler's not from here. He's an Essex man, some say; or a Kentishman. An incomer. And what would an incomer care about Flemings?

Why would an incomer, and a man on a mission of his own, someone with so many other demands on his time and attention, care enough about Lyons to lead him personally to his death?

Chaucer groans out loud. He's remembering what Alice told him last time they met, when they sat up for a night and a day talking, about why she'd charged in and disrupted proceedings at the King's Bench all those years ago. That was the one ill-considered act the Parliament managed to get her for, in the end; and for years Chaucer hadn't understood why she'd been so rash. When he finally asked her, her answer was simple enough. Because Lyons asked her to, she said. It was Lyons' man, caught in some dishonesty at the ports. That was it . . . Lyons firing the man later; the man weeping drunkenly at the Dancing Bear; talking about Alice. Yes, it's all coming back now . . . Chaucer even remembers the suddenly impish grin on Alice's face, when she said, with a bit of her old defiant insouciance, 'I agree, it was madness, but I don't really care. Because what came out of it wasn't all bad. The man turned out to be someone I grew up with and hadn't seen for years. My brother from the tilery. Wat.'

Wiping his mouth, straightening up, Chaucer tries to see reason. There must be a lot of Wats and Walters out there in Essex. It's a common enough name. But – he's still feeling dizzy – Wats who are tilers? And tilers with a grudge against Richard Lyons?

If . . . then . . . could Alice herself somehow be tied up with what started, back in Essex, as an uncannily well-planned attack on state finances, but, here in London, is blossoming into a gigantic act of hatred against the Duke and his allies?

His stomach churns again. He puts hands on his knees and surrenders to nausea.

Chaucer's still emptying his guts on the stinking cobbles when he feels hands on his shoulder.

492

Rough hands.

They pull him upright.

They're all around him. They stink. Their laughing eyes mock his fear.

'What's this, then? Delicate stomach not enjoying our justice?' a taunting voice comes from behind the wall of muscle. And, as Chaucer's hair is pulled back to force him to stare straight ahead, he sees the stringy, red and brown-streaked Wat, grinning at him with wild eyes.

'You a Fleming?' Wat says.

Chaucer doesn't like that grin. He shakes his head, or tries to; but he's held too tight. He can only move his eyes. He mumbles, 'No.'

'Just a sympathiser, then?' Wat says, sticking his face right near Chaucer's, so Chaucer can see the bloodshot whites of his eyes, and smell the black teeth and the wine.

Wat's got a blade in his hand. Chaucer's head's so far back that he can't get it properly in his sights. It's flashing around just below where he can focus.

'No,' he says. Wat only grins wider. There are guffaws from behind.

Chaucer thinks: Is *this* Alice's brother? He also thinks: Am I going to die?

The grinning stops. Chaucer didn't think it was possible for Wat to get any closer, but the face is right up in his now, eyeball to threatening eyeball.

'Your name, citizen,' Wat rasps. 'And your calling.'

They're still wondering, Chaucer sees, with the strange calm that has come over him since he felt the first hand on him, whether they haven't caught another foreigner, or at least someone in the Flemings' pay. Wat wants to kill again. But, Chaucer also sees, he's not far gone enough to do so without an excuse.

'I'm the wool comptroller at the port,' Chaucer forces out, gambling that the impeccable Englishness of this calling will work in his favour. 'Geoffrey Chaucer.'

It doesn't go down well with Tyler's men. 'Baa, baa!' one of them starts yelling, and they all burst out laughing. The others take the cry up. They start singing, 'Baa, baa, black sheep!' They're grinning at him. They're coming closer.

But Chaucer hardly hears them. He doesn't understand the look in Wat's eyes. A blink or two, as if astonished. Then the face pulls back, to maybe a foot or two away, far enough to focus, anyway, and Wat Tyler actually looks at Chaucer, seemingly searching for something. The blade goes out of sight.

'Not Alice's Chaucer?' Wat says in what sounds like a stunned, slack-jawed sort of question. 'The dad?'

The men behind and in front don't know how to respond. The jeers die away. The hands half pulling out Chaucer's hair loosen. Taking advantage of that, Chaucer shakes his head loose.

After another wondering shake of the head, Wat comes to. He waves a curt hand. The men drop Chaucer altogether.

'Go,' Wat tells him. And Chaucer walks.

It's only when Chaucer's moved his legs, one in front of the other, with excruciating care, all the way to the Catte Street turning, that he starts to shake. He leans against a wall, in blissful solitude, waiting for his jelly legs to regain their bone and muscle.

He let me go, Chaucer tells himself, over and over again. His teeth are chattering; he's cold and hot. Because I'm Alice's Chaucer. The dad.

He's too joyful at just being alive to wonder overmuch, for now. But he knows, at least, that he was right: Tyler is Alice's Wat.

She's not here, though. This can't be her doing. She's not here. Chaucer's too overwhelmed to do more than repeat that to himself for a few more moments.

But he hasn't got time to think of Alice now. He'll have to save that for later.

It's the thought of Wat pushing Lyons forward to his death – of those bulging eyes, and the darkness in them – that's propelling him. With the heat and excitement of that last encounter still on him, he sets off at a crazy pace, arms swinging, legs covering seven leagues with every stride, faster than he's ever walked before, to find Walworth; to stop the man with the murderous eyes.

The day and night that follow are the time of the Beast.

The chroniclers, locked away wherever they're hiding, will spill almost as much ink on their descriptions of the horrors that follow Corpus Christi as the rebels are now spilling blood.

Brother Thomas Walsingham, who, today, is not writing his usual spiteful chronicle in the scriptorium at St Albans, because, along with Abbot de la Mare, he's being frogmarched to London by rebels, will call the rampaging men the whores of the Devil, and describe the way they invade Princess Joan's bedroom in the Tower as if it were a rape. They search the most secret places there at their wicked will, he'll say; they lie on the fainting Princess's bed and demand she kiss them. They drive their swords violently into the bedclothes, over and over again.

> These and other atrocities they committed, sparing none of any degree or order, whether in churches or public places, or in houses or the fields, and wherever they raised a clamour against anyone, the rest quickly gathered, knowing that he would be beheaded, without either fear of God, or reverence for Holy Church. And when they had spent the whole day in those and many other execrable deeds, at last they wearied of such work, and being flown with un-accustomed and immoderate quantities of wine, and the night approaching, they might be seen lying scattered in open places, or under walls, like so many slaughtered swine. And indeed during the night, many of them, in their drunken state, secretly slew companions against whom they had grudges, so that there was much bloodshed that night, among their own number as well as other people.

No law-abiding person goes out on the street, because there is nothing down there but the smell of blood, and the sound of burning, and the sting of smoke, and the crash of collapsing buildings, and noises round corners. Rumours pass from window to window. Tyler is going to light fires at the four corners of London and burn it down. Tyler will tie up the King to a horse and parade his prisoner around the shires. Tyler will abolish the Church and execute all lords and bishops. John Ball will be Archbishop. Tyler will be King of the Commons. Fear paralyses so many people. But does hiding from the Beast do any good?

At dawn on Saturday, the mob bursts into England's holy of holies, Westminster Abbey, and corners the fugitive Marshal of England, Richard Imworth. They find him hiding behind the marble pillars at the tomb of King Edward the Confessor, clinging to his belief that sanctuary won't be desecrated.

An hour's forced march later, his head joins the others lolling wide-eyed at the corner of Cheapside and Milk Street.

'It's not too late,' says Walworth the merchant, with iron in his voice. 'Attack.'

Chaucer's standing quietly behind him, his sallet chafing at his neck, trying not to feel sick. Walworth has no doubts. Walworth's plan is the last chance. But can it work?

Half of the noble lords whose job is to fight, but who yesterday counselled appeasement, are dead. The rest are too frightened to speak.

The young King takes a moment to put aside the belief of his entire short lifetime that the nobility is the only order of society with God's grace to defend the realm. Then, still doubtfully, he puts his faith in the merchant Mayor, and nods.

Preparations. The King at desecrated Westminster, praying with the hermit of the abbey gardens. Walworth, in London, repeating his instructions to Chaucer. Chaucer, slipping from one great house to the next, with his heart in his mouth, murmuring Walworth's instructions. Inside the courtyards, hushed clanking and whispers.

The sun hangs low and red and glowing in the sky by the time two hundred noblemen, on horseback, in velvets, make their way behind the boy-King to Smithfield, where, long ago, in the grassy space between the walls of St Bartholomew's Priory and Hospital and the Charterhouse and the Mortality mass graves, and the sluggish waters of Faggeswell Brook and the river Holborn, Alice Perrers once reigned for the day as King Edward's Lady of the Sun.

The rebels have been called to one more meeting. This time, Tyler has come.

The King's party draws rein on the east side of the square, in front of St Bartholomew's. Walworth's in his long merchant gown behind the King. Chaucer, in another long gown, behind Walworth. All along the western side, with the rivers behind them, are the tousled, stinking others, thousands of them, roaring.

Of all the royal party, it is Walworth who's ordered to ride across the empty space in the middle, and shout out for Tyler to present his demands to the King. Wat Tyler rides forward on his little hackney.

All eyes are on him.

Chaucer's whole body has become a drum beat. It's so loud and insistent that he can't think. So much could go wrong.

The rebels have been drawn outside the walls of the City. So far, so good. There are hundreds of mercenaries, armed and quietly waiting, inside those courtyards back there, ready to prevent the men's return, or come out and finish off Tyler and his men if need be. But the King doesn't want that. He wants the day to end without bloodshed. He wants to persuade these men to go home peacefully.

Everything depends on that. Because if they don't, if they won't . . .

The King and what's left of the nobility are out here, around Chaucer, utterly exposed to the enemy . . . endangered . . .

If the men won't go, it will be up to Walworth to change the strategy and attack. But Walworth's only a merchant. Because of the King's wish that there should be no bloodshed, Walworth's refused even to wear fighting clothes. It was all Chaucer could do to persuade him to put on a discreet metal breastplate under his gown, invisible to everyone, as Chaucer himself has done.

When it comes to it, does Walworth have the killer instinct? Will he dare attack?

Chaucer tries not to let his body tremble. He clenches his hands more tightly together. Don't give way to panic, he tells himself. Don't give way.

But he's scarcely breathing as the supremely confident Wat Tyler dismounts in front of the King, holding in his hand a dagger. The rebel leader half bends his knee, then takes the King by the hand, and shakes the boy's arm forcibly and roughly, saying to him, 'Brother, be of good comfort and joyful, for you shall have, in the fortnight that is to come, praise from the Commons even more than you have yet had, and we shall be good companions.'

Chaucer quakes at the brutal good cheer in that rough voice. The man's talking like a victor already; he dared call the King, God's anointed, 'brother'. But the King, small and young though he is, does not appear intimidated. All he says is, 'Why will you not go back to your own country?'

Chaucer can hardly hear the answer for the rush of blood in his ears. The man in front of him, in the pulsing centre of Chaucer's field of vision, starts ranting threateningly and waving his arms about and talking, on and on, in that strange, grating, rustic voice, about the charter that he and his fellows want, with all their demands met, before they'll go away. Only snatches of the wild demands come through the roar inside Chaucer's head: '. . . the Law of Winchester . . . no more lords, barring only the King . . . Church lands to the people . . . only one bishop to remain . . . the serfs to be freed . . . all men to be free and equal . . .'

Chaucer sucks in more air just before the last threat. 'You'll rue it bitterly if you don't settle this to our pleasure . . .' he hears, almost fainting with disbelief.

The menace is enough to make Chaucer splutter out that breath, near-choking on it. All around him, he's aware of the darting eyes, the panic.

Only the King remains calm. He inclines his boy head, and replies, without emotion, that Tyler can have all that he, the King, can fairly grant, saving only the regality of his crown – whatever that means. Chaucer can't imagine. Perhaps that's the point.

'So now,' the boy adds, level-voiced and majestic, 'go back to your home, without further delay.'

It seems to Chaucer that the two sides have reached stalemate.

The King has told the peasants what to do. He has no more to say.

Tyler has no more to say, either. But he won't go. He's swaying, on his feet, in front of the King, as if he doesn't understand what's been said to him.

Walworth's doing nothing.

Time is suspended.

And, far away, the thousands of men on that side of the field are waiting and watching, as intently as the two hundred men over here.

'Water,' Tyler croaks. But when it's brought by a pageboy and he's gargled it down his throat and chin and front, and spat some of it out, it still doesn't seem to have refreshed him, or resolved him to obey his King. 'Beer,' the rebel leader calls hoarsely, and spits near the King's feet.

Then, ignoring the horrified murmurs, and the hands going to belts and blades, he gets up on his knock-kneed pony again, and looks around, seeming dazed.

It's only afterwards that Chaucer pieces together what happens now with his mind: the various rushes of movement.

First, the pageboy, retreating to beside Chaucer, whispering loudly, 'No, it's him! It really is! The Canterbury highwayman! The greatest thief in Kent!'

Second, the skirl of horse-legs and harness, as Tyler lunges forward, apparently straight towards Chaucer, with death bulging from his eyes, bawling, 'You little fucker,' and Chaucer ducks and dives for the ground. It's only a moment later, when nothing further has happened to him, that he looks up, feeling foolish, and sees that it's the boy Tyler was after: the boy Tyler's now got by the front of his tunic. And Tyler's got his knife arm up, ready to strike.

'Stop,' says someone else. A deep voice. A tall man, in a long robe streaming down his horse's side, steps forward into

Tyler's long shadow. Walworth, taking command at last. As Chaucer scrambles back to his feet, Walworth intones: 'I'm arresting you for drawing your weapon before the King's face.'

Tyler drops the boy, not out of respect for the other boy, the royal one, and not out of fear of the man, but just because he's obviously going to try to kill Walworth. He stabs at him. Hard, upwards, under the ribs. In the stomach.

The blade screeches against something hard, and sheers off. Thank God for that hidden breastplate, Chaucer thinks. He looks down at his hand in surprise. His own dagger is drawn. He's moving forward.

Walworth's cutlass is out before he even feels the dagger blade slide over his body armour. He brings his weapon down on the brute sitting on his shaggy little horse. It hits the man's shoulder. A jarring of bone. A blush of red. Tyler dropping on to the animal's neck. A groan.

Tyler isn't dead. He backs off the blade, with sick eyes. He turns his little horse. It sets off across the tussocky grass towards his kind, with the rebel slumped on top.

But then, midway, he falls. He lies flat. Walworth breathes.

But the undead rebel rises.

He gets to his hands and knees. In a voice loud enough for Walworth to hear, so maybe loud enough for the others to hear, too, he quavers, 'Treason.'

And then he collapses again.

Chaucer's blade is still out.

Chaucer is one of half a dozen men who turn to Walworth with the beginning of disbelieving euphoria in their hearts, and on their faces. They've beaten the darkness. A merchant's led them to victory. We've won, Chaucer starts to think.

But only for a moment.

Because Walworth's not looking around, offering sweet praise.

Walworth's off too, up on his horse, with no more than a curt nod to the King, with his men streaming behind him. back to the City, leaving behind a company of men who, now he's gone, don't know whether he's following some plan of his own, or has just cut and run, and are beginning to remember, with dread, the thousands of men on the other side of the field, still watching and waiting.

The rebels don't know what's happening, or what to do, any more than Wat did. They haven't been able to follow what their leader's been saying to the King's men. They're too far away.

But they can see something's wrong now. Why is he lying there, so still?

In the half-dark, they stir, with confused questions, then the beginnings of anger.

What did he mean: Treason?

If they've learned anything in these last days, it's to be brave. No one helps you unless you help yourself. You can always do a bit more. So some among them start to bend their bows and untruss their sheaves of arrows, ready to shoot into the royal party. What have they got to lose?

But then another horseman comes out of the reddish glow of the cortège at St Bartholomew's gate. A boy, in gold, with golden hair, riding at a thunderous canter, with his right hand raised. A boy followed by a smallish man in long merchant robes, who's wobbling in the saddle, holding tight to the leather with one hand, a dagger as well as reins fumbled in the other.

The men ignore the retainer. It's the King they stare at. They pause. They waver.

This is what they wanted: the reward for their courage, the reward for their journey. The King. God's anointed. He's come to them at last.

'Sirs, will you shoot your King?' the vision shouts boldly into the great shaggy Beast-shadow of the thousands of men, and his voice is just as you'd imagine a boy-king's voice: strong, and pure, and fresh, and as English as theirs.

'I will be your chief and captain,' the boy shouts. Only a boy, but with all the presence of mind and courage of his hero father, so beloved by them all. 'You shall have from me all that you seek, only follow me out to those fields there,' he finishes, and he points, decisively, to a place beyond the smoking ruins of St John's Clerkenwell, a mile further from the City.

Then the boy who is King of England turns his horse, and sets off there himself, at a walk, as if he's never even imagined fear, or an arrow in his back. After a quick glance back at the crowd, the retainer turns his horse and goes after him. After another moment, the bewildered men start following too.

They're sheep without a shepherd. They don't have a better plan.

They'll follow their chief and captain's plan. The trudge into the dusk becomes more certain, more rhythmic. How pink and white and fresh the King's cheeks are, in the red of sunset; how bright the gold glows, the gold of God.

The rescuers find them in the trampled wheat of Clerkenwell fields half an hour later: a sea of adoring men, clustered around their monarch, still shouting about their rights to fish in the rivers and hunt in the forests. King Richard hasn't lost his nerve. He's still talking back. It's nearly dark.

Chaucer looks up almost disbelievingly at the measured thud of approaching hoofs. He's been standing very still beside Richard, with his dagger arm up, for so long that his weary muscles are aching – for so long that, even if they did attack, he doesn't know whether he'd still have the strength to strike back as they took him down. But there's been no need. They've ignored him all this time, King and men alike, just as they've ignored the other members of the King's party, most of whom have, gradually, and far behind Chaucer, reassembled somewhere near their master.

Through the shadows, Chaucer sees Walworth's eyes seek him out and, for a moment, rest on him with approval. He thinks he might see a flicker of surprise in that other face too, for who'd have thought that, of all the knights and lords in the royal entourage, it would be quiet little Chaucer standing guard, and with that unlikely weapon, too?

502

Walworth's brought forth an army: seven thousand men, riding out of Aldersgate to rescue the King. He and Brembre and Philpot are each at the head of a cavalry of property-owners, each under the banner of a different London district, and Sir Robert Knolles' one hundred mercenaries are deployed at the flanks, pushing forward as if to encircle the rebels. Walworth hasn't lost his nerve. This is the end for the rebels.

When they reach the King, a band of lances pushes through and ranges itself around him: a wall of shining points. Chaucer lets his arm drop. In the midst of this glittering battle scene, he feels strangely at peace. He's done his duty; more than. He steps back and sheathes his dagger. The boy is safe. Not that the boy seems to care. He's a lion in a child's body.

'It would be easy to kill them all,' Knolles murmurs to his monarch. There are maybe twenty thousand of them, three times his own numbers; but they're on foot, without proper weapons, and tired, and muddled . . . lost.

But the King calmly shakes his head. He murmurs in reply, 'No: they've spared me . . . and three-quarters of them were brought here by fear and threats. I won't let the innocent suffer with the guilty.'

He turns to the crowd. Ringingly, he shouts, 'I give you leave to depart!'

And, quietly, the tramp of feet starts again, as the former rebels obey their King, and turn, and head out to the fields, for Essex, for Hertfordshire, for home.

As the multitude begins to disperse, watched by a slight boy on a charger, Walworth dismounts and fumbles with his saddle-packs.

Walworth has brought something with him to Clerkenwell fields: Wat Tyler's head on a lance. He plants the lance in the ground beside the King. The head stares back: a man too brave; a man who didn't know when to stop. A man who brought forth the Beast. The crowds avert their fearful eyes.

When the fields have emptied, and the King has returned to his overwrought, overjoyed mother at the Royal Wardrobe, this head will go to London Bridge, and Archbishop Sudbury's, with its nailed-down mitre, will come down.

Before that, while they're still watching the streams of humanity drain away from the dark earth among the midges, the King will call Walworth and Brembre and Philpot to him: men of courage, despite their servile rank; men of the sword. He will knight them all.

But, even before the knightings, Chaucer has slipped back from the jostling, triumphant throng around the King, and started walking his horse slowly back towards Aldersgate and the City.

He's more tired than he's ever been. And he doesn't want to be here, or be part of this celebration. He looked into Walworth's eyes as the merchant leader drove the lance with that bloody head on it into the earth. And what he saw frightened him. He's had enough of bloodlust.

Besides, Chaucer needs to be alone. He's got something else to think about.

In the uncertain light of dawn, the law-abiding citizens of London cautiously put their noses outside their doors, and form groups to inspect the damage all around, and stand in knots on street corners, still looking over their shoulders, muttering, comparing fearful notes, but getting braver.

St Helen's is safe, though still barred. There are two ruined houses smouldering on Aldgate Street, but no more flames. Down at the Savoy, people say, there are still men screaming in the collapsed wine cellars. *Those* men.

But there are no markets working. No food coming into the City.

There are men barricaded inside a house in Milk Street, still fighting.

There are bowmen still picking off victims from the Guildhall roof.

Yet Mayor Walworth's guards are already going round the wards making arrests. There'll be executions soon enough. Exemplary ones, they say. Arms and legs chopped off. Quarterings. They say he's going to let the widows of the

504

Flemings who were murdered kill their husbands' killers with their own hands.

But you still don't want to go too far afield. Not yet.

You certainly don't want to go outside the City walls. Because even if London's almost safe again, out there, all over the east, and to the south, and up in the Midlands, and beyond, who knows? They wanted the Duke, *those* men. And he's still out there, on the loose. Who's to say *they* won't still get him?

Chaucer is one of the first out into the changed City.

He's lost his fear. He's made up his mind.

Before other Londoners are up, before the dawn's even properly broken, he's already picked his way through the rubble to the Customs House, checked it's safe, picked his way through more rubble in Vintry Ward to his father's neighbour's house, banged, got a sleepy Henry Herbury up, asked the bewildered old man to stand in as his deputy at the Customs House for a few days, and got him to sign a document temporarily taking control of Chaucer's property (including old Chaucer's large and gracious house, currently rented out), with instructions to pass it on to Geoffrey's children in the event of his death, just in case anything goes wrong. He leaves a letter for Elizabeth. In exchange for signing over his property, Chaucer also gets Herbury to sign a letter of credit for ninety pounds. Cash money wouldn't be safe, not today. He scarcely draws breath.

'But . . . where are you going?' Herbury says. 'You must be careful, my boy. These are dangerous times.'

'Do what I can to make things safe,' Chaucer says tersely.

Herbury nods sagely. 'Ah, joining a guard, eh? Admirable . . . admirable. I've heard Walworth's calling for volunteers,' he says. 'A great day for Walworth, this. And all of us Londoners. Splendid.'

'Out of London,' Chaucer says, reaching for the paper. But Herbury's got his hand on it. Herbury wants to talk. 'They say the Earl of Kent will have the Governor of Dover to help him calm Kent . . . Trivet, isn't it? One of the old *condottieri*?'

he muses, happy at the thought of order being restored. 'Suffolk's off to Suffolk with five hundred lances . . .'

Chaucer reaches again for the paper, and then pulls back.

'And everyone seems to be going to Essex – the King's going himself, the Earl of Buckingham's being brought back from France . . . I also gather there'll be an army under Thomas of Woodstock . . . I've heard Sir Thomas Percy. And the usual suspects, too, of course. Locals like Fitzwalter; tough old war-horses like William of Windsor. They'll give those creatures something to think about. Brutes, one and all.' He chuckles.

'Me too,' Chaucer says, almost snatching the paper from under dear old Herbury's palm. He's heard the same stories on the street since last night: the same commanders' names.

'What, a brute?' Herbury asks.

'Off to Essex,' Chaucer says as he leaves.

FORTY-ONE

Chaucer glides by the hallucinatory landscape of Essex: in smoke, with splintered trees, quietly burning houses, and, every now and then, an unexplained body, lying half-in, half-out of a fishing boat or swinging, peacefully, from a tree.

He could have ridden, of course. He could have passed through Stratford, West Ham, Barking, on up to Hornchurch and Romford, then to Brentwood and Upminster. Or he could have taken the longer northern route, the courtly route, along the good wide road through Edmonton and Chingford and Waltham forest to the palace at Havering-atte-Bower, then cross country through Romford to Upminster.

But he doesn't want to go through the forests, with their green twilight and great silences and disconcerting sounds. Not now.

Who'd want to be stopped by strangers, sweating strangers, the kind who might ask, 'Halt! With whom hold ye?' He would have no idea who would kill him for answering, 'With the King and the True Commons,' and who would kill him for answering anything else.

He's heard the local landlords are out with loyalist thugs retaliating. And he's heard the rebels are still desperately calling men to arms south of Chelmsford, the county town, at Great Baddow and Rettendon and Billericay. So he's better off by boat. Even with the price he had to pay for this ride, since there are hardly any fishermen out.

'Nasty, out Essex way,' the thieving boatman says gloomily, as if trying to make up for his greed earlier on with a running commentary. 'Every big 'ouse torched, seems like. Half the villages gone, just like that. And the forests crawling with outlaws. And now this Buckingham, back from France to sort 'em out: they say he's well 'ard. And plague, too, I've heard: up Colchester way. A punishment for our sins. We'll be having a hot summer out 'ere all right.'

Chaucer nods, and nods again, trying to look calm, just in case the man sniffs fear on him and tips him over the side to steal his purse.

Still, his heart's in his mouth when the boatman, who's never once indicated where his own sympathies lie or asked Chaucer what he's doing heading out into this mobsters' heartland, steers him up to a sandy creek and says, roughly, 'Right, Rainham Creek, out 'ere. Up the little river there. Upminster, eight miles north, Gaines, maybe six,' because the smooth marshy coast turns, almost at once, back into forest.

In the embrace of the green, he hears men. He hears hogs. He hears deer. There are ghosts, and clatterings, and the breaking of branches just out of sight. Birds cry in alarm. A fox screams. It takes a good hour to cross the forest, and there isn't a moment when Geoffrey Chaucer, Esquire, isn't scared half out of his wits.

But he keeps going, up the splashy little river, jutting his jaw, puffing up his chest.

Nothing will stop him getting to Alice now.

Elizabeth is safe. It's over. She's alive. They'll be opening the doors of St Helen's any time. The worst that's happened to the women inside is a couple of sleepless nights; oh, and they might be hungry. But Elizabeth doesn't need him right now.

Chaucer has to come here, because Alice is the one who needs him.

Chaucer's known he'd have to do this ever since he heard the first rumours that Walworth would be organising his own punitive bloodbath in the City, and all those noblemen would be going out to put the provinces to fire and the sword.

He's always known there's a hard streak in Walworth. Those half-starved Flemish tarts, opening their legs for a penny: weren't they proof enough? The parliamentary attacks on Alice? But now the man's tasted blood. He's out to prove himself a grandee; a noble knight in deed as well as word. And Chaucer doesn't want to see any more blood flow, or any more men turn into brutes.

He doesn't want to be part of the reprisals, either. And this is going to be a time when loyalties are tested; when Walworth, who's grown fond of him, might conceivably want him to do ... well, something, to help the authorities in their clamp-down. Or the Duke might. Or any number of other noble lords who have a claim on him. And if they asked, he might not have the courage to refuse.

Most importantly, he doesn't want Alice to be part of the reprisals. If she *has* been— He stops himself on that naive thought. Because of course she has been. The early stages of this rebellion, at least, have her handprints all over them. Before the bloodletting began.

She's been sitting out there in the wilds, alone (for Chaucer doesn't think for a moment that she'll have taken his advice and fetched her children back). Brooding. And she'll have been going over her humiliation with ... Chaucer can't bring himself to think the name of Alice's near-brother ... *that man*. Obsessively. She'll have made another of her plans; trying to get her own back on the Duke. And now it's all gone so terribly out of control, and *that man* is dead, she's got no one. No one but Chaucer can save her.

He's got to save her, and himself.

He's going to take her away. Far away. On that pilgrimage, maybe. He's got that letter of credit here. It'll pay for years of travel.

If he hurries, he'll be with her before William of Windsor gets near Essex.

Eventually the trees thin out, and there's Upminster town-ship smoking on the horizon, and a hodge-podge of patchwork fields, and closer up a collection of burning village houses, and more roofs closer still, the only unburned roofs in the

509

whole ruined landscape, which must be the manor of Gaines.

Chaucer isn't frightened when at last he does see men, and they're scuttling around just outside the gates at Gaines, even though they're low men, in ragged clothes, with cut faces and bruises. He only hesitates a moment when, as he passes through the gates himself, a pair of them, busy poking papers into the end of a bonfire, look up, straight at him. He sees the fright in their eyes at the sight of a stranger. He has no monopoly on fear any more. Even when one of them growls, with what's supposed to be a fierce look, 'Oi, you! With whom hold you?' he scarcely misses a beat, because, after that last hour in the greenwood, he trusts his instincts; he knows whom he's dealing with. 'With the King and the True Commons,' he says evenly. 'I'm here to see Alice Perrers.'

The man doesn't deny she lives here; he only shakes his bandaged head doubtfully. The lid of one eye is twitching. Chaucer steps closer, and sees what they're burning: letters. The kind that were nailed on trees, that say, 'To John Sheep, from Jack the Lad: rise up!' He nods, and the sadness grows. Letters she wrote, he can guess. Oh Alice, he's thinking. You fool.

'Will you take me to her?' he presses gently.

The man says, 'She's not at the house. There's only the women in there. The . . .' His face twists bitterly. '. . . the *ladies*. The ones she took in. 'S why we're out here, innit?'

Chaucer looks from one to the other. He doesn't understand, or perhaps these men don't. Then he puts the flicker of doubt out of his mind. They're just peasants, these men. He needs to find Alice. 'Well, where is she?' he persists.

The other man puts a last handful of letters on the big pile of burning embers. Quickly they flare up; glowing ash flies out. 'We're off now,' he mutters as the flames die away.

They don't want to help. They're too scared, Chaucer sees. They're longing to lose themselves in the forest. Two days ago, they might have been in the mob in London. They might have killed him, with gleeful yells on their ugly lips. But looking at them now, Chaucer finds himself almost pitying their wasted, skinny limbs; the years of rye bread and watered-down milk; the missing finger on the taller one, the mark of a wood-worker; and their dull, hopeless fright. They know there's nothing ahead for them, he sees. They just don't know how the darkness will come.

He sets off away from them, towards the manor house, along the avenue of slim young beeches someone (Alice, he presumes) will have planted for shade in years to come. It's an incongruously pretty sight that meets his eyes, after every-thing he's seen today. There are scented roses and gillyflowers in bloom in the garden, and beans and salad leaves and herbs sprouting in the kitchen garden, and vines tumbling over a barn with a new roof. There's a new section built on the tilting old house, too, with spacious doors and windows, smelling of fresh wood and straw. He can guess at the high ceilings from outside. And he's almost soothed by the low crooning of doves, and the buzz of bees in the lavender hedges, and the brightness of the well-tended fields all around. He can guess at the energy she's brought to the project of renewing this place in her short time here; shaking his head, almost laughing, he wonders how the locals coped with her energy.

He offers the fidgeting men a last scrap of help over his shoulder. 'They say the King and his army are heading out of London for Waltham Abbey,' he says calmly as his feet scrunch, left, right, over the bits of stuff. 'So don't go north.'

There's a crowd of women at the back of the manor house, when he reaches it. Ladies patching well-made but torn skirts, and quiet, quiet children. They look at him with fear as he comes around the corner. Two middle-aged servants come towards him, trying to look threatening, with big sticks in their hands.

'I've come from London to look for Mistress Perrers,' he says to reassure them.

'London,' they sigh, calmed by his gentleman's voice, craning closer.

'It's over,' he says, and they sigh again, and their faces relax in well-bred relief.

Who are these ladies? Chaucer's wondering, suddenly made uneasy again by their reaction. They're no rebels. What are they doing here at Alice's home? He can't, can he, have been wrong . . .?

'Mistress Perrers?' he nudges.

'She's up at the farmhouse,' the lady in the far corner with the beaten-up face says, looking curiously at him. 'Since the sickness started. They're all there.'

All? Chaucer thinks, feeling his heart sink. But he shuts his mind to the question of how both those men outside, and these women here in the courtyard, can be connected to Alice. She'll explain it all when he finds her. Hastily, he sets off in the direction the lady points him towards.

It's quiet in the farmhouse. There's no fire burning on the kitchen hearth. Just embers.

He looks around, wondering where to go. It's well appointed downstairs: neat, simple furniture, clean rushes on the floor, silver and pewter in the cupboard.

But it's too neat . . . and so quiet . . . as if there's no one left.

He can hear his own footsteps, heavy as a threat. He can hear his own breathing. But that's all.

Chaucer only hears Alice when he opens the inside door: quick breathing, damped behind wool. Sobs, even, maybe. She'll be scared, too.

There are two big beds, with their curtains drawn around them.

'Alice,' he says. 'Come out. It's me. Chaucer.' His voice is soft.

He isn't expecting the look on her face when she pokes it out from between the far bedcurtains: the drawn whiteness, the indescribable relief, and the shining, grateful love in those reddened eyes.

'You,' she whispers, staring at him as if he were God himself.

He isn't expecting, either, the next thing he hears, from the other closed bed: a baby's awakening, experimental whimper; the prelude, he knows from experience, to loud shouts of hunger.

('Alice's Chaucer? The dad?' suddenly echoes in his head; dead Wat's voice.)

There's no time for Chaucer to ask about the baby.

Alice's face crumples into fretful helplessness at the sound of crying. 'Oh no . . . I can't . . . not now,' she mutters, pleating her fingers together, scrunching up the wet rag she's holding. To Chaucer: 'Please, will you get the baby?' Then, as if to herself: 'No, no . . . he'll wait.'

She gazes at the stunned Chaucer, as if she's made her mind up to something. And Chaucer, for all his resolve, for all his certainty that this time it's he who will set the agenda, put his case to her, and insist that she does as he says, finds himself drawn in, as usual, to the world according to Alice. He waits. 'Please,' she says, quickly, 'tell me what you think.' She puts a finger up to her lips, muttering, 'Shh.' And then she pulls him inside the bedcurtains, into the half-dark, and sits him down by the side of the bed.

There's a boy under the quilts. A youth, a bit taller and skinnier than Thomas, but then Thomas has always been small, so they might be the same age. This boy has freckles and black hair. Just like Alice's.

It takes Chaucer's eyes a moment to adjust to the dimness; his heart a moment to adjust to the darkness closing in on it.

It's Alice's son. She's had her children with her here, all along . . . and if she has them with her, then what good is it that he's turned up to save her from her solitary fate? He's misunderstood. He doesn't know how, yet, but he can see that he's got it wrong, all wrong . . .

Then he sees that Alice's son's hair is plastered to his skull, and sweat's dripping off him, and his skin is whiter than it possibly could be in nature, healthy nature at least, though he's not dead, because he's still moaning under his breath.

In the middle of his private sorrow, Chaucer's overcome by a father's tenderness. He leans forward and puts his hand on the lad's forehead. It's raging hot. The boy – John; Johnny, Chaucer remembers he's called; Sir John, now – moans again.

'Thirsty,' he whispers, in a dry little voice, a child's voice, though the boy must be well into his teens by now. 'So thirsty.'

Chaucer turns to Alice. He can see the fear in her face. He can feel it in his.

The boatman told him. It's back in Colchester. He can see Alice already knows it's the Mortality, even though there are no buboes at his neck, and no blackness where the skin has started rotting around his fingertips.

'Plague?' he mouths, so the youth with the closed eyes can't hear. She'll want him to say what he thinks. Alice has never shied away from knowing the truth.

From beside him, she nods. She isn't surprised. Without a word, she bends down and scoops up water from the bucket on the floor. There's infinite tenderness, and infinite sadness, on her face as she puts the cup to her son's lips. Johnny swallows. Then he starts to cough. There's panic on her face as she pulls out the other cloth she's been pleating, and puts that to his lips. When the spasm's exhausted him, and he drops it back on the quilt, Chaucer sees, as bright as roses, the blood in the slimy spit.

Chaucer puts a hand on Alice's. He can sense the galloping beat of her heart; and sensing it calms him. There's no reason for him to be here, he can see that now. But he can't leave her like this. He'll have to stay and help.

Just outside, the baby's cries are getting louder and more fractious.

'Calm,' he mouths. 'Be calm. I'll sit with him for a minute. You feed the baby.'

She nods, and for a second the terrible weight of love and care lightens, and she manages something like a smile of gratitude. 'Oh, Chaucer,' she whispers, 'thank you,' and she's off.

A familiar kind of bewilderment settles over Chaucer in this unfamiliar place, but there's a warmth, a softness, too. He's come here with his certainties, and she's overturned them in an instant. He can't believe he's here, doing this, tending to her son, while she nurses a baby he knows nothing about. He can't believe he feels so tender towards her.

He takes a corner of the quilt, and dips it in water, and

514

wipes the boy's sweating face clean. 'You'll be all right, Johnny,' he whispers. 'It's not so bad, this kind. Just hold on. You'll be all right.'

He only wishes he could be sure it was true.

She comes back. The baby's quiet behind his curtains. Johnny too, on his pillow.

Before anything else, she checks the boy. She's got an ear cocked, listening for his breathing. He's asleep; or passed out. You can't tell which.

'Do you think he'll . . .?' she begins, bravely. Then she wrinkles up her face. 'No, don't answer.'

So Chaucer says nothing. He puts his hand on hers again. She lets it stay there, on her dry, cool, unresponsive skin.

'I sent the girls away with Aunty,' she says reflectively. 'Up north. A week ago, when he began to sicken. When I brought Johnny up here. I didn't want them to get ill . . .'

Helplessly, Chaucer pats her hand. He can't help admiring her hollowed-out calm. If this were his child, he knows he'd never be this self-possessed.

'Or all those women who'd turned up,' she goes on. 'Once all the fighting started. Sewale's wife; Ewell's widow. And all the rest of those women at the big house. They've had enough misery without this, too.'

'You took them in? Refugees?' Chaucer says, still not understanding, but lost in admiration. 'In the middle of all . . . that? You gave them your home?'

'But,' she replies, and she doesn't flinch from what she's going to say next, 'I was the one who caused their trouble in the first place, wasn't I? Because I helped start it, you know,' she goes on, in the same flat little voice. '*That*. I wanted to scare the Duke.'

Chaucer looks up. A thousand things fall into place. He's been right, after all, to think she's been involved. He says, 'Oh.'

'But it was never supposed to be like this,' she says, a bowed head before him. 'I wish I hadn't. What happened out there, afterwards – what they did to Mary Sewale's home – London

515

– it's not what I meant. Not at all. That's the world gone mad. Wat gone mad.'

He keeps his hand on hers. Like her, he clings to that thought. She's done wrong; but not all wrong. She's had a change of heart. She's seen the error of her ways.

'Wat's dead,' he says.

She nods, and her head sinks lower. Is she sad? He can't tell. 'He went mad,' she repeats. Then she adds, 'But I made him. He'd never have done it if it hadn't been for me. I only realised that when the women started coming, with their stories; when I saw the way Johnny was looking at me, as if it was all my fault. And it is, Chaucer. It's all my fault.'

'Your husband's being called back to England . . . the Earl of Buckingham too . . . to suppress the revolt,' Chaucer says awkwardly. He doesn't know how to answer her directly, because he's realising, painfully, how her change of heart has come about – out of love for her son – and the knowledge that Alice now sees the world through her son's eyes is making him sadder, yet also gladder, than he's ever felt before. 'They say both of them will be sent to Essex. The King's on his way already.'

Her head droops even further. 'What can they do that's worse than this? I'm being punished, even now,' she says in the unbearable monotone. 'With this . . . It's the worst thing of all – that it should be *him* who's paying the price for my wickedness. My stupidity. Johnny.'

She raises those red eyes to him.

'Do you think God does bargains, Chaucer?' she asks, and even now, even here, there's the ghost of a miserable laugh in her eyes. 'Because I've been praying and praying that if only He'll let Johnny live, I'll do whatever I have to, for the rest of my days. Have William back, when he gets here; pretend none of this had anything to do with us; it doesn't matter, anything; as long as Johnny's here. I've been praying like a fool. I'm just not sure He hasn't given up on me already.'

She shakes her head. 'You've always known, haven't you, Chaucer?' she says, and turns her hand up so it's holding his. 'How you love your children?'

That's enough to remind Chaucer of the futility of his being here. Wearily, he nods. 'I just never thought,' he says miserably, 'that you'd realise it too.'

It's only then that she seems to become truly aware that Chaucer is actually here, in the flesh.

'You haven't said,' she asks, soft and defeated against the arm he's just put around her back, 'why you came?'

Chaucer gets up and walks her over to the window at the far end of the solar. It's almost dark on the ground, but the evening sky is still luminous.

He needs a moment.

A thousand thoughts are running through his head.

'I came . . .' he says, wondering whether he shouldn't just go, now his foolish idea of rescue has been superseded by reality. Then he shrugs. There's nothing left to lose. He might as well explain. At least she'll know he cared enough to come; at least she'll know he loves her. 'I came to ask you to go away with me.'

Her eyes turn up to him: great dark pools of misery.

Then she looks back at the bed, where Johnny's lying so still, and shakes her head.

They both know.

But still she says, 'Where?'

Chaucer falters; but then gains new strength: 'That pilgrimage we once talked about. Jerusalem. Antioch. Malta. Or Italy. Rome. Does it matter where? Canterbury would do, if I could save you from yourself there; if it wasn't in England. Away, that's the point. That's what I wanted to offer you.

'I brought money,' he adds defensively, as if she's going to chide him for having a poetical flight of fancy. 'It wasn't just a thought. I came ready.'

She smiles; almost smiles. For a moment.

'Thank you,' she says, 'for the thought.' It's a no, of course; he doesn't expect anything else. She's staying here with Johnny, and waiting for William. They both know that. But it's a recognition, too. She takes his hand and squeezes it very hard; her eyes are wet.

'I never cry,' she mutters after a while, though Chaucer's

seen her in enough hard places by now to know that isn't always true; then, with a choked, whispery laugh: 'But you're not usually so brave.'

It's a few minutes more before she speaks again. Hesitantly, she says, 'There's something I should probably tell you. Something else.'

Chaucer says, almost at the same instant, 'I think I might know.'

She's surprised at that. 'You can't,' she says.

Chaucer says, 'Well, something I was going to ask you . . . when the moment was right.' He swallows. The moment's not right. It's an effort to go on. It's such a wild leap of the imagination, when she's got so much else to think about. When this could be anyone's baby: Wat's; the maidservant's; who knows? What if he's wrong?

'I met Wat, your Wat, in London. It might have been nasty. But he let me go when he heard my name. He said, "Alice's Chaucer . . . the dad . . ."' he stumbles.

He hardly dares look at her.

But when he does, she's nodding. And the look in her eyes is soft.

'You always know everything, Chaucer,' she whispers. 'I've called him Lewis. I thought you'd like to have a son whose name meant glorious warrior.'

And then the baby stirs, and starts to cry again. With a helpless, anguished look, Alice ducks away from Chaucer, and vanishes out of sight into the bed-tent. Through the curtains, Chaucer again hears the quick, uncertain breaths that might, just might, be sobs.

The near-silence goes on for a long time. The curtains stay shut. Chaucer lights the only candle he can see. When the youth on the bed groans, it's Chaucer who goes back to sit with him; mops timidly at him. The boy might not die, he thinks, clinging to that faint hope. If there's no blackness; no buboes. If it's gone on for a week, and he's still only spitting blood-flecked sputum, not gushing blood from his throat.

518

Chaucer thinks: And me, what will I do? It's dangerous to be around the plague. He should run off back to London; save himself for the children who don't need him any more, whom he loves. But he's needed here. He's lost the power to leave.

He wakes up with Alice shaking him. The candle's at its end, sputtering. He must have been asleep.

'Don't lie with him,' she whispers. 'Too dangerous. I will. You take Lewis. Here.'

He's too heavy with sleep to argue. He takes the baby, and stumbles away, and lies down on the other bed with the little swaddled form tight against him.

It's the first chance he's had to look at the infant Alice has been nursing. Lewis . . . he's heavy with milk and sleep too, Chaucer sees, and feels, as the weight's transferred to him. He's got long eyelashes, sweeping his cheek, and fat little hands curled outside his blanket. My son, Chaucer thinks, mine, and warmth spreads through his heart before sleep claims him again.

When he wakes, Alice's head is there, sticking in through the bedcurtains, with grey light behind her. She's transparent with it; she doesn't seem to have slept.

'He's no better,' she whispers of the supine form in the other bed. 'But he's no worse either.'

Chaucer sees she's trying, desperately not to let hope in. But it's just possible . . .

'Sleep,' he says. 'I'll . . .'

'No,' she interrupts. 'You have to go. You and Lewis.'

He opens his eyes wider. Properly awake now, he stares at her.

'I can't go,' he says, knowing it's true only as he speaks; knowing how desperate he'd feel if Johnny were his daughter, or his son; realising how his heart's been torn to shreds afresh at this careworn, love-worn new Alice. 'You can't stay alone.'

'You must,' she insists. 'I've been thinking. It's not safe here. Not just him . . . Johnny . . . the sickness . . . but whatever comes next, here. Or whoever. You shouldn't be here when that happens. Nor should the baby. Take him away.'

Her eyes go diamond-shaped with unshed tears. 'Please,' she adds wearily; then, with a strange new strength in her voice: 'You'll look after him better than I can.'

Chaucer sits up, putting his hands to his head. His head is whirling.

He has no idea what to do. Even if he could leave Alice, the baby he's had sleeping up against his chest is a stranger to him. He still hasn't taken off the swaddling bands on the infant; examined him, inch by inch, for points of similarity, for his father's eyes, or nose, or leg shape, to celebrate his being. It's in Chaucer's nature to be moved by the child's very existence in all this: for, in among the ruins, there's a new beginning. He just doesn't know what to do with him.

But before he can do that, or anything else, she's talking again, too fast. 'There's no point in your staying,' she's gabbling. 'You know that. There's no future for you here. This is my battle, and Johnny's. I'll cope. I always cope. You know that. Just keep the baby. I know you'll love him, bring him up right, keep him safe. And I can't. You must see that. You say William's coming. If they don't get me for . . . *that* . . . if they never associate me with any of it . . . if he just moves back in and takes me back while they do whatever they're planning to do' – Chaucer sees that Alice is, even now, making plans and contingency plans – 'well, I'll do whatever I have to . . . for Johnny, for the girls. I'll have him back. He's my husband. But how would I explain a baby?'

You can't just give your baby away like that, without a second thought, Chaucer reproaches her in his mind. But a moment later, he's already realising, she's right. What else can she do?

He nods. 'If I do,' he muses aloud, peering into a future for Alice that might, yet, not be as dark as he's feared, 'things just might work out for you. Mightn't they?' He adds, 'God willing, for Johnny too . . .' and crosses himself. She does the same. She sits down beside him.

520

'There'll be a dozen women around, when William gets here, who'll say you took them in and looked after them in their hour of need,' he says, drawing comfort from the thought. 'That will stand you in good stead. And there'll be no one left to connect you to what went before, either. The men will be long gone. I saw the last of them making off into the woods yesterday.'

'There's still Aunty,' Alice mutters. Then, stricken: 'And Johnny . . .'

Chaucer shakes his head. 'She'll keep quiet,' he says, with conviction. 'She loves the kids.'

That's true enough.

Leaning forward, taking her hands in his, he adds, 'And Johnny will keep quiet too.' She looks expressionlessly up at him. Chaucer says, 'Because he loves you.'

After a moment, Alice nods.

'And then,' she says. Not quite a question. 'The rest of my life.'

Chaucer has tears smarting in his eyes. It's killing him to think any of this, after the wild hopes he came here with.

But he goes on, stoutly enough: 'You already know what you'll do, don't you?'

Because, even in the sadness of farewell, he can see she does. She's changed. She's steadier, more stable, than he's ever known her. She has her brood to care for; she wants what's best for her son. She knows her mind.

'You'll do what we talked about once . . . what you were already doing, before *this* happened,' he says. 'You've built up Gaines; now you're going to make it better still, for your children. There's never been anyone like you for organising and planning, Alice. You just needed to know what – who – it was for. Now you do.'

Her eyes shift sideways to the other bed, where Johnny's lying. She crosses herself again. Then, almost guiltily, she looks back at Chaucer, without forcing the softness she feels for her son off her face.

'You know,' she confides, a little unsteadily, trying to smile, 'it's madness, I suppose, but before he got sick, there were

521

two days when we were fetching and carrying for those poor women all day long; and Johnny was so kind to the Ewell girl . . . She, her husband, killed; she . . .' Alice chokes on whatever it was that was done to the Ewell girl. After a moment, she goes on: '. . . that I couldn't help imagining: that girl's only a year older than Johnny; one day soon, after her mourning's over, they might . . .'

Chaucer's heart wrenches. There's no place for him in these dreams. But it's right for him to encourage Alice in them, for this is where her future must lie.

'You see?' he says, as heartily as he can. 'You're already beginning to imagine it. Why wouldn't they marry? You've earned the lifelong gratitude of those women out there. You've saved them. You'll be a pillar of Essex society before you know it, with that lad a strapping young courtier, in the pink of health, with title to half of Essex, and the Ewell widow his bride, and your girls married to the finest young lords of the county after him.' He manages a watery smile.

'And a pack of grandchildren at my knees,' she replies, and she's almost smiling too, doing her best to enter into the spirit of the thing, just as he is, though her voice is as shaky as his. 'Each with an estate half the size of France, and a golden gown . . .'

She makes a little noise: a kind of sobbing laugh.

'And you, what will you be doing?' she asks, in that same trembling tone, stealing a glance at him that he's aware of, but can't bear to return. He knows what she's doing. She's memorising him, for all the tomorrows.

He swallows. 'Me,' he says. 'I'm going to try to teach this boy the most important thing his mother taught me.' He can't get rid of the lump in his throat.

'Finance,' she prompts, almost playfully.

He shakes his head. No, he won't be doing any more accounts. He already knows he'll never sit miserably at a desk adding up other people's numbers again. 'Courage,' he corrects her, and the word hangs in the air, opening new possibilities before it that he's not even thought, until now, that he might consider. Life's too short for all the cautious

522

career-building he's gone in for until now; and where's it got him, anyway? He'll leave London; get away from what he saw in Walworth's eyes. He'll take the child out to some fresh air, and spend the money he's raised on the house giving his new son a braver and more honest life. It's time to follow his heart and devote himself to his child, just as Alice is going to do. And he thinks it will make him happy to sit in the sun writing his poetry and watching this little Lewis grow.

She deflects the compliment with a blink. 'Just don't make a poet of him,' she says, trying for brightness.

'One day,' he replies, almost to himself, 'I'll write a poem about you.'

She shakes her head, but gently. 'Let's just hope it's not a tragedy, then,' she whispers back, still trying to be pert; still failing. 'We've had enough of those.'

There's nothing more to say after that.

And when Chaucer stops talking, and she reaches down, and picks up the baby, and holds him for a long moment, rocking him, just a little, before kissing the top of his milky head and passing him to the still seated Chaucer, and says, very quickly, 'Now go; and God speed,' in a choked voice, and turns away, vanishing back behind the curtains where her older son is lying, Chaucer finds that there is no reproach left in his heart, and no regret, and no fear; all he feels is love.

He stands up with the baby, looking, for another moment, at the spot where Alice has just been standing. While he's there, he's still suspended between two worlds, half thinking he'll ignore all this and go after her and see if Johnny's better or worse, half wondering, dully, whether if he walks down to Rainham Creek, he'll find a boat before the baby gets hungry and starts to cry, and whether the baby will be satisfied for a few hours by damped-down bread crusts, or whether he'd be better heading for a village, and chancing his luck that there's a functioning inn somewhere near, or at least someone to give him milk.

And then he makes up his mind, and takes his first step

towards the door before the pain of parting begins; and says, over his shoulder, as he moves away from her, the only blessing that his stunned mind can think to make: 'I wish you well.'

EPILOGUE

A World Begins

There's constant noise outside: men's heavy feet, tramping in and out of the barn where the soldiers are being billeted, and the kitchens, where the big cauldron is boiling with some greasy, stinking army stew, and the shouting of orders, and the jingle of harness.

But it's faded into the background. Alice doesn't notice it any more.

She's hovering around the bed, whose curtains are open to let some air circulate in the heat of midday.

She's watching her sleeping son. She's watching the dust motes dance around his face.

His coughing and sneezing and spluttering stopped yesterday. His fingers and toes never went black; no buboes ever developed. His fever seems to have passed, too. She changed the top sheet two hours ago, and it's still crisp and fresh. He's pale, but he's breathing regularly.

It doesn't hurt to hope. Or it shouldn't.

She gets up, tiptoes around to the bucket of water, dips the cup and puts it, full, by the bed. She's been piling up the drenched sheets in a corner for the whole of the past two days to keep out of the way of Will's soldiers. She still doesn't want to go downstairs, except in the quiet of the night. But she does want to get the odours of sickness out of here. So she picks up the whole armful, and takes it just outside the door, and drops it, quietly, at the top of the stairs.

When she comes back into the room, Johnny's eyes are open.

He's looking around, not moving his head. Just those quiet blue-green eyes. He looks puzzled, as if he doesn't understand something. He's still not quite a man. But illness has made him a child again.

'Mam,' he whispers when he sees her, and his face is transformed by the dawning trust in that small smile, which is all he can manage.

She goes to the bed; sits down on the edge of it. As she sinks down, she suddenly feels her legs might not support her any more, she's trembling so much. She leans down and burrows her arms around the weakened body on the cushions, burying her face in his neck.

'Mam,' he whispers, 'you're crying.'

'Oh,' she mutters, smelling his skin, 'it's nothing.'

It will take a lot of explaining before Johnny understands how much everything has changed since he fell ill; understands what he's allowed to remember from the recent past and what he'd be better off forgetting. Alice will have to school Aunty and the girls, too, once they're back, to forget anything they ever knew about the rebellion Will's returned to crush. Just as she's schooling herself.

So much has gone. Her little Lewis, whose entire tiny hand curled around just one of her fingers, whose baby head smelled of milky innocence when she kissed it . . . and Chaucer too, with him (though there's sweetness in her pain, at least, at the thought of the two of them together). Wat's dead; and if they grieve for him, after this, she and Aunty, it'll have to be in secret. Gone, as well, the Tom Bakers and Piers Plowmans and Jack the Lads of the rebellion, the ordinary men of England she's listened to, and the heroic versions of them she's made up in her letters; gone with all their songs and dreams and grievances, being hunted down and exterminated. So many hopes. So many vain hopes.

It strikes Alice now, in the strange peace she's finding as she holds her near-miraculously living son close, that the turmoil she's suddenly so weary of has been going on since long

528

before this revolt. Upheaval has been part of life since that first Mortality, the plague she was born in. It's a sickness that's never abated; a sickness that's made its delusional sufferers go on grabbing for dead men's gold, go on being feverish with ambition, go on burning for land and change. But maybe it's all burned out now, not just in her own heart, but throughout the land. Alice still can't help hoping, somewhere inside herself, that this last great outbreak of public loathing and derision for the court will, somehow, have damaged the Duke she hates. But the intensity of even that desire has faded. It's a wistfulness, now, a memory of mischief; no longer strong enough to act upon – just as the physical plague that started it all seems to have weakened enough to let its sufferers occasionally, by some miracle, survive, as Johnny has. Maybe life will quieten down for all those who've made it through these years, and who now choose peace, rather than adventure. Maybe, if it stops seeming to the toughest that anything is now possible, some gentler order will prevail.

Perhaps even Aunty, to whom Alice has been writing, while she waits for Johnny to wake up, to tell her to bring the girls back – Aunty, who's always been so keen on her girls and boys going out to grab whatever they can, whenever they can, for as long as Alice can remember – will be relieved if that's the way things turn out. It's conceivable that Aunty wants nothing more, now, than to sit at home, contentedly watching her children's children live uneventful, but happy, lives. That might be all she's wanted for years, even, if Alice had only been willing to see it: a quiet life, with her family, at Gaines.

For the first time, Alice lets into her head the thought of herself, an older, calmer version of herself, watching Johnny take the place she's earned for him in the life that lies ahead for them all, standing at the altar with the Ewell girl, perhaps, and her, afterwards, bursting with pride, sipping apple wine with one or other of the Sir Johns as their children ride out past the terrace, laughing . . . of herself discussing pasturage rights, or the details of marriage contracts, or the latest developments in the law courts, with the fathers, politely, gently, without ever again going too far in pursuit of gain.

That's not a picture for now, of course. For now, there's just Will, with a fierce gleam in his eye, marching around and barking his orders, too busy to pay much mind to wife and child in the sickroom above; too busy enjoying the cruelty of his calling. For now, just him and these other men in the kitchen, made in his mould.

She sighs. But then she brightens again, and hugs Johnny closer.

For there's this, too: the treasure she's not counted until it was nearly too late. This boy, limp against the bedding, looking at her from that wasted face in which she sees both him and herself, with trust in his eyes. With concern. With love.

In that moment, with the dust motes lit up like gold, that seems more than enough.

'Happy,' she says indistinctly. 'Why I'm crying. You've been so ill. I thought you might die. I thought I'd lost you.'

Then Alice raises her son's head and shoulders, very tenderly, and begins moving the cushions around behind him to prop him up a little, so he can begin to take in the world he doesn't yet know has changed. As she tries to make him comfortable, she murmurs, 'But you're back. And it's all going to be all right.'

HISTORICAL NOTE

It took the rest of the summer of 1381 to clean up the last flickers of the Peasants' Revolt.

The peasants lost everything, even the vaguest hope of liberation from serfdom. 'Villeins you are, and villeins you shall remain,' King Richard II told the sullen, scared men of Essex as the royal armies began to pacify the shire, and the executions began. The young King grew arrogant and capricious on the memory of his success in crushing the uprising. Eighteen years later he was forced off the throne by his cousin Henry, the eldest son of John of Gaunt, Duke of Lancaster.

John of Gaunt escaped the uprising with his life. So did his wife. Still, he was so shocked and terrified by the hatred of him that the uprising revealed that he made a public confession of immorality and renounced his mistress, Katherine Swynford. He called her a 'she-devil'. He changed his mind several years later, after his wife's death, and married Katherine. But he never rebuilt the Savoy.

Sir William Walworth served on two commissions to restore the peace in Kent, and died, at the peak of his powers and reputation, in 1385. His fellow-merchant, Sir Nicholas Brembre, whose fortune amounted to £10,000 (the equivalent of almost £3.9 billion in 2007) by the time of his death, had a less developed sense of when to stop. Brembre became close to King Richard II in his last years. He also tyrannised the City, stealing two mayoral elections in 1383 and 1384.

He executed opponents, some without trial, regularly accused opponents of treason and crushed dissent by filling London with armed men. His relationship with the King ultimately cost him his life, after lords hostile to Richard took control of government. Brembre was hanged at Tyburn in 1388, on the treason charge he'd so often levelled at others.

The de la Mares lived out the remainder of their lives more peacefully. Peter de la Mare served in several further Parliaments in the 1380s. He is last heard of as a feoffee to Richard Burley in 1387. Thomas de la Mare remained at St Albans after the Peasants' Revolt, serving as Abbot until his death in 1396.

William of Windsor, who returned to Essex from Cherbourg in the wake of the revolt, was part of the King's force that put down all traces of rebellion in East Anglia. He did this with his usual severity. His reward from the King was to be made a baron. He did not spend his last years with Alice or the children. Within a year, he returned to his family home in the North to die in 1386, in debt.

Alice Perrers lived out her days at the Essex estate at Gaines, dying nearly twenty years later, in 1400, in the same year as Chaucer. She married her son and two daughters off to local landlords when they came of age and stayed geographically close to them for the rest of her life. Alice also campaigned, with only limited success, to get back the property she'd amassed in her glory days. Richard II never really helped, but, after the death of his mother, Princess Joan of Kent, in 1385, he did at least allow Alice back on occasional visits to court. There is no evidence that Alice ever saw Geoffrey Chaucer again.

Geoffrey and Philippa Chaucer lived apart after the Peasants' Revolt. A few years after entering St Helen's in Bishopsgate, their daughter Elizabeth transferred to Barking Abbey to be with her cousin, Margaret Swynford. Geoffrey Chaucer left his job as comptroller of wool customs in the City for good in 1382, and went to live in Kent, where he stayed for the rest of the decade and served as a parliamentarian in 1386. He later held office as Clerk of the King's Works between

1389 and 1391, and as deputy forester of the Royal Forest at North Petherton in Somerset from 1391, and he was still active on the King's business in 1398. A year later, when Henry IV, John of Gaunt's son, seized the throne, he renewed Chaucer's grants from the previous King and added forty marks a year for life. Chaucer died in October 1400. In his later years, he devoted more and more time to writing poetry.

In 1391, ten years after the Peasants' Revolt, Chaucer dedicated his *Treatise on the Astrolabe* to 'lyte Lowys my sone, of the tendir age of ten year', and wrote the child an affectionate foreword. Lewis Chaucer, whose birth date suggests Philippa was not his mother, was listed in public records just once more, in a retinue roll at Carmarthen Castle in 1403, which listed him next to his elder brother, Thomas Chaucer. Thomas, Geoffrey Chaucer's eldest son, did go on being mentioned in the records. He was to become one of the most wealthy, influential and distinguished men in England. Through his daughter Alice's marriage to William de la Pole, Duke of Suffolk, he was the ancestor of a future heir to the throne of England.

After the death of Philippa Chaucer (probably in 1387, accompanying her Duchess to Castile for John of Gaunt's last unsuccessful outing overseas), Geoffrey Chaucer went on a pilgrimage to Canterbury in 1388.

His writing is oddly – or perhaps diplomatically – short on references to the turbulent current affairs of his time. Yet there are hints of the upheavals Chaucer lived through in his work.

His greatest comic creation, in his unfinished poem about a pilgrimage, *The Canterbury Tales* (which he wrote in fits and starts over the rest of his life), was the Wife of Bath. This portrait of a rambunctious, wise-cracking, irreverent, independent-minded, profit-seeking female, who's buried five husbands and may be out for a sixth, who has no time for priests yet loves nothing more than a good pilgrimage, is often said to be based on the character of Chaucer's sometime patron, and King Edward III's last mistress, Alice Perrers.

ACKNOWLEDGEMENTS

Many thanks to Susan Watt, Katie Espiner, Clare Hey and everyone else at HarperCollins Publishers for all the work that went into this book, as well as to Tif Loehnis and her colleagues at Janklow & Nesbit Associates, my kind and patient workspace colleagues at 115 Bartholomew Road and, of course, my lovely family.